MARIENNA'S FANTASY

Rosemarie:
I hope you enjoy this.
John.

Marienna's Fantasy

John Sheffield

iUniverse, Inc.

New York Lincoln Shanghai

Marienna's Fantasy

iUniverse books may be ordered through booksellers or by contacting:

iUniverse
2021 Pine Lake Road, Suite 100
Lincoln, NE 68512
www.iuniverse.com
1-800-Authors (1-800-288-4677)

ISBN: 0-595-33345-1 (pbk)
ISBN: 0-595-66855-0 (cloth)

Printed in the United States of America

Contents

▼

Acknowledgements

I owe my interest in Greek mythology to the boarding school I attended from age 10 to age 18. Life in a boarding school can get boring, and I read most of the books in the school library during this period. To me, the Greek and Norse myths and legends were the most exciting books. "Marienna's Fantasy" is the product of this passion and a most enjoyable period spent at the University of Texas at Austin, from 1966 to 1971. To find out about the Greek gods, I recommend the superb "Greek Myths" by Robert Graves. The Labors of H.E. Festus owes much to these books:

> *"He has pillaged our graves*
> *For legends and deeds.*
> *The reader should judge*
> *If the author succeeds."*

I am grateful to Jason, Suzanne, iUniverse, and Valerie Clarke for their valuable help. I am most deeply indebted to my wife, Dace, for providing encouragement, critical commentary and sound advice.

H. E. FESTUS

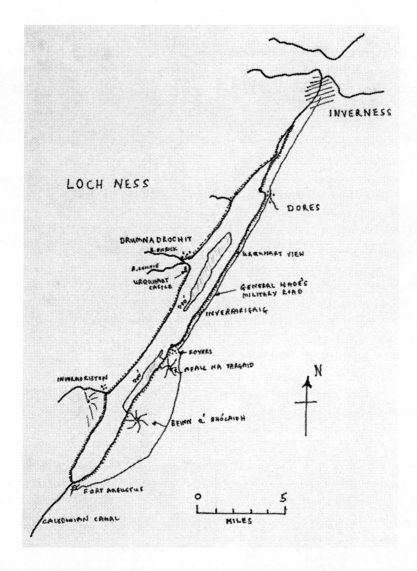

Loch Ness has been isolated for twelve thousand years. It is hard to explain how Monsters could have survived in that land-locked stretch of water for so long.

1. Oil

Henry Everett Festus sat on the hilltop overlooking the oil field, where arrays of rockers nodded contentedly as they extracted more wealth for Argos County. A peaceful sight, he thought. It brought back memories of a very different time— August 1929. Could it have been thirty-one years ago? He remembered the scene. He had climbed the hill with his father to get a view of the solitary well that his father had erected on Cronson land. They could see the operating field on Old Max's land, a quarter mile down the valley.

"The drill should have got there by now." His father sounded worried.

"Are you sure there's oil there?"

"There's oil all right. We'll find it soon." Argos Festus patted his son on the back. Then removed his hand quickly, pointing at the rig. "What the hell!"

It was an amazing sight. The top of the well blew off and a fountain of bright pink mud streamed high into the air and showered over the roustabouts.

It worked, Dad!" Henry jumped up and down in excitement.

"Damn!" Argos Festus said, grabbing his son and pulled him to the ground. "One of Old Max's crews must have detected the drilling slurry."

"What's it got to do with Mister Maximos?"

"We were bias drilling Old Max's field. He must have found out and closed off his wells. I should've guessed."

"Why would he do that?"

"So he could shove mud in our faces. That's the reason for those pumps over there. The old bastard! Come on! Let's see what's happening!" They crawled to a better view- ing point.

The Cronson roustabouts were busy capping the well, and did not notice the arrival of Old Max's men. From the hill, the two groups of men looked like pieces at the start of a board game. The Cronson set were pink. The Maximos set, wearing blue denims, were more or less blue. They did not remain separated for long, but merged into a brawling mass. From time to time men fell out of the muddy arena; tired, bruised and bloody individuals, who sat out a while before returning. Henry wanted to get a closer look, but his father restrained him.

"Only fools fight, son."

Henry realized it was not a question of fear of fighting. If you were smart, there were always ways of getting back at people who had hurt you.

The two sets of players soon lost their distinctive colors—like a child's play-dough. Nevertheless, each player seemed to know his enemies and, though tired, continued to

Agamemnon Cronson (Kronosakis)
+ 1. <u>Olympia Platon (1)</u> (m. 1894)

Georgiou	Marienna	Panou (Pan)
+		+
Christina Platon		Maria Novas
V		V
Persephone (Peri)		Rosalie (Rosie)

+ 2. <u>Penelope Zolatas</u>   (m. 1913)

Zachary		Aristotle	Angelica	Dawn (adopted)
(Zack)		(Ari)	(Angel)
+		+
Elena Maximos		<u>Yianna Patillis</u>
V			
Deucalion	Demosthenes	Samantha
(Duke)	(Demos)	(Sam)

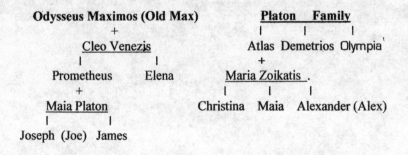

Odysseus Maximos (Old Max)   <u>Platon   Family</u>
+ | | |
<u>Cleo Venezis</u>   Atlas Demetrios Olympia
| | +
Prometheus   Elena   <u>Maria Zoikatis</u> .
+ | | |
<u>Maia Platon</u>   Christina   Maia   Alexander (Alex)
| |
Joseph (Joe) James

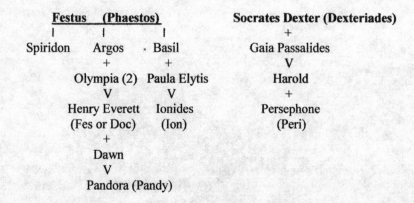

<u>Festus   (Phaestos)</u>   **Socrates Dexter (Dexteriades)**
| | | +
Spiridon   Argos · Basil   Gaia Passalides
+   +   V
Olympia (2) Paula Elytis   Harold
V   V   +
Henry Everett Ionides   Persephone
(Fes or Doc)   (Ion)   (Peri)
+
Dawn
V
Pandora (Pandy)

+ 1. Olympia Platon (1) (m. 1895)

| | |
     Deucalion   Demosthenes   Samantha
      (Duke)   (Demos)   (Sam)

Odysseus Maximos (Old Max)   Platon Family
        +
    Cleo Venezis   Atlas Demetrios Olympia
                                        +
  Prometheus   Elena   Maria Zolkatis
        +
    Maja Platon   Christina Maia Alexander (Alex)

Joseph (Joe) James

Festus ("Phaestos")   Socrates Dexter (Dexteriades)
                                              +
Spiridon   Argos   Basil   Gaia Passalides
                     +   V
      Pandora (Pandy)

thrash away at them. Just when there appeared to be no basis for ending the fight, a shiny model-T Ford rolled slowly to the edge of the arena and stopped. A small man in a black suit got out and took a shotgun from the passenger seat. He fired the first barrel. The surging mass of men slowed, momentarily. As the action accelerated, he fired again and reloaded. The fighting slowed to a halt, like a carnival ride preparing to disgorge its passengers. The indistinguishable players regrouped, one set around the oilrig, the other by the model-T Ford. A few of them still lay on the ground. From the oilrig set, a mud-encrusted man emerged. It was Agamemnon Cronson. He approached the Ford; his gesture acknowledged defeat. He stopped short of the model-T, standing upright with difficulty, waiting for Old Max to come to him. It was a question of honor and pride. Old Max set down his shotgun and walked to him.

"Old Max has won. Next, everyone will find a reason to blame me," Argos said, speaking in Greek.

"How can he blame you? You only did what Uncle Agamemnon said?" Henry replied in English.

"I know Henry, but in my job, and it will be yours some day, when things go wrong for the Cronsons the men in our family pay a price. Of course, everybody's happy to take the credit when things go well. When I developed that bias drill, I didn't reckon to use it for rustling oil. Unfortunately, I don't decide the grand plans."

Henry stroked his father's gnarled hand. "It's not fair!"

"That's the way it was in Crete, son—vendettas. I guess your Uncle Agamemnon is right. That's how it will continue in Argos County. He would never have bias drilled for the oil if Old Max hadn't cheated him out of the land. The whole affair's senseless really. I wonder," he stopped, staring vacantly into the distance. "The players may change but the main plot and sub-plots remain the same. Just as in Crete. Sometimes, I wonder if we're acting out the plays in real life."

Henry Festus remembered how the mention of the plays had stilled the multitude of questions in his head. They had walked to the oilrig in silence. The plays were a fantasy world in which his imaginative mind could roam. The shelves in his childhood bedroom had bulged with books on legends, adventure, travel, and science fiction. Between the shelves, the walls had been covered with pictures of dragons, castles, space ships and, what remained a favorite topic—the Loch Ness monster. He still had the faded photograph of the small terracotta disk unearthed at the palace of Phaestos on Crete. His godmother had given him the picture, explaining that the inscription, in strange symbols that spiraled around each side of the Disk, had never been translated. Now, with his godmother's help, he might get a chance to solve the two mysteries. He thought about this as he made his way to the theater to get ready for the play.

2. Samaria Canyon

Festus looked across the stage to where Zeus was shedding the bindings that had tied him to a pillar. He wished that Zeus would hurry up and deliver his lines. His uneven legs hurt from an hour of balancing on the buskins—the stylized elevated boots traditional in Greek tragedy. The play, "Zeus Bound," was performed for the first time, in 1928. The plot irritated him. Hephaestus is trapped in a losing situation by the need to serve the Zeus, while trying to help the War-god, Ares. Hephaestus makes some trick bindings to trap Zeus. He plans to wait until the last minute to see whether Ares or Zeus will win, before deciding whether to use them. Unfortunately, the wily Zeus is not fooled. He realizes what action his brother Ares is considering, and talks him out of it. He fears the Smith-god more, and decides to teach Hephaestus a lesson. Zeus forgives Ares, making him chief of staff, thereby ending the traditional battle between the sacred king and his tanist. The Smith-god's power is weakened.

Zeus, alias Zachary Cronson, took his time. He smiled, a grim knowing smile, savoring the moment, before speaking. Hephaestus answered him, and Zeus replied:

Zeus:

Ares is gone now to tend to matters of his own.

He will protect me now.

For you a task to set my mind at ease.

Prometheus remains a greater threat.

Is he still firmly bound or, soon will he be free?

Hephaestus, bid farewell to Aphrodite

And journey to far Scythia.

Confirm for me that Prometheus yet is bound.

(Zeus departs. Hephaestus follows slowly.)

Chorus:

Poor Hephaestus. Zeus trusts neither him nor Ares.

It is clear he fears Hephaestus.

So he sends him away on this futile task.

What will Ares do?

Marienna's Fantasy

Henry Everett Festus is miserable working for Zachary Cronson, padrone of the Greek families of Argos County, Texas.

Marienna Cronson, Henry's godmother, comes to his aid. Frustrated by their male-dominated society, she has written four plays about the Greek gods, in which the Cretan-immigrant families have established roles.

Marienna—Athena—believes their roles may be real. She plays out her fantasy through the plays and through persuading Henry—the god of technology, Hephaestus—to repeat the "so-called" Labors of Heracles. Henry sets out to find the Loch Ness Monster. Other Labors interrupt his quest. Finally, his translation of the Phaestos Disk leads to a treasure hunt on Crete.

Henry's selfish focus on work and a cruel trick he plays on his wife, Dawn, drive her and their daughter away. While completing the Labors, Henry strives to recover his family and be free from the domineering Zachary. In the background, Marienna manipulates their lives.

He lusts for Aphrodite, and he may succeed.
Will Hephaestus prepare, and wreak vengeance
On the two of them when he returns?
Dear gods, why, if his powers far outreach theirs,
Does he remain the servant of them all?

The stage lights dimmed save for a spotlight that briefly illuminated the departing smith-god, Hephaestus. The chorus exited, continuing its chant of "Poor Hephaestus." The audience applauded. The sound echoed in the natural bowl, that formed the Greek Theater set in Samaria Canyon, Argos County, Texas. As the audience left, the actors took the path from the orchestra, around the proscenium, to the changing room in the skene building.

Henry Festus remained, standing in the shadows at the edge of the stage. He was still immersed in the play, thinking about a different ending in which Hephaestus would triumph. A light touch on his arm brought him back to reality. It was Marienna Cronson. She was wearing a white, high-necked blouse, and tailored blue trousers that flattered her tall slim figure. Her graying hair was in a bun. Very Katherine Hepburn, he thought. Bless her! She was carrying a drink for him.

"Thanks," he said, taking a sip. He did not know what she put in it, but the tart taste was always refreshing.

"Henry! I'm glad to see you take your role seriously, but you shouldn't get so depressed. Hephaestus will win in the end."

"I wish I didn't, but I've done this cycle of plays so many times, I guess it's more than just acting now. I resent the way all the men chase after my...his wife Aphrodite. Dawn plays her so damn well and I feel sorry for him. Why is it that smiths and wizards have to be so subservient to the gods and sacred kings, who they have the misfortune to serve? I daydream of a time when Hephaestus could achieve the glory he deserves."

"So do I. Like Hephaestus with the gods, your poor father suffered at the hands of us Cronsons. Don't let it happen to you." Marienna retorted. "I'll see what I can do. I'll have to be careful. As it is, I get enough complaints every two years for my minor improvements." She chuckled. "Incidentally, I have an idea for an improvement you might like. That damned male domain, the "kinotitos", can take it or leave it." She hugged him, and rushed away to congratulate other players before he could ask what it was.

Festus had not given it much thought, but Marienna was right. Their community was an anomaly with its kinotitos—the ruling body of elected male representatives who traditionally, in Greek communities, watch over the welfare of the community, and sustain the school and church. It must have been very frustrating for Marienna to be denied election to the council. Just like the "Foreigners" who were disenfranchised because they could never gather enough votes to be elected.

Nevertheless, he was convinced that the kinotitos had served Argos County well. At the end of the First World War, Odysseus Maximos had retired to his ranch, some twelve miles down the road towards Lampasas. A few of his close relatives had followed and so the rival village of Arcadia had been born. Nevertheless, the population of the county had not been sufficient to support more than one High School; consequently, there were two distinct groups within the school, one from Argos and the rest, who by default became associated with Arcadia. The rivalry between the two groups mellowed with time, until it became only a basis for forming two teams to compete in the annual mini-Olympic Games. Fortunately for the community, the Maximos clan remained involved in the kinotitos and its activities. These included the Argos Play Cycle, and Festival of Greek Dancing, Singing and Crafts, that were the foci of social activities on May Day and around the Fourth of July.

Shortly after the discovery of oil on the Cronson's land, the kinotitos established the Eurysthesian Foundation. The Foundation took over the sponsorship of the Plays, the Festival and the Games, and it paid for the Greek Theater in Samaria Canyon.

Zachary Cronson, who had overheard the interchange, stuck his head around the backdrop. "You want Hephaestus to stop workin' for Zeus? You gotta be kidding."

"Oh no, he'd never do that," Festus replied, without thinking. Then, realizing Zack was joking, sought to disentangle himself, commenting sharply, "You pretend you're joking, Zack, but don't tell me you don't identify with Zeus sometimes? For example, how many lightning bolts did you fire this week from your summit in our 'kinotitos'? How many unfortunate debtors did you strike down from your position in the bank?"

In an attempt to cover his irritation Zack laughed uproariously, throwing back his head in a characteristic gesture, as if this was a wonderfully funny idea. Those close to him recognized the gesture as a sign of anger. Those, who did not know him well, found the gesture appealing; in keeping with the impression he gave of strength and trustworthiness. His classic features with their frame of thick, brown hair—the natural looking color a credit to his barber's skill, enhanced the image. Zachary camouflaged his unimpressive stature with elevated boots and carefully tailored western suits, in pale, "good guy" colors. Most important to his image, however, was his bearing, his direct way of looking at people that automatically made him the focus of attention.

"Not fair! People here rely on my bank, and that gives me a good deal of power. It's not my fault that Old Max doesn't come to the kinotitos very often. I hope I use my immense power more responsibly than some of the gods." His reply sounded pompous and defensive.

The comment about the gods resonated with half remembered stories, and Festus retorted without thinking. "Remember what they used to do to the sacred king. The minute you show any signs of decay you'll be replaced."

Zack pointed a finger in warning. "I haven't forgotten that unfortunate time your father Argos conned Marienna into trying to get Ari promoted over me. When my father was dying, for God's sake!"

"My father was only trying to support Marienna."

"Don't blame my family, Fes! Marienna doted on Agamemnon."

"I don't believe it. Dad would never have done something like that on his own."

"You were young," said Zack. "You don't know what happened. Whether you like it or not, Argos Festus, screwed up. He waved his hands irritably, dismissing the topic. "Incidentally, I've been thinking about your suggestion that the Foundation should sponsor scientific research. I'm still not convinced, but Marienna seems to think it has merit."

"What are you going to do, Zack?"

"Talk to a few people. Then maybe we could have a broader discussion at the Breakfast Club. I'll let you know," Zack added, emphasizing his authority.

It was too late to discuss it. Zack had gone. Anyway, none of it made any difference, except for the implication that his father was dishonest. Festus had loved and respected his father. Consequently, he had followed in the path of Argos, in working for Cronson Enterprises. Continuing his father's work had been easy. It allowed him to stay within the Greek community. It paid well. On the down side it meant that, since completing college, he had worked for Zachary Cronson.

Sometimes, he managed to escape from this trap to work for himself. Escape! He thought ruefully. It had become a chore, running the light-engineering works he took over when his father retired; an enterprise primarily owned by the Cronsons. He spent most of his time dealing with problems in their various businesses—oil, agriculture, and transportation. He managed to find a little time to do short-term, research projects. Those, and adding to his complement of qualifications, rounded out his life. In his heart, he knew that he was underachieving.

He could tell that his friends at the University of Texas in Austin had a mixed view of him. They seemed to appreciate his imagination and technical skills, but viewed him as a dilettante—like a Victorian, amateur, gentleman scientist. Some of them had even suggested that, with his talents, he could find a more interesting job outside of Argos. Festus knew this in his heart, but admitted to himself that working for the Cronsons had become too comfortable from a financial point of view. Marienna was the only person to whom he had confided his concerns.

"Maybe I should leave Argos? I know I could get a good job outside. I'm bored. I don't feel creative. My life is slipping by and I have haven't done a damn thing!"

"Henry, don't do anything rash. I know it's frustrating, but we need you in Argos."

"We Cronsons?"

"No, our whole community. You have a responsibility."

"Like my father? Look what it did to him."

Marienna looked hard at him. "I know. Let me get something I've been working on." She returned with some papers. "Maybe now is the right time to tell you about some ideas I have. If we can persuade the kinotitos, I think they'll give you what you want. Have a look."

"You think they'll buy the idea of a Trust to support me to do research?"

"Yes, if we appeal to their greed."

"Redo the Labors of Heracles?' Festus chuckled. "I can't wait to see their faces."

"No, redo The Labors of Hephaestus! In the myths, Heracles was a shambling idiot, who hardly had the wits to tie his sandals. He could never have done the Labors without the help of Hephaestus." Marienna had sounded angry. "We'll show the world who really did them."

"You were the one who made my name a pun on Hephaestus—H. E. Festus. Now you're casting me as the god in real life?"

"Why not?"

Festus hoped she was right. He removed his buskins and placed them beneath the long communal dressing table. As always, he was the last to remove his make-up. He was glad that Agamemnon had been obliged to involve all of the Greek families of Argos in order to fill the large number of roles in the play. The plays remained a joint effort, since no family was prepared to give up its role, notwithstanding the friction between Agamemnon and Old Max. Moreover, as in the Passion Play at Oberammergau, families had become associated with particular parts—father handing over to son, mother to daughter.

The gradual loss of Greek names had not affected the commitment to the Greek activities. During a period of anti-Greek sentiment, Kronosakis became Cronson, and Dexteriades became Dexter. Henry's family name, Phaestos, became Festus. Not by choice, but for the prosaic reason that the immigration officer had spelt it that way.

Festus looked in the mirror to check whether he had removed all of his make-up. It was a good thing that Marienna had forsaken the traditional masks of Greek tragedy; somehow, it was more satisfactory to use make-up. He needed little. The saturnine face of Hephaestus still looked back at him. His large dark eyes were set wide apart. He had the pale skin of the scholar; black curly hair, now showing a trace of gray; and a moustache in the Cretan style, a wide triangle of hair, with its apex under the nostrils, fanning out beyond the mouth and trimmed level with the upper lip.

Tell me what you are thinking Hephaestus! Tell me the truth about Aphrodite! Is she unfaithful to me? He willed the face to answer him. The face smiled back—a mustachioed Mona Lisa on a billboard, divulging nothing.

"Fes, are you still in there?" It was his wife, Dawn. "Come on now! We've got to get home. I don't like leaving Pandy alone this late." A second face appeared in the mirror. A beautiful face framed in thick blonde hair.

"Aphrodite says, go home Hephaestus!" The blonde head shook in mock irritation. "You always seem so spacey after a performance. The play's over. Come on!"

Hephaestus was tired of orders, he thought, watching his wife's face through misting eyes. For a moment, the features distorted, like the dial on a Salvador Dali watch. He refocused. Her big green eyes were smiling fondly. She kissed the back of his head.

"We really must go Fes. It's not just for Pandy's sake. I have plans for you." Her hands stroked suggestively. She turned and was gone.

The lone face looked at him. "Go home to daughter Pandora!" Hephaestus says. "Go home to your beautiful, sexy wife and let her magical touch turn your frustration into ecstasy. Your problems will go away. Come on, you silly bastard, stop mesmerizing yourself. If anyone could see you they'd think you were mad." Hephaestus grinned broadly at the thoughts and released him.

As he walked to his car, Festus remembered the mention of the Breakfast Club. He would have to see Marienna as soon as possible to work on strategy. It would not be an easy sell.

3. The Breakfast Club

It was ironic, thought Festus, as he drove into to the square, that oil had played a role in the creation of the Breakfast Club. Following the influx of wealth, it was no longer necessary for all the men to rise early to attend their crops and flocks. They could employ others to do these chores, while they engaged in the luxury of their beds and their wives. Perversely, as is the nature of the human race, it seems that all women are not as easily aroused as men, first thing in the morning. Some men had an excuse to get up anyway, that is, out of bed. The creation of the Breakfast Club grew out of this reality. It was a main point of contact for the men of Argos County.

Festus soon reached the First Argos Hotel, which some wag had pointed out was also its last. He did not want his friends to know he had arrived first and parked on the other side of the main square. He walked towards the hotel—a three-story, red brick building from the early 1920's, that filled a corner of the square. In it was the First Argos Grill, the only restaurant in town that served breakfast. The commercial minded additions of the 1950's could not disguise the charm of its veranda and rocking chairs. A mismatched collection of rectangular brick and stone-faced, one and two storied shops and offices spread from the hotel around three sides of the square. They catered to the needs of Argos in hair-cuts and saddles, insurance and beauty, lingerie and legal advice, cosmetics and clothing, and included further relaxation for the men in the—"Kaffenion"—the coffeehouse in which men debated endlessly, as if they would explode in silence.

At this time of day, the Knossos Kaffenion harbored a rare silence. Through the window, Festus could see that its marble topped tables and twisted wire chairs were against the wall, a clue to the dancing of the previous night. The pastries were covered and the coffeepots cold. Around the wall, the pictures of the founder, Agamemnon Cronson, the revered Cretan and Greek leader, Eleuthe-rios Venizelos, and of that good friend of Argos, Lyndon Baines Johnson rested between the maps of Crete and Greece, and the paintings of Cretans beating the daylights out of the Turks.

The enterprises of the Cronson and Maximos families filled the remaining side. They included a litter of small offices for oil-related activities, and the bank—a miniature copy of the Alamo. The town hall occupied the island in the center of the square. It was a fanciful edifice of pink granite from nearby Marble Falls, with a contrasting blue-capped clock tower and a myriad of interlocking peaked roofs. Around it, there was a wide grass and tree-covered area with benches and an octagonal, brightly colored bandstand.

Just before seven o'clock, the lights in the hotel restaurant came on, and men slipped in through the open restaurant door. Festus was waiting in the men's room. He could hear snatches of their conversation, as Joe Maximos, Old Max's grandson, greeted them. As he ushered his friends into the dining room, Joe embraced them with the litany of small talk that marked his trade. He worked for one of his grandfather's enterprises, Maximos Insurance.

"Hi, Ion."

"Mornin', Joe."

"You're here early, Harold." There was no reply.

"Do I smell steak?"

"Naturally, it's the first Tuesday in the month, Zack."

"God! Is it another month already?"

"Glad you could make it Ari."

Festus entered quietly, at the back of the dining room," and sat with his cousin Ionides. He saw that Joe, a short, plump, dark-haired man, was smartly dressed in his standard attire for a Breakfast Club meeting—blue suit, subdued orange tie, white and blue shirt, and alligator skin boots.

"Good morning gentlemen. I call this business meeting of the Argos Lake Breakfast Club to order. I am the secretary of the club and chairman for social affairs." Joe paused, looking expectant.

"We know all about your affairs. Didn't realize you did them on behalf of the club."

"I don't know why I slave away on behalf of y'all—shrimp bakes, barbecues, heaven knows what all. When all I get are ungracious comments like that...I don't want to keep you away from all this good food for too long, but I've an announcement to make; the results of our election for treasurer. Very appropriately this has been won by Harold Dexter, and he has undertaken to do the job." He paused, again receiving hoped for laughs, and appreciative groans.

Festus watched from the back of the room as Harold Dexter, proprietor of the Argos County mortuary, stood and nodded gloomily to the assembly. His somber clothes, the trademark of his profession, contrasted strangely with the gaudier western dress of his colleagues. He peered hesitantly at his audience, his head bobbing up and down.

"Thank you for your vote of confidence. I undertake, as is my profession, to treat this position seriously and look forward to working on the committee." Harold sat to the accompaniment of scattered clapping.

"Looks like a vulture," Ionides whispered.

"Yeah." Festus smiled.

"Glad you could make it, Doc," Joe said, seeing that Festus was in the back of the room.

Festus nodded self-consciously, lowering his head and giving a lopsided smile. His moustache exaggerated this expression and, as his wife had explained to him often, gave him the slightly nutty look, which made some people uneasy. He had tried practicing different smiles while looking in a mirror, but it did not seem to have helped. In this case, it and his limp, more pronounced than usual, betrayed his secret. Festus had arrived early and had made adjustments to the cruets and the head table.

Joe sat down, resting his elbows on the head table. It rocked ominously. He looked sharply at Festus, who stared back, with a peaceful, wide-eyed, and innocent look. It did not fool his good friend. Festus knew what Joe was thinking. Joe had told him many times, *"Festus you're wasting your brainpower on practical jokes, what looks like random research, and getting endless qualifications."* Festus hoped that this new deal with the Foundation that Marienna and he had cooked up would help change the view.

The members of the Argos Lake Breakfast Club finished their remaining scrambled eggs, breakfast steak, and biscuits—an American breakfast was the only deviation from a traditional Greek menu for the First Argos Grill—then sat back, lighting cigarettes and getting refills of coffee. Zachary Cronson was talking excitedly about his recent trip to visit relatives in Crete. He acted as if he had discovered something interesting but, irritatingly, would only hint at what it was.

"We need to get on with the program!" said Joe, interrupting the flow of Zack's story.

Zack looked at his watch. "My God! Is it seven thirty already?" The background chatter, which had underscored Joe's opening remarks, quieted. "The blackboard's from Argos High. I'll be throwing various numbers at you and I think they're important enough for you to consider them carefully, so we all have the same picture. My topic is tax and the legal methods of avoiding it. In particular, I'm going to float an idea, originally suggested by Marienna, and brought to fruition by Alex Platon and myself. I think it may be of some interest to you all." Zack paused. "Do you know what the gross product of Argos County is?" Zack did not wait for an answer. "No?" He continued. "Well, our county has a population of some fourteen thousand, and from local enterprises, agriculture, and the oil business we made roughly ninety five million dollars last year." He wrote the number in large figures on the blackboard. "Of this money about forty four million was taken as private income. We spent approximately sixteen million on running the county, including our schools, supporting our local hospital and maintaining the various other activities. Our local businesses reinvested about sixteen million in agriculture, oil and so on."

He paused for effect, while subtracting the expenses. "Gentlemen, the remaining nineteen million went in taxes, either federal or state. We estimate at least seven million in direct federal tax alone. O.K., I know what you'll say. We get it back in federal and state aid, and we must pay for the armed forces and the defense of our great country. Sure, but we calculate our return in social security, welfare, agricultural supports, oil depletion allowances, etc, at eight million and our contribution to the military at seven million, so they owe us four million dollars every year." He wrote 4 million on the board and drew a circle around it. He paused again, before finishing with his punch line.

"What's your point?"

"The only sure way to get some of this money back is to not pay it in the first place, Harold. That's the point!"

Festus watched the reaction to Zack's final statement. It ranged from glee to apprehension. Zack responded first to those who were apprehensive, raising his hands to still their questions. "Please don't be concerned that we're going to try and cheat the government. Alex and I are not so foolish as to risk the wrath of the IRS. We propose to work well within the law. How shall I put it? The law just begs us to take every advantage of it we can. For many years, the Foundation has underwritten the Greek Festival and the Play Cycle and, in the past, these activities used up the spare cash. In recent years, though, these enterprises have turned a healthy profit. We have a large cash surplus. The work on the medical center is nearly complete and we need something new to fund. The bottom line is that we propose to expand the role of the Eurysthesian Foundation to include a Charitable Trust that will support scientific research."

During Zack's speech, Aristotle Cronson, Zack's younger brother had shown a growing irritation. Ari's large, broad shouldered, nearly triangular, body shifted restlessly—like a caged gorilla—hinting at his feelings. *It was typical of Zack to keep him in the dark. He had surmised, correctly, that the suggestion to put his money into scientific research meant supporting Henry Festus. Festus made him feel inadequate. As deputy to his brother in the family enterprises, he was concerned about his image.* Anger won out over fear of his brother.

"For God's sake, Zack! Why compound problems. Take chances with IRS? Risk money. Cockeyed plan of Henry Festus to do scientific research? Pay only…twenty percent or so in federal tax. So Foundation puts up most of the money. Bet we'll have to put up own money. Will scheme work? Don't see extra benefit from other eighty percent. Mine already." Ari snapped. The clipped sentences were an affectation he had acquired during his service with Patton in the Second World War. He still served as a colonel in the Army Reserves.

"Good points. Thought I'd explained it all," replied Zack. "Suggesting those who pay most tax should invest most. Will clarify proposal." Ari's style of speech was catching, Festus thought. Zack succeeded in shaking it off. "It's really the business taxes we're looking to save rather than personal income tax. Yeah, it's still true that we will have to commit some real money. I agree also that, on the surface, scientific research is a risky business and it would be easy to lose money. Ironically, that's what led Fes to the idea in the first place."

"Don't support it. Henry Festus too immature. Look what he did to our salt-shakers. Loosened the caps. Nearly ruined my breakfast. I saw Alex Platon cross himself. Throw salt over his shoulder. Typical stupid-Festus practical joke!"

"For God's sake, Fes, why do you do these dumb things?" Festus hung his head in mock apology.

"It would have to be Henry! Wouldn't it?" Harold Dexter exclaimed, emphasizing the first name.

"Let me pose a question! Where would such money get lost to?" Harold looked to be preparing for another outburst. Zack raised his hands in supplication. "Don't answer that! I'll put my rhetorical question another way. Can we guarantee that the money gets lost to somewhere we can use it? The answer is yes."

Harold looked unimpressed. "You're still being too vague. Give me a clear-cut example of the benefit to me and maybe I'll support the plan."

"Fair enough. Let me postulate that we send a research team to study the possible uses of the poison secreted by the stonefish. For example, this venomous creature lives around in the Cayman Islands. The Trust would purchase or rent a boat and housing for the team—us. Do you have any idea of what it costs, just to get there? The savings to each family would be incredible and all they would have to do in return would be a little fishing."

"Zachary! Are you trying to tell me that this whole deal is being set up in order to get cheap vacations?"

"No, Harold," Zack said firmly. "It wouldn't be good enough if the whole deal were set up solely to provide cheap vacations. However, that is proposed as only a modest part of the work of the Trust." Zack paused for a moment to find the right words, and then emphasized each point by ticking it off on the fingers of his left hand. "We have three main goals. One is to expand our contacts beyond the little world of Argos, and broaden our minds. Two is to search for new products that would allow us to diversify our work. I worry that we're too dependent on our oil revenue. Three is to allow us to relocate some of the tax dollars in safe havens as a hedge against future problems at home." Zack had left this point until last, knowing it would appeal to many of the members of the Breakfast Club. He waited for a response, but not even Harold spoke.

"All right then, since y'all are tongue tied today, let me continue. I should point out that the Caymans are a tax haven. Let's imagine that we did research the stonefish and in the end found no use for its poison. We would make a loss, apparently. Yet, in reality, the venture would in part be tax deductible and there would be some tangible assets left in the Caymans. Clearly, at some point, we must have profitable ventures or, as Harold points out, the whole exercise will become merely a complicated way to take vacations. Here, all I can say is, you must put your faith in old Fes as I do."

"You need to comment on the question of expenses that the Foundation can't pay! How do we cover them?"

"Thanks for reminding me, Alex. The idea is for the Foundation to underwrite most of the work. We will issue shares, and try and raise a hundred thousand dollars immediately as a float to cover expenses that fall outside the domain of the Foundation. If, or rather when, we make a profit, the bulk of the money will go to the Foundation with a moderate amount for the Trust." Zack stopped and looked around expectantly. Whispered discussions, some of them heated, were taking place at each of the tables.

Ionides Festus broke the quiet buzz of conversation. He was a gangling youth in his mid-twenties, with an untidy shock of black hair, a prominent Adam's apple, and bright brown eyes that gave him a permanently eager look. Following graduation in engineering from the University of Texas, Ionides had joined Festus in working at Cronson Enterprises. In honor of the meeting, he was wearing a white shirt and tie. "Say Mr. Cronson, what are you going to put up? I'll be happy to follow suit." He tugged nervously at the tie, which appeared to be strangling him.

"Why, thank you. I hadn't realized you were so wealthy or so generous. Festus can't be as mean as I've heard. We'll all look forward to receiving your ten thousand dollars. Just make the check out to my bank." Zack grinned at his audience, who laughed at Ionides' apparent discomfort. "I hope the rest of you will follow this fine example?"

"There's one small thing, Mr. Cronson. Can you lend me the money? You see I'm temporarily out of funds. Fes doesn't pay me until the end of the month. I don't think I can handle ten thou, maybe if you can give me a deal I can manage a hundred bucks."

Zack shook his fist in mock anger.

Throughout this exchange, Aristotle Cronson glowered at Ionides. His daughter Samantha and Ionides were dating.

"Young Ionides makes a good point," Zack continued, emphasizing the young. "Maybe ten thousand is too high. Let's agree to take smaller sums. Joe and Alex, you work it out!"

Alex Platon took the lead. "As you heard from Joe I've been involved in working up this concept. I really believe it's a good idea, though I think we need to do more homework on the details. In particular, I need to get more advice on the tax aspects. It's a gray area. As in poker, you can get away with a lot, until someone in the IRS calls your bluff. We're going to write it down so that y'all can study it. In the meantime, it would help us if each of you could give us some idea, privately, of what you might be prepared to commit. I plan to support it at a similar level to Zack." He looked around, "and it seems that my table is generally supportive too. One person we should hear from is Fes. I really don't know enough about the details of his plans."

"Thanks for your support. Let me say just a few more words before handing over to Fes. I hope you won't think I sound pompous but I believe this could be a turning point in the development of Argos County. We are about to prove that a small group of people within a country, as large and as great as ours, can still have a major influence on their destiny by working effectively within the system imposed on them."

"And if nominated I will not stand. If elected I will not sit," muttered Harold.

Zack glared and continued. "Alex, Fes, Joe and I feel, and we hope you'll agree, that it is totally appropriate to use names and aims relating to our Greek ancestry. We named our Foundation after King Eurystheus and the twelve Labors that he gave to Heracles. By the same token, we plan to name the operating arm of our activity 'Olympic Services.' It will support new Labors for our community and," he looked hard at Festus, "do other research, for our benefit and for our great country."

Festus had been listening but only half seeing, his mind was fixed on steadily sexier images of his wife. Dawn had wanted sex, just when he was ready to get out of bed. He had this strange vision of her poised on the bed her breasts in his face, and lower down a softness waiting to envelop him. They had wrestled quickly and unsatisfactorily. His mind had been preoccupied with the plans for the Breakfast Club. With exquisitely bad timing, the image generated a stronger erection than the one that had failed earlier. His erections often appeared inconveniently. Dawn usually had that effect on him—on most men. Her smile, the touch of her hand, the way she posed in conversation, all seemed like invitations to bed. For the first years of their marriage, he had enjoyed the envious looks and reveled in the wonder of their sex life. Dawn's social life, tennis, card games, had expanded in response to his long hours at work. There seemed to be a never-ending stream of eager young men ready to escort her when her tennis partner, Ari, was unable to play. He did not know whether it was innocent or she was simply a flirt. Recently, his feelings had turned to jealousy. He was unsatisfied with his work, and sex and other pleasures had soured. One way or another, the Cronsons seemed to have him by the balls. He grimaced at the idea.

"Fes will be our Heracles, heading this service organization and, undauntedly, facing every challenge issued by King Eurystheus," added Zack, with gentle malice. "He will have one advantage over Heracles. Fes will play a key role in identifying the Labors." There was muffled laughter as Festus stood.

Festus was wearing a suit. Both he and the suit looked uncomfortable; the jacket was creased, and the cuffs on his pants were uneven. He tried to lift his left foot enough to stop the scuffling sound of the shoe on the wood floor. Festus knew that his infirmity was a continuing source of embarrassment to Zack, since he had been responsible for the accident that had caused it. His brother Ari and he were climbing a tree and the younger, twelve-year old Festus, who at the time still idolized Zack, insisted on following. Zack had shaken the branch, in irritation, causing him to fall. The height was not great but he had fallen awkwardly, suffering bad fractures of the bones in his left leg. The available medical facilities were limited, and a poor job was done in resetting the leg, leaving Festus permanently lame.

He averted his eyes as club members moved chairs, unnecessarily, to let him pass. On reaching the front table, Festus acknowledged Zack and turned to face his audience.

"Gentlemen, I have the problem, which I'm pleased to share with you, of finding projects—Labors—that will be beneficial to the Eurysthesian Foundation," he said. "There are a number of factors that bear upon this choice and I'll remind you of them first. The projects must be viable in that they should be interesting for the participants. I was going to say they should be fun, but I don't want to antagonize Harold. They don't need cast-iron, scientific justification, but they do need to be plausible enough to withstand the scrutiny of the IRS. From my selfish point of view, they should be scientifically interesting. This may be a more demanding challenge than satisfying the IRS. They also have to satisfy Zack's desires…er…the combination of these factors compounds the problem of finding good projects."

"Keep hearing what projects aren't. What are they?" Ari growled.

"I've identified three possibilities. Two of which should provide travel and entertainment for our members. Neither is in the Cayman Islands. Though I should point out that there are some interesting possibilities in the Caribbean area."

"I don't mind, anything for the cause, except Greenland in winter."

"I'll try and avoid it, Alex. In the meantime let me continue to give you some of the flavor of our plans."

"Tell about projects!"

"In a minute, Ari."

"We'll set up a laboratory in Austin as a base for Olympic Services."

"Why Austin? What's wrong with Argos?" snapped Harold.

"It'll be easier for us to use consultants from the University in support of our research."

"Research! From what Zack said I had the impression you were going to don a lion skin and roam the countryside beating people over the head with your club."

"Very funny, Harold," Joe interjected, waving his hands in a calming motion to quiet the background of bantering talk and muffled asides which had marked much of the proceedings. "Please give Fes a chance, to explain."

Festus nodded his appreciation. "I'll have to give cut back on my part-time research, and employ a full-time manager for the tool shop in Argos, in order to do work for Olympic Services. So it isn't a simple matter." He paused, on the pretext of taking a sip of water, using the opportunity to gauge the response of his audience. Gratifyingly, they appeared eager to hear more.

"Our longer-term research at home will be on topics that fit in well with our oil business: the use of bacteria and enzymes to control oil pollution, for example; and techniques for extinguishing oil-well fires. Now, let me tell you about the first project. Lights please!" He signaled to Ionides who was ready with a slide projector.

"What's your first Labor, Heracles? The Hydra?"

"Yes, in a way it is the Hydra. Very good Harold."

"The picture shows a small submersible exploration craft. I have information that one is for sale in England, and I can get a good price for it if we move quickly. Yes Ari, that means submarine."

The tension, which had built again during the interplay with Harold Dexter, evaporated. Alex Platon, who was suffering, incongruously for a lawyer, from a fit of the giggles, bellowed out, "I've just got to ask this Fes. Why, in heavens name, do we need a small submersible exploration craft—type submarine? Don't tell me! We're going to float it down the Colorado to the Gulf and then sail in it to the Cayman Islands." Like a colony of cicadas, his audience resonated with his giggles, as he collapsed holding his sides.

Harold's face took on a grimmer look, and he appeared to have an attack of hiccups. It was his form of uproarious laughter.

"I'm glad you raised that point," Festus replied, with a straight face. "I must admit I hadn't thought of using it in the Caribbean. No, I want it to help us find the Loch Ness Monster!"

4. Loch Ness

Festus and Ionides arrived in Inverness in late July, shortly after Festus had succeeded in persuading the Trust to buy a miniature submarine. Festus still had a vivid memory of the heated debate.

"Come off it! The Loch Ness monster! You can't be serious," Alex Platon exclaimed. "I am."

"You've had that monster on the brain since you were a little kid," Harold muttered.

"So?"

"You had pictures on your wall." Harold continued. "I remember reading in the National Geographic that the Loch's been isolated for twelve thousand years. It's hard to explain how the Monster could have survived in that land-locked stretch of water for so long. You've got the damn thing on the brain. Why should we pay for you to play out your childhood passion?'

Festus recalled his response. *"I've read the article too. You could have added that it's known the Loch has a very low quality of life. There's only a minimal supply of eels, arctic char, salmon, and undersized trout to support the beast and its family. It's also curious that nobody has found bones or carcasses. That isn't a proof the monster's a fantasy."*

"Expect damn thing doesn't exist. Wild goose chase. No clear evidence of existence," Ari answered, with irritation.

"Come on! It's hardly surprising people haven't found solid evidence. The water's really murky because of the peat washed down from the neighboring mountains. The Loch's very deep too—as much as one thousand feet at the deepest point. Anyway, I've got a theory." Thinking back, Festus knew he should not have said that. Harold had reacted immediately.

"Oh, God! Henry has a theory. Naturally, there are numerous theories to explain each point. I've read that maybe there are only a few monsters and though the quality of life is poor, the Loch is more than big enough to support them. Some people believe there are extensive cave networks, connecting to the sea. The monsters live in them and have access to sea fish and distant breeding grounds. What's your fantasy?"

This time, he had been smart enough not to argue. However, in his opinion, most of these theories were either incorrect or at best, touched only lightly on the truth. He had replied, quietly. *"Interesting points, Harold. Are there other concerns?"*

"We'll look stupid," said Ari, loudly.

"I am prepared to look stupid on behalf of us all, Ari, and you don't have to come."

"Peace everybody," Zack interceded. *"You're forgettin' the purpose of the research. It doesn't have to work; it only has to be plausible. That's the point. You can fish or play golf, Harold...or..."*

"I'm not going," Harold said, stubbornly.

"Let's get back to the point. Why do you need the sub, Fes?"

"I'll need it to search for...maybe capture...the monster."

"Capture it? You're kidding! How the hell are you going to find the damn thing?"

"I've got a plan."

"Tell us about it!"

"I'm not ready, Zack."

"No explanation, no sub!"

"I've studied the sightings. I think there'll be a birth soon. I've decided to name the beast Hydro-phoenix Nessius.' It's a clue to..."

"If it's as large as its name you'll need a battleship not a sub," Alex laughed.

"How soon?"

"A year or so, Joe."

"Jesus Christ, Doc! Can't you narrow it down?"

"It took a lot of analysis to get it down to this decade."

"So! There's going to be a birth?"

"Creatures emit pheromones, particularly during that period. I plan to look for the monster's pheromones." Festus remembered being glad they weren't scientists. His reply had not been quite the truth, but it had been necessary to shut them up.

"If it's so obvious why hasn't somebody else done it?" Zack asked.

"It's not so obvious, and it wouldn't have been possible until recently. The development of the liquid chromatograph has changed things. Though it may be hard to get hold of one"

"Pheromomes or whatever, Fes? Liquid chromomomes? Nobody gives a shit about your Goddamn science! We need a project now! Let's buy the fucking sub!" Zack snapped, his face reddening.

"Thanks Zack."

Festus grinned at the memory of Zack's childish reaction, and gave Ionides an affectionate pat on the back. Ionides looked puzzled by the gesture, but smiled anyway. Festus could tell that he was enjoying his first trip abroad, and each bend in the road revealed something new. Ionides had not said anything, but Festus knew that this was no compensation for the absence of his girlfriend, Samantha Cronson.

Loch Ness is situated at the northern end of Glen Mor. It is connected to the sea, at the south, by the river Oich and the Caledonian Canal. To the north, the river Ness drains it into the Moray Firth. The City of Inverness, long ago capital of the Picts, stands at this junction with the Moray Firth. Its orderly rows of gray stone houses, set on the slopes alongside the Ness, rise up in a challenge to the weather that comes from the Arctic, across the North Sea, and hammers up the Firth. While to a casual observer—particularly a southerner—it is gray and fore-boding, it is in fact a comfortable and friendly place. Festus and his young cousin, Ionides, coming from far to the south, were very conscious of both aspects. For now, as they walked down towards the docks, the prison gray walls were a wel-come protection against the wind.

McDougall's yard had the job of modifying the submarine to meet the needs of the monster hunt. Argos 1 was in a converted aircraft hangar, a relic of some long forgotten flying boat service. Festus had been doubly lucky in getting per-mission to buy a submarine, and in hearing about a failed venture in the North Sea that had left an unwanted miniature submarine at the Vicker's yard in Bar-row in Furness. The dumpy, burnt-orange submersible squatted, gazing expect-antly at the doors, as if it were eager to get to the water. Extendable lamps, portholes, and the first of two clawed arms projected from the bow.

"Looks like a crab," Ionides had remarked to Hamish McDougall. "At least now it's a Texan color crab," he added, pointing at the fresh, burnt-orange paint.

Hamish, the younger partner at McDougall's, and Ionides had become friends, and Festus had decided that the three of them would be a good choice to man the submarine. Hamish was an ideal partner for the venture, not only because of his engineering abilities, but also because of his dual experience as an operator of underwater craft, and as a diver. Hamish would train them to scuba dive.

The fitters were working to attach a new device, which consisted of a tubular canister on the end of a moveable arm. Festus waited for Ionides to ask for an explanation.

"Okay. I'm a sucker for saying this, but what the hell is that Rube Goldberg device?"

"I'm glad you asked. That brilliant invention is a self-propelled net. It has a range of a hundred feet underwater and it can be opened remotely. We'll use it to trap the monster."

"How does it work?"

"The net is in that canister at the end of the arm. It's bunched up into a ball and surrounded by an airtight bag, with a quick-release seam. The bag will be pressurized. Following ejection from the canister, it will be propelled at the target by a small compressed air turbine. As long as the bag is closed, it will move rapidly through the water. It may be opened, either by a signal from the submarine or by a sensor if it hits something before the operator can react. When the bag is opened, the net blows out like a flower, enveloping what ever is in front of it. A short time later, it's pulled back in by a drawstring and closes around the netted object. When they've got it all rigged, we're going to take it out in the Firth and try it against an underwater target." Festus turned to the foreman. "Will it be ready by next week?"

"Yes, *sorr*, but the other arm is *nae* finished yet."

"Don't worry about it! More important to do it right." Festus continued his inspection of the submarine. Like most engineers and scientists, he treated all his new toys with the persistent attention of a child. He overheard the foreman talking to Hamish. "They're all the same *sorr*, these scientists, him more than the rest. Can't wait to try it out. I'll *hae* to reschedule Charlie to do the welding. I guess we have to humor him?"

Hamish smiled. "Keep him happy, or he'll get even more impatient. We'd better recheck that the dolly and crane can be used to launch the sub."

In fact, they had to wait for two weeks, because the weather closed in, and the waters of the Firth were too choppy to risk the trials. Ionides and Festus spent the time, touring around the Loch, looking for a base from which to work. They had not been successful in finding a base close to Inverness. Festus had not told Ionides, but he was facing up, reluctantly, to following a suggestion of Marienna's.

They were returning to Inverness on General Wade's military road, which runs along the eastern side of the Loch from Fort Augustus at the south to Dores at the north. They were about half way between Inverfarigaig and Dores, on a stretch of road where a line of firs blocked their view of the water, when Festus prodded Ionides. "Stop the car!"

"You want to contribute to the precipitation?"

"No. I want to investigate a track back there that heads toward the Loch. It looks unused but, in fact, there's a house at the end. Marienna bent my ear about it."

Ionides turned the car around and they drove down the track. Beyond the trees, there was a large area of uncut grass reaching down to the water. Positioned to their right, and fifty yards back from the water, was an old Victorian house with stone walls and a slate roof. The white paint on its window frames and door was discolored. The flowerbeds were running wild; the roses were overgrown and falling away from the porch. It was late in the year and a few flowers, with long, spindly stems, remained, peering out of the undergrowth. They parked the car and walked toward the lake, passing stables, which Festus eyed appreciatively. A sturdy boathouse and a small dock extended over the rocks to the water. The wind had dropped and the drizzle had abated, temporarily, and from the dock, they could see to their left, across the Loch, the ruins of Urquhart castle and the little bay leading to the village of Drumnadrochit.

"This place is perfect, isn't it?" Festus asked, mainly to himself.

"Sure is."

"It seems to be derelict. I wonder why Marienna thought her friend still lived here?" he muttered. Festus took one last look across the Loch, in the hope of seeing a disturbance in the water, but it remained irritatingly flat. Looking up from the water, he saw some sturdy brogues, a long tartan skirt, and a high-necked blouse covered by a wool cardigan. They clothed a tall, aristocratic, elderly woman. She was leaning on a shepherd's crook. She waved it at them.

"What are you and your cohort doing on my land, young man? I do not take kindly to having my property described as derelict."

"My apologies, Ma'am. I didn't hear you come up. We've been looking, without success, for a house by the Loch for our studies. I saw your drive and took a chance on finding the place we needed. Y'all have a magnificent situation here, and a beautiful home. I am Henry Festus and this is my cousin, Ionides Festus. We're visiting from Texas."

She looked at them, intently. "Did you say Festus?"

"Yes Ma'am."

"My hearing is not so good any more." She paused, looking undecided, and then nodded her head to no one in particular, as if she had reached an agreement with herself. "I have been expecting you. I will…"

"What?" said Ionides, sharply. "Sorry Ma'am you surprised me."

"But not your cousin, Dr. Festus."

"How did you know?"

"Come back to the house! I will give you a tour and then we'll have tea and you can tell me about your studies. Possibly, when you see inside my house you will understand how I know who you are, and why I invited you in instead of throwing you off my land. I am Georgina MacLeod…Mrs." She gestured imperiously at him. "You may take my arm!"

Inside, the house was in better condition than the outside, though most of the rooms had an unlived in, musty, feeling. Like the house, most of the furniture was Victorian in style, with white antimacassars protecting the chair backs in the living room. The decor of the study was surprisingly different. The furniture was Spanish in character, the chairs covered in leather, embossed and with brass studs. On the wall were horns and stuffed heads of various animals.

"Please sit down in here, while I make the tea. You should feel at home."

"It's like Zack's den," Ionides whispered. Look at those paintings of western scenes!"

"I think that's a Salinas over there. See the bluebonnets and Indian paint, dotting the field?"

"She's been to Texas, hasn't she?"

"Yeah, and met Marienna, during a Festival."

Ionides looked irritated. "If you knew that, why didn't we come here straight away, instead of stumbling all over Inverness looking for a place? This is great?"

In truth, Festus did not know why he had been reluctant to take Marienna's advice. Was it because he felt she was manipulating him? Or, simply, that he did not like taking instructions? "I wanted to see for myself. Marienna's too pushy sometimes. I didn't fancy being stuck with one of her old buddies. Maybe she was right."

Mrs. MacLeod returned with scones, a trolley of cups, plates, butter, strawberry preserves and tea. Festus smiled at her, gesturing at the paintings. "I assume you bought those in Texas, Ma'am."

"In fact, I lived in Texas, briefly. It was my husband's home. He was born in Scotland but immigrated to Texas as a boy. He lived and worked there and made his fortune. We two old people met by chance when he came to Scotland during the war. For my sake, he retired to this home of my family. He died here. I keep this room as he liked it. You are honored to be the first gentlemen to enter since he died."

"Where did he live in Texas, Ma'am?"

"Houston but eventually he settled in San Antonio. Not so far from your hometown."

"Yes Ma'am."

"We visited Argos. That's where I first met your aunt. No, your half-sister I believe. The age difference confused me." She smiled. "I took to Marienna immediately. She has such an interesting background, coming from Greece and writing those plays."

"When did you visit Argos?"

"It must have been in 1946. We were on our honeymoon. We came to a festival, and saw a play. My husband and I went backstage to congratulate the director, and that is when I met Marienna. We have corresponded erratically ever since. I can still recall images of the Greek gods and goddesses in that wonderful setting of Samaria canyon." She paused. "My husband enjoyed the bawdiness. Was either of you in it? I recollect that all the parts are played by locals."

"I think Ionides would have been too young, and I didn't take over the role of the smith-god Hephaestus, from my father, until 1948. I'm still playing it. You know, Ma'am, it's a pleasure to meet someone who has actually visited Argos. I've the impression that the only people who know of our existence, outside of Texans, are those who've read that old National Geographical article on Argos County."

"I am acquainted with that article."

"You said the first time you met Marienna." Festus sounded surprised.

"Yes, she often stays with me when she is in Europe. I recall that, recently, she was in southwest England and was then going to the Continent."

"Oh, I remember now. She did the grand tour last year. Came back with all kinds of souvenirs. Gave Aristotle's wife a ghastly statue…a Cornish Piskey, she called it. It's in their front yard. Ari hates it. But, of course, that was the point of the gift." Festus chuckled.

"I recollect that she then went on to Italy and Greece…that is Crete." Mrs. MacLeod paused, and then added, using her deliberate manner of speech. "Now, your visit has occurred, apparently, as a result of some studies you are making. She smiled. "Can you tell me more?"

Her amusement stimulated Festus to tell her about the Trust and how he planned to hunt the Monster.

"A submarine! Do you really have to hunt that poor beast?"

"Yes Ma'am. I think we do. If we can track her down and understand how she survives here, then, hopefully, we can act to prevent anybody doing anything harmful. As long as it is unclear whether she exists, it is possible that someone will do something foolish, changing the natural balance of the Loch."

"You used the word 'she' as I did. Do you have some idea about her?"

"Yes, I do. I think I understand how she survives. I've studied the records of sightings and I think there's a pattern to them. Soon, maybe within a year she'll make a transition. I'm guessing it's the best time to find her"

"You act as if there's only one monster. Surely there must be at least two of the species?"

"Conventional wisdom would say so."

"You have a different view?"

"Let me just say I've got some new ideas."

"You seem very confident."

"In research you've got to be confident, Ma'am, or you'd never start. In reality, I'm scared stiff. I hate to fail, and I've surely stuck my neck out on this one," he replied, not sure why he was making such an admission. Ionides nearly choked on his scone, as Festus expressed a lack of confidence.

"Realism is a key to success my husband used to say. I am sure you will succeed. The thought leaves me with mixed emotions. It may take much longer than you think," she added, showing a remarkable prescience.

"I will not ask you now what your ideas are, but I hope that when you and your party are staying here, I will be able to understand them. I assume that you do wish to use this house as a base for your operations?"

"Does that mean that we may buy this property?"

"Oh no, young man! I do not know what Marienna implied, but this is my house. You may stay here as guests. It is time I came out of mourning, and having you young people around will be the tonic I need. Obviously, I realize that the house and gardens need some work. We Scots are known for being canny in business, you know. I would hope that your Trust might see fit to make some improvements. Do we have a…a deal?"

"Yes Ma'am, I think so. You do understand, I hope, that we would need to rebuild the dock for the submarine, and I guess convert the stables into laboratory areas. Also, I don't quite know how to say this, but…er…we may need to add to and improve the bathrooms."

"I see. You will need to work out the details with my lawyers. Now, tell me what Texas is like today."

The days passed quickly. Festus returned to the house for final discussions and, as Mrs. MacLeod had indicated, she and her lawyers did strike a canny bargain. The Trust would pay a monthly rent for using the house, starting in October. She would arrange for a cook and other staff to look after the Texans. The monthly cost would be renegotiable after one year, if the search should extend that long. In addition, the Foundation would pay for refurbishing the dock, the conversion of the stables to laboratories, and for modification and improvements to the house and grounds. On her part, she gave them complete freedom of the house, buildings and grounds, except for her late husband's study and her own quarters.

Christmas was approaching, and Mrs. MacLeod and Festus were sitting in the study—sipping tea with milk, which he did not like very much, and eating scones and strawberry preserves, for which he was acquiring a taste.

"Please pardon an old lady for prying, Dr. Festus, but you seem preoccupied and, if I may say so, unhappy. Your cousin Ionides seems out of sorts too. Surely you are both enjoying your studies?"

Her question surprised him and he sat in embarrassment, drumming his fingers absentmindedly on the arm of his chair, as she repeated it.

"I'm very sorry, Ma'am, I was day dreamin'." He decided to concentrate on Ionides' problem. "Ionides has this girlfriend, Samantha. I know he misses her. It's selfish of me to keep him here at the moment, though I will need him later."

"How about you then, Dr. Festus?" Mrs. MacLeod prodded gently. "Is everything all right with you?"

He shrugged. "I miss my family. My wife, Dawn, is in Texas with our daughter, Pandora. However, I enjoy my work. I find it hard to take care of both, and my priorities may be wrong. Hearing you reminisce about the happy times with your husband, struck a chord." He didn't know why she was able to affect him like Marienna could, but he felt obliged to answer her. Festus continued, reflectively. "I guess I'm inherently selfish, when I'm doing projects that interest me. Unfortunately, most successes seem to have a price. The trick is obviously to strike a good balance. I'm not good at it." He paused in embarrassment. "May I have another of your fabulous scones?"

"You may, and let me say this. Since you understand the problem, I cannot believe that you are entirely responsible for any troubles you have. One word of caution from an old lady, though. The children are the most vulnerable. I haven't met Pandora, so I can't comment on her needs, but you should send Ionides back to his girlfriend," she paused, for emphasis. "It is not in my nature to interfere, Dr. Festus, but you too should go home for a spell. It will soon be Christmas. A man should be home with his family."

"You're right. Ionides has a few more tests to carry out, before I can send him back to Texas." Festus continued, speaking mainly to himself. "I must make my hunt successful. I can't afford to fail in this…this Labor. I can only go back to

Argos for a short time. There are so many things to do here, but I guess I should go back too. Anyway, I need to put my friends in the picture, personally."

Festus returned to the Yard. He decided to wait to tell Ionides of his decision to send him back, until the test of the submarine was completed. In the meantime, he kept Ionides busy, completing the work needed for the test. His main task was the construction of a model monster for use as a target. He had asked for the test to be made before the interior fittings of the submarine were complete, feeling there would be plenty of time for that work later.

Saturday, the day of the test, eventually arrived. It was a calm day and a low mist clung to the surface of the Firth. Festus watched as the orange submarine was lifted by a jib crane and swung out over the water. Two anglers, rowing out of the dock area, saw the strange sight of the disembodied submarine descending like a flying saucer into the water. They stopped rowing and stared in bewilderment at this apparition.

It took another hour for the motor boat to tow the submarine slowly out of the dock area and down to a small bay. On the way, they passed the anglers, who waved half-hearted manner of people who did not appreciate an intrusion on their fishing grounds.

"The water here is much clearer than in the Loch, Fes," Hamish commented. "This mist will be useful. It'll reduce the visibility. Of course it doesn't help when you're trying to find a small buoy!" He circled the boat a few more times before they found it. "Fes, as you wanted, the model is down at a depth of about fifteen feet. Ion has painted a face at each end so, hopefully, we'll be able to see it. Come on, Ion, let's get after your monster."

Hamish handed the controls of the boat to the foreman, and he and Ionides boarded the submarine. Festus watched them close the hatch, as the foreman backed the boat away. They sat in silence, the rotund foreman, taciturn; Festus silently bound up in his impatience. He had wanted to operate the net himself, but had seen the expectant look on Ion's face and suggested that he do it. In the meantime, the anglers reappeared, drifting and fishing. Eventually, the submarine moved and started to submerge. Its light from its searchlights was visible, dimly, through the water. The next event was not what Festus had planned.

Ionides told him later what happened. Hamish managed to maneuver the submarine towards to face the model monster. It was turned sideways and one of the faces, painted by Ionides, leered idiotically at them. Ionides aligned the canister on the face, and set it for an automatic opening on impact. He fired! The net enclosed in its bag, shot out of the canister propelled by the blast of the compressed air and the turbine. Unfortunately, it did not travel horizontally, but rose rapidly toward the surface of the water as it progressed. It bounced off the top of the model monster and shot to the surface, opening as it went.

Festus watched in amazement as the net billowed out like a great flower and enveloped the boat in its fine mesh. The drawstrings operated automatically, and left the anglers struggling helplessly.

"Damn! Why didn't it work?"

"It did Dr. Festus. Indeed it did," the foreman chuckled. "You got *yuirself* two beautiful monsters. Oh! My sides…Just listen to *em*! What a sight, I…" He had to stop, he was laughing so hard.

In the submarine, Hamish could tell from the taut line that they had caught something, but it was clear from the angle of the line that it was not the monster. He brought the sub to the surface and opened the hatch, to be greeted by a storm of abuse in raw Scots. After a moment, even the prisoners were laughing! For good reason, the net had brought with it a present of a few fish.

"Ah well! Back to the drawing board," the foreman muttered. "It's lunchtime. Pub's open. A wee dram of whiskey wouldn't hurt any of us while we dry out these *puir* gentlemen."

The pub had a few customers at the bar. A middle-aged woman with peroxide blonde hair and a full figure was warming herself by the fire. Her sharp eyes brightened at the infusion of new talent, and she made a great show of moving to accommodate them, trying to start a conversation. Unfortunately, she concentrated on Festus, as an obvious foreigner and the most likely candidate.

"*Wudya git me a wee drink, dearie,*" She smiled. Her teeth were uneven and tobacco stained.

Festus shrugged and turned his back, indicating that he could not understand her, which was nearly true. He was both repelled and, to his horror, illogically aroused by the sexual advances of this caricature of Dawn. Hamish, seeing his discomfort, changed places and was able to dislodge her. She moved to the bar, muttering angrily to herself.

The incident disturbed him. He had immersed himself in work, suppressing thoughts of sex. The chance meeting with this apparent prostitute had aroused erotic images of Dawn. He concentrated on his beer, whiskey, and sandwiches.

The foreman, mellowed by the whiskey, unwound and related numerous fanciful tales. Festus could see that the whiskey was making Ionides steadily more morose. "Ion, I have to go back to Texas for a few weeks; to brief Zack, and help make travel arrangements for the full party that will come here in late spring. I'm looking forward to spending Christmas with Dawn and Pandy." Ionides looked forlorn. Festus smiled. "Oh, incidentally, thanks for your help. You won't have to stay in Scotland. There are things I need done at Olympic Services. Just be ready to come back in May."

Ionides stood still for a moment, interpreting the message, and then he let out a loud whoop and ran out of the pub, performing an odd Indian-like dance.

"I've seen whiskey have strange effects," grinned the foreman, "but I've never seen anything like that before."

The two damp anglers looked at each other, communicated silently, and sidled out. Festus watched them leave, glancing surreptitiously at the woman. She gave a knowing look.

Festus and Ionides flew back to Texas, just in time for Christmas 1959.

5. The Hunt

Festus returned to Scotland in January. Christmas in Argos had started well. Pandora had met him at Austin airport, long blonde hair flying. In her face, burgeoning breasts and elegant legs, she was beginning to show some of he mother's beauty. Dawn had been affectionate, clearly pleased to see him. They had talked and laughed a lot, and their sex life had been formidable. Yet, over the few weeks of his stay, her unhappiness with life seeped out. Pandora was behaving like a typical adolescent; insecure, she agonized over her appearance, and her weight. Her pretty face was marred by a perpetually sulky expression—a mark of her insecurity. Dawn resented having to take all the pressure of this transitional period. As the only parent present, she had become the immediate focus of Pandora's misery.

Feeling trapped, alone, and lonely, Dawn had turned to her adopted family for reassurance. She had explained what little help they had been. Festus remembered listening to the unloading of her unhappiness, realizing how he had contributed to the problems but not knowing what to say.

"Zack is too busy."

"As for my sisters, they're too bound up with schoolwork and, besides, they've resented me from the day Mom and Dad adopted me."

"Come on! You're being unfair. Marienna always says nice things about you. Like yesterday, when she helped me work out a fix for the problem with the net."

"Sure Fes, when you're around. Don't trust her. She's a scheming old bitch."

Festus had not realized the level of discord. 'Surely you don't feel like that about Angel?'

"I guess not. You know, she's a bit odd. Those clothes and stuff."

"What about Ari?" he had asked, tentatively.

"Ari tried, but he's so demanding." She did not elaborate. Festus had felt uneasy hearing the comment, but he had not questioned her.

"Anyway, Ari's wife, Yianna, hates me, and so Ari is not available often. Against Yianna's objections, Ari has pushed Samantha onto Pandora."

"Sam's nice," he had said.

"Yes, but what about her brother Demos he's weird. He always seemed to be hanging around, and Pandy is so impressionable." Dawn replied.

That had worried him too. She had continued, saying that only her older brothers, Panou and Georgiou, had ever really cared for her, and Georgiou had died when she was little, and Pan didn't live in Argos anymore. Festus had held her as she wept deep, wracking sobs; feeling helplessly inadequate to deal with the problems. The thought that he should give up the hunt had crossed his mind, but he had rationalized it away, quickly, arguing to himself that he couldn't let down the Trust. In truth, he had been waiting to find the Loch Ness monster nearly all of his life. He decided that Dawn would have to cope a little longer, but it was hard to forget her impassioned outburst.

'I'm not just a pretty toy, I've got brains!'

Heaven knows it was true, Festus had thought. Dawn was smart enough, but had not managed to apply her talents. Before they were married, her family had kept her in Argos. Festus wondered sometimes whether Dawn had married him to get out. She had been taking courses in Liberal Arts at the University of Texas, when they were first married. Then, shortly afterwards, they had moved to California, where he had obtained his Ph.D. in the College of Engineering at Berkeley. Dawn had continued course work at a local college until Pandora's birth in 1945. She had not completed a degree.

Festus had turned the discussion to the upcoming trip to Scotland in the summer, and to suggestions about how Dawn might return to college on a part time basis, to finish her degree.

"You've got a real gift for interior design. Why don't you get back into that?"

"Fes, the work's sporadic. I only have a few friends who want help in remodeling. I'm tired of redecorating our house. You know what people say about me."

"Yeah, I suppose," said Festus looking at the den, rearranged yet again. "Then, why don't you go back to college and get a degree."

The idea of college resonated with suppressed longings. Dawn began to apply herself to the task of finding courses at the University. She seemed to be satisfied, at least for the time being.

Pandora was another matter. For the first week, she had clung to his side, endlessly asking about the hunt or gossiping about her friends. She had seemed excited about the foreign trip. Then, as he began to take more time to handle Dawn's problems, Pandora seemed to distance herself from him. Festus would see her sitting quietly, looking wistfully out of the window or, apparently, deeply immersed in a book. He was relieved, choosing to believe her quietness to be a sign that she was content, and not recognizing the sign of depression. Festus was impatient to try his new ideas, and left shortly after the New Year.

Back in Scotland, in his quiet moments a feeling of loneliness overwhelmed him as he looked ahead to the dreary winter months he would spend without his family. Though he suppressed the thought, he was scared of failure. Georgina MacLeod provided encouragement. It was like having a clone of his godmother to talk with. She too seemed lonely and they provided company for each other.

"What on earth is that contraption, Dr. Festus," she exclaimed, pointing at the net launcher. It was the first time he had persuaded Mrs. MacLeod to come to the boatyard.

"That's the canister that holds the net," Festus replied.

"Oh, I see. The one with which you captured those fishermen." Mrs. MacLeod chuckled. "I wish I had seen it. Do you think you will do it again?"

"Not by accident," said Festus, thoughtfully. "The problem was that the compressed air was causing the net to rise to the surface before it hit its target. We fixed it by putting some fins on it and angling the launch down a bit."

"We?"

"Your good friend Marienna helped me," Festus said. Mrs. MacLeod, smiled.

"We also have the remote handling arms operable. This afternoon, I'll try them out. It'll be my first lesson in piloting the submarine. That way I can be a back up for Ionides."

Meanwhile, the builder remodeled the interior of the house, repaired the dock, and converted the stables into laboratories. All the subsidiary equipment arrived. Festus spent much of his time unpacking and checking echo sounders, underwater cameras, scuba diving equipment, and his prize possessions, a used liquid chromatograph, bought from a research laboratory, and a mass spectrometer. He also pottered around in the garden, preparing a flowerbed in the front lawn.

The day arrived for transporting the submarine from Inverness to the Loch. Festus had discussed it with Hamish McDougall.

"I've been over it a number of times, and I reckon the transporter should just be able to negotiate the drive from General Wade's military road to the boathouse. What do you think?"

Hamish shook his head. "It looks awful close."

"It'll be okay," Festus replied confidently. Fortunately, Hamish remained less confident about the venture. To ensure success, Hamish had small modifications made to the drive—a tree removed here, an extension to the hard surface there.

By now, the press, both local and national was aware that a new monster hunt was on. Numerous jokes were made about this Texan madness. However, one astute reporter for the Financial Times wrote an article, pointing out the possible tax benefits that could accrue from indulging in even whimsical scientific projects.

The reporters were present in force when, finally, the transporter arrived at the Loch. Mrs. MacLeod and Festus walked behind it as it started down the driveway.

"Oh, my goodness. Do be careful!" Mrs. MacLeod cried, as the unwieldy vehicle removed shrubs and trees not anticipated by Hamish. "Dr. Festus, I am disappointed in you and Mr. McDougall. I had not expected this level of destruction. Look what it has done to that poor rhododendron."

"I'm truly sorry, Ma'am. Its turning circle is worse than I expected," said Hamish, who had just joined them. Festus, seeing that Hamish was dealing with the problem, muttered that they would replace the bush, and hurried down to the dock. Shortly afterwards, the submarine arrived at the water's edge and a crane lifted it off the transporter and lowered it towards the water. The photographers took many photographs as Festus and Hamish tried, hurriedly, to clean off the branches stuck on its various appendages.

"Dr. Festus, shouldn't you be adding more of that most effective camouflage," a local reporter, laughing. "That orange paint is going to be a real giveaway to the monster."

"What's the reason for the color?" asked a reporter, new to the story.

"University of Texas at Austin colors," said Festus, removing a twig from one of the remote handling arms. "I'm an alumnus of that fine institution." He continued. "Ladies and gentlemen, this is a great moment for all of us. I've been fascinated by the legend since I was child. To be here in Scotland and at Loch Ness is just great. I'm only sorry my family and friends from Texas can't be with us. It's taken longer than we had estimated to get things ready and..."

"When will they get here?"

"We're planning for July. Now, where was I? Oh, yes. We would not have been able to achieve what we have without the help of Hamish McDougall and his crew, and, of course, Mrs. MacLeod, who has kindly allowed us to use her house and grounds. This will be the center for our activities. Mrs. MacLeod, please do the honors. Hamish, the champagne!"

"I name this craft the Argos 1. May all who sail in her have safe passage." Mrs. MacLeod broke the champagne bottle across the bows of the submarine.

The riggers lowered the small craft into the water. The orange blob floated, its window staring balefully at the crowd through the water, and its stern pointing across the lake at Urquhart Castle.

"Dr. Festus, that thing looks more like the monster than the Monster. Is this the Texan plan—to add a monster?" The reporter did not wait for answer. "More seriously, can you say something about how you plan to track the Monster?"

"That's a good question, sir. The short answer is modern detection techniques. I'll say more at the airport, when my colleagues arrive." Festus avoided saying more by passing the buck. "You should talk to the head of our Foundation, Zachary Cronson. He's responsible for everything."

"Dr. Festus, when we were at the sub launching, you said you'd tell us more about your plans for catching Nessie when your friends came." The reporter looked expectantly at Festus. "Well, the plane just landed. What's the story?"

"You'll understand more when they arrive," Festus replied, turning to watch the plane taxi to the terminal. "See! There they are." The Eurythesians, as he thought of them, were easy to identify, looking like they had been displaced from a western movie.

Pandora and his godmother emerged first from customs. A caravansary of equipment followed them. Pandora rushed into his arms. He hugged her. Marienna was smiling at the sight of his saturnine face framed in Pandora's streaming blonde hair. He tried to ask Marienna about Dawn. The tendrils of hair got in his mouth and brushed his nose. He sneezed, stopping Marienna's explanation about Dawn's absence. She was about to continue when the reporters intruded.

"Do the golf bags and fishing tackle have something to do with the hunt?" a reporter shouted, reaping laughter from the onlookers.

"This is Scotland," said Festus, as he watched the group disappear into the building. "The connection should be obvious."

"Which one is Zachary Cronson?" asked another reporter, after consulting some notes.

"Brown hair, probably wearing a white suit and Texan boots," replied Festus, looking around. "See! He's over there."

"Mr. Cronson, Press here, can you come over," shouted the reporter, muttering to Festus, "From our discussion, I had the impression he'd be taller." When Zack arrived, they surrounded the two of them and barraged them with questions.

"From the look of this sophisticated scientific equipment, sir, it would seem that you plan to challenge the monster to a sporting competition?"

Zack, laughed, and deflected the comment. "No, I can assure you that this is a serious scientific venture. We golf and fishing enthusiasts would be pretty dumb to come here for the whole summer, and not take advantage of your wonderful Scottish courses and lakes…what? Oh, lochs."

One of the reporters returned to the question of how the monster would be found, hoping that, with the other Texans present, Festus might unbend. "Could Dr. Festus tell us something about the techniques that will be used for finding the monster?"

"Well, gentlemen, you see it will be like this. Every day, various members of our group will be staked out around the lake, fishing. They will act as spotters. We all know how anglers can sit for hours contemplating their navels. Our fishermen will be equipped with hollow golf balls and drivers. When one of them spots the monster, he will write a note on a specially prepared piece of paper. He will pop it into a hollow golf ball and drive the ball towards his neighbor, shouting, 'monster ho!' as he does it. In addition to this approach, we also have a few odds and ends such as our submarine, support boats, echo sounders, underwater television cameras, and so on."

"As Doctor Festus has indicated, we do have hopes of locating the monster and if it seems appropriate, we will attempt to capture it for limited scientific studies," added Zack. "In these studies, we expect to work with the Royal Zoological Society, and of course with the local authorities."

"What if you don't catch it?"

"We will have enjoyed the golf and the fishin' and your wonderful Scottish hospitality." Zack glanced out of the rain-flecked window. "I'm hopin' the weather will cooperate. Thank you gentlemen. We'll see y'all later." He tipped his Stetson, indicating the end of the interview.

"Where's the snake oil, Zack, now's the time to sell a few bottles."

"Thank you sir. I shall take that as a rare compliment, comin' as it does from an old bullshai-it artist like you. Shall we join the ladies?"

Zack turned and faced the group, which had at last assembled around the mountain of luggage. "We're going straight to the house now. Is that right?"

"Not exactly. It's not far, but on these roads it will take a few hours, so we'll stop for a snack on the way." Festus grinned. "A side of Haggis washed down with whiskey should do the trick."

While they waited for a break in the steady drizzle to board the coach, Festus greeted his other colleagues. Joe Maximos grasped his arm warmly.

"Good to see you, Doc, and good to be here. The wife has been going out of her mind waitin' for the chance to play the Scottish courses."

Joe's wife was standing ten paces behind him, keeping an eye on some expensive-looking golf bags. She was a quiet woman who always blended into the background. Even though she was a native Texan, to the close-knit Cretan clan she would always be a 'foreigner'. Her main passion was golf and Festus could not recollect hearing her comment on any other topic except, maybe, her children. She repeatedly changed the color of her hair. This time it had a green tinge. Ghastly! He always had difficulty remembering her name. It irritated him and his brow wrinkled with the effort of recalling it…Mary Jane or something. It did not sound right.

"The rain does stop sometimes doesn't it?"

"Sure, Joe. At least once a month."

"Zack ain't gonna to like it. He's a warm weather person."

"Screw, Zack! He can just get used to it," Festus replied, looking around quickly to check that Zack was out of earshot.

"Right." Joe laughed.

"Right of what?" asked Marienna.

"Our great Leader, Zachary, will just have to get used to the rain."

"Where's Dawn?"

"Henry, she tried to call."

"Our telephone's been out of order. Couldn't she write or send a telegram?"

"You know Dawn doesn't write letters. She just found out that UT was offering a summer course she needed. She's taken an apartment in Austin to use during the week…to avoid that long, daily drive from Argos"

"Shit! How am I going to look after Pandora and do all my work?"

"I'll watch after her, Henry. Don't worry about it."

Festus mumbled his appreciation. The appearance of Ionides stopped further discussion.

"Hi, I've got something to stir up Hamish McDougall." He waved his bottle of bourbon so excitedly that it slipped and smashed on the pavement.

"It looks like gravity has saved Hamish from his fate."

"Oh shi-it!" said Ionides. Then his face brightened. "I've got reserves in my golf bag." He picked up the glass and disposed of it in a trashcan, did a small dance, bowed to the spectators, and rushed off to help load his precious possessions.

A number of hours later, having passed through the ominous Glencoe to Fort William, they were following General Wade's road on the south side of Loch

Ness. The weather had cleared and the Loch lay calm and still before them. The Texans crowded to the windows, causing the coach driver some problems.

"Can there really be a monster?"

"Sure, and we're going to find it," Festus answered.

Joe looked at him. "You talk like you know something. I'm here to help, but I still cai-in't take it seriously."

Festus looked enigmatically at him and shook his head. "Have faith!"

A short while later, they pulled into the drive of Urquhart View House. The gardens had been re-planted and a lawn now stretched from the front of the house, down around a few grand trees, to the Loch and the boathouse.

Mrs. MacLeod came out and embraced Marienna, who introduced the rest of her guests. She took them in for tea. As they were entering the house, Zack took his arm. "I think we should have a few words privately, Fes. I'd like to get an up-to-date picture."

Festus escorted him upstairs, happy to be able to talk about their successes. "It's all coming along very well, Zack. All the equipment is here now. We tested the sub, successfully, in the Moray Firth. It's ready for its final tests in the Loch. The support craft are ready. All the road transports are here. We leased a couple of cars and some bicycles and mopeds to use in distributing people around the Loch." He paused to grin at Zack, gesturing at his waist. "That should get a few of you in shape."

"My dedication to science, Fes, is such that I'm prepared to spend hours contemplatin' the surface of the lake. The idea of pedalin' all around it, however, doesn't quite seem to have the same appeal; further, Elena says she prefers a man of substance." Zack paused, and looked out of the window, studying the garden idly. It was raining again. He peered more intently at the central flowerbed as if it had a strange look, shaking his head in irritation that it did not come into focus. "There still seems to be some activity going on around the house. How do we stand on that?"

"The workshops will be completed in a few days. We had some delay with materials. We've prepared the cameras and recording equipment, and some of them have been installed around the Loch. We even have some preliminary data. Finally, all the staff is here and seems to be very competent. Mrs. MacLeod is doing a fine job of keeping them on their toes."

"Do we have to call her Mrs. MacLeod all the time?" Zack asked, petulantly.

"Not exactly. She indicated to me recently that it would be proper now, since we had known each other for some months, if I called her Georgina; but not in front of the staff. Who knows, if you stay long enough, she may extend the privilege to you." Festus replied with a grin.

"A snobbish landlady! Great! What about the cost?"

"We're keeping to our expected budget; slightly over if anything, I guess, due to the usual unanticipated problems. We got a great deal on an early model sub."

"How much, then?"

"Slightly more than I'd told you. Just under six hundred thousand"

"Shit! Dollars or pounds?" Zack looked startled.

"Dollars. Then the work on the house, payments to the shipyard and the rest of the equipment has cost about the same. I estimate by next autumn, we should be at close to one and a half million...dollars, including the travel expenses, operating expenses, and staff costs."

"How are your finances if we don't find the monster?"

"A lot of the money is tied up in the equipment. We should view it as an investment. Hell! We can always sell it. As for the rest, we can legitimately subsidize some of our travel expenses. So we'll get something back. We're in pretty good shape, I reckon; though, it would be bad if none of our ventures paid off."

"Tell me again, Fes, how do we justify this fishing as being part of a scientific project?"

"In two ways. First, we need watchers to give us a good idea of the general activity in the lake. Of course there's always a remote chance they will see the monster."

"Sure, but do they have to fish? How do we explain the fishing in the neighboring lochs and rivers?"

"We need the fish for comparison. I was lucky to be able to pick up a recent model, used chromatograph, and a mass spectrometer that will allow us to analyze as little as a millionth of a gram of a sample. Remember what I told you before? All fish, and probably all creatures, emit very particular chemicals, which identify them."

"Yeah, yeah, you said something earlier." Zack waved his hands in an irritated fashion, not wanting the lecture. Festus ignored the signs.

"In the case of fish, these are used to mark the way to the spawning grounds, and to bring the male and female fish together over what, in the ocean, can be vast distances. These chemicals can be identified at incredibly high levels of dilution. Now, while our understanding of these processes is very poor, we nevertheless have some idea of what type of compounds to look for. It's possible—a long shot certainly—that we might pick up some trace of the monster by this procedure. However, we can only determine this if we eliminate all the other types of chemicals detected. We'll attempt to do this by analyzing fish and eels taken from Loch Ness itself and from surrounding lochs and rivers. Either way, the 'revenooers' cai-in't prove otherwise."

"Do you really think it'll work?"

Festus was silent for a moment. "I don't know how to…"

Zack interrupted him, laughing. "Why don't you just stick with your first words? 'I don't know'."

"It's not like that," Festus expostulated, rising to the bait. "I'm cautious. This is research. Nothing's certain. If it were, why would we need to do it? We've got a hell of a lot better chance than those amateurs who've been thrashin' around, stirring up the Loch."

"Okay. Peace. As you explain it, we cain't lose anyway."

Festus looked out of the window. I can, it's my reputation, he thought, worriedly.

Zack passed on the information to Joe Maximos' wife at dinner, adding. "Obviously, the golf cain't be justified by any invention we can come up with, but certainly all we participants are entitled to some time off. Weekends and a few working days seem like a reasonable time for relaxation. Hamish has all that side of it organized."

At that moment, he realized what had seemed strange about the flowerbed. "Goddamn it Fes! Can't you ever be serious?

"What are you talking about Zack?" Joe's wife asked.

"Go look at that flowerbed in front of the house. The flowers spell FES WINS."

In deference to Mrs. MacLeod's old-fashioned ways, after dinner, the men retired to the study for a drink. Over a glass of remarkably good single malt, Joe also broached the subject of justifying the play side of the hunt. Even after hearing the answers, he was still puzzled. "It still seems incredible that Uncle Sam allows the Trust to pay anything for all this. Anyway, I'm not going to turn my back on it. This is the life for me."

"You did work for it, Joe, remember that! You'll work some more, too," Festus responded. I expect you're all suffering some from that tiring trip, so I'm going to give you maybe two days to recover, but followin' that we start work in earnest."

Festus had arranged a simple regime for the 'Eurysthesians.' Every day, they had to fish for a half day at the observation posts spread around the Loch. "Who knows? If you're lucky, you'll spot the monster," he said laughing.

The kitchen staff organized by that inseparable pair, Georgina and Marienna, prepared lunches and snacks. Half the weekends and the last week of their stay were free for playing the tourist. For most of them, it was relaxing, and the strange surface patterns on the Loch helped to sustain the belief in the monster's existence. Festus dutifully recorded all quasi-sightings.

Unfortunately, it rained remorselessly, until everything and everybody was damp. The purple of the heather covered hills and the green of the trees changed to a depressing gray. The whiskey bottle received greater and greater use. Zack Cronson was in a permanently foul mood. Only Joe seemed immune to depression. He sat, quietly fishing, occasionally playing his harmonica. On misty days, boat travelers passing close to him must have wondered if they were hearing correctly, as the "Eyes of Texas" floated across the water.

They brought all of the fish to the laboratory for analysis. Festus and Ionides extracted the various chemicals, and compared them with those found by the detectors. For amusement, Festus also analyzed the catches to determine who were proficient at fishing. Ionides lacked the patience, and Zack's mind was apparently on other things so that their catches were small. Elena Cronson and others in the group were faring tolerably well, and Joe and Mary-Beth Maximos were returning large catches. To compensate for the imbalance in performance, Festus rotated the participants around the various sites.

Pandora entered into the hunt with enthusiasm, fortunately, because Marienna neglected her totally.

"Look Dad!" Pandora thrust her catch in front of him. "Joe and I caught three fish."

"Great, honey!" Festus smiled. "Let me have the eel!"

"It's slimy. Yuck!"

"It's okay. I'll take it."

"What are you going to do?"

"Take a sample of its gut and test it for various chemicals."

"Can I watch?"

"Sure, if you'll let go of my shoulder."

At first, he was amused by her antics. However, a tinge of irritation crept into his response as the results of his analysis became successively more confusing. As he gave her less and less of his time she latched on to her cousin Ionides, who kept her entertained. He was happy to have someone to talk to about his girlfriend Samantha.

Hamish took the submarine out for its final commissioning tests. These took very little time because of the previous work in the Moray Firth. For the amusement of the Eurysthesians and the staff of Urquhart View House, who had all heard from Ionides the story of the first trial, Festus arranged for a demonstration of the net. On one of the few days when the rain subsided, a stationary target was set up just below the surface a short distance from the jetty at Urquhart View. Hamish and Festus piloted the submarine into the Loch, keeping the hatch at the water line. In the meantime, Ionides took a dinghy and rowed Zack to where he could get a better view. Festus switched on the searchlights. Hamish turned the submarine slowly until Festus could see the target. He was about to fire when the bottom of the dinghy came into his field of view.

"A little to the right, Hamish...Yes, that's great. Hold it!" He fired.

Festus sat on the dock gazing across the Loch to where it was raining on Glen Coiltie. He'd been looking forward to showing off his work to Dawn and Pandora. It was bad enough that the results of the tests made little sense. Why, now of all times, did Dawn have to decide not to join him, but still send Pandora? Why did the University offer summer courses? They should give the faculty a break. An apartment in Austin too. He didn't like the idea. The rain clouds were drifting in his direction. He shivered. The surface of the water reflected a mildly choppy version of the advancing front. It gave him the impression that there was no water at all, merely a mirage. Like sightings of the monster, he thought, unhappily.

"This is a damn mess, Henry!" said Zachary, using his first name for emphasis. "Let's not waste any more money."

"Zack!" pleaded Festus. "I'm making good progress."

"Show me!"

"Come and look at the chromatograph outputs! They're very interesting."

"Screw the outputs! Where's the monster?"

"I don't know yet"

"That's the problem."

The search continued into mid July, with breaks for golf and touring. They caught and analyzed numerous fish and eels. Festus and Ionides tracked down the sources of many of the chemicals they had detected. The group consumed considerable quantities of scotch. However, after numerous dives they had not discovered large underwater caves and had made no sightings of the monster on the sonar screen in the support boat.

Nevertheless, at the end of a month, Festus was beginning to feel that he had some evidence for the existence of the monster, and on occasion some idea of where it might be. Unfortunately, as new results came in, this location changed.

"It's infuriatin', but typical of research," Festus explained to Zack. "You start with a theory which the first results don't fit. So you modify the theory as new results come in. In the end, you may well end up with what is in essence the original theory, but in some subtle way the basis for it is different." Festus took out a map of the lake. "The marks on the map show where we've had detectors, or fished, or traversed with the boats. We've got our measurements. As you can see there are traces that may relate to the monster, but the patterns, even after exhaustive analysis, make no sense."

"Well I hope you get somewhere soon. I can't piss away the time around here much longer," replied Zack, uncharitably.

He's still angry about the net, thought Festus, as he answered. "I'm doing my best. Research isn't simple."

"I know. If it were simple it would have been done," said Zack, doing a fair imitation of Festus's pedantic style of speech. "Do you still think you know what the monster is?"

"I don't think I know what it is, but I think I know how it is."

"Where's the most likely place for its lair?"

"Across the Loch under Urquhart Castle…I guess. A lot of sightings have been made there and it fits the data as well as anywhere."

Zack acted as if he had not heard the hesitancy. "Well then, go for it!"

"But I'm not ready."

"Ready or not, I'm up to here with this mess." Zack patted the top of his head. "Get everybody out! At least, we can film the hunt."

The attempt was doomed from the start. The submarine controls behaved erratically. The sonar stopped working for a time and, just when Festus, Ionides and Hamish had got the equipment repaired, the wind came howling down the Great Glen. Then it rained; sheets and sheets of viciously biting drops, which penetrated their oilskins and soaked them to the skin.

Zack stood the discomfort for two days before confronting Festus. "Time's up Fes. I'm turning into a fuckin' puddle. I can't afford to hang around anymore. I've done some sums. By adding existing footage of Loch Ness to our new material, we can fake up a movie. That'll be good enough for television. Then if we sell the equipment, like you suggested, we can recoup most of the Trust's outlay. Pity! But that's the way it goes."

"Zack. Let's not be too hasty to sell the submarine. I still think we've found something. I've got all the data I need. It's just that…Oh, hell! I don't know, there's something missing from my analysis. I'm sure in time I'll work it out."

"I don't know. We've got a lot of money tied up in that sub. Christ, man! We hardly used the damn thing! I'll think about it." Zack left, abruptly.

Festus turned back into his lab and slumped in a chair. With no sub, he was doomed. His godmother, Marienna, was the only one who could help. She had bailed him out before, but would she take on her half-brother Zack again?

"The only things I've caught are a ton of fish and two angry Scottish fishermen," he kicked the table in frustration as he waited for her answer, "and Zack." The memory brought a brief smile.

Marienna listened to him patiently. As she told Georgina later, *"From the moment Henry started explaining his problem, I knew what I must do. Henry must never guess my plans. I made sympathetic and encouraging noises of support, suggesting that in Argos he would have plenty of time to rethink the problem and prepare for next year's Play Cycle."*

"How did you deal with Zachary?" Georgina asked.

"I dressed carefully for the assault, wearing my most austere clothes, and tying my hair into a severe bun. I wore no make-up. I took Zachary by surprise. I lectured him in my most schoolmistress-like manner, on the need to protect the Cronson name, to protect the investment of the Trust, and to work to ensure the success of the hunt. I told him he should not sell any of the equipment."

"Did he listen?"

"I nearly messed it up when I told him he was getting back at Henry because of that business with the net—thrashing around getting more and more tangled. Poor Ionides, trying to calm him down. It took ten minutes to free them."

"What did he say?"

"Damn your precious Henry! Is that it? No way am I going to let all that money be tied up in useless equipment."

"Seeing that it was not having the desired effect, I played my trump card. Let me be blunt, Zachary, I said. If you don't leave the equipment alone I will tell Henry and Harold about your plans for Crete."

"Do you know what they are?"

"Only a little, but Zachary doesn't know that. He raised his hand as if he were about to strike me. I stared him down. His anger appeared to wilt as quickly as it had arisen.

"Okay, Marienna," he threw back his head and laughed. *"I don't know what you think you know. Just forget about it! Tell Henry he can store the equipment for a year!*

God knows what Harold will say? You deal with him! I have more important things to worry about. You win, as always. I really don't care." Then he stalked out of the room.

Georgina MacLeod let Festus leave his equipment at Urquhart View House—for a fee! Even her good friend Marienna could not talk her out of it. Hamish returned the submarine to the Yard for storage.

In September, Festus returned to Texas. For the first time in his life, he dreaded the thought of being in Argos. He had considered staying in Austin to work full time at Olympic Services, but Dawn had preempted this possibility by signing on for another year at the University. Neither of them was prepared to take Pandora out of the Argos school system. They had accepted the offer of Dawn's sister, Angelica, to take Pandora for the brief period between when Dawn went to college and Festus returned to Argos.

Festus always felt uneasy in Angelica's presence. The atmosphere was charged with some unspoken emotion. Angel was his age yet, with her athletic appearance, she seemed much younger. With her broad shoulders, narrow hips and long legs she was even boyish looking. She exaggerated that impression with her predilection for short hair, and a leaning towards clothes of a masculine appearance. Like many others, he had wondered whether she was a lesbian. He accepted that it was his turn to stay in Argos and look after Pandora, and that he would only be able to make limited visits to Olympic Services. His return started badly, again!

6. Austin

Aristotle Cronson was at Austin Municipal airport to meet his plane.

"What are you doing here?" Festus asked. "Where's Dawn?"

"Couldn't make it. Be back at the apartment later. Asked me to pick you up." Festus's looked bewildered. Ari hurried to explain. "In town, been doing some business for Zack. Dropped in to see her. Good thing. Was rushin' off. Offered to help."

"I see. Where do we go now?"

"To the apartment."

"Let's go."

The drive was short. Ari hefted Festus' three bags out of the car with ease, as if they weighed nothing, and strode up the stairs to the apartment. He handed over one bag while he searched for the key. "Got key from Dawn to let you in." He put it back in his pocket. "Must go now. She'll be back later."

Festus settled back in the chair, cradling the coffee cup in his hands. Its warmth was comforting; nothing else was. Why were there two tennis rackets in the hall cupboard, a man's clothes—Ari's perhaps—on a chair in the living room?

During the latter part of the Loch Ness fiasco, a state of depression had descended on him. Like a gathering fog, its tendrils had closed tighter around him, as he brooded over his failure. Now this. He was not in a state of mind to examine the evidence impartially.

Two hours later, when Dawn arrived, Festus had worked himself down to a new depth of misery. She was wearing sneakers, baggy linen pants, a loose, high-necked blouse, and a long blue jacket; a motley collection of apparel designed, apparently, to conceal her figure. She had pulled her thick blonde hair into a bun, and she wore no make up. He had heard that the look was the most recent extension of her efforts to get people to take her seriously. He wondered where it would end. In an all-encompassing baggy dress, like Afghan women wore, with only her hands and eyes showing. Of course, she would probably wear gloves and glasses too. Her face was flushed from tearing up the stairs. Despite the dowdy clothes, she looked good.

Dawn was sensitive to his feelings about the hunt, but her excitement about her recent successes at the University of Texas came first. She rushed into his arms, hugging him enthusiastically, and feeling to see if he was undergoing his normal reaction. He was not. She stroked him vigorously, whispering in his ear. "I have plans for you."

"Where have you been? I didn't expect to see Ari."

"I'm sorry darling. I had to see my professor. Ari had just dropped by on his way back to Argos. I was stuck. It seemed the simplest thing to do."

"Does he come here often?"

"No-oo. "She leaned back and looked at him. "You found his tennis racket, and tennis cloths, didn't you? What were you thinking? Zack's had him doing some project in Austin. Sometimes he has to work late. He's my brother."

"Adopted," retorted Festus, without thinking.

Dawn's body tensed and she let go of him, turning away. "What do you mean?"

Her drawn look startled Festus. Was it guilt? If so, he'd deal with it. For now, he was unsure how to interpret her expression, and changed the subject. "So the courses are going well?" He asked, smiling.

"Yes. I guess so," replied Dawn, uncertainly. "If I'm lucky, should be able to graduate by the summer."

"So, you'll be able to come on my next...er...Labor?"

"Sure, Hephaestus," said Dawn, recovering her composure. "What is it?"

"A secret."

"You're terrible! I don't know what you think, or even, sometimes, what era you're living in." She hugged him and this time he responded following her into the bedroom.

The winter months passed slowly. Dawn stayed at the University, returning to Argos on weekends. Festus remained in Argos, looking after Pandora, and occasionally venturing to Olympic Services in Austin, to work on the Eurysthesian Foundation's long-term projects. To relieve the boredom, he bought a polygraph and took training in how to use it. The polygraph was a critical part of his next Labor.

"You need to come to the Breakfast Club and tell us about your plans," Zack told him. "I know Joe has reminded you of the attendance rules."

"I will, but I need to be sure I can operate the polygraph properly."

Festus went to see his godmother. "I'm embarrassed by the failure at Loch Ness, and by the sarcastic descriptions of my work in the press. I don't want to go through that again."

"Henry, I can sympathize, but you'll have to face people sometime," said Marienna. "Why don't you start by giving a talk on Loch Ness to our Argos Ladies Society? I know they've asked you. At least you won't have to deal with Harold."

"Okay. Tell them I'll be at the next meeting!"

"Don't look so gloomy. Unless…that isn't the whole story." She looked at him, sharply.

"What do you mean?"

"That's not what is worrying you?"

"I guess not. Marienna, how can I balance my work and my family? Right now, it's not going well. I know it's my turn to look after Pandy. I know Dawn needs to "do her thing," but I'm frustrated that I can't do more on Loch Ness. I've thought a lot about the data. I'm convinced it holds the answers, yet something is missing and I can't identify it."

"It seems to me that, since Dawn is pursuing her career, you could spend more time on your research. You have too good a brain to waste it. Frankly, Pandora needs to grow up. Get her involved in your work!" Marienna counseled. "On the subject of getting out, why don't you go to the Kaffenion now? I hear that the regulars are upset you haven't been in for a chat."

Festus followed Marienna's advice, devoting more time to his work, and communicating reluctantly, with Dawn and Zack. He spoke to Ionides, only when he needed some work done at Olympic Services. With Pandora, he was less remote. They were companions by virtue of proximity, and he needed her to help in his study of the polygraph.

In the early spring, Festus was ready to rejoin the world, and arranged to talk at a business meeting of the Breakfast Club. While Ionides organized the slides, Festus watched Harold Dexter. He knew that Harold had heard bits of the latest plan in a secondhand way at the Kaffenion, and that he was upset that he had not been formally consulted. Harold was such a pessimist, Festus thought. He had been loud in his criticisms of the Loch Ness affair. Zack had explained the problem.

"Fes, he says it's an embarrassment to Argos. Secretly, I think Harold takes pleasure in the lack of success, because it makes you look foolish."

"Oh God! Why?"

"Harold resents your offensively superior attitude," Zack replied. "His words."

"You're kidding!"

"No. You've got; God knows how many degrees, including a Ph.D. Harold never attended college. So to compensate he reads voraciously. But, as we all know, his encyclopedic knowledge isn't a compensation for a formal education."

"I'm usually impressed, Zack."

"You're being kind. Most of us are sick of his interminable lectures, when he unloads sections of this library of shit on us."

"I can see what you mean."

"It's sad. Harold believes we look down on him. You know we don't. He's got a cold but steadily, logical mind. We just don't want lectures on subjects that don't interest us. It's a pity he feels that way about you. He tries to hide his snipin' behind some imagined cloak of affability. I think he has the naive belief that nobody has noticed. Fat chance!"

Zack had been right. This time, Harold was so angry he made no attempt at politeness. When the lights dimmed and he saw the picture of a dirty gray stone wall, he erupted.

"When are we going to stop this nonsense? I mean, what the hell is that thing? Do we really have to support Henry Festus in another of his damn fool plans? Haven't any of you learned anything from the Loch Ness fiasco?"

"I had a great time. I don't blame the Doc for the rain. What's the complaint? We'll get most of the money back, one way or another. Listen to the Doc! This one's a great idea," Joe replied. "Carry on Fes."

"That, Harold, is the Blarney Stone, which is part of the battlements of a castle in Southern Ireland. You're seeing a picture of the battlements, taken looking down. You can see the metal grill that's designed to stop visitors from plunging to the ground. The Stone is set just above it. It is said that anyone who kisses it, while leaning over backwards, will be given the gift of the gab." Festus stopped and grinned.

"You'll not get me to go to Ireland to kiss that thing." Harold thrust his jaw out belligerently.

"Not just you Harold. Everybody who comes will be given the opportunity to kiss the stone. We will encourage you to kiss it leaning backwards and forwards or even sideways, if it amuses you. Before and after these osculatory efforts we will test you with a polygraph—a lie detector—to find out if the Stone has any affect on your abilities. It could transform you into an even more charming and articulate person. Does that answer your questions?"

"I know what a polygraph is, Henry. I'm not totally uneducated." His audience applauded. Harold got the message and continued in a more conciliatory manner. "What I mean to say is…What are the benefits of this grand plan?"

"Surely there's something he likes?" Zack bent down and whispered to Joe.

"Fishing," Joe whispered back. "I've often wondered whether he carried on his dad's funeral business because the cemetery is by the river."

"Yeah, Harold's so gray looking, I forget he goes outdoors. I can remember seeing this ominous looking, black figure sitting on the riverbank, hunched over a fishing pole. You know, Joe, even as a child, he rarely ventured out without a large black Stetson."

Zack stood. "Not even if it means a subsidized opportunity to fish those fine Irish trout streams? You missed out on the Scottish trip. Which surprised us all. Come on Ion! Show him the pictures of those Irish rivers and lakes! I don't think you'll have to twist his arm much more, Fes. His will is wilting already. Okay everybody we need to hurry up, our time's nearly over."

Harold merely grunted, uncompromisingly, but his eyes followed the slides with interest.

Because of the longer time between Festivals, Marienna had arranged for the Play rehearsals to start early. Festus still had mixed emotions about playing Hephaestus. Nevertheless, rehearsals for "Hephaestus and The Cretans" were fun with attractive young Cathy Schmidt playing the mortal love interest of the god. Cathy was a colleague of Marienna's at Argos High School and seemed to be a particular buddy of his godmother's, despite their difference in age. She came from Lampasas. Cathy was often at Marienna's house when he went to help with fixing some problem and they had talked a lot about the plays.

"Watching you at rehearsals, I get the feeling you don't really enjoy your role?"

"Cathy, how can I put it?" Festus replied. *"On the one hand I was unhappy when the Festival and Play cycle was delayed a year. On the other hand, there's an element of masochism in doing the role. Hephaestus, is a key role but he's a non-hero, and his abilities are resented and mocked."* He hadn't added that it mirrored his own life; maybe that was why he related so strongly to the part. Even worse, Dawn played Aphrodite.

"You do it so well. When we're rehearsing, you are a Greek god, er…if you know what I mean?" Cathy looked embarrassed.

"Have you ever seen the karagiozi? *It's a popular Greek form of entertainment. We had it at the Festival one year."*

"I don't think so."

"Well, Karagiozis is a puppet made of goatskin and cardboard. Puppeteers manipulate him using long rods behind a backlit screen. Karagiozis has huge bare feet, a bulbous nose, a black moustache, and a hunchback. His right arm is longer than his left, giving the impression of a crab. He spends his time feeding his voracious appetite and belaboring Turkish foes, whom he outsmarts by lying, cheating, boasting, and stealing."

"Sounds like fun."

"It is. The kids love it, and laugh, but he's an idiot and that's what I feel I like."

"Oh Fes, you don't come across like this…Karag…"

Cathy had hugged him, and then stepped away quickly. He had gone back to repairing the light switch as if nothing had happened.

Festus continued to brood about Hephaestus, finally blurting out his unhappiness to Dawn. "I hate the way Aphrodite fools around with Ares and those other men in the plays. It's not fair to Hephaestus, even when he gets revenge. Don't you feel that too? You should know."

"No, Fes, I don't see it that way. You take us Cronsons far too seriously. Zack, Ari and I have hammed it up ever since we were kids. You worry too much." She smiled, hopefully.

Damn the Cronsons thought Festus, uncharitably, wishing that Dawn had been from some other family. Dawn was a born flirt. Did her relationship with Ari go beyond that? He had a fleeting image of the play with the couple entwined on the bed. Damn it! The evidence was there. He tried to turn his thoughts to other matters but, willfully, they returned to the performance of "Aphrodite and Ares" that had just ended. In the play, Hephaestus, returning from Scythia, discovers he has been made a cuckold. With the aid of a cunningly modified bed, he traps his wife Aphrodite with her lover Ares. From its premiere in 1930, this play had been immensely popular, particularly because of the special effects. It was viewed as too bawdy by some of the non-Greek audience, who tried to have it closed. They were unsuccessful in persuading the local judge to take action. Nevertheless, it left the play with a certain notoriety that did not hurt at the box-office. Some lines of the chorus were still ringing in his head:

This is a fine mess, and who can tell where it will end.
Hephaestus has exposed the lovers in all senses of the word.
He has proved his point but what good does it do him.
We will accompany the lady Aphrodite to Paphos.
There, she will renew her virginity in the sea.
If we are lucky, some of us may receive that privilege too.

Festus mentally exited the play with the chorus, though there was more to follow concerning the maneuvering of Artemis to ruin the marriage. Well! She's succeeded, he thought. What Hephaestus can do, I can do. Marienna brought him her customary after-performance drink, interrupting his thoughts. Recently, she had forsaken her trouser suits for embroidered Cretan style skirts and blouses. It was an age thing, returning to ones roots, he guessed.

"Good job, Henry. Try to be a little quicker with your lines. You spent far too long staring at the bed. You looked very convincing. What on earth were you thinking about?"

"Oh, nothing…I guess." He was lying, for he had seen the way in which Ari had surreptitiously managed to trap his hand on Dawn's left breast, out of sight of the audience. Dawn hadn't seemed to mind.

"You don't sound very convincing. I think you were upset seeing Dawn and Ari in that bed. You shouldn't be. Whatever happens is only acting. They've always been close. As I told you before, he was a pillar of strength in your absence."

"That's good to know." Festus replied, taking a long sip of the drink to hide the sinking feeling in his gut. Unwittingly, Marienna had confirmed what he feared. What he planned for Blarney would fix it. "I'll try to speed it up next time. Got to get changed."

"You'll be ready for the dance won't you?"

"Oh! The dance! Yes, I guess so." He wanted to say that he hated the so-called Royal Cretan Dance that Marienna had created some years earlier for the Festival, but she looked so excited about it, he couldn't. He always had difficulty remembering the pattern he had to follow on what Marienna called the dancing floor. With his impediment it was hard to get the timing right and avoid collisions with the dancers and acrobats.

7. Blarney

Festus waited impatiently at Shannon airport, watching planes tucking in their wheels as they left—like cats folding their paws, he thought. He'd worked hard preparing this project for the Eurysthesian Foundation. Now it was August, in the first year of Kennedy's presidency. He had talked to Marienna about this new Labor.

"Between you and me, I think it should be the Labor of the Nemean Lion. Though I can't see a good connection between going to Blarney and the capture and slaying of that poor beast by Heracles."

"Maybe the connection will become clearer when you complete it?" Marienna replied. *"In my experience these kinds of things work out eventually."*

"Since it's in Ireland I'll call it the O'Nemean Lion," Festus said as he watched her leave.

Now he was distracted by the memory and stood quietly, idly thinking of puns connecting the Labor to Ari Cronson—that conniving bastard! From there he turned to mulling over his plan. It would require careful timing, but he reassured himself, there was enough flexibility to cope with a wide range of possible outcomes. He nodded his head in agreement with himself.

"Did you say something Dr. Festus?" The burly, red haired man standing next to him leaned across to hear well.

"Sorry, Seamus. I was probably talking to myself," Festus replied. He had forgotten about his companion. Seamus O'Flaherty was a graduate of Dublin Law School, a county rugby player, a man involved in a number of enterprises that included being the new agent in Ireland for the Eurysthesian Trust. Festus was glad to have his help.

The plane bringing the Eurysthesians was now on the final approach. With a little jiggle, an adjustment of flaps to limit the rocking motion caused by the slight wind, it settled down on the runway. As it taxied towards the terminal, Festus pressed against the window, his forehead bearing on the glass, his hands clasped tightly in front of him. He prayed that the entire group had managed to come. No last minute illnesses or cancellations. The ground crew wheeled up the steps. He studied the disembarking passengers carefully. A group he didn't know—presumably some other charter organization—then Peri Dexter with Marienna Cronson, a start at least. Zack was involved in an important business deal and he and Elena could not come. That was not important. His plan required witnesses from Argos. It did not matter which ones. Ari Cronson, looking athletic as ever, bounded down the steps. A plump, dark-haired girl followed him. She waved. Festus realized with a shock that it was Ari's daughter, Samantha. How quickly they grow up, he thought. Damnation! Why had Ari brought her? Black-suited Harold Dexter appeared with Joe Maximos and with his wife…Mary Lou or something. It did not help that Joe usually referred to her as "the wife." What had she done to her hair? Orange! Surely, it had been blonde. Joe neatly dressed, as always, saw Festus, and doffed his Stetson.

Another unknown set of people emerged, and—he hugged himself inside—his wife Dawn on the arm of Alex Platon. The beautiful people, he thought, wryly, realizing that for the moment she was not attempting to disguise her good looks. Curious? As she walked towards him, he felt a surge of weakness, and held more firmly to the rail that crossed the window. Even from a distance, he could see the effect she was having on the men.

"Are you all right, Dr. Festus? You seem a bit faint."

"I'll be fine, Seamus. It's just my leg giving me a bit of trouble and I guess relief that my wife got here safely." He flapped a hand in the direction of Dawn.

Seamus resumed his watch of the arrivals. The ground crew had stopped working and caps pushed back, were staring unashamedly as the Dawn glided towards the customs area, leaving a trail of unfulfilled desires. She was wearing a thin dress, and the light breeze was molding it against her body. Her thick blonde hair fell across her face. She brushed a tendril away in a sensuous movement. Some weeks later, Seamus confided his thoughts to a good friend while they downed beers in a pub.

"You should have seen her, Patrick. Incredible! I didn't believe the Doc. 'Jasus', I thought, if that's the Doc's wife, I can understand why he has problems."

"So you fancy her then?" Patrick peered over his glass.

"Yes sir. You know, with my job an all, I imagined being in a 1930's private eye movie. She would be like the gangster's moll."

"And you'd be 'loik' the 'toff' private eye from LA then?"

"Yeah," answered Seamus, continuing with an Irish sounding American accent. "To say that she was sexy was like describing the blue whale as quite a large mammal. She moved, her arm snuggly enfolding the Capo's arm, her body pressed against him.

In her stiletto heels, she was as tall as her companion. He walked, apparently ignoring her, but stiff backed and self-conscious like a man with a pitchfork pressed against his backside."

"*You should be a writer," said Patrick. "Come on have another beer."*

In the meantime, the first of the Texans had worked their way through the immigration area, and were standing in a disorganized group, waiting for their luggage. After a slight delay, the bags arrived and following a frantic search for the women, lost in the bowels of the powder room, the Texans cleared customs and reached the main concourse. There, a large sign suspended from the roof proclaimed, "The Irish Republic Welcomes the Eurysthesian Trust."

Festus and Seamus were standing under it. Dawn rushed up and embraced Festus. Alex Platon interrupted her attempt to talk to him.

"Your assistant reporting for duty, Sir!" Alex was wearing a pale blue western suit, with a fancy shirt and bolo tie, held by an onyx and silver clip. He looked very handsome and elegant.

Samantha Cronson followed Alex. "I'm sorry Pandy couldn't make it, Uncle Henry. It would have been neat with her here."

"So am I, Samantha, but it wasn't convenient. She had...er..." He used Alex's presence as an excuse to change the subject. "Glad you could make it, Alex. I'll need the help. You'll need to change into something scruffier. If that's possible. I'd like you all to meet our agent, our good Irish friend, Seamus O'Flaherty. Seamus has set up the whole deal for us here and will assist you if you have any problems."

Seamus looked around. "Is all the party here?"

Harold Dexter, who was officiously shepherding people, answered. "All here."

Marienna Cronson looked at him pityingly. "Not quite, Harold. We seem to have lost your wife again. Has anyone seen Peri? I don't see Aristotle or Mary Beth either."

At that moment, Aristotle appeared from the customs area, staggering under the weight of a number of suitcases. Festus could not suppress a smile. Ari did not have his normal, well-groomed presence. With his long arms extended, he looked more ape-like than normal. Catching sight of the group he bellowed, "Might help, Henry? Presumin' not too busy. Could help with Dawn's bags."

A search party found Peri Dexter talking to Mary Beth Maximos outside the terminal. They were admiring a flowerbed in which the flowers were set out like a clock. "I can imagine young maidens tending the arrangement; fresh faced in their white tunics with flowers in their hair," Peri said, wistfully.

Mary Beth squeezed her arm. "You're such a romantic."

Seamus herded his flock towards the bus, made sure that they had all of their luggage. The bus followed a route that took them from Shannon to Limerick, and then on through Roth Laire and Mallow, on the Cork road, to Blarney.

"We have just entered the fair town of Limerick, and to celebrate your arrival, I have composed one," said Festus.

"Wonderful!" said Joe, leading the chorus of groans. "The main reason the wife and I came was to hear your poetry."

"Good. Then I'll recite it for you," Festus grinned.

"Twenty Texans went on a trip
They went by plane, not by ship.
Does one mean lyin' by blarney,
Was the question to answer?
Or simply a little tongue slip."

"The poet laureate of Argos strikes again," muttered Harold Dexter, sarcastically.

"Come on, boys, be fair. That was clever, though I must admit the scanning is somewhat contrived. And we are not twenty."

"Poetic license, Ma'am and, strictly, it should be I am not twenty."

"Henry, don't try to be too clever," Marienna snapped. Later on, she described to Festus how Aristotle had looked during the exchange.

"He was glaring at you, Henry. You should have seen his face."

"Why? What did I do?"

"Henry. You know he doesn't like you," Marienna replied. "And he is angry about the whole trip. I had a brief chat with that ghastly wife of his a couple of days ago. Aristotle did not want to come. Zack told him to. Then he wanted to bring that unpleasant son of his—Demosthenes. Nevertheless, Yianna insisted he bring Samantha instead. She didn't want Demos going abroad. They pamper that child."

"I don't think Demos likes me either," said Festus.

"Certainly not since Pandora refused to go out with him." Marienna laughed.

"I didn't know that. Good for her," Festus showed his relief.

"In private, Yianna admits that Demos is a little wild. She thinks it's a passing phase and it will go away when he goes to Stimpson College. She and Aristotle believe he will graduate with honors."

"Good luck!" Festus groaned.

The bus threaded its way along the Cork road to Roth Laire. It was one of those rare summers, which occurs maybe every seven years, when for most of each day only a few fluffy, friendly clouds obstructed the warmth of the sun.

"My, it's gorgeous. If only I could live here forever. I hope Harold will like it." Peri's expression changed. "Marienna, I'm worried the trip will bring trouble for Dawn and Henry. I tried to tell Harold but, as usual, he wouldn't listen."

Marienna looked amused, briefly. The rather strange existence of Peri and Harold was a well-known feature of Argos life. At least once a year in the spring, and usually for more than a month, Peri would escape from the home-cum-funeral parlor she shared with Harold, and visit relatives in Greece. "I'm convinced that when I'm away Harold goes downstairs to the store and sleeps in one of the coffins," she had confided once to Marienna, in an uncharacteristic fit of pique. Marienna spoke sharply. "You're so sensitive to everything, Peri, such a contrast to Harold. I'm sure you're wrong."

As they passed down the main street of Blarney, Seamus pointed out its key features. "There is a variety of shops and, I expect of interest to the ladies, a number of antique shops. Of possibly greater interest to the men, there are a number of pubs. We are just coming to the most interesting one, on your left." Heads turned obediently and swiftly to see this important institution. "You can see the sign with a painting of a yellow jar on it. That's the Brass Jar Inn and I recommend a visit. It's a typical Irish pub. A word of advice to the ladies. How shall I say it? It is more or less the custom here that women use the lounge or snug as it is called, rather than the bar."

Alex Platon nodded approvingly. Seamus spread his hands deprecatingly. "I don't make the customs, sir, but I have to tell you what they are." The first sight of Blarney castle saved him from the need for further defense of his position. "Ah! Now you can see the castle. Those gray battlements up ahead, peeking over the trees. We will be staying just outside Blarney. But, let me reassure you that, we'll be within easy walking distance of both the castle and the town."

At this point, the bus turned off the main road onto a gravel drive that wound around the fairways of a golf course to arrive at the nineteenth hole, a rambling country house.

"We have arrived at the South of Ireland Country Club and Hotel," proclaimed Seamus, grandly.

The South of Ireland Country Club and Hotel, known locally as the Club, was a converted mansion. The main building was of red brick construction, and from the seventeenth century. Around it were the outbuildings that now served as the golf pro-shop and clubhouse. The restaurant was in the clubhouse. At the back of the house was a manicured lawn, a formal garden in the English style and beyond it the golf course. The ground floor of the house had been modified to provide a lounge, a small library, and an area that could be used for dining and dancing, known grandly as the ballroom.

"Welcome to Blarney. Doctor Festus, some of your apparatus has arrived and we have started preparing the ballroom to take it," explained the manager. Festus introduced him to the Eurysthesian group and he fussed over each new arrival with a plethora of words that were a credit to the legend of Blarney.

While the manager was talking, Alex Platon was pointing out the virtues of the golf course to Harold Dexter.

"You can have your golf," Harold replied. "Look at that little stream and the lake. I reckon I could fish there."

"Sure looks like it. Not all bad then?" said Alex, smiling.

"I guess not," Harold gave a rare grin. "There was an undertaker back in town. Near the pub. That should be interesting too."

The manager noticed that people were starting to collect up their belongings. "Come, have some tea! *Whoile* McCarthy takes care of everything."

"Here we go again, McCarthy," he muttered as the Texans left. "We make a good profit from these American tourists, but is it worth the hassle? Iced water at every meal. The kids complaining that there aren't any hamburgers."

"Good tips," McCarthy, volunteered.

"You're right, but I worry about this lot. Dr. Festus seems reasonable, but wanting to check out the efficiency of the Blarney stone. Can he really be quite normal?"

"That Mrs. Festus looks normal."

"McCarthy, right to the point as ever. It'd sure be nice to be married to that one. Ah hell! I'd probably be her personal secretary. It deserves a little fantasy, eh?" McCarthy tapped him on the shoulder. Peri Dexter was watching him. "Yes m'lady, how can I help you?" he asked, still in his daydream.

"Kind sir, could you show me the way to the powder room please?" Peri asked, in the same vein.

Powder room? We have no armory, m'lady…Oh! I see what you mean. I'll take the ladies upstairs and show them the facilities," he said, recovering quickly. "Mr. O'Flaherty, please show these gentlemen the ballroom, restaurant and bar?"

"Fes, I feel a wreck after all that traveling and while taking tea sounds real nice, I think I'll have a bath instead." Dawn looked at Festus, hopefully.

"All right I'll see you later. I just want to explain the set up in the ballroom." Dawn made a face at him and left.

The men, following the hint of a drink, followed Seamus into the east wing of the house, to what was normally the ballroom. There were two sturdy wooden tables and some portable, Japanese lacquered screens on a small stage at the far end of the room. Beside the stage were the packing cases containing the polygraph, and associated equipment. The curtains were pulled back and, through the windows, they could see the top of Blarney castle rising above some woods.

"The working area will be on the stage, where the subjects will be hooked up to the polygraph. I will ask the questions. They'll wear earphones, to cut down the audience noise. Those Japanese screens will act as an additional barrier. We'll use closed-circuit television with projection onto a screen at the other end of the ballroom so that the audience can watch the proceedings without causing too much of a distraction." Festus turned to see if there were any questions to find that even Seamus and Alex were on their way to the bar. He called them back in a peremptory manner, and concluded his comments.

Festus worked for a time checking the packing cases to see that the last of the equipment had arrived. He delayed facing Dawn, fearing she would weaken his resolve to put the plan into action. Finally, as he felt more and more nervous, he stopped the work. Seamus and Alex watched him leave.

"He seems uptight, Mr. Platon. I guess it's excitement at being close to doing the tests."

"Maybe? It could be because Dawn's here. Oh! Call me Alex, Seamus."

"This business of Loch Ness. I read it in the papers. Does he really believe in Nessie?"

"Absolutely! He's been fascinated with it since he was a little kid. It's amazing how quickly he's got over the disappointment of not finding anything. I guess scientists are incurable optimists, unlike us lawyers."

"One other thing, Alex," Seamus sounded hesitant. "Miss Cronson said she wanted to talk to me. Do you have any idea what she might want?"

"Tough looking lady with gray hair." Seamus nodded. "I've no idea. Probably she wants help visiting somewhere?"

"Yeah. That could be it." Seamus smiled. He seemed pleased with Alex's response.

As head of the party, Festus had the suite of rooms—reception, bed and bathroom. As he crossed the reception room, he could hear Dawn splashing in the bath. He went over to the bed and sat down. He felt tired. He removed his coat and tie, and loosened his shirt, and finally took off his shoes. It was always a relief to remove the surgical uplift shoe that compensated for his shorter leg. He lay back on the bed and closed his eyes.

"Is that you, honey?" his wife's words drifted lazily around the door from the bathroom.

"Yes. I'm just resting, thinking about the tests."

"Have we got long before dinner?"

Festus glanced at his watch. "Six fifteen, about an hour, I guess."

"I've missed you, Fes. It gets lonely when you're away. Do you want to use the bath? Come on in now."

Festus was about to say no. His feelings towards her had been almost totally negative since Marienna had let slip another clue that had confirmed his fears. He remembered how Marienna had been strangely evasive in answering questions about Dawn and Ari's relationship.

"Did they get on well, as children?"

"Oh yes, Henry. They've always had a very affectionate relationship."

"I see. Ari doesn't strike me as an affectionate person. He looks like a gorilla. Hell! He's even got a gorilla haircut."

"Gorilla's are gentle creatures," Marienna retorted.

"He looks like a junior King Kong."

"Well, there you are. King Kong was in love with that pretty girl, Faye…somebody or other, and would do anything to protect her, keep her for himself."

"Sure, honey. Give me a second to get these clothes off!" He mustn't give any sign that might allow Dawn to sense his plans. She might sometimes affect a helpless image but this was only her way of using people. She had a quick and, as he had discovered early on, a devious mind.

"I'm waiting," Dawn cooed.

Dawn rose out of the bath, the ends of her long blond hair clinging to her breasts. Festus knew her timing was deliberate. Dawn was too finely tuned to him to have missed his frosty attitude. With luck, she had interpreted it as his normal nervousness at the start of a project. Though he had seen her naked many times, he reacted automatically. He felt a hardening sensation and a strange embarrassment at this sign of weakness. He turned away and stepped sideways into the bath. As he lowered himself, Dawn leant over him, her breasts brushing his shoulder as, awkwardly, he tried to sit down. She kissed him on the top of his head. He slipped and for a second, was immersed, helpless, his legs threshing wildly. Dawn helped him up, her soft body enveloping him. This time he could not contain the overwhelming sexual urge that came over him. Hurriedly, they dried each other, and rushed into the bedroom.

Later, lying together, he wanted to tell her of his plans, ask her forgiveness, and cancel everything. He was fighting this out in his mind when she whispered in his ear.

"Honey, why don't we go out tonight, not eat here." Dawn continued, "It would be more fun to go into Blarney. Alex and Sam and Ari could come with us, and that nice Irish guy, Seamus, could show us where to go."

Festus felt cold, the warm soft wetness became clammy. The letdown was complete in all senses. With great difficulty, he controlled himself. He waited, so that his words would not sound like an outburst.

"Some other night, Dawn. I arranged for Alex and the others to help set up the equipment. If only you'd told me earlier."

Dawn pouted sulkily and rolled away. "You and your damned work, you never think of me. Someday, I'm going to walk out on you."

Someday, thought Festus. You did it years ago. He dressed quickly and went in search of Alex before Dawn found out that he'd lied.

Dawn did not appear at dinner, so Festus ate with Alex. They drank a lot of wine, and had brandy with their coffee. He tried to draft them into setting up the equipment. They declined, so he worked on his own, taking occasional sips from the bottle.

Finally, unable to focus clearly on the equipment, he reeled back to his suite. Dawn had locked the door to the bedroom and its bathroom. Festus undressed automatically, taking off his shoes and folding his coat and trousers neatly. He wandered down the hall in his underwear, unselfconsciously, found a bathroom and washed. That night, he had to resort to the sofa in their reception room, with only a small carpet to keep him warm. He slept fitfully, his mind returning in a distracted fashion to Loch Ness. It was a tiring yet productive night, for in the morning he had new ideas for hunting the monster. He decided to call Zack that afternoon.

8. Blarney Castle

After a number of abortive attempts, Festus succeeded in persuading the Irish telephone system to connect him to Argos.

"I've been thinking about the monster. I've got an…"

Zack interrupted him. "I've been thinking too. You didn't find the damn thing. I'm worried the whole idea of the Trust is dumb. When you're done with Blarney, we'll need to reconsider everything. You need to get back to your real job, working for Cronson Enterprises."

Shit! Festus thought hard before answering. How the hell was he going to get out of this mess? Zack would be even unhappier after the Blarney. He remembered a discussion with Marienna. She had cautioned against telling Zack. Now he had no choice. "I'm not ready to deal with it yet, but I think the Phaestos Disk may hold the secret to a treasure on Crete. We'll need the Trust to provide a cover when we look for it." There was along silence.

"Maybe I'm being too hasty." Zack sounded cautious. "I guess I could support a second hunt...if there are ways of making money out of it. No fucking rain though! Don't you go telling anyone until I've fixed it! Harold and Ari ain't goin' to like it." He hung up.

Festus shook his head wearily. No rain in Scotland! What had he let himself in for now? He soon got over his depression and, elated by the prospect of a return to the Loch, worked his friends hard. They were sweaty and tired from rearranging chairs an, tables and electrical cords, when Seamus appeared with Dawn.

"Hi there." He glanced approvingly at the rearranged ballroom. "We seem to have arrived at a good moment. Good, you've finished. I have a reward for you all. We'll be going to the castle this afternoon. *Oi* suggest that first we pay a visit to the Brass Jar for a drink and *lonch*. I'm sure Fes'll be pleased to treat you all after such sterling efforts?"

"My pleasure"

"What's lonch? Dawn whispered to Alex.

"I think it's food," he whispered back.

The Brass Jar Inn was an integral part of a long line of shops and businesses making up one side of the main street. From the front, it had a drunk and surly look. Above the door, the bright Inn sign was swinging gently. Inside, there was a passage, off which was a bar on one side and a snug on the other. Seamus directed them to the snug.

"With the ladies here, we would be more welcome in the snug. You would call it a lounge. It will be more convenient for lonch, too. I've arranged for sandwiches and bread, cheese and pickles."

The snug was a dark room with a small bar in the left-hand corner facing the window. Bench seats were set against the walls, except where an old dartboard hung on a pockmarked wall—a witness to the uncertain accuracy of tipsy players. There were stained tables in front of the benches. A few chairs were scattered by the tables and in front of the bar were three leather-topped stools.

Seamus reached the bar and tapped lightly on the counter. The publican, who had been quietly working below it, rearranging his bottles, appeared like a jack-in-the-box, causing Seamus to put his hand to his heart in mock alarm.

"After that shock I need a drink. What are you all having?"

Alex Platon spoke up quickly. "I don't know about the rest of you but I want to try that draught Guinness I've heard so much about."

"I'd rather have a gin and tonic, with lots of ice and a slice of lemon", Dawn said, watching the black foaming liquid being poured into the glass.

The publican raised his eyebrows at this remark and kept on pouring. As he handed the glass to Alex, he whispered, "I can surely do the gin and tonic, sir, but we don't have much call for ice and lemon around here. I could send the boy out to find some."

"Don't bother. Just fix the gin and tonic and leave it to me. I expect she can handle it," Alex replied, his green eyes reflecting his childish pleasure in thwarting Dawn. He was immaculate as always, in cream white pants, pale blue loafers, a blue blazer with brass buttons, open necked shirt, and a red neckerchief. Dawn and Alex had the same startling, blonde, good looks, hinting at their distant Circassian ancestry, which was in marked contrast to the swarthy looks of the majority of their clan. It was well known that Alex was a favorite of hers, like a brother. Like a brother and sister, they needled each other remorselessly. Consequently, when he brought her the warm glass, she accepted it with good humor and ostentatiously took a sip.

"This sure is an unusual drink, but I guess a girl could get used to it." She leaned around Alex and flashed a brilliant smile in the direction of the bar.

To the amazement of the publican, a few of the locals drifted in. He looked at them quizzically, wondering what could have driven them from the bar to the snug. They indicated, by their expressions, that Dawn was the reason. Three of them arranged themselves at the bar, half turned so that they could take surreptitious looks.

Ari Cronson was sitting with Alex and Samantha. She was chattering excitedly about a proposed shopping expedition to the nearby town of Cork. Ari looked, and clearly felt, very much at home.

"This is the life. Real fine place to be." Ari raised his glass and wandered over to the bar. "Your health. What will y'all have?"

The locals to a man responded. "Sure and you're the visitor here, you have one on us."

Seamus intervened quickly. "We can only stay for a short while and we have to visit the castle in a sober state, all those steps and the dizzy height, you understand. I'm sure we'll be back. Let me get a round for everyone this time—on behalf of our leader Dr. Festus." He turned to the publican, "what's your pleasure?"

"A Guinness for everyone, sir. It would do me a lot of good while I fetch the sandwiches." He paused, then reassured by the friendly gesture, asked the question that was puzzling him. "Could you explain, sir, what your group is doing here? We've heard some strange stories."

"Festus, these good people want to know what we're doing here. You explain it!"

"Sure, Seamus, on condition they'll play darts with me."

The trade was agreed, and Festus started to explain how they were going to try and to find out whether kissing the stone made any difference to people's ability to embroider the truth.

"As soon as we leave here, we'll pick up the rest of our party and go to the castle, just to show people the stone. At this time, we won't kiss it. Then we'll return to the hotel. There…"

Alex interrupted him. "We're going to connect them to a lie detector and ask them questions. We'll give them the answers too. Some of the answers will be the truth and some will be lies."

"Thank you Alex, for clarifying the situation." Festus failed to mask his irritation.

Alex Platon, amused at having caught Festus off balance, rose to his feet and continued for him. "Then we'll take a two week break so that we can go sightseeing in your beautiful country. Doc Festus here will analyze the polygraph output. I'm planning to go trekking in one of those fancy caravans." He paused and sat down. "Why don't you finish the description Fes? Otherwise they may not play darts with you."

Festus, who did not like being upstaged, took a careful swig of Guinness, pretending briefly that he would not continue. His bluff didn't work. Alex cleared his throat and started to rise again.

"When we come back is the time we'll all kiss the stone, and repeat the tests. To put it simply, we will look to see if there is any detectable difference in people's ability to fool the polygraph." Festus stooped and smiled. "Now, who's going to play darts?"

When he had been a small boy, Festus had owned a dartboard. Hour after hour, he had practiced in his bedroom. Now, he wanted to show off. Unfortunately, too many years had elapsed and Festus could not match the languid practiced style of the local player. Nevertheless, he put up a creditable performance much to the surprise of his friends.

While they waited outside the castle for the guide, Seamus reminded them again that, on this occasion they would not kiss the stone. Nevertheless, they would go and see it so that all aspects of the two tests would be the same, except for kissing the stone. Peri Dexter, who was admiring a large horse chestnut tree that sat in front of the castle, was still confused by the whole exercise.

"Why not, dear? I thought that was why we came here?"

Seamus patiently explained it to her yet again, but she appeared unconvinced, and resumed her study of the scenery, until the guide arrived.

There is something about the accent in the southern part of Ireland that lends itself to story telling. The Texans were soon under the spell of the guide, as he launched into his story.

"Ladies and gentlemen, the castle was once the fortress of Cormac MacDermot MacCarthy. This gentleman, who lived in the time of Elizabeth the first of England, was asked repeatedly by her deputy Carew to acknowledge the sovereignty of the Queen. I don't need to tell you this sovereignty was not a good thing. People wanted the old system whereby the Irish clans, alone, elected their chiefs."

"You mean the Irish didn't like the Queen?" Peri sounded surprised.

"Ma'am, she was English."

"Oh, I see."

"So, on each occasion, by the use of carefully chosen words, he avoided committing himself. Finally, Elizabeth, irritated by this persistent procrastination exclaimed, 'He never says what he means; his words are all blarney.'"

"What does that have to do with stone," asked Harold.

"Sir, this ability to misuse words was subsequently attributed to the stone that supposedly conferred the gift of blarney. I like to quote these lines, attributed to Father Prout. The guide struck a pose and recited:

> A stone that whoever kisses
> O, he never misses to grow eloquent.

"So you see, ladies and gentlemen, this is a truly remarkable place. You can believe what I tell you about the stone because though I show people how to kiss it, I have actually." He paused for effect, looking wide-eyed at his flock. "*Oi* never kissed it *moiself.*"

Mary Beth turned to Dawn. "Obviously some people were born with the power."

The guide gave then a moment to recover from the one hundred and twenty seven step climb, and to look at the view over the Muskerry Hills. Then he showed them the stone—a lipstick and hair-oil besmeared oblong object—set below foot level in the battlements, where a cavity gave a view, through the grill, to the ground eighty-five feet below. The guide illustrated how to kiss the stone, by lying on the footway and leaning backwards, while grasping the guardrail. "As you noticed, I myself did not kiss it," he pointed out again.

"Do you disinfect the stone?" Mary Beth asked, oblivious to the obvious answer.

"Madam. The *Oirish* government ensures that all proper precautions are taken so as not to endanger the wellbeing of the public," the guide hastened to reassure her, carefully avoiding, in the tradition of Blarney, answering the specific question. "You can see we have even put iron bars across the bottom of that hole to save you from falling through."

After further inspection of the stone and a tour of the castle and its dungeons, the party returned to the country club. Seamus reminded them. "We will have a brief pause for tea and to allow the ladies time to powder their noses before the tests begin, but please, all be in the ballroom by three."

Alex took his Seamus' arm. "Did Marienna talk to you?'

"Sir? Oh, you mean, what did Miss Cronson want?" Seamus hesitated. "It was nothing much. She wanted to do some shopping in Cork. That was it."

At three, most of the Society's members were seated in the ballroom facing a large screen. The area for the tests was behind them. Festus paced impatiently and eyed his watch. Finally the latecomers appeared. Peri Dexter looked flustered. Dawn sat with Alex.

Festus was excited. The months of preparation was now going to pay off. His enthusiasm, about his work, rubbed off on his audience and they, like he, began to feel excited about the tests as he explained them.

"This is a big moment for the Eurysthesian Trust. We have arrived at the second of our scientific adventures. While, originally, blarney meant only speaking carefully to avoid answering a request, it is now given a broader meaning than simple evasion."

"Is this going to be like Loch Ness?"

"Loch Ness isn't finished."

"Just kidding, Doc."

"Very humorous, Ari. I don't know what the results of our tests will be, but I reckon they'll be interesting. I should warn you, it will take today and tomorrow to complete the first set of tests, and I must insist y'all come. Please bear with me in this; I'm trying to accomplish a number of things here. Incidentally, I will try to publish the results, though I'm not sure whether there's a journal that will take them. At the moment, it's a toss up between the Journal of Applied Psychology and Mad magazine."

"Could you explain, first, what a polygraph is, Fes? Peri requested. "I think I'd like to know before I'm enveloped in it."

Harold answered for him. "Let me explain. The idea of testing for truth or innocence is an old one. The concept, that the bodily functions reveal all, has been around for a long time. In the Far East it was, at one time, the practice to place a small amount of rice in the mouth of a suspect. If he could spit it out easily, he was innocent. If it stuck to his tongue or palate, he was judged guilty. In the late 19th century, Lombroso, an Italian criminologist, used a device that monitored the pulse and blood pressure, during interrogations. However, it was an American entrepreneur, one William Marston, who really brought it to public attention in the States, around the time of the First World War. More important, his activities prompted the police in Berkeley, notably a gentleman called Larson, to develop what is the present polygraph. It's been widely used in the States ever since."

"Thank you Harold. I couldn't have explained it so expertly." Festus continued. "Peri, as far as the tests are concerned, you'll come to the stage one at a time. We will connect you to the polygraph. Let me use Alex to demonstrate what I'll be doing. I'm going to attach some simple monitors to you. These two rubber tubes, placed on the stomach and on the chest, are to measure breathing; this cuff, wrapped around your upper arm, measures blood pressure; and these two metal caps, which will be attached to two fingertips, measure electrical response. They won't hurt a bit. I guarantee it. Now, let me just illustrate in a simple way how the device works!"

Festus produced a pack of cards from his pocket. "I'm going to ask Alex to take a card, and then I'm going to use the detector to find out what it is. I'll ask you a set of simple questions, Alex, and we'll monitor your responses.

"I want you to answer no to each question. Okay? Take a card!"

"Is it black?"

"No."

Festus looked intently at the chart recorder, after each answer.

"Is it a picture card?"

"No."

"Is it the king of spades?"

"No."

"Is it the jack of clubs?"

"No."

"All right Alex, you can hold up the jack of clubs."

Festus didn't wait for the audience reaction to die down. He had succeeded in the purpose of the exhibition, which was to show that the detector worked. He didn't want to give anyone time to wonder whether the deck had been fixed—it had. All of the cards were the same.

"You see it really does work. Let's continue! I can assure you that during these tests I will not ask any embarrassing questions. I will hand you a sheet of paper with both the questions and answers on it. Naturally, some of the answers will be lies. It is your reactions during questioning that we want to compare with your response in about two weeks' time, after you have kissed the Blarney stone. We will televise the interviews and show them to the rest of the group, so please be quiet." He paused.

"Finally, I should encourage you with the thought that for the next week we'll be enjoying the recreational part of this trip. The weather forecast is surprisingly good. Seamus has completed the arrangements for all the side trips that you've requested. There'll a trip to Killarney, of course, and golf and fishing, Harold, and Alex has rented a gypsy wagon."

"I'm an old romantic," Alex smiled. "The local priest's agreed to bless it. I should be safe," he added.

"A wise move. I've heard strange tales about the Romanies. Who can tell what evil deeds that caravan may have seen?" Festus took the opportunity to play on Alex's superstitious mind.

"What do you mean?" Alex asked, worriedly.

"You'll find out," Festus replied, turning quickly back to the test. "Marienna has agreed to be the first subject. She has already received her questions, which I hope she's been studying. Sam will work out with the rest of you the order in which you want to go. I'll leave her to do that and start the first tests. Alex, you come with me."

"Who's going to be the second contestant?" Samantha asked, smiling. "Don't be bashful, now. Come on, Dad, lead the way!"

Ari declined the offer, volunteering that it should be ladies first. Dawn offered to go second and the rest, one by one, signed on to the list.

Marienna Cronson reached the stage and went to the test area. An upright chair faced a television camera. Around it, some of the Japanese screens hid most of the apparatus.

"I hope this won't be intimidating."

Marienna gave him a steely smile. "I don't know how the others will react, but you seem to be forgetting that I helped you learn how to use this contraption."

Festus was engrossed in attaching the monitors and did not pay attention.

"I wonder if we'll find out about any of Marienna's little secrets." Alex whispered to Joe as they left the stage. "She uses that icy schoolmistress image very effectively to hide what she's really like."

"I've heard she was slightly crazy when she was young," Joe replied.

"Slightly doesn't match what I've heard," Alex added. "Schizo's more like it. Boyfriends couldn't keep up with her personality changes or her intellect. It's why she never married."

"It was the Doc's father, Argos, she really wanted, wasn't it?"

"That's right Joe. Doc is a substitute son for her. If anybody could get her to talk it's our Dr. Henry." Alex continued. "It's sad you know. When Marienna was young, it was not fashionable in our Cretan community for women to be educated; nor was it acceptable for them to have authority. She wanted to become "padrone" on her father's death. I've heard that she even tried to install someone she could easily manipulate."

"I heard that poor Argos suffered for helping her," Joe added.

"Just like in the play. Strange isn't it?" Alex smiled. "Zachary, like Zeus does in the play, thwarted the plan and become padrone."

"They seem to work together okay?" Joe queried.

"There's an uneasy truce I think. She rarely interferes in his plans and, in turn, he puts up with her little manipulations. I wonder sometimes…" Alex's comments were curtailed by an announcement from Festus that he was ready to begin.

"Can you hear me now?" asked Festus.

"Yes, Henry, it's a little loud though."

"Okay. I'll ask you a question. After a slight delay, to allow you time to digest it, you give the answer on the sheet! You should read it, understand it, and then give it!"

"That's fine, Henry. I'm ready to start."

The questions began. "Where do you live?"

"Argos, Texas, U.S.A."

"Are you a citizen of Mexico?"

"Ye…es."

"Did you enjoy the flight over?"

"Yes"

"Are you enjoying your visit to France?"

"Yes."

"Is the Eurysthesian Trust a purely philanthropic organization?"

"Yes."

"Are you a member of the Argos Lake Breakfast Club?"

"No."

"Are you a member of the Argos Lake Ladies Club?"

"No."

While some of the questions were common to all of the subjects, their answers were varied. Other questions were specifically aimed at the subject, about whom Festus, Alex, and Joe had compiled a file of information. Finally, there were control questions for which the answer could be either yes or no depending on the subject's personal likes and dislikes. Questions such as, "Did you enjoy the flight over?" came in this category.

"Do you have a pet dog?"

"Yes"

"Do you have a pet cat?"

"No."

In total, Festus asked sixty questions. The answers contained twenty truths, twenty lies, and twenty random responses. He allowed some fifteen seconds between the questions to let the graphs equilibrate.

It was a surprise to some of his colleagues that they were allowed to watch the tests. They felt that it might help them prepare for their own questions. Festus explained that this was a deliberate effort to find out whether people could learn to cheat the polygraph. This rationalization covered up the main purpose, which was to maximize the effect on his quarry. Nevertheless, he did not let people see their own tests.

Festus watched with irritation as Dawn played up to the camera. It was a relief then to work with Samantha who answered the questions calmly. He allowed a brief break, and then continued with Joe's no-name wife, who was interviewed by Alex. Finally, by popular demand, their guide from the castle took the test. Then Festus, noticing that his audience was becoming restive, called a halt.

Marienna stayed behind. When everyone else had left, she went backstage to where Festus was tidying up the equipment. "Henry, you're up to something aren't you?"

Festus looked puzzled. "What do you mean, Marienna?"

"You can't fool me Henry. I know how devious you can be. I remember how you set up Aristotle when he wouldn't stop bullying you. Made sure that old Constantine caught him with the peaches, didn't you? Constantine paddled his butt."

"How did you know?" Festus asked, in surprise.

"I saw it happen. Reckoned you had a right to protect yourself. Said nothing. So where are the peaches this time?"

"I'm just doing this test for my Labor," Festus expostulated.

Marienna said nothing. When she turned to leave, she was smiling.

The tests resumed the following morning. Alex Platon seemed able to control the response of the machine. Harold Dexter, taking the questions too seriously and trying to give different answers, was a nuisance. A confused Peri Dexter took the test and created some very erratic chart recordings, which left Festus and Alex gaping. Joe, Seamus, and Ari followed her and, finally, Festus was tested.

It took six hours to complete the session, including two long breaks. "It's been a fascinating experience," Festus said, "very interesting; some results were really quite unusual." He looked sideways at Peri Dexter, who blushed. Thank you for making it possible. I know it must have been very tiring. To show my appreciation and to celebrate our progress we will have a special dinner tonight. Seamus has arranged for an Irish folk group to entertain us, and I guess there may also be dancing. So, see y'all this evening."

The dinner passed smoothly. Festus, sitting at a table with Dawn, Alex and Seamus, was witty, charming and attentive to his party. About halfway through the act of the folk group, he told Dawn he had to leave to start analyzing the tapes. Alex, who was discussing clothes with Dawn, looked stunned. Dawn turned away and pointedly continued her discussion with Alex. As Festus was leaving, he passed Peri Dexter. She held out her hand, motioning him to stop.

"What are you up to, Fes? I overheard you say that you have to start on the tapes. I can't believe that it's so critical that you have to spoil this beautiful party."

Festus looked embarrassed. "I'm not a great one for dancing, Peri, and I am very curious about some of the responses. I need to get a head start on the work. We…uh, we don't have much time, someone has to do it." He looked back at Dawn, who was being escorted to the dance floor by Seamus. For a second, he hesitated, then stiffening his resolve, walked out.

When Dawn came to their suite, Festus was still working, systematically sorting the tapes and charts and beginning the analysis. He looked up, distractedly, when the door opened. She stood in the doorway, briefly, then leaned through it into the hall and gave an audible, long, passionate kiss to someone standing there. Festus couldn't see who it was.

"Good night…sleep tight…see you tomorrow. Thanks for looking after me!"

"God, you're a drag, Henry."

"What!"

"Oh, forget it!"

She went into the bedroom and shut the door, making a great deal of noise out of locking the door.

Festus tried to work but couldn't concentrate. He was too embarrassed to ask the hotel staff for a blanket, so he picked up the small carpet from the parquet floor and went to the sofa. Here we go again, he thought. The carpet pressed heavily on his legs and he slept uncomfortably, wracked by nightmares of being interrogated in a police station. The guide at Blarney Castle held the stone over his head, the whole time repeating the words, "if you tell a lie, I'll have to drop this *blody* stone on you. *Sorr*!"

9. Killarney

Festus woke early in his makeshift bedroom. He lay on his back, brooding about his plan. Then, his personal demon brought Dawn and Ari into focus on the back of his eyelids. In Argos, he had seen them in animated discussion. They had appeared conspiratorial, heads close together, turning to give him that amused and, for God's sake, pitying look, which caused his chest to tighten until he felt he would choke. The sight had hurt him. The hurt had soon turned to anger and to thoughts of revenge. Who were they to make a fool of him? Therefore, he had concocted his plan. It was a fine madness. He suppressed concerns about consequences.

Now he had to consider the next week. They would all take various trips. Joe and Harold would fish near Blarney. Peri, probably relieved to get away from Harold for a short while, would go sightseeing in Killarney with the Cronsons and "what's her name" Maximos. He and Dawn would accompany them. Alex planned some incredible caravan trip. His mind wandered back to the point of the trip. Maybe he shouldn't go, but that would look odd. No, he would go for the first few days, and then make an excuse and return to work on the tapes. As for dealing with the present problem, he would apologize to Dawn for last night, when she eventually emerged from the bedroom.

He traveled to Killarney with Seamus and Dawn. Glengarriff was so beautiful and Dawn, trying to make up for screaming at him, so accommodating, that his resolve was weaker by the time they reached Killarney. However, the sight of the town itself—a tourist trap—reconfirmed it. After they settled in their hotel, he announced his intention to return to Blarney the next day to work on the data.

Dawn turned white with fury. She rose to her feet, mutely pointing at Festus—imperiously—then strode out of the room. Festus sat on the bed and worried. Had he overplayed his hand? Would she stay in Ireland? He picked up his bag and went down to the lobby. Dawn was in the bar with Marienna, Seamus and Ari. She was wearing tight jeans and an open necked shirt, deliberately unbuttoned to display her cleavage to advantage. She had the men's full attention. Festus approached apprehensively. Dawn turned to him, speaking evenly.

"This is the first vacation we've had in years, and after a few days you can't stand to be with me. Maybe I'll be better off without you?"

"It's not like that," Festus protested. I have an obligation to make this project work and someone has to analyze the first set of data to get ready for the second set."

"I know it's difficult for you, Dawn, but we have to make this project go," Marienna said, quickly. "Henry is the only one who can do it, and without him we wouldn't be here in the first place. He's making a big sacrifice in giving up his time."

"Bullshit!" Dawn muttered, angrily. "Work is being here with us. He gets his kicks from the project. Don't kid yourself."

Festus shrugged his shoulders in a "What can I do about it" appeal to the assembly. Seamus O'Flaherty, taking the hint, crossed over to him and put his arm around him. "Don't you worry, Fes, I'll look after Dawn. He leant conspiratorially towards Festus, and whispered, "Jasus, Fes, I'd just be happy that she cared whether I was here or not."

Festus turned and looked searchingly at him. Seamus inclined his head slightly. "Come on, cheer up folks, we're here to see the most beautiful lakes in the world. Finish your drinks and we'll collect everybody and go sightseeing. I've got my camera. I'll take superb pictures of you riding in a pony trap. Festus doesn't know what he's missing." Seamus took Dawn by the arm. She made a face at Festus. "What the hell! Let's go and see your dumb pony trap. Then I'm going for a walk with Marienna and Ari. Sam's going shopping with Peri."

That evening, Peri took Dawn by the arm. "Is something else worrying you?" Peri asked, perspicaciously."

"Not much. Just things and Fes as usual. I wish Marienna had come with Ari and me for that walk."

"I wish I'd come with you too. Was it a great view?"

"Yeah, I guess so. It was a good thing Marienna lent us her water flask. It was quite a climb to the top of that hill. Then…I don't know." Dawn rubbed her eyes. "It got very hot. I felt dizzy. Ari...I...it's a blur. The next thing I remember is Ari helping me down the hill."

"All right then?"

"Yes," Dawn did not sound convinced.

"What about Fes?"

"I could kick him at times. He can be a real shit, hiding in his damn science, but then he'll look vulnerable, and...I don't know if I should make up with him, again."

Peri smiled sympathetically. "Dawn, I know he loves you. He gets so distracted when he's doing research. Go on, make up!" There was silence.

Festus was in the ballroom, working, when the first group returned. He was tired, but happy he'd completed his analysis. Now all he needed was the final piece of the puzzle, and they could complete the test.

The returning travelers were also relaxed. Harold embraced Peri passionately when she returned, belying the normal impression of coldness that he fostered. Ari Cronson watched his daughter pensively as she entered the hotel. "I guess I should have spent more time with her in Killarney," he whispered to Joe.

"Don't worry about it man. She did fine." Joe laughed, "I seem to have lost Mary Beth. Let's find Seamus and see if he wants to join us at the pub."

"He can't. Festus sent him to Dublin on some fool errand."

"Wait! There's Alex. Do you want to come to the pub with us, Alex?"

"Can we get a ride? I'm not sure if I can make it on foot, Joe." Alex was walking with a significant limp.

"What happened?"

Alex, who was concentrating on negotiating some steps, smiled ruefully.

"Oh hi, Ari, let me just say that there's not a lot of room in a tinker's caravan." He paused. "Maybe it was because I washed my hair on Sunday?"

"Come off it, Alex. You don't believe that crap?"

"You can't be too careful, Ari. Maybe that priest put the hex on me?"

"You can tell us all about it in the pub," Joe grinned. "I'll get a taxi."

Dawn peered around the ballroom door. Festus was sitting, hunched over a mound of papers. His right hand was turning pages. His left hand was worriedly playing with his tousled hair. He was wearing his favorite cowboy shirt and his oldest jeans, with one leg of his jeans tucked inside a boot, and one leg outside, in the traditional Texan manner.

She put her arms around him, pulling his head back against her breasts. He didn't turn but pulled her hands to his lap, then put his hands behind him to stroke her thighs. They stayed like this for a few moments, until he could stand her expert manipulation no more. He rose and they embraced, a slight desperation marking their moves as they tried to prove a normalcy to their situation. Dawn took him by the hand, indicating the need to get to their bedroom. Festus protested unconvincingly that he needed to work. After what had happened, he still wanted her, yet it was an uneasy, ambivalent feeling. He made a joke of it to hide his unease.

"We could do it on the stage. Nobody would hear through the curtains." He grinned evilly at her.

"You're awful, Fes, but what I have in mind would better be done behind locked doors."

When Seamus returned, the group made the final visit to Blarney Castle. The conversation at breakfast was excited and agitated. Peri Dexter was fluttering about, hovering over Harold as he slowly finished his coffee. "Come on Harold, we don't want to be late for the bus."

Harold, somberly sipping, would not even look up. "Stop flappin', honey. It's nine-twenty. The bus doesn't go until ten."

With a withering look, she left him and joined Marienna. They discussed the problem of bending over backwards in a decorous fashion while kissing the stone. Festus, for once in a chatty mood, was frivolously entering into their discussion. Peri stopped him briefly, putting her hand on his as he gestured with his knife.

"Fes, you really have a captivating personality when you try. I think you're far too serious normally."

Dawn smiled, wryly. Festus was embarrassed, but recovered a little ground. "You're right, but sometimes I do things that might surprise you." He looked wide-eyed at Dawn.

The bus slowed to turn into the parking area. A mist still hung around the castle and the wetness of the trees and the hanging lichen gave it an eerie look.

"I wonder if Dracula's still up?" whispered Peri.

Harold Dexter, overhearing the remark, sought to put the picture straight. "I think you are confused, Persephone. If you were to read Bram Stoker's book you would discover that Count Dracula inhabited Transylvania, not Ireland." He looked around triumphantly for support.

Peri, in an unusual display of irritation, retorted sharply. "I was joking, Harold."

"Oh, I see." Harold sounded unconvinced.

The guide arrived and, for the second time, conducted them to the top of the castle.

"Mornin', ladies and gentlemen. I won't tell you the history of Blarney again, but when we get to the stone, I will repeat my demonstration of the way of kissing it. This will be for me," he paused, theatrically, "the first time. I know that there are men of science here," he nodded towards Festus, "who do not believe in the magical action of the stone. Let me say that you will be surprised when you complete your scientific tests. You will be amazed at the difference in me. I shall be eloquent and at the same time moving. Following the ceremony, I will be pleased to take the interested parties to the Rock Close to see the Druid's Circle and the dolmen. It's not in my normal duties." He looked hard at Seamus. "But, for such a group as you, I would feel it my honor."

Dawn lay on her back and inched towards the battlements. Festus and the guide assisted her while she held onto two railings and bent backwards. A small crowd had gathered. Her jeans were tight between her legs, showing a tantalizing cleavage. The men in the audience stood quietly, transfixed by the sight of the body symbolically laid out before them as Dawn stretched to kiss the stone.

"Oh Jasus," murmured Seamus. "It's not fair to test a man like this."

The guide seemed less reluctant to take advantage of the situation. The men watched in amusement as he managed, under the excuse of helping, to grope every woman.

Sam followed, aided by Ari, who indicated firmly to the guide that his help was not needed. In quick succession, they all kissed the stone, finishing with the guide and Festus.

By the time they returned to the ballroom, a few attempts to test the efficiency of the stone. Peri came lose to success in persuading Harold that he had been invited to a convention of undertakers in Cork. The publican listened resignedly as Ari explained that he had lost his wallet. "Ah, m'boy, even if I didn't know you'd been to the stone today, I could have guessed." He chatted about the many other attempts to get free drinks, and in the end, with typical hospitality, offered Ari a Guinness. Then, Ari was allowed to find his wallet and the drinks flowed.

Ari tottered unstably, with the concentration of the truly drunk, as he weaved his way to the hotel, arriving just in time for the final tests. Festus was speaking.

"We've come to the final stage of our second project. I will call you, one by one, to the stage. I will ask you simple questions, to which you will have read the answers. Please use the answers given to you. It is a waste of everyone's time if you try to be subtle. We'll go in the same order as last time, except that our guide has to get back to work, so I'll take him first. Marienna, you can come with me now! We'll do some tests today and the rest tomorrow."

The guide's test was finished and Festus shook his hand warmly, passing him a ten-pound note. It took a few minutes for Festus to usher him to the door, so fulsome were his thanks. Alex turned the camera and Marienna and Festus came into view. Festus connected the monitors to her chest, fingers, and upper arm.

As Festus was about to attach the earphones, she reached up and held his wrist. "Henry, since your mother died I've taken a particular interest in you. Behind the scenes, I've tried to help. I do understand your problems with Dawn and frankly, though she's my sister, I have little sympathy for her. You could have made a better choice."

She caught Festus off balance. He grabbed for the loudspeaker switch. It was off. He recovered quickly while pretending to fuss with the apparatus, holding up his hands in supplication. "Marienna, I appreciate your help, but could we...discuss it...some...other time." His voice slowed as he began to understand the drift of her conversation. "That's a...curious remark. Did you have any particular girl in mind?"

"Not really." She paused. "Well, if it were today, I guess I would be thinking about someone like Catherine Schmidt."

Is that why Marienna had gotten Cathy a role in the plays? Festus hid his discomfort by making fun of the suggestion. "You know it's a nice thought, if you like the cheerleader type. You've persuaded me. I'll return to Texas tomorrow and we'll elope. On reflection though, she only teaches arts and sports. Now, if she were like you and taught science, I might be interested. Anyway, aren't I a little old for her? And she's a foreigner."

It was Marienna's turn to be flustered but she recovered quickly and retorted, sharply. "Don't make fun of me Henry."

He showed her the first questions and answers.

"Are you a citizen of Spain?"

"Yes"

"Where do you live?"

"Argos, Texas, U.S.A."

"Did you enjoy the flight over?"

"No"

"Are you a member of the Argos Lake Breakfast Club?"

"No"

"Have you kissed the Blarney Stone?"

"No."

The test continued until the sixty questions were completed. Many were a repeat of those in the first test. Festus concluded the day's work with a test of Dawn, who played to the camera, and Samantha, who answered calmly.

The following day, testing started with Mary-Beth. Alex came after her. He was well in control, lying or telling the truth with apparent ease, except when he was asked whether he was superstitious. Peri, who remained flustered by the whole business, followed overly serious Harold. Joe and Seamus came next. Then it was Ari's turn.

It was obvious that Ari was still feeling the effects of another lunchtime binge. He wobbled unevenly to the stage, brushing aside the attempts of Seamus to help him. Ari slumped in the chair and Alex connected him to the detector.

"Do you live in Argos County?"

"Yes."

"Did you enjoy the flight over?"

"No."

"Do you like zoos?"

"No."

The questions moved slowly as Ari's brain foundered in a sea of Guinness. He was having difficulty in reading the answers on the sheet of paper. Festus prodded him occasionally to reactivate him.

"Is your wife with you?"

"No. I mean Yes."

"Did you enjoy your trip to Killarney?"

"No."

"Are you having an affair with Dawn?"

"Yes…Wait a minute! No! You're crazy"

The pens on the chart recorder were moving jerkily. Ari started to rise then sat back, partially regained his composure.

"Lyin' bastard," Festus shouted, switching to a second camera, and handing Ari some photographs. In the ballroom, a shot of Killarney came on the screen. In a series of still photographs, the camera zoomed in on a secluded hollow in the bracken. It showed Ari and Dawn. They seemed to be wrestling. The following shot showed part of Ari's backside. Dawn was facing the camera, her shirt was open and her brassiere was loose, exposing one breast. Her face had a wild look to it. The penultimate shot showed them in each other's arms, before they disappeared from the camera's sight.

Ari Cronson leapt from the chair, pulling over the recorder, as the tapes holding the electrodes split. He ran from the stage and out into the gardens.

Dawn's cry broke the silence. "Oh, my God! Festus, what have you done? It's not what you think." She slumped in her chair ashen faced, in her panic, further speech deserting her.

Peri and Mary-Beth rushed to help her. "Come on, Dawn, we've got to get you out of here." Marienna followed them. The ballroom emptied except for Alex, Joe and Seamus.

"How did y'all enjoy our home photo show?" asked Alex, faking a laugh.

"Shit, Alex. It's not funny. The Doc's flipped."

"I know that, but there were some good pointers for you and Mary Beth."

"Very humorous Alex." Joe continued reflectively, "now, what do we do?"

"Let's leave him for the moment. We'll need to get a few of us together and come up with a plan. Zack will go vertically when he hears. I'll start on it while you talk to Fes. Wait a second!" Alex's legal mind came back into play. "Incidentally, Seamus, where did the photos come from? What exactly is your job?"

"I think you've guessed it; part-time, private detective, and not very proud of it at the moment. Come on, Joe, let's start cleaning up.

Joe and Seamus found Festus sitting in the chair facing the camera, eyes closed. He was clenching the arms of the chair as if he was frozen. Any pleasure in the revenge he had taken on Dawn and Ari had gone. He now saw the void that faced him. Dawn would go. She was too proud to accept such an insult. He would have time to immerse himself in research, but would it be enough? He looked up. Joe faced him. "I had the feeling that you and Seamus were up to something, but I never thought it would be like this. They shouldn't have done what they did, but to show Ari up like that in front of Samantha was cruel."

"I didn't plan for her to be here. I thought that Ari would come alone?"

"Well, you should have cancelled your stupid stunt!" Joe left.

"I couldn't," Festus cried.

"In any war, there are civilian injuries," Seamus reassured him.

"I know, but it's the saddest part of it all. I guess I didn't have to use all the shots you gave me. But, somehow, showing them like that seemed right; historically right, you see?" Seamus, who was not versed in the Greek legends, did not see, and remained silent.

"What did Dawn mean? 'It's not what you think.'"

"Look Fes! I was quite a distance away. As I told you, it wasn't clear what was happening, but she didn't scream or anything. Then they disappeared, so I left. It's difficult when you're trying to take pictures." Seamus sounded embarrassed.

"You did the best you could, Seamus. The pictures are clear." Festus paused, as if he was thinking of a question, and then changed the subject abruptly. "Connect up these leads, will you? I still have to take my test. You can give it to me."

"You're kidding!"

"No. I need all the data I can get. Please sit down." Festus connected the polygraph and they completed the test. Seamus left, shaking his head.

The senior members of the group were gathered around Harold Dexter in the hotel bar.

"Festus set us up. There's no doubt about it," Harold muttered angrily, looking around for confirmation.

"Surely Harold, you don't think it was the only motivation for organizing the Trust's research at Blarney? We were all...Zack and all of us, involved in that. I guess he saw the opportunity to trap them and couldn't resist it."

"Don't be so sure, Alex. That man's arrogance is incredible."

"I tried to phone Zack but he's gone hunting for a couple of days, so let me speak for him," Marienna added, taking charge. Her aggressive move came as such a surprise that nobody argued.

"I agree with Alex. Henry has taken advantage of us, but we have too much invested in this research to stop it now. We need Henry, but he's got to agree not to do anything like that again as a condition for us allowing him to continue. He can be devious, but this seems out of character. There's one other thing we need to discuss before we deal with the mess—Loch Ness."

"Goddamn it! Haven't we had enough of that man's fantasies?"

"I know that Zachary has already decided that the Foundation and Trust will support another hunt. I must insist that Henry go to Scotland as soon as everything's wrapped up here. The last thing we need is to have him moping around Argos." Marienna looked at Harold, who seemed prepared to argue. Her hard, dark brown eyes expressed a confidence to which he had no answer. His head dropped in submission.

"Well then, seeing as we all agree. Alex! Why don't you go and speak to Henry! I'll go and help deal with Dawn. Mary-Beth will look after Samantha. Harold, you'd better try and find Ari, get Seamus to help you."

They went on their various errands. Harold and Seamus collected all of Ari Cronson's belongings and scoured the village. They tried the Castle first, following Seamus' hunch that in his hung-over state Ari might have gone there to hide.

"As I said before, I suspect he's at the pub," said Harold, pompously. He was right.

"You go in," said Seamus. "Best keep it a family affair. I'll be outside if you need help."

Harold found Ari, embedded in his favorite corner of the snug at the Brass Jar. He looked up glaze-eyed as Harold entered. The publican sounded worried. "What the hell's the matter with him? Hardly spoke a word except 'give me another one.'"

"Problems at home", Harold replied. "I'll take him off your hands."

"Thanks. I don't like to see a fine drinking man in a state like that. Mind you look after him! Maybe we can meet again when all's well?"

"'A woman should be everything inside the home, and nothing outside it.' Euripides wrote that," said Ari, cryptically. "Stupid bastard. What did he know about women?"

"He's on his fifth." The publican said. "I told him it was the last. What happened?"

"Bad news," Harold replied. "Time to go, Ari. We need to get you home." His dour face showed his concern.

"Don't remember what happened," Ari sounded distraught. His cheeks were tear-stained from crying. "Like a bad dream. Walking up hill with Dawn. Hot day. Glad Marienna lent us her drink. What did I do? Those photographs."

"It's done, Ari. You'll have to deal with it when you're sober." Harold spoke more curtly.

"God! What's Yianna going to say?" The fear showed in Ari's face. "Be silent—at first!

Make me pay. Little things. Smoke two cigarettes before sex. Lie there like a sack of potatoes. Hate it. Minute I finish, she'll start talking at me." Ari tried to smile. "Sermon on the dismount I call it."

Harold looked uncomfortable. "Can you stand?" He took hold of Ari's arm.

"Did Dawn say anything?" Ari lurched to his feet. "Festus is a shit," Ari shouted, his face suddenly red with anger. "She should never have married him."

"It wasn't Festus in those photos?" Harold snapped. "How about Samantha?"

"Oh, God! I'd forgotten about Sam…and Demos. What will he think?"

Festus was still filing charts, when Alex found him. Alex came straight to the point. "You conned us, Fes. That was unfair. We're your friends."

"I'm sorry, sorry for everything, particularly for hurting Sam. I couldn't stand Dawn's affairs any more. You know, in Cyprus it was the custom for the women to prostitute themselves at the temple of Aphrodite to ensure fruitfulness of the ground. Dawn seemed to want to carry on the tradition," he added, distractedly.

"Fes, I don't think Dawn has been having affairs. Are you sure this wasn't all Ari's doing?" Festus did not appear to be listening. Alex looked worried.

"She uses lures you know, even with me. He probably didn't stand a chance." Festus wiped his eyes. "Ari deserved to be exposed. That arrogant bastard has made a play for nearly every woman in Argos; successfully too…and she's his sister!"

"His adopted sister, Fes. It's not the quite the same thing."

"Are you sure? He shouldn't have done it."

"I know. There's been something odd about their relationship…ever since we were kids. I thought everyone knew. I paid Ari once, to see Dawn's, you know what." Alex stopped. "Did you hear what I said?"

"I wish I hadn't." Festus squinted his eyes, trying to stop the tears. "I know I shouldn't have manipulated the Foundation to make a trap. It won't happen again. To be honest I hadn't expected to catch them, red-handed, quite like that. All I'd expected to film was a little necking," he said wistfully, adding, "the weather's been so good…"

"I didn't pay much attention to their hands. I hope they didn't get sunburned in any awkward places, Fes," then, seeing the hurt on Festus' face, added, "I'm sorry, that was insensitive. So, Seamus took the photos?" He reflected for a moment. "It seems out of character for a lawyer?"

"He's a lawyer, specializing in divorce cases. Not a particularly good business in Ireland, I guess. So, on the side, he's also a private detective—a 'Shamus.' It seemed funny when I hired him."

"Jesus Christ, Fes, you're incorrigible. To be more serious, the message is simple. If you're to continue in this work, you must guarantee never to act on self-interest again!" Festus nodded agreement.

"What about Dawn?" For the first time, Festus showed emotion. He turned away and with a slight break in his voice, whispered. "Tell her to file for a separation order. I won't file for divorce yet. I'll go straight to Scotland. Now, let me get back to my work!"

Alex was about to leave, when Marienna came by.

"Can I help?"

"I'm off. You talk to him," Alex said. "Oh, incidentally, Marienna, did you find anything good in the shops in Cork?"

"What?"

"Nothing, I'd heard you'd been shopping." Alex looked at her, thoughtfully.

"Nonsense. Well, Henry, what have you got to say for yourself?"

"Marienna, look at this!" Festus flapped a hand, excitedly, continuing his comparison of the results of the two tests. Marienna's face showed her shock at his appearance. His hair was ruffled, and his face had an unhealthy pallor. He had been crying. Finally, he finished, leaning back in his chair. "Marienna, I never seriously expected to get anything out of these tests, the statistics are lousy. Nevertheless, these results are incredible. I've normalized the responses of the lies and truths and truths to the control questions. The correlation is around seventy percent or more. I can hardly believe it, but there is a difference emerging, showing that most people were better able to fool the detector after they'd kissed the stone. That is, except for the output from our wonderful guide, who appeared to be lying even when he wasn't. Result of overexposure, I guess? My success is a good omen for Loch Ness. I reckon I'll find the monster this time." His attempt at a grin looked strained.

10. Interlude

Following the final analysis of the results of the tests on the effectiveness of the Blarney stone, Festus shipped the polygraph and other equipment to Argos. He then traveled to Scotland.

Throughout the winter and spring, Festus stayed at Urquhart View House. He completed an article on the Blarney findings, and submitted it to the Journal of Applied Psychology. He then set about gathering additional facts on the inhabitants of the Loch. He was making good progress up to the day when he heard the phone ring. It was Zack. Georgina came by as he replaced the telephone.

"You look pensive," Georgina said. "Is everything all right?"

"Zack, and then Elena, wanted to talk to me," Festus said. "Pandora's acting up."

"She's very young. She misses you. I'm sure it will turn out to be just a phase," Georgina said, reassuringly.

"I expect so," Festus replied, though he was not so certain. He had brief thoughts of returning to Argos, but embarrassment, and a desire to complete his work squelched the idea. Then, his efforts took on a manic quality. Finally, he entered a mood of depression. When Dawn had been with him, though he had felt insecure in their relationship, his work had been fun. Now he felt frustrated in his work and, in a perverse way, sexually too.

What had Marienna said in Blarney? At the time, it had given him hope. Oh, yes! Catherine Anne Schmidt who played his—Hephaestus'—love interest in the play, "Hephaestus and the Cretans." He fantasized briefly about Cathy Schmidt, daydreaming about her athletic body and bright young face. It was comforting to think about her, yet she seemed unattainable. Images of Cathy and of Dawn appeared in quiet moments. Images of the prostitute who lurked in the pub were remorseless in supplanting them, until he could think of little else.

On his occasional visits to McDougall's Yard to check on the progress of further improvements—by bus, for he had no car—he would walk by the pub keeping to the far side of the road, half hoping to see her, half not. Once he had seen her entering and once, when she was leaving, she had stopped and waved suggestively. During a period when progress on the analysis was slow and the weather was cold and depressing, she appeared as he passed the pub. This time when she beckoned, he followed at a distance, watching her large hips swaying under her short coat. Illogically, the sight aroused him.

He followed her into a house in a terrace of gray slum buildings. The house smelled damp and the floral wallpaper hung in patches like a section of a decaying garden. A door was open at the top of the stairs. He entered slowly closing the door behind him. The woman had removed her coat, blouse and skirt, and was washing herself; apparently, she did not wear panties, for there was none in the pile of discarded clothes. Her grubby white garter belt and brassiere straps were pressed into her puffy white skin.

"It'll be ten pounds. Now!" she said, sounding more confident than she looked.

Festus removed his reefer jacket and gave her the money in a disinterested fashion. He was beginning to feel uneasy. "Would you help me with my bra 'dearie'?"

Festus fumbled with the clasp, unleashing two, deflated and blue-veined breasts. She turned and placed his hands under them, squirming against him as she reached down to his jeans.

"Ooh! You are ready, dearie, and such a big one too." Festus turned his head away from her whiskey soaked breath. The woman shrugged, handed him a contraceptive and sat on the bed. As she lay down her breasts puddled on her chest and slipped over the sides of her ribcage like errant saddlebags. She opened her legs; her pubic hair was turning gray.

If she had hoped to arouse him, it had the opposite effect. Suddenly she was in focus, not simply on his retina but in his mind. Festus was appalled at himself. How could image of Dawn and Cathy have translated into this creature? Frantically, he picked up his jacket and fled, dislodging wallpaper as he took the stairs two at a time.

"Filthy Yank!" she screamed. "I'm not good enough for you. Bastard!" He was gone. The ten-pound note lay on the bedside table. She rolled on the bed reaching for it with one hand, while with the other hand she searched for the half bottle of whiskey she kept under the bed. Festus kept clear of the pub for the rest of his stay, and soon afterwards, the submarine was shipped back to the Loch.

Ionides sent him more data from the first phase of the hunt. Festus soon had so much data that it was no longer amenable to a hand analysis. Fortunately, he had been able to buy time on a computer at the University of Aberdeen. Computing was a new experience for him, so he took a course and, with help from his instructor, he succeeded in constructing a deck of punch cards to feed into the computer for analysis of the combined data. Developing the program was a slow process. His first output placed the monster in Honduras. It was well into the spring before he succeeded in moving the monster from the environs of Tegucigalpa, across North America and the Arctic, to Novaya Zemlya, and on to the vicinity of Loch Ness. Even with his improved analysis technique and the enhanced data set, he could not reproduce his earlier result that the monster's lair was near Urquhart Castle. The target area now appeared to the southwest, near Foyers. Festus worried that his interpretation of the data could be so variable. It was a comforting thought that at least many of the sightings had been made near Foyers. It was clear he needed greater accuracy, more helpers, and more data. The new echo detectors would help. Until that time, when his colleagues returned, he and Hamish McDougall would spend more time cruising the Loch. Maybe they would see the monster or find a likely cave? It was not to be. They saw a fair number of fish, old shoes, bottles, even rusted bicycles and an encrusted baby carriage, but no Nessie and no lair!

Zack and the first group of Eurysthesians arrived in June of 1961. Zack wasted no time in cornering Festus, remaining silent until they reached the den. His experience told him that silence was the most effective way to unsettle someone. Certainly, with someone as intelligent as Festus, it was necessary to gain the maximum advantage before starting the lecture.

"You heard the views of your friends some months ago. As President of our Foundation, I'm goin' to say it again. I know you were very hurt by what Ari and Dawn did…but you took advantage of us, your family." As Zack spoke, he began to show his suppressed anger. His face reddened. "There fucking well better be no more silly games, like in Blarney." To emphasize the point he turned Festus to face him.

"I know. I'm sorry." Festus acted contrite. In fact, he no longer felt guilty; time had washed that away. He wanted the sermon to end.

"Now another serious matter," Zack continued. "I telephoned you about the trouble we were having with Pandora. She's a very mixed up young girl. Angelica did the best job she could while you and Dawn were in Blarney. It was obvious even then, that Pandora resented you leaving her. Then, Pandora heard what had happened."

"Did she say anything?"

"No. Angelica and Elena tried, but she wouldn't talk to anyone about it."

"So she was okay then?" said Festus, in a pathetic attempt to make light of the problem.

"For Christ sake, Fes!" Zack's face seemed to bulge with irritation.

"I see. I'm sorry. Carry on…please."

"In the meantime Pandora started seeing this young man. He wasn't a bad kid, though he was quite a bit older than Pandora, and not one of us. It was all right, I guess, the guy was like a substitute father. That is, until he made a pass at Dawn."

"Jesus Christ! That woman is insatiable. I thought Blarney would teach her a lesson. I might as well not have bothered."

"I didn't say Dawn did anything. It's not her fault if some guy makes passes at her."

"Crap!"

"Don't be so damned self-righteous Fes! In your own way, you're as bad as she is; with your work, I mean. And let me tell you somethin'! Even I feel guilty, because I encourage you." Zack did not sound very convincing. "I tried to call you a number of times but the damn phone was out of action every time. So, seeing I'm Pandora's godfather and you were absent, I talked to Elena and we decided to take action. There seemed no point in getting you back to Texas at this stage of the hunt."

"What action?"

"Dawn couldn't handle the pressure. Said she needed time to get her life in order. Angel had as much as she could take, so Elena offered to look after Pandora for a few months. Dawn's staying with friends of y'alls in Berkeley. Elena tried to get Pandora to discuss her feelings. But she wouldn't say anythin' and became more and more moody."

"I don't know what to do." Festus sat with his face in his hands. His shoulders were shaking.

"Self pity is no damned good, Fes. You and Dawn have a lot in common. In your own ways, you're both self-centered. You've given Pandora little but looks, affluence and neglect."

"I know it, Zack, but I'm driven to compete. You never needed to compete. You started at the top. Look at your poise, your confidence! Do you have any self-doubts? It's tougher for people like Dawn and me. We're always trying to prove ourselves; working for a pat on the back. Is it so uncommon?"

"No, Fes, it's not uncommon," Zack reassured him. "We talked about bringing Pandora here, but Elena reckoned you would probably ignore her. Elena remembered that Dawn had mentioned sending Pandora to Greece to visit family so, I've sent Pandora to stay with my cousin Nicholas."

Festus nodded wearily. He felt he should be angry—Dawn had pissed off and Zack had sent his daughter to Greece—but he only felt resigned. "Nicholas Kronosakis? Yes, I remember him. He has a villa outside Athens…near the sea. Right?"

"Elena and Marienna took her there. Pandora can lie on the beach, swim and help with Nico and Maria's children. I hope the change of scene will do her good. Marienna stayed for an extra week until Pandora settled in."

"With Dawn gone it sure sounds like the best solution." Festus tried to sound thoughtful. His feeling of resignation had turned, rapidly, to relief that it would not interfere with the hunt. He could see Pandora when the hunt was over. From then on, he would make up for his neglect. "Where is Marienna now?"

"Touring somewhere in Italy, I think?"

"I hope it wasn't too much trouble for Elena."

"No problem. Elena planned to visit Duke. He's stationed in Germany now. You know how she worries about him."

Festus suppressed a smile, picturing Zack's son Deucalion, named after the Cretan Heracles, a giant of a man, affectionately known as "Little Duke."

"I worry too," admitted Zack, uncharacteristically. "I still see the small boy playing in the yard but, like Pandora, Little Duke was getting into trouble. Typical teenager. That's why Elena and I persuaded him to join the army, hoping that the army would…give Duke the discipline he needs until he matures."

"One other thing, that research you started on bacteria-enzyme mixes is going quite well, I hear."

"Yes, Willard wrote me a note," said Festus, his face brightening.

"I have some ideas we should discuss at a more opportune moment."

"Oh! I see. I'll look forward to it," replied Festus, failing again to hide his unease. His hope that working for the Trust would cut back on his work for Zack, did not seem to be working.

"Good. Now tell me about Nessie!" Zack smiled.

Ionides and Samantha Festus arrived near the end of June. On his return to Argos, Ionides had proposed to Samantha. Ionides did not know that his proposal was accepted, in the face of opposition from both of her parents, only because of the combined efforts of the three Cronson women, Angelica, Elena and Marienna. Festus was not invited to the wedding. Samantha distanced herself from Festus, showing her anger about what had happened in Blarney.

Catherine Schmidt accompanied Marienna. Festus looked quizzically at Marienna, as he greeted them.

"Catherine met me in London. She is here to keep me company, and help me get around for the fishing. I don't like to admit it but I'm getting old." She had a walking stick and waved it at him.

Festus shrugged as if it was not important. Secretly, he was pleased. Cathy played the role of the mortal girl loved by Hephaestus in "Hephaestus and the Cretans." She was often at Marienna's house when he went to visit. In looks and bearing, she was a younger, softer version of the stern, spinsterish, Marienna. Consequently, her passion in their brief embrace in the play had startled him. On reflection, he had concluded it was simply acting. However, he felt unsure of himself and while they were friendly to each other, it was a distant friendship. Festus believed that Cathy liked him but suspected his marriage was a barrier between them. Their coy interactions were a visible source of irritation to Marienna. Her frustrations were to continue, for the next day Elena Cronson arrived and distracted Festus' attention.

After the normal opening pleasantries, Elena came straight to the point. "I expect Marienna has already told you. We think Pandora will be fine with cousin Nico, Fes. She helps in the house and baby-sits their two young children.'"

"Great. Thanks. I really…"

"I don't want to preach, but Pandora needs you. She's still very lonely. I considered bringing her here. Zack reckoned you couldn't handle it with your work. You really should go to see her as soon as possible."

Festus had the feeling he should respond enthusiastically, yet his words sounded shallow. "Elena, I wish you'd brought her here. I could show how much I care. Do you think I should leave the project and go to Athens? I could bring her back with me. There'd be plenty for her to do. We still need more fish caught and she could help Ion keep up with the notes." Festus spoke wistfully as if the whole matter were outside his control, so that some other Festus would have to perform this task.

Elena looked at the set expression on the dark face. "That's a very theoretical discussion about what you might do, Fes," she replied, pursing her lips disapprovingly. "You need to be clear about your priorities. The good thing is that Pandora seemed all right when I left. But you really must get out to her as soon as the project's over."

"Elena, I'm close to locating the monster's lair." Elena looked irritated. "Oh yes, of course I will go to see her." Festus finished, lamely.

To celebrate Marienna's arrival, Georgina MacLeod organized a special dinner with her best red wine—vintage Chateau Margaux. On the previous trip, the Texans had become accustomed to the old British system where, after dinner, the ladies retire and the men get drunk passing the port.

Festus was not ready to lie down; knowing it would make him nauseous. The Loch was an attraction and he headed to the shore. Vague thoughts of seeing the monster circled his brain, coupled with double images of his surroundings and of the women in his life—his mother, a faded memory, then Dawn, Pandora, Marienna, and…Cathy.

Afterwards, Festus could not recall how he had arrived at the small headland a half mile from the house. A confused stumble along the stony shore and a few bruises and cuts were evidence of it. He did remember throwing stones into the Loch and watching the ripples spread in neat circles; at the middle of which the head appeared—a sleek grayish-green head. It was hard to tell the color in the dim light of the moon. The big black eyes stared at him in a puzzled fashion as if to ask, "Why did you drop a stone on me?" It looked quite like one of the pictures he had pinned to his bedroom wall as a child. Festus rubbed his eyes. When he looked again all that remained were a few circular ripples. He imagined he could see a wake as it retreated, but the image did not stick. Was it the drink? Was the whole idea of the monster wishful thinking? Slowly, he walked into the water. The gently shelving beach rapidly steepened, and before he reached where the epicenter of the ripples had been, his feet could no longer touch the bottom. The shock of the cold water and the fear of the bottomless pit sobered him. He scrambled from the Loch and stumbled, dripping water, back to the house.

Next morning, Festus took a very long shower, picturing Georgina MacLeod bitching at him in her high Scots accent for wasting hot water. "What is the matter with you people? You must feel very dirty; you stay in the shower so long." He was not the only one suffering that morning.

At the breakfast table, Zack and Elena sat idly forking the scrambled eggs and kippers. The pungent smell of the kippers did not fit well with a hangover. Zack was complaining about the un-American plumbing; his shower had oscillated between icy cold and scalding hot. Many of the new arrivals had also not made it to breakfast and only Cathy, who drank little, took much notice of his arrival.

Festus unwisely chose the opportunity to mention that he was close to finding the monster. He did not mention the previous night's vision. If his clothes had not been soaked, he might have believed the whole episode to be a dream. He was received politely but without enthusiasm. Zack mustered enough strength to say, "Get on with it, Fes. I'll be with you later."

"It's down the lake, near the hydro-works at Foyers."

"I hope you're right this time. Look, I'm a bit overwhelmed by that port. What the hell do they put in it? Fortified is the wrong word, booby trapped would be better." Zack stood.

Ionides stared out of the window, sipped black coffee, and said nothing.

"I'm sure everybody will rally around later, but you sure picked a bad time to tell us," said Cathy, coming to his side.

"Yeah, I guess I did."

"Come on, Fes! Let me get you some food! You look ghastly." Cathy put her cool hands to his forehead and pulled his head against her. It was an unconscious motion, as if he were a child in her classroom. Like a child, he put one arm around her and held on. They clung together for a moment.

Elena turned her head away and pretended to see something interesting through the window. Zack had seen Festus and Cathy too and muttered, "We don't need more complications. What was Marienna thinking, bringing Cathy here?"

"I think she's trying to match them up," Elena whispered.

"God! That woman meddles. What can we do?"

"Let's go for a walk so we can talk. It's awkward in here." Zack nodded agreement.

Georgina MacLeod had also watched the interplay with interest and later put her thoughts in her diary. *It is fascinating how women seem to be attracted to Henry Festus. His intellect can be off putting but his disability makes him appear vulnerable. From all accounts, his wife Dawn is a rare beauty, maybe this is what she found appealing. Marienna dotes on him, as if he were her son. She does not seem to like Dawn Festus. It is as if the two women are battling over him. If so, it looks like Mari-*

enna's proxy is winning. Georgina put the diary into the secret drawer in her bureau and locked it.

It was not a good time for work, so Marienna, Cathy and Festus spent the morning walking the hills behind the house. It was surprising how easily Marienna made the hike, thought Festus. The walking stick seemed to be used mainly for his benefit. They chatted idly about the plays and the hunt, as they made their way towards Tarn Bailgeann, the heather springy beneath their feet. The sky was a surprisingly sharp blue. It was a beautiful day for clearing a hangover. As noon approached, they returned to the house, fitter and hungrier for lunch.

"Come on, Fes, we're all ready now, tell us what you know. Are you sure it wasn't the port?" Zack raised his water glass, mimicking the drinking of the previous night.

Festus held up a map of the lake. "After that vote of confidence from Zack I guess I'll settle for him holding this map. For those who weren't here before I'll point out that the marks on the map show where we've had detectors, or fished, or traversed with the boats. We've used chemical analysis in the hope of finding traces of some compound that might be associated with the monster. In my original crude hand analysis with part of the data, I showed that the monster's lair was most probably across the Loch near the Castle. We looked. Didn't see anything."

"Don't remind me about it. It pissed with rain. Only other time I've been so wet was when I fell in Lake Travis. Why do you think it moved?"

"It didn't move, Zack. This year I managed to gain access to a small computer at Aberdeen University. I got help to write a program to analyze all the data on a common basis. As I told you, I now reckon its lair must be on our side of the Loch near Foyers."

"What a pity, I won't be able to watch from the dock," said Georgina MacLeod. "Mind you, last time I could hardly see anything either."

"Can we start tomorrow?"

"Not exactly, Ion. I need a little more data from a couple of places, including your favorite, the pier at Inverfarigaig." Ionides groaned, remembering how he had fallen off the pier in his eagerness to unhook a large fish. "Also I need more fish from across the Loch at Altsigh, and at Foyers. That should be enough to pin it down."

It took three weeks of intensive fishing and analysis before Festus was prepared to move to the next stage. During this time Cathy was his constant companion, helping with the work of recording the catches and preparing the data for the computer. For some reason, Marienna had suddenly decided she didn't need

Cathy's help after all; making it clear to him that her story had been a pretext for getting Cathy on the hunt. When he was finally satisfied that there was no more to be gained by further analysis, Festus directed Ionides and Hamish in positioning sonar detectors underwater off the shore near Foyers. Unfortunately, the day the hunt started Zack received a telegram from his cousin, Nicholas:

> PANDORA RUN AWAY STOP
> NO TRACE STOP
> IS ILL STOP
> WORRIED HER SAFETY STOP
> NICHOLAS STOP

Zack went immediately to Festus and showed him the telegram. "You'd better get your butt off to Athens right now."

Festus protested weakly, but he knew he had to go. "What about the hunt?"

"Leave it to me."

The hunt proceeded under Zack's direction. He managed it efficiently. He got Hamish to give reporters tours on the submarine. For a short time, he even seemed to enjoy the experience. Yet his frustration, when there was no sign of the monster, showed in occasional bursts of anger. After a week, he abandoned the search.

11. Athens

The world was a black place, a disaster, thought Festus as he withdrew from it. He brooded about his brief telephone conversation with Nicholas Kronosakis. The line had been very noisy and he was not sure that he had understood the full story. His daughter had run away with some hippies. She was ill. Nicholas had not said exactly what illness, but he, Festus, was convinced from the tenor of the discussion that it was a venereal disease. His mind continued to the next unpleasant thought, Pandora was sexually active. He did not like the idea, and switched his thoughts to Dawn, seeking a reason to blame her for the situation but finding fault with himself. He had humiliated Dawn in front of her family and friends, and she had left him. Festus guessed it was final.

His problem was clear. Even when his work allowed him a small success, in some subtle way, he remained dissatisfied. He continued to blame the Cronsons for his unhappiness. Nothing he had done was his own. The Labors had not solved the problem—yet.

The analogy between his work for the Trust and the Labors of Heracles seemed weak. His second Labor—the Nemean Lion—did not connect well, except in a punning way "One mean lyin" bastard'. The uncompleted first Labor—the Hydra—had some resemblance to the original. Now, this third Labor was supposed to relate to the capture of the Ceryneian Hind. Heracles hunted the poor beast from the Ceryneian Hill to Istria and to the land of the Hyperboreans, before capturing her by the river Ladon. He recollected that Hephaestus had made the tools of her capture.

His mind was a confused muddle of thoughts. His wife had left him. Now his daughter had run away to Greece…in Greece. How could that be? He knew that he must take action; forget about Dawn, she was out of reach anyway. Find his daughter that was the first priority. Chase after her like Heracles after the Golden Hind. No! That did not sound right. It should be like Hephaestus chasing the Golden Hind. He settled back, content with the thought, and slept for a while.

Waking up, Festus read the telegram again. Finding flights had not been easy, and it was now three days since he had first seen the words, "Pandora run away. Pandora ill." He watched the wing, and the engines suspended from it, flex in the air currents. He tried to visualize Pandora as she was now nearly grown up. No, grown up! Yet, all he could see was the little child who would come into bed with Dawn and him when she could not sleep. A memory of a collection of discarded bedclothes laying a trail from her bed to theirs; a small figure with long blond hair clutching her toy animals like a passenger leaving a sinking ship.

Damn it! Why couldn't life be simple? Was it the reality that all he wanted to do was his research? That he could take interpersonal relationships as the mood suited him? It was an ambiguous feeling. Fate and sex had saddled him with Dawn and Pandora and he had not found a way to balance their needs against his need to be creative. He still felt pangs of longing for Dawn, and guilt when he thought of Pandora. Had he and Dawn, like many Greek couples, wanted a boy and been disappointed when Pandora came along? A little maybe, at the beginning, but it was not the main problem. He had to admit that selfishness was the problem.

Cathy Schmidt sat next to him. Marienna had turned down his plea for help. *"I'm too old to be traipsing around the islands, Henry. Try Elena."*

In the end, Marienna and Elena Cronson had descended on Cathy.

"Henry will need help," Marienna said.

"I agree," Elena adding, *and I think Angelica would agree if she were here. Fes will need a woman around when he finds Pandy and you're nearer her age than the rest of us."*

"You think so," Cathy asked, uncertainly. "Angel wasn't happy when I came here."
"Please help. You have to stay in Europe anyway," Marienna pleaded.
"I suppose so."

Cathy glanced at Festus. He looked pensive. She reached over and patted his hand. He turned his head wearily, gave her a wan smile.

"Pandora wasn't in any of my classes," Cathy said. "But I know she's pretty bright. Takes after you. She's acting the rebellious teenager. I know a lot about that." She smiled, reassuringly. "Some of it is an act, you know."

"Yes, I suppose I do know, but she's at a vulnerable age," Festus answered, remembering Elena's comment, *'Pandora's emerging from the chrysalis of puberty with her mother's beauty, but she lacks experienced to handle opportunistic men.'* He wished he hadn't heard the comment.

"Do you think Pandora might have VD?"

"Yes," Festus said, edgily, turning to watch the wing. Cathy withdrew her hand but continued to study him.

The plane flew low over the bay giving glimpses of the Acropolis before, in its final swoop, it settled on the runway. The sight of the Acropolis reminded Festus of his first visit to Athens with his father in 1949, on Argos's final journey to his homeland, Crete. The excitement had been hard to bear. It was like his first glimpse of the sea on a childhood trip to Galveston to meet the "new Greeks" who had settled there.

On this earlier visit to Greece, the weeks spent on boats traveling from Galveston to Miami, to New York and then to the port of Piraeus had seemed, in his impatient state, to last nearly as long as the rest of his life. The smell of Athens, the throngs of people who were like him, the sound of Greek spoken naturally by all around, not simply by the elders, had caused his eyes to mist. His father, an old man then, gray hair thinning around his weather-beaten face, had hugged him. His callused hands, still strong from a life of metalwork, had reached out and cradled his head. It strengthened further the bond that had grown between them since his mother had died. When he thought of his father, he could still feel the rough palms against his ears.

From Athens, another boat had taken them to Khania in Crete and there, after a few weeks, he had left his father with their remaining elderly relatives. His father had died suddenly, a month before he was to have returned to Texas. Festus's only memento of this journey was a letter; the final words, an allusion to their servitude to the Cronsons—"be your own man!"

He wished he knew how. Thank God, his plans were being followed by the Trust, but he knew he would have to change them if Zack demanded it. Moreover, what else would Zack demand in payment for supporting his, Hephaestus's, Labors, and as atonement for his actions in Blarney?

Festus still mourned the loss of his father. His older relatives in Crete were gone too, and that left only his cousin Ionides to carry on the family name. To succeed him there was Pandora, and little chance remaining for a son to continue their role in the plays. Dawn had wanted their first child, but had suffered badly from postpartum depression, and refused to consider having another child.

"Nicholas Kronsonakis greeted them as they cleared customs. When he smiled, a fleeting impression of Zack Cronson appeared, but he was younger and his stature and bearing were altogether different. The worry over Pandora expressed itself in his manner as he grasped Festus with both hands and embraced him. "What can I say? She just left. No warning." He looked distraught and on the point of tears.

Festus put his arm on Nicholas's shoulder. "We'll discuss it later." He introduced Cathy, diffidently, taking pains to explain that Marienna had asked her to help them. "She can only stay a few weeks," he added. "Then she has to start teaching at the U.S. base in Mannheim.

Nicholas said very little until he and Festus were sitting on his terrace, shaded by an old vine. Nicholas stared out across the sea at the island of Salamis and talked about Pandora. His wife and Cathy tactfully busied themselves in the kitchen and kept the children away.

"We try my English," Nicholas said. "Maybe better than your Greek."

"No argument, Nico."

"I am honest with you, Doctor." His dark eyes looked intently at Festus. "You know this, I guess. Pandora is unhappy, lonely and, how do I say it, feelsa unloved." He paused to let this sink in. Festus nodded his head slightly. "Honest Doc, she's selfish," he continued in his broken English. "Maria, Elena and Marienna try to help. She not listen. Not reliable. We hoped for older daughter for us…with Christos and little Maria. She started okay. Then she changed. Sometimes she played with them. Another times ignored, special if there is young man. No could leave alone with children."

"What men?" Festus asked hesitantly.

Nicholas looked straight at him, obviously having made up his mind to come directly to the point. "Men…ah men! She flirt all time—shopping, beach, young man for our garden. I fire him. Marienna go, Pandora worse. Can't watch all the time." He paused.

"She need love. Is dangerous." He turned away. "Hell of a body, Doc, tanned, curves," his hands moved expressively to emphasize the point. "Long blond hair, she's beautiful."

He paused, then tried, unsuccessfully, to make light of his story. "Good thing, Maria keep me in line."

The comment did not help Festus. "I know now, Nicholas. I hadn't realized she'd grown up. It's just six months since I saw her. She's only sixteen. I...my work occupies me; I don't always see the obvious. You said she was ill, but on the phone I couldn't understand...a venereal disease?"

Nicholas looked uncomfortable and hesitated for a second. "I told of gardener, Christos. We fired him. He said...uh...sex with him. Said unkind things to Pandy. Maria heard it. Tell her she the problem he lose job. Tell her she useless. Pandy very crying and no talk with us. Big problem we hear, after she ran away. Here, everybody knows everything. He's at doctor's for syphilis. Pandy too? We doesn't know. She not know too."

Festus' face crumpled. He remained silent. Nicholas took this as a sign to continue. "I hear that local boys say she have sex with anybody."

The full impact now struck Festus. He put his head in his hands but otherwise remained motionless. His mind worked rapidly, trying to come to grips with this new understanding of the reality of his family life.

Nicholas put his arm around him comfortingly. "Come on, Doc! Sorry I put it to you straight. Now, try find Pandy. Get medical for her and all her boys."

How could I be so ignorant of my family, Festus thought, I just switched them out when they were not convenient. Nicholas was right; it was his responsibility to clear up this mess. He concentrated on thinking of solutions to the problem as if it were a scientific project. As if it were such a project, even the small action of taking up the challenge, made him feel better.

Festus looked up at last, his face set. There were no tears. The time for tears had passed. "Do you know where she went?"

"I asked around. Not call police yet. Good you get here quickly."

"Please don't call the police. This is a family problem."

"I find, maybe, she took bus to Khalkis. With foreign kids, probably American. My guess is they go to islands."

"I suppose the best thing I could do is take the same bus to Khalkis, then try and pick up her trail," Festus asked.

"I feel bad about this thing, Doc. I promise to look after her. Let me come with you."

Festus reacted quickly. The idea of being alone with Cathy appealed to him. "That's kind of you, Nico, but I'd rather you stay here. My Greek's good enough and Cathy will be a big help. What I really need is someone to find a good clinic, and act as a contact for the kids who need medical help. You're much more valuable to me in Athens. You'll do it won't you?" He was pleased with his rationalization.

"Okay if that's what you want, Doc." Nicholas' face showed his relief. "Good thing, Marienna get Cathy to come. Need her when you find Pandora." He paused. "Er…I hear rumors about you and Dawn. Elena not say much. You separated? What's deal with Cathy?"

Festus did not reply, for the simple reason that he did not know the answer.

Nicholas interpreted the silence to imply he was offended. "Sorry Doc, forget it."

"No, no, don't worry about it! I've been so busy with my work, and then the business with Pandy. I just don't know the answer about Dawn. Cathy's a friend of Marienna's. I'm glad she's prepared to help. Anyway, we didn't come this far just to sit in the sun and gossip on your terrace."

"Okay, then, rest today. Take bus tomorrow morning. Your suitcases gonna be…how do you say…big pain in the butt. See, I know English good. Get back packs for your stuff."

The bus rattled down the dusty road, through the lemon groves and vineyards, with the passengers clinging gamely to the inside. The bus driver was a friendly man with a large drooping moustache, which served as a cover for his undesirable teeth, and which, fortunately, filtered out some of the garlic that appeared to be a substantial part of his diet.

"Do you get many tourists on this bus?" Festus asked in Greek.

The moustache lifted, and Festus turned slightly sideways, supposedly to get a better view of the lemon groves.

"Not many. Most of them are on organized tours and have their own coaches."

"What about foreign kids?'

"Now that's another matter. When they can't hitchhike, they go by bus. They're pests. They try not to pay, or slip me foreign money. Why, there's one of them on the bus today, an American…like you? He paid!" He gestured towards the rear of the bus.

Festus turned, but could see only a guitar, with some long brown curly hair and a bit of blue denim collar showing to one side of it. He gestured at Cathy, who was lost in contemplation of what appeared, through the dust, to be a monastery set on top of a hill by the road. "We're looking for my daughter."

"Good luck."

"Have you seen her?" Festus produced a photograph of Pandora on the beach with Nicholas's children. The driver t ogled it.

"I wouldn't forget that one if I saw her dressed like that," he chuckled. "They usually wear more on my bus. The police would pick them up if they didn't."

"Well?"

"Yes, I've seen her. Good luck." He rolled his eyes. "She was with a group of three or four of them—all hippies. I remember now, she spoke a little Greek. Wanted to know how to get to Karystos."

Festus surreptitiously handed him some money. "Thanks, have a drink on us."

The driver felt he ought to volunteer more information. "If she's yours, you've got real problems. If I remember right, all the boys were after her and the other girl didn't look very happy about it."

"Great, thanks a lot."

"I see a lot more on my bus than the passengers realize. I don't normally let on though." He turned towards Festus, laughing through a cloud of garlic. "How old is she?"

"Sixteen. Well, nearly seventeen."

"Sixteen! My God, what are we coming to? They didn't have them like that when I was a young lad. Sorry, no offense meant."

The bus stopped to pick up more passengers and he was unable to continue. Festus passed on the essentials of the conversation to Cathy and went to the back of the bus.

"Any room for me?"

The young man did not look up, but involuntarily edged slightly sideways, pulling his knapsack, guitar and boots towards him leaving barely enough room for Festus to sit. He must be tall or bulky, thought Festus, looking at the hunched body in the corner—bulky, he concluded. He tried for some minutes to attract his attention. The boy ignored his coughs and restless movements. Festus decided speak, but phrased his question badly.

"Young man, could you help me please? I'm looking for a young girl."

"You're what?" waking up, and laughing as he turned to look at Festus. "Listen man! We may have a free life style by the standards of your generation but that sure as hell doesn't mean we want to share it with you. You're looking for a young girl. What do you take me for…a…a pimp?" He turned away and stared out of the window.

Festus blushed. "I don't mean that. I'm looking for my daughter. She ran away. I'm worried."

The boy looked at him. "Sorry, you caught me by surprise. You'd be surprised how many dirty old men pester us." He paused. "Sad thing is some kids do pimp for them. There really are some mixed up bastards around. You'd be surprised." He turned to the window, then back to face Festus. "Okay, I'm sorry again. Too close to the truth, was I? Hey, wait a second!" He looked searchingly at Festus. "Don't I know you?"

He rummaged around in one of his bags and pulled out a copy of the Herald Tribune, turning to the front page. The headline of an article read: 'Texan Hunts Loch Ness Monster'. Below it was a photograph of a number of the Eurysthesians; at the front was Zachary Cronson.

"Can I look at that?"

"Be my guest."

Festus read the article with growing irritation. Apparently, the New York Herald Tribune reporter had talked mainly to Zack. Zack's role as president of the Eurysthesian Foundation figured prominently. Near the end of the article Zack was quoted as saying, "He regretted that Dr. Henry Festus, who had provided technical assistance to the expedition, was not present to add to his comments." In an inset on an inner page was a second photograph of Festus captioned, "From Blarney to Loch Ness, fun and games for scientist and inventor, Dr. H.E. Festus." It referred briefly to Festus' role at Loch Ness, and commented humorously on his tests of the Blarney Stone, making him look like a nut case.

Damn Zack! He hadn't wasted any time taking credit for what wasn't his work.

"You're Dr. Festus, aren't you?" The boy's deep-set brown eyes looked at Festus searchingly. Then he seemed to have changed his mind. Holding out his hand he said, "I'm Chuck Steeger. It says in here you come from Texas, from Argos. I guess I've heard of you before. You see, though I'm from San Angelo, I'm doing engineering at UT in Austin. Hope to graduate in a couple of years."

"What brings you to Greece?"

"I made some quick money digging ditches. Had to stop," he laughed, and held out his hands. "The digging nearly ruined these good guitar picking hands of mine. Now I'm spending it, bumming around Europe for the summer."

"I see," said Festus, showing his disinterest.

"We Texans should stick together. Maybe I can help a little?"

Festus was pleased at the offer, but concerned about appearing too anxious; he took his time in responding. It was hard to tell what Chuck was like on such a brief acquaintance, yet he had to find help somewhere. With his sunburned face, shoulder length hair and denims he looked like a modern Christ. Maybe that was a good sign.

"I sure could use help. My daughter's called Pandora. Our only lead is a suggestion that she's gone to Karystos. This is why we're on this bus." Festus waved in the general direction of Cathy, before handing Chuck a photograph.

Chuck studied the photograph. "Can't say I've seen her. I surely wouldn't forget if I had. Pandora, you say. Now, wait a minute! I have heard of her, sir." There was a long pause. Chuck seemed to be having trouble deciding what to say and continued, picking his words carefully. "Well sir, she has a bit of...a reputation. You have a problem there."

Festus winced. "So everyone tells me Chuck. I wish...I wish I'd realized before."

Chuck looked sadly at the bowed head. "I'll tell you what I can do. I'm going to Karystos. Plan to spend a day or so checking it out. I doubt Pandora stopped there though. It's more likely she went to get a boat to the islands. I'm doing the same thing. I could make inquiries. I'll stand a better chance than you of finding things out. I could leave messages in the post office each place I stop."

"We're going to check briefly in Khalkis. Then, assuming she's not there, carry on to Karystos. It would be a great, if you could help us."

"I don't mind stopping off in Khalkis, but not for too long."

"I should introduce my friend." Festus pointed to Cathy. "Miss Schmidt...er...Cathy is a teacher from Pandora's school. She's helping me look for Pandora."

Chuck looking knowingly at him.

"It's a long story," added Festus in embarrassment. "Thanks for the offer. It would be great if you could help. We're not sure how to start. I would be happy to pay for your trouble. Incidentally, Chuck, people call me Fes."

"You don't need to give me anything," Chuck said. "I'm happy to help."

The bus climbed up the final hill and then descended towards the swing bridge that crossed the Euripus to Khalkis. The brightly colored houses around the harbor mirrored sinuously in the waters of the bay. The blue hills of the island of Euboea shimmered as a backdrop to the town.

At the bus station, the driver offered to question other drivers about Pandora during his lunch break. They arranged to meet him at his cafe at two o'clock. Festus handed Chuck and Cathy a photograph of Pandora. They looked good together he thought, jealously, realizing he was staring at her. She didn't seem to mind. Cathy's slim body, still brown from the Texas sun, was lean and athletic-looking in her short denim dress. Her brown hair, curly and tangled from the sweaty hours in the bus, framed her quiet face. A steady face, he thought to himself, a controlled person, looking out from behind the slightly prominent blue eyes. Cathy grinned, glanced at Chuck, and shook her head, smiling. Festus acted as if he had not been looking at her. The moment passed quickly.

At the harbor, his inquiries among the crews of the small boats were fruitless. No one had seen Pandora. The general advice was to check the buses and the square. "You'll find all the young people there, sitting around the cannon balls—drinking."

Sure enough, when Festus entered the square, there was a group of kids showing their independence by wearing the standard uniform—tee shirts, blue jeans, floppy hats, guitars, the girls braless, the boys bearded with long hair. Chuck and Cathy were talking to the group.

"We couldn't find anybody who knew Pandora, but some of them had heard of a group which came through within the last few days. Apparently, there was some sort of fight with local kids over one of their women. From the description, it sounded like Pandora. Unfortunately, they didn't know for sure where the group went, but they agreed it would probably be Karystos," said Cathy.

They decided to leave further inquiries until after lunch. Following a meal of lamb cooked over a charcoal brazier, a salad, bread, and a few belts of the local wine, they felt better equipped to continue the hunt. Festus found the cafe frequented by the bus driver and his friends. Fortunately, one of them recognized Pandora from her photograph.

"It was about four days ago. She took my bus to Aliverion with another girl and two boys. There were three boys at first, but there was a big argument as they were boarding the bus, and we nearly had a fight on our hands. One boy left before any real problems occurred."

"Do you think they stopped in Aliverion?"

"No, I kept an eye on them. They took the bus to Karystos. I guess you want to follow them. In about ten minutes, I'll be going to Aliverion. My bus is just over there."

After a very long ten minutes, the bus finally lumbered off. The road skirted the sea, before taking a route that passed through eucalyptus and olive groves to reach Aliverion. There, the conductor located the appropriate bus, for they were determined to press on to Karystos.

This bus climbed shakily out of the village into the Euboean hills. Then it descended to a marshy area before climbing once again. Festus was tired, uneasy about their ability to track Pandora, and absorbed in his thoughts. Only Cathy and Chuck noticed the strange beauty of the dry, heather covered hills that rose from the road. Festus sat silently, in a daydream until the bus reached the fishing port of Karystos—near the southern tip of Euboea. It was now late afternoon. They found a hotel, a cool oasis from the sinking but still blazing sun. Chuck declined the invitation to stay with them.

"I'll camp out," he said. "Most of the kids camp just below the Castel Rosso. The authorities don't like it, I hear. From time to time, they eject everybody. I'll take my chances." He indicated writing on the walls of the bus station. "You see, we leave signs like hoboes and gypsies, to help each other. You can see the castle from over here. I'll see you tomorrow."

Cathy preempted any discussion of sleeping arrangements by stating that she wanted her room to have a shower. Festus did not know whether to feel relieved or frustrated. He had not worked out how to handle this self-contained girl; sexy one minute, prim the next—a miniature Marienna Cronson. At least he had not made a fool of himself by proposing a double room.

12. Chuck

Chuck strode through the village and up the hill to where tents were pitched below the castle. The sound of an inadequately strummed guitar, and a familiar herbal smell, wafted towards him. He pitched his tent a little way from the others. He ate some food and sat quietly puffing on a cigarette and sipping wine, until he could sense acceptance; then, guitar across his back, he sauntered over to the other tents. He approached a fire, around which a boy and two girls were cooking.

"Hi," he said, "I'm Chuck. Can I join you?"

The boy, a skinny sandy haired youth with freckles, looked up warily, and glanced at the girls. They smiled so, satisfied with what he saw, he moved over symbolically to make room.

"Sit down, mate."

"I'm Beth, and this is Kay. Kay's boyfriend here is Bob." Beth grinned, "I'm with me," making it clear she was unattached. "We're from Wisconsin. If you haven't already guessed, Bob's from Australia. Where've you come from?"

"I left Athens this morning and came through Khalkis."

"That's moving pretty fast," muttered Bob.

"Sure, but I met these characters, who were looking for someone and I said I'd help them."

"Police?" Kay asked, suspiciously.

"Good grief no!" Chuck said, laughing. "Just some Texan who's mislaid his daughter. He seemed a nice guy and pretty desperate."

"Is he traveling alone?"

"He's traveling with this lady...who's like...a teacher."

"No mother then?" Beth queried, knowingly.

"I guess the parents are sort of separated. His daughter Pandora was staying with this Greek guy's family. Her Old Man got delayed on business and his daughter just lit out."

Bob reacted quickly to this information. "Pandora, eh! I've not had anything to do with her, unfortunately. She was here a few days ago and I have the impression that nearly every other guy...how should I put it gracefully...came across her?"

"That's an unkind thing to say, Bob. You never saw anything happen." Beth was incensed.

"Sure, but the truth is I've never seen a girl who seemed to want it so much."

"It's true, Beth. Let's face it, the stupid little cow made a play for everyone. Don't you remember Bob here with his tongue hanging out?"

"I thought she was with some guy. Surely, he wouldn't have just sat around and let the other guys screw her. Who else was there?"

"You didn't see her mate," answered Bob defensively. "Or you wouldn't be asking. Well, maybe I'm exaggerating and it was just an impression she gave?"

"Where is she now?"

Bob shook his head. Kay shrugged. Beth on the other hand seemed to know, but was cautious. "You're telling me the truth about her old man, aren't you?"

Chuck nodded.

Beth looked intently at him. "Why do you care?"

"He seems like a nice guy. Really worried. Made me think of my parents and what they've done for me. I guess it's a chance to give something back," Chuck spread his hands, expressively, "and, maybe I'm an idiot?"

"All right, I believe you. She's with two guys and another girl. One of them is crazy about her and the others are friends of his. They only stayed here a day," she giggled. "You can see what a big impression your Pandora made."

"Wait a second. She's not mine. I've never met..."

"Just kidding. They left for Andros the day before yesterday. Or, maybe, it was the day before that? I don't pay much attention to time, you know. The boy who's crazy about her is called Joe. I don't remember the other guy's name. The girl is called...oh shit! What's her name?"

"Mo…no…Mildred. She's called Millie," Bob answered. "They're all from California."

So he would go to Andros, Chuck thought. Dr. Festus could wait until morning to hear the news. He felt restless and eyed Beth. She turned away slightly. He picked up his guitar and sang some Dylan songs to her. After a while, Beth stood and pointed at his tent, smiling. They moved off together, silently, his arm around her. Her body, all curves and shadows, melted into his sleeping bag. He snuggled against her and whispered, "I'm glad I was a scout. It taught me to be prepared. So I brought a double sleeping bag."

Beth chuckled against his cheek and pressed against him. "I'm tired of being alone in my tent listening to Bob and Kaye."

In the morning, Beth made coffee and they ate dry bread and honey and grapes. She tried to persuade Chuck to stay. He was tempted. Beth was attractive and pleasantly experienced. Yet some inner urge told him that he must move on. He held Beth, briefly, before packing up and making off down the hill to Karystos.

She watched him go, a wistful look on her face, and then made her way back to her tent, where Kay and Bob were huddled around the fire. "Let's go to Andros," she said.

13. Andros

Chuck found Festus and Cathy at breakfast. "We need to go to Andros," Chuck said. "Pandora left a few days ago with two boys, one of them called Joe is with her. There's a girl along called Millie."

Festus looked anxiously at Chuck. "They…up there, knew her, did they?"

Chuck stared into his coffee. "Yes, they knew about her. In a place like this, people get to know each other pretty quickly."

"Do you think you can trace her through the islands?"

Chuck hesitated. "Yeah, I think so. I guess our movements are predictable—a campsite here, a beach there. The only problem comes if there are options. Like this island or that island."

Festus sat agonizing whether to mention the syphilis possibilities. Cathy could see he was having trouble fighting his conscience and made the decision for him. "Chuck, I think we should tell you something. We're not sure, but there is a possibility that Pandora has VD. We think she may have had a liaison with a rather undesirable young man in Eleusis."

"Syphilis," added Festus.

"Oh!" said Cathy. "I didn't know it was that."

Chuck reacted quickly and angrily. "You should have told me before! I could have warned people here. I've got to go back to the camp and spread the word. Damn it!"

"I've no excuse, Chuck, except embarrassment. I find it hard to think about it, let alone talk about it." Festus' drawn face mirrored his feelings.

"I left Beth for this," Chuck muttered to himself. Aloud he said, "You go on to Andros. Leave a message for me in each post office. I'm going back up to the camp. I'll probably catch up with you tomorrow or the day after. Don't wait for me!" He picked up his backpack and guitar, and left. He did not look back. Festus watched him leave, guessing he would not return. It would be harder to find Pandora now, thought Festus, sadly.

Cathy and Festus boarded the boat, with a mass of islanders and a few tourists. The quay at Karystos, with its line of trees, the domed church in the background, and the Castel Rosso, seemingly perched on top of the highest dome, dwindled into the distance. The sea was choppy, and the boat lurched sickeningly all the way to the small port of Gavrion on the island of Andros.

The motion of the boat remained with them for a short time after they reached a café by the harbor. Festus ordered ouzo for himself, lemonade for Cathy, and a snack of olives and feta cheese. When the waiter returned, Festus asked him about the movement of young foreigners on the island. "Do they stay in Gavrion or in Port Andros?"

The waiter raised his hands, expressively. "They come here, with little money. They rarely use the cafe. They take all the benches intended for the old people. No, they don't stay in Gavrion, except to buy food and drink. You'll find them down on the beaches. They sleep in caves. Neanderthals! There are usually a lot of them just beyond Bastios, on the Road to Port Andros."

"How can we get there?"

"You've missed the bus, but my cousin has a taxi. If I can find him, he'll take you. Surely you don't intend to stay there, on the beach?"

"I don't know. We can always walk back to Bastios, I guess?"

The waiter shrugged. "It's your affair. I suggest you take some food with you. It's further than you imagine, and maybe you'll get hungry."

He gave them a menu. "You can order in the kitchen, while I go find my cousin."

"How can a man with such business acumen be just a waiter?" Wondered Festus aloud, explaining the conversation to Cathy.

They left a message for Chuck in the post office. Following the waiter's advice, they bought bread, sausage, fruit, wine and water. The cousin deposited them by the side of the road just beyond Bastios. He grasped Festus by the shoulders and turned him towards a path. "You'll find them camping down there. Do you want me to come back tomorrow morning?"

"Please come about nine."

The path led to a low cliff. Below it, there were some small rocky beaches separated by promontories. A number of the sunbathers, nude or semi-nude, turned away or covered themselves. Others, less self-conscious, turned directly towards them. There were curious, and suspicious stares, as Festus and Cathy approached.

Festus grinned at Cathy. "Now I really feel hot. Whew!" He loosened his shirt. One of the boys, offended by this intrusion, moved into their path. He was blond, his hair bleached nearly white by the sun. It appeared that his shorts did not mark the limit of his suntan. "Can I help you?" He asked in halting Greek.

Festus, judging that English might be a better compromise, answered. "Yes, we're looking for my daughter."

The boy studied them suspiciously, and some of the girls, pulling on clothes, came to his side, effectively blocking the path. "You're not police then?"

"No," said Festus, "I'm looking for my daughter. She ran away, and I believe she's ill. I need to find her."

A blonde, Scandinavian-looking girl, who appeared to be little older than Pandora, sniffed in disbelief, and spoke, hesitantly, in English.

"Parents! Why you not leave us alone? We want to do our own thing." She turned deliberately so that her shirt hung open, exposing her young breasts.

Festus looked away.

"Why won't you listen?" asked Cathy angrily. "He's trying to find his daughter!"

"So what?" the girl replied. "Let her do her own thing!"

Festus responded angrily. "No, damn it, no!" Forgetting himself, he blurted, "My daughter's name is Pandora. She's not well and I must find her...and get treatment for her. Please help me."

When he said Pandora, they went into a huddle and consulted. In the meantime another boy appeared. He looked curiously at Festus and Cathy, then more searchingly at Festus, and joined the huddle.

The first youth looked up. "Pierre thinks he recognize you from newspaper pictures. You're Dr. Festus, aren't you? You look for Loch Ness Monster, right?" He grinned.

Festus acknowledged it and introduced Cathy.

"Oh! I see," said the boy. "We guessed she was Pandora's sister."

Cathy snorted and squeezed Festus's arm.

They consulted again. "Okay we'll help and say what we know. There is a girl here who was with Pandora—Millie. She'll be back later. Where are you going tonight?"

Festus suggested that they would walk back to Bastios, because they needed to leave a message for Chuck.

"No need to do that. Stay here. We'll tell you about Pandora if you'll tell us about Loch Ness."

Festus, surprised at the sudden turn in attitude, nodded his agreement. What he did not realize was that he had become a kind of folk hero. From the time he had taken over the hunt, Zack had been publicizing the work of the Foundation. Articles on the Loch Ness hunt had been widespread in the world's press. This impression that Festus was a brilliant but entertainingly, nutty scientist had broken down the barrier to Chuck, and it was working well again.

"That's settled. We must find you a place to stay. I'm Helmut." He indicated the younger girl. "This is Astrid."

"Helmut, let me speak to you for a moment." Festus took him by the arm and walked him away from the group. He explained Pandora's problem. Helmut looked shocked.

"What are you going to do about it?" he asked.

Festus had expected the question. "I must admit that until we got to Karystos I hadn't faced up to that. Since Karystos, though, I've talked to my friends and we think the best thing is for anyone who had sex with her to go to Athens. A clinic there handles such cases. My cousin will fix it. I'll pay."

"Sounds good. I'll bring Millie along later."

Festus followed them down the path. "I can offer you a fine room, Dr. Festus. The bridal suite is taken." Helmut grinned at Astrid.

"Most people call me Fes or Doc. I would prefer it if you did too. Being called Dr. Festus makes me feel old."

"Okay Doc. Now, I guess you'll need something to sleep on."

"Where…" Cathy stared hard at Festus, for a second. "We'll be fine in here."

Festus looked at her sharply. She held his gaze and he remained silent. He had the fleeting thought that he shouldn't agree, but suppressed it rapidly.

"It's too hot for more talk now," Helmut said. "We swim first, cook later, and then talk. I'll let you sort out your fine apartment. Cathy, come with me and see what we can find."

Cathy returned with a blanket and one ratty looking sleeping bag. "I'm embarrassed to explain it to such a distinguished person as you but there's a trick to this bag," she said, as she showed Festus how to zip it up.

"What about you? Is the blanket enough?" Festus worried.

Cathy looked intently at him, her blue eyes evaluating him, carefully.

"Maybe we can work something out?"

Festus started to question her, but again she held his look steadily and in turn, he held himself in check. For the first time in days, he felt relaxed. "Yes, that would be good." He said.

She smiled at him. "Come on, let's go for a swim."

Cathy took off her dress. Underneath she wore only panties. Her breasts were white. "There's a first time for everything," she said, laughing.

Festus suddenly felt very unsure of himself—illogically so. Dawn was as good looking as any woman he'd ever known and he'd seen her naked, made love to her for many years, yet at the sight of this girl naked he…Cathy interrupted his thought. "It's okay Fes; you can keep your shorts on."

"I'm embarrassed. I have a bad leg."

"I know. You limp. It doesn't matter. Anyway, that's not what you're thinking about." She laughed.

Festus grinned, and dropped his jeans. "Let's swim."

Cathy took his hand and led him, like a small boy, down to the water. In the water, Festus was a different man. His bad leg was less of a problem in the water, and with his powerful shoulders, he swam well. They splashed, shouted, and dunked each other like children, until exhausted, they returned to lie in the sun and rest.

Sitting by the fire, Festus told the group, assembled from up and down the shore, about the Loch Ness adventure. He found it surprisingly difficult to talk about Loch Ness. Failure was a new experience, and he had no prepared response to the question of what he would do next. What if there wasn't a next time? What if Zack had sold the sub? For the next hour, he answered their questions patiently, and then he looked appealingly at Helmut to fulfill his part of the bargain. Helmut turned to a short plump girl sitting on the outside of the group.

"Your turn, Millie. Tell Doc about Pandora." He signaled behind his back for everyone else to leave. "I didn't tell anyone else yet, Doc."

Millie sat next to Festus, looking into the fire. She looked untidy, used and unsure of herself. "Pandora picked us up on the beach near Eleusis. I guess about a week or so ago. She was with some children. Came over and sat with us—that is, Frankie, Joe and me. I remember her words, 'Can I make up the set', she said.

Frankie and Joe didn't waste time agreeing. She's sexy." Millie paused. "We thought she was kidding but, when we said we were going to Khaklis, she arranged to meet us the next morning and we all went on from there."

"Why did you stay here?" Cathy asked.

Millie was silent for a while, thinking of an answer, anger building up inside as she felt for the right words, then she poured it all out, not caring. "The little bitch...no apologies...I found her screwing Frankie."

"Oh!" said Festus involuntarily. Cathy squeezed his hand. He lowered his head.

"Then it didn't work out with Joe. I was sick of traveling day to day, anyway, and there's a good group here, so I left them."

"What did Joe do about it? He must have been upset?"

"Upset sure, but Frankie bosses him around."

"How long had Frankie and Pandora been...you know...?"

"I don't know."

"This may seem like a strange question. Did you and Frankie, or Joe...uh...after she had been with him?"

"What kind of a question is that? Oh...oh! You mean she's got something, don't you? Oh, shit." She began to cry. "The bastards!"

"I guess the best thing I can do is put it to you directly. We are not sure, but it's possible that Pandora may have syphilis."

"Oh, Jesus!"

Helmut, watching from a distance, sauntered over. "It'll be okay, Millie. Fes wants to help you," he said.

Festus motioned him to sit. "I told her about Pandora's illness." He had difficulty continuing.

Cathy took over. "It seems that after Pandora slept with Frankie, Frankie slept with Millie, once, and then Millie went with Joe. "Millie, can you come with us to Gavrion tomorrow?"

"I don't know. I..."

"Millie, the symptoms won't show for a few weeks. It'll probably be best if you go back to Athens so that treatment can start as soon as possible," Cathy said. "We'll finalize the arrangements to get you treated, if it turns out you've got it."

Helmut reached out and took her hand. "Have you been with anyone else since then, Millie?"

She shook her head, crying softly to herself. "I'll come with you," she whispered.

"Good."

Festus waited until she had recovered her composure and then asked the question he had been holding back.

"Do you know where Pandora went?"

"We were all going to Tinos, Siros and Naxos then on to Santorini. Frankie was interested in stories about Santorini being connected to Atlantis—archaeology and that sort of thing. He was going to try to get work on an archeological dig. Is that enough?"

Festus thanked her and she went away to be comforted by Helmut and Astrid.

He clambered along the steep rocky path worrying about Pandora. How could she be so promiscuous? Dawn was the problem he rationalized. However, the sight of Cathy and his response to her, forced an acknowledgement that he was as much the problem. We all need attention, he thought. Pandora and I are both reaching out for it. A modicum of sex doesn't hurt either. Unfortunately, she's not mature enough to be discriminating. He reached for Cathy and she took his hand and helped him down to her side.

"You look worried, Fes. Tell me about it!"

"I'm not sure I want to. Oh, what the hell! Dawn and I are both selfish. Only reach out to each other when we're both depressed. It's not a good environment for a child to grow up in. Dawn flirts. I reckoned she was having an affair. Trapped her and Ari in Blarney. I had photos. Showed them to everybody. Ari's daughter Sam was there. Pandora found out. It's a mess."

Cathy, who had sat quietly until this point, sympathetically stroking his hand, pulled away in shock. "You really did that? I believed Marienna when she said you were vulnerable. Good grief! Poor Dawn. I'm not surprised y'all have problems." She looked as if she had just eaten something distasteful. Her eyes seemed more prominent than normal. "It's incredible I never heard about that in Argos. Of course I'm a foreigner aren't I?"

Festus looked embarrassed. "It's difficult to be a successful scientist...or for that matter to be a success at anything, without being a little arrogant. The problem is that it carries over into other facets of ones life. After Blarney, I was initially very pleased with myself. That changed to depression, though I'd recovered more or less by the time this business happened. You know, I was really angry. Angry with everyone, especially Dawn." He paused and reflected a while. Cathy let go of his hand. "In reality, I was angry with myself. I can admit it now. I hope I can help Pandy...and Dawn."

Cathy stopped further talk. "I may be back later," she said, picking up her tote bag.

Festus watched her leave. He suddenly felt apprehensive again. Somehow, everything had changed when he had told the truth about Blarney. Damn!

She did not return. Festus tossed and turned in frustration. Had he misunderstood her? He lay on the sleeping bag, pushing himself hard into the hard ground to relieve his frustration. God! He'd go to church and light a thousand candles if she would come back.

After a while, he slept. She did not appear but his dreams invented her return...*Hephaestus moved carefully, raising his legs to hide his excitement. He felt very foolish sitting there with his arms around his knees. A misty looking mortal girl looked at him knowingly but warmly.*

"Have you been preparing yourself?" she asked, laughing. "Maybe this will keep it up." She stood at his feet and pulled up her tunic, wiggling her body suggestively as she did it. Hephaestus watched as the tunic rose. Her long slim legs blended into a lean body, the dark shadow of her pubic hair standing out as the dress pulled across her hips. Her hard nipples caught the tunic as she pulled it over her head. She posed in front of him, spreading her legs suggestively.

At that critical moment, the Chorus from the plays minced into the cave. They were wearing old-fashioned swimming costumes and had buskins on their feet. "Oh Lord Hephaestus, you seem to be up again? Just what are you up to? Is this mortal trifle a substitute for the glorious Aphrodite? Woe to you! Woe! Woe!"

"Not again, dear Cronos, make them leave. Go away you morons! Don't ruin this for me!" His stomach hurt with frustration as he willed them out of his dream. She mocked him. "Your mortal slave awaits your desires."

Hephaestus suddenly felt no embarrassment. He unclasped his arms, pulled his shorts down and let his legs lie flat. "Wench, can you do anything about this problem?"

"Oh, yes, Lord Hephaestus, I can." She knelt in front of him and slowly moved up his body, gently kissing him until she lay on top of him. Hephaestus closed his arms around her. His hands molded to the firm roundness of her thighs and he caressed up them to hold her to him. They made love, slowly and with care for each other.

The images of his wet dream flickered to a close and he fell into a deep sleep. In the morning, he had difficulty knowing whether it had been real, but only for a moment. Cathy wasn't there.

Festus slept until light filtered into the cave. Cathy was kneeling beside him looking down at his face, when his eyes flickered open. She held out a mug of coffee. Festus turned over onto his elbow, scratched his head and motioned her to set the mug aside. He tried to caress her and she moved away.

"You've got to get dressed. The taxi will be here soon. Millie is ready. Drink you coffee!"

"Cathy, what went wrong? Last night, I thought…"

"I don't know you well enough, Fes. You scare me. How could you do what you did at Blarney?"

"I don't know. It just seemed like the right thing to do when I thought of it."

"Do you have to do everything you think of?"

Festus reflected for a moment. "I suppose not, but at the time it seemed right."

"The play cycle?"

"Why did you think of that?"

"Last night I had this weird dream," Cathy replied. "I didn't sleep well. I'd rustled a blanket and slept in Millie's cave. It smelled of Millie." Her nose wrinkled in distaste. "I got to thinking about the Play cycle. I could see you. Wearing a white tunic, god-like. You were working on a piece of metal, crafting it to form the arm of a chair, a bronze chair. I brought you wine. You looked up and smiled at me. You took a sip and handed it back, indicating I should drink. I was frightened."

"What happened," Festus asked, grinning.

"We talked. It went something like this."

"I, a mortal girl, must not drink the wine of the Gods."

"Do not worry. I will protect you. Drink!"

"When my lips touched the rim, the sky darkened, and a roll of thunder broke the silence. You, Hephaestus, looked up angrily, and raised your fist. 'Leave me alone, Aphrodite!' you bellowed. 'I care for her.'"

"Then you put your arm around me."

"And?" Festus asked, impatiently.

"I woke up, abruptly."

"Damn!" Festus laughed. "I had a dream too. Better ending. What a coincidence."

"Look, Fes. I don't understand what's happening. I know you've got to find Pandora, and then go on from there. I've enjoyed being with you, if only for a short time. I'm scared of becoming too involved. You don't have Dawn out of your system yet. I don't want to be hurt." Thereafter, she kept a distance between them.

When Millie arrived, clutching her few belongings in a backpack, they started the climb back up the cliff. His mind returned to Pandora and he tried to work out how he would treat her, when they met. If they met, he thought unhappily.

They waited for some while for the taxi, which took them back to Gavrion. Festus spent an impatient day, torn between wanting to move on to Santorini with Cathy, and waiting for Chuck.

Chuck arrived soon after Millie had left for Athens. Chuck appeared to be in a better humor since they had left him in Karystos. Later, Cathy asked him why he had decided to rejoin them. *"Not sure," Chuck replied. "Opportunity, curiosity, and an illogical desire to meet Pandora. Who knows? There was this girl who was not happy at my choice," he added.*

They boarded the first of a number of boats, which over the next few days took them hopping from one island to another. Tinos was a waste of time. In Naxos, they tracked Joe to a pretty ravine, filled with a river of oleanders. Joe was not a pretty sight. He was broke, drunk, and nearly suicidal.

"They dumped me. Frankie's a bastard."

"Where did they go?"

"I don't give a fuck! Frankie's a bastard and..."

"I heard you. Some people need to talk to you."

"So what!"

"They'll pay for information."

"I need help." Joe's head sank.

"Did you sleep with Millie?"

"Once. We were drunk."

"You may have syphilis."

"Oh, shit!" Joe began to cry.

Chuck settled his bill, helped him to his feet and managed to drag him back to the hotel. They waited until he was sober. Joe confirmed that Pandora and Frankie had gone to Santorini, where they planned to obtain work on a dig. He thought it was a few days earlier, but his mind was hazy on that score.

When they left the next day, Joe had begun to recover from his alcoholic daze. Festus gave him some money and advised him to go to directly to Athens where Millie would be waiting. Joe accepted the advice gratefully and they left him on the quay, grinning and waving; a man reprieved from the gallows.

14. Pandora

It was late morning when the steamer entered the Bay of Santorini, the most southerly island of the Cyclades group. The glimmering white town of Thera was perched on the cliff that towered over their boat. A thin layer of bushes and trees skirted and infiltrated around the lower houses like an unshaven chin. Behind a small jetty, brightly painted rowing boats rocked gently in a floating sea of pumice. Festus and Cathy mounted donkeys, which carried them up the zigzag path to the town. The ride was accompanied by much muttering and blaspheming when the donkeys, clinging close to the upper side of the cliff, persistently grated them against it. Chuck disdained to take the ride, preferring to walk and protect his precious guitar. They found a *pensione* quickly and, refreshed by drinks, some food and more drinks, they prepared to start their inquiries.

"There are two possible digs," Festus said, "the continued excavation of the site of the old Thera, and the excavations started by Professor Marinatos near Akrotiri. Why don't Cathy and I go to Thera and you, Chuck, go to Akrotiri? We can all take a taxi and it can drop us off on the way to Akrotiri and then return to pick us up later. If our search is unsuccessful, we'll come and join you."

Festus and Cathy walked down what had been the main street of the old town of Thera. It was a magnificent site, seemingly floating above the sea. Their questions had unearthed nothing and they were idling the time away, taken up with their own thoughts. Festus, brooding about Atlantis, bent down to pick up a dried flower stem from between some stones. He would like to spend time to study Atlantis, he thought. Nowadays, it seemed to be generally believed that Atlantis was Crete, whose civilization had been destroyed by the eruptions of this volcanic island that had been the center of what was known then as Kaliste, 'the most beautiful.' It seemed to fit in with his memories. How could he have memories? His daydream continued…

In the street people were moving now. It was a market area. He stopped and purchased some grapes. The farmer selling them greeted him with respect.

"Something else for your lady, Sir?"

The mortal girl touched his arm. "I need nothing." It seemed she was about to add that she wanted him, but an image of Artemis appeared warning her to be silent. "Remember your Sapphic vows!" the goddess ordered. Hephaestus offered her a grape. She reached to take it. There was a loud clamor.

Their taxi had arrived. Festus lifted his hands, as if expecting to find in them something more dramatic than the dried grass he was holding. He looked to see if Cathy had felt anything. She was staring in puzzlement at the piece of grass he had given her. They looked away from each other and remained silent all the way to Akrotiri, where Chuck rushed up to greet them. "They've been here," Chuck said, "but, a few days ago, Frankie was fired for being drunk."

"Where are they now?" Festus asked, worriedly.

"As far as I can tell, we're in luck. They're in a hut near the sea below Kamara. It's about one kilometer from here." He pointed to the south, where a track wound down over the gravel topped pumice to the sea. "I think it…"

Festus hardly waited to hear him before heading off down the track. His limp was very pronounced as he tried to move faster. At the top of the final descent, he paused to look down. His face was grim. The blue sea glinted harshly against the stark white cliffs. Poised above the sea was a small hut of dark pumice. He moved blindly towards the hut.

Cathy restrained Chuck. Festus opened the door slowly. He stood transfixed by the scene inside. The room had a rancid smell. Empty wine bottles and one partly filled, gave witness to the state of the naked couple sprawled on the bunk that faced the door. Cathy came to his shoulder. "Oh, my God!" she gasped.

Pandora, her blond hair spreading over the floor in supplication to them, lay on her back moaning in climax. Her face hung upside down over the side of the bed. She was facing the door, but did not see them, her eyes closed as she concentrated on her orgasm. A boy with straggly dark hair knelt on the other side of the bed. His head was buried between her legs, and his hands were massaging her breasts. His dark moustache moved feverishly, above her blond pubic hair as he excited her.

Festus staggered forward. In one movement, he grabbed the boy by his hair and an arm and swung him off the bed and against the wall. Frankie half rose, grasping his bruised shoulder.

"What the fuck do you think you are…?" Frankie stopped as Festus went for him again, his face a mask of hate and pain. Cathy, suddenly aware of the danger, grabbed his arm.

"Leave him! It won't do any good!"

Festus glared, and then pulled Frankie away from the wall and pushed him out of the hut. He fell to the ground and crawled a few yards before collapsing in a dazed state, too drunk to run. Chuck, who had been about to enter the hut and help Festus, stood guard over him, relieved at being able to stay outside.

Pandora continued to lie in front of Festus and Cathy, her eyes blearily opening and closing. Festus moved towards the bed. In her drunken state, she knew only that more people had arrived, but could not understand who they were.

"Come on, Frankie, don't stop, please." Her arms reached out pathetically towards Festus. He couldn't see Pandora, in some strange juxtaposition of images she had become the Inverness prostitute. He stepped back, shocked, shaking his head as if to clear the scene from his mind, turned and stumbled out of the hut past Cathy.

"Please help her. I'm no use." He carried on down to the seashore and stood looking blankly out across the sea. In his shocked state, he reverted to his earlier daydream…

The earth shook, and the clouds from the volcano filled the sky, moving south towards Crete. "Oh Atlantis, where are you now?" He cried again, out across the waves.

Cathy took charge. She went to the door and shouted to Chuck. "Grab that creature, tell him the facts of life, get him dressed, sober him up, give him Nicholas Kronosakis' address, and get him off this island and back to Athens! I'll deal with Pandora. Here's some cash. Take the taxi, and then send it back for us! We'll meet it on our way back."

"Tell me what?" Frankie said drunkenly.

"She may have syphilis."

"Oh, shit!"

Cathy found a bottle of water in a corner, and with determined pleasure poured it over Pandora, who was single-mindedly trying to masturbate to a further orgasm. Pandora fell off the bed spluttering and leaned weakly against the wall. "Wha shit's happenin'?"

Pandora peered at Cathy through narrowed eyes. "Mis-sss-us Schmidt, wha're you doing here?"

"Your father's here. We've come to take you home."

"Oh Jesus…Jesus…leave me alone?" Pandora turned her head wildly, looking for Festus, and catching instead a glimpse of Frankie, being bundled away. "Where're you going, Frankie?" she wailed. He didn't hear.

Cathy looked at her sadly. "We'll talk later. Let's get you dressed. We've been tracking you down for days. Your Dad's real upset." Pandora looked disbelieving. "Get it into your head! He loves you."

Pandora, finally awake to her situation, collapsed in tears on the bed. "He doesn't care shit. You want me to tell you what he did to Mom?"

Cathy ignored the question. "Let's get you fixed up some before he comes back." She pulled Pandora to her feet, cleaned her, combed out her tangled hair, found the cleanest of a heap of clothes and dressed her. She came out into the sunlight, clutching her few belongings, a scared child with a drawn and frightened face. Festus stood, his feet leaden, wanting to take her in his arms, but his horror at what he had witnessed was preventing it. Cathy settled the problem, taking Pandora by the hand and bringing her to him. Hesitantly, Festus reached out for her hand. Pandora did not take it and looked away. They walked in single file, silently, back towards Akrotiri.

The next day, Festus tried to explain about Blarney. Pandora listened stony faced with no comment. She would not say much about what had happened in Greece. Fortunately, she was more forthcoming with Cathy, who then passed on the story to Festus. It seemed that she had not had sex with Christos—Frankie was the first and only one—"useless, stupid little virgin, nobody will love a loser like you." Pandora had sobbed out the Christos' parting words. It was much crueler than Maria had overheard. It was enough, in her depressed state, to cause her to run away. Frankie had been kind and loving at first, she said, and that was what she had needed.

Festus, while relieved that some things were not as bad as he had been led to believe, was having a hard time coming to terms with the change in his 'little girl'. Nevertheless, he agreed with Cathy that Pandora should go to a doctor for a checkup. Just in case Frankie wasn't clean.

While Cathy took Pandora to the doctor, Chuck sat with Festus, who was drinking morosely. By an unspoken mutual agreement, they had not talked about Pandora or, for that matter, at all.

"Would you like me to leave?"

"What? No, I don't want to be alone. Let's talk about something." Festus did not volunteer a subject. They sat in silence a while longer.

"Is it generally agreed now that this is the area where Atlantis existed?"

Festus woke from his thoughts. "Er...not exactly here. The current theory is that the Minoan Empire, centered in Crete, was the Atlantis referred to by Plato." He paused, it was hard to think straight. "The civilization was wrecked when this island suffered a series of eruptions, starting around 1400 BC—creating tsunamis and covering an enormous area, including Crete, with tephra.

"The newspaper mentioned this Foundation of yours. Could you investigate it as part of your work?"

"Yes, maybe. I've thought about it."

"Maybe, you could research something before you return to Texas?"

"I'd like to, but hell! I'm responsible for what's happened to Pandora. I neglected her because of over commitment to my work. I just don't think I could justify it."

"It could be a good idea to wait a bit before returning to Texas? Give Pandora a chance to recover. If you take her back now, with everything fresh in her memory, she may have difficulty in dealing with her friends." Chuck volunteered, diffidently.

Festus brooded over it. "You may be right. It's a good idea. Stay over a couple of weeks before going back. I guess I can afford to."

"There you go."

"I need time on my own with Pandora. We could go to the palace of Phaestos in Crete." Festus looked thoughtful. "Also, there's this tablet, the Phaestos Disk. There's no, generally accepted, translation." He paused, thinking about how to repay Chuck. "Our company, Olympic Services, is in Austin. Would you consider working for me part time?"

"Thanks for the offer. I'll think about it." Chuck replied, cautiously.

"Let me give you a note of introduction. Just in case I'm not there," Festus said.

"Okay." Chuck started to leave. Festus motioned him to stay.

"Pandora's still not talking to me. I'm not sure what to do."

"Let me try. Maybe she'll open up with someone nearer her age."

The following morning, Festus came down to find Pandora on the terrace. She was absorbed in the view of the bay and the still smoldering Kameri Islets. He came up behind her and touched her lightly on the top of her blonde head. She stiffened, then turned and hesitantly wrapped her arms around his neck— saying nothing, holding briefly, and then moving away. She was very different now from the creature he had seen in the hut the previous day; a sight he was trying to forget. She was again the girl he liked to remember, with her mother's fine-drawn features beginning to emerge.

She was still wary of him, he realized. "I missed you. I'm sorry I was away for so long."

"I missed you too," Pandora replied, quietly, then added, apprehensively, "Are we going straight home?"

Festus felt his way. "Would you like to stay in Greece a little longer?"

"Yes, but not here, with Miss Schmidt…Cathy. I'd feel embarrassed with her around."

"No, sure, I understand," Festus replied quickly, sensing the slightly jealous tone to Pandora's request, though he didn't like the idea of losing touch with Cathy.

"Not too long. I want to see Mom."

"Sure." Festus replied, uncertainly, not knowing when Dawn would return to Argos. "I thought of going to Crete, to Phaestos. Our name comes from there, you know."

"Yes Dad, I know. You've told me every year since I was little."

"We've got your Mom's relatives there. I could arrange something there."

"I know, Dad. I really don't want to see any relatives."

"Okay."

Cathy stepped onto the terrace. "I overheard some of that. It's a good idea. Don't forget to wire Marienna, call Nico and let them know what you'll be doing. Also remember to tell Nico that gardener lied about Pandora."

"Yes Ma'am. Pandora could you go and sort through your clothes? See what else you need. I'd like a couple of minutes to talk to Cathy."

Festus waited to make sure Pandora was out of earshot. "Cathy, about us…"

Cathy did not wait for him to continue. "Fes, frankly, I'm not sure that there can be an 'us.' What about Pandora and Dawn?"

"So you'll go to Germany?"

"Yes. You need time alone with Pandora. I've got to get to my job in Mannheim. I'm packed." She gave Festus a quick kiss, turned on her heels, stopping briefly at the door. "When you get your act together, y'all give me a call! Marienna knows where I am. Write anyway!" She left before her tears gave her away.

Festus remained on the terrace, watching her leave. He wanted to follow and beg her to stay. But she was right, having time alone with Pandora was more important.

Chuck walked Cathy to the boat. "Fes offerd me a part-time job. Any advice?"

"From what I hear he's a brilliant man. He's great in the play we do and very considerate when we help his godmother. But I don't know what he would be like to work for."

"What about Pandora." Chuck looked sheepish. "Do you think I would get to see her?"

"Interesting question." Cathy grinned. "Will Fes ever let her speak to another man?"

Festus and Pandora traveled to Crete, spending the first few days around Iraklion, playing at being tourists.

Pandora watched her father with amusement. They were in the Museum of Cretan antiquities and he was absorbed, studying a case of artifacts from the palace at Phaestos. The reflection of her face in the glass of the showcase suddenly came into focus.

"I can see you. What are you grinning at?"

"Oh, Dad! The way you get into this kind of stuff."

"I'm sorry I'm neglecting you again. Let's move on."

"It's fine. You might find out somethin'. You're so clever."

"I wish I had your confidence," Festus smiled.

"Hey! Look at this! Neat-o!" Pandora had found the case containing the Phaestos Disk, a brownish circular slab of terracotta. "Look it's got lots of symbols on it. This is the one you've been talkin' about, isn't it Dad?"

Festus peered in. "The Phaestos Disk!" he exclaimed. "Years ago, Marienna showed me pictures in a National Geographic. It's always fascinated me. The photographs don't do it justice." He stopped. His heart was pounding, and his legs felt weak. For a moment, he felt as if he ought to be able to read it. He mouthed words that had no meaning.

"Dad! Are you okay? You look ghastly."

"Sure, honey. I felt faint for a minute. I've been on the road too long. I'll be fine. Yes, that's the Disk. I've wondered for some time what it means."

"Take it on as challenge."

"Yes, maybe I should." He took a last look. "Let's carry on upstairs. See the frescoes. Then get some lunch."

"Look at those ladies!—*La Parisienne*. Isn't she elegant? I wish I could look like her." Pandora pulled her hair into a high ponytail, held her head high and arched her back. "What do you think?"

"Cretan girls have always been elegant, but nowhere near as pretty as you."

"Dad! You old flatterer." She kissed him lightly and swayed down the stairs.

From that day on, Festus had the look of someone with an idea on the tip of his mind. Apparently, it was something he could work on while relaxing. The look increased in intensity after they moved to Matala, on the southern coast, to be close to the ancient palaces of Phaestos and Hagia Triada. In fact, they spent little time looking at the remains of the Cretan civilization and more time lazing on the beach. For the first time in years, Festus felt relaxed. The stark gray and white, mountains contrasted with the greener villages. The olive trees, cypresses and oleander, shimmered in the bright sun. He was reborn. It was not, however, until their last week on the island that the idea clicked into place, and his inner smirk became nearly unbearable. Pandora pulled his leg mercilessly about it, but he would not divulge his idea.

Stuck in a plane waiting to take off, he thought. Fumes from the engines permeated the cabin. Disjointed background music prompted a concern about the overall engineering of the system. It did not worry Festus; he had learned to live with the limitations of engineers. As the engines roared during takeoff, he was smiling happily at the thought that this Labor had been completed successfully. Pandora oscillated between affection and wariness, but they now understood each other a little better. The episode on Andros had forced him to rethink his priggish conception of morality and sex, and he was more understanding of Pandora's needs. He hoped that Pandora had a better understanding of the inner conflict, between work and family that raged within his mind. He glanced at her surreptitiously. She was contentedly reading a book—in Greek for God's sake! Festus was elated. He had recovered Pandora and he, Festus, had started another long-term project, to translate the Phaestos Disk. Maybe it really did hold the secret to the treasure he had mentioned to Zack? The excitement allowed him to forget Loch Ness for a brief time.

15. Argos

Pandora was chattering excitedly over the sound of Elvis Presley coming from the radio. Festus hardly heard these background noises. He was eager to return home, and concentrating on the scenery. The long absence had sharpened his appetite for well-remembered sights. He glimpsed the track that led to the abandoned settlement of Mormon Mill, just south of Burnett. Lyman Wright, a Mormon apostle of Joseph Smith, had taken his flock there following the murder of Smith in Chicago in 1844. The small community had lived at Mormon Mill from 1851 until 1853, when Wright again felt the call to move on. The thought led his mind to make the connection to his own family, a unit apparently as fragile as the Mormon Mill community. He had recovered Pandora, but he had lost his wife. His emotions surfaced and his eyes were watering. He closed them and concentrated on imagining the road.

We're on the final section now, close to Arcadia, he thought. I make a slow right here. Sure enough, he could tell it by the sulfurous smell of the oil fields that permeated the car. He sat back savoring it. Funny though, it was more acrid than he had remembered. "The smell seems stronger than it used to?"

"I didn't say anything, Doc. Wondered when you'd notice. One of the wells on the Everyman Field has blown its top," Joe Maximos who was driving, answered. "You'll see it in a minute."

Sure enough, in the distance was a pall of smoke. Great gushes of flame shafted up from the ground. It had been raining. The glinting, puddles of water made the conflagration look huge.

"Old Max can't be happy about that," mused Festus, smiling to himself as he pictured the patriarch of the Maximos clan; a miniature man in a black suit, with bright black eyes framed by a wing-necked collar and a shock of thinning white hair. In all of Festus' forty odd years, Old Max had not changed much, except for shrinkage. At the age of ninety-six, he still held considerable influence in Arcadia, though his son Prometheus, Joe's father, now managed the family enterprises.

As a teenager, Odysseus Maximos fled Rethymnon in his native Crete, still under Turkish domination, for the Greek mainland. In Athens, he found work with the import-export firm of Ralli Brothers, who dealt in cotton. An opening for the position of senior clerk in the New York offices of the company had led him to the United States. A short while later in 1892, at the age of twenty-five, he opened a new office for the company in Galveston, Texas. There he worked for eight years expanding the firm's dealings in the Texas cotton trade. It was a time marked by substantial migration from Greece and Crete to the United States. As Greek consular agent, Odysseus Maximos was a focal point for many of these emigrants. His business expanded beyond the horizons of the Ralli Brothers, until it included a restaurant, a shoeshine parlor and a kaffenion.

The main rival for authority in the Gulf Coast Greek community was Agamemnon Kronosakis, once an employee of Ralli Brothers like Odysseus and owner of a bank. Kronosakis was a fellow Cretan, from the province of Sfakia.

Their rivalry rose to its peak in the infamous incident, when Agamemnon attempted to steal oil from a well on Old Max's land known as the Everyman Bore.

Joe interrupted Festus' thoughts of Argos. "Old Max is really pissed off, Doc. He's harking back to the old days. I think he believes the fire was Zack's doing."

"You've got to be kidding," said Fes. "All of that died out years ago. Hell! We're all kin."

"Apparently, my 'nonos' has flipped. Zack's really worried."

"So Old Max is reverting to his youth?" Fes shook his head, smiling at the contrast between Joe's nearly childlike use of the Greek name nonos for grandfather, and his own image of the ruthless patriarch. "Next thing you know somebody will be pumping mud again."

"What do you mean?" asked Pandora, who had been ignoring the conversation to that point.

"We're getting old," said Festus, glancing at Joe. "Honey we were referring to that famous incident in the thirties when a large oil strike was made right back there on Old Max's land. You tell her Joe!"

"It was like this, Pandy, our foreman noticed that the drilling mud coming back was different from what they were using. Old Max guessed the cause, immediately. The only other well they could see was on Agamemnon Cro...your other grandfather's land, close up to the boundary between the two properties and about half a mile away. From their tests at the time, Old Max was convinced that the oil didn't go in that direction, so he guessed that the Cronson's had found a way of drilling sideways."

"You mean they don't just drill straight down, Dad?"

Joe was reasonably sure that Pandora knew the answer and watched amusedly as Festus launched into a more detailed explanation.

"Heavens no, Pandy! That would mean putting drilling rigs all over the place. With bias drilling or extended reach drilling, you can cover a large area from one place—as much as 10,000 acres or more, if you can drill at sixty degrees. There are all sorts of tricks used to increase the angle: special drilling mud with oil in it to decrease friction; eccentric tool joints to reduce differential sticking of the drill string; hydraulic collars to grip the walls of the hole; and so on. These are replacing the more conventional approach that was used to tap the Maximos well. Sorry for the lecture. Your granddad invented a type of bit used for bias drilling the Everyman field. Sad thing is he didn't want it used for that particular bit of piracy."

"I bet it's worth a lot of money," Pandora said, calculatingly.

"Yes. Unfortunately, there wasn't much for us. The Cronsons set up the engineering works. They own many of his inventions, or take most of the royalties. Agamemnon needed to appease Old Max, and forced my father to share the rights with him. Even so, Old Max blamed your granddad for the incident. They never spoke to each other again. It's a bit late but, for my father's sake, I'd like to get some kind of reconciliation."

"It doesn't seem fair. You wouldn't get caught like that, would you?"

"I try hard not to, honey," Festus grimaced, remembering what had happened after the Loch Ness Labor. Zack better have a damn good explanation for that newspaper article.

"To get back to the story," Joe continued. "Old Max came up with a solution. He closed off all his wells except the one that showed Cronson slurry. He attached all of his mud pumps, put on full power, pressurizing that well. He colored the mud as a joke. When Cronson's crew withdrew their drill to change the bit, a shower of mud—pink mud—sprayed all over them. The pressure laid Agamemnon flat on his back."

"I bet he was mad."

"I was only a little kid then," said Joe, "but I must have heard the story a hundred times. I think your granddaddy, Agamemnon, was more embarrassed than mad. Unfortunately, it really screwed it up between my family and you Cronsons. You saw it, didn't you Doc?"

Festus nodded uneasily. He had not thought of himself as a Cronson. Maybe it was true.

"It didn't help that they were sharing a common boundary, at a time when boundaries were not always recorded," Joe added. "There were serious fights during the next couple of years. Fortunately, oil was discovered on Agamemnon's land and things eased up."

"I haven't seen mister Maximos often, but he always seems to be such a sweet old man. What could he do?" asked Pandora.

Festus considered the appalling thought of what Old Max could do. "He knows a lot about us. He can cause more trouble than simple violence." He didn't elaborate on this point, though Pandora quizzed him on it. "We've gotta do something, Joe. I'll offer to help. Surely they've called in experts."

"They have," Joe said. "They've tried everything. First, bulldozers to close the well, then explosives, but that only made it worse. It's such an old field, and the fire is in the middle of it. There's a hell of a lot of rockers and pipes and tanks. They're scared of setting of everything in sight, in a chain reaction. Zack offered help, but Old Max won't have anything to do with him."

Festus brooded about the fire. He supposed this must be his fourth Labor. In old times, the capture of the Erymanthian Boar that had been ravaging the country around Mount Erymanthus? It was strange how the Labors kept on appearing, one after the other, as if it was planned. What was the connection this time? The fire was ravaging the oil field, and it was a Bore? He giggled to himself at the stupidity of the idea. Did it matter? Not really, all he had to do was think of a way of putting it out. What would Hephaestus have done? Probably use bias drilling again.

Naturally, Zack would expect him to solve the problem. Here I go again, he thought; technological mercenary solving problems for Zack, like a performing dog. It wasn't obvious that either his father, or Hephaestus for that matter, had ever overcome that dilemma. Some day, some day he would show Zack, but not this time, the challenge was too intriguing. He muttered some thoughts aloud.

"If we could think of some new technique, we could do it through the Olympic Services as a project. It might reestablish good will, eh Joe? I don't like this feud, it's pointless."

"Yeah, that'd be great. Got any ideas?"

"H'mmm…maybe. We'll see," Festus said, smugly.

Pandora patted his shoulder. "You'll think of something, Dad, you always do."

"I'll surely try, Pandy."

"My! Look! There's Maria and Greg. He's let his hair grow. It looks real neat. Hi!" She screamed, oblivious to the fact that she was inaudible.

"Can you take care of Pandy, Joe? She doesn't need me at the moment. I've gotta talk to Marienna and then I'd better check on some things with Zack before I go home. Just drop me off at the next corner! I'll call you later."

"Sure, Doc."

"Yeah, fine," Festus replied, in a distracted fashion. He was worrying about how people had reacted to his trip with Cathy. By now, all of the Argos clan would know.

He felt better after talking to Marienna. Their chat had helped. He suddenly appreciated how much he owed to the tall, angular, iron gray haired woman. A cold, logical, and intimidating figure to most people. Festus knew a different person. Witty, imaginative, even nutty and, as time has passed, becoming slightly nuttier. Her cactus garden summed it up—a reflection of her prickly personality. He could see it as a rebellion against the pitiful attempts of her neighbors to have a 'conventional' yard with, for God's sake in this climate, lawns and roses. His godmother encouraged him to make use of his fantasies. In fact, he owed many of these to her. Mind you, she sometimes went too far. Like with this business of her relatives being the characters in her Plays. But life was never dull with her around. These thoughts occupied him until he reached the bank. Customers and tellers alike looked up as he limped across the floor.

"Why, it's Doc Festus!" a beaming matriarch exclaimed. "My! Are we glad to see y'all. You must come to the Argos Ladies Society and tell us everything that's been happening at Loch Ness! You will now, y'hear?"

Festus regarded her ample mid-portion nervously. "I'll try and arrange it," he mumbled, before fleeing to the safety of the executive section of the bank. Zack's secretary opened the door, stepping aside as Festus escaped past her into the office.

"Zachary has been waiting for you, Doc. He'll sure be glad to see you. Please go on in."

Zack Cronson was already around his desk and halfway to the door when Festus entered. He strode forward to grasp him with both hands.

On the surface Zack appeared at ease, but Festus knew him well enough to spot that underneath the controlled exterior he was a very worried man.

Zack did not voice his concerns immediately, but arranged for coffee to be brought in, courteously expressed his relief that Festus had found Pandora. He answered the queries that Festus had about Dawn before unloading his own problems.

Yes, Zack confirmed, Dawn had returned to Argos. The news gave Festus a sinking feeling. "Where is she staying?"

"In your house, naturally!" Zack seemed surprised by the question. "You're still married, aren't you?"

"I guess so. Separated might be a better description." He paused. "What am I supposed to do?"

"I think that's up to you Fes. I'm not getting in the middle. Maybe Marien…?"

Festus interrupted him. "I don't think that will work."

"How about you just go and talk to her? You've been married for years. Surely you can still talk to each other?"

"I guess so. How are things here? There seems to be some slight problem with a fire back down the road a bit."

Zack warmed to the new topic, quickly. "You saw it? Presumably, Joe waxed eloquent on the problem. It's in the Everyman field. It would be. Old Max is up in arms about it. From what I hear, I gather he blames us. He won't let us help. I'm very worried about what he might do, and what some of the young bloods, seeking to impress him, might do. The former is the worse, though. That old man is crazy."

"When Joe told me I had the same thought. What exactly is your main concern?"

"Unfortunately, when we decided to set up the Trust and do these scientific ventures we offered Old Max a part of the action. I'm sure you remember that we told him something about the way we'd work, and I'm sure he knows a lot more now. For some reason, I don't know what, he turned it down. I have a feeling he may provide information to the Feds, the Internal Revenue Service! I know what you're going to say. We're strictly legal. Right!" Festus nodded. Zack continued. "As far as we know, that's still true. But it's nevertheless a somewhat new wrinkle in the world of foundations and trusts and, to date, in our contacts with the IRS. We haven't worked out a complete deal. Oh! One thing is important. Hurry up and publish our findings from Loch Ness and Blarney in some reputable journals. The IRS views that as a prerequisite for them to accept a project as bona fide research."

Our findings, thought Festus, with irritation.

"Tell me what happened after I left Loch Ness! I…"

Zack didn't let him finish. "You saw one of those damn articles. Right!"

"New York Herald Tribune. What the hell was all that about?"

"Fes, believe me I tried. Those damn news hounds, they don't listen. They talked to everybody, and put together what they thought the public wanted."

"Technical support was provided by Doctor Henry Festus. Fuck it, Zack! It was all my idea. All of it."

"Sorry, Fes."

"Well what did happen after I left?"

"We continued doing what you'd set up to do; monitored the echo sounders, sent the sub down and watched. God! How we watched, and the news media watched us. There was nothing. Absolutely nothing...unless you count the hoax by the students from Aberdeen University."

"What hoax?"

"They floated a dummy monster off Urquhart Castle. You just missed seeing it."

"Why were the news people suddenly so interested? Most of them left us alone after we launched the sub?"

"It wasn't a secret, what we were doing?"

"Yeah. But why all the attention? The minute I left."

Zack looked embarrassed. "Well the student thing got it moving, and...I guess I hinted we were close to finding the damn thing to a guy from Inverness."

"It was in the Herald Tribune soon after I left."

"News moves fast."

Festus was silent. Zack filled the void with words. "We have a provisional agreement with the IRS, based on what we've divulged. It isn't clear to me that all the ramifications of our...your projects have been appreciated yet."

"Obviously not."

"Now, if someone as influential as Old Max were to stir things up, it could shift the balance against us. He has many contacts through his friends in the Texas Legislature and the Congress—not to mention our powerful friend to the south. Max is like Lyndon—one of the great manipulators. Frankly, he wields nearly as much power as I do. So, I'm looking for some kind of miracle to get us off the hook." Zack stopped in his pacing and passed by his desk, fiddling with an ornate pen set. "It's history repeating itself. The Everyman Bore all over again, and you know what problems that created."

Festus gave up on discussing Loch Ness. He was tired of brooding about it. This new Labor needed his attention. "I gathered something of this from Joe," Festus said, anticipating Zack's question. "I thought about it the last few miles into town. I don't want to give you the idea that I have just, in those few minutes, found a solution, but I do have a new technique that might put out the fire. It's something I've been working on with friends at the University. I might have mentioned it before."

"Maybe? You're into so many things I can't keep track."

"We never had any occasion to try it, and so we kept it on a back burner. Your problem, Zack, is to persuade Old Max to let me try the technique."

"You need to think about what to do if he won't except help! How much time will you need to set something up?"

"If we move fast, I might have something ready in a week or two. It depends on how far the improvements at Olympic Services have progressed."

"It's all arranged. Your consultants appear to have done a good job. Incidentally, you may be surprised by one of your new employees."

Festus could not draw him out on the final comment and took the opportunity to mention that he had offered a part time job to Chuck Steeger.

"I hope that's okay, Zack? He helped us find Pandy. Could be a useful addition."

"Sure, that sounds fine. In fact, I heard he dropped in on Olympic Services last week with some note from you. Ionides hired him."

"Great."

"You oughta go straight down to Austin and check out what's happening at Olympic Services. What will you do about Pandora and Dawn?"

"I know Pandora misses her mother, and I'm sure Dawn will want her to be here. Judging by Pandora's excitement on seeing her friends, I suspect she would prefer to stay in Argos for the moment. I'll just pray that she doesn't get bored too quickly. I don't know about Dawn."

"I'm sure it'll work out." Zack dismissed the concern. "Back to business. I think you understand your priorities. Got any questions?"

"How do we stand for funds, Zack?"

"No worries on that account. At the moment, if anything, we have an embarrassment of riches. We're anticipatin' considerable revenue from the Loch Ness film. It seems that even failure fascinates the public. Strange isn't it?"

"I guess."

"Are you going to claim any of the Greek trip?" Zack asked. "I don't think I can swing the hunt for Pandora as a Labor."

"I see."

"You don't sound happy about my decision?"

"I guess it has an historical precedent."

"What? Oh! You mean Zachary Cronson's acting like King Eurystheus with Heracles?

"Yes."

"You take the analogy to far, Fes. This has to do with the IRS. Greek gods didn't have to mess with those suckers."

"All right. Let me claim a small part, because it gave me an idea for a project and we can put it down to advance expenditure."

"Fine, Fes."

"To get back to the main subject, you realize that this new project will be expensive we'll need about one hundred thousand dollars immediately, and as much as a million dollars finally?"

"Fes, you worry too much. I'll say it again; the Trust is in good shape."

"You haven't sold my equipment have you? The sub…"

"So that's what you're worried about," Zack chuckled. "No. Marienna twisted my arm again. It's all stored at Urquhart House. Now, I'm going to call Prometheus again and offer him our help. Before I do, can you give me some idea as to what you propose, so that I can convince him. Also, what you'll do if he turns me down."

Festus outlined his plan, reluctantly, stating firmly that it was restricted information, and he didn't want anyone, other than Prometheus, told until he had conducted some tests. He managed to keep a straight face while he talked.

Zack stopped his pacing and slumped back in his chair, drumming his hand-crafted boots on the desk with glee. "Whoopee!" he hollered. "Oh shii-it! Fes, when y'all have an idea it sure is a beaut! Ain't no way I'll tell him thai-it. Ah'll simply say that y'all have some new kind of explosive." He roared with laughter again and Festus, who could not restrain himself, started to giggle until he too, weakened by laughter, collapsed back into a chair holding his sides. "I had a feeling you might appreciate it, Zack."

"I'll probably regret saying this, but I'm glad you're back to doing your practical jokes."

"I guess since Blarney I haven't been in the mood," Festus said, ruefully.

"Except for that damn flowerbed in Loch Ness. FES WINS!"

"That was just therapy. Pity I was wrong. Er! One other thing Zack, when this…er…Labor is over I do want to go back to the Loch."

"You fix this little problem, Fes, and you can have anything. Even Catherine Anne Schmidt."

"I didn't know you'd taken up pimping."

"I haven't. I leave it to Marienna."

"Shit! There's nothing there."

"You're kidding."

"No."

They discussed details of the plan for a further hour, and then Festus phoned Ionides at Olympic Services, explained his ideas, and asked him to start tracking down the key equipment required. Zack called in his secretary and started the arrangements from his end. When Festus left, Zack was talking on the phone to Prometheus Maximos.

Festus walked to his house, a neat single story building a few blocks away from the river. It was a chilly day, and few people were about, but those who knew him, inquired about the Loch Ness project. Thus, he made slow progress.

There had been plenty of time for Dawn to worry about how to greet her husband when he returned. In fact, ever since the time she had returned to Argos and Elena had broken the news about Pandora's disappearance…

"Festus and Pandora are in Crete, Dawn," Elena said, abruptly, when Dawn arrived on her doorstep.

"Damn!" Dawn replied, looking downcast. "I'd worked out what I wanted to say to him." She was silent for a while. "When will they be back?"

"Are you thinking of making it up?" Elena asked.

"Hell no! But we've go to make some arrangements and settle on Pandora's future. Why are they in Crete?'

"After I called you about things not working out with Angel and about the opportunity to go to Nico's house, Marienna and I took Pandora to Athens.

"I felt bad about leaving like that. I just had to get out." Dawn held out her hand as if expecting sympathy. "I'll be staying here now so Pandora can come back to live with me and I'll help her. You see, Elena, I've been living in this commune and I've learned how to meditate and control my emotions. I'm a much calmer person now. I'll teach Pandora." She paused, savoring the thought briefly. "You know it might be a good idea if, later, we both went to live in the commune."

"She ran away in Greece," Elena said, sharply.

"She what! Who with?" Dawn cried.

"Some hippies. It seems Pandy was upset by some young man she'd been…fond of?"

"Where were you?"

"Well I'd gone on to Loch Ness. I never conceived she'd do anything like that."

"It's my fault. I'm to blame. I never should have left her."

"I'm afraid it gets worse, Dawn."

"Worse! How could it get worse?"

"At first they feared she had contracted syphilis. Happily, that turned out to be untrue."

"She what! You mean she'd been with a man…She's so young?"

"Older than you were?" Elena said, fishing.

"How could you know?" Dawn cried. She recovered her composure. "I never gave myself to a man before I married Fes."

"Oh!" It was Elena's turn to sound startled. "Dawn, I'm so sorry about all the things that have happened," Elena patted Dawn's shoulder. "That's why we need to think hard about how to help Pandora"

"Who found her?" Dawn asked, having trouble holding back her tears.

"Fes left Loch Ness the minute he heard." Elena reflected. "One of the few really unselfish acts I've ever seen him do.'

"Oh, Fes. Why do you do things like that? Just when I'm ready to call it quits," Dawn said, nearly to herself.

"That young Cathy Schmidt went with him."

Dawn jumped to her feet. "Jesus Christ! The man's insatiable. She went to do what?"

"To help with Pandy when they found her. Marienna and I talked her into it," Elena added, quickly.

"So it all worked out." Dawn had calmed down and looked sad. "What should I do now?"

"Talk to them when they get back. Let Fes come to you," Elena answered. She laughed. "He'll be unsure of himself. Don't lose that advantage!"

Festus looked apprehensively at his house. His crippled leg ached. This reaction had been with him since his childhood. He was looking down at the path thinking hard of what to say, when he heard the door open. Dawn was standing in the doorway. She had lost weight and her striking features were more finely drawn than before. She'd look good with spinach stuck on her front teeth, he thought. He was as devastated as the first time he had called at the Cronsons to take her out, when he was a teenager. Festus reverted to that time and stood gawping and nervously fingering his jacket.

As he looked at her, another image appeared, of Cathy standing in the cave entrance on Andros. *She smiled at him. "Come on, you'll be fine," Cathy said. "Don't worry, I know you limp. It doesn't matter."* The moment passed and now, he saw Dawn differently—a woman, worried, beautiful, but no longer young.

"So you managed to get here, eventually, Fes."

"I had to speak to Zack."

"Naturally."

They were sitting in the parlor, stiffly facing each other, like parodies of their Cretan forebears in the sepia photographs that looked down on them from the walls. At the start, Festus against all his logic would have taken her back, but he had convinced himself that Dawn could not want him so he misinterpreted her attempts to be conciliatory. The conversation degenerated,

"How's Ari?" Festus asked, regretting his question the minute it he said it.

Dawn's face went white. "Fes, how could you?" She seemed close to tears. "You don't understand. Nobody does."

Festus could have been sympathetic and asked what had really happened but, in his mind, he could still see the images of Dawn on a hillside in Killarney. "Cathy was a great help with Pandy, Dawn. I really appreciate Marienna persuading her to come. Next time you see her, you should thank her."

"Cathy Schmidt!" Dawn cried. "That bug eyed scheming pawn of Marienna's. I'm sure you thanked her well enough."

"Nothing happened," Festus snapped back, sounding defensive.

"Maybe she's smarter than I thought," Dawn fired back. "I hear she didn't continue on to Crete with you?"

"No-o, she wanted to get ready for school. I guess she felt that Pandy and I needed time alone."

Festus let the discussion die. His life was confused enough, with the precarious state of his marriage and with Cathy in Germany. He knew, selfishly, that he didn't want their problems to interfere with the new Labor. If he succeeded in dealing with the fire, he would be able to go back to Loch Ness. The hunt wasn't over!

There was a long silence while each of them calmed down. In the end, they compromised on an arrangement in which Pandora would stay with Dawn. Festus agreed to move out in a formal separation. By mutual consent, divorce was not an option until Pandora had grown up.

They engaged in small talk for the long half-hour until Festus made his good-byes. Pandora seemed to be happy with the arrangements. She and her mother had enjoyed a tearful reunion. Pandora spent the rest of her morning on the telephone. She was still occupied, gossiping with various friends, when Festus left. Pandora kissed him, gaily; sufficiently wrapped up in the attention of her peers that no thought of neglect entered her mind.

16. Olympic Services

Festus took the Triumph sports car. When he turned the ignition, the radio blared rock and roll—Pandora! He reset it to country music. Instead of heading for Lampasas, he drove through Llano and south of Marble Falls and Lake Travis to Austin. He thought about his ideas for dealing with the fire. Lateral thinking, that was his forte. The ability to tackle a problem, not step by step, methodically building up on sound knowledge, but the ability to jump from the present position to the solution, as if by magic. He recalled the ancient tunnelers who, millennia ago, had bored a tunnel through the mile of rock in the center of a Greek Island, to bring water to a town. They had met in the middle, but not exactly; the tunnel jogs about a foot or so sideways. A small mismatch can be allowed for, he thought, but unfortunately the brain sometimes plays tricks and the blinding flash of inspiration is only a mirage. He hoped the latest idea was not like that. It seemed a good idea, although there were a few tests to be made: on the marker, to color the flame when contact was made; on the chemicals added to quench the flame.

He was still going over his plans as he crossed Tom Miller Dam and drove to north Austin and Olympic Services. It consisted of a group of buildings off Research Boulevard, opposite a new shopping center, built in what the architect imagined to be the Moorish style. The coupling of a few tawdry minarets and fake wooden embattlements with the generally low quality of the products on sale—plastic flamingoes, cheap clothes, plastic back scratchers, freezer pots with inadequate lids, and the like—had spawned the name, "the Taj Banal." Festus eyed it with dislike, as he pulled over to the space reserved for Dr. H.E. Festus, "noted fisherman."

"Good to see you back, Fes. You're looking fit. Let me show you to your office." Ionides was grinning a self-satisfied grin.

The buildings looked drab from the outside. Inside, the reception had modern furniture, some good prints and a jungle of plants. A girl was busy behind the reception desk. She was bent over a filing cabinet drawer, muttering to herself angrily about the recalcitrant files. When they approached, she turned. "Hi, Uncle Fes, I'm your receptionist-secretary." It was Samantha! She looked at him warily.

"Well, Sam. Zack said I'd have a surprise. I'm real pleased." No way she has forgiven me, Festus thought.

It didn't seem to worry Ionides. He had obviously talked her into taking the job. "Isn't it great, Fes? All of us working together." Ionides beamed in triumph.

"It's great." Festus smiled, in spite of the additional uncertainty as to whether the Samantha he had known would have the maturity to handle the job. He recognized that he might have to be tolerant for the sake of Ionides.

"One other thing, Fes," Ionides said, cautiously. "Chuck seems like a neat guy. Sam and I think he could be good for Pandy."

"What? Oh, yes, he could be." Festus looked thoughtful.

The offices were behind the reception area. Covered walkways led to the other buildings that housed the laboratories and the stores. Festus was pleased to see that all of his favorite belongings had been installed in his new office. He was not so happy that Zack had taken the opportunity to add some executive touches to impress visitors. There was a bar in one corner and some modern art on the walls that offset his ratty old armchair. An ancient school blackboard faced the armchair. Behind his desk were the painting of Texas bluebonnets that had won him a prize at school, and the remains of a model airplane. It had a surrealistic air, so that a visitor would be uncertain whether it was simply a child's toy or a major advance in art. Festus was dubious about this treatment, but decided to leave it.

He started to wade through the pile of paperwork, and was making limited progress when the intercom buzzed and Samantha called. "Chuck's here to see you."

Festus pushed the work aside. "Send him in." At first, he didn't recognize Chuck: the fashionable haircut, the trimmed moustache, and the flared pants, a button down shirt and tie, no less, and brown leather loafers. Chuck still needed to lose a little weight.

Chuck smiled. "I decided a new image was needed to fit the job, Dr. Festus."

"Come on, I'm Fes, right!" He gestured at Chuck's new clothes. "I'm pleased to tell you that very soon this job will have us back where we started, in jeans."

"That's a relief. Ion said we have to put out an oil well fire…within the next few weeks!"

"If they'll let us."

"What do you mean?"

"Nobody's told you about the feud between Old Max and the Cronsons?"

"Sure, a little, but it can't be that bad?"

"Oh yes it can. The fights over the oil were really bad."

"My great grandparents came with Count Carl von Solms-Braunfels in the 1840's and were with him when he founded New Braunfels and Fredricksburg," said Chuck. "I've heard, they were tough, but that patch in Argos County was too rugged for them. How did your families survive before the oil?"

"When we left Galveston in 1901, we were looking for somewhere like home—Crete." Festus replied, thoughtfully, "scrub-covered limestone hills…and those little green sanctuaries in the shaded river-beds. Your German culture didn't include olive trees and goats. Ours did. We spread into San Saba and Lampasas counties, and achieved county status following a realignment of county boundaries a short time later."

"Why did they leave Galveston?"

"I'm surprised you can't guess," Festus said.

Chuck looked puzzled for a moment. "Of course! The famous 1900 hurricane."

"They should have seen it coming. Galveston was built on a sandbar a mile wide but it was a mere nine feet above the nominal high-tide mark. The hurricane hit with little warning. The electricity failed, the water rose above the sand bar and the wooden houses began to collapse. Then the broken houses acted as battering rams. Thousand of people died. It was devastating for our community."

They talked a short time further about the working arrangements. Chuck asked about Pandora, making it clear that he would like to see her again. Festus determined to help him. He prodded the intercom. "Sam, can you send in Ion?"

Festus went to the blackboard. He sketched the layout of the Everyman Field, indicating the property boundary and the position of the runaway well. He explained the problems and some of the history of the oilfield, and covered in detail the actions he proposed to take.

"So you see," he concluded, "there are maybe three problems. The first of which is that we need a really experienced drilling expert."

"We don't have anyone good enough, do we Fes?"

"Zack employs some good people but this is special. I know just the man, Ion. He's been barred for a number of years now, but he could put a drill anywhere you wanted it. Of course, that was his problem." It was a wonderful thought. His grin showed it.

"Who?"

"You know him. Our main problem will be to persuade him to come to Argos."

By now, Ion was also grinning. "Zack goes along with his coming to the play cycle, but God knows what he'll say about this." Festus tilted his head.

"You're serious, aren't you, Fes?"

Festus nodded. "Thar ain't nobody better, Ion. Y 'all know it."

"Who're you talking about?"

"We're talking about Panou Cronson. Ion, you tell him!"

"He's Zachary's half-brother. He was mixed up in the Everyman fiasco. My dad used to tell me stories." Ion grinned at Festus as they silently shared the joyous devilry of the situation.

"Come on, fellows; let me in on the secret. What did he do?"

"You remember I was telling you about Old Max's well being bias-drilled. Well, Uncle Panou was the guy who did it."

"I see."

"Panou had to leave Argos to appease Old Max and save face for his father. They made out the whole thing was ordered by him, but everyone knew that Agamemnon Cronson did it."

"Bringing him back would sort of be poetic justice."

"Yes. Panou drifted around for some time. Naturally, his services were in great demand. Some of the oil companies eventually bought him off, to get peace. He has numerous small businesses and this club near San Antone. I worry less whether Zack will agree, than what Old Max will do if he finds out."

"What do you want me to do first?"

"Now Chuck, the second problem is to find a suitable marker to show when we have made contact with the shaft and, obviously, we will need a flame suppressant. I hear Prof. Eckerman's made real progress on it. Y'all should try to finish the tests in a week or so. Let him have the final say on the matter. I know he seems out of touch, but he's one smart old guy."

"That leaves you, Ion. How are you doing on getting the equipment Zack asked for?"

"It's being shipped up from Houston, Fes, and should be here tomorrow."

Festus drove down the interstate into "German country;" Fredricksburg, Albert, Schulenberg, and New Braunfels, where he'd been many times to the October Fest. It reminded him of Professor Eckerman, who had emigrated from the "Fatherland" many years earlier. The "Prof." liked Texas except for his one complaint, the lack of proper bread in Austin. Festus could hear the Prof. delineating, in a thick German accent, the cure for his irregular bowel movements…

"I need a good rye bread. Heavy! Gritty! I need to feel it settling in my stomach, and working its way through my digestive system, cleaning things out. This soggy, expanded plastic, you Texans call bread, is an insult."

Eventually, after a brief sojourn of thirty-one years, he returned to Germany and proper bread. But this was before that time, and Festus, like everyone else, ignored his bitching assuming he would stay forever.

Festus pulled his car off the Interstate. The New Braunfels bakery produced really good bread, in the old style—nearly to Prof. Eckerman's standards. He bought a selection of breads to give the old man later. From experience, he knew that they were robust enough to keep.

Pan's Palace, on the outskirts of San Antonio, was a drab, part stone, part corrugated iron structure, immersed in a large dirt parking lot—a typical country boozer. A hitching rail leaned wearily outwards from the building—relic of the past. Neon signs flashed, with arrows leading to the entrance. The front of the building was devoid of windows. As he parked, another neon sign came on. It depicted a stylized Greek god, head shrouded in grapes, lifting a glass with one hand, while his arm encircled the waist of a neon girl with pronounced physical attributes. Appropriately, the lights flickered drunkenly.

He pushed open the door and stood acclimatizing his eyes to the dark. The interior was quiet. It had the dirty-clean smell of a place in which antiseptics could not hide the history of smoking and drinking. The smells were now percolating into the room, bringing Pan's Palace back towards the eye-smarting level that it would achieve later.

"Is Pan here?"

The pretty boy bartender looked suspicious. Festus didn't match the normal customer image. "Who wants to know?"

"Tell him Fes is here!"

"Fes?" the boy smiled. "What a pretty name."

Festus reached across the bar, and twisted the brightly colored bandana. "Now! Okay."

"My you're strong. Don't get your pants in a twist! I'll do it." The boy disappeared through a door behind the bar.

It had always astounded Festus how Panou Cronson was able to project the appearance of size. A small giant, not so large, but with a walk, posture and attitude that made him appear bigger than the reality. A pair of large, high-heeled, ornate, Texan boots aided this impression. Festus recollected that there were animals that had the ability to appear bigger than they really were. His thoughts were broken by the appearance through the door of the boots, followed by a thick belt that hung below, and supported Pan's central section and jeans, a colorful shirt and, finally, the grinning face of Pan arrived. He looks larger than reality, because the eye is drawn from one part of him to the next, Festus realized.

"*Hi'yar thair, Fai-is. Y'all sure looo'ok fai-at.*" Pan's exaggerated drawl hung lazily in the air, like smoke. "*What are y'all doin' ha-ir?*" The voice rumbled up from the depths of the tent-like Hawaiian shirt. It was a deep voice, and though roughened by years of smoke and booze, it retained a honeyed rhythm and appeal. After a while, though, it seemed natural, and blended in with the rest of the conversation. "Hell, sit down. This calls for a celebration. Let me get you a drink—*beer and ouzo all right?*"

Festus tried to decline the *ouzo*. Pan ignored him. He waited patiently for the formalities to be concluded, while Pan reminisced over the good old times. He realized that Pan, whose capacity had always appeared limitless, was deliberately plying him with drink, and was resigned to it. Fortunately, Pan held to the Greek custom of snacking, while drinking. Festus was happy to help him demolish the plates of tomatoes chopped with potatoes—meze—that were ferried to their table with the drinks. Customers started to drift in, and the bartenders and waitresses were busy. The atmosphere was smokier now and noisier. There was a dance floor, and the jukebox gave way to a country band. Pan left him for a while and Festus relaxed, sipping his beer. The band was playing the current pop success, a local song much overplayed around Austin…

> *Austin Tai-x-as U.S.A.*
> *I'll come back again some day*
> *When I do, I'm gonna stay.*
> *In Austin Tai-x-as U.S.A.*
>
> *A and M and Razorbacks*
> *Take right off along the tracks*
> *Sure as h-ll they'll rue the day*
> *They came to Austin, Tai-x-as, U.S.A.*

It was a catchy song, written by a booster for the University of Texas Long-horn football team. Festus hummed it as he watched the dancers cavort in the stylized way of the country scene.

Pan was dancing, his arms enfolding a pretty, young girl who clung around his neck—a different kind of dancing, more lust and less grace. The other dancers studiously avoided them. Pan's latest acquisition, thought Festus. He wondered how Pan, who was paunchy and debauched looking, could attract such girls. Boys too, he'd heard; the young bartender was glancing at the dancers. He looked jealous. The only signs of Pan's youthful good looks were his thick, curly, but now iron gray hair and his strange pale brown eyes. Festus put the success down to reputation and confidence.

> *UT Longhorns we all hail.*
> *Driving down the Chisholm Trail.*
> *Chasing all their foes away,*
> *From Austin Texas, U.S.A.*

When the band finished the song, Pan returned, the girl in tow tripping along behind him. He sat down. She remained standing.

"Fes, I'd like you to meet Cindy, a girl with a lot of talent."

Cindy simpered and shook hands in a disinterested fashion, her eyes always on Pan. She was a medium height, leggy girl with dyed blond hair. About twenty-two, thought Festus, then on looking closer, revised that down to nineteen. Her slim legs were tightly encased in jeans that looked like they had been sewn in place. Festus realized he was staring, and shifted his gaze upward only to avert it again from the breasts that swelled out of her open-necked shirt. He turned away and saw that Pan was eyeing him knowingly. He realized this was an intended distraction, designed to unsettle him.

Pan shoo'ed Cindy away for more beers. "Found the Loch Ness monster ya-it?"

"No."

Pan grinned, impishly. "Reckon it's there?"

"Yes, and I could find it, if damn stupid things didn't keep distracting me."

"Sure, Fes. If you're a good boy Zack might let you play some more. Has he sold the sub yet?"

"Fuck off!"

"All right, that's enough of the niceties. What do y'all want?" His pale brown eyes twinkled at Festus from a deeply tanned round face. They had the innocence of a child's eyes.

Festus outlined the plan. For once, it was Pan's turn to be startled. Then as the enormity of the proposal hit him, he began to roll in his chair, great bellows of laughter shook him, his eyes crinkled, tears, seeping from closed lids, trickled down his cheeks. He could be heard even above the band, and a silence descended as the patrons paused to watch him. He flapped his hand angrily at the dancers and band to continue.

"Oh that's good," he bellowed. "That's good—a new kind of explosive. Oh, I'd like to see his face." He sat back weakly, breathing heavily. Cindy hovered anxiously in the background while Pan calmed enough to ask Festus to go over the plan again.

"Young Festus you've done well. I remember when your dad made me that bias drill. History coming round again in a circle, eh?" He stopped and thought for a long period.

"I'll do it but Zack's got to ask me. Make him crawl. Though how you'll persuade Old Max, god only knows. If that works, I'll need to talk to y'all again. When I call, you get your butt out here pronto!"

"I'll tell Zack tomorrow."

Festus managed to escape Pan's attempts to drown him in beer and to find him a girl. "Cindy has a cute little girl friend, boy. No tits to speak of, but very active I hear. Do you fine."

"Thanks for the offer. I'd better go now while I can still stand."

Outside, the cold winter air amplified the effects of his drinking. He spent an hour or so lumbering around the parking lot to shake of the drunken stupor, arousing curious stares and comments. His head hurt too much for him to care.

"Which race has Pan got you in?"

"It's two years to the Olympics, boy. Stay off the beer."

Festus staggered around the parking lot for the umpteenth time, his head at last beginning to clear. Finally, judging that he was sober enough to drive, he proceeded carefully to Austin and collapsed into bed.

Festus opened one eye, cautiously. A headache and a dry mouth reminded him of the previous night's beer and *ouzo*. He was horrified to see that it was already nine twenty. Coffee, a cold shower and a quick breakfast made him feel considerably better. He reached Olympic Services at ten-forty. Ionides and Chuck were in the workshop checking the equipment that had arrived from Houston.

"Morning, Fes," Ion said. "You look like you had a good time with old Pan."

Festus shook his head wearily. "Every sentence with him is another drink. It took half a barrel of beer and too many *ouzos* to get to brass tacks. The bottom line is he agrees to do it, provided I can get Zack to ask him. How's it going?"

"We've made some progress, though there's more work to do on the flame inhibitor," Ionides replied. "I've got people working on the attachments."

"Great! For the marker we can use a potassium salt and feed it in here." Festus pointed at a tube on the slurry pump. "Chuck, you continue with that! I'll do a few sums to check out the alternatives." Festus paused. "I'll see you for lunch, Chuck. There's somebody you should meet. Now I must have a clear understanding with you that what you will hear is not for other people to know. Is that clear?"

"If it's not illegal, I guess so," said Chuck, cautiously.

"It's not illegal. It's family sensitive. I am going to get into trouble for involving you, but it fits with things that need doing. Chuck, you sound equivocal."

"I meant yes. Unequivocally."

"All right. We'll go to the best hamburger and chili joint in town," Festus laughed. "Incidentally, get your tie back on." Ion grinned. Chuck was bewildered, but they would not enlighten him.

"Ion has talked about lots of your relatives. It's hard to keep track of them all. If I knew who was in Galveston, maybe I could make sense of it?" said Chuck, as they drove to the downtown.

"Let's see. I'll get back to the Cronson and Maximos families. There was Socrates Dexteriades—the undertaker. His son Harold Dexter continues the business in Argos. Then there were the Platon brothers, Demetrios and Atlas and their sister Olympia. At the time, she was married to Agamemnon Cronson. Demetrios accompanied Bishop Nicholas to set up a Russian Orthodox Church in Galveston. Other members of his family followed and they generally found work with Old Max. Demetrios officiated at the marriages, christenings and funerals of the Greek community, while Socrates rounded out the process by burying them. You'll be meeting Alexander Platon. Alex's father, Atlas, operated a restaurant and shoeshine parlor for Old Max."

"How about your family?"

"There was my father, Argos Phaestos, and his two bothers, Spiridon and Basil. They were metal workers from Khania on the north shore of Crete. Through contact with the Kronosakis family, they found work in the Galveston shipyards. Our name got changed to Festus by some civil servant who couldn't spell," Festus laughed. "It has nothing to do with 'Gunsmoke'."

"Did many of your relatives die in the hurricane?"

"A number died, including my uncle Spiridon and Uncle Basil's wife. He married again. Ionides is the result."

"I didn't know. It must have been a hell of a mess."

"It was really bad, Chuck. People could not face the possibility of going through it again. They salvaged what they could, sold their land on Galveston Island, and moved the Hill Country. Only Demetrios Platon and Olympia Cronson and her children, Georgiou, Marienna, and Panou remained. Demetrios was ordered by the church to stay and re-establish his parish. My mother was waiting the birth of her fourth child."

Chuck looked puzzled. "So Olympia was your mother? Did I miss something?"

"Let me just say that the baby died, and my mother and Agamemnon divorced. She married my father in 1917. I came along in 1920."

"It's like a soap opera," Chuck laughed. "Sorry. I wasn't thinking. Back to Old Max. What happened there?"

"Old Max's first wife had died and he was courting this girl in Crete. Agamemnon, now divorced, moved in and married her."

"I can see why they didn't get on," Chuck laughed."

"They only agreed on 'uncontroversial' subjects such as American politics," added Festus, sarcastically.

"Democrats."

"Yes. It pays in Texas. There was one odd thing. No rift in religion, despite enormous battles for supremacy between our Russian Orthodox Church and the royalist Church of Greece, which was expanding in the early days of Argos."

"What kept them together?"

"I guess, in the early days, it was respect for their old friend Archimandrite Platon. Poor old Demetrios, he found it harder and harder to make the journey to Argos. It was a tough trip back then. Eventually, he stopped coming, and I suppose that's why religion's not a problem today? Making money, the Games, the Festival, and the Plays, took its place."

By the time Festus finished talking, they had reached a tall building near the State Capitol in downtown Austin. They stepped out of the elevator into the plush surroundings of a private club. Facing them were a lounge and bar. As Festus had explained in the car, this was the rendezvous for state legislators, lobbyists and the business elite of Austin and of the rest of the state. Numerous people nodded to Festus, and a few, including the Chancellor of the University and the Lieutenant Governor of Texas, came up to ask him about the Loch Ness project. While they were getting a drink, a young-looking, smartly dressed man joined them.

"Hi Alex, it's good to see you again," Festus said. "Chuck, I'd like you to meet Alex Platon. He's an attorney…at least, when he's working."

"That is an unkind commentary on the days that I spent on your damn projects in Ireland and at Loch Ness. I'm sorry to rush you, but at the last minute, something came up and I have another appointment. Let's grab some food and talk over lunch." Alex led them into the dining area, where there was a buffet of hamburger fixings and steaming chili.

"Down to business now," Festus said. "You phoned me, Alex, because you had some worrying news."

"Yes, Fes," Alex answered. "A friend in the IRS has told me confidentially that an investigation of the Eurysthesian Foundation and its Trust has been started. I'm not clear what has motivated this, whether someone has complained about us or it's simply that this is the first time they have had a deal like ours. Clearly, in dealing with the financing of scientific projects for philanthropic reasons, we are in a gray area with respect to tax liability. I don't believe that it's ever been done before in quite the way we are trying to do it." He paused, looking worried.

Festus was watching Chuck. He had been listening intently but was distracted by of one of Alex's strange nervous habits. Alex played incessantly with a string of beads, while he talked.

Alex continued. "Frankly, there are some reasons for concern. So it's very important that you keep me up to date on your activities. I guess that's where Chuck comes in?" He had been surprised when Festus had enlisted a foreigner for this delicate liaison job and questioned the idea. But a censored version of how Chuck had helped in the hunt for Pandora had eased his concerns.

"I've said a little to Chuck about the subject and it seems to me that it fits in well with our needs and his long-term plans for a Ph.D. topic."

"It looks like it could lead to a good career. Can you clarify what I'm supposed to do, sir?" Chuck continued. "For example, should I send Alex a weekly report on our progress, flagging such things as major expenditures, giving a scientific justification? In addition, should I see Alex regularly for further briefings on the situation vis a vis the IRS?"

"Yes! It's particularly important to be systematic about things. Also, if either of you has worries about the credibility of the work for the Trust's, please let me know immediately," Alex replied.

"Okay."

"I'd like a word with you, Fes, before you go," Alex pulled him aside. "There are things about that business in Blarney with the photographs that worry me. Are you sure you got the whole picture of what happened from Seamus?"

"I don't know what you mean. I paid him enough."

"I talked to Dawn. She said that, out of the blue, Ari attacked her. He seemed deranged. She didn't understand why the photos didn't show it. It seemed like they had been selected to make her look bad."

"But, why would Seamus do that?"

"I think that Marienna may have got to him."

"Come on, Alex, you can't be serious?" Alex shook his head and kept silent.

"That's ridiculous. Marienna wouldn't do that to me," Festus was shocked.

"It wasn't done to you," Alex replied, curtly.

Festus grimaced and left to join Chuck. When they were alone in the elevator, he quizzed Chuck. "So, what do you think of Alex?"

"He looks like a film star. Please understand I'm not a connoisseur of men. I like the ladies." Chuck sounded embarrassed, then recovered quickly and continued, grinning. "It took me some time to work out that Alex is as old as you."

"Shi-it!" Festus replied.

"What about the beads, is Alex a Catholic?"

"No, Chuck, it's common for Greek men to have worry beads, 'komboloia'," Festus explained. "Alex is somewhat superstitious. Typical Greek. Broken mirrors, spilt salt, opening an umbrella indoors are bad luck. You shouldn't cut your nails on Wednesdays or Fridays. There's a nearly endless list of do's and don'ts. Perfect background for the law or the church," Festus added, sarcastically. "He nearly went into the church. His Uncle Demetrios got him into Pomfret College when it opened in…I guess…1937. It was the first Greek Orthodox Seminary."

"What happened?"

"He liked jazz, he fooled around too much, and was politely requested to seek other educational opportunities. That's when he came back here to UT and the law school."

Festus studied the exterior of Pan's Palace dubiously. Not wanting to go in. Why wouldn't Pan deal with him by phone? The tricky bastard must want something, he thought. He wasn't given a choice. Pan's spies had seen him coming. The door opened and a voice boomed out of the darkness. "Come in little Fes. Don't be scared!"

Pan was seated at the same table. He had changed his Hawaiian shirt, and moved Cindy to the bar.

"Good to see you again Mr. Cronson," Festus said, with exaggerated politeness.

Pan chuckled. "Mr. Cronson! I'm surprised at you Fes. You need a drink." He pushed the *ouzo* bottle across the table, and indicated the glass and water jug. "Bring food!" he bellowed to Cindy.

Festus, realizing he was in for another long evening, poured a small amount of *ouzo* into his glass, and added a lot of water. Pan watched in irritation, grabbed the bottle and strengthened the cloudy liquid. "Don't be wet. You're a Cretan!

Now to business, I want more details about the fire and your plans for putting it out. I've been thinking about something you can also explain to me. What's happened to my sister, Dawn?"

Festus was relieved. He was to realize later that it was only a part of the game.

Pan listened in silence until Festus finished explaining what he had done in Blarney.

"You're a real shit, Dr. Henry Festus. You know that?" He spoke steadily, emphasizing his anger.

"I had to do something?"

"About what?"

"Dawn's affairs."

"Flirtations, Henry. What proof do you have of an affair?"

"What do you mean?" Festus remembered Alex's comments. "Surely it was obvious?"

"You have photographs. They show my stupid brother Ari molesting Dawn. What's new? He's had evil thoughts about her since he was ten. You're assuming Dawn encouraged him?"

"She'd got half her clothes off, and…Hell! Dawn's shirt was torn, and she was stripping her bra off." He stopped. "Or was she trying to put her clothes back on?"

"Not so sure now, eh!" Pan asked.

"You can't tell from the photographs."

"So your private eye didn't stop to see what happened?"

"I guess not." Festus wondered what Pan meant. "Makes no difference. I found Ari's clothes in Dawn's apartment."

"So what? He's her brother."

"When I asked her about it she lied. I could see it in her face. Absolute panic."

"There could be another reason for it, Henry. Going back a long time. You're jumping to conclusions. Fine in science. Damn stupid with human beings," Pan muttered.

"Talk, Pan. Just talk. Give me a reason?"

"I'll give you a reason. I can feel Marienna's hand in this and Zack may be too bound up in his deals to act like a true padrone, but you'll answer to me on this if Dawn suffers any more. Y'hear!" He prodded Festus in the chest.

"It all adds up." Festus hoped he did not sound as uncertain as he felt.

"If Marienna can play games so can old Pan," he chuckled, mischievously. "Got you worried haven't I?"

During their ensuing discussion, a girl had joined Cindy at the bar. They were talking, animatedly. At first, Festus did not pay her much attention, but as his alcohol intake increased, he became steadily more aware of her. Her pretty face and thick black hair were her best features. They distracted the eye from her skinny body. He could tell from Pan's sideways glances, that Pan had deliberately placed the girls in plain view. Pan beckoned them to the table.

"Linda, I'd like you to meet my cousin Henry Festus. You can call him Doc."

Close up, Festus could see that Linda's eyes were a deep blue. Her long eye-lashes, short and straight nose and loose, green and blue, sweater accentuated their color and size. Her smile illuminated even Pan's seedy room. She also wore tight satin pants. At the table, the girls sat quietly, like geishas, murmuring agreement with each point the men made, and topping up the glasses.

"Come on, let's dance," said Pan.

Who is taking photographs? Festus wondered idly, as Linda wheeled him around the floor; her body seemingly welded to his.

He was not surprised when Pan, suggested that Festus should take Linda to bed. It was not altruism. It was a test, Festus guessed. A test of whether he would be faithful to Dawn. It would also give Pan a hold on him, to be saved and used later. He did not ask himself why Linda would want to do it.

"Upstairs. Take the second room on the left! She's got no tits, you know. But she's very athletic, I hear." The girl showed no overt emotion, but the hand that Festus held clenched tightly, and as they climbed the stairs, she said, softly, "damn him! I'm not a professional. I don't have to do this. I just like it, and you're available, okay"

"Look", said Festus. "You're a real attractive girl, but I'm married…more or less. Please show me how to get out of here without Pan seeing.

As he was jogging round the parking lot to clear his head yet again, he thought he could hear Pan laughing and shouting. "Chicken, squawk, squawk, squawk."

Ionides led a convoy of transporters, cars and tankers, out of Austin, carrying the various liquids needed in the assault on the fire. To avoid Arcadia, they went through Llano, passing over the bridge into Argos and in the early afternoon reached Zack's ranch; fancifully named Rancho Sfakia. In the distance, was the Everyman Bore fire, just beyond the boundary between the ranch and the Maximos spread.

"Hi, Fes. Hi, Ionides. My Samantha, you look pretty. Chuck, I've heard good things about you. It's good to see you all. Come on in." Elena Cronson greeted them, warmly. "It's real nice to see you all together." Elena looked relieved. As she told Festus later, she and Zack had discussed the wisdom of Samantha working at Olympic Service.

"*Zack, after what Fes did in Blarney, do you think it'll be okay?*" *Elena asked.*

"*She'll get over it because of Ion,*" *Zack replied.* "*I can't say the same for Ari and Yianna. From what I hear they hardly speak.*"

"*I don't think they talked much before,*" *Elena laughed.* "*That woman lives only for her children, poker and rummy, or I should say "koum-kan". And I'm not sure in which order.*"

"*Demos first, heaven help her,*" *Zack said.* "*I hope it works out at Stimpson College. That kid's got problems.*"

"*At least Sam is doing well. Ion's a nice man. I'm glad I was able to help get them together. Ari didn't like it.*" *Elena paused.* "*Maybe that was why Yianna agreed.*"

"*What about sex?*" *Zack asked.*

"*You mean right now? Zachary Cronson, what are you thinking?*"

Zack laughed and patted Elena's backside. "*It's a thought. I meant Ari and Yianna.*"

"*I hear that Yianna performs her wifely duties but not enthusiastically,*" *Elena said.*

"*Gives Ari an excuse for philandering,*"

"*As if he needs it,*" *Elena replied, scornfully.* "*You men may think it's funny, if he's not after one of your women, but I know what we women think.*"

"*To hell with Ari! How about it then?*" *Zack took her hand and led her to the bedroom.*

Elena apologized for the fact that they had a full house, with relatives from Crete visiting so that Festus and Chuck would have to stay with the riggers and technical support staff in the bunkhouse.

Festus was pleased to see Elena again. A comfortable woman, he thought, good looking. He approved of her working boots, jeans, checked shirt and practical hairstyle, not like those scruffy young things who had invaded Austin. Strong willed too; a woman who, behind the scenes, wielded a lot of power.

Ionides helped unload the equipment, and then went with Sam to her parent's home.

Festus took Chuck with him when he went to see Zack Cronson. "I'll be interested to hear your opinion of my family," Festus said, as they approached the bank.

Inside, they were ushered in to Zack's office. Zack raised his arms in greeting. The arms were hairy, muscular and contrasted with the delicate fingers of his broad hands. A heavy gold ring and inset green stone dominated the left hand.

There was another man sitting on a small wooden chair in the corner of the office, his body overflowing the edges of the precarious structure—Panou Cronson.

Chuck was offered the customary cup of strong Greek coffee. Festus knew that, despite a summer in Greece, Chuck did not like the drink. Festus was pleased when Chuck accepted it graciously.

"Pan let me introduce my assistant, Chuck Steeger."

"Good to meet you, Chuck," Pan rumbled. "I used to educate your boss. I told him, you gotta drink or dance boy. He sure couldn't dance much, so I used to give him some of my beer. Helped him out with women too. I've got some real good photos," he added, maliciously.

Zack moved quickly to cut off the interchange. "Fes, I'm still having trouble with Old Max. Prometheus would have agreed, but neither he nor Joe could persuade the old man. Elena even tried. It didn't work."

Zack turned to Chuck "I guess you don't know the intricacies of our extended family hierarchy, Chuck. Prometheus is Old Max's son, Joe's his grandson, and my wife is his daughter. The bottom line is that we may have to move without his agreement."

Festus looked worried. "That means doing the job from your side of the boundary. Damn! Pan, is it possible from that distance?"

"Difficult, yes, but possible." Pan was more serious now. "The greater distance will cut into our accuracy. I hear that y'all have some new technique, Fes, and some tricky way of guiding the drill. Convince me it'll work!"

Festus refused to be drawn into an argument. "I have a plan."

"Naturally."

"The solution to our problem here is not quite the same as bias drilling to reach a general area. What we need is more like a technique used in navigating. Say you wanted to fly to Bermuda. If you aimed your plane at the island, by the time that you'd gone far enough to reach the island, you might be either to the left or right of it. If you couldn't see it by then you wouldn't know which way to turn. A trick, developed to overcome that problem, is to deliberately aim to one side of the destination. Then, when you've covered roughly the correct distance you know which way to turn." He proceeded to outline his approach and as the account proceeded, even Pan was nodding appreciatively.

Pan looked at Festus, smiling. "That's clever, Fes. You always were a smart kid. I'll buy you a beer on it. When do you want to start?"

"Tomorrow. There's no point in waiting. If we have to do it from the boundary, so be it."

The meeting broke up, with Pan trying to persuade them all to come for a drink. Chuck and Fes declined the offer, agreeing only to meet at six the next morning for breakfast and an early start. Pan's face reflected his disgusted at their refusal. He looked happier when he heard some that some relatives from Crete were staying at the ranch.

"At least we'll have some proper Greeks in our crew. A pleasant change from you milksops." With this passing shot, he ambled off, pausing only to make a lukewarm pass at a secretary. As they left, Festus rushed after Pan in an attempt to talk to him privately. "Wait a second, Pan. I've got a question."

"I thought you might have. Photos worry you, huh! You and Linda look real good together."

"I didn't do anything. We were just dancing. You know that. Give them to me?"

"Hell no! Now you know how Dawn feels. You think on that, right!"

"What did you think?" asked Festus, as he and Chuck walked to his car.

"Mr. Cronson, Zack, is sure an interesting guy," Chuck replied. "I wouldn't want to mess with him. Incidentally, that ring he wears. What is the pattern? It looked like an axe."

"That's the labrys," Festus replied. "The twin axe symbol of the royal house of ancient Crete. Anything else?"

"I don't know if I should say this, but you asked," Chuck answered, cautiously. "You all seem wary of each other. Like, you acted apprehensive with Panou Cronson. Then he seemed nervous too—scared isn't the right word—and that's why he needles you. I wouldn't want to mess with him either." Chuck laughed. "Ion told me about these plays you all have roles in as Greek gods. It was like being on Mount Olympus."

"God help us!" Festus exclaimed. "Middle aged Greek-Americans is more like it."

17. Prometheus Maximos

"*Mah, thai-is shu-ure looks goo-d, Elena,*" Pan rumbled, as he surveyed the breakfast buffet.

"It's along time since we've seen you here, Pan, and I want y'all to remember us. Start the day with a good old Texan breakfast and y'all finish it with something better still, a proper Greek dinner." For some reason Elena did not associate Panou's club with Greek food, or maybe couldn't believe it would be adequate.

"*Ah'll gai-ve urp mah plai-ins to lose wai-yet.*" Pan piled his plate high with food, and wandered across the room to join the riggers."

During breakfast, Festus reviewed the plans and made the final arrangements for the working groups. Pan would supervise the setting up of the mobile rig. Fortunately, the firm renting the rig also provided the riggers and the supervision was mainly a question of siting. Pan and Festus had studied a map of the area, looking closely at the geological formation. They had identified a point, near the boundary, suitable for the job. "An historic site," Pan said. "A bit *murddy*, eh!" He gurgled happily over his coffee. "Do *y'all remaimber* Dad, Zack? Covered in *murd* from head to toe. That old bastard Max had *dahd a-it pai-nk*." He could not continue he and Zack collapsed in paroxysms of laughter, remembering the sight of their muddy pink father stomping and swearing.

Festus, Chuck, and Ionides set off to start assembling the peripheral equipment. It took them two days but, at the end of that time, they had all of their paraphernalia arranged around the new oilrig, which stood close to the boundary between the Cronson and Maximos properties. They were ready to drill.

Pan, who was supervising the drilling, called to Festus for confirmation. "We agree then. Go down a thousand feet, and then put on a bias bit and swing across the boundary to the left of the flame? Right?" Festus nodded, amused by how Pan's exaggerated Texan speech came and went depending on the type of discussion. "Now, the next stage ain't clear to me. When do I put in your transverse bit?"

"Stop when you reckon you are about two or three hundred feet short of the well. We have sensors in the drill and can make a fair estimate of our progress. We'll put an initial guidance sensor down and try to measure accurately where the bit has reached. If it seems all right, we'll then put in the transverse bit and sweep across. Remember, we can pull back and try again, or go forward and try again if we get it wrong the first time." The drilling started.

Some hours later, Zack arrived looking worried. "I don't understand why we haven't had some kind of visit from Old Max's men. They know we're here. I tried to speak to Prometheus, but he won't answer the phone. I kept getting excuses. I can't believe they'll simply ignore us. Look over there; you can see them around the fire! We gotta talk to them before we start the final stages of the project."

The day passed uneventfully, and the drilling proceeded well. Elena kept her promise about providing Greek dinners. They were lively affairs, especially for the Cretans, involving long, drunken discussions with Zack's Sfakian relatives about the problems of modern Greece and Crete. In particular, the Turkish problem still weighed heavily on the minds of the Sfakians. Festus was unable to find out the purpose of their visit. It didn't seem to be just a vacation.

On the day that would ultimately bring a resolution to the problem with the Maximos family, he broached the subject over dinner.

"Your relatives, Zack, why are they here?"

Zack looked up so quickly he missed his mouth with a forkful of hot saganaki. "Damn it, Fes you should know better than to interrupt a man while he's eating this good stuff." Zack wiped the soft cheese from his chin. "What a dumb question. They're relatives. What other reason do we need? Here, have some salad!" He shoveled cucumbers, tomatoes, olives, and feta cheese onto Festus's side plate. "Tell us about your business, Pan! How's it going?"

The dinner, which continued with stifado and eggplant, fruit and coffee and Cretan white wine from Gortys, was completed with no further reference to the relatives.

Festus, Pan and Chuck returned for the first part of the night shift in Pan's station wagon. They were at the point of extending the drill, when a number of grimy-looking men surrounded the rig.

A tall, gray haired man walked forward. "What the hell do you think you're doing? We said we didn't want help."

Festus had difficulty in recognizing that this tired man, covered in dust, was the normally elegant Prometheus Maximos. He started to reply that they were simply trying to help, but Prometheus motioned him to be silent. He continued. "Now! It will all be peaceful! Y'all just sit over there, away from the rig, and we'll just make a few adjustments."

Some of the men were carrying explosives, others firearms. Festus could see that he was trapped and signaled to the riggers and Chuck to back off. The continued absence of Pan was puzzling. He kept quiet in case Prometheus spotted it.

"Like hell I'll sit over there. It's more than my job is worth. You blow up this rig and my company will sue you for everything you own."

Festus restrained his foreman. "It won't come to that; we'll pay for any damage. I told you that before. We guaranteed to cover any losses when we rented the rig. We'd better do what he says."

They had all filed away from the drilling area and Prometheus and his gang were preparing to dismember the rig when they were stopped by a shout.

"Hold it, everybody!" The voice came from the shadows by the station wagon. As they turned towards the voice, Pan, who had spotted the trouble coming and hidden in the wagon, emerged. He leaned on the hood, holding a submachine gun, which he trained on the invading group.

"Y'all are *traispassing*. Put those explosives down, then move slowly to the right and lie face down. This is Pan Cronson speaking. Prometheus, I thought you might try something. I came prepared. You know me. I've dealt with situations like this before. Tell your men not to chance it."

Before Prometheus could give his advice, one of the men on the outside of the group started to move. A stream of bullets ran into the ground in his path. The shock froze them all and, like automatons, they did what they were told.

Pan came out from behind the wagon. "You take this!" He slung a handgun to the foreman. "Take a couple of men and check the area! Make sure there aren't any more of them skulking in the brush!" He walked over to the prostrate party. "Turn around! Put y'alls hands behind y'alls backs and listen up to Doc Festus! Particularly you!" He prodded Prometheus.

Festus spoke to them. "I have a technique for putting out the fire. It's unusual."

Pan chuckled, "it sure is."

"But it should work," Festus continued, "We want to help. Can't you understand? We're repaying an old debt. That goes for Pan too."

Pan looked dubious. "I'm not repaying a debt. I'm returning some mud they left here." He kicked some mud in the general direction of Prometheus.

"We're bias drilling down to the left of your shaft. In a day or so, we should be ready to add a new transverse drilling system and bit. This will be moved back and forward and drift-drill across your shaft and cut into it, assuming my calculations are correct."

Prometheus was interested now. "But how can you drill transversely? Is it similar to bias drilling? I guess it could be?" Prometheus added. "But how will y'all know whether you've hit the right shaft?"

"As to the second question, the drilling mud is a special mixture. We've added a potassium salt to it. If we hit, this will mix with the oil and the flame will change color slightly. A spectrometer and photomultiplier here will detect the potassium lines and indicate success. In fact, it may well be visible to the naked eye and the flame will turn violet. We have a special high pressure pump to prevent a blow back."

"So assuming you intersect. What can you do about the fire?" Prometheus asked, skeptically.

"When we intersect, it may take more than one try, we'll add a considerable quantity of another chemical to the mud." Festus pointed to the tankers, standing by the rig.

"This chemical is a flame inhibitor, a deionizer. We'll apply full pressure and blast mud and inhibitor back up the shaft. If we're lucky, we'll put out the fire and the inhibitor will prevent it re-striking for a short time. The main problem is that we have only a limited amount of the mix and we must succeed the first time."

"It could work. That's a lot better solution than the explosives we've been trying," Prometheus said, thoughtfully. "All we've done so far is to make a bigger and bigger mess. We run the risk of setting off another rig." He paused and after some seconds reflecting, continued. "All right, I agree. Y'all go ahead! Dad'll be all fired up about it." He gave a wry smile as he tried to relieve the tension with that small joke.

"If ah let you go, do y'all guarantee no double cross?" Pan asked, wary about the sudden change of attitude. He waved the gun threateningly.

"I guarantee it. I wanted to go along with you earlier but my first duty is to Dad, even when he's wrong. I'm afraid he's reliving the past. One favor I ask is that we all try to keep the truth from him. I cain't tell how he might react to the y'alls practical joke."

The confrontation over, they worked up a plan. Prometheus agreed that the area around the Everyman Bore should be cleared as if the Maximos team was setting up a new batch of explosives. This pretence would allow them to be ready to cap the well if the plan was successful.

The bias drill started to bite, steadily eating its way below the burning rig. It was a slow process. Periodically, Ionides would monitor the special sensor in the head that assessed the position. He called out his interpretation of the position to Pan. On one occasion, it was necessary to replace the bit to correct the alignment of the hole. Eventually, Ionides calculated that they had reached a position just in front of and to the side of the burning rig and he called a halt. The transverse drill was installed.

Zack joined them, bringing breakfast from the ranch. The weather continued to be unseasonably cold and wet for October and a pale wintry looking sun afforded little relief from the damp air. The men around the Cronson rig were muffled in thick clothing. In contrast, around the Everyman Bore, the workers were sweating from the humidity and the oppressive heat of the fire.

The transverse drill worked in and out, edging sideways, towards the target. Festus ordered the introduction of the marker into the drilling mud. Both groups watched silently as the well continued to belch out orange colored flame...ten minutes…thirty minutes passed and no change occurred. They withdrew the drill sixty feet and traversed again, with no success.

"We seem to have missed it," said Ionides, who was plotting the position of the drill. "The sensors say we passed directly underneath some time ago."

Festus was worried. He had convinced himself it would work the first time. He did not like being wrong, and was about to order another try along a different line, when he realized that there was no gain in being proud. He was not the expert, Pan was. I'm learning, he thought to himself as he asked for advice. "What do you think, Pan? Where do you think it is? Forget about sensors. What does your experience tell you?"

Pan pulled out a scrap of paper and did some calculations. "To tell the truth, Fes, I don't agree with young Ionides. I think we went maybe three hundred feet deeper than we intended. The way the drill was working a day or so ago, it seems to me that we hit a soft patch, and the drill dropped at a steeper angle. Knowing the length of the drill and allowing for this, I think we still have a way to go. It's worth some more drilling with the bias drill."

Festus nodded in agreement. "Change the bit. I reckon Pan's right."

Drilling continued further into the Everyman area. They reinstalled the transverse bit then watched impatiently. Still nothing happened. Ionides monitored the sensors. In the meantime, Festus opened the valves to add the chemicals from the tankers to the slurry.

"If Pan is right, we surely should be…" His voice trailed off as a shout went up. The flames slowly changed from orange and red to violet. Pan reacted rapidly to increase the pressure of the drilling slurry. The bit spun and gouged out the bore, opening a better passage for the mud. The flame increased in height and intensity as the mud ejected the oil above it at a greater rate. The noise and the light were noticed as far away as Argos and Arcadia. Suddenly, the flame broke away at the base and disconnected like a rocket at take off. It shot up into the air, gradually diminishing in size until there was no more flame, only a great gusher of mud and oil. The Maximos team rushed in quickly to cap the well the instant the flame died.

"*Tha-it's a thang,*" Pan exclaimed, in amazement. "*Fa-is, y'all da-id ait.*" He ran to his wagon, and hauled out a case of champagne. The sprayed champagne in all directions until common sense mandated it should be drunk.

In their excitement, they forgot their promise to Prometheus Godson to hide the truth from old Max. "Let's go over to the Everyman," Zack shouted. No more encouragement was needed. They piled into every available vehicle and tore across the open land to the Maximos well, where the crew was closing off the flow of oil. Standing by the remains of the rig were a number of figures, ankle deep in muddy oil and covered in it.

One of them was Prometheus. He embraced Zack and patted Festus on the back. With suppressed emotion, he spoke. "Thank y'all. Maybe we can act civilized again." He paused. "There's someone who wants to see you." He pointed to an old pickup, covered in mud. They could see a face in the open window. "We couldn't stop him. He knew something was going on, and came here just as you put the marker in. I had to tell him the truth. I just can't tell how he's reacting. He's said nothing."

Prometheus opened the door of the pick up. A very old man sat on the edge of the seat. A blanket covered his knees, his hands sheltering under it. Bright black eyes peered out at them from under bushy white eyebrows. A shock of white hair stood up stiffly from his head. He wore a black suit, white shirt with a starched winged-collar and a black tie. There was silence.

The old man eyed the group, one at a time, slowly. He looked particularly hard at Zack and Pan. His thin voice croaked out. "Panou Cronson, you come here!"

Pan shambled forward, still holding a bottle. The old man smiled a wintry smile. "We should drink on it. I have glasses by my feet, if you could reach them for me."

Pan reached forward. As he did so, the old hands came out quickly from beneath the blanket and slapped a great glob of mud in his face.

Pan staggered back and sat in the mud. "You old bastard," he screamed as he fell. Pan sat in the mud, his head in his hands.

"Sorry Pan, I had to give him the mud," Prometheus moved to help him up, but Zack restrained him. No one else moved. Pan sat for a long time, his shoulders hunched over, then his body began to shake, and he rolled on the ground, slapping the mud and laughing, uncontrollably.

Old Max was cackling, hoarsely. "Now we're all square! Now we're all, square!"

"Quick," said Zack. "Pass out the rest of the booze before he changes his mind. It's a cheap price to pay to settle this damn stupidity."

The champagne was finished quickly, and they retired to Old Max's ranch to celebrate further and sample his famed Greek style chili.

Later that evening, the old man asked to see Zack alone. "Your father and I feuded, Zachary," Old Max said. "I have never forgiven him for stealing Penelope from me. I loved that woman. You know she was the most beautiful creature I ever saw. Then you came along and stole my beloved Elena. I'm a vengeful old man." He paused. "I have a confession to make. I was so worked up about the fire; I convinced myself you were to blame. When you are old, Zachary, events get jumbled up and it is difficult to keep the chronology right. I gave the IRS all the information I had on the Eurysthesian Foundation and Trust." He paused. "I tricked Joe into telling me about the latest trust stuff, on the pretext that I wanted to make it up to you. I don't know that it matters much. From what I hear you're on pretty good ground, unless somebody gets too greedy."

Zack understood now why Joe had studiously avoided him in recent weeks. It confirmed Alex's worries, but the problems it might cause were minor, compared to the gain of peace between Argos and Arcadia. "What's past is past. It will cause us some problems, but we've just solved a worse one. I surely would appreciate it, if you would tell me everything you know." Old Max talked for fifteen minutes, and then he and Zack shook hands.

The executive committee of the Foundation and its Trust discussed the matter at length. Zack advised them to be cautious in their action. "The problem is not that we're doing anything illegal, but it's a fine line between tax avoidance and tax evasion," he said. "I recommend, strongly, that everyone contact Alex if they have any doubts as to the legal position of their work for the Foundation and Trust." Zack turned to Festus. "I think we've covered that well enough. Maybe before we close, you could say a few words about future projects."

Festus hesitated, and then gave a partial answer. "I have a few ideas; two in particular that I'm pursuing actively. The long-term one is a project that will take us to Crete. I would prefer to say nothing else at the moment. It'll require a lot of my time to get ready. In the near-term, we'll continue one that I started at the inception of Olympic Services. It relates to some interesting developments in the field of biochemistry. In fact, it involves the use of mass-produced enzymes and bacteria for making massive amounts of some products. For example, as used in the tanning industry, in corn oil production, paper manufacture and drug manufacture. Our particular interest is in using bacteria-enzyme mixes to clear up oil spills. We've been funding Willard Mowlin at the University to research the subject for us, and he's been doing some tests. While I'm in Scotland, he'll direct our efforts."

"I hear there might be some military applications? I'd like the opportunity to get some of those *de-fiance* bucks."

"I don't know of any, Zack. I'll look into it, when I've finished with Loch Ness." Festus responded calmly. Goddamn it! He thought. Why does Zack have to reduce everything to money? I don't want to do military work, and I certainly don't want it rammed down my throat by a money grubbing banker, when what we've got right now is some great research.

"I've tried to forget about the monster," Zack asked, brusquely. "Do you have to go?"

"You know the answer."

"Yes, unfortunately, but if this bug thing breaks I'll want you back here," replied Zack ungraciously.

"Yes, sir!" Festus turned away to hide his anger.

18. Battleships

Cathy Schmidt returned for Christmas. Festus had mixed emotions about seeing her. Since she had left him on Santorini, they had communicated by letter. Her personality was distracting—hinting at romance in one sentence, curt and dismissive in the next. Maybe that was what had kept his interest. Would she ever go out with him? God! He hoped so. After walking away from Linda, he seemed to have developed a fixation on slim women. He had talked Cathy's parents into letting him pick her up at the airport. He even had faint hopes that he might persuade her to spend the night in Austin.

"How were the flights? Tiring?"

"Yes, but it's great to be back. I can't wait to get home." Cathy looked at him. "How's Dawn?"

So that was it, Festus thought. She knows Dawn's back. How? Angelica he guessed. He was convinced there was something strange going on between the two of them. "She's fine, I guess. We're separated now. I don't see much of her, except when I visit Pandora. Can I come and see you?"

"Sure, you know my number. Give me a call."

"How about tomorrow for dinner? There's that great barbecue place off Redbud Trail?"

"Not tomorrow. I promised to see Angel. How about Thursday?"

The dinner went well. They had a lot to talk about and were able to keep off the subject of Dawn. On their third date, Cathy spent the night with him in Austin. Festus was elated but, that morning, as they ate a light breakfast on the patio, she raised the question of Dawn. What did he plan to do?

The problem was that he did not know. He mumbled some words about it being difficult with Pandora still so young. He feared driving her away again.

Cathy listened, her lips pursed in obvious irritation. "I see," she said. "You'd better get me home. I told my Mom I'd go shopping with her." The change in mood was as meteoric as the tone of her letters.

They spent their final few dates arguing. Cathy wanted a commitment from him that he could not bring himself to offer. He tried weasel words, but she saw through his ploy and became more and more angry with him. After the New Year began, Cathy returned to Germany and Festus returned to Loch Ness. She had not slept with him again.

It was great to be back in Scotland, thought Festus, looking at the sun-dappled Loch. There was a light breeze and the few clouds scudding across the sky raced their shadows on the gray, snow-capped hills. He was standing on the dock at Urquhart House with Georgina MacLeod and Marienna Cronson. They were chatting quietly about Texas. The submarine had been given a 'winter cleaning' and its bright orange hull oscillated gently in the water below their feet. A beautiful, crisp winter day, yet somehow frustrating. Beyond the submarine, the scattered reflection of the sky from the Loch's surface gave the impression that they were sitting on the end of the world. The Loch had no depth. Therefore, there could be no monster. Festus thought about his sighting the previous year. Had it been real, or merely a drunken fantasy? He was close to telling his companions when Marienna interrupted his thoughts.

"Georgina and I were wondering whether you have all the information you need? Now that you have had time to use that new instrument of yours, the chromatograph."

"I guess so. I can't think of anything else to do. It always helps to have as much data as possible. I might have missed something. The problem is that even with the new data and better chromatograph the computer program still indicates that the Loch off Foyers is the place to look. Yet when we hunted there before there was nothing."

"You had to leave, Henry," Georgina said, sympathetically. "Maybe the rest of us were not smart enough to find her. Or for some reason she was not there at that time."

"I appreciate those kind words Georgina, but I've had the sensors mounted in the Loch for some time. A month, I guess. We've seen some faint signals. They're probably noise." He was silent for a moment. The wind had died and the image of the sky had softened. He studied the surface of the Loch intently as if his eyes could penetrate its depths. "It's like a game I played as a kid—Battleships. Do you know it?"

Georgina nodded. "Maybe I do. I've seen my grandnephews drawing squares on pieces of paper and marking in ships. Is that the game?"

"Yes, that's it. The two players take a piece of paper each and draw two sets of a hundred squares on it; the grids are ten by ten, A-J and 1-10. Each player then takes their paper and secretly shades squares on their own grid to represent their fleet: one square for a submarine, two for a destroyer, three for a cruiser and finally four for a single battleship. The shaded squares must be in line, either horizontally or vertically. Each fleet has, say, ten submarines, three destroyers, two cruisers and the lone battleship. Ships aren't allowed to touch. The other, initially blank, hundred square diagram is used to represent the opponent's sea. The game allows each player, in turn, to 'drop a bomb' on his opponent's fleet by calling out a square, C8 for example. If it lands on part of a ship or submarine, the victim says hit, otherwise miss. Eventually, after some large number of tries, it is possible to sense where the enemy fleet is situated and tracking down the remaining ships becomes simpler. Sometimes, you've peppered your opponent's sea with bombs, but you can't find the battleship, even though it seems impossible that you could have missed it. Until, suddenly, you spot the blotch of four unmarked squares and then, 'bingo', you've got it. Of course, this situation is like the reverse of battleships. I'm looking for the most marked area." Festus paused, his face suddenly excited, eyes sparkling from the recollections of his childhood, then clouding rapidly as he returned to the present.

Georgina looked at his fox-like face with amusement. "You're still the child playing battleships, aren't you?" She chuckled. "And yet you're the one leading this incredible enterprise. You clearly feel that this hunt is like battleships, but somehow you can't find the great boat itself. What if your opponent cheats?"

The excited look disappeared and his face darkened as Festus remembered playing with Zack. He cheated, not much, but just enough to stay on top. In battleships, he would record Festus' bombs in the wrong squares. Festus recalled the frustration he had felt as a child. He knew he had won but Zack would shrug his shoulders and make some remark like, "you got it wrong again, Fes. Why can't you little kids learn to count? You may have meant B-9 but you said C-9."

"We ought to get everybody to play sometime," said Marienna, interrupting his train of thought. "On one of those terrible, gray, drizzly days when the monster's retired to its lair."

Festus looked at her, tiredly. "Yeah. We could have a competition," adding sarcastically, "if Zack were here, I'd have to let him win. He expects it."

"You may have to, but I don't!" Marienna snapped.

"Nor do I, Marienna," added Georgina. "The idea of it! Letting Zachary win!"

"I'm beginning to feel that we're being cheated here, but if that's so, it's because we're cheating ourselves." Festus took a piece of paper from his pocket, and sketched a map of the Loch. "Maybe I can show you why I'm so confused." Quickly, he marked on the paper the positions where fish had been caught, where detectors had been located and the lines that had been traversed by the surface craft and by the submarine. He then shaded the areas that included detection of chemical compounds that were not due to the fish and eels in the Loch or in the neighboring streams.

"It seems that you have dropped all your bombs, Henry, and the signs all point to Foyers." Marienna commented with a smile, looking at the map, which was nearly obliterated with pencil marks. "Maybe the monster is moving all the time?"

"We thought of that, Marienna!" he retorted. "Obviously, like most animals, it will move about but also it has nowhere to migrate to so it's likely to return to some home base regularly. That should show on the map. I have a couple of places, which I may not have analyzed right. We'll get new data. It'll probably turn out to be in one of them."

Festus stood up, angrily screwed up the paper and threw it into the Loch. The paper slowly drifted further away. He watched it for a minute then, without another word, he turned and walked back to the house.

Marienna and Georgina watched him leave. "I hope you don't take his anger to heart dear," Georgina said, kindly. "He must be bitterly disappointed."

"I don't," replied Marienna, wearily. "But, when you've had to put up with it for nearly forty years, it can get very tiring. I wish he'd grow up."

The few Eurysthesians, who had ventured to Scotland, were driven hard by Festus in his efforts to find a solution; fishing, watching, and helping in the analysis. It was as if he did not know how to stop. Zack solved the problem for them all. He telephoned and told Festus to return to Argos. One of his contacts in the oil industry had found out that a breakthrough in the fight against oil pollution would be announced soon in a public meeting. Zack wanted Festus to attend the meeting.

It was sad Festus thought. The game of battleships was played out. There was not a blank space on the grid. He had peppered the Loch near Foyers with bombs, figuratively speaking, and had seen nothing. Ionides, Hamish and he were sore from cruising in the cramped quarters of the submarine. The new chromatograph was a wondrous instrument, but it could only analyze the data it had, not interpret it. Festus had to admit to himself that he had not a clue where the monster was. The image of large curious eyes haunted him. Why had he chosen that moment to rub his eyes? For when he had looked again, only a ripple remained on the surface, and that could have come from his stone. Shi-it! What monster, he thought? No, damn it! There was something unknown in the Loch, the signs were there in the chromatography, and maybe he had seen it. Something was screwing up his analysis. He had fought of attempts to end the hunt, but now he had no ammunition left. The data was there. He had analyzed it as well as he knew how. Yet, something was missing.

He lay on his bed in that half-and-half world which is reached by a staircase of bottles. Following dinner, he had remained behind in the study slowly finishing the bottle of brandy. His head swam and he felt so nauseous that he had to stand up and walk around the bed. Occasionally, he would stop at the window and press his forehead against the cool windowpane. Through the window he could see Urquhart Castle and, beyond it, the villages of Lewistown and Drumnadrochit, sitting on the banks of the rivers Coiltie and Enrick. It was a clear night with a nearly full moon. The moonlight reflected off the rivers and gave them the appearance of silver ribbons flying off the silver tunic that was the loch itself. Festus returned to bed, his mind still active and reeling from thought to thought as he drifted into sleep. He found himself playing battleships with Zack Cronson and the omnipresent Chorus lined up behind him. This time they were wearing kilts that looked completely ludicrous when combined with their buskins...

"Do you want to know what we hae neath our kilts laddie," the chorus chanted.

"Go away! Please leave me alone," Festus cried. The Chorus turned away and bent over in unison. Festus averted his eyes and found Zack, larger than life, swimming in a great silver sea. Zack was chanting all the time, "You'll never find my battleship. I'm moving it under water all the time." In his mind, Zack reached out of the water and pulled at a silver ribbon, which floated up in the air from the loch, moving it quickly to another spot just as Festus was about to drop a bomb. Festus, trapped in the nightmare, tried to follow, but his body was leaden and he struggled in frustration. "I've got to cut the ribbons," he said to himself, but as he reached for them, Zack would move them away. Festus had just worked out a plan to get the ribbons and trap Zack when, finally, he was too tired to follow the dream any further and he fell out of it.

When he woke, the daylight was filtering through the windows. The ache in his head had subdued to a low murmur and he sat up in bed, looking at the window. In his mind, he could still feel the frustration of the nightmare, but as he lay there, it seemed more and more the frustration in tracking the monster. He analyzed the nightmare, and remembered that, in his sleep, he had formulated a plan. What was it? It was a plan to cut the ribbons, the silver ribbons. He smiled to himself. What the hell was he doing, thinking about silver ribbons? Did the monster decorate itself? But wait a minute. He forced himself to concentrate. There were silver ribbons. He put his hand to his forehead. The pressure took him back to his ramblings around the room. His head was pressed against the cold glass. That felt good. In his mind, he could see silver ribbons linking up with the silver body of the Loch. He sat back on the bed, unsure of himself. For a moment, he had seen the answer. Now think again, the silver ribbons, what were they? He forced himself to concentrate on the dream. He imagined driving around the Loch. As you come out of the bend following the castle, you come to Lewistown and then to a low area with a river, maybe two rivers. His mind raced. That was it; the silver ribbons were the rivers. Festus opened his eyes. They were there. Not as clearly as at night when the moonlight reflected from their waters. Rivers gave the flow of water to the Loch that had caused the map to drift, when there was no wind.

In analyzing the data, he had not allowed for the currents in the Loch. They would redistribute the chemicals. How could he have missed something so obvious? Unfortunately, blind spots were typical of research. The exhilaration he felt, at having solved the problem, even overcame his hangover for a brief moment.

Festus announced his discovery at breakfast. "The data clearly showed Foyers to be the place, but we didn't find the monster. It made no sense. Now I can see I missed a crucial ingredient—the currents in the Loch. The water flows from Loch Oich to the west through Loch Ness into the river Ness to the Moray Firth. Coming in from the side are numerous rivers which cause local currents."

"So he's going to rewrite the program to include the currents, and then find Nessie." Ionides finished the point for him.

"Indeed, I shall do just that. Starting as soon as my head clears. Assuming I can persuade the diabolical telephone system to connect me to Texas, and I can get Zack to agree that we don't need to return."

Zack did not agree. "I'm tired of hearing your latest fantasies about the how you're going to find the fuckin' monster!"

"Well, Zack. I'm tired of hearing you ignore every fuckin thing I suggest. I can do what the fuck I like." Festus regretted losing his temper the minute he said it.

"With whose money, Dr. Festus? Remember who supports you!"

"I could try to raise it privately."

Zack was brief and to the point. "Get your fucking butt back to Texas right now! Or I'll instruct Hamish McDougall to sell the equipment. It belongs to the Trust, not to you. Or, maybe, I'll replace you with Dr. Erhard Mitterer. He seems to be smarter than you. He developed these new bugs to deal with oil-spills."

19. The Augeian Affair

The auditorium at Gum Oil headquarters in Houston was full. The public relations officer for the company, a past master at timing, allowed a further period of anticipation. At what he judged to be the correct psychological moment, he mounted the stage. The newspaper and television reporters, the researchers and oil company representatives became still.

Festus sat at the back with Willard Mowlin, a biochemist at the University of Texas in Austin. They had the common bond that both loved practical jokes. Willard was a plump untidy looking man. His disorganized manner belied a brilliant mind. He was the prime consultant for Olympic Services for studying the use of bacteria and enzymes in the oil industry. He had a good idea what the press release concerned, and was worried about it.

"Welcome to Gum Oil. We appreciate your interest in our development work. I will say a few words, and then I'll hand the session over to Dr. Erhard Mitterer." The middle-aged man, sitting at the side of the stage, nodded cursorily. In contrast to Willard, Erhard Mitterer was a caricature of the scientist as a steely-eyed, omniscient being. "One of the main areas in which oil companies are criticized is that of pollution, particularly of the seas. We have been caught on the horns of a dilemma. On the one hand, it is our business and, in fact, our duty to extract and deliver oil. On the other hand, under the arduous conditions in which oil is often obtained, some oil will be spilled. We all regret this and do our utmost to deal with it. Certainly, it is of no advantage to my company to be classified as polluters. We've felt so strongly about this that we have, as many of you know, invested considerable amounts of money and brainpower in looking for solutions to the problem. We have tried special chemicals to break up the oil. We've tried plastic mesh absorbers to contain the spills. There is a long list. Now we've arrived at what we believe to be the ultimate solution. We hope that when you have seen our demonstration, you will understand the advances that we have made." The PR man turned to look across the stage. "I give you Dr. Mitterer."

Despite his German name and Germanic looks, Erhard Mitterer was a second generation Texan, as became evident when he spoke. In fact, he was of the same vintage as Festus. They had competed for state science prizes at high school level. A rueful smile crossed Festus' face as he remembered losing to the smooth talking Mitterer. Festus had little respect for Mitterer's intellect. He had an uneasy feeling that Mitterer's research could be as glib as his way of talking, and that he lacked the ability for self-criticism. Erhard projected an image of cold, intellectual virtue. As pure as the driven snow, and as intelligent, he thought, unkindly. Zack's suggestion that this "foreigner" could replace he-Festus as the Trust's chief scientist had weakened his determination to rebel and continue the hunt for the Loch Ness monster. He knew the threat was a ploy, yet he hoped he would be able later to ram it down Zack's throat. If his judgment of Mitterer was right, there would be something screwed up. He would find it.

"I will be brief, Ladies and Gentlemen," Mitterer said. "We have telescoped in time this demonstration. Like a television cooking class, where you see a series of dishes presented in rapid succession, each representing a stage in the preparation of some culinary masterpiece. In such demonstrations, the real cooking time is compressed to fit in the few minutes left by the advertisements. The difference now is that we will show a meal being eaten." Like a magician, he pulled from under the lectern a large beaker full of water. "This is sea water." He then produced a second smaller beaker. "This is crude oil."

With a flourish, he poured the oil carefully onto the water, until a thick black-brown layer was formed. He left the beaker on top of the demonstration table and produced a plastic bottle, which he waved at the audience. "In this bottle, I have a truly remarkable development." He paused for effect. "Bacteria that eat oil. At present, they are living in a nutrient solution. This solution sustains them but it does not encourage them to breed too much. You have all seen, at least on film, the mess that is left by an oil spillage. If I remember my Greek mythology correctly, an Augeian mess might be a proper description. This liquid, containing bacteria, will clean up that mess. In deference to our Greek scientific forebears, we've called it Heracles."

He poured a small amount of the liquid from the bottle onto the oil, adding liquid from a second bottle. "It requires only a small quantity of this bacterium to deal with the oil because I added a special enzyme from this second bottle, which enhances the process. The amount you put on depends upon how long you are prepared to wait." Mitterer produced a second large beaker. "We prepared this in a similar manner two hours ago."

The audience could see that some of the oil had disappeared and a brown suspension was sinking to the bottom of the beaker. Even Festus was impressed. A third large beaker was produced, which represented a twelve-hour delay. In it, nearly all of the oil had disappeared. Erhard Mitterer held the final beaker aloft. Prepared the day before it showed no trace of the oil and only a small quantity of brown sludge remained. His look was triumphant. "There, ladies and gentlemen, we have the answer to the problem of oil pollution. Are there any questions?"

"I represent the New York Times, Dr. Mitterer. Are there any toxic waste products?" asked a reporter.

"Thank you. I was waiting for that question. I am happy to say that we've done exhaustive tests and can find no toxic waste products."

The reporter from the Dallas Herald was not satisfied with the answer. "Frankly, that sludge may not be toxic, but it sure as hell looks like shit to me." He sat down enjoying a wave of laughter.

"Of course it does," said Mitterer, with equanimity. "Because that is precisely what it is. Thank you for the prompt. You see the trick was to find a way to prevent this bacterium from being poisoned by the waste products of its interaction with the oil. Here we have soluble, non-toxic…um…feces. That brown suspension will break up in about a week, under the action of the seawater."

"What happens to the bacteria?" another voice asked.

"The bacteria are produced by manipulation…uh, patented processes in our laboratory," Mitterer replied. "As I said before, they are sustained, until use, by a nutrient solution. They and another enzyme are then added to the oil. The bacteria multiply rapidly and eat the oil. The enzyme acts as a catalyst. Fortunately, the whole process stops when the oil is eaten up, and then the bacteria die. As I indicated, we've done many, many tests to verify this."

There were numerous other questions, checking on the uses of this new wonder cleanser, and some questions about future plans.

"What future tests do you propose and has the Department of the Interior requested any tests?"

"A good question. I've been waiting for it," Mitterer replied, smiling. "We've made numerous satisfactory tests in large tanks of sea water. Now we propose a test on a controlled spill at sea. The Agency is very interested in this, and tentatively has agreed to support the test and provide assistance in its analysis. It will be a few months yet before we are ready. Probably it will take place in May or June. We intend to make a small spill somewhere off the Louisiana coast, near one of our oilrigs, and then clean it up. This should dispel any doubts anyone may have. We have complete confidence that this test will prove to be successful and will be a milestone in the control of pollution."

Festus and Willard had been exchanging comments throughout this demonstration, much to the annoyance of those around them. Now Festus was prodding Willard to ask a question. Festus still resented Mitterer's past victories. He did not want to contribute to his moment of glory. Willard, who was surprisingly shy for a professor, rose reluctantly and posed his question with diffidence.

"One last question, if I may?"

Mitterer turned towards him, recognition showing on his face. Festus ducked down so that he would not be seen. "Certainly, Willard. What can I tell you?"

"Is the bacteria and enzyme mixture safe in the sense of…what happens if some is left over at the end of the oil dissipation?"

"That's the kind of intelligent question I expect, and always get, from you Willard. Professor Mowlin is a distinguished member of the faculty of the University of Texas." Mitterer emphasized Professor. "The fact is, we've arranged an extra protection, which ensures that the mix self-destructs as soon as the oil is eaten up. It, how shall I put it, turns on itself and becomes neutralized. However, this is another of our patented processes that I can't discuss. If that is all, then let me thank you for attending."

The audience rose and applauded in appreciation of the impressive demonstration. Festus had a further hurried discussion with his friend, and then they walked to the front of the hall where a crowd had gathered around the beakers. Mitterer was holding up the first beaker to show how effective the bacteria had been, when his arm was jogged. Though he managed to hold onto the beaker, some of the mixture splashed onto the table. Festus started to help clean it up, using his handkerchief, but was brushed aside as assistants rushed to remove it with chemical cleaners. In the confusion, as Mitterer apologized for the mess, Festus popped the rolled up handkerchief into his pocket and sauntered away. Mitterer, recovering from the incident, saw Willard leave and greet Festus on their way out. For a moment, he did not recognize him. Recognition brought a worried look to his face. He made a move to chase after them, but the crowd still pressed around him and he was bombarded with a string of questions.

Willard glanced at Festus. "I don't think anyone realized that I jogged him on purpose, Fes. Did you get a sample?"

Festus grinned and nodded. "Willard, why don't you tell the folks at work what happened. Get them started! I need to be in Argos.

"Okay, Fes. Are you sure?" Willard looked amazed that Festus would delegate such an important task. He did not know that Cathy had returned home.

After only a day, Festus was not so sure her return was a good thing. Their interactions were still lukewarm. Cathy had made it clear that their relationship would be platonic as long as he and Dawn were still married. Somehow, he had imagined it would be possible to have Cathy and hang on to Dawn. Should he have asked Dawn for a divorce? Would she agree? He had heard she had been seen with Alex Platon. Even though he knew that Alex's sexual preferences lay elsewhere, he felt uneasy; a selfish feeling, like he was losing a precious possession. It made him think hard about whether he wanted a divorce. Then there was the problem of Pan, and his damn photographs. It had not been a joke. Pan had sent him one every month. They were not particularly provocative but they made him look bad. The old bastard! Strangely, anger at Pan had not prevented his subconscious from giving him a hard time, and he no longer felt so self-righteous about Dawn. What could he do, the whole affair was a mess.

Willard described the Gum Oil demonstration to his co-workers. "It was very impressive. The bacteria-enzyme mix cleaned up the oil with remarkable effect," he concluded.

"Tell me again what the problem is, Willard, and why we should get involved!".

"Fes and I are worried, Ion, about the secondary effects of this technique," Willard replied. "The bacteria eat oil, which is fine, but it's a mutant strain of another bacterium. Normally, its rate if consumption would be small, however they have found, by trial and error, this catalyst and enzyme that speed up the process. Mitterer maintains that the bacteria gorge on oil, while multiplying ferociously. Then, apparently, they self destruct, leaving only the waste products that they claim are harmless."

"So, what's the problem?"

"We're very concerned about what would happen if the bacteria evolved further. If for some reason, it was not destroyed but started to breed again. The possible consequences would be frightening. The tests I've been doing for us, which have been on similar substances, have shown odd effects which may be generic to the whole concept."

"Can we do anything about it?" Chuck asked.

"As you know, Fes and I succeeded in getting a small sample of the mixture at the end of the demonstration. There should be enough for testing in a day or so. We are feeding it carefully. The fact that we've been able to keep it going is worrying."

"I heard how you got it. Neat job." Ionides applauded.

"Thanks, Ion, a very professional exercise, though I say it myself. I think we'd make a good dip team." Willard beamed, and scratched his left calf with the toe of his right sneaker. His students wagered on the gesture—how many times would he do it during a class. The smarter students would generate the action, asking loaded questions to ensure he matched their bets.

"Watch it! Willard, habitual thieves like you end up on the most wanted list." Ionides chuckled.

"You don't think so really, do you? I'd like to do it again. It's as good as practical jokes." He scratched his calf again. "Where was I? Anyway, back to your question. Fes wants you and Chuck to start analyzing this sample. Fes has asked Panou Cronson to take on the job of finding out about any field tests that Gum Oil makes. He's got heaven knows how many contacts."

When Festus appeared, Willard quizzed him about the Trust. "One thing still puzzles me, Fes, and this case is a good example. What will the members of the Foundation get out of this work?"

"I've been curious about that too," added Chuck.

"A fair question. To be honest at the beginning of such a venture it's not always clear. Generally, I try to combine something scientific and saleable with travel and business opportunities for the members. In this case, if we can find out what the substances are, we may be able to anticipate problems and produce, how shall I put it—an antidote? Less seriously, when Pan finds out where in the Gulf the tests will be held, we'll need people to sample the sea water over the whole area to check for any changes."

Festus chuckled. "Naturally, at the same time, they might just get in some good fishing and have an excuse to lie on the beach. If we're to take this job seriously, then we will require samples all the way round from the Florida Keys to the Yucatan peninsula."

Willard nodded appreciatively. "Boy, you really do have all the angles covered."

"Don't be misled, any of you, by the fun aspects of our work. We may not have to make a profit and we, at Olympic Services, can all act in a godlike fashion trying to sort out the problems of these poor mortals, but it can be a serious business, and never more so than this time."

Festus settled back in his chair. "Willard, have you got the samples here? Good. Would you go over your proposed program, briefly?"

Willard rummaged in his briefcase and extracted a plastic box. Inside, was a ratty looking bologna sandwich.

"Now, that looks dangerous," Ionides laughed.

Willard hid the sandwich quickly and found the correct box. In it, securely clamped, was a Petrie dish. "This is the bacteria-enzyme mix. I have another portion back in my lab. This sample we will divide into ten portions. Two, we will refrigerate as a further safety precaution. Two, we will analyze immediately to be sure that we know which of the bacteria we're dealing with. I've some ideas on that. The topic is not new. With another two we will try and track down the enzyme."

"Good, Willard," said Festus. "The remaining four dishes we'll divide into very small portions and test what impact different environments have on the bacteria and their waste products. We'll be able to speed up the process if Pan can find out what kinds of plants and materials Gum Oil has procured recently. Presumably they are setting up for increased production."

At first, the work progressed slowly. Pan, despite his many contacts, had difficulty in obtaining information rapidly on all of the materials passing through the Gum Oil receiving department. When he was successful, Willard supervised Chuck and Ionides in assessing them.

"I wish I could be more than a glorified technician, Ion," Chuck said. "I'm enjoying the research, but it's sure tough to do my engineering studies, and work for Alex."

"Be patient! You haven't earned your union card yet."

"Tell me about it. More than a year to go."

"Hang in there!"

"I'm having a hard time concentrating on all this work in Austin, while Pandora's in Argos."

"Better than her being away at college. I hear she'll be going to Stimpson." Ionides laughed.

"Ain't that the truth, boy. It'll be a lot tougher than worrying about high school jocks. Pandora's too exper...you know what I mean."

"I know what you mean. Tell me," Ionides paused. "I probably shouldn't ask. Oh, the hell with it! Has she er...reformed?"

"Fortunately, and unfortunately, the answer's yes. She's still an outrageous flirt. Other than that she's been on the wagon since we found her in Santorini."

"What really happened? You've never told me."

"Not going to either, old buddy. Best forgotten."

"That bad."

"Yes."

"How are you managing...without you know what?"

"Ionides Festus!" Chuck exclaimed, in mock horror. "How could you ask an innocent young man a question like that? I'm shocked."

"Well?" Ionides demanded.

"Ion, you know how I feel. I don't want my frustration to come between us. Pandy still has real problems in that area."

"Sorry."

Finally, the team's efforts were rewarded by a lucky break. Pan tracked down the source of the enzyme. He was very coy about explaining how he had managed this feat and deflected all questions. The enzyme and bacterium were identified in early May; leading them to concentrate on tests for side effects. Quite early on, they saw worrying signs when they used the oil eater in different environments. Festus phoned Mitterer the minute Gum Oil announced that the first test on a controlled spill would take place in June. He attempted to persuade Mitterer to delay the tests. Unfortunately, it was already too late. The publicity machine was wound up and Gum Oil had too great an investment to delay the schedule.

"What did he say?" Willard looked worried.

"I tried to talk him out of it. I guess he's got too much riding on it. Ego overrides objectivity again!"

By the day of the test, the Trust had mustered an armada of long-range pleasure boats in which they could couple the joys of fishing and sunbathing. Their excuse for using the Trust was that they needed water samples from around the Gulf, before during and after the test. In reality, the important samples would be from the sea near the test area. Marienna and Angel Cronson went to St. Petersburg in Florida. Harold and Peri Dexter stayed with relatives in Galveston. Ionides and Samantha covered the area around Port Aransas, Texas, while Zack and Elena Cronson handled the south Texas area from Port Isabel. Finally, Alex Platon vacationed in Vera Cruz, Mexico, with the supposed purpose of obtaining long-range samples. Willard was happy to remain behind to continue the laboratory tests; the sea made him queasy.

Dawn, Pandora and Chuck made their headquarters in Port Arthur, Texas. Festus went with them. He was uneasy being near Dawn, but it was a better solution than her original proposal, that she and Pandora should join Alex. To the amusement of Pandora and Chuck, their interactions were coy yet friendly, as if they were on a first date.

The test was carried out on the floating oilrig, "Betsy Ann Gum Oil II;" moored some miles off the Texas coast between Galveston and Port Arthur. It was a calm day. The oil was spilt on the surface, to make an unlovely flat black carpet covering about one thousand square yards. Mitterer supervised the spraying of the bacteria-enzyme mixture from a helicopter. He was pleased with the rapidity of the operation and requested the helicopter pilot to circle the area for a time, so that he could study the site. As he circled, he noticed without curiosity, two boats, off in the distance, apparently cruising for fish. He hoped they would stay away from the oil and observe the warning markers, otherwise he would have to shoo them off, which he did not want to do because of possible adverse publicity. However, they showed no signs of trespassing on his preserve.

Chuck steered the boat, while Festus, Dawn and Pandora pretended to fish. Chaos ensued when Chuck misjudged the distance from a marker buoy and fouled the lines. Meanwhile, Harold and Peri decided to motor over and socialize, because Harold had discovered that Peri had forgotten to load his beer. The two boats closed on each other, and Harold on his first pass signaled his intent to jump into the other boat from the aft deck, where he stood holding onto a small mast. He instructed Peri to bring his boat alongside. Unfortunately, as they came parallel and he jumped, Peri's hand slipped and pushed the throttle full forward. Harold sensed the surge while he still held the mast. His body swung out towards Festus and then, clinging to the mast with one hand and drawing upon that superhuman strength that can come with fear, he swung back into his own boat, where he landed on the aft deck in a disjointed heap.

"What the hell was he thinking about?" Festus shook his head at the sight of Harold trying to regain his feet and Peri gamely trying to slow down their progress out to sea.

"Oh! I wish I'd been quicker," said Dawn, taking photographs of the retreating boat. Harold never mentioned the incident, but Chuck, Dawn, and Festus had a field day with it.

"I hope Mitterer's crew didn't see it."

"I don't think so, Fes. They're still fussing over the oil." Chuck pointed at the rig.

Over the next hours, the oil broke up, leaving patches of brown sludge on the surface. Peri and Harold, with his arm in a sling, returned the following day. By then, most of the oil and sludge had disappeared, and at a rate entirely consistent with the laboratory experiments. By noon on the third day, the wind had freshened and the test was terminated, as nearly all of the oil had disappeared and the waves made it impossible to monitor progress further.

The test was claimed as a great success. As far as the press was concerned, that was the end of the matter, at least until the technique could be tried seriously on a major accidental spill.

Festus phoned to congratulate Mitterer, though he retained an uneasy feeling about the technique. Later, when they analyzed his own collection of samples, taken from the area following the test, he had to admit that there were no apparent side effects, and all the bacteria they recovered were dead. Nevertheless, he remained concerned enough to push on with the laboratory tests. They had now produced useful quantities of the bacteria and enzyme and were able to conduct a variety of tests on materials that theoretically might affect the mixture.

His concerns turned out to be correct for, towards the end of June, they began to find positive effects from certain types of chemicals. Small effects to be sure, but ones that intensified their anxiety.

Festus considered his situation. Family affairs seemed to be more or less in order. His relationship with Cathy was going nowhere. He and Dawn had even gone out for dinner together a couple of times. Pan seemed to know, for he had stopped sending photographs. Chuck and Pandora were dating. It was clear that Chuck was having a stabilizing influence. Pandora would graduate next year from high school, and enter Stimpson College in South Texas. Life was good.

Dawn had a different view and berated him about it. "Fes, I'm very worried about what Pandy might do without us…and Chuck. You're back deep in your science again and not paying attention."

"You worry too much, Dawn. It's a year away. Pandy learned her lesson in Greece. Anyway, she's got Chuck now. He's a good kid."

"Sure, but I don't think he can handle Pandy when she's at Stimpson and he's in Austin, doing his degree and running around for you and Alex. Be realistic!"

"I'm trying to be."

"Fat chance!" Dawn sniffed, contemptuously.

Festus stayed in Argos through most of July, to take part in the play cycle. Since there had been only a little time to rehearse he had accepted only one role; playing Hephaestus in the satyr-play, "Aphrodite and the Cretans." The play described an interlude at the court of King Minos of Crete. A jealous Zeus has banished Hephaestus from Olympus. Now, he is resident at the court to help Heracles in the capture of the Erymanthian Boar. Aphrodite is also present, incognito, with the initial intention of repairing her marriage to Hephaestus. Unfortunately, King Minos has fallen in love with Aphrodite, who is disguised as a mortal. Minos asks Hephaestus to help him gain her affections. Hephaestus is horrified by the request but does not wish to antagonize his new master. Hephaestus, aided by the satyr Slienus, does a masterly and amusing job of procrastination. Finally, King Minos, in frustration, threatens him with death if his inaction continues. Hephaestus persuades Aphrodite to submit to Minos, and both appear heartbroken. In reality, she has become unhappy again with Hephaestus and is using Minos, to whom she is attracted, to regain his attention. Hephaestus, believing she has betrayed him, has designs on a mortal girl. Each of them is trying to make the other feel guilty. In the final scene, the satyr Silenus elicits the truth about their affairs, and makes fun of them.

The satyr Silenus would be played by Panou, with Zack as King Minos, and Dawn as Aphrodite. Festus was uneasy. After Marienna had persuaded him to play Hephaestus, she had told him that Cathy would return to play the mortal girl. "Marienna you're interfering again!" he expostulated angrily.

"The idea, Henry! Of course, Cathy should play the part. She's done it for a number of years."

It was all too close to life, Festus worried. Nevertheless, he realized he would have to face the problem sometime. In the event, the rehearsals went smoothly as Dawn and Cathy kept a wary and courteous distance. Acting in the play, before a live audience was different, and it was a relief when play-cycle ended. He found it difficult to play Hephaestus as an arrogant fool. He even felt some sympathy for Heracles, sworn to do the bidding of king Eurystheus. As Hephaestus, he could happily hand over Aphrodite to the king and settle for the mortal girl's favors. Life did not match the play. As Henry Everett Festus, he did not want to lose his wife. An image of Linda came to mind, reminding him of Pan's photos, and then of Cathy. Hell! He still didn't know what to do about her. Festus carefully avoided looking in the mirror as he removed his make-up. The last thing he needed now was for Hephaestus to confuse the situation.

He need not have worried. Cathy returned to Germany early. The brief affair with Cathy was definitely over. A few weeks later, Festus received a letter from her that said she would not be coming back at Christmas. She was dating some-one else. Apparently, they had a lot in common; sports, dancing, and Billy was nearer her age. Festus reread the closing sentences a few times then tore up the letter. He did not reply to it. The bitch!

Festus was happy to return to work. Progress had been rapid. Willard tried hard to persuade him to publish their results. Festus was unwilling to risk the scandal that might result if someone detected how they had obtained the sample, particularly, because there was still no evidence of ill effects. Instead, he pushed the group to find ways of handling the bacterium if it should get out of control. By now, the oil pollution control approach was receiving a wider, though still limited, application. A real oil spill in the Gulf and a crashed oil tanker truck in Mississippi were among the first clients.

In the middle of November, the first hint of disaster emerged. Painters, work-ing down near the water line of the oilrig, noticed some brown sludge floating around the hull. It soon dissolved and they made only a passing comment to their foreman that someone should dispose of sewage further away. More precisely, as one of them explained, "Some bastard ought to chuck that 'friggin' shit further from the rig."

Preliminary drilling from B.A.G.O.2 had looked encouraging. Some time after the test, the oil became harder to extract. Moreover, a small motor, used for hoisting provisions from the service boat, seized up. The shift engineer was quite upset when it was suggested that this was a result of sloppy maintenance. Then, the service boat packed up, followed by the power supply for the drill itself. By this time, knowledge of the events was not confined only to the hierarchy of Gum Oil, and scientists from Gum research and from a Government Agency were rushed to the rig. It did not take a genius to remember the bacteria-tests, and further work soon confirmed that a mutant strain of the bacterium was to blame.

The armed services announced "Operation Big Sweep" to deal with the problems. They explained the operation as a test of defensive measures against an invasion. The Administration did not support the ultimate option, mooted by a few knowledgeable people, of classifying the research area and anything connected with it. The decision displeased Zack Cronson, one of the knowledgeable people.

Quarantine regulations were introduced to contain the bacteria, both at the oilrig and around the crashed tanker. The ploy worked for a short time. There was little coverage on television, because no filming was allowed. However, a few enterprising reporters were creating steadily larger headlines as they homed in on the truth:

CUBAN INVASION A HOAX!"
"BIG SWEEP—BIG MESS?

The potentially most damaging headline was:

MUTANT MADNESS IN MISSISSIPPI!

It was relegated to the less significant pages by the stark news:

"PRESIDENT KENNEDY ASSASSINATED IN DALLAS!"

It was a troubling time, but Zack Cronson took comfort in the fact that the strong hand of his good friend, to the southwest of Argos, would now be at the helm. Festus persuaded Zack to offer the assistance of the Eurysthesian Foundation and Olympic Services to Gum Oil. Initially, there was resistance from the oil company executives, who viewed the offer as a ploy to make them divulge their research secrets. Festus dealt quickly with this obstacle by making it clear that he already knew the bacteria and enzyme types, and by describing ways in which the bacteria could mutate. Cooperation was soon assured and this led to a second meeting and demonstration at Gum Oil Headquarters in Houston. It was not exactly what Festus had wanted.

The lecture-theater was only a quarter full. Uniforms were mingled among the business suits of the sparse audience. There were no representatives of the Press. The Biological Defense Act, rushed through Congress efficiently by the new President and a select group of Congressmen and Senators, had taken care of that.

The public relations officer for Gum Oil, a master of timing, allowed them a further period of waiting to heighten the tension. At what he judged to be the optimum psychological period, he mounted the stage. The hall became still. Festus and Willard were standing off-stage, worrying about whether the demonstration would be effective.

"Ladies and gentlemen," the PR man said. "I give you Dr. Festus, chief scientist and a director of Olympic Services, which is an arm of the Eurysthesian Foundation and Trust, and Professor Willard Mowlin of the University of Texas at Austin. It was with foresight that our company employed these eminent gentlemen and I'm sure that their revelations will be a relief to us all."

Festus looked sharply across at him at the mention of foresight, but the PR man merely signaled that Festus would take over. "It was remarkable, ladies and gentlemen, that Gum Oil had the foresight to give a demonstration of their pollution cleanser some months ago," Festus said, looking hard at the Gum Oil executives. "It was fortunate that Willard Mowlin and I also had the foresight to be there, and to take the action that I will relate to you. We are faced with a severe problem. The bacteria and enzyme mix developed by Gum Oil scientists is remarkable in its ability to clean up oil." He looked across at Erhard Mitterer sitting to the side, with his head resting in his hands. "I think we should all be clear that this cleanser was the result of a brilliant piece of research by Dr. Mitterer and his colleagues. Unfortunately, as we are all aware, there have been side effects and now the mix is turning on us. While it appears that the Corporation and Government Authorities are getting the matter under control, it is essential that we understand how the bacteria mutate and how to handle the mutants." Festus paused for effect. "The civilian and military implications are considerable if we fail. Even before the time when Willard and I saw the first demonstration, we were uneasy. I should point out that Willard and his Department had been working in this area for some time, using a grant from the Eurysthesian Trust. We

worried that, while the possible benefits of this kind of technique were phenomenally good, there were also substantial dangers inherent in it. I can own up now
that Willard and I attended the previous meeting with the intention of purloin-
ing some of the mix."

There was a titter of laughter from the crowd.

"We succeeded. Willard jogged Doctor Mitterer's arm, causing some of the
mixture to spill. I collected some on my handkerchief and then we transferred it
rapidly to a Petrie dish. A very professional and I must say satisfying, engagement
for both of us." The tittering turned to outright laughter. Festus let this noise
subside. "From that time on we have conducted a vigorous research program and
I must acknowledge at this point the help of our colleagues Ionides Festus,
Chuck Steeger, and other friends from UT for their work. Our first efforts were
to find out what bacteria and enzyme were being used."

Festus looked across at the Gum Oil executives again. "Our...farsighted...
present colleagues were not so forthcoming then. Finally, we succeeded in identifying the components of the mix and we then looked for agents that could cause
undesirable mutations of the bacteria. I should say right now to save further
uncertainty that we found such agents, though whether among them are the ones
responsible for the present crisis I cannot guarantee. We will now demonstrate
one mutation effect and show the effectiveness of an antidote for this particular
mutant variation."

Ionides produced a beaker of seawater. He poured oil onto the surface and
scattered bacterium-enzyme mix over it. Chuck brought a second beaker, representing a two-hour delay. In this beaker, most of the oil had disappeared and a
brown sludge was settling to the bottom.

"Let me now introduce an extra factor," Festus said. He inserted a red painted
metal plate into the liquid. "We believe that the cause of the trouble in the Gulf
may have been the anti-fouling chemicals in this corrosion proofing paint."

Ionides produced a beaker representing a week's delay. There was no sign of
the oil and the brown sludge had dissolved, but the paint on the metal plate was
marked with a green discoloration. Festus removed the plate and put it into a further beaker containing oil. A beaker representing a delay of one day showed clear
and strong activity. The surface of the oil was broken up by a green slime that was
clearly living on it.

"I think this indicates the type of problem we face and in this instance, we
have an antidote which I can demonstrate." Festus poured a colorless liquid into
the beaker and then presented earlier samples in which the slime had disappeared.

"Ladies and gentlemen, it is clear that no effort should be spared in searching for any additional mutation and in developing their respective antidotes. I can assure you that the Eurysthesian Foundation will work wholeheartedly with Gum Oil and the Government to this end. If we don't all work together, then you may be sure that we will end up with another mess. But this time, if I may quote from the classics, it will be of truly Augeian proportions."

Zack Cronson visited Olympic Services, when their research was completed. He must want something was Festus' immediate reaction. He was right! After receiving a tour and making numerous congratulatory remarks, Zack worked his way around to the purpose of his visit. "I've been talking to my friends in Washington. Naturally, there's been a lot of interest in these bugs, mainly concern to stop them getting out of control. Now people have had time to come up with other uses. They're thinking of dropping it all over North Vietnam." He waited for a response. Festus could guess what was coming and remained silent.

"A couple of guys are coming to visit you next week. Give them any help you can! There's the chance of a very good contract. Incidentally, you need to write a paper on what we did on this, in a way that'll satisfy the IRS. Touring around the gulf taking water samples and so on."

How many years had he worked for Zack? Festus thought. Too many! The tone of the requests—commands—had changed. He could hear them. *"Fes, it would be great if you could look at this problem."* Which had become, *"You give it a try, old buddy,"* and then evolved to, *"I need this in a couple of weeks. See to it! Please."* And now had become, *"Give them any help you can!"*

"Goddamn it Zack! Vietnam!" Festus exclaimed. "That's the dumbest idea I've heard in years. It won't hurt them. They hardly use vehicles. But it could ruin our highly mechanized forces. I've told you a dozen times I'd prefer not to work for the military if there are other options. I won't do it."

"Don't be so damn precious! Who the hell do you think you are?" Zack's voice rose. "One of those fucking pinko-students. This is in the national interest. Do you want the Commies to get an edge? Why do you think I got this area classified?"

"So that there wouldn't be any competition," Festus snapped back. "What about Gum Oil Corporation?"

"I had the foresight—a popular word—to buy into that company. I own this place too," Zack replied, emphasizing the 'own.' "If you won't do the work I'll take you out, and find somebody else. Mitterer will do. Gum Oil knows most of it. Remember the deal you made in Blarney!"

Festus hung his head. The same old arguments, he thought, wearily. What could he do? Zack had him by the balls. He knew there was no way he could get back to Loch Ness, let alone finish his projects, without the Foundation's support. It wasn't just the money. For some reason, he needed the Eurysthesians to help in the Labors—and Zack was the Foundation. And he had made a deal. "Shit! I'll give them the bloody stuff. Let them handle it,"

"Not exactly. They would surely appreciate help from you and Willard." Zack backed away a little from his previous hard line.

"Okay I guess so. I don't know about Willard?"

"You'll persuade him, Fes. Raise his consulting fee!"

Festus realized he had no choice, other than to resign and he was not ready to do that. At least he would try to get something out of it. "I want to ask Hamish McDougall to do some tests of currents in the Loch. Will that be all right?"

"You're not still on that kick are you?"

"It's there, Zack."

"Come off it!" Zack's laugh was derisive.

"I saw it," replied Festus, angrily, seeing an image of the dark eyes of the monster.

"In your dreams, Mister, or you were drunk. Work up something with the military and then maybe you can get the tests done! That's the real world."

Festus did not reply, remembering the plays. Sometimes it was hard to know what was real. Maybe reality was what you believed in? Well, he believed in the monster. When Hamish sent him the data on currents, he would modify the computer code and find its lair.

20. Stimpson College

Stimpson is a small town in south Texas in a surprisingly unfertile, marshy part of the Rio Grande valley. Stimpson College occupies the middle of the town and is the main reason for its existence. Certainly, the quality of the area itself is not sufficient, otherwise, to justify such a population density. The College was founded in 1922 by Colonel Robert J. Stimpson—silent p—who had the misfortune to return from the First World War with an insubstantial pension, an inheritance that consisted only of a large plot of this infertile land, a small homestead and his self-inflicted title. The Colonel, whose statue dominates the center of the campus, was not a man to be thwarted by such minor problems. After considerable thought he arrived at the idea of providing further education based mainly on self-help, and started his college. At the beginning, the students were all male and the environment was somewhere between that of a summer camp and a military school. Stimpson, plus a few ex-army officers provided the education, in sport, mechanics and agriculture. In their turn the boys helped to run the establishment and, in fact, to build it. The college, because of its Spartan lifestyle, was not badly affected by the minor perturbation of the Depression. In fact, it even experienced a small boom during this period as a last resort, cheap, junior college for the offspring of the recently impoverished middle class.

From these meager beginnings, the institution had grown into a four-year college, and had acquired a good reputation for hard work, a good education, discipline and later—girls! Sport was the major activity of the college, ahead of education and discipline. Football in the fall semester, basketball in the winter, tennis, swimming, baseball and track in the spring and golf all of the year, were a serious business. The rivalry with other small colleges was intense. The annual "friendly" football game against the University of Texas Longhorns junior varsity, a part of summer training, was a major event. Pageantry was a significant component of these games.

"Does Pandy really have to go to Stimpson," Chuck asked worriedly. "Why not UT?"

"Afraid so," Dawn replied, smiling. "Austin's too close to home for her."

"But she's bright," Chuck argued.

"Yes, but she needs a year or two to…mature." Dawn paused. "Frankly, the business between her father and me hasn't helped."

"That place has a reputation, you know?"

"I've heard—Girl City." Dawn laughed. "Don't worry! A lot of it is talk."

"I heard it used to be men only. What happened?"

"You can thank Colonel Stimpson's wife, Miss Molly," Dawn replied. "If I remember right, the first girls arrived in 1936. Changed the place totally. You know, the Stimpson College cheerleaders are renowned throughout the State of Texas for their beauty, artistry and precision and…"

"Conceit among other things," Chuck said, adding, "and Pandy's tried out and has been accepted into the squad. "Great!"

"All the high schools and colleges have cheerleaders." Dawn giggled. "Come on Chuck, lighten up. Going coed has been good for Stimpson. Some of the early graduates married and stayed on to work at the college or open businesses. So the college grew and they renamed the town after the good Colonel."

"No problems at all?" Chuck queried.

"I think only the Second World War and a rather thorough tax investigation in the late 1940's rocked the Colonel's life." Dawn smiled. "He survived. From what I hear, the Colonel, despite his title, isn't a great believer in government control—even of the armed forces. Do you have any other questions?"

"Festus is up to his chin in bacteria-enzyme mixtures and wants me to take her," Chuck said, tentatively.

"Typical," Dawn muttered.

"Zack's putting a lot of pressure on him."

"I know," Dawn sighed. "Maybe some day he'll refuse."

"Will that be okay?"

"Yes, and I'll come with you. At least her mother can show up."

"Thanks," Chuck said. "I'd like support. I've heard worrying things about how the new girls are met."

"Don't worry. It can't be that bad.

On the first Saturday in September of 1964, Chuck and Dawn took Pandora to Stimpson. After a vigorous argument over the choice of music on the car radio, the Beatles or a memorial program for Jim Reeves, they departed. On the journey from Argos, Pandora bubbled with excitement. Chuck and Dawn looked worried. The reality they encountered was worse than they had imagined. Traditionally, the new girls were known as "birds" because, some long time ago, someone had made the remark that birds were now migrating to Stimpson for the mating season. Despite the moralizing of the Colonel and his good wife, the comment was close to the truth. Signs directed them to the meeting place by the open-air theater where a gaggle of birds was clustered in a bewildered group with their luggage.

Pandora stepped out of the station wagon to the accompaniment of "I Want to Hold Your Hand". The song was picked up rapidly by the group of boys, fighting for the privilege of helping with her luggage. The singing intensified when Chuck joined her, and rose to a fever pitch when Dawn emerged.

"Are you a new bird, Ma'am?"

Dawn shook her head in amusement.

"Are you staying, sir?"

Chuck reddened. "I'll be gone in a minute. How about letting me say goodbye to my girlfriend?" He said, angrily. He turned to find Pandora—too late!

"We'll look after Pandora now," said a boy who had been smart enough to check the name on the luggage. Chuck watched in hurt bewilderment as Pandora's belongings were added to the pile. Pandora turned, smiled reassuringly and was gone. He started to follow. Dawn restrained him gently.

"I know it isn't easy, Chuck, but she's got to do this on her own."

"I guess," said Chuck, his face tight with worry.

At this point, they were approached by an elegant youth. His pale washed-blue eyes scanned Dawn's face searchingly while he smiled in commiseration. He proffered his right hand to Dawn, while his other hand brushed back a recalcitrant part of his sleek blond hair. He was looked closely at Dawn's left hand, which was bereft of rings.

"Ma'am…Sir. Please don't be offended by the guys. They mean well and this is a sort of tradition with us. I'm Wendell Jameson, chairman of the student entertainment committee."

"Sir! Shit!" Chuck muttered under his breath.

"I guess you can blame all of this commotion on me. I'll make sure your daughter," Wendell looked questioningly, "will be fine. If there's anything I can do, anytime, please let me know."

"Sure," growled Chuck.

Wendell ignored the anger. "An administrative matter. Those freshmen are so impulsive. Rushing the birds away before I can get their names." He held out a clipboard. It looked official. In fact, it was a trick he used to get information. "What is your daughter's full name?"

"Pandora Olympia Festus," Dawn replied.

"What a pretty name."

Chuck's irritation became more visible.

"Did you say Festus? By any chance, is she related to Demos Cronson, a sophomore here? I've heard him mention his uncle, Dr. Festus, who was in on the Loch Ness monster hunt."

"Yes, Dr. Festus is her father. We're…" Dawn's lips pursed. Wendell dipped his head, acknowledging what he took to be a signal.

"Since you know Demos, maybe you could find him and he could look after her? We thought he'd be here to meet us."

"Well see, Demos, now he's a busy guy, yes indeed a busy guy. He has his business to attend to."

"I didn't know he had a job. His father will be pleased. What's he doing?"

"Oh, working around campus. That's all."

"But doing what?"

Wendell shrugged his shoulders. "Various things." He left.

"That Wendell's something, isn't he," Dawn said when they were out of earshot.

"I was ready to slug the bastard," Chuck replied. "What was that business about Demos? I know Pandy can't stand him."

"I wish I knew," Dawn answered. "When they were young they played together a lot. Demos was a bad influence. More recently, and don't tell anyone I told you, there have been drug problems. Fes and I debated whether we wanted Pandy to go to Stimpson with Demos in residence. Pandy thinks he's reformed. Huh! What did Wendell mean with 'he was doing various things'? What things? I suppose he's like his father." Chuck looked curious but Dawn went silent. Chuck was in no mood to talk more, and only the gentle sounds of Jim Reeves filled the car on the drive back to Argos.

As soon as they were back in Argos, Dawn went to see Elena Cronson.

"I've got to talk to someone, Elena," Dawn said, immediately Elena welcomed her. "It's silly. I was listening to Jim Reeves when I was coming back from Stimpson. That song "I Love You Because," made me think of Fes. It was hell watching that skinny, bug-eyed bitch, Catherine Schmidt hang all over him during the play."

"It's only acting," Elena cautioned. "From what I hear, Cathy's interests lie elsewhere."

"I've heard. Angel, you mean? Is it true?"

Elena nodded. "Look Dawn! Any normal man would like the attention of a pretty, young girl. Even if she's suspect."

"Sure and has he slept with her?"

Elena shrugged. "There's gossip but I don't know."

"If I could get the old goat back in bed, he'd soon forget Miss Frogs Eyes."

"You go for it girl! Elena laughed.

"Will he want me?" Dawn asked, her eyes misting.

"He's an idiot if he doesn't," Elena replied encouragingly.

Despite all of the male attention at Stimpson, Pandora had managed to remain faithful to Chuck. In fairness to her, the environment was not one to encourage chastity. She kept her promise to herself and did not sleep with anyone; however, she remained an outrageous flirt. Her most persistent admirer was Wendell Jameson.

Pandora commented, when she telephoned a girlfriend in Argos, "the other girls think he's a really neat guy, blue eyes, sun-bleached blond hair, and buns, wow!"

"So what's the problem?" asked the friend.

"He's a complete bastard and I wish he'd leave me alone," Pandora replied.

Wendell was often successful in using his position to seduce new girls. He concentrated particularly on the cheerleaders, who were usually the prettiest and most versatile girls. In fact, his reputation was such that the presidency of the committee was generally known as the seventieth position. There was curiosity about his progress with Pandora. "How's it going with Pandora, Wend?" a friend asked.

"Slow. I'm making progress," Wendell lied. "She acts like a little virgin but I'm sure she's hiding something."

"We all know what she's hiding." His friend laughed.

"Demos will help me, when he gets back from Mexico tomorrow."

"What's he doing there?"

"Stuff," Wendell replied, winking.

Demos had also tried to date Pandora. But, though he had matured since leaving Argos, he had led her into various scrapes when they were younger, and she remained wary of him. Nevertheless, with his unruly mop of black hair and his engaging smile he remained the charmer with whom she had once played.

Fall and spring semesters passed quickly. Pandora prospered in her course work and as a baton-twirling cheerleader. Wendell smarted under his failure, and Chuck, accommodating his uneasiness and frustration, became resigned to trusting Pandora.

The Augean affair came to a successful conclusion, as the antidote for the oil bacterium was commercialized, and Festus set about worrying over what to do for his next project.

At Stimpson College, Founders Day, May 21st, approached. It was the custom to celebrate it by a wide range of festivities, including a parade, beauty contest, charity golf tournament and numerous publicity stunts. The college was now run by his son, Robert J. Junior and the Colonel, in his eighties and retired from active participation in college affairs, was literally wheeled out for these events. He took a keen interest in the golf and in the beauty contest.

Wendell's sole success with Pandora had been to talk her into persuading Festus and the Eurysthesian Foundation to support Founders Day. Festus did not like the idea, but Pandora's relentless pressure, by letter and telephone, eventually wore him down. With considerable reluctance, he agreed to try to get Foundation funds to support the event and to play in the tournament.

He called Zack and passed on Pandora's request. "What do you think Zack?"

"I like it, Fes. There's a banker in Austin, I've been having trouble with, Howard Clements, fancies himself at golf. By pure chance, I heard from Marienna that he'll be there."

"What do you want to do?"

"Fix it that he and I get to play against each other. I can take him easily."

Festus passed on the message to Pandora. She called back to say that Wendel Jameson had offered to help. After Festus talked to Zack, he replied to the invitation from Robert J. Jr.

"The Eurysthesian Foundation would deem it a great honor to assist in the celebration of Founders Day. Our Foundation is a charitable organization and members of our associate company, Olympic Services, will be happy to contribute to this renowned event. Colonel Aristotle Cronson, Dr. H. E. Festus, Mr. Joseph Maximos and I look forward to participating in the golf match. We understand from your letter that the golf is viewed as part of the entertainment and will not be played at the same level of seriousness as the Masters. Sincerely yours, Zachary Cronson, President of the Eurysthesian Foundation."

Founder's Day was the climax of a weeklong holiday for a number of Eurysthesians. Prior to it, Peri Dexter and Elena Cronson toured the Rio Grande Valley, shopping across the Mexican border in Reynosa and visiting Port Isabel and South Padre Island. They were alone, because Harold, could not be bothered with such a frivolous trip, it raised again all his misgivings about the Foundation. Ari and Yianna came to visit their son Demos and brought Rosie Cronson with them. Rosie, the daughter of Panou Cronson, planned to join Stimpson College the following year. Pan agreed to the visit but was not prepared, as he put it, "to come and put up with all that crap". Zack spent all his time with Ari and Demos pounding balls around the golf course. Elena complained to Peri that the brothers took the game far too seriously.

Festus and Joe Maximos, who were neither as dedicated nor as competent at golf as the Cronson brothers, spent a short time pottering, putting, and driving. The rest of the time, Joe took his wife and two kids to the beach, while Dawn and Pandora dragged Festus and Chuck on loathed, sightseeing and shopping excursions.

Festus discovered, to his delight, that the local general store, "Happy's Emporium," was run by his old college pal, Jonas "Happy" Hapgood; so-called because he kept as straight a face as any mortal man. However, the stone face hid the fact that Happy truly lived up to his nickname. During the six years he spent at the University of Texas, he was happy to be there, and happy to have had a brainy ally like Festus to help him to execute his wild practical jokes. He was very happy that fate had directed him from UT to Stimpson, where he had married the store owner's daughter. He was particularly happy to see Festus again.

"Let me show you something, Fes." Happy opened a door at the back of the store. It opened into a Black Museum of practical jokes. The room was filled with whoopee-cushions; wineglasses with cunningly placed holes; a plethora of strange electrical gadgets; and a bewildering array of potions and powders that could cause discomfort.

"I bet you do a lot of business with the students," Festus chuckled.

"Only those who are smart enough to not boast about what they've done."

IHappy regaled Festus with stories of how; one Founders Day, he and his accomplices had modified the good Colonel's statue with fluorescent paint, emphasizing his manhood. How, on another occasion, they had arranged for the football field to flood in the middle of the game with the University of Texas team. He was proudest of the fact that, through all the years, his role as the mastermind of these events remained undiscovered.

"Will I see you at Founders Day?"

"Hell, no! I've had enough of them. I'll be here, doing stocktaking."

Before Festus left the store, Happy loaded him with a bag of gadgets to use, as he put it, in emergencies.

The festivities on Founders Day began with an assembly in the Football stadium, with addresses by Robert J. Stimpson Jr. and local dignitaries, including the mayor, the local state senator, and the local U.S. congressman. The celebrities, including Zack, Festus, the Austin banker and a semi-well known movie actress who had passed through Stimpson some time back, were all paraded past the audience to the sound of polite applause. Festus was the best known, owing to the numerous sensational and inaccurate profiles in the National Investigator and other similar publications. He was notorious for testing the efficacy of the Blarney Stone using a lie detector, and for his continued, unsuccessful attempts to find the Loch Ness monster.

During all of the activities, the Colonel huddled in his wheelchair, nodding approvingly as the program progressed in the time-honored manner.

Following the opening ceremonies, the college marching band gave an exhibition of close order marching, while playing the "Yellow Rose of Texas," and finished with the College Commemorative March. For the latter song, everyone stood, except the Colonel, and sang the inevitable, trite, self-congratulatory lyrics.

Accompanying the band, in their natty scarlet, gold and white uniforms, were the twelve cheerleaders. They wore jackets of scarlet with gold trimmings, very short white skirts, scarlet panties and short white and gold Texan style boots. Pandora was one of the twelve.

Peri, watching them, drifted away into her customary trance like state, and saw them as a flock of birds as they strutted and pranced across the field. "They look like storks, or flamingoes," Peri said, thoughtfully to Dawn. "So elegant with their long legs and darting motions." A worried look crossed her face. "Why were they so pretty but so menacing? Zack should be careful," she continued grasping Dawn's arm.

"Peri, you're day-dreaming again. Wake up," Dawn said, seeing the glazed look on Peri's face.

"No, Aphrodite! "The Birds". They are the Stymphalian birds. Zeus is in danger."

"Why did you say, Zeus?" Dawn looked at her, searchingly. "You think Zeus…er…Zack could be in danger from the Birds? You mean this is like one of the Labors?"

"Yes. I can feel it."

"Did Marienna put you up to this?"

"No! No! It's not from the plays."

"Pandy's one of them. What could happen?"

"I don't know. I just have this feeling of evil." Peri looked embarrassed. "I feel so silly. I always seem to be seeing things as if we're acting out the plays in real life."

"You've got too fertile an imagination, hon." Dawn hugged her. "You've got it the wrong way round. God help any of those creatures if Elena sees them make a play for Zack."

The band and the cheerleaders left the field and the spectators were entertained for the next hour and a half by track competitions, gymnastics and an eight minutes a side tag-football match. Zack was paired to play with the Austin banker, and was engaged for most of the time in earnest and sometimes heated discussions with him.

Wendell Jameson was in his element, organizing the students and socializing with the more important dignitaries. He was studiously attentive to the U.S. Congressman, the state senator and the banker, who was a potential employer.

The beauty contest was a sedate affair. Miss Molly had accepted having the leggy cheerleaders, but the Colonel had not persuaded her to accept a bathing beauty contest. Consequently, the girls were demurely dressed in the Southern Belle style that appealed to her as being suitably dignified. The contestants

paraded, curtsied, said a few inconsequential words and swept off. The committee to select the winner consisted of the local congressman, the Austin banker,
Zack Cronson, Wendell Jameson and Mrs. Robert J. Stimpson Jr. The banker,
who was the chairman of the committee, announced the winner.

"The girls are all so beautiful that we find it nearly impossible to select a winner. But since we are here to do just that, we will honor this obligation and I have
pleasure in naming Amanda Ellesmere as the winner of this year's Stimpson College beauty pageant."

Amanda Ellesmere, a statuesque brunette from San Marcos with an excess of
teeth, embraced the award. The majority of the crowd who had favored other
girls, including Pandora, responded lukewarmly to the choice, but encouraged by
Wendell and the committee picked up their applause enough to prevent embarrassment. Coincidentally, Amanda was Wendell's current girlfriend.

Pandora came in fourth and put on a brave face but offstage, after the ceremonies, she cried openly in Chuck's arms. There were two hours before she needed
to appear as a cheerleader for the golf match. "I need to get out of here," Pandora
whispered. We've got two hours. I'm feeling sexy." She hugged Chuck.

During the drive, Pandora's unhappiness had translated into hunger. They
came to a gas station-cum-village store and a scruffy Southern Fried-Mexi-
can-Fast Food joint serving hamburgers, hot dogs, fried chicken and tacos. Set
back from the gas station was a dilapidated motel, consisting of a row of small
huts. Its main business was accommodating one-night stands for Colonel Stimpson's sex-mad students. She persuaded Chuck to stop.

"I could kill that cow, Amanda," Pandora said again, eyeing Chuck over her
Dr. Pepper and licked her corndog, suggestively. "God I'm frustrated."

"Want to do something about it?" Chuck asked, hopefully.

"Yeah! Race you to the motel." She beat him.

The clerk eyed them wearily.

"We'd like a room. Our luggage is in the car."

"I'm not a bell-boy."

"We'll take it in."

"How long will you be here?"

"An hour or so. We need to rest up. Long drive ahead," Chuck explained.

"Can you be out by six? I'm expecting a lot of business. Founders Day you
know."

He said this litany of words nearly without a breath and handed them a key.
Chuck signed as Mr. and Mrs. L. Johnson. The clerk's final comment was, "It's a
pleasure to have you back again, Sir."

The room was starkly furnished, the sheets none too clean. They didn't notice. She lifted her arms to help him remove her shirt and bra. Her young breasts were inviting. He buried his face in them, biting at her nipples. Pandora grasped his head and pushed it down to where she had loosened her jeans. She fell back onto the bed, as he rolled the jeans down her thighs. Her legs were parted and her panties were skewed, provocatively.

Afterwards, Chuck lay limply for a while, then lifted up to look at her. "The timing wasn't quite right, Pandy. Sorry we didn't make it together. I've needed for you so long, I couldn't stop."

"Chuck, you worry too much. It was great. Jesus! I've wanted you so much. I'm tired of lying to my friends about our sex life." Pandora chuckled. "I felt so randy it was killing me. You made it work, one way or another. Will you be able to get it up again, before our friend throws us out?"

"In a bit. I'm not through yet. Tell me! What turns you on?"

"You."

They rested for a while and talked about their future, then made love again. Chuck was gentle, patient, and contained himself through Pandora's orgasm. They slept until a banging on the door woke them. "Is nearly six you must get out," shouted the clerk.

"Oh, shit!" cried Pandora. "We've missed the golf match. They'll fire me from the Birds."

"I'll get hell from your Dad," muttered Chuck, adding. "I don't care. Damn! It was worth it. Hey! Maybe we've got time for a quickie?"

"No more quickies," Pandora said, lying back seductively. "Take it slowly. Burn off some of your puppy fat." She giggled, pulling him down on top of her. Later, as the clerk banged on the door again, and they rushed to dress, she stopped, kissed him passionately and whispered, "Don't change anything. I love you like you are."

"I don't plan to." Chuck laughed.

Meanwhile, back at Stimpson College, the charity golf matches had started. The first tee was just below the clubhouse that was set on the largest "hill" in the area. From this point, there was a panoramic view of the golf course. It was built upon land reclaimed from the marsh and the fairways wended their way through a complex arrangement of lakes and channels. The addition of small wooden bridges and trees gave the picturesque scene a resemblance to an extended Willow Pattern plate. From the golfer's view, the scene was less attractive. The course was a testing one and many of them would have substituted willingly some sand traps for the numerous water and reed traps. Most of the reeds had been cleared but the clumps remaining presented a considerable hazard to a low flying ball.

A large crowd had gathered to watch the matches, willingly paying the few dollars to enjoy the pageantry. Yes, pageantry, for an event like this could not go unsung. The marching band sent off each twosome at both the first and tenth tees. Because there was little room at the top of the hill, the marching band roamed up and down its side.

"It's like that old song," Peri said to Elena, singing the words to herself as she watched the band march. "The grand old Duke of York. He had ten thousand men. He marched them to the top of the hill, and he marched them down again." Peri stopped in embarrassment, realizing that others were listening.

Festus was competing against the local congressman—a jovial, quiet-spoken man who gave the impression that he was no particular hand at golf. In fact, though he was out of practice, he had competed for Stimpson during his college years. Festus was no great player but he was generally methodical and patient. Sometimes he was daring in his shots, but lack of experience often let him down. They were the first pair to tee off, and the cheerleaders celebrated their departure by chanting the Stimpson fight song. The marching band paraded on the hill, yet again.

"Where are Pandy and Chuck?" Festus asked Dawn, who was walking with his twosome.

"I don't know. I guess she's upset about the beauty contest. Let me get Ion and see if we can find them. You play well, honey!"

The match progressed evenly with both Festus and the congressman settling into their game. At the fifth hole, with the congressman one up they heard the cheerleaders and the band signaling the somewhat delayed start of the third group, a two man, best ball, game, which matched the state senator and semi-well known film star against Ari and Joe.

Demos Cronson arrived as they were leaving, muttering apologies for his tardiness. He was caddying for his father. Dawn considered him handsome, but to Festus he looked like Norman Bates in Hitchcock's film "Psycho".

The players continued around the course, ending back on the hill at the ninth green, where Festus holed a magnificent, if totally misjudged, chip shot to even the score. They took a short rest then drove off from the tenth tee. The cheerleaders and the band, led by Wendell Jameson, apparently not one wit affected by their strenuous efforts, erupted once again into a paroxysm of leaping and playing. Zack and the Austin banker were in the final group and were waiting impatiently to leave. Festus and his companion wished them luck. Strangely, they had completed the eleventh hole before the band signaled the departure of the last pair.

As they progressed back towards the clubhouse, they could hear the noise from the cheerleaders and band continuing, sometimes distant, sometimes close. Apparently, the cheerleaders had left the hill and were following the final pair around. Festus glimpsed them, looking like brightly colored red birds as they stalked the fairways and perched on the bridges. Occasionally he could hear their raucous chatter. Odd during a golf match, he thought.

The congressman had played well but without luck. Festus had played badly but the gods had been on his side. The tide turned at the seventeenth hole, a significant hole for the Eurysthesians, as it turned out later. Festus hit into a very bad lie, and while he could see a potential way out of it for a very skilled player, was not prepared to make a fool of himself by trying it, he played safe and lost the hole. On the eighteenth and final hole, the congressman, seemingly remembering his college form, played superbly, and birdied the hole to win the match. Throughout the match, Festus and his opponent had been exchanging comments for the benefit of the small crowd following them. The congressman not only won the match, but to Festus's chagrin got in the last jibe.

"Doc, you play well for a Longhorn," he said, grinning.

"It's been a long time," Festus replied, shaking his head.

"I suspected so. Now, if you'd attended this fine college, and practiced regularly, you might have amounted to something."

Festus was reaching for a retort, when Ionides rushed up.

"Zack's in trouble," he said breathlessly. "He made a large side bet on his game with that banker from Austin and everything is going wrong".

"In what way?"

"Well, for example, on one occasion, when he was about to take his shot, the cheerleaders started to dance and he put his ball in the water. Another time just as he was about to hit, the band started up. It's as if he has been set up. The coincidences are too great. They're at the seventh and he's already two holes down."

"How much did he bet?"

"I don't know, but he's obviously very worried, so it must be big. His game is going off rapidly." He stopped briefly. "It's funny really except for the bet. Another time he was in mid-stroke when a cheerleader nearly fell of a bridge. I've left Sam and Elena to keep an eye on things. We've got to help him."

"All right, I wonder what's up?" Festus looked thoughtful. Dawn had told him about Peri's daydream. The Birds were attacking Zack. It would make sense if this was the sixth Labor—the Stymphalian Birds. What could he do? He needed time.

"Go back and tell Zack to slow down the pace of the game! Also, observe the band and the cheerleaders carefully! See if they are being directed, or are just over enthusiastic to make the game entertaining! Oh! And find Chuck for me."

"Dawn and I couldn't find him…or Pandy."

"Get Joe then!"

21. Trick Shot

Festus was lost in a daydream, muttering to himself.

"What are you going to do, honey?" Dawn asked, worriedly.

"Eh! Oh! Sorry. I was thinking about how to help Zack. It looks like he's being set up. I'm thinking about what to do." Festus grinned. "You can help."

He whispered his idea to Dawn. She giggled appreciatively and gave him a big hug. "There are times, Fes, when you remind me why I married you. That's a marvelous idea." She pressed harder against him. "Maybe we can find time for…you know…later?"

"Find time for what?" Festus, caught off guard, looked at her distractedly.

"Surely, you haven't forgotten? We used to do it. Pandora's the evidence."

"Oh! That 'you know'." Festus looked at her, thoughtfully. Frustration was mounting and Cathy had not worked out. While he and Dawn had interacted platonically, since her return to Argos, erotic memories of her occurred more and more frequently.

"I take my clothes off, and lie on the bed," Dawn whispered. "You do wonderful…things to me…"

"Dawn you're terrible," Festus said, cautiously. "What about Alex?"

"Henry Everett Festus, you're a damn fool! Alex is an old friend, and a sympathetic listener."

"You wanted to go to the Yucatan with him when we were chasing the bugs."

"I only proposed it so you'd invite me to join you."

"You did what?"

"Fes! Alex, as you ought to know, is of the opposite persuasion."

Festus was about to respond, when Joe arrived.

"What's the problem, Fes? I got some weird story from Ion."

Festus explained the problem and sent him into town to see Happy Hapgood.

The final group walked to the ninth green. Zack was already two down. Festus watched the cheerleaders, who were along the side of the fairway, keeping pace with the players. The band had stopped playing now as they were approaching the hill and the girls were keeping a quiet and respectful distance behind the players. Wendell Jameson was also watching. Festus moved to study him more closely. Yes, that would be it, he thought, a favor for a favor. It had to be Jameson who was causing problems for Zack. He was the only one who could have organized the whole deal—but why? Maybe the beauty contest, was the reason? Certainly, Zack had indicated that the Austin banker had favored Amanda Ellesmere and had voted down strongly on Pandora, as had Jameson. However, that would not be enough reason to set up such a complicated charade. Festus wondered what Jameson was majoring in, commerce, banking, maybe? He would ask Demos. Also, where were Pandora and Chuck? Festus was impatient, waiting for Joe to return. In the meantime, Zack managed to tie the ninth hole. He looked relieved as his putt sank.

"I've been conned, Fes. It's not even very subtle, and since this is a fun charity match, I can't complain."

"How much did you bet?

"Don't worry," Zack answered, hurriedly. He looked embarrassed. "It's the honor of Argos I'm concerned about."

"Just hang in there, Zack, don't lose many more holes! I'm working on a plan to deal with the problem." Festus reassured him.

The game restarted and both players drove the ball well, reaching the fairway on the far side of the lake. Zack had out driven the banker and waited while he took his second shot. When it was Zack's turn, the band decided to celebrate the time of day. Festus could now see that Wendell was directing them. Zack's stroke faltered and he sliced the ball, luckily not quite far enough to reach the water. He scrambled hard for the remaining strokes but the Austin man, playing a steady and uninterrupted game, won the hole. The banker was now three holes up with eight to play, and he looked triumphant.

Meanwhile Joe returned from his errand. He was carrying two brown paper bags.

"You were right, Doc, the store wasn't open, but he was checking his inventory. As soon as I gave your name, he let me in. He's a *terch* strange, isn't he? That room of his is somethin' else. I've not seen *serch* a collection before. He gave me these. He said he'd like to help except he has to watch out for his reputation. Anyway, he'll be along to watch the fun."

"Fantastic, Joe. What would I do without you? Now I think the best thing to do is share them out with your kids, Ion, Elena, Peri, and Sam. Dawn and I'll go along and do some distracting, separately."

"Okay, Doc. The kids are going to love this."

"Wait a minute! Leave me just a couple of powder sprays. Dawn, I think it's time to fix Mister Jameson and start some problems for the band." Festus handed a small canister to Dawn, keeping one for himself.

The Colonel was sitting on the verandah at the front of the clubhouse and, to all appearances, oblivious of all around him. Festus waited until Wendell signaled again for the band to march up the hill, and then used the noise to drown out his approach. He came up behind him and sprayed a small puff of dust at his neck. Wendell was so deeply absorbed following the golf and directing the band that, by the time he reacted, Festus had limped away. The band started down the hill again, stamping their feet in time to the music. They were too distracted by the sight of Dawn standing aside for them to see the small clouds of white dust rising from the ground by their feet.

The golfers were at the twelfth tee by the time Festus and Dawn arrived. Zack had scrambled to tie the eleventh, but he was three holes down with only seven to play. The banker was about to drive. Dawn, in a low cut dress, chose the moment to lean forward. She had removed her bra and her full breasts swung gently forward. She smiled sweetly, and stood back, but though the banker averted his eyes and steadied himself, the distraction caused him to top the ball. While he was lucky that the ball remained on the fairway, it went only a short distance. Zack smiled appreciatively. His troops were hitting back. He addressed the ball confidently. Amanda Ellesmere signaled to her fellow Birds and they lined up behind Dawn. Zack noticed them, his smile dropped and he made a few tentative practice swings. The cheerleaders posed with one leg slightly forward, as if they were about to start a routine. Amanda raised her hand and kept acting as if she were about to signal. Zack tried to concentrate but like the banker, he was distracted and also fluffed his shot. He looked bitterly at the cheerleaders, who smiled back sweetly. Then Amanda gave the signal, and they went into their routine of high kicks and a rousing Stimpson chant. A flying boot caught Dawn.

"What the hell...?" Dawn staggered forwards and fell into a bunker.

"I'm so sorry, Mrs. Cronson. I slipped." Amanda Ellesmere tried to brush sand off Dawn's dress. Dawn pushed her away, and turned to Festus.

"I'll be back in a minute." She gathered the Eurysthesians and discussed tactics, before returning with them to the fairway. Zack was standing in the shallow water of a small lake. His ball lay just below the surface on a shelving gravel beach. He decided to play it from where it lay. The twelve Birds were all perched on the small wooden bridge that crossed the water behind him. They were idly drumming their feet on the bridge—a noise that irritated Zack and many of the spectators.

"Stop that damned noise!"

"It's all part of the show, honey," Amanda laughed.

Dawn signaled and the Eurysthesian sauntered onto the bridge behind the Birds. The drumming increased in intensity and when Zack swung, the Eurysthesians squirted powder into the golden boots and on the back of the cheerleader's necks. Zack missed the ball completely, lost his balance and sat down. In the excitement, the Birds did not notice what had happened. The spectators roared with laughter, as Zack rose out of the lake. His efforts had not been in vain, however, as he had hit the ball out of the water. Ionides helped him to his feet and retrieved his club.

"Hang in there, Zack! Fes has got some stuff to fix the Birds," Ionides whispered, smiling.

Zack glanced casually at the Birds, who were peering at him from the bridge. Small specks of white glinted against the tan of their legs and necks. He grinned at them and began to laugh, re-igniting the spectators as if a dam had burst. The Birds were giggling and as they giggled, Zack's laughter increased.

On the bridge, the drumming started again. The Birds were shifting their legs, anxiously looking at each other. First one hand came down to scratch, then another, and soon they were all scratching frantically, oblivious of the spectators, who stared in amazement at the spectacle. The boots came off and were hurled away, some splashing into the water. First one girl, then another, leaped off the bridge into the water, tearing at their clothes to find relief from the terrible itching powder.

"It worked, Dad! Look at them!" Joe's children were ecstatic.

"Come on kids! We've got to go."

"Oh, Mom! Why do we always have to go when it's real fun?" Mary-Beth Maximos embarrassed by the sight of the semi-naked Birds rolling in the shallow, muddy water, bustled her offspring away.

"You too, Ion!" said Samantha, giggling.

"Oh, Sam. Do I have to go when it's real fun?" laughed Ionides, ogling the Birds in an exaggerated fashion. "Look at that redhead! She's got weeds caught in her..."

"Ion!" Said Sam, firmly, handing him a brown paper bag. Ionides collected the empty itching powder sprayers, and walked away laughing.

At the base of the hill, the entire marching band, followed by Wendell Jameson, marched and then ran into the nearest lake, stripping as they went.

Zack battled resolutely for the twelfth hole. He lay three strokes behind the banker when he emerged from the water, nevertheless, encouraged by the belief that he could play a straight game now, he succeeded in pulling back to tie the hole. From then on, the game swung his way, he won the thirteenth and four-teenth, tied the fifteenth and won the sixteenth. As a result, he reached the seven-teenth tee with the score tied and two holes to play.

The seventeenth hole was a monster five hundred and seventy-yard par five that took a dogleg turn to the right and ended close to the bottom of the hill. The final hole was then a short but awkward par four to a raised green on the hill below the clubhouse. The difficult part of the seventeenth was the wide channel of water that cut across the fairway just in front of the dogleg. The far bank of this channel, except for the gap where the fairway broke to the right, was lined with high trees making it impossible to cut the corner of the dogleg, in any nor-mal sequence of shots. A phenomenally long tee shot would put the ball over the channel, and permit a single shot to reach the green. A bad tee shot on the other hand could put the ball in the channel or on the bank that sloped down to it. The conventional approach was to hit short, and with the second shot to put the ball high over the trees across the corner, leaving a reasonable shot to the green.

Zack took a mighty swing at the ball. Unfortunately, he didn't have the strength to carry the channel and, in his effort to gain length, lost control of accu-racy so that the ball drifted to the right, its speed carrying it onto the down slope of the near bank of the channel. The slope of the bank, coupled with the position of the trees on the far side of the channel meant that he could not hit his ball across the corner of the dogleg. The banker smiled and hit his ball short of the channel in the middle of the fairway. The jaunty spring in his walk suggested that he believed he had the match sewn up.

Zack was grim faced, as he walked down the side of the fairway with Elena and Festus. "I've lost," Zack said. "If he plays carefully, he's gonna win."

"But you still have the eighteenth hole, Zack," Elena said. "You can tie the match."

Zack looked embarrassed. "He made me so angry I bet him I would beat him in eighteen holes. If I lose the seventeenth, I've lost the match. I…uh…forgot to tell you that part."

Elena shook her head, in irritation. By now, they had reached the ball. Festus could see that it was in a similar lie to that of his second shot in the earlier game. He remembered his idea of a way out of the problem. He was unsure at first whether to tell Zack his idea, but weighing it up he realized that Zack had no choice if he wanted to win.

"There is a shot you could try, Zack, which would get you to the green. I landed in the same place but I didn't have the skill or the balls to try it. Nevertheless, out of curiosity, I checked the rules. It's in bounds and quite legal."

Festus explained to Zack what he would have to do. He could not afford to follow the fairway around the trees to the green. The trees were too high to go over since he would have to hit from a down slope. But there was another way. Festus pointed down the channel to where, in the distance some one hundred yards away, they could see the edge of the seventeenth green coming down to a thin layer of mud by the water. Between them and the green, high trees overshadowed the water from both banks and a bridge crossed the channel some fifty yards away.

"It's impossible, Fes. I've skimmed stones like that when I was a kid, but, if you think I can risk it here, you're crazy."

"All you have to do is hit it hard enough and top it. It will bounce off the water and, if you're lucky, skip onto the green."

"Yeah, right! Is that all?"

Festus kept up the pressure. Zack remained unconvinced until he turned to see what other shot was possible and looked straight into the triumphant face of the banker. "All right, Fes, I'm convinced. Anything to beat that...that...smug shai-it."

Zack carefully selected his club, a three wood and moved to address the ball. The noise of the crowd rose as he took up a position facing down the channel.

"Where the hell do you think you're hitting?" exclaimed the banker.

"Are you trying to put me off my shot?" Zack retorted sharply. "We've checked the rules, it's legal to hit down the channel."

The banker studied the proposed shot. From the top of the bank, the trees and bridge looked impenetrable. He couldn't see the green. "You'll never clear them. It's your funeral"

Zack steadied his feet, and then took some practice swings, hitting the top of the ball-high grass. He did this a number of times raising his head slightly as his club reached the bottom of its swing. Then he positioned himself over the ball, lining up with the small patch of green at the end of the channel. The crowd hushed. Elena clutched Festus, and Dawn looked away. Zack hit at the ball, rising deliberately in the middle of his swing, so as to top it. The ball shot off on a low trajectory, hitting the water just below the bridge. As it dropped towards the water, his opponent laughed.

"Are you going to try another one, Cronson? We all have plenty of time."

As he spoke, the ball hit the water spinning. It was on a low trajectory and didn't sink, but skipped across the surface. So it carried on, skipping on the water until, sliding over the mud, it rolled onto the green.

Zack, who could see the green from his position, turned to Festus. "Thanks."

There was a moment of silence, and then wild applause as the spectators and the Eurysthesians realized what Zack had achieved. Elena and Zack were waltzing. Dawn hugged Festus, Peri, and anyone else in range. Samantha and Ionides were doing a war dance.

The conclusion of the game was a formality. The banker's game collapsed and Zack won both the seventeenth and eighteenth holes. After a terse acknowledgement of his defeat, the banker ungraciously ripped off a check that he handed to Zack. With a hard look, he then made off in the direction of Wendell Jameson and the waterlogged marching band. The bedraggled Stimpson Birds could be seen in the distance, fluttering their way back to the main part of the campus.

The Eurysthesians celebrated their victory in the clubhouse with champagne as they pieced together what had happened.

Ari grabbed Demos by the arm. "Do you know why Jameson tried to fix Zack's match?"

"Wendell's majoring in public relations. I've heard that he hopes to work in that guy's bank." Demos replied, cautiously.

"Anything else?"

"Amanda's mother is a "lady friend" of the banker. Amanda's very jealous of Pandora." Ari's tightened his grip. "I didn't hear this until near the end."

"How come Amanda agreed?" Ari released Demos. "It was easy for Wendell to persuade Amanda to organize the cheerleaders to harass Uncle Zack. I think she believed Uncle Zack was a part of it and doing it for charity. She must have thought him very convincing." Demos smirked. "Pandy not being there made it easier."

"Incidentally do you know why the hell Pandy wasn't around," Festus asked. "I'm worried; it seems like a strange coincidence."

"Maybe she was unhappy about the beauty contest? You could ask her boyfriend, but I haven't seen him either."

Festus changed the subject. "What about the band then?"

"Wendell spun them the same line, and anyway, when they were playing they couldn't really pay much attention to what was going on."

Zack thanked them for saving him. "The Eurysthesian Trust has struck again. Festus, I just don't know how you do it. Just tell me what you want."

"Loch Ness."

"What the hell man! I think you're crazy as a drunk rattlesnake, but I'll come with you. After the play cycle's over."

"I'm not planning to do them this year. I want to get back to Loch Ness."

"Marienna will be furious. Who's going to play Hephaestus?" asked Elena.

"Ionides. It's time he learned the part."

"Boy I wouldn't like to be there when you tell Marienna."

"I don't plan to be either. I'll leave it to you and Ion."

"God help us!" Zack laughed.

"So, how do you feel about golf now?" Elena asked.

"It's a great game, but I've learned a lesson. Maybe, just maybe, I won't be quite so dumb again."

"Oh, Zack," Elena said, brusquely, "I hope so."

When Pandora and Chuck returned, Festus asked them sharply where they'd been. Chuck replied diffidently that they'd been for a drive. Festus looked at his watch, shook his head but made no comment. The awkward moment passed as they were bombarded with descriptions of the events they had missed.

Zack and Festus went off in search of Colonel Stimpson. He was still on the verandah, observing the scene.

"Sir, I would like you to accept this check donated to me by our Austin colleague," Zack said. "I hope that it may be used to improve the standard of the college entertainment."

The shrunken figure of the Colonel was shaking. This worried the Eurysthesians for a minute, until they realized from the shine in the beady eyes that he was laughing. "I saw it all. No damn ball gowns. Tits and ass everywhere. Molly's having a fit. The funniest thing I've seen in years. I wouldn't have missed it for the world. Maybe we should make it an annual event. The Stimpson College Itch, eh? Heh! Heh! Heh! How did you do it?"

For a moment Festus was undecided what to reply. But, to protect Happy's reputation, he decided to give the Colonel an explanation. "I just happened to have some itching powder with me, sir. It's hard to find these days, and I must admit I take a childish pleasure in practical jokes. I've been waiting for the right opportunity to use it. It's made in England. It's a mixture of ground stinging nettles, talc, and white hellebore—popularly known as itchweed. It works fast. Don't worry about it! The effects go away in a day."

The Colonel looked at him shrewdly. "It was lucky for you, young man, that Happy had some in his back room, eh! I don't miss much, you know. I saw him lurking around enjoying the chaos." He started to say more but seeing the amazed look on Festus' face, he convulsed with laughter again, and couldn't continue. When they left, he was still cackling to himself.

"It's a long drive back to Argos, Fes...to an empty house! I could sure do with a drink," Dawn pleaded.

"This is a dry county, Dawn, except for today's event. I guess Reynosa, over the border, is as near as anywhere."

"Okay."

God! He wanted her. Yet, something, thoughts of Cathy maybe...no way! Festus hesitated, but not for long. Why not, they were still married. "Let me just deal with some loose ends! I'll be right back."

Festus headed the car towards McAllen and the bridge across the Rio Grande to Reynosa. During the drive, he quizzed Dawn about her time in San Francisco. Dawn, leaning back in the passenger seat, played up to him, fending the questions with suggestive answers, as he drove. Her long legs were exposed by the action of the seat belt, which had caused her skirt to ride up. Dawn made no attempt to rectify this situation, but made sure he noticed by fingering the seat belt absentmindedly from time to time. At the frontier, the Mexican border guards paid them particular attention, and ushered them through, directing flattering comments at Dawn.

The market in Reynosa was crowded. Yet they were so engrossed in their sexual game that it might have been empty. The contrast, between the plethora of goods and the relative poverty of the inhabitants, made no impression on them. Their progress towards one of the better restaurants was marked at all stages by a movement of the crowd away from them so that people could see Dawn. Outside the restaurant, the splayed, smoked carcasses of small goats hung, advertising the specialty of the restaurant, El Cabrito.

In a secluded corner, they sipped large frozen Daquiris, silently eyeing each other over the mounds of ice. Festus knew that Dawn wanted to sleep with him but, uncharacteristically, was acting as if it was their first date. Festus had reached the point where the drink had relaxed him sufficiently to pop the question when he took too big a sip of the ice cold drink. The freezing liquid hit the roof of his mouth, sending a shaft of pain up through his head. He dropped his drink and to the astonishment of Dawn, clasped his forehead with one hand, with the other pointing at the drink. She burst out laughing and reached over to him. At this moment, a Mariachi Band opened up at full volume with its trumpets and guitars. Festus, his moment of decision interrupted, sat back and listened resignedly to the music, his frustration building with every bar. Only after Dawn slipped a couple of dollars to the lead trumpet player and indicated that they should transfer their attentions to another table, did the band leave.

Dawn took advantage of the moment to lean across, take his face in her hands and kiss him fully and softly on the mouth. For a moment, he tensed, then his arms folded around her and he responded eagerly. Dawn, her tongue working wildly, encouraged him then she moved away gently and held his hands. "We can move into a hotel, here, tonight, Fes. It seems silly to go back now. Any suggestions?"

"Sounds good to me." Dawn stayed in the car while Festus booked a room.

"By the way, what name did you give?" Dawn asked curiously.

"Dr and Mrs. Henry Everett Festus. It sounded good."

"Fes, I love you," chuckled Dawn, kissing him. "Go take a shower! I'll get some ice from the front desk. We may need something cool later."

Festus showered, wrapped a towel around his middle and stepped cautiously into the room. The lights were turned down and Dawn was standing by the window. She brushed past him quickly, kissing him lightly on the shoulder as she went by. "Get into bed" Dawn said. "I'll only be a minute."

He waited apprehensively, as Dawn showered and dried. The comforting thought came to him, that he'd made love to this goddess before. He pulled the sheet back for her. "G'god you're beautiful!" he stuttered.

"Fes, you make it sound like the first time." Dawn chuckled, posing for him; her long blond hair had tumbled down over her breasts and her tanned body was naked. They took thier time, returning to previous pleasures. He succeeded with a great effort of concentration to hold off until tshe climaxed. Dawn gave a contented sigh and continued to hold him.

Festus waited, and then spoke in a rush. "I've missed you. I want to come home."

There was a long silence. "What about Cathy?"

"It didn't work very well."

"You mean sex?" Dawn held him away.

"I couldn't keep up with her changes in mood."

"Poor you!"

"She's got a boyfriend."

"I don't think so," said Dawn.

"What do you mean? His name's Billy."

"Her name is Billy, Fes."

"You're kiddin?"

"No. Angel found out. She's really pissed off."

"Oh, I see. I thought it was because I was too old for her."

Dawn rolled on the bed laughing, pinched his behind and kissed him passionately. "Too old for sex? That'll be the day. I'll show you what erotic means in a minute when I've recovered my breath."

Festus held her close, hesitating about asking the question that still burned in his brain. Hell! Let it all hang out.

"What about Ari?"

He could feel her become tense. "Fes. Ari still makes passes at me. It's more a habit with him than serious. I learned to handle him years ago."

"He's your brother!"

"Fes, I'm his adopted sister. It's wasn't like…incestuous."

"Why didn't you tell him to leave you alone?"

"I have, but I don't think he can help himself. Ari and I go back a long time. There's too much history."

"What history? Like he used to sell a look at your pussy when you were kids?"

Dawn turned away. Her eyes were cloudy. "Yes. I was lonely, Fes. He protected me from my sisters. They hated me. It didn't seem bad at the time. I had to repay him."

"Was that all?"

"No," she whispered, turning back to cling to him. She was crying softly. "He used me. I was so scared someone would find out."

Festus held her, stilling her shaking body. "We only did it when I was a kid," Dawn cried "Do you forgive me?"

"There's nothing to forgive. You were only a child. It's over now." Festus paused. "What happened in Ireland?"

"Ari told me he'd found a real pretty cottage. Would I like to see it? I needed to get out. I was unhappy with you. Then he attacked me. He was different, completely wild. Like on drugs or somethin'. Those photos. You shouldn't have done that, Fes. I kneed him in the balls. That's when he fell down, grabbing me on the way. I guess Seamus didn't catch that part."

"Yeah, Seamus! There's something odd there, but it's too late now to do anything about it. I'm sorry. It was stupid. I convinced myself you were having an affair and I had to deal with it."

"I love you so much, honey. Don't leave me again!"

"Never."

Festus dragged himself wearily out of bed. He needed to pee. It was going to hurt, he thought as he walked stiffly to the bathroom.

Dawn smiled knowingly at his discomfort. "Let's take a quick shower, and get out of here. We can get breakfast in McAllen. Then we can go home."

"That's the best idea I've heard in years," Festus smiled, happily.

When Festus returned to Austin, Chuck was waiting to see him. Festus motioned him to sit, but he continued to stand. His inverted eyes betrayed his embarrassment.

"I'm sorry about Stimpson, Dr. Festus. I didn't know you'd need Pandy and me. She was upset at losing and we went for a drive."

Festus remained silent but continued to look inquiringly at him.

"Oh, hell! It was my fault. One thing led to another and…you know…it was six before we realized it."

Festus worried about what he was not being told. Did Pandora and Chuck have sex? He still couldn't get used to the idea of Pandora having a sex life. He was about to comment when an image of Dawn came to him. "It's all right, these things happen. It wasn't your fault."

He waved Chuck out of the office. How can I be self righteous, he thought, I'm no different. It was a good thing Pandora had Chuck.

Festus unlocked the top drawer of his desk. The only item in the drawer was a neat bundle of the letters that Cathy had written him. He removed the elastic band and scanned them. Notwithstanding the outcome of Hephaestus and the Cretans, maybe the play cycle would not dictate his life anymore? At least, in his relationship with Dawn he seemed to have broken its grip. Four Labors were completed for the Trust and Zack—Nemean Lion, Erythmanthian Boar, Augeian Stables, and Stymphalian Birds. Five if you counted finding Pandora as the Golden Hind Labor. That Zack-Eurystheus wouldn't allow him to claim finding Pandora as a Labor didn't bother him. Now he had a chance to complete the sixth Labor—the Hydra. It was in the wrong order, but who cared? The most important fact was that he had his family back together. Festus shredded the letters and dumped them in the wastebasket.

22. Chekush

"So you see it made no sense until I added the crucial ingredient—the currents in the Loch." Festus said, coming near the end of a long explanation of how he knew where to look for the monster. He looked at Dawn, expectantly.

"You are very clever darling. I guess I'm going to have to stop being jealous of science—your real mistress. But I want you to know. She's a real bitch."

Festus was trying to think of an answer, when Ionides took the opportunity to finish the point for him. "So he rewrote the program to include the currents, and then found the monster."

"Indeed I did what my eloquent and bashful assistant has just indicated. The answer is simple. The majority of unassigned chemicals seem to emanate from our side, the eastern side of the Loch, to the south of us near that steep part of the shore, opposite Alltsigh."

"I hate to say this, Fes, but we've heard you make similar statements before." Zack sounded resigned. Why is it a better place than Foyers or near the Castle?"

"It really is the most likely place for the monster."

"If it exists, and I mean if, why wouldn't we be able to detect it anywhere in the Loch? It must roam around looking for food?"

"In principle, no reason we shouldn't detect it sometime. However, it's a low probability unless it likes feeding somewhere in particular, or has a lair. That's what I've been trying to find. We've had unexplained signals on the echo sounders."

"Like when you saw it? Zack said.

"What's this? You saw it and didn't tell me. Hell, Fes! Secrecy can go too far," Ionides said, angrily.

"Thanks Zack for telling everyone. I'd had a few drinks, Ion. Maybe it was those damn students playing a hoax again. I don't know."

"You didn't explain why this new place is better than the others."

"For a number of reasons, Dawn," Festus replied. My analysis is much better now, and it's one of the least accessible and least visible parts of the Loch. The old echo sounders wouldn't work well close to these steeply shelving cliffs. The depth in-shore is six or seven hundred feet. Finally, of course, the currents are strong there. We have to go back and try again. You tell them Hamish. You've been doing most of the work recently"

Hamish stood up. "As you know, Ladies and Gentlemen, we have had an inkling of the solution for some time now. Ion and I have been working with our technicians preparing equipment in anticipation of the results that Fes has described. We've modified the echo sounders so that they don't suffer so badly from the cliff reflections. We expect to have our first trial in the target area today. I'm using a larger support boat, so everybody can come along. You'll have a grandstand view of the proceedings."

"How long will we be out there?" asked Marienna.

"Don't worry, Ma'am! The support boat has the necessary facilities," Hamish chuckled. "With the food and drink, Mrs. MacLeod has prepared, it should be a hell of a party. That is the impression we want to give to outsiders. You can never tell when the news media will take it into their heads to descend on us again." He paused, grinning at Festus. "I remember all the questions after they found out about Doctor Festus's tests in Blarney. I must admit, I wondered if he'd got a wee screw loose. I think that's all, Fes."

"Thank you for those revealing comments, Hamish. I've nothing to add except let's all meet down at the dock, in say half an hour, and get out there."

Their boat passed the tree-covered southwest slope of Meall na Targaid. There was a narrow rocky beach by the Loch. Then it continued south, to the steep part of the eastern shore and cruised along it. Georgina made sure everybody had plenty to eat and drink. The submarine was in the water, drifting slowly in the middle of the search area. Its fuel tanks and range were limited and, when the time came, they did not want to be messing around fueling it. The Loch was mirror calm. Hamish and Ionides, wearing wet suits, perched impatiently, one on the bow and one on the stern of the small craft, watching their reflections as they awaited instructions.

For two hours, nothing showed on the modified echo sounders, and then a faint trace appeared. "I think there's something alongside the cliff," Zack whispered, trying to hold his excitement in check.

Festus, who had been keeping an eye on both their own position and that of the sub, rushed over. He looked for a few minutes at the trace. "That could be it," he shouted. "It's about fifty feet down. We've got to get the sub moving."

Festus signaled to Hamish to start the submarine. After some confusion that this was a serious request, Hamish and Ionides clambered in. The submarine moved towards the shore. The trailing aerial allowed them to keep in contact with Festus. Festus instructed them over the intercom to descend to the same depth as indicated by the trace and then, watching the scanner, he directed them towards the cliff face. On the support boat, the chart recorder showed the submarine and another shape ahead of them up against the cliff.

"Hamish, are your cameras set up?" Festus asked, speaking into the microphone.

"Yes," Hamish answered, patiently.

"Then start them rolling. I think you know its position, right?"

Hamish, keeping an eye on the detectors, turned the sub slowly. He held it on course at the cliff, then spoke softly to Ionides. "Lights, now!"

Ionides switched the searchlights fully on. There was nothing in front of them except the blank face of the cliff.

"What happened, Hamish?" Festus sounded impatient.

"I don't know, Fes. Maybe the other signal was some reflection from the sub? We're very close to the cliff."

They patrolled for another ten minutes, but saw nothing. They surfaced.

"What do you mean, nothing? I could see that other trace on the sonar." He took a sip from Marienna's flask.

"Could it be a reflection?"

"I don't think so."

"What can we do?"

"Get the damn scuba gear! I want to look more closely at the cliff. Hamish, you come with me!"

"You're the boss. I hope it's not there."

"Ion. Lower the television camera and a light as we go down!"

When they had swum down to thirty feet, Festus signaled to move slowly along the cliff face. The visibility, even with their hand held lamps and the television light, was not very good and progress was slow. After a long and fruitless time of finding only the unchanging rock face, Festus signaled that he wanted to go deeper. Hamish shook his head. He pointed at the low reading on his air gauge. As they rose, the water swirled below them. A mass of bubbles clouded the water as something brushed past, pushing them violently against the cliff face. When the water cleared, Festus could see that Hamish was dazed. He quickly put a mark on the cliff, and then he helped Hamish to the surface, where Zack and Ionides pulled him onto the support boat.

"What happened?" asked Zack. "Is Hamish okay?"

Hamish answered, groggily. "Something banged into us. Did you see it Fes?"

"I saw a strange shape and felt something hard and leathery but I couldn't see with all those bubbles," Festus said.

"That's what we saw on the television monitor. A moving shape, obscured by a mass of bubbles," said Zack.

"I was looking at the surface. There were bubbles and bits of wood and weeds," added Ionides. "You can see some of it floating over there."

"That may explain it," said Hamish. "It could have been rotting vegetation."

Festus shook his head. "I think I saw more than that. Maybe it was eating and we disturbed it."

"Where would it find anything to eat here, in this depth of water?"

"Maybe stuff falls in the Loch and gets stuck against the cliff," Ionides volunteered. "What do you want to do, Fes?"

"We'll check after we've taken a harder look at the TV pictures. I'm hoping they'll show something."

Dawn looked sympathetically at Festus. "Do you think you saw the monster?"

Festus grinned and rocked his hand in a sign of uncertainty. In fact, he was feeling light headed and steadily more convinced he had met the monster.

"Hamish, when you've rested, I want you and Ion to take the submarine and check that part of the cliff," Festus said. "I made a scratch mark. It should be visible."

The steep face of the side of the loch rose up in front of them. The poor visibility in the water made it difficult to see much detail. The wall seemed to continue uninterrupted. They edged closer and a few feet below the mark Festus had made they saw an overlapping rock that hid a fissure. "It's not surprising that nobody ever found this place, Ion. If we hadn't had that experience, we would never have located it," said Hamish.

They maneuvered as close as possible, but could see only the blackness of a cave extending deeper into the cliff. Hamish called up to the surface. "There's a cave. Nothing we can do now, so I'll put another mark on the cliff. We can use one of the remote arms. Then I'm going to surface. Please get the cameras ready. Ionides and I will put on scuba gear and set them up by the mouth of the cave. Can you find a photocell and light to use, or an alarm to switch them on when, whatever it is, comes back? Frankly, I want to get this over with." A muffled squawk from Ionides interrupted Hamish. "Ion has misgivings, too."

"We'll be going into shore when you've finished," Zack cautioned them. "Don't let anyone know until we get back to the house! Since you've been down there, a number of boats have pulled over to see what we're doing. One of them is still lurking about, supposedly fishing. Let's go to the beach and have our picnic."

Ionides fiddled with the television system. Zack had seen nothing of interest on the tiny monitor screen in the support boat. Now, when the lights were out and the same pictures were shown with a good contrast on a large screen, there did appear to be a shape, or shapes, amidst the bubbles.

As they reran the pictures, Festus commented, pointing out that the changing forms might be the head and neck followed by a fat body and tail. "Assuming the movement of the bubbles gives us an idea of the speed of the body, and knowing the field of view, I guess the thing is ten or more feet long."

"Fes, Aren't you reading an awful lot into those fuzzy pictures? You're acting as if you know what it is and it must be there," argued Elena. "I just see a mess of bubbles and, frankly, what looks like garden trash."

"I didn't just see it, I touched it too, Elena. It felt like skin," Festus replied, defensively.

"Should we try and capture the creature now?"

Festus looked concerned. "No, Zack, first we need to set the cameras up in that cave"

"Hey, wait a minute, Fes! Who's going to do that?" Ionides looked worried. "Where's the father? If she's that big, what about him?"

"I'm not sure there is a father in the normal sense. I believe the explanation is parthenogenesis."

There was a stunned silence. Festus continued. "Anyway, I thought that you and Hamish might enjoy that small chore, Ion. I'm not so proficient at diving."

Ionides, his macho image in question, looked over to Samantha, who pursed her lips and nodded. "Okay, I'll do it if Hamish will." Hamish also nodded agreement.

"We'll have to wait a week or so until we are sure she has stopped leaving the cave. You'll have to check the television cameras and reload the tapes daily. We can go out tomorrow morning for the first check. We will only need the support boat. I think it would be better if there were not a crowd. We don't want to attract too much attention. I suggest some golf or a visit to Balmoral, or whatever, for the rest of you. Samantha, could you set that up please?"

After a few days, they had seen no sign of the monster; leading to numerous questions about whether it existed. Festus agreed it was time to set up the cameras inside the cave.

Maneuvering the submarine wasn't so difficult, Festus thought as he practiced in the lake away from the cliff. He felt himself in control and took a swig of his drink then descended, steering slowly towards the cliff and the opening to the cave. Above him, on the surface, Zack Cronson steadied the support boat, while Hamish and Ionides finished putting on their scuba gear. The cameras and some other heavy equipment for mounting them were below water attached to the submarine. The divers rolled backwards off the boat into the water and swam down holding onto a line strung from the boat. It took a few minutes, in the murky water, before they found the submarine. They tied the line loosely to the sub, and banged on the side. At this signal, Festus turned on the searchlights and worked the vessel nearer the cave, illuminating the fissure from the side to minimize the light penetrating deep into the cave. Zack steered the support boat to keep plenty of slack on the line.

Ionides swam down in front of the porthole and signaled to Festus; before he and Hamish swam into the cave on a first reconnoiter. Festus watched them anxiously until, with a last flip, they disappeared, and then even the light reflected from their feet flickered away. He sat in the near silence, sipping from the flask Georgina had given him. Only the faint hum of the quieted submarine engine and the murmur of the support boat engine penetrated the still, tomblike chamber. He felt very satisfied. He had nearly accomplished his sixth Labor. The analogy to the original Labor—the killing of the Lernean Hydra—was much more satisfactory than the punning connection he had made in the Blarney affair—the O'Nemean lyin' bastard. He giggled nervously and thought about Nessie. It was a pathetic name. He needed something that reflected the way in which the beast reproduced itself, like the Hydra re-growing its heads. He came back to Hydra-phoenix, why not Hydro-phoenix Nessius, even if it guaranteed the risk of contraction again to Nessie? He watched the stone cliff, trying to see her through it. He returned to a childhood game. I'm Mr. X-ray eyes, he thought, I can picture what is happening on the other side of the wall. He visualized the men swimming cautiously into the cave, but the scene changed subtly. *He was swimming towards some dazzling white cliffs. No, it was a beach. A girl was waiting. Her face came in and out of focus.*

"Is it you, Aphrodite?"

She did not answer, but handed him a tunic and spoke urgently. "The gods will talk to you now, Hephaestus." Then, conspiratorially, "I think they'll give you another chance."

Another chance for what, he thought. A chance to prove himself, maybe? Above the beach, facing the sea, was the palace. Its white walls glistened in the sun, the dark maroon pillars stood out like sentinels. He followed the path. I must get there soon, he thought, if only my legs would work properly. His limp became more pronounced as he tried to run,. I must seem like a bird hopping was the last though before he reached the door. He raised his hand to bang on it but the banging started before his hand moved.

Festus sat immobile, puzzling it out. Where was he? A face appeared at the window in the door, and a hand was rapping on the glass. It was Ionides. What did he want?

The spell broke. There was no palace, just the light reflected from the cliff face. Ionides signaled him to surface. The hatch was unbolted. Festus leaned out of it to hear Ionides and Hamish who were clinging to the sides of the submarine.

"We swam into the passage. It's much wider than it looks from the outside. Hamish went first. The passage rises above the surface, maybe thirty feet or so. We came around this bend. We were swimming awful slow…you know…both of us thinking, what if it came back?" Ionides paused for breath. "It was creepy."

"There wasn't anything there Fes," Hamish added.

"I hope you didn't frighten her away."

Ionides gasped and took in some water, which was nearly his undoing. Hamish moved over to steady him while he recovered. "Fes, you've got to be joking—frighten her?"

"Did you go to the back of the cave? Are you sure she wasn't further into it?"

Hamish thought for a moment. "There's a flat area out of the water that extends to the end of the cave. There are some fissures in the walls, which could explain why the air is quite fresh"

"Damn! Damn! Damn! I was sure she would be there. We may be too late and she's moved on."

Ionides looked hard at Hamish, willing him not to say anything.

"I know what you're thinking," Festus continued. "I'm kidding myself. A perfectly rational explanation is that it doesn't exist. Fellas, it's not just that odd encounter we had. It's all the data that doesn't fit what we know is in the Loch." Festus' face showed his frustration. "I have to believe in it, or give up. We need to go back and set up the cameras in the cave. Ion I'll do it with you. I really believe there's no danger. Hamish, can you help me get my gear on."

"Are you sure, Fes?" Ionides peered at him nervously from under the face-mask. "If you're correct she could turn pretty mean."

"Don't worry about it! I'm sure there'll be no problems."

"I'll follow you," Ionides laughed. "After I get a new tank."

They set up the cameras and lights without incident. Festus climbed onto the flat dry portion of the cave. The floor was mainly rock, with a few stones scattered over it. He put a few into a pouch to study later. As they entered the water, their movement triggered the camera lights. Ionides, who was ahead of him, suddenly dived, returning with a handful of small bones. Festus added them to his collection.

During the following days, Festus gave priority to the search with the submarine. The main finding was an indented part of the cliff, underwater near the cave, in which tons of debris had collected—a mass of fresh and decaying, water plants and tree limbs. Festus decided it was caused by a combination of currents and wind. They could see some eels weaving in and out of the vegetation. He viewed it as a good sign. "It's a miniature Sargasso Sea," Festus said. "I bet this is where the monster feeds."

The stones he had collected were a puzzle. They appeared to be fossilized remains of something. What were they? Festus sent them by express mail, along with a few of the bones, to a friend at the University of Texas for analysis and dating.

The cameras in the cave had nothing to show. Therefore, Hamish and Ionides moved them to view the trapped vegetation. After they had finished, Festus returned with Ionides to look at the underwater floor of the cave. It was covered in bones. Was it a fish graveyard, or the remains of some animal's meals? The fact that many of the bones were broken and there were no live fish suggested the latter.

Three days later, Festus reviewed all the data for his colleagues. "We've not explained what happened to Hamish and me with that eruption of bubbles and stuff. The rocks and the bones in the cave are peculiar. It could be that the cave was the monster's lair some time in the past. It will be weeks before we hear results of the analysis."

"What's the bottom line?" Elena asked.

"Elena, there is some circumstantial evidence, but in reality we're still in the same position as previous hunters—nothing definite," Zack said, before Festus could answer. "I say we wrap it up, folks. I'll get the company that put the package together last time to make a new film. We're going to get our money back."

"I can think of other things to do," replied Festus, showing his reluctance.

"I think, Zack's right, Henry. We should declare victory and move on." Marienna did not wait for an answer. "Henry. I know you were waiting to give detail of your theories until after you had proof, but we're coming to the end of the hunt. Why don't you tell the others your theory about how the monster survives?"

"Simply put, there is only one monster. When the time comes to pass on the baton, she-he goes into a cave and gives birth to the next one. Then she dies."

"Where does the baby get its food if she dies at birth?"

"A good question, Hamish. I speculate that the skin acts as a container and I suspect that all of the body, including the bones, will convert into food for the baby—a supply for many months, protected internally by preservative chemicals. Initially, this allows the baby to grow in the protective environment of some cave. Probably, not the one we found. Finally, it will be a supplement while it learns to feed itself in the main body of the lake. Eventually, the young one will consume the entire carcass, which is why nobody has found remains. Then in turn, later on she-he will reproduce and continue the cycle."

"Henry, we have debated this before and you know my opinion." Marienna sounded sad. "Yes, there are lower life forms that procreate like this, parthenogenesis, but nothing of the scale of the monster. How could the genetic information be preserved?"

"I agree it's improbable," Festus expostulated. "But, if the monster exists, give me a better explanation. Are there dozens of monsters? We haven't proved there is even one."

"So, Fes, you think we have come at precisely that phase of the cycle when a birth occurs. Sounds like a fluke. Frankly, in the limited amount you told us about your plans it was never clear that there was any reason for the timin' except that we needed a task. To be honest I really didn't believe we would find anything. It just seemed like as good an excuse as any to visit Scotland." Zack paused briefly then slumped back in his chair. "Folks you might as well sit back I've just earned y'all one of Fes's famous lectures. You can blame me for questioning the master."

Festus, uncertain how to take the remark, smiled. In the back of his mind, he realized that he did have a tendency to lecture people. "Even if I am right, I'll admit to a measure of serendipity. Come on now! I didn't just say, whoopee; let's go hunt the Loch Ness monster. I studied the history of the monster, the reports of sightings and realized that they were cyclical. I analyzed the sightings. It seemed to me that either we were approaching a birth or the creature was in the middle of its life. There was a fifty-fifty probability that a new birth could occur around the year of the hunt."

"Wait a second! We started a few years ago?"

Festus grinned. "Give or take a year or so."

"It's too flaky for me. Let's go home. Can you give me any reason to stay?" Zack's voice rose—a prelude to a temper tantrum.

"Zack, will you let me do one last test? I'd like to try the net again."

Zack threw back his head and laughed. "Hell, why not. It'll look good in the movie. Which boat are you going to attack this time?"

"Very funny, Zack! I'll try it where the cameras are—the Sargasso Sea."

"What will you do if you capture it?" Elena asked.

Festus looked startled. "I hadn't thought of that."

"So you really don't believe you'll catch it?" Elena said, laughing.

"Elena, give him a break!" Dawn snapped.

"Sorry Fes. This whole Loch Ness monster business is too weird for me."

Hamish helped him out. "I'll get the men to build a wire-mesh tank where there's a gentle slope into the water. Say about twenty by twenty? We've got some chicken wire at the yard."

"Before we break up, I have a suggestion. Let us come up with a decent name for the monster. It could help 'sell' your project."

"That's a great idea, Georgina," Festus responded enthusiastically. "I suggest we give it a scientific name: Hydrophoenix Nessius: hydro for water, phoenix because it was reborn from its deathbed, and Nessius for obvious reasons."

"I hope I don't sound too negative, Fes," Hamish volunteered cautiously. "While Hydrophoenix Nessius may be fine for erudite scientific articles, it doesn't role off the tongue too easily for simple folk like me."

They discussed numerous names, but none seemed right. Ionides fancied the obvious name Nessie. Festus liked it too since it fitted in with his suggestion. Georgina MacLeod found the solution. "I really don't like Nessie. It gives me the wrong image. I just see an overweight and, as you might say, over the hill, music hall star. In Gaelic, it's called Chekush, or water horse. Why don't we keep that name, Chekush, or 'Che' for short?"

The news that the Texans had built a tank in the Loch traveled fast and aroused a lot of speculation. Zack was unable to hold the press at bay. A flotilla of other craft followed the submarine when it appeared for its final dive.

Hamish and Festus floated in the submarine in front of the dark mass of vegetation. It was hard to see anything without the lights that would only come on in response to significant movement. It was boring and both of them, in a distracted fashion, nibbled the food and sipped the drinks that Georgina and Marienna had prepared. Their colleagues gathered around the television monitors on the support boat,. There was little to see. They also ate and drank to while the time away. After two hours, Zack was becoming more and more edgy, calling Festus every fifteen minutes to ask if he had had enough.

Festus was about to give up, when one of the lights came on. The vegetation was stirring. Festus grabbed the controls for the net. He and Hamish watched in a daze as a bunch of small eels raced in front of them and took cover. Suddenly, all of the lights came on showing the tail end of a creature, whose body was buried in the vegetation. There was an explosion of bubbles and debris enveloping a dark shape. Festus pushed the button. The net bag shot forward. The sensor reacted and the net blossomed out, enveloping the shape. Hamish rapidly brought the submarine to the surface and towed the net to the tank.

On the surface, the onlookers had seen the eruption of bubbles and a dark mass that appeared briefly, then sank. One of the reporters described it as many waving arms like an octopus. There was no lack of believers at the scene. The flotilla joined the support boat in the rush to see the catch.

"This is insane," cried Georgina MacLeod, watching the reporters jostling to get the prime positions around the holding tank. "Have these people no decency at all?" She waved her stick at them. "Keep back," she shouted.

The reporters and their cameramen ignored her. The efforts of Hamish with the submarine and the captain of the support boat were more successful than her pleas. They blocked two sides of the tank, eventually confining the press to the deepwater side of the tank. Workers from McDougall's yard held them away from the shallow water end, while Festus and Ionides swam to the tank.

"We didn't get Che," said Festus sadly, as he removed the net from their catch. A massive ball of weeds stuck around a piece of decaying tree trunk. "I know there was something else. I missed it."

"What about that wee monster there," shouted one of the reporters, pointing at a purple and green rubber dinosaur that had just surfaced.

Festus grinned sheepishly. "I didn't want to disappoint y'all."

"You caught a lot of eels, Fes. That one's quite large," Dawn said, pointing at a five-foot giant, apparently too fat to escape the tank like its smaller brethren.

"Oh! You mean Elmo," said Festus, laughing. "Ion, help me catch him!" He climbed into the tank.

"It was a bonus for the cameramen, as Ionides and Festus floundered around in the mess of weeds, trying to capture a reluctant Elmo.

"Round one," shouted one of the reporters. "Eel ten, Texas six"

"Funny," spluttered Ionides, trying to hold onto the tail, while Festus took a skin sample.

There were loud cheers, when they released the weed-covered eel to the Loch. Clear pictures of the toy dinosaur and fuzzier pictures of a wriggling Elmo were highlights of the news reports.

"We should have kept him," Dawn shouted.

"Great Dawn. We could have had eel pie." Festus looked tired, but he was smiling. "Is that what we saw, Hamish. That eel feeding?"

"It looked bigger to me, Fes. Do you want to try again?"

"After this fiasco, I'm not sure."

"Ion! Take some pictures! Hamish, when he's finished, please get this mess cleaned up. Let's call it a day."

"You did fine, Fes. You know, there was something else there," said Zack. "We all saw it on the monitors. Great stuff for the movie. In fact, your failure to prove it exists will keep the air of mystery. I can see the headlines, 'Che escapes again.' Now, the press wants to talk to us. Leave it to me!"

"I think it worked out well Henry," said Marienna, who was sitting with Festus and Georgina on the dock at Urquhart House.

"I agree," added Georgina. "Except for that ghastly scene with the press. Some good came from it, I suppose. You have tantalizing evidence that Che exists. A fascinating theory as to why it can keep going. It may even be a good thing that the authorities have seen fit to ban further attempts to catch Che. The bad part is that now you will leave me. Life will not be the same. I will miss you all."

"Come to Argos, Georgina. I could use your help again."

"You mean help provide the food and drink, Marienna?" She giggled.

Festus looked up sharply. Had he heard Georgina laugh? Marienna was smiling. Incongruous! They were acting like a couple of schoolgirls. "Am I missing something?" he asked.

"Henry, believe me, you did not miss anything."

"I saw Che. I really saw her."

"I am sure you did. We all saw that strange tail on the monitor."

"You don't think it was an eel?"

"No, there was something different about it," Marienna shook her head, trying to remember.

"What is Zachary doing now," asked Georgina.

"Being a help. It seems that the authorities will take a hard line in controlling future hunts. I don't know if it was because we're foreigners, or they felt we went too far. As you said, that scene when we opened the net was crazy. Either way, they were not keen on us investigating the 'miniature Sargasso'. It took Zack's persuasive powers to get them to agree to allow the studies to continue through the University of Aberdeen. It means I'll have to leave most of the research to my Scottish colleagues. At least I should get some good papers, even though I'll be a secondary author."

In fact, Zack did more than that, surprising all of them. He announced that, while the Trust needed to make some profit to support future work, nevertheless they would make a sizeable contribution to help protect the Loch Ness environment.

Hamish returned the submarine to the Yard and sold it. He got a good price. Ionides was sad to see it go, and sad that they had not caught Che. "I wonder where she is?" he said to Hamish.

"Festus might know. I'm not sure he told us everything."

"You're right. It's a pity he and Dawn have gone to Crete."

"I love you Dawn. I'm sorry about my...you know selfishness."

"It was my fault too, Fes. I couldn't handle the little housewife role. I was jealous of the fun you were having."

"And I resented your effect on men. It's crazy. You can't help being beautiful anymore than I can help being..."

"Clever."

"I was going to say too damn imaginative. I got worked up about Ari. The fact is the man's an idiot."

"I should have told you about Ari. I was so scared, embarrassed. I never told anyone. Alex guessed. My family too. They protected him. He was tied by blood. I wasn't."

"Are you sure you're not related?"

"Not really. I could be Agamemnon's illegitimate child. I'll never know. Anyway, I felt just as guilty as if Ari was a real brother."

He put his arms around her. "Now to the future."

"What are you going to do, Fes?"

"I've completed, more or less, six Labors. There ought to be twelve. Don't laugh! I'm waiting for the next one to be handed me by King Eurystheus, you know...Zack...Zeus."

"Are we becoming our characters in the plays?"

"What do you think, Aphrodite?"

"In the last few years it's been like we were living out the plays. It could be coincidence, or Marienna manipulating us."

"That's what I used to think, Dawn."

"Something changed your mind?"

Festus looked uncomfortable. "There's no question that Marienna's been playing little games with us, but...I'm going to tell you something I haven't told anyone. I've been worried that the line between life and my daydreams is disappearing."

"What do you mean?"

"On a number of occasions. Most recently, in Loch Ness. I reverted to the past. I see things as they were. I am Hephaestus."

"You're not alone in seeing visions, you know."

"You mean you too?"

"Not me so much as Peri. She's a very sensitive person you know. When we were at Stimpson, she knew the cheerleaders were dangerous to Zack. I told you. She saw them as birds of prey. The Stymphalian Birds she called them—like in the Labors."

"Yes. Thank god it isn't only me."

"To be honest, Fes. I've sometimes had a strange feeling come over me when you're around."

"Like what?"

"You're so sexy," she smiled.

"Very funny. You know. You were there in Loch Ness."

"I remember, honey. We just left."

"No! I mean as Aphrodite."

"I never knew. What did I do?"

"I was in the sub, except, suddenly, there we were on a beach. In the distance was this palace. I had to go there. You said something like, 'the gods will talk to you. Give you another chance.'"

"Do you understand what I meant?" Dawn asked.

"Ion banged on the side of the sub. I woke up before I could get to the palace."

"Does it matter?"

"I guess not, except for the final play—'The Goats.' I'm struck by the coincidence that Rhadamanthys, king at Phaestos, sends Hephaestus to recover a treasure from Tartarus that, supposedly, he wants for defense against the Hittites. Remember Apollo's words near the end of the play? I know them well."

> *You create the weapons for your master,*
> *Zeus or Minos or Rhadamanthys or Eurystheus,*
> *Or whatever he called himself at the time.*
> *Wake up to yourself!*
> *It was Hephaestus who brought the sword to man.*
> *It was Hephaestus who invented the shield*
> *To protect against the sword.*
> *You bring both the benefits and the problems*
> Then, right at the end, Athena speaks.
> *Dear Hephaestus, I, Athena, have protected you*
> *Through all of your troubled years.*
> *Now you have won your treasure, and proved to all it was not Heracles,*

But you, who masterminded the Labors.
From now on, let them be known as the 'Labors of Hephaestus.'
Yet, at the same time, you have lost.
In reality, you have no control over your inventive genius.
So the world will careen on its merry path, staying one step ahead of disaster;
While you and your fellow technologists will attempt to invent
The way out of each crisis as you invented the way in."

Dawn and Festus were silent for a while, thinking about their words.

"I don't want to remain the little helper of Zack-Minos. I didn't want to develop those bugs to drop on Vietnam. It was destructive, and anyway," Festus laughed. "It didn't work. Closed down two of our battalions when they lost the antidote."

"Why don't you quit? We're not poor."

"I've thought of it. But, without the Trust, Zack's support, I could never complete the Labors. He made that very clear."

"And you've got to finish them?"

"For most of my life I've wasted my talents. Never finished anything of substance; until the last few years working for the Foundation. Yes, I want to finish the Labors."

"And that's why we came to Crete." Dawn smiled.

"Oh! You guessed."

"It seems to me that if we're acting out the plays in real life, so is Zack-Rhadamanthys."

"Yep. My guess is that he's searching for some treasure on Crete. There is a Sfakian legend of treasure buried in a cave…like in the play."

"I bet you could probably find such a legend anywhere."

"When I was dealing with the Everyman fire, he had Cretan relatives staying at the ranch. They and Zack were very secretive."

"It could have been some business deal? Zack's always got a lot of deals going on."

"True, and if it weren't for the plays that would be my interpretation."

"So we're here to look for the treasure?"

"Not exactly. I wouldn't know where to look. No. I want to study the Phaestos Disk. It's never been translated to everybody's satisfaction. I've convinced myself that it and the plays hold the clues to our past and our future. Don't ask me how I know. I couldn't tell you, anymore than I can tell you why I am redoing the Labors of Heracles. Will you help me, Aphrodite?"

"Hephaestus, I would go to the very depths of Tartarus with you."

"To hell with Tartarus!" Festus laughed. "How about bed?"

FESTUS THE GOD

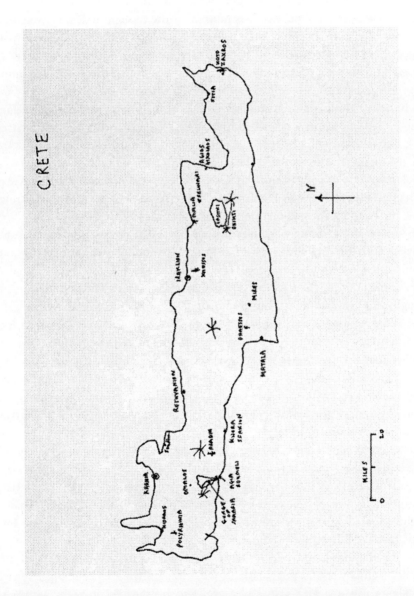

The Phaestos Disk is a terracotta tablet that was found at the Minoan palace of Phaestos in Crete. There is no accepted translation of the symbols that spiral out from the middle of each side.

23. Festus the God

In the 1930's, Americans would flock to hear Albert Einstein lecture in German; not understanding a word, but mesmerized by the thought that they were in the presence of genius. Possibly, they believed he would perform miracles or, suddenly, all of his science would become clear to them. More likely, they were attracted by his kindly face and cuddly appearance; so different from the humorless, steely-eyed, caricatures of scientists seen in the movies. In the 1960's Festus also became famous. His four publicized Labors had captured the imagination of the public. One reporter described him as Eli Wallach with a Cretan mustache. Zack helped the media in recognizing this new "genius." Zack also made sure that the National Press realized the connection of the luminaries of Argos to the Greek pantheon of gods in the Play Cycle. There were numerous sidelines about his name H. E. Festus and Hephaestus. There was less interest in Zack's role as Zeus; the reason Zack had mentioned the plays.

Festus worried about what they would have said if they had known about Blarney and his unwilling contributions to biological weapon development. Would it have destroyed his image? It became irrelevant, for following his adventures in the hunt for the Loch Ness monster his fame was secure for all time, even though people knew he had not found it. The "miniature Sargasso Sea" was an unusual environment that supported a number of species, and aroused a lot of scientific interest. The stones and bones that he had collected from a cave were another matter. The stones were fossilized feces. A colleague carbon dated them to the sixteenth century. What animal the feces came from was not clear. The fish bones were scored with teeth marks. They were from the twentieth century. This information was sufficient to perpetuate that the monster might exist. Certainly, Festus was now sure of it.

The Loch Ness Labor was very appealing to young people, who chose to believe that the Loch Ness monster's nickname "Che" was an allusion to the South American revolutionary, rather than an abbreviation of the Gaelic name, Chekush. His movies were added to the roster of unclear findings, taken seriously by the Monster cult, now known as Chekkies. The movies had made a lot of money for the Eurysthesian Foundation.

Under the influence of Zack's flattery, he had begun to believe the publicity, and his brainpower and imagination gave him a growing satisfaction. Exercising his talents was a nearly sexual pleasure, and he pursued it again with a single-minded attention that sometimes submerged the love for his family.

One way or another, the Cronson clan dominated his life—Zachary, its padrone; Marienna, who had mothered him since the death of his real mother, Olympia; and Dawn. His was a self-inflicted bondage, brought on by his desire to complete the Labors. Festus was uneasy about doing the occasional, profitable, defense work that Zack thrust upon him. Nevertheless, he suppressed his convictions and did what he was told. He used Cronson power and wealth, and through this unholy alliance, the Cronsons used him. As to his next Labor, the Phaestos Disk, he was close to starting it, but fate had other plans.

24. Munich

There is a small bar in the basement of a five-story, nineteenth century, town house, on the Occamstrasse in Munich. A fanciful painting of primitive figures of a knight in armor, a damsel in distress and a dragon covers the window by the front door. Multicolored light from the window provides some illumination in the bar that is down some steps. A few tables crowd this dimly lit area. On this day in early 1966, a large man sat with his hands clasping a beer mug. His legs draped, protectively, over two large cases. His clothes, sweatshirt, jeans, and hair, cut very short, marked him as an American soldier.

The barman, a slight queer, looked up when he hears the scuffing of shoes as a girl with red hair came down the stone steps. The hunched figure rose to meet her. They embraced; the huge figure of the man dwarfing the girl, the top of her red head reaching only to his shoulders. The man indicated to the barman that he had left money on the table. Then he lifted the cases. The larger one, obviously custom made, was new and unmarked. The other was old and liberally bespattered with labels. They climbed the stairs to the street. Although the girl lead the way, the man still loomed over her. The barman glanced at them briefly. He knew that American soldiers came to Schwabing to pick up girl students. He returnsed briefly, to polishing glasses before glancing at his watch. It was midday and there were no other customers. He reached under the counter for his lunch.

Earlier that day, at 8.26, the Orient Express from Paris had pulled into the Haupt-Bahnhof in the center of Munich. It did not carry mysterious blondes or mustachioed, balding, Belgian detectives. It disgorged tired looking students who had sat up all night, and businessmen, refreshed from a wash, shave and breakfast in the first class sleeping cars. The train remained for only nineteen minutes before it pulled out on the final leg of its journey to Bucharest.

A few hours later, the large man and the red head arrived at the station. They waited for the Tauern Orient express. It went to Belgrade and connected to the

Athens Express and to the Marmara Express that completed its journey in Istanbul.

The man slouched in his seat, an arm across the girl's shoulders. His feet rested on the two cases that project into the gangway. They received a few irritated glances from people skirting the obstacles, and paid tno attention until an officious assistant stationmaster, making his early afternoon prowl, had words with them. The man rose briefly and then, still holding the girl, pulled the cases towards the seat, barely acknowledging the official presence. They remained, with the girl making one brief foray for some drinks and food, until the departure of the Tauern Orient Express was announced. They boarded a second class carriage at 17:10 and the train departed on time at 17:30.

25. The Bullroarer

A few days later Zachary Cronson received an urgent call came from a friend in the White House. He left immediately.

"What the hell's happening?" Zack asked, as he entered the office at the Pentagon.

"Your son Deucalion has gone A.W.O.L. from the U.S. 7th Army Base at Badgarten, sir," the official replied. "We wouldn't normally bother you, sir, but it seems your son has taken some army property with him—the Bullroarer. I'm with an Agency that worries about that kind of stuff. What I am going to tell you is off the record. Information about the Bullroarer is classified. If it were discovered that we had one in Germany, it could be an embarrassment to your neighbor—POTUS one. Before you leave, I'm going to get you to sign a security form. Do you understand?" He looked at Zack for agreement.

"The what?"

"The President of the United States."

Zack inclined his head slightly, but said nothing.

"Your son went missing last Monday but it wasn't reported until Tuesday," the official said, looking at papers in a folder. "He had a weekend pass."

"Doesn't sound like Duke," Zack commented. "He's always been reliable."

"Possibly, Deucalion…er 'Duke'…has changed, sir" the official said. He read from a paper,…'disregard for regulations and punctuality have been noted'…It goes on to say that he might not retain his rank for long."

"But Duke gets on well with people."

"Apparently so, sir. His friends covered for him. It says here that he's on the 7th Army football squad. Socially, well regarded and…"

"What is this Bullroarer? Zack interrupted.

"I'll get to that. Coincidentally, the report that your son was missing reached the commanding officer at the same time as another report, which covered the disappearance of the Bullroarer and its ammunition from the field-testing laboratory on the base. The commanding officer didn't connect the two incidents for a further day; until at a meeting to investigate the loss, it turned out that your son had been in charge of the guards on the day in question."

"So, what does that prove?" Zack asked aggressively.

"I'll get to that too," replied the official, patiently. "The Chief Security Officer made discrete inquiries through the local police and sent his operatives into Munich. There they set about contacting Deucalion's friends and investigating all his favorite haunts. Meanwhile, the commanding officer called the head of U.S. Forces, Europe. In turn, he contacted Washington. At that time, they were not concerned about your son. One sergeant, more or less, made little difference. They were however extremely disturbed about the loss of the weapon."

"Yes the weapon."

"It's a new anti-personnel flame projector. This device sends out balls of incendiary material, like a Roman candle. It can clear a wide area of a battlefield by catalyzing the combination of the nitrogen and oxygen in the air, rendering anybody in the vicinity senseless. Very few examples of the weapon exist. Frankly, in the eyes of some authorities, it should never have left the testing grounds in the U.S. The deployment of this chemical device might be viewed as contravening international agreements. Its existence was a secret kept within the army. Some upper level maladministration, in fact, led to the weapon reaching Badgarten. A recall notice had been issued, but it had been delayed in the administrative line."

"Typical bureaucratic incompetence," Zack muttered to himself.

"Not to mention the role of your son, sir," the official reminded Zachary gently. "A preliminary report reached the commanding officer a couple of days later. They found your son's Jeep at Munich's airport. The name, Deucalion Cronson, appeared on a flight to Frankfurt for the Friday on which he had started his weekend leave and a man had taken the flight. It took a day or two to prove that it was not your son."

"Oh!" Zack frowned.

"As you can imagine, sir, this worried the security people. It looked like clear-cut evidence of a conspiracy rather than simply a random AWOL situation. Inquiries around student hangouts in Schwabing revealed further disturbing news. Deucalion was seen regularly in the company of a radical group of students. The police were informed and set out to question the group, but they were gone. It was known, however, that they included both Greeks and Germans, and some had fled Greece to escape imprisonment. The Greek connection led to renewed inquiries at points of departure for that direction. Eventually, the police tracked down an assistant stationmaster at the Haupt-Bahnhof who remembered a large man and a red haired girl with the two suitcases who got on the Tauern Orient Express. Operatives took the Express and talked to staff, but though they located a few people who remembered Cronson and the girl, they could not be sure where they had gone beyond Belgrade.

"That's where our troubles start. We can't get the Yugoslavs to cooperate, officially. About all we know for sure is that your son and the girl aren't there."

"What girl?" Zack looked startled. "Duke's never mentioned a girlfriend. God knows what she might persuade him to do." He paused for a long time, as if he were considering all the ghastly possibilities. "That is, he didn't talk about one in his letters," he finished, lamely.

The official looked surprised by Zack's vehemence, and wrote a note on the folder. "We've established the name of the girl and some information about her. She is known simply as Europa. She was a student activist in Greece, and fled before the authorities could arrest her. Europa has a reputation as a revolutionary, but not communist as far as anyone knows. She's very nationalistic."

"What hold does she have on my son?"

The official paused before answering. "Love, Mister Cronson, leads to strange bedfellows, if you'll pardon the expression. We can only guess that she persuaded your son to help her with some deal in Greece. We reckon they took the Athens Express in Belgrade, but where from there remains somewhat of a mystery." He wiped his glasses and carried on. "Your family is of Greek origin, I believe?"

"Yes, my parents came to the States from Crete, to be precise."

"That's what I had heard. One possibility is that they went to Crete. We have a difficulty. Since we cut economic aid in 1962, and then Papandreou became premiere, our relations have become somewhat tense. We daren't take any overt action, even though there have been worrying rumors stemming from that area. We're concerned about a possible incident at the NATO base on Soudha Bay."

"What kind of rumors?"

"Oh! Odd bits and pieces, Mister Cronson," the official replied. "There are, as I'm sure you know, longstanding grievances on many of the Mediterranean islands. Look at Cyprus, for example, after Makarios took over from the British." He paused. "Anyway, back to the purpose of our discussion. Can you think of anything that might help us locate your son? You have relatives on Crete. Could he have gone to them for help?"

"Offhand, I can't think of anything. I doubt he would go to our relatives when he hasn't contacted me. I'm still stunned by what you've told me. It seems out of character for Duke and this business of the girl revolutionary is very worrying." Zack was silent for a moment. "Let me ask you a question. If I were to go to Crete, assuming he's there, and if I could recover this weapon, would it be possible to get some kind of deal for my son?"

"I understand your desire to take some action, Mister Cronson. However, it would not be wise for you to get involved. Some of these young revolutionaries are…crazy. You could be in great danger."

"He's my son. I can't just sit here while some crazy young girl is perverting him. How about my question? If I can return the weapon, will you get him a deal?"

"It's not up to me, you understand. My advice is to leave it to the professionals. Of course, I can't prevent you going to Crete." The official did not look upset by Zack's request, as he put a tick on a list. "Would you be taking anyone with you?"

"So, it's okay for me to deal with it?" The official raised his eyebrows and smiled.

Zack smiled. "Good, I have a way of doin' this through our Trust, with my family."

"So you'll have to tell them about the Bullroarer?"

"I suppose so," Zack said, thoughtfully.

"Then you need to work out who you'll be taking and let me know immediately. You'll get a visit from one of our agents. Each of you will have to complete a security form."

"Okay, I guess"

"I'll see what we can do for your son, in the event that you recover the weapon. We like to look after our supporters and we appreciate all the things you've done for the party, Mister Cronson."

"Thanks. I will. I'm sure he will want to see this worked out to everyone's benefit."

"So I've been told," said the official as he showed Zack to the door. He mouthed the conventional pleasantries and returned to his desk, writing a number of notes before calling his the CIA.

On his return to Argos, Zack called Festus. He swore him to secrecy, on the subject of the Bullroarer. "It was strange. At first, this guy acted as if he didn't want me involved. But, when I offered help, he didn't look disappointed at all."

"It sounds like that's what they were after," Festus laughed. "That's quite a shocker about Duke. What do you need?"

"I need to bring enough people to Crete to have a chance of finding Duke. We must have a cover story for the Trust. A couple of years ago, after you'd chased Pandora around the islands, you went on with her to Crete. You charged some of the costs to the Trust, and mentioned the…Phaestos Disk. Did you find anything we could use?"

Festus tried not to show his excitement. "I think so. I've been working on it for some time. I'm convinced that the Phaestos Disk hides some secret that's important for us. We could split the group up to visit archaeological sites across the island. They could be looking for other examples of the Disk's symbols."

"Hasn't someone done that before?"

"Certainly, but I'm not satisfied they did a good job."

"Cunning." Zack laughed. "I'll set up a meeting, and you can explain it to everybody. I'll have to tell people we're looking for Duke and about the Bullroarer. We're all going to have to sign some damn government secrecy paper."

"That's not surprising."

"Incidentally, Ari's going to come. I hope you two can work together?"

"Oh!" said Festus. His face showed no expression.

"We need Ari. He's got the military experience. Somebody's going to have to deal with this contraption. Ari understands army instructions."

"I see."

"Hell! Zack laughed. "The man thinks like an army instruction manual."

"No choice. Have to do it. Duty, you see," Festus said, mimicking Ari's clipped military style of speech. "Have you contacted the relatives on Crete? Surely, they're the best bet to find Duke. I mean, he may have gone to them for help?"

Zack answered defensively. "Oh, I don't think they could help much. The man I talked to in Washington seemed to think he would be in the Soudha Bay area, around Khania. Unfortunately, if I remember right, we don't have any close relatives left there. I've talked to my synteknos' son. He's old and sort of out of it. I've asked him to set up accommodation, and a few other simple things, but I don't want to worry him unnecessarily. He lives a simple life. It wasn't easy to explain it to him without mentioning the Bulllroarer." Zack looked worried. "Fes, God knows what this girl's got Duke doing!"

Festus was amazed that Zack did not plan to ask his Cretan relatives for help. The synteknos' son was an old man, but he had a sharp mind, and considerable influence. It sounded like Zack did not want him talking to his relatives. He gradually forgot about it as he concentrated on how to capitalize on this opportunity to test his theories. To his own surprise, he spent as much effort on this as he did in preparation for this next Labor. In the legend, it was the capture of the Cretan Bull, ferried across Europe to Crete by Zeus. If he took the parallel seriously, it implied that Zack had arranged the theft of the Bullroarer, and the relatives were involved!. What could be the reason? He dismissed the idea. It was too preposterous.

26. Spiros

Spiros rested in the taverna, taking advantage of the shade offered by the vine-covered trestle. He sipped at his small cup of thick black coffee and, occasionally, he drank from a glass of water as he looked past it at the sea. The boat to Khora Sfakion was leaving, taking away a few of the tourists to Crete who had completed the trek down the Gorge of Samaria. Other tourists, tired from the jolting they had received on the Gorge's rock-strewn path, were soaking their legs in the clear sea. Spiros wore baggy black trousers with a ballooning seat that betrayed the earlier Turkish domination of the island. They were tucked into swash-buckling black leather boots. A black sash, around his middle, held his white blouse and the trousers in place. He wore a fringed black scar around his head. It was a heroic mode of attire when worn by an eagle-eyed, mountain man. On Spiros, it was a somewhat outfit that highlighted his small skinny frame. Compensating for this failure was a magnificent, thick black moustache.

Spiros turned lazily to look at the village, Agia Roumelli. It had two tavernas and a number of small stone houses, which snuggled around the base of the cliff and up the entrance to the gorge that cut deep into the White Mountains. A deep emotional feeling brought the hint of a tear. This was his land and no one would take it away. His people had fought for independence against the Venetians and the Germans. Between those two occupations, his hero, the great Sfakian, Daskaloyiannis, had led them against the Turks. Today, people said there was nobody to fight, but he had read about problems in Cyprus. After Cyprus, would Crete be next? Who was going to stop the Turks trying to reoccupy Crete? Certainly not those mainland Greeks. The tourists were not a problem it seemed to him, but a welcome source of income. He was proud to show his beautiful country, but what if some of those supposed tourists were Turkish spies. His chest swelled with pride, he was a Sfakian. He and his comrades would be ready for them, ready for any invasion for that matter, and very soon, when they found the treasure.

27. Crete

It was April, and the Eurysthesians were lunching under the trees in Eleutherios Square in Crete's capital town of Iraklion. Marienna was eating 'bougatsa,' a flaky pastry filled with soft cheese, and drinking her favorite white wine—Cava Minos. "It's a pity that we're not what we seem," Marienna said to nobody in particular, "a simple bunch of tourists enjoying this glorious scene."

"Marienna's right. I'm really enjoying the opportunities provided by our Trust. It's a pity the serious side of the work takes away some of the fun. Mind you," she looked sideways at Harold, "Harold enjoys the exercise. Like when we went fishing near the oil rig and he tried to jump into your boat. Oh, Harold don't glare so!"

"I'll drink a toast to all of that," Alex Platon echoed, nodding agreement and succeeding in spilling his wine. A worried look crossed his face, and he muttered "gouri", as he quickly dabbed a spot of wine behind his ear.

"*Gouri*," Festus laughed. "Boy, you're superstitious."

"Better to take precautions than bring misfortune on us all."

Festus changed the subject quickly. "While we're all together let's me go over our plans."

"Well grounded. Hardly see reason do it again," Ari Cronson growled.

"Some of us aren't as well prepared as you, Aristotle," Peri Dexter answered gently. "Right. I see."

"Ari, why don't you explain the plans,? You're the military strategist," Festus said, keeping a straight face.

"Good. Happy to do it. Look for Duke and girl. Important characteristic, red hair! Crisscross island essential. Best chance of discovering Duke, if he's here. Right, Doc?"

"Right, Colonel."

Ari continued in his telegraphic style. "Two points. One, don't let natives know about…" Zack coughed. "Oh…I see…Two, fit to mission of Trust. Tricky to organize. Hope it works out. Need map, Doc!"

Festus took a map from his knapsack, and spread it on the table.

"Next, characteristics of Crete. Skinny island, runs approximately east to west. Iraklion on north coast, about a third of the way from the eastern tip of the island." Ari paused to allow questions.

"Get on with!" Zack muttered.

"Relatively easy to follow north coast. Mountains also run east to west. To approach southern coast better to cut between mountains." Ari stopped and held up his large left hand, carefully tucking in the thumb and closing the four fingers. Achievement of goals requires dividing you in four task groups."

As he described each of them, he studiously unfolded another finger. Another technique from an army manual, thought Festus. "The first task group. To be known as group one will be Zack and Elena and myself. Action one: take bus along north coast to the west, through Rethymnion to our main base at Khania. Duke may be in the Soudha area. Action two: from Khania take number of side trips. Ancient settlement at Polyrhinia recommended, after Khania investigated."

"Do we really have to do this temple bashing, Ari?"

Zack Cronson answered for him. "I know it takes time from finding Duke, Elena, but it's important for our cover. Everybody, please remember to look for anything that looks like a symbol from the Disk. Take notes! When this is over," he looked away for a second, "Festus will write some kind of a paper."

"We must take lots of photographs too," Harold added.

"Second task force. To be known as group…"

"We understand the system, Ari. Just summarize who and where!"

"Got it, Zack," said Ari, uncertainly. His speech became even more tele-graphic. "Group two: Harold, Peri, Marienna. Tour arranged to east. Palaces at Knossos, Mallia, then go to Agios Nikolaos! Find transport back through Iraklion to Khania! Questions?"

He should not have asked. Harold and Peri kept him busy for more than twenty minutes worrying about details of their tour.

"Group three. All young folks, includes Alex." The joke fell flat. Nevertheless, he joined in the expected but nonexistent laughter.

"More energetic schedule. Explore the far east of island and southern coast! All end up at Matala." Ari pointed at the map. "Southwest of Iraklion. Alex! Proposal made that you hike up into Dhikti Mountains. Visit Lasithi plain! Check for sightings of Duke! Have to return north before going south to Agio Viannos. Goal, visit as many villages as possible on way to Mires.

"Second part of group three, Samantha and Ionides. Take bus to Ayios Nikolaos! Explore the east end of the island! Important to visit palace at Kato Zakros! Here on map, right near eastern edge of island. Then, go to Ierapetra. Take the bus back through Ayios Nikolaos and Iraklion to Mires. Meet up with Alex…Now, where am I?"

Festus was weary of Ari's clipped delivery and grasped the opportunity to take over the discussion. "It's very important for you to make inquiries among the for-eign kids, who tend to gravitate to the sea. So go from Mires to Matala. A lot of the…I hate the word…hippies…camp out there. Don't forget to see the palace at Phaestos on your way."

"Alex says the girls go topless," Ionides grinned. "I'll take lots of photos for the record?"

"Over my dead body," Samantha snorted.

"I'm group four. I'll start here, in Iraklion. I need to go to the museum first, and then I'll inquire at the airport and docks. The museum's just across the road. You can see it over there." Festus gestured vaguely with his hand. "I'll meet you later in Khania, Zack, in a few days time. That's all I have to say except, have a good time."

It was a hot day, and Festus took a sip of Marienna's drink as he walked from the restaurant to the Archeological Museum. He walked through the Museum in a dream, absorbing the atmosphere of ancient Crete. He drifted past the Neolithic pottery from Knossos, Phourni and the Cave of Eleithya, past the jewelry from the Leben tombs, and past the votive figures. He enjoyed the beauty of the Kamares ware, with their light paintings on a dark background. The first time around, he bypassed the Phaestos Disk and lost himself in a study of the royal gameboard, an inlaid ivory piece from Knossos. As he walked, time retreated around him. By the time Festus reached the white sarcophagus from Agia Triadha, it seemed as if he were back acting in the Argos Play Cycle and his role as Hephaestus had taken over. He stopped. Memories flooded into his mind, the Disk and the Dancing Floor. Why did he think of them? He couldn't remember.

It seemed as if his legs were being drawn up to his chest as the undertakers lowered him into the sarcophagus. It was a cold and lonely feeling. Two thoughts battled for his consciousness; a fear of dying before his mission was complete; and a fear that he would lose Aphrodite.

When he came out of the trance, his face was gray and beads of sweat dotted his forehead. The Minoan frescoes, showing the bull leapers and the elegant women tried to call him back. Festus fought back, struggling out of the grasp of the many fleeting images that tried to hold him. The business of the bull and the acrobats fascinated him. Why did they do it? Was it simply an entertainment or was it an important ritual? Was it a right of passage for the young men and women who dared to confront the awesome beast? Could it be a part of the challenge of a tanist to the king? He had the feeling he ought to know the answer, but it escaped him.

Festus returned by a circuitous route, stopping to look at some tablets inscribed with Linear A and B script, the gameboard, the Phaestos Disk and eventually arrived at the office of the Director of the Museum. He had arranged to photograph the Disk, the gameboard, some other tablets, and sealstones that the Museum's Director had suggested might be of interest, for though they were not of the same form as the Disk, there were similarities in some of the symbols.

"Frankly, Dr. Festus, I am disappointed you will not divulge your ideas about the Disk," the Director said, as they walked to look at the Disk. "I am sure you are aware that there are many suggestions. Possibly the Disk is a hymn or, maybe, it is some kind of list, or details of a business transaction, and that it is not Cretan at all but written in a variant of Hittite script. The forty-five pictographic signs imprinted on the two sides do have similarities to symbols in other languages."

"Thank you for reminding me." Festus nodded. "I might add that it remains unclear whether the signs are ideograms or syllables, or for that matter both. Now, may I inspect it?" The Director looked uneasy but he opened the case and let Festus pick up the brown terracotta tablet, some seventeen centimeters in diameter. The minute he touched it, Festus had the feeling he had held the Disk before. Hazy images appeared in his mind.

He was in a workshop—his workshop? He was holding a tablet in his left hand. It had not been fired. The spiral of symbols was incomplete. He laid the tablet with care on a folded cloth on a wooden table. In his right hand, the stylus was ready to complete the writing. As he lowered the stylus, he realized he did not know what to write.

The image cleared he was back in the museum. His legs felt weak and he was grateful for the arms that held him.

"Are you all right, Dr. Festus?" the Director asked, releasing him.

"Yes, thank you," Festus replied, recovering quickly. "Too much sun I guess. I should have sat in the shade over lunch." Festus smiled at the sigh of relief as the Director returned the precious artifact to its rightful place.

"I expect that was it." The Director called for one of his assistants to come to his office, and then reached into a drawer of his desk. With a flourish, he produced a brown paper parcel that he placed on the desk. "My aide will take our photograph while I make this presentation." Before Festus could react, the Director grasped him firmly by the arm and struck a pose. "To the man who hunted the Loch Ness Monster, the Archeological Museum of Iraklion has great pleasure in presenting this fine replica of the Phaestos Disk."

"Director! You are too kind," Festus thought quickly. If he were open about his study, the director might be persuaded to hold the photograph, until the Deucalion mission was completed.

"Thank you for this magnificent gift. As one scientist to another, let me say something about my ideas. I'm working on the assumption that the symbols are an old form of Greek, rather than some other language, such as Hittite. I suspect that the Disk is connected in some way to the bull ritual and to the motion of the dancers and acrobats. If we could understand this relation, then we could decipher the Disk. We must find the right place. I sense we need to find the "Dancing Floor", Festus said the last words at a rush as if he had difficulty uttering them.

The Director looked surprised. "How curious. Just yesterday, there was an American woman in here asking the same question. She was from New Orleans, I think." Festus looked startled, but remained silent. The Director continued. "I am sure you know that he phrase "Dancing Floor" is used sometimes for the open courtyards," he said. "At Aradin, on the south coast between Khora Sfakion and the Gorge of Samaria, there is an area called the Dance of the Hellenes. I'm not sure it's as old as the Disk. Though at this site, as at most ancient sites, the construction of one era covers another, going back in time."

Festus nodded. "I've read of the place. Maybe I should go there?"

"Perhaps you recollect that, in the Iliad, Homer says..." the Director paused reflecting on the correct words:

> Daedalus in Knossos once contrived
> A dancing floor for fair haired Ariadne.

"I have some memory of it. I've read that the ritual partridge dance followed the pattern on the dancing floor."

"Yes, and Daedalus is a later version of the smith-god, Hephaestus. The smiths were often ritually lamed, you know. So they hobbled like a partridge." The Director showed his embarrassment. He had forgotten Festus's disability.

"I think it was more likely to prevent them running away," laughed Festus. "They were too valuable to their masters."

"Yes. I'm sure that was the reason."

"Director, I have two small requests."

"Feel free." The Director raised his hands sympathetically.

"Please keep this conversation to yourself. I would like the opportunity to discuss the Disk with you further as our investigation proceeds. As with all such studies, it will take some time, and as I have other work to do. Finally, please could you hold the photograph for some weeks; otherwise, I'll be at the mercy of the press and the tourists. As far as I can tell, my presence here isn't widely known yet."

"I'll certainly not do anything to embarrass you, Doctor Festus. I would deem it an honor to work with you on this project and I will do some research on my own that might be of some small help."

"Thank you, Director. I'll be in touch," Festus replied, as he left. "A woman from New Orleans, you said? Strange!" The Director shrugged.

Festus ate dinner alone, brooding about the strange happenings in the museum. It wasn't the first time. Something similar had happened in Loch Ness and on his previous trip to the Greek Archipelago. What if he really was the reincarnation of the Greek god of technology, Hephaestus, returned to complete some mission. What mission? A fine madness to think about it. Unfortunately, there wasn't anyone to take his mind of the fantasy. He wished Dawn or Pandora could have come, but he couldn't take Pandy out of school and Dawn's work kept her in Texas. Screw Women's Lib! Not really, he smiled to himself. Irritation was a good way of blocking the dream world.

28. Knossos

To the south of Iraklion, Harold, Peri, and Marienna were enjoying their tour. The bus had taken them to Knossos along with a bunch of tourists and they had all entered the West Hall of the Palace. Like Festus on that same day, these Eurysthesians were seduced back in time by their surroundings. They wandered, oblivious to the other tourists.

"I'm going to find the tombs," Harold said.

"I'll give them a miss, dear," Peri said. "Far too gloomy, don't you agree, Marienna?"

"Yes, but I am sure they will be most interesting for Harold," Marienna replied.

Harold found his way to the tombs, and mused about how the ancients would prepare for the burial of the dead. It was a subject he had studied at length. The ancients knew how to honor the dead, he thought. His funeral home in Argos did a good job but a wooden casket, a modest headstone, and a simple ceremony could not prepare people adequately for the afterlife.

Peri was with Marienna in the Central Courtyard, absorbing the atmosphere. Rounded hills formed a backdrop to the east and south of the site. Yellowing scrub lightly dusted the slopes above a band of silver gray-green olives, vines, and the dark cypresses. They could see the double peak of Mount Iouktas through the sacred horns that mark this southern end of the palace. "I wish there were more flowers."

"I'm sure there are, Peri," Marienna said, reassuringly. "Why, on the way here I saw lilies and violets by the side of the road and I know crocuses and narcissi come out at this time of year. We'll go for a walk later and find them."

"Later in the summer there will be red poppies. I can put them in my hair."

"Flowers are important in the dance," Marienna said very quietly.

"The dance and the labyrinth. Is that why we came?"

"Peri dear, there never was a labyrinth, but only the maze of corridors in this large palace and possibly also it referred to a complex pattern on the courtyard floor," Marienna explained.

Peri looked at the floor, dreamily, and started to sway. "I am beginning to remember. The dancers must follow the pattern on the dancing floor. I can see my path. Look! My symbol points the way." Peri started to move across the floor. "The bull is near, bedecked with flowers, uncertain, snorting its bewilderment. Pray that that the acrobats will distract it! I must follow the pattern." Peri swayed gently, shuffling along the chosen path. "The bull is coming," she cried. "The acrobats have failed." She fainted.

When Peri woke, she was sitting in the shade of a wall. Marienna's was saying, "It's all right, Peri dear. The heat, the bus fumes, you fainted."

"The dancing floor, the bull came. I couldn't move."

"Could you see it all as real, Peri?"

Peri nodded. "We all can sometimes," said Marienna, patting her hand. "Don't worry. With your imagination, you may be more inclined to revert than the rest of us. Tell me about it." They sat, talking quietly.

Meanwhile, Harold had reached the throne room. It had been hot in the sun and he took another sip of the drink, Marienna had given him. He waited for his turn to sit on the throne.

He felt drowsy and his eyes closed. The gypsum throne seemed to grip him. The weight of his gold crown was oppressive. Some people approached the throne. Servants, he thought. What were they saying? The bull has injured a girl dancer. Sad, but what could he do about it? Tradition insisted upon the ritual. Nevertheless, he would go and console her friends. He would use all the conventional words, honor, glory, beloved of the gods. He went over suitable phrases in his mind as the throne released him and he walked past the people to the antechamber and up the steps to the Central Courtyard.

Harold was still in this dream when Marienna caught his arm and stopped him. "It's all right," Marienna said, "Peri will be fine."

Harold looked confused for a moment. "Fainted, did she?" he said, caustically. "Should have worn a hat. I told her." He looked worried. "I took photographs. Nothing useful. Heaven knows what Henry will be able to do with them."

On the way to Ayios Nikolaos, they stopped at the chapel of Saint George in the Monastery of Selinaris. From the terrace below the Monastery, there was a beautiful view down a gorge to the sea at Sissi. Peri held firmly onto Harold and propelled him into the chapel. Harold resisted at first until he saw the look in her eyes. She is scared, he thought. Scared of what happened at Knossos. Just like me, he admitted to himself. In the center of the nave was a large brass candlestick, its sand-filled top supporting rows of brown candles. It looked unstable. Still holding hands like a pair of small children, they walked around it cautiously to reach the iconostasis, which divided the nave from the sanctuary. The icons, mainly depicting the patron saint, were in various poses as Saint George slew the dragon. There were also Taximata, small silver simulations of parts of the body on which the supplicant wanted a blessing. They watched as the Cretan pilgrims kissed the paintings and crossed themselves\

The bus climbed out of the ravine and descended around hairpin bends to the town of Neapolis. "I should have prayed for a safe journey," said Harold, with an uncustomary grin.

"I did," said Peri. "Look at all that wayside shrine!" She pointed at a small, glass fronted shrine, perched like a bird house on a post."

"All crash sites, I suppose," Marienna added.

"They usually contain a painting of Christ and a set of offerings such a jar of olive oil and in some cases a lighted candle, dear," Harold said.

Peri clasped his hand fondly and rested her head against his shoulder. "We know, dear."

Marienna, watching them, smiled. A small curly haired boy moved down the aisle to sit with his sister. She pointed, "He looks just like Deucalion did, when he was little," she said. "I wonder if we'll find 'Little Duke?'"

29. Khania

Zack Cronson and his entourage were more successful in their trip to Khania. Roaming from their hotel on the quayside, they had already disposed of the local tourist sites—the old ramparts, the mosque, the market, the church of St. Francis and the museum. Then, in the picturesque narrow stone covered streets behind the port, they came upon gypsies hawking their wares. After they had made numerous purchases, the gypsies told them that a large man with short dark hair and a red-haired woman had danced in a Romany bar. They remembered the incident not only because of the size of the man, an American who spoke Greek badly, but also because the girl had danced improperly. She was drunk and insulting. Maybe more than drunk they hinted. The gypsies were not prepared to divulge more.

"They know something else," Ari muttered, menacingly. "Let me lean on them!"

"Let it go!" Zack cautioned. "We can try again later."

Elena squeezed Zack's hand, showing her support.

"We gotta get out of here," Zack said. "Fes suggested we should visit Polyrhinia. Let's do it. Anything's better than sitting here twiddling our thumbs."

They reached the site in the early afternoon, high above the gulf of Kisamos. Zack wiped his forehead "Elena, is there any more of the drink left." Elena took a sip from the bottle and passed it on. Ari nodded approval, returning his military style flask to its position on his belt. "Good procedure. Getting hot. Keep fluid levels up."

Zack studied the scene. He felt strangely comfortable.

Time passed hazily he could see the walls rising around him, the weeds disappearing from around the stones of the courtyard. He turned to his war chief. "Tell them to start the parade."

The troops marched by, silently. In his mind, the whole scene appeared to float above the sea. The ladies of the court sat talking quietly, admiring the youths marching by in their smart tunics. His war chief advised him of their strengths and weaknesses.

A sudden sound broke the spell. It was a herd of goats scuffling in the brush. Zack, to cover his embarrassment, turned quickly and walked away, as if he had just thought of something important. The goats continued foraging.

Festus was waiting when they returned to the hotel. Zack passed on the limited information they had on Deucalion. "I think we've just about run out of good will," he added, suggesting that Festus should try to find out more.

"I'll do it. Just show me on the map here where you met them."

"Do you want any of us to go with you?"

"No, it'll be easier if I'm on my own. I know I'm going to regret this."

"What does he mean?" Elena asked.

"Poor Fes still remembers the drinking bout he had with Pan, at the time of the Everyman Bore fire," Zack replied. "With that happy thought, why don't we head up the street to that good looking bar on the corner, and have a few?"

They didn't see Festus until late the following day. He was exhausted and his pale face indicated a formidable hangover. "I've got to tell you this quickly," he said, "I need to get to bed." His friends smiled sympathetically.

"I thought I knew what it would be like." Festus shook his head, wonderingly. "I had to buy a drink for every sentence. Eventually, I found this Romany youth. He and his entire family, it seemed to be most of Khania, sat around and let me ply them with booze. Finally, they told me what they knew. I've no idea how much I spent."

Zack motioned that it was unimportant.

"I showed him this recent picture of Duke. He said, if you added a mustache and imagined longer hair, this would fit. He also agreed there was a girl with him. Referred to her as *fraulein*."

"Did he know where they were going?"

"He wasn't sure, but he thought the girl was going to Iraklion. That's not the interesting part, though. Apparently Duke rambled on about a Turkish invasion."

"Turkish invasion!" Zack expostulated. "Ridiculous!"

His outburst was not convincing Festus thought.

"This kid obviously thought Duke was either mad or just drunk." Festus continued. "Duke tried to get some of the men to join him. To train to meet this danger. Would you believe it? When they refused to join him—they were never sure if he was joking or not—he changed the subject. Their best guess was that he might have gone to the south coast. They suggested the Gorge of Samaria. Zack I really think we should talk to Uncle…"

Zack interrupted him. "If we have to go to Khora Sfakion I guess I'll have no choice. Until then I want to leave him out of it."

30. Matala

Ionides and Samantha spent an idyllic few days exploring the eastern end of the island. They passed quickly through the "Cretan Riviera" to Sitia and then more slowly explored the less populated area out to Kato Zakros, before hiking and busing back to Ierapetra. From there they took the bus west to Mires and met Alex.

"Ion took lots of photos," Samantha giggled. "The ones without scantily clad girls are for Fes. How did it go with you?"

"Entertaining and tiring," Alex replied. "I trekked around the Dhikti mountain area. The Lasithi Plain—great windmills. Visited the Dhiktian Cave. It's reputed to be the birthplace of Zeus, you know." He laughed. "They'd never heard of Zack! More important nobody in my wanderings had seen Duke."

"Were people friendly?"

"Great, Ion, just great. They're really poor, but often, when I stopped to ask about Duke and the girl, they would invite me into their house for a drink and a snack. Good thing I had my guitar. It's funny, they liked old cowboy songs and I was ready to play a Cretan ballad; a mantinadhe, you remember?" Ion and Sam nodded. "I did meet this musician with a lyra. We played a joyful ballad to celebrate our encounter. Then, at a funeral in the village of Exo Potamies, I got to hear the other, mournful aspect of that kind of music."

"We came up with zip," said Ionides. "We should follow the plan and move on tomorrow."

They left at dawn and hiked down the road to the sea. They stopped briefly at the Palace of Phaestos, before pressing on to sea at Matala.

By the time they reached the beach, they were dusty and tired. After a leisurely swim they sat in the shade offered by the cliffs, drank wine, snacked and idly scanned the promontory. Many of the tourists lived in the multistory caves that riddled the slanting yellow rocks above them. Tanned and tanning bodies, some nude and not all young, were taking a maximum advantage of the midday sun. Alex went off alone to explore the coast. Ionides and Samantha wandered slowly, sunbathing, swimming and chatting to groups of sunbathers as they went. Ionides in an illogical, prudish, Texan way, seemed to be embarrassed at first by the sight of the naked bodies. His sideways glances evolved into overt staring.

"If you want to see boobs, look at these!" Sam said, removing her bra.

"Sorry, Sam. I'm not used to this," Ion laughed.

"Don't push it!" Sam punched him lightly.

When Alex rejoined them, Samantha posed proudly to show her new liberated self.

"Very nice," said Alex. "Ari will be ecstatic. Why is Ion still wearing his shorts?"

"He's chicken," said Samantha smiling.

Ionides changed the subject quickly. "It's clear that Duke hasn't been here. Nobody could forget seeing old Duke."

"We did see a few redheads," Sam added. "But none of them was Europa."

"You know, while she's Greek, she's been living in Germany. If she's not with Duke, she's quite likely to be with Germans," Alex mused. "We should concentrate on them."

"Why don't we have another go around tomorrow taking the opposite sides of the cove and see if we can find her," suggested Ionides. "It won't be as easy as finding Duke, but it's worth a try."

Sam and Ionides followed the path that meandered precariously up the cliff above the last houses in the village. A woman, hanging clothes to dry on her patio, turned briefly to look up. She did not appear pleased to see them. They soon smelled the reason. The path was soiled with human waste and trash. Rounding a bend in the cliff, they came upon the source, a cave with a number of kids sleeping in it. Beyond the cave, the path dropped down to a flat rocky area by the water. A disused holding tank for fish was carved in the rock. A boy was lying by it, sunbathing. A girl floated below them in the transparent blue sea. As they approached, she swam lazily to the shore and clambered out of the water, picking her way carefully over the shellfish covered rocks. Her face was hidden by long red hair. She stood over the sunbather deliberately dripping water on him. He turned and shouted at her in mock anger. They did not understand the German, except the one word—Europa!

"We think we've found her!" Sam shouted to Alex, as they approached.

"I think you should go to Khania at once, and tell Zack," Ionides said. "If this is the real Europa, Duke may not be far away. We'll watch her."

"You be careful." Alex grinned. "I've got something else to tell Fes. I just came across an old friend of his. She's an attractive lady, works in Germany at the moment, teaching at a U.S. air base. She's in Crete with a girlfriend—Billy something."

"Cathy Schmidt? Oh, shit! This could be trouble." Ionides made a face.

"She plans to be in Crete for another week, so they're bound to get together." Alex paused. "You know, it's strange. I had the impression she knew we were here."

Alex reached Khania that evening. He found Harold, Peri, Elena and Marienna Cronson sitting outside the Mouragio. The sky was a clear blue and a light breeze fluttered the cafe awnings. The harbor was vibrant with activity. By the quayside, the multicolored boats bobbed gently in concord with the wake of each passing craft. It was lost on the Eurysthesians, who were listlessly debating what to do and looked relieved to see him.

"What did you find out?" Harold asked.

"We think we found Europa in Matala." He didn't mention Cathy.

"That's great. Bless you." Elena hugged him. "No Duke?'

"No Duke, I'm sorry. Ion and Sam are keeping tabs on Europa. Where's Zack?"

"Zack and his motley crew, by which I mean Ari and Fes, have gone off to the Gorge of Samaria to find Duke."

"What should I do?" asked Alex.

"That's what I'm pondering," replied Harold, importantly. "I think you should follow them and tell them about Europa. It seems clear the action is on the south coast. Anyway, they might need more help. I'd be happy to go with you but I've been ordered to stay here and look after the ladies. From what we hear, Duke is trying to form a small army.

"I have trouble admitting it, Alex, but he's been handful since he turned fifteen. Frankly, I'm a little scared of him. Not that he's done anything. It's more that he always seems about to explode. Hormones, I suppose. I don't understand him anymore. He's closer to his father. Zack shouldn't have any trouble. I mean, he's been talking to him on the phone regularly." She sounded uncertain. "This whole business is a great shock. Zack is really upset that Duke never mentioned this girl Europa. I guess she must have talked Duke into doing what he did."

The brief silence that followed Elena's admission was broken by her sister-in-law, Marienna, "I don't like to raise it, Elena, but does Zack know more than he's telling us? Not just what the army's really wor..." Marienna's voice trailed off.

Elena looked thoughtful for a moment, apparently considering her response. "I..."

"I'm sure the whole business has been cooked up by that girl," said Peri soothingly, interrupting her. "He doesn't sound like the Duke I knew. I hadn't realized you were having such trouble with him."

"Damn!" Marienna muttered. Elena looked surprised but said nothing.

Alex changed the subject, abruptly. "How can I get to the Gorge?"

"Your best bet is to take a taxi up into the mountains to Omalos. I have the map here," said Harold. "From Omalos it's a short distance to the Xyloskalon. It means the place of the Wooden Steps. They lead down into the Gorge." He explained carefully,

"I think the taxi driver will know the way, dear." Peri nudged him gently; concerned that Harold would start one of his interminable lectures. "Alex really should go quickly. That way he might catch them not too far into the Gorge. They'll not be moving very fast, you see." She looked embarrassed at the implied comment on Festus' disability. "Well, they have to look for Duke," she said defensively.

Harold succeeded in offering one more piece of advice, before Alex left. "Remember to stop in Omalos! There's a small cafe. They offer a very good mizithra—sour cream served with honey. Give you plenty of energy for your hike. The honey's local. If you keep a sharp lookout, you'll see colonies of bee-hives alongside the road. They're easy to recognize, box shaped, blue or white, and usually have a large stone on top to keep their little roofs on. Now, I remember, when I was young…" Peri tapped him gently on the knee and he stopped. "Oh yes, I see. I suppose you know all that. You really should catch that taxi."

31. Samaria

The wooden steps of the Xyloskalon, situated at over four thousand feet on the edge of the Plain of Omalos, mark the start of the Gorge of Samaria. The Plain is high in the White Mountains—Lefka Ori—that rise to a height of eight thousand feet from the Libyan Sea. The Gorge slashes like a knife-cut into the mountains as it descends for twelve miles to the sea at Agia Roumelli.

Alex paused to consult the map of the Gorge, which he had bought in Omalos, near the restaurant where he had stopped for some mizithra. He licked his lips for a final taste of honey and started down the steps. The path dropped rapidly, for two thousand feet, down to the bed of the Gorge. The tall trees that shaded the steps stood in a pleasantly fertile contrast to the barren mountains that towered above them. It was late in the day. A few tourists who had come from Agia Roumelli at the other end of the Gorge were climbing slowly up to the Pavilion to spend the night. A guide, shepherding them from the rear, saw Alex descending and explained that it was unwise to start so late. Alex indicated his backpack and said he would camp for the night. The guide looked disapproving, shrugged his shoulders and pressed on after his flock. Alex soon appreciated why the guide was concerned, for in the Gorge it rapidly became dark. He stopped by the small chapel of St. Nicholas, deciding to camp in a grove of pine trees and cypresses rather than carry on to the deserted village of Samaria—his initial plan.

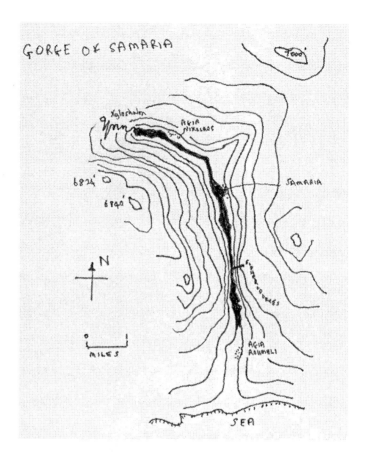

The flashlight, which he had tied to the branches of a low tree, spotlighted his dinner of bread, sausage, grapes and wine set in the middle of his ground sheet. Alex ate in a leisurely fashion admiring the pinpoint pattern of starlight in the dark sky. It was a pity there was no bright-eyed youth to share this experience, he thought. After dinner, they could have dipped briefly in the ice-cold stream and…His thoughts were interrupted by a brief, bright glow, which lit the Gorge to his south. Startled, he jumped to his feet. There was a rustling of wind, not towards him as in an explosion, but away from him, a faint grunting inhalation as if he had happened suddenly on the remote edge of a vacuum. The Bullroarer! Duke must have used it! Alex packed quickly and with the aid of the flashlight set off down the Gorge. He moved slowly, partly in deference to the roughness of the path, and partly out of a nagging worry that he might meet Duke. He felt very lonely and exposed.

It took Alex nearly twenty minutes to cover the mile to Samaria. The air had a strange acid smell, reminiscent of a chemistry class in high school. He could not identify it immediately, but there was something else strange about the place. He stumbled across Ari on the outskirts of the village. Ari was kneeling with his head bent to the ground and his hands clasping his ears. Nearby, was Festus, semiconscious and breathing hard. They were covered in leaves. The feature that had been puzzling Alex came into focus; there were no leaves on the trees.

"Are you okay?" Alex asked, realizing immediately it was a dumb question.

Ari struggled to his feet, shedding leaves as he rose. "Zack...went to check...Duke hiding here...one of houses...we stayed...block path...while he went...check. Found him, I guess...Great ball of fire...like Roman Candle. Way up above us...air seemed to disappear. Choking acid fumes. It was hell."

Alex patted Ari on the shoulder. "You hang in there! Check on Fes! I'll try and find Zack."

Alex turned off the flashlight as he approached the first house in the village. The sky was clear and the moonlight bright enough, in this more open area, for him to pick his way through the village. He checked the houses; all were empty. A quarter of a mile below the village, he came across two isolated stone cottages. The furthest from the bend of the Gorge had been lived in. He saw the remains of a fire, and some cans and other trash littered one room. Where was Zack? Puzzled, he looked across the Gorge. Moonlight illuminated the Church of Saint Maria. He picked his way over the riverbed and reached the church. He peered in. A figure was kneeling in front of the icon-covered screen. Alex spent a moment listening for the presence of a second person, before moving to the still figure. He shone his torch on the face. It was Zack! His mouth was gagged and his hands and legs were bound. The single word, TRAITOR, was written in blood on his forehead.

"My God, Zack! Let me get these ropes off." Alex released Zack rapidly.

Zack struggled to rise, stuck out his left leg and fell back. "Jesus Christ!"

Alex helped him to massage his legs, to restore the circulation.

"How do y'all feel?" Zack asked.

"Fes and Ari are okay. Dazed and breathless, but they'll survive. I was further away."

"Duke must have set the fireball to go off high, up the Gorge from the village, because he wasn't exactly sure where Ari and Fes were. I guess that saved them. Further away, by the church, we still felt the effect of the implosion. In fact, it caused Duke to fall over. He cut his hand on a rock. It was after that when he came back and wrote on my forehead. "You're a traitor, Zeus," he said. "I leave you here as a warning to all other traitors who follow. Next time I may have to kill you."

"Did he mean it?"

"I don't know." Zack sank back to the ground. "Now we have to start all over again to find him."

"There's some good news, Zack," Alex said.

"Like what? It didn't blow Ari's balls off?"

"Sam and Ion think they've found Europa in Matala." Alex continued. "I'll bet Duke will go down the Gorge to Agia Roumelli and work his way east to join her. That'll take time and we can catch up with him."

"Great!" Zack smiled. "We need to get away from here. When the word gets out about all those leaves being blown off the trees, the police and the press will be here. I don't know how long the Army investigators will keep out of it. I want to find Duke first."

Ari and Fes arrived.

"God, y'all look a mess!"

"Thanks a lot. Wait to talk. Still difficult to breathe," Ari rasped.

"Okay. I'll give my side of it. At the moment, Duke's nuts," Zack said, wearily. "He thinks we're here to hand him back to the Army. That girl Europa's got him all screwed up. Duke believes he has the divine duty to protect this island against the invaders. It's difficult to know even which millennium he inhabits. For God's sake! Sometimes he refers to them as Turks, sometimes as Hittites. I don't know what's happened to him. Maybe he has pressure on the brain from an accident or a tumor. Maybe that girl Europa's fed him drugs."

"Could be like a reaction to LSD?"

"I reckon so, Alex. I tried to calm him down. For some of the time he was rational. I felt I was making progress when suddenly he looked up at the Gorge. He was hyperaware, like an animal. Ari, Fes, I guess he saw or heard y'all. He knocked me down, tied me up and took me to that church. He said. 'You can't trick me, Zeus. I'm smart enough to outwit you.' Then he fired that device. It's got to be the plays…and the dance. He started when he was real young."

32. Phaestos

Alex waited until he could speak to Festus alone, and then whispered. "Something else came up at Matala which might interest you, Fes."

Festus looked at him patiently, waiting for the revelation. Alex smiled impishly. "Cathy Schmidt's there, camping with a girlfriend."

"What!"

"You're ex-girlfriend."

"I know who she is, for Christ sake! What's she doing here?"

"Marienna?" questioned Alex.

"Yes, that would make sense." Festus stopped to think. "What the hell do I do?"

"How about nothing? Let Marienna deal with it."

"I didn't mean that. Marienna may not let me do nothing."

"Fes, you're a big boy. You've got Dawn. You don't need to play around with little girls."

"How about little boys, Alex?"

"Cheap shot, Fes. I'm not married, and they're not little."

"Sorry. I'm still dizzy. Not thinking straight." Festus clasped his hands to his forehead, as if to press out his memories. "She helped me find Pandora. I can't ignore her."

"Fes, be careful!"

"About what?"

"You've got a good family life now. You may think clearly with the brains in your head, but you've a poor track record of thinking between your legs."

"Pan showed you the photos of me dancing at his club, didn't he?"

"Yes."

"But I didn't do anything"

"Just like with Seamus's photographs of Dawn?"

"Thanks for reminding me."

They rose early, and made their way slowly down the Gorge, passing through the Sidheroportes—Iron Gates—where the Gorge narrows to a few tens' of feet, and the cliffs tower a thousand or more feet above the riverbed. Festus had a brief feeling that he had been there before, but thoughts of Cathy distracted him. For the final mile to the village of Agia Roumelli, the Gorge widened to encompass a welter of oleander bushes. By the sea, near the ancient city of Tarrha, they had breakfast at a small taverna—goat's cheese, bread, grapes, tblack coffee and cool glasses of water.

Zack questioned the owner about Duke. Apparently, he had come crashing through the village sometime after dark, carrying two large suitcases. He had demanded a boat to take him to Khora Sfakion. They had told him there were no boats that late. However, he'd bought wine and had persuaded Spiros to take him.

"Where is Spiros?" Zack asked.

The owner shrugged his shoulders. He would be back later, he supposed.

"Did the boat, in fact, go to Khora Sfakion?" Alex questioned.

The owner shrugged again. "Why not?"

Festus managed to elicit one further piece of useful information, a description of Spiros' boat.

"All we can do is go on the assumption that he plans to join Europa near Matala. We can catch the first boat. They tell me it leaves around ten," Zack said.

Some hours later, they reached Khora Sfakion. In the harbor, snuggled against the quay, was Spiros' boat. Spiros was lying on the deck, snoring loudly. He was so drunk that it was only after extreme jostling that Ari could get any statement out of him, and then it was only the one slurred word, Phaestos.

The group conferred rapidly, and it was agreed that Festus and Alex should go on to Matala and investigate Phaestos from there. In the meantime, Ari would return to Khania to join Elena, Marienna, and the Dexters. There he would wait for a phone call to advise him whether to escort the Eurysthesians to Matala or to return to Iraklion. Since Zack had relatives in Khora Sfakion, it was clear that he had no choice but to visit them. Festus indicated that he and Alex would welcome the chance to rest before proceeding to Matala the next day. It seemed to him that Zack didn't like the idea, but Cretan traditions of courtesy prevailed, and so they accompanied him to the home of his godfather's son.

The gleaming, white, house was an extensive single story dwelling, perched high on the hill that rose steeply from the harbor. They entered through a door cut into a high stone wall to discover a small courtyard, ablaze with colorful plants. Leading off this courtyard, were a number of doors, a sure indication of the wealth of Zack's relatives. Festus wondered how much of the wealth derived from Texas. One of the doors led to a delightful room, bright with the color of woven rag rugs. The window offered a panoramic view of Khora Sfakian. The customary photographs of the family dotted the walls. Zack drew their attention to an ancient sepia colored print that showed Agamemnon Cronson and his first wife Olympia, the mother of Marienna and, later, of Festus. Festus had the eerie feeling that her eyes followed him around the room, as if she wanted to tell him something. He backed away, through an archway, into the kitchen, and was amused to see that its traditional, whitewashed, open-fireplace had been supplemented by a less traditional butane gas cooker.

Though their hosts were charming, and inundated them with food and drink, Festus could sense that they were uneasy. Zack steadfastly refused to discuss the real reason for their presence in Crete, and Festus gave up trying to introduce the topic. It was a pleasant night, warm and not particularly humid. Since the house was full, Alex and he followed the Cretan custom and slept on the flat roof, sharing it with a small field of drying almonds. He lay for a long time, looking up at the stars, worrying about Zack, and trying to work out what he could be hiding. He slept fitfully until, suddenly, his dreams drifted into soothing images of Cathy. The images still dominated his thoughts as he descended sleepily to find breakfast. He was surprised to find Spiros, who was snacking on bread and smoked fish.

"Hey, Spiros! I want to ask you something."

Spiros looked uneasy and pushed past Festus as he ran from the house.

Zack came in as Festus was finishing his coffee.

"I just saw Spiros."

"What did he say?"

"Nothing. He ran away."

"I see." Zack selected some food, sat down, and started eating. He remained silent. Festus shook his head and left.

By late afternoon, Festus and Alex reached Matala and the spot where Ionides and Samantha were camping.

"Have you seen Duke?"

"No." Ionides shook his head.

"Taking everything into account, we expected him to come here."

"Well, he may be coming," said Sam, "but Europa has gone. She moved nearer Phaestos. She's on her own, though."

Festus seemed relieved. "That makes sense. Spiros, the boatman, mentioned Phaestos."

"There has been talk around here about a strange wind that blew all the leaves off trees in Samaria. Did Duke use the Bullroarer," Ionides asked.

"Yup," Festus said.

"Oh, sha-it! I hear the police are investigating"

"We reckoned they would. That's why we need to work fast. Get everyone to come to Phaestos." Festus paused. "I hear Cathy Schmidt is here?"

"We haven't talked to her for a couple of days, Fes. She and her friend Billy may have gone to Iraklion. I think Billy has to get back to the army soon."

"Oh! I see. What's Billy like?"

"Pretty solid looking. Reminds me a bit of aunt Angelica. If you know what I mean?"

"That adds up," said Festus, thoughtfully.

In the late morning, the group gathered at the foot of the northwest staircase in the palace of Phaestos—the sometime home of King Rhadamanthys, brother of King Minos of Knossos. It was becoming hot and they were grateful for the cool fruit drink that Marienna had brought. She had disappeared on some errand. Minutes earlier, they had stood in the shelter of the tourist pavilion watching Europa arrive and descend the steps into the palace. She moved slowly, apparently studying each aspect with great interest.

At the bottom of the staircase, Festus turned left up the Grand Stairway and climbed to the Propylon. He followed Europa through the double porch of what had been an impressive entrance hall. She hesitated then turned right down to the central courtyard. The Eurysthesians, approaching from different directions, followed her in sheep-like fashion. She stood in the middle of the courtyard—her head bowed, as if in prayer. The Eurysthesians filed around the outside of the courtyard, uncertain what to do.

"It's like performing in one of Marienna's plays or that Royal Cretan dance," Elena whispered to Zack, "but without Marienna's directions."

"It looks like we all feel the same way," Zack replied, watching his family spread out as if it had been choreographed.

Zack and Elena took up a position at the far northern end, backing the corridor that leads to the quarters of the king. Ari was to their left and beyond him were Ionides and Samantha. Harold and Peri moved down to the right hand side. Festus and Alex moved slowly to the southern end of the courtyard and turned to face Europa. Alex crossed himself, surreptitiously. Some way behind them, Marienna approached quietly with Cathy. Marienna signaled to Ionides and Samantha not to give away their presence. Zack broke hthe silence. "Where's my son, Duke." He moved at a steady pace towards Europa. For Festus, this one action altered the atmosphere of the palace. The temperature seemed to drop. For a second the scene became still while, to him, all of the players made the transition to the past.

He could hear a rhythmic drumming. Pipes picked up the insistent rhythm. The girl turned and looked at the king. She smiled triumphantly. "He's not here. He was never here. We tricked you." As she spoke, her body swayed gently, rhythmically. She hummed the repetitive melody and turned, shuffling her feet, to face each side of the courtyard in turn. Her action strengthened the fantasy and the palace itself appeared to reconstitute around them. To the east, the pillars, alternately round and square, stood supporting the multi-storied buildings. To the west, the walls rose up. A gentle wind rustled the tunics of the spectators.

Hephaestus watched as King Rhadamanthys returned to the raised section near his quarters. He stood majestically, his crown high on his leonine head. "Would you defy your king?" He said. "Deucalion must answer for his crimes."

"My lord Rhadamanthys, he seeks only to protect the kingdom from those Hittites who would invade it," said the girl.

"Nobody would dare attack," said Ares, grimly. "We are too powerful. Such an attack would mean only destruction for the invaders."

"You have grown fat and weak and careless, Ares," said the girl scornfully. "Look at you—an overweight soldier, an aged embalmer, a crippled smith. We are young and strong. We have weapons. We will repel the Hittites."

Rhadamanthys winced. His face showed his pain. "You know what action I must take to test you," he said, wearily.

The girl's face whitened. "Yes," she whispered, "the dancing floor…but who will dance with me?"

Another mortal girl walked forward. "I will take the other side."

Hephaestus started forward involuntarily, and then turned away. Tears coursed down his cheeks. He felt helpless.

"So be it," said the king. "Clear the area."

The two girls moved to the center of the courtyard. They were dressed in flounced skirts, with bodices that caused their breasts to thrust out suggestively. In contrast, they bowed their heads, demurely, so that the spectators could see only their elaborately curled hair, and the gold filigree thath adorned it. The spectators retreated to the refuge offered by the pillars. There was a hushed silence, from which a slow rhythmic chant grew in consonance with the pipes and drums. The girls began to glide gracefully outwards, first diagonally and then parallel to the sides on an apparently predestined motion, away from each other and away from the center. Their skirts swung gently in sympathy with the rhythm. As each progressed, she dropped flowers to mark her spiral path.

They had completed two tight spirals when the rhythm of the chant changed. The atmosphere became tense. At the northeastern end of the yard, bronze doors opened slowly. Hephaestus saw a shape emerge from the dark void. The massive shadow remained still, except for a pawing motion. Suddenly, irritated by some combination of color and shape, it charged. The acrobats, who had appeared from behind the pillars, moved quickly, luring it away from the dancers. All the time, the two girls, their eyes downcast, shuffled rhythmically on their preset pattern. The dark shape cavorted and joined in the mad dance. The acrobats worked hard, distracting the "Bringer of

Death". The spectators and courtiers, held by the spectacle, stood frozen in their places, willing their favorite to complete the dance.

The whole mad scene came to an abrupt stop when a group of people, seemingly oblivious of the danger, walked onto the dance floor and gazed curiously at the king, the acrobats and the dancers. They seemed unaware of the "Bringer of Death" and, curiously, it was no longer there.

Europa disappeared back through the western court. Festus fainted. The Eurysthesians looked at each other in bewilderment.

"Are you okay, Fes?" Zack said, helping him to his feet. Marienna joined them.

"I'm still too shaken to think straight. I saw the dance and the bull, but it wasn't there."

"You weren't alone, Henry," Marienna interjected. "I sense that some part of the ordained past was missed and it's waiting to take its rightful place in history." She paused. "You know. I had that feeling when I was writing the plays."

"I wondered why you dressed like some modern day goddess," Zack snapped. Flowing robes and the like." He threw back his head and laughed. "Hell! Maybe you are Athena?"

Peri, prompted by Marienna, told of her reactions on the dancing floor at Knossos. "It was terrible. I knew I had to follow this pattern, but I couldn't remember it all. So, I did the steps from your dance, Marienna. I remember you told me it was important in the old days, otherwise the acrobats lead the "Bringer of Death" in the wrong direction. She shook her head in a bewildered fashion. "What do I mean by Bringer of Death?"

"You mean the bull," Harold said, softly.

"Oh, Harold!" said Peri, taking his hand, "I'm glad you understand. I was worried it was just me." For once, Harold did not make a sarcastic comment but smiled understandingly at her.

"One thing that surprises me," Festus added, "is how Europa and Cathy became involved. "Can you tell us how you felt, Cathy?"

"I didn't feel anything. I just tdid my part in Marienna's dance."

"Duke must have put Europa up to it. He's been in the dance. They were making fun of us, I guess." Elena sounded unhappy. "Alex, how about you?"

"It's hazy, but there was something. It's as if I'm acting out the plays and the dance in real life." Alex looked around. Ionides was scratching his head. "How about you, Ion?"

To cover his embarrassment, Ionides answered with an exaggerated Texan accent. "Ah don't know what y'all's talking about. I was wurtching Europa and she started this real weird dai-ance. Like tha-it daince of Aunt Marienna. The rest of y'all acted real strange too. Nobody spoke. Thai-n Europa ran away and Fes fainted. I reckon Fes got a terch of the su-rn."

"Any other thoughts," Zack asked. Nobody responded. "I don't like to disturb you, but we gotta return to our quest. We didn't find Duke. Do you have any ideas, Fes?"

"It goes back to our encounter with Duke. I was so dazed I wasn't thinking straight. The question to answer is…why was he in the Gorge of Samaria? He wasn't just camping there for the hell of it. He must have been waiting for somebody or some people. He made us think that he was coming here to Phaestos. This means that Spiros, that apparently drunken Sfakian fisherman, is in on the game. Now, it makes sense if Duke, with his Sfakian heritage, has persuaded some of them to join him in his crazy venture. Sfakians have always been ready to fight invaders—pnotably the Turks. They murdered our hero, Daskaloyiannis. Right, Zack? From all this I conclude that Duke was in the Gorge waiting for recruits and waiting for his nationalist or terrorist allies. It would be easy for them to come in unnoticed as tourists. That leaves us with the question of where he was going to take them. My guess is somewhere between the Gorge and Khora Sfakion, up in the mountains. Probably not too far from the coast to allow them to ship in arms easily." Festus looked at Zack searchingly. "Did your godfather's son know anything?"

Zack took a long time answering the question and, when he did, he sounded apologetic. "He's an old man Fes. I really didn't discuss it much. As to my other relatives, they're just simple folk, you know. I don't want to worry them." Zack changed the subject. "I suggest that some of us go to Khora Sfakion and look around. I think we should camp because I'm convinced that eventually we'll have to go into the mountains to find Duke. We don't have enough camping equipment so I recommend that the women go back to Iraklion. Alex and Harold can accompany them."

"No! That's not acceptable, Zachary. Hell! I may be old, but I'm quite capable of walking a long way, if I take it steadily." Marienna continued in a slightly more conciliatory tone. "You seem to forget, I'm family."

Zack smiled sympathetically at his half-sister. "You're right, Marienna. We Cretans tend to be too protective of our women. God knows why? You're tougher than we are. Let's all go. Is that agreed?"

Harold Dexter looked dubious. "I'm not sure Zack. After that performance…" Peri glared steadily at him. "Okay, I guess I'm overruled. We'll all go."

Zack continued. "It's not practical for all to go immediately. I think most of you should remain near here for the moment. Let Festus, Ionides, and Sam go to Khora Sfakion. I'll go back to Iraklion with Ari and buy some camping equipment. We'll all meet in Khora Sfakion in a couple of days."

"Cathy can you come with me? I can use some help."

"I'm not sure, Marienna," Cathy answered. "I'll have to check with my friend. What do you think, Fes?"

Zack saved him from having to answer. "Cathy, I would sure appreciate it if you would stay with us to help Marienna. I'll arrange for your friend, so she's not bored. It'll only be a couple of days." He turned and whispered to Ari. "Gotta keep her away from other people." Ari nodded agreement.

33. The Dancing Floor

"We're camped down by the sea just beyond Loutro, Zack," Ionides said on meeting him. "We're in the ruins of the ancient port city of Phoenix."

"Yeah, whatever!" Zack growled. "It was a hell of job findin' more camping gear. Had to go to Iraklion. I'm tired of luggin' it around. How do we get there?"

"By boat to Loutro." Ionides explained.

"Why Phoenix?"

"I'm not sure why Fes chose the spot except that he's been studying some maps and history books and has convinced himself that it's the place to be. I'm skeptical. The whole area is quite wild, a lot of it is barren and the few people that we've seen don't look to me like the makings of a revolution. But far be it for me to disagree with the master." Zack looked at Ari and raised his eyebrows. Ari glowered.

After they reached the dock at Loutro, there was a trek of a mile to the camp. They were all exhausted from the weight of the equipment and the heat by the time they reached the three tents, perched on a small promontory above a sharp drop to the sea. Cathy came out of one of them, blinking in the sun. She was wearing shorts and a bikini top. A few seconds later Festus emerged and flapped his hand. He appeared uneasy.

Ari greeted him warmly. "See you're organized, Fes. Look after him, Cathy! Undomesticated on his own."

Festus pointed at the other tents. "This is Marienna's and Cathy's tent and I think Ion and I can look after ours. Thank you."

"Whatever," Zack showed no interest.

"Let me summarize our situation," said Festus, sipping some wine.

"Leave us alone!" Alex muttered. "Marienna had the right idea, bringing this great red wine from Gortys. I don't even mind the plastic bottles."

Festus grunted. "I believe Duke will be found somewhere near here between Agia Roumelli and Khora Sfakion—but where? It seems he was camped in the Gorge of Samaria waiting for recruits. Would they come? Certainly, the gypsies in Khania didn't take him seriously. I guess there may be a few, though that fisherman Spiros is the only one we've seen." Festus paused, searching for the right words. "Zack, are you really sure he hasn't contacted your relatives? I find it..."

"I told you before Fes. I don't want my relatives brought into this," Zack replied, angrily. "Our job is to find Duke and...you know...before that girl Europa makes him do something stupid."

Festus wasn't happy with the response. Every time he raised the question of the relatives, Zack evaded giving an answer. He waited, hoping that someone else would challenge Zack. There was silence.

"Well, seeing that's all clear, let me move on to the next point," Festus continued. "I can't believe that his main camp was in the Gorge. It's far too public. Samaria may be abandoned, but there is a continuous stream of tourists passing down the Gorge right now. Remember that Duke's a professional soldier. He'd never leave himself so open all the time."

Zack looked troubled. "Are you saying that he could be anywhere up in those mountains behind us? Goddamn it! We'll never find him."

"No, I think that there are only a few places he could be. I believe history will guide us to him." Festus paused. "I should level with you; otherwise you'll believe I can work magic. There's a boat in the next cove. I think it's Spiros' boat. Duke will need a route out of here if there's trouble. If I work back from the coast up into the hills, I come to Aradin. See here?" He pointed to the map.

"So what?" Ari argued.

"So, tomorrow we'll go there and hopefully we'll be able to find him. I'm particularly curious about the site the Dance of the Hellenes. I should warn you, it's going to be quite a climb. So rest well!"

The morning sun had not appeared when they rose and started their trek up into the hills, carrying their camping gear. The track was rough and the going arduous in the deep ravine that led to Aradin, two thousand feet above the sea. Zack walked sulkily, showing his frustration by kicking stones off the path. His tent had collapsed during the night, as he and Elena were engaged in some serious lovemaking. He had not been able to finish. He and Elena concluded it was one of Festus's idiotic practical jokes. Damn him! In fact, as Elena would find out later, Alex Platon had rigged the tent pegs to fail.

"Won't he know we're coming, Fes?" Asked Harold, incredulously. "A party of…uhm…middle-aged relics like ourselves can hardly have gone unnoticed. Surely he has contacts in Loutro and Anapolis?"

"I'm sure he does know, Harold, but he doesn't know what we're going to do. We do know Duke. Zack, Elena and I reckon he'll wait."

"Do 'we' understand what you've asked us to do?" Harold asked.

"Yes, Harold, I think you do. Please trust me!" Harold looked unhappy, but under warning glances from Zack and Alex, he kept quiet.

"We're being watched," said Alex, quietly, as they worked their way up the ravine.

"Ignore it!" Zack replied. They continued in single file, their heads lowered, like monks in meditation. In fact, the only visible signs of life were the ever-present goats, black ones, brown ones, white ones, and ones with every conceivable combination of those colors. Goats, it seemed, were occupying every nook and cranny of the hills and cliffs that surrounded them. Just before they reached the head of the ravine, Alex handed Festus the extra backpack he'd been carrying for him and then dropped back. The rest of the party carried on, picking their way over the stony path until finally they reached the small village of Aradena and beyond it found the ruins of Aradin.

There were the remnants of walled fields and a few scattered stands of firs around the site. The ground, red clay covered in rocks and scrub was a contrast to the smooth chalky peaks that overlooked them from the north. Holes marked the place occupied, originally, by a majestic stand of pillars. Behind these holes was a large, flat, circular area that had recently been cleared. The cleared surface was made from large, worn stones. Some showed signs of a pattern. Some stones were missing so that the floor had the appearance of a patchwork quilt and the original pattern was hard to see.

The Eurysthesians followed the earlier instructions of Festus. Zack and Elena moved to the northern end of the circle. Ari, Ion and Sam carried on into the hills above the ruins, Harold and Peri took a place around the circumference to the east, with Marienna to their right and Cathy to their left. Finally, at the southern end of the circle, Festus stood, staring grimly up at the sky. His open backpack lay by his feet. Faint sounds came from their surroundings, indicating the watchers were approaching for a closer look.

As the sun rose, the shadows withdrew across the ring. Zack looked up and spoke. He had difficulty with his speech, initially, stumbling over the half-remembered words that Festus had suggested to him. "My kingdom is troubled. Rumors of invasion are being spread." To Festus the scene flickered, the outlines of ancient columns appeared, and it was Rhadamanthys speaking. "*There are those who say the Hittites will invade. Others say that these stories are lies put about by those who question my authority. Some say that my son is involved.*" His eyes shone as the sun caught them. "*There is a way to test this, laid down by the gods. We are here by the dancing floor. Who will dance for me?*"

The young girl looked uncertainly towards Hephaestus. He motioned her to be still. There was a long silence. Then, Persephone, ignoring the imploring glances of her husband, swayed forward to the center of the circle and faced the King.

"Who will challenge me?" Zack spoke quietly. There was no reply. The scene flickered between past and present.

He repeated the question, louder. "Who will challenge me?"

There was no reply but there were shuffling sounds. Suddenly, there were more spectators gathered around the edge of the circle, interspersed with the Eurysthesians. Their tunics were rougher, denoting a lower station in life.

He shouted again. "Who will challenge me?"

Hephaestus watched as, from out of the shadows to the, west a giant of a man emerged. He was dressed in a purple tunic. A golden skin was draped across his back and a wreath of olive leaves circled his tight black curls. Europa stood by his side. She was wearing a simple white tunic with flowers garlanded across her shoulders and in her hair.

"*She will challenge you. I Deucalion say it. She will challenge you.*" *The ritual test was accepted.*

Europa, like Persephone before her, swayed gently to the center of the ring. The floor appeared smoother now and Hephaestus could see patterns spiraling from the center. The acrobats materialized out of the sun's rays to the east and stood expectantly by the side of the ring. Rhadamanthys raised his arms. "Let the dance begin!"

Hephaestus could hear a rhythmic drumming. The pipes echoed the beat. The spectators chanted with the music. The two women, swaying gently, glided out on the spiral path away from the center and away from each other. The spectators marked their progress by the symbols on the floor, the first sickle, the first soldier, the first sheaf of corn, and so on. They had reached the first soldier, as tradition required, before the large dark shape emerged from the shadows. The garlands of flowers around the massive neck only served to make its presence more ominous. It stood uncertainly in the sunlight. The eyes picked up the movement of the dancers and it glanced up balefully, shuffling its front feet in irritation. The great head lowered again and the sunken eyes peered out from under the dark hair. For a moment, it stood motionless. At this time, the acrobats, experienced in judging the critical moment, moved into their positions on the grid, spaced out on circles about the center of the ring. The creature reacted and charged at the nearest girl. The crowd hushed. Hephaestus could see that Persephone had sensed their reaction and was aware of the threat that approached her. Persephone looked pale and was having difficulty moving along the dancing path. The acrobats worked hard, running across the path of the bull, flaunting themselves. The bull appeared to be confused and stopped uncertainly, snorting with fury. A young girl vaulted over the lowered horns. She was naked except for a loincloth and halter, with flowers in her hair and her breasts thrust up by a halter. She lay briefly on its broad back before flipping off gracefully. Hephaestus prayed that Persephone would follow her pattern and not falter. He knew that if she stopped then she would lose and certain death would follow, for all the other players would leave.

The bull showed its anger. It charged again, blindly. More garlands, placed by the acrobats, flew up in front of its eyes and obscured its sight. The bull barely missed Europa. It was distracted when an acrobat jumped on its back. His lithe brown body clung to the bull's neck. His bracelets and necklace, and the sealstone, attached by a cord to his wrist, glinted wildly in the sun as the beast reared. He pulled on the left horn, causing it to veer back into the center of the floor. The bull, furious at the weight of the acrobat, tossed its head angrily and then made the move, which held terror for the players. It rolled. The boy, still off balance, scrambled to get away—no longer elegant, just fighting for survival. He nearly succeeded but the massive head had trapped his legs. The Bringer of Death came to its feet quickly. It swung around and gored the prostrate figure, viciously. At the north end Persephone, unnoticed by the bull, was about to finish her pattern. The bull turned to the south end of the ring, where Europa, head bent, was also near to completing her orbit. The acrobats, spread to thinly across the dancing floor, did not divert the bull when it charged again. The spectators and the helpless acrobats froze in fear. Only Persephone and Europa moved.

Hephaestus could see that Europa would die and Persephone would finish her dance. Rhadamanthys smiled triumphantly and raised his arms in triumph.

Europa could feel the creature bearing down on her. Her time had come. She sank to her knees, waiting for the inevitable.

The heavens exploded with a brilliant light. A great wind rushed upwards from the ring. A cloud of dust rose. Hephaestus, his eyes lowered, his hands over his mouth and nose, ran towards the prostrate figure of Europa. The creature, its breathing labored, struggled slowly forwards and sank to its knees beside them.

Festus put his arms across the massive shoulders, and pushed his oxygen mask onto the lowered face. "The game's over, Duke. You've got to go. Quickly, before they all wake up."

"Dad always wins. You know, I did it all for him. The Bullroarer was payment for the secret." Duke laughed, bitterly. "It's all crazy. They don't know the secret. Nobody does anymore. It's all talk."

"No Duke, I'm not sure it's all talk. Some other time we'll discuss it. For now, you need to get out of here. I'm worried there may be agents of the U.S. army around. I'm amazed they've left us alone. Take Europa and go! Spiros is waiting below." Duke nodded his head slowly. Festus handed him the oxygen mask that had protected him this time from the ravages of the weapon. "You'll need this to help you carry Europa. We'll return the Bullroarer. Your father thinks he can use it to help get you a deal. Whatever you may think, Zack loves you, Duke. Never question that!"

Deucalion looked at Festus anxiously. "I don't know whether to believe that." He picked up Europa and staggered down the path to the sea. Festus watched him leave. In fact, Festus was certain that Zack cared for nobody except himself when the chips were down—not Elena or even little Duke. Why should Duke believe it?

Some time passed. Duke's few followers reeled away, carrying a boy with a twisted ankle. There was no interest or ability to chase them, for breathing was too difficult. Ari, Ion and Samantha appeared. Ari was carrying a large case. They looked for Festus and were surprised to find him lying in the ring. Ionides and Ari rushed to his side. Festus was reclining on the ground, his head propped up by his right hand. He glanced around when they approached. "It went well. That Bullroarer's really sumthin'. Thank God, I was ready for it! Any trouble finding the thing?"

"Did what you said, Doc," Ari replied, looking pleased with himself. "Watched where Duke came from. Tracked back from there. He'd left it back of Dancing Floor, by some trees. Didn't bother about old Aristotle. Instructions on lid. Typical army jargon. Simple for soldier like me. Set it to go off high up. Like you said."

"You did it just right."

"It was weird," said Ionides. "All I could see was a burnch of silly looking people cavortin' spastically on the floor. With Duke, tearing around like a drurnk animal. One of those Sfakian collided with him and seemed to twist his ankle. Duke kicked the sha-it out of him. He's crazy. I thought of doin' somethin'. Then you signaled and Ari fahred. Were people in a trance again, like at Phaestos? Didn't y'all see it like tha-it, Ari?"

It was curious that he and Ion did not see the same images, Festus thought. Maybe, Ion had not spent enough time in the play cycle, and he had never done Marienna's dance.

"Don't know what I saw," Ari replied. "I was concentrating on the weapon. Can Marienna explain it? I think Duke accepted a challenge and lost. Now he's gone. We have the Bullroarer. That was our mission. We can go home."

Zack and the rest of the Eurythesians came up. "Who fired the Bullroarer?" Zack asked, angrily.

"Ari did," said Festus quickly. "We have it here."

"Why the fuck did he do that! I was winning."

"We agreed, Zack. Win what?"

Suddenly Zack looked bewildered and old. "I don't know, Fes. Where is…"

"Duke's gone down to the sea with Europa," Alex said.

"I guess it's too late to follow."

"I think so," Festus commented, curtly. "It's too late for many things. One day you're going to pay for your grandiose schemes, Zachary Cronson, or Rhadamanthys, or Zeus, or whoever the hell you are. God knows what you'll lead us into."

"Lay off, Fes! I don't need a lecture from you. Particularly now, when I don't know where the hell Duke's going. Just remember who supports your research! I think you'll come to see it my way. There's a great treasure here." Zack strode away, imperiously giving orders to show his power. "I'm going to find it, and you're going to help me, Henry Everett Festus, or Hephaestus, or whoever the hell you think you are. Just be ready when I need you!"

Festus joined his fellow Eurythesians and they returned to the campsite above the sea. In the distance, a small boat was disappearing towards the horizon. Those with good eyesight claimed they could see Deucalion and Europa aboard.

Festus and Cathy walked down to the beach. Laid out on the path to the cove that had sheltered Spiros' boat, were gray pebbles marking the words "Farewell Phaes". By it was a crude drawing, scratched in the dirt, of a bull with a girl astride its back. Festus stood looking at it distractedly. Patterns on the ground, he thought. "The pattern on the dancing floor, Cathy. It's trying to tell me something. All of this is planned." He stopped, remembering the girl acrobat on the dancing floor. "You knew what you had to do in the dance, didn't you?"

Cathy looked uncertain. "I felt really light headed. Like I'd had too much to drink. I seemed to be following a pattern I'd learned." She laughed. "Sort of a cheerleading routine."

"You looked really sexy." Festus motioned with his hands, indicating how he had imagined her breasts in the dance. "It reminded me of the first time we did 'Hephaestus and the Cretans." I…"

"Fes, is there an 'us' in real life, or is it only in the plays?"

"I've sometimes had trouble in telling what's real. Not this time. Dawn and Pandora are real, and I don't want to screw that up again." He tried to make it easier for her. "I'm a lot older than you. You hinted at it in your letter. Do you really want an old cripple like me?"

"Don't be so silly! My letter was stupid. Your athletic prowess is not in question. I had a hard time keeping up with you in bed. I suppose I owe that to Dawn. Shit! What a ghastly thought." Cathy looked at him sadly. "The bottom line is that you won't leave Dawn!"

"Dawn and I are back for good. I made a lot of mistakes. What about you and Billy?"

"Oh! You know. It isn't working out. I'm so confused." Cathy started to cry, then regained control. "I'm going to chuck my job in Germany and return to Texas. Marienna says she'll help me find a job. I guess I'll see you in Argos." Cathy left abruptly before he could say anything."

Marienna Cronson, yes that makes sense, thought Festus. He could picture her translating the plays, subtly changing them and in so doing manipulating their lives. Could this puppet mistress get him a release from Zack's clutches? Not yet, he guessed. Not until the Labors were completed. He, Festus, had to solve the puzzle of the Phaestos Disk. Find the treasure for Zachary-Rhadaman-thys—but what treasure, and why the Disk?

34. Nightmares

The Cretan business was over. At least for the time being. However, Duke was still missing. Zack had told Festus that the army was so relieved to see their weapon returned that they were prepared to deal somewhat leniently with him when he resurfaced. His life was back to normal, Festus thought, contentedly. He was doing research. His marriage was going well. Dawn was happy studying part-time at the university and doing some interior decorating projects. Pandora was now finishing her second year at Stimpson College. She would transfer soon to the University of Texas in Austin, to be near Chuck. Festus and Dawn approved of him. He was a steadying influence on their daughter. However, Dawn was not happy that Ari's devious son, Demosthenes, was involved in one of Pandora's activities—the Central America Club. She mistrusted anything involving him.

Demos had discovered a fascinating book, from the 1920s, in the library at the University of Texas. In the book, two newlywed teachers described their trek across the Isthmus of Tehuantepec in southern Mexico. They were weak from some illness, when they chanced upon a remote village. The villagers welcomed them as if they were gods. The headman treated their illness with locally developed drugs. While recuperating they made their discovery; a fabulous, ancient city existed near the village. They villagers gave them gold ornaments as parting gifts.

The Club members analyzed the book carefully. The young couple had landed in Puerto Arista on the Pacific Coast of the State of Chiapas. Their adventures occurred in the northern end of the mountains of the Sierra Madre, as they tried to reach the state capital, Tuxtla Gutierrez. They had left whatever road there was and had tried to take a more direct route over the mountains. It seemed that they might have found their way to the valley of the Suchiapa River. It descends on the eastern side of the mountains to join the Grijalva River, near Tuxtla. The members decided to explore this river valley and look for the lost city.

The Club decided to sponsor a few members to make a quick, two to three week search, after the spring semester. Pandora and her cousin, Rosalie, the daughter of Panou Cronson were included. Festus was nearly as excited about the expedition as Pandora.

Unfortunately, Dawn's concerns were justified. Two days after the expedition returned, she had not heard from Pandora. She telephoned a number of times before Pandora answered. Pandora had been generally vague about the trip, except to say they had seen some ruins. She apologized for not calling home. "We've been working on our report…sorta."

"Why, sorta?"

"Some of us have been ill. It's only a minor fever, Mom."

"I talked to Pandy," Dawn said, when she called Festus at his office.

"How is she?" Festus asked, continuing his study of the Disk. "Did they find any ruins?"

"I think so," Dawn said, uncertainly. "But Pandora was very vague about it"

"Oh," said Festus, continuing his attempt to assign meanings to the symbols.

"She's ill," Dawn spoke sharply, realizing that Festus was not paying attention.

"Ill! That's curious." Festus sat up. "What do you want to do?"

"Go to Stimpson as soon as possible."

"I agree. Pack some stuff for me in case we have to stay the night!" Festus shouted into the intercom. "Sam, get Ion! I have to go out of town."

Some five hours later, Festus and Dawn reached the apartment that Pandora and Rosalie shared in Stimpson.

"We found it, Dad," Pandora said, pride showing in her voice. Festus was about to ask what they had found when Pandora's eyes became vacant. "They wanted to sacrifice us. Keep it away!" she cried weakly and fell back onto the sofa, apparently asleep.

Dawn rushed to Pandora's side and felt her forehead. She was not feverish. A moaning sound coming from the bedroom interrupted their attempts to wake Pandora. Dawn held Pandora while Festus went to investigate. As his eyes became accustomed to the dark, the scene came into focus. Rosalie lay, apparently naked, under a tangle of sheets. Her open eyes stared through him. As if his entry into the room were a cue, for which she had been waiting, she began to move her hips. "Take me," she moaned. "Take me now, oh great god. I am prepared and cleansed, I await your embrace!"

"Dawn, get in here!"

Suddenly, Rosalie stopped writhing. Now she was looking at Festus. "What the hell are you doing in my bedroom?" she shouted. "Get out…you Peeping Tom…you." Rosalie's voice tailed away as some memory of the previous scene filtered into her consciousness. "Oh God! What happened to me?" Rosalie looked frightened and curled up protectively, trying to cover herself.

Dawn peered round the door. "It's me, Rosie. Dawn. We've come to help you."

"Oh! Dawn. The nightmares, are they real? I'm so tired." Rosie looked distressed. "We found the city, you know. Then, all of tour tapes and films were destroyed. No one will believe us."

"Fes, we can't handle this. It looks like they've been on drugs."

"Demos?"

"Could be."

"I want to get them back to Argos. Deal with it in the family." Dawn nodded.

"What about the rest of the expedition?"

"They've got problems too," Pandora answered.

"Does Chuck know about this?" Festus asked. Pandora shook her head.

"Has he been down to see you?"

"He wanted too, but I told him I was too busy. He was pissed off."

"Hmm. I think you did the right thing. It's probably better not to say anything. I'll assign him stuff to keep him busy in Austin. Better to keep things in the family."

"Chuck is sorta family, Dad."

"Not yet."

Festus telephoned Zack and spoke at length. He called and asked Ionides to come to Stimpson immediately. By the time he had made these and other calls, Pandora had recovered slightly.

"We need help. There's something terribly wrong with all of us. The boys don't show it as badly as Rosie or me, but we're all getting these nightmares, and they're getting worse."

Dawn put her arms around Pandora and comforted her. "I'm amazed Panou hasn't found out, he's so protective of Rosie. Do any of the parents know about this?"

"I don't think so. They all knew we'd be at Stimpson's to write our papers and then stay on into the summer semester. The boys are seniors and sort of independent of their families. Even Demos, except you know how Aunt Yianna fusses over him," Pandora laughed, "but Greek girls like Rosie and...I...are still watched closely by our families."

"Can you think of any reason why the nightmares are worse now?" Festus asked.

"It's weird, but it does seem to get worse when I try to write up our discoveries," she laughed, nervously. "It wasn't too bad when I tried travelogue. When I try to concentrate on what we found, my mind goes fuzzy and I see these awful images. I'm getting to the state now when I can't remember what's real and what's a fantasy. Maybe the whole thing was a fantasy brought on by our illness?"

"Why didn't you call us?"

"Oh, Mom, that's simple. We thought the nightmares would go away and we agreed to handle it ourselves. The state you're seeing Rosie in is something new. She was fine when Uncle Pan phoned, soon after we came back. He's away on business now, which I guess is the reason he hasn't called again. I was getting round to calling you, but somehow I got confused. I'm glad you're here."

"I'm still surprised some parents haven't found out."

"Come on, Dad, who's going to tell on us. We thought we could handle it. We were wrong. Can you help?"

"I hope so. Zack has agreed that you can all stay at his ranch for a few days while we try to work things out. What I need is for you to get hold of those other two boys and persuade them to come. They can tell their parents you've invited them to Argos for a bit of relaxation and to finish their reports. I'll work on Demos.

Ionides arrived and took the girls and Dawn to Argos. The boys agreed to the plan. Festus had no success with Demos. Unfortunately, Ari Cronson was still away on business. Festus, who did not want to deal with Demos's mother, Yianna, made a call to Zack. Fifteen minutes later, Zack called him back.

"The little bastard will be here."

"What did you say?"

"Enough. I got hold of Ari and Pan, they're coming."

"What about medical help?"

"Elena called Doc Maximos. He deals with drug problems all the time. He's on his way from San Antone."

"Thanks."

"That's what family is for, Fes. We all have to help each other. Don't forget it!"

The padrone has spoken, thought Fes. He is right.

The members of the expedition gathered in the den at Zack's ranch. Pandora and Rosie were on a sofa. Demos Cronson, Jack Mathews and Dieter Newhart were slouching in easy chairs. Dawn shared another sofa with Doc Maximos. Elena, Yianna, and Ari were sitting to the side. Ionides was hovering in the background, tending to some hidden tape recorders. Zack and Festus stood by the fireplace. Panou Cronson had not arrived yet. Festus brooded over the comments made by Doc Maximos, after he had made a brief examination of the members of the expedition.

"I treat far too many of the kids who go down to Mexico to try some dumb mushroom or cactus. They think it's fashionable. Generally, they don't have much and there are no long-lasting effects. These kids seem to be in deeper trouble. The symptoms are similar to prolonged use of something like LSD. Hallucinations are generally temporary but they do reoccur. In this case, it's like a mixture of drugs and brainwashing. From what I've heard, the nightmares may be triggered by any attempt on their part to remember too much about what happened." Doc shrugged, expressing his concern. *"Hopefully we can learn more from questioning them. Be careful to build up to the final part of their trip slowly or you may push them into hallucinating! Unless you can come up with some clear answers and a solution to the problem, I strongly recommend we send them for tests at a center specializing in drug problems. I'm not sure how much I can help."*

Now, seated in the den, Festus watched the young faces closely, looking for clues, as the questioning began. Zack placed one of the Spanish chairs in front of the fireplace and straddled it, his arms resting on the back. "We'd better start now. Jack, you were leader of the expedition. Why don't you kick off? The rest of you should leave. It'll be more useful if each account is independent. We'll let you know when we're ready for you."

Festus watched Jack straighten up in his chair. It was interesting how Jack's small, neat appearance gave, at first glance, the misleading impression of softness. Yet, Festus could see that the clean sneakers and well-pressed jeans and shirt covered a tough, wiry physique. The carefully combed brown hair, soft brown eyes and smiling face hid a tough and determined personality. Jack started slowly, recounting how they had analyzed the book and narrowed down the area where the explorers might have traveled. "We got a lot of support from the College." Jack smiled. "The bursar was as excited as we were about the possible findings. We also got funding from a Mexican archaeological society."

"That's interesting Jack, but can you say something about finding the book and getting the grant.

"I'm sorry, Dr. Festus, I should have given credit to Demos for setting this up. He has a small grant to study Southern Mexico and its languages and customs. He did a fantastic job. Why, the society even provided a guide."

"Thanks, Jack. I just wanted to be sure that I'd got it right. Please carry on."

"We drove down in two, four-wheel drive, Jeeps. We left early and took a small detour so we could visit the Olmec remains at Tres Zapotes and La Venta. Pandy and Rosie hadn't seen them, and those sites are fantastic. We were ready for action when we reached Tuxtla Gutierrez. I…"

Jack's thoughts seemed to be wandering so Dawn quickly asked a question to focus his attention. "Did you go to any ruins from Tux…that place?"

Jack laughed. "Yes ma'am, our start was not particularly auspicious. It took us a little time to track down our guide. So we visited Chiapa de Corso. Jack continued meditatively. "Three thousand years ago they were making beautiful pottery. It's brilliant white and red with patterns imprinted on it. They still make these painted gourds for carrying various kinds of produce. I'm wandering. Let me…"

"Tell us about the gourds!" Doc Maximos asked quickly, to keep the conversation going.

"They sand it and grease it with crushed insects. Then the girls color it inside and out, usually a black color, though occasionally it's red on the inside. Finally, they polish it and often paint it with brightly colored flowers. Where was I?" Jack rubbed his eyes. "Oh, yes. We also went to the Santa Marta rock shelter, which is older still, from around 7,000 to 5,000 B.C. All of this helped us feel that we were near the cradle of Central American civilization. I'm now convinced that this civilization started there, somewhere in the Grijalva valley, rather than near the coast or in the valley of Mexico. I'm daydreaming." He held out his hands helplessly in supplication. "I'm so confused!"

"What you said is fascinating, Jack" Elena said, quickly. "You seem to have the feeling that someone told you all of this. Could you tell us more?"

"Did Demos have this feeling?" asked Yianna. "You said that he was interested in the history of the area. Maybe he told you?"

"It's possible, yes." Jack's head started to drop again.

"So you spent a day or two soaking up the atmosphere of the area," Zack interjected. "Where did you go then?"

"Our guide tracked us down in Chiapa de Corso. It was odd you know. He wanted us to look at villages in the Grijalva valley. We told him we didn't have time and needed to get to Suchiapa right away." Jack laughed. "Heraclio wasn't happy."

"Please, not Heracles!" Festus shook his head. "Tell us about him!"

"His full name is Heraclio Balaam"

"Means jaguar," Ari interjected. "Balaam that is. What did he look like?"

"He was tall for the people of the area—maybe five foot ten. We guessed he was part Spanish. He didn't like that suggestion. He was adamant that he was purebred. Whatever that means. Rosie reckons he's a Zinacantecos. They're taller than the other Indians in Chiapas." Jack paused, closing his eyes as if to see Balaam. "He had the right characteristics for a Zinacantecos—not just the height—a long thin nose, widely spaced brown eyes, and a broad thin mouth. Aristocratic looking for an Indian." Jack opened his eyes. "Where was I? Oh, yes! He's in his early fifties, I'd guess. Dieter reckons he's like a…banker"

"A banker! Great!" Zack snorted. "How did he act with you?"

"He took money from us, for acting as our guide, though he made it appear that we were privileged to give it to him. In all the villages, the people seemed to defer to him. It was a subtle and maybe I just imagined it. Although he was deferential to the village, er, headmen I suppose is what you'd call em, it was like a game they were playin' for our benefit. Jack stopped, apparently absorbed by this image.

Doc Maximos could see that Jack was flickering into his other world and spoke to him sharply. "Enough about Balaam. Tell us more about your expedition!"

Jack's eyes jolted back into focus and he continued as if he were describing images that were flashing rapidly in front of him. "That's really nearly all of it. We decided to hike so that we'd see more, and parked the Jeeps some way beyond Suchiapa. Then we carried on up the valley, making occasional side trips into the smaller valleys. We didn't find anything. Each little valley seemed the same. A small stream descending from the high mountains, brown volcanic rock on top; thickly forested with pine trees, and cedar; and in the denser parts, the only flowers are orchids, which are usually high up in the trees. Things grow quite well on the volcanic soil. What else can I say? Well, generally, a small village by the side of the stream. Some farming, often slash and burn it seemed. Though, in the bigger villages, there were regular fields."

"How far did you go?" Ari asked.

"Hard to tell exactly. The river's got to be at least 50 miles long. We didn't reach its source. With all the side trips, who knows how far we walked. We could understand how that young couple who wrote the book would have had trouble, coming over the mountains from the Pacific. We became very frustrated. Still, at each bend we expected, subconsciously, some revelation, a magical city springing out of the woods. Certainly, that book implied it. The further we went the less useful it all seemed. We were close to agreeing with Balaam that we needed to stop the aimless wandering and go back to one of the villages. We might have if it hadn't been for the accident. While Dieter and Demos were carrying a load across a stream, Dieter fell and banged his head. Balaam wanted to go back to Tuxtla immediately. It would have been a hell of a hike. Dieter had recovered a bit and said he just needed to lie down. By chance, we'd spotted a village way up on the mountain. It was the closest one to the spot where he fell. Balaam didn't like the idea, of going there. We ignored him. The village was roughly in the area that we'd established for the ruined city from reading the book. Later, we concluded…to be accurate, I should say that Demos concluded it was the best place to study. Heraclio seemed less sure. I remember him muttering scornfully, "what could these peasants have which would be of interest to you?""

"What was the village called?" Festus asked.

"It had a Spanish name Santa Cruz, but that wasn't what the locals called it in their language. Their name wasn't written down, you understand, but it always sounded something like that Scottish hat. Anyway, that's how I remember it— tam o'shanter."

Ari jerked forward. "You sure? Seems coincidental. Could it have been Tam'oan Shan?"

"Yes, that's it," Jack looked surprised. "What do you mean by coincidental?"

"Oh! Just remembering some ole legend," Ari replied. "What's the climate like up there in the mountains?"

"In the valley it's damp and towards the end of our stay it rained most mornings but it usually cleared up by mid day. There was a lot of mist and it was easy to imagine that shapes looming ahead were more significant than reality." Jack paused. "You're right. It was Tam'oan Shan. I should have realized!"

"Can you tell us some more about the place?"

Jack did a double take, squinting. "The track winds upwards beside a stream."

"What's the village like?"

"I remember banks of houses. Most are thatched, a few have red tiles." He shook his head, as if to make the image clearer. "We saw so many villages, it's a blur."

"Do you remember anything else?" Zack asked.

"I think there was a larger house with gardens descending to a small lake by the square. Yes, that's right. We decided it was the assembly building for the elders of the village.

"I'm curious about…"

Festus interrupted Elena. "Tell me about their water supply! Do they take it from directly from the lake or was there a well?"

"Water supply! A well and some terracotta pipes, I think.

Festus appeared to be strangely pleased by the answer.

"If Dr. Festus has quite finished," Elena continued. "I am curious about two things. It sounds like quite a large village. First, was it on your map?"

"You know. It was strange. There was a dot but no name and we never heard about it in any of the other villages."

"Can you find it again?" Elena asked.

"I think so. On the maps, it's in an area with very little detail."

"Good. Second, whereabouts is the church?"

Jack seemed surprised. "There was no church."

"No church! Is there any structure that has some religious significance?"

"There was another building across the stream from the assembly house." Jack passed his hands wearily over his face. "I can't remember any more, I'm tired."

Ionides and Elena helped him to his feet and half carried him out of the room. Elena indicated a door at the end of the passage. "He can sleep in there. You'd better stay with him for a while, I need to go back."

"We're going to have to move slowly when we ask sensitive questions," Zack commented reflectively, as much to himself as to anybody in the room. "Let's get on with it. Who's next?"

"Dieter Newhart, I think would be best," Doc Maximos answered.

Zack started the questioning. "Dieter, please sit over there! Let's have a bit of background first. Where are you from?"

"Round Rock, sir. My grandparents came from Germany in the late 1800s," Dieter answered. He was a big old Texan boy, with broad shoulders, sun bleached hair and blue eyes. There was a faint scar in a small shaved spot on the back of his head.

"Nearly local then." Zack smiled, encouragingly. "I think we have a pretty good idea from Jack how the early part of your expedition went. What we'd like is some better idea of your experiences in the Suchiapa valley."

Dieter's story followed closely that of Jack. Under the guidance of Heraclio Balaam, the team had trekked, from each small village, along seemingly endless numbers of small tributaries. There were no signs of ruins of any kind. The trek had been harder going than Jack had indicated. They had not been adequately clothed to handle the rough, rarely used trails. They suffered very badly from insect bites and particularly from clouds of ticks—pinolillos. This was a key reason that they had decided to stay at one village, and explore out from it. By coincidence, his accident had led them to this particular village.

"Jack described a track to the village. Could you have driven there?" Ari asked.

"Not easily. Generally, we were glad we'd left the Jeeps behind. The road got pretty ratty as we went up the main valley. We didn't see any vehicles anywhere near Santa Cruz." He smiled. "Then, when I got hurt, we wished we'd kept ours."

"Jack said there was no church. The assembly building, did you go in it?"

Dieter looked embarrassed. "Mr. Cronson, I know this'll sound strange, but my memories of the village are real hazy. I think they…uh…showed us the food store there. My memory is terrible, sir. Demos would know."

"How did Demos get on in the village?" Ari asked.

"I only saw him near the end. Of course, the main language isn't Spanish. It's a local language, different even from the Tzeltal or Tzoltal that thay speak in some parts around there. I did catch him, once or twice, speaking to some of the younger men. I wondered whether Demos had picked up some of their language. He's good at languages."

Yianna reacted angrily. "I did catch him! Do you mean he was being furtive about it?"

"Demos and the villagers. At least, it looked like it to me."

"Can you say anything else about the village? Is it rich or poor?" asked Ari, changing the subject, quickly.

"There was no obvious poverty, yet nobody seemed to work very hard. When I was getting better, they moved me to a bed near a window. I remember there was a continual coming and going from that assembly house." Dieter pointed to his head. "You know, they were very kind to me. The local voodoo man did a fantastic job fixing up my head."

"Did you ever find any ruins?" Dawn asked.

"Balaam toured the team all over the mountains. They didn't find squat. By the time, I was feeling well enough to get up; they had decided to spend the last couple of days researching the village.

"How was that decided?"

"Jack and Demos thought it would be useful. Demos secretly bugged one of their houses. Although, how we would have translated the stuff, we didn't work out. We took pictures of the village and villagers right up to the time when we were hit by the illness."

"I heard that all your tapes and films were lost?" Festus said.

"Yes. When we left, some of the villagers helped us back down the road. We were still a little weak from the illness. It was embarrassing." Dieter flexed his large frame to emphasize the point. "Unfortunately, the guy carrying those items, slipped! He fell in the stream and we watched him dfisappear round a bend. We never saw the records again."

"Do you think it was an accident, Dieter?"

"I don't know, Mr. Cronson. At the time, we were too tired to think about it. Later we wondered whether it was deliberate. The stream wasn't that violent. We were ahead of the rainy season."

"Please tell us about this illness." Doc Maximos asked.

Dieter's face tensed with concentration. "The illness..." He seemed to have difficulty recalling it. "Yes, I think I remember? It was after Pandora conned her way into one of the houses. She moved a chest to get a better angle for a photograph and a book fell out. Pandora slipped it into her backpack. Later in the day, there was a lot of scurrying around. From then on the villagers appeared to be watching us with greater intensity."

"You didn't offer to return it? They didn't ask for it back?" Elena queried.

Dieter looked embarrassed. "I don't know why they didn't ask for it. Pandora wanted to look at it, and Demos persuaded us that we could give it back after we'd photographed it."

"What was in the book?" Ari asked.

"It was old, and probably written on treated fig tree bark, like a Mayan, Codex. It showed pictures of people, gods and animals, and some kind of hieroglyphic writing."

"Why didn't you study it more?"

"Because after the feast, that evening, it was gone."

They all looked curiously at him, so Dieter continued. "That evening, we were invited to a special feast at the big house. This was unexpected. After the celebration, we felt ill. The room started spinning and I don't know, I guess I felt feverish. I think I saw an ancient…It's all hazy. I guess I passed out."

Ari sat up abruptly. "So you don't know what happened to the book?"

"Book? What book?" Dieter looked puzzled and his eyes became dreamy.

Zack and Elena exchanged astonished looks. "But…you said. Wait a minute, play the tape back!" Zack motioned to Ionides, who quickly rewound and turned on the tape.

"*…I Pandora conned her way into one of the houses. She moved a chest to get a better angle for a photograph and a book fell out. Pandora slipped it into her backpack…*"

Dieter stayed in his dreamlike state, but his own voice played back to him, triggered speech. "She should not have taken the book. She shouldn't have been in the house. It was the wrong house. I sinned." Dieter collapsed in a huddled mass on the floor.

"Shit! I've never seen anything as bad as this." Doc Maximos moved quickly and checked the prostrate body. "Carry him to a bed and keep him warm! I'll fetch sedatives."

"What's next?" said Zack, as he returned with Ari and Doc Maximos.

"I'd like to get back to Tam'oan Shan," said Festus. "Ari, you've always been interested in Central America. That village name meant somethin' to you. What, exactly?"

"Tam'oan Shan is the legendary name of the ancient holy place of the Olmecs," Ari replied. We know of it from Mayan writings. It means, 'land of rain and mist'. The conventional wisdom has been that it referred to the area around La Venta. I've never heard of it in relation to the Suchiapa valley. If the village really is close by the 'Tam'oan Shan,' I'd expect to find some substantial ruins. Dieter seemed to be about to say something. Maybe they did find Tam'oan Shan."

Festus smiled. It was always a surprise when Ari lost his normal clipped style of speech. He even sounded smart. As far as Festus knew, only four things interested Ari, sport, his children—mainly Demos—women, and pre-Columbian, Central

America. Why ancient Central America? Festus suspected it had started in a fasci-
nation with the violence of the Aztecs, and spread from there to be nearly a religion with him. "It's as if they've been allowed to remember some parts and not
others. You see…"

Zack interrupted. "I'm getting the idea that, somewhere in this valley, there
may be the remains of the ancient Olmec city of Tam'oan Shan. The people
there, or at least some of them, know of its existence. They're protective of this
knowledge, so they feed hallucinogenic drugs to anyone who gets too close to the
truth. To prevent the information getting out or, rather, to make the stories
sound like wild ramblings. How then do we explain the book at the University of
Texas? A simple slip up?"

Ionides raised his hand and Zack motioned for him to speak. "Mr. Cronson,
I've got information on the book. At Fes's request, I asked a friend at U.T. to
borrow it from the library. He tells me it's not there. There's no record of such a
book."

"Great!" Zack snorted in disbelief.

"So then we're left with a number of puzzles," Festus said, before Zack could
give his opinion. "The book that the team saw has gone or, apparently, didn't
come from where Demos says he got it. Tam'oan Shan exists somewhere in the
Suchiapa valley. However, except for that odd comment by Dieter, and a strange
remark Pandora made to me, it seems the expedition saw no ancient remains.
Most significant, the village has no church!"

"What the hell has that got to do with it?"

"I'm not sure, Zack," Festus replied. "Why don't we speak to Pandora and
Rosie next I would prefer to take them separately, but Pandy insists that Rosie
can't handle the questions on her own."

"Okay," Zack agreed. "Then, we'll leave Demos till last. Frankly, Ari, there are
aspects of his involvement that er…puzzle me."

"Me too," Ari said, grimly.

"Ari! What do you mean by that?" exclaimed Yianna, defensively.

"Yianna. Face the facts! Demos is right in the middle of everything."

Pandora and Rosie came in together, looking apprehensive. Following an
affectation of the time, each wore her hair in a ponytail, and a check shirt, jeans
and sneakers. It made them look very young and innocent. They confirmed most
of the earlier part of the story, but did not seem to remember that Pandora had
found an ancient book. It was noticeable that, at first, Pandora answered for both
of them. Elena asked some non-provocative questions to put them more at ease.
She finished her questioning with, "What does Heraclio Balaam look like?"

"Oh! He's a good-looking man, taller than average. His face is…very Mayan. Rosie thinks he's a Zinca…something or other."

"Zinacantecos," said Rosie, speaking for the first time.

"Yeah! That's it. He's got jet-black hair and an aquiline nose and his eyelids droop in a really sexy way. He speaks very good English when he wants to. He can be very funny."

"What does he wear?" Dawn asked.

"Let me see." Pandora closed her eyes. "Starting at the top, a hat, naturally, the brim was white once I suppose. Usually, he wears a white shirt with no collar, open at the neck, and white trousers. They're clean. He must have had clothes stashed in a number of villages. I never saw him wash anything. He tucks his trousers into lace-up boots, as protection from the pinolillos. We knew all about them," Pandora shook her head, "but we just didn't take them seriously enough. My legs were a mess. Where was I? Oh yes, and a thick leather belt and a machete. That's Heraclio Balaam."

"Great description, Pandy." Dawn smiled. "Now, Rosie, can you describe the local people? What did the women wear?"

Rosie appeared calmer now. Nevertheless, when she spoke it was nearly in a whisper. "Around Tuxtla, the Zoque women, the local Indians, wear a white cotton blouse, and a dark blue skirt wrapped around the waist. They have this strange shawl on their heads. A 'huipil de tapar' it's called—usually blue or white. The Indians modeled it on a Spanish child's shawl that, years ago, they mistook for headwear. I'm going to write about the women's clothes for my project. Her voice rose as she became more animated. "In contrast, the Zotzil women look drab. They wear clothes made from a dark, striped, woolen material sort of bundled around them in a blouse and skirt. Frumpy looking." Rosie paused. "I didn't really pay as much attention to the men. They dressed similarly, I think. Some of them dressed like Balaam, except I suppose they couldn't afford boots like he had. Balaam is gorgeous. I…I just love him."

Festus decided to change the subject. "Tell us about this special feast the villagers gave you?"

The girls exchanged looks, each waiting for the other to speak. Pandora answered. "We went to the large house on the square. They had this big room. There were wooden tables forming a semi-circle and within the arc of this semi-circle was our table—like at the focal point. They laid out the food in beautiful patterns—tortillas, beans, portions of goat meat, squash, guacamole, fruit, water and so on. The arrangements were…well, sort of ritualistic. Behind us, there was a large stone table. Carved from volcanic rock, I think. It was the only really old-looking thing that we saw, except the cups. I remember Demos muttered something under his breath about it."

"We were the only women," said Rosie.

"Where was Heraclio Balaam?" Elena asked.

Both girls looked puzzled. Pandora answered. "I don't think...he was there?"

"It was odd," said Rosie.

"So you ate the meal. Then what happened?"

We ate in silence. Except, before each course one of the elders would say something. Demos looked very uncomfortable each time this happened," she made a face. "I guess he understood more than we had realized. He even tried to leave, I remember, but the elders looked hard at him and he stayed."

"Did you drink anything other than water during the meal? You mentioned some cups." Festus interrupted.

"Not until right at the end, then they brought in these stone cups. They were ornately carved and I guess they were old. We all stood and drank. Like...a toast. It was silly because we didn't know what we were toasting. Dieter said 'Remember the Alamo,' and gulped his drink."

At this point Pandora stopped. Her eyes were glazed; she stood silently, going through the motions of drinking, as if in a ceremony. Rosie stood too. "The jaguar has come," Pandora screamed. "He stands before us." There was a shocking change in her appearance. "Oh, great God, take me, forgive me my sins!" Pandora raised her arms in supplication. Rosie fell to the floor. For a second, nobody moved. Doc recovered first, rushing to check Rosie's pulse. "Dawn, Elena, help me get them to a bedroom."

Festus was scared. His Pandora was losing her mind and he did not know what to do about it. Up until this point he had assumed, arrogantly, that as with most problems he had faced, there would be a straightforward solution. This area was outside his experience. He tried to help Dawn but she restrained him. "You'd get in the way, Fes," she said firmly. "Let us handle this! Talk to Demos. Find out the truth! God! It's a good thing Pan isn't here to see Rosie in this state."

Demos came in with his father. He was a tall boy, slightly built and swarthy. Demos wore white. Trying to be Balaam? Festus wondered idly. A shock of black hair hung straight around his head, seemingly coming from the center of his scalp. His piercing black eyes stared out from under this fringe of hair. He appeared very calm and moved rapidly to take control of the situation, turning to Zack as he sat down. "I hope I can help you Uncle Zachary. I'm as confused as the others. We've all talked and talked about this trip and none of us can explain what happened."

"I hear that the idea for the expedition started with a book you found in the UT library?" Zack looked hard at Demos.

"Yes. I guess I was lucky to find it."

"Can you explain why the library has no record of such a book?'

"What the hell! I returned it before we left." Demos exclaimed. "That's where I got it. I swear!"

"You can't explain it?"

"No." Demos looked worried.

"Well I guess we have to put it down as another mystery. So, tell us about the expedition from the time you left Tuxtla Guiterez!"

Demos looked relieved and started confidently. "We picked up the guide after we left Tuxtla. He agreed to take us up the—"

Zack interrupted him. "Why did you need a guide? Mexico, even southern Mexico, isn't so far off the beaten track these days."

"I managed to get some help, and a little funding from the Mexican Society for the Protection of Antiquities. They use the funding as a lever to persuade you to take one of their guides. That way they get some protection against expeditions that come in and rip off the old sites. They proposed Heraclio Balaam," Demos replied, smoothly. "As to your second point, there are tourists who visit Bonampak, but they don't just wander over there. The forests are pretty wild. I agree around Tuxtla isn't like Bonampak, but we needed a guide for this area because it's not traveled much by foreigners, and certainly none of us could speak the dialects." Ari looked like he was about to question whether this was true in the case of Demos, given the earlier comments of Dieter and Pandora. Zack, apparently seeing the question coming, shook his head.

"So this Balaam worked out well then?"

Demos looked uncertain. "He worked out all right, I guess. He seemed to know all the villages, but we wasted a lot of time going up side valleys that had nothing of interest. I reckoned he was trying to slow us down.

"How was it you stayed in Santa Cruz, the locals call it Tam'oan Shan we hear?"

Demos looked surprised. "So you understand about the name? We were tired of traveling and some of us were in bad shape, the ticks and cuts and so on and so we'd decided to concentrate on one area—a consensus of sore feet. Then, as I'm sure you've heard, Dieter hurt his head. He slipped as we were crossing this stream. I tried to catch him, but I'm afraid I made his fall worse. The village was close by. It seemed to be as good a place as any." Demos smiled wryly. "I mean there were no fewer ancient ruins than in the other places we'd looked."

"How did Balaam react?"

"He seemed angry, Uncle Zachary. He flared up occasionally and usually got his own way. We ignored him. Dieter needed to rest. He stared hard at us, shrugged his shoulders and said something like 'As you will."

"Did you find anything unusual?" Festus asked.

"Nothing really, except the village was attractive. We studied it carefully, but there wasn't anything ancient. Pandora found some kind of book. I wanted to take photos, but we got ill. It disappeared."

"I presume you did study the house of worship?" Festus asked, casually.

"No we weren't allowed to go in," Demos caught himself. "But I'm confusing things. I was thinking of a church in another village. It was interesting but the roof had been damaged by an earthquake and it was being repaired." Demos wiped his forehead wearily. "Please excuse me, I get confused sometimes." His voice trailed off and his head bowed.

"Crap!" shouted Panou Cronson, who had entered the room, unnoticed. "You're talking crap, boy! What have you done to my Rosie? Stop swanning around like a pansy, wiping your brow. You're not drugged as bad as the rest of them!"

Demos looked out sharply from underneath his thatch of hair. Then as Pan stared him down, his head drooped and he turned to his father, Ari. "There's nothing I can do about it. I'm sorry." He ran out of the room before anyone could move to stop him.

There was silence. Everyone had turned to look at Pan. The object of attention shuffled his feet and looked defensive. "Hell! Someone had to say it. I guess I'm sorry I wrecked your polite little chat, but you weren't getting anywhere." Then, with more anger, he added. "That little bastard's responsible for what's happened to my Rosie. He'd better come up with something more substantial."

Ari responded quickly, glaring at his wife who was about to protest. "You did the right thing, Pan. Someone needed to shake him up. Now, can see what part he had in it."

"Has he been on drugs for a long time?"

Ari looked shamefaced. "Yes, Pan. My fault. Should have kept him under control when he was younger. We've sent him for treatment, but it only works for a short time."

"What do we do now?" Festus waved his hand vaguely. "Do we take the stories at face value? The story about the ancient book that Pandora found for example. Could it have been a set up? Something to arouse their interest to keep them in the village? Is it another example of Demos manipulating them?"

"Demos used the expedition as a cover to get drugs. I'll bet you that this Balaam guy runs the local drug operation?" Pan muttered.

Zack shook his head. "It's an apparently convincing explanation Pan, but it's too glib for me. There have to be deeper reasons."

"Whatever these kids were given, it wasn't simply drugs in the sense you mean," added Doc Maximos. "You asked me here to help. I'm embarrassed to say I don't know what to do, other than recommend obvious medical precautions. Keep them quiet. No alcohol or drugs! Psychotherapy might work, but if it's voodoo drugs, they may need voodoo medicine."

"I think you're right Doc. Regardless of what Demos did, I still think the main clue, to understanding the problem we face, is the lack of a church. If the Spanish missionaries didn't succeed in penetrating to this village, it must have been a remarkable place. Sure, it's a little isolated but certainly not inaccessible. Remember what Jack said about the people further down the valley not mentioning the village." Festus stopped. He felt that he had enough information that he ought to be able to unravel this puzzle, but the pieces did not fit yet.

Meanwhile, Pan had moved over to sit with his half-brother Zack and they were talking earnestly. Zack stood. "There can be only one course of action for us. We've got to go to this village and find out the truth. Whether it's drug running or an 'ancient civilization' is irrelevant. Their illness came from there and we must go there to find the cure. We need to take all of them. Demos, certainly, is central to the whole problem. Ari you've got to make him tell you what he knows! I hope you'll all be able to come." Zack spoke sharply. "I guess we can do it through the Foundation and Trust?"

Festus nodded absently. Then, understanding the question, he reacted quickly. "I doubt we can make a profit for the Foundation from this, we're going to have to fund a lot of rain gear," Festus laughed, uncertainly.

"I wasn't looking for a profit. You should know me better than that."

"Yeah! I guess I should."

35. Tam'oan Shan

His lame leg was a nuisance, Festus thought wearily, as hiked the last miles to Tam'oan Shan. Jack had made a couple of wrong side trips, before finding the correct stream to follow. Even Pan, gross Pan, seemed to find the going easier than he did. Festus had covered up well to protect against the insects. Consequently, he was sweaty and the straps of his backpack had chafed his shoulders. The rain that had fallen nearly continuously since their arrival had abated. There was a break in the mist. Butterflies were cavorting in the green foliage. He saw Pandora, Rosie and Pan, who were waiting for him at a bend in the track, and pushed ahead faster.

"You go ahead. I need to rest. Just leave me something for lunch."

"We'll stay with you," said Rosie. "This workout is good for my waistline, but I need a little sit."

"Fine with me too," said Pan. "I could do with a rest before I start sorting people out." He grinned in anticipation.

"Don't try to be too smart, Pan. You saw what happened to the kids." Festus sat on a rock and watched the rest of the group crossing a bridge further up the track. He could see that Demos was hanging back. Hardly surprising, he thought, his peers weren't talking to him. His thoughts turned to Dawn.

"Penny for them, Dad?"

"I was just thinking it's a good thing your mother didn't come." Festus giggled. "Sweaty. Hair tangled."

"Dad, you're awful," Pandora laughed. Actually, he had been thinking how glad he was that he hadn't exposed both of them to this risky situation. Festus added another thought. "I was also wondering how many people have crossed that little bridge. Like the honeymoon couple who wrote the book, if they existed. Like your expedition, and like us." He stopped talking, abruptly.

"And wondering how many came back like us, and in what condition." Pandora finished the thought for him.

"Yes and wondering not only that, but what to do about it? Heracles must have felt like this when, for his eighth Labor, he went to the court of the Thracian, King Diomedes, to capture that maniac's savage mares. Unlike me, Heracles didn't lack confidence he could fix things."

"Still on that Labors of Heracles kick, Fes. Get real." Pan shook his head. "This is a damn bunch of peasants with some stupid mushroom. There never was an ancient city, except in their addled brains.

Rosie spoke hesitantly. "Dad. If you believe something's a temple, you'll see it as a temple. I saw something."

"I'm sure you did, Rosie." Pan looked worried and patted her shoulder, consolingly.

The bridge was made of wood, but it rested at each end on concrete blocks.

"So much for your ancient ruins, Rosie," Festus chuckled.

Pandora glared at him. "Why spoil her illusions Dad?"

"Why indeed, when so much of this problem may be illusion."

The woods had returned to life now that the rain had ceased. They could hear the chattering of howler monkeys. Festus glimpsed the iridescent green feathers of a quetzal. It was flying with characteristic undulating swoops. It brought to mind a gaudy, paper airplane. He signaled to Pandora, who was too slow to see it.

"You keep seeing quetzals Dad. Who knows, soon you'll come face to face with the Olmecs. Are you sure you're not on something stronger than Dr. Pepper?"

The mention of the Olmecs triggered the thought in Festus' mind that the expedition seemed to be free of the hallucinations. "How are you doing?" he asked Pandora, diffidently.

"It's strange. The nearer we get to Tam'oan Shan the better I feel."

It is as if she's been conditioned to forget so that she can't tell the outside world anything, Festus thought. Near Tam'oan Shan there was no need to forget. He wondered how Balaam, or whoever—he didn't like to think about that—had accomplished this subtle piece of brainwashing.

The mist hung low for the next half mile. There was a subtle change in the type of tree and undergrowth. Land of mist and rain—Tam'oan Shan—could this be it? The mist ceased as suddenly as it had appeared. Here, at some hundreds of feet above the valley, there were walnut, mulberry and fig trees.

The track continued up by the side of a small waterfall. At the top, he saw the first of a series of lakes. The stone dam showed that it was man-made. Higher up the mountain, above a small cliff, the village glittered in the sunshine. The houses were built in terraces, like layers of an ornate wedding cake. There were petal-shaped fields, one above the other, up the side of the hill to the base of the cliffs, with avocado and papaya orchards beside them. After a tortuous climb up the side of the cliff, they reached the top and found the expedition waiting the bridge that led into the village.

"We decided to wait here and all go up together," said Zack. "There's something creepy about this place. It's like a museum, wet clothes left by the stream, clothes hanging out to dry; smoke from a few fire places over there, but no people."

"They may be getting instructions on how to greet us." Festus turned to Jack. "What was it like when you came before?"

"It was different. We were with Balaam," Jack replied.

"Don't worry about it," said Pan. "There's a delegation coming to meet us."

A column of villagers walked slowly through the village and onto the bridge, stopping in the middle, waiting silently. The column parted and a man, taller than his companions, walked forward. He wore white, except for his Mayan sandals and a flat straw hat that was held by a strap to the back of his head and tilted forward at a jaunty angle. The hat had a black ring around the brim and two small red ribbons on top.

"That's Heraclio," Jack murmured.

"I guess we'd better go and do the introductions, Zack waved his group on.

Festus studied Heraclio Balaam carefully. Another Heracles to battle. Was this Heracles, the prototypical tanist, waiting to oust Argos's king—Zachary/Zeus? Was he-Festus, expected to protect the king. Could he win? He hoped his plan would work. Was it too simple-minded? Time would show.

"Welcome to Tam'oan Shan. We have been expecting you." Balaam removed his hat with a swirling gesture and spoke in precise, cultured English, colored by only a faint accent.

"Damn it! A Harvard man." Pan muttered. The younger members of the group tittered nervously, reassured by the joke.

"Correct," said Balaam. "Class of '32.' Does it surprise you? I graduated in among other things, American." He paused, "Culture."

"How did such a well educated man as you become a guide?" Festus asked, grateful to find out that Balaam was probably not a scientist.

"I have many roles Dr. Festus, as do you," Balaam replied. "One day a guide, the next a movie director."

"A movie director?"

"The next, a priest." Balaam smiled. "A number of us are priests. It is not easy for some. Farmers, for example, cannot work their land while they serve—losing money. It is the only way to rise in the hierarchy. Now, I come from a relatively wealthy family. It has been easy for me to rise far." He raised his scholar's hands expressively, to emphasize the point. "You appear tired. I see you have tents. That will not be necessary. We have rooms prepared. We can talk, after you've rested."

"Thanks. I don't fancy a tent right now. You were expecting all of us?"

"Mr. Cronson, your party has not been invisible!" Balaam took Zack by the arm and walked him through the village, speaking quietly. "I prefer not to discuss money, but it is better to clear it up right away. Though this is a moderately afflu-ent village, you are a large party. You and I, Mr. Cronson, should discuss some reasonable level of remuneration."

Zack smiled and nodded.

At the top of a flight of stairs, they came to the square. It was crowded now. Under cloth awnings, produce was on sale, chickens, cloth and hats, and wicker-work baskets. Women were preparing food for the shoppers. It appeared that Santa Cruz—Tam'oan Shan—was the local marketplace. Even more amazing that there was no name on the map, thought Festus. Above and to the right was the assembly house. By it, another bridge led to a windowless white building. In the middle of the square, a woman was drawing water from a well She turned and looked at them curiously. Beside the well, a raised platform supported small fountains and pots of flowers. Festus scrutinized the buildings, looking for the other water supply that Jack had described. Sure enough, threading between the upper buildings and, in some cases, over them was a system of pipes and he could see the cistern that fed the assembly house.

Balaam had arranged accomodation, and a villager escorted Festus and Pandore to their room.

"What do we do Fes?" Zack asked in frustration, after waiting a day with no further sign of Balaam. "They seem to be tryin' to wear us down, but I don't see why. I don't like sittin' around without a thang to do. What does fuckin' Balaam want?" Festus shrugged noncommittally. "I think about food too much. The only entertainment around here is watching the women cook. I reckon I could make a tamale." Zack mimicked the voice and pose of a small child, showing his irritation, while reciting the recipe. "Take one banana leaf, and heat over fire to toughen. Spread with fresh, mashed corn. Cover with small pieces of chicken, almonds, raisins, and olives. Grind tomatoes, onions, chili peppers, and other spices in a metate, to make a sauce. Pour sauce on tamale, and then fold it over. Steam for about half an hour then eat. Hell! I'll write a cookbook when we get home."

"I'll buy it," Festus said, laughing at Zack's petulance. "Please be patient. All the kids seem to be in good shape…except Demos. He seems very edgy."

"Yeah, I'd noticed. Odd isn't it? I've seen him talking to some of the young men. I wonder what the little bastard is up to," Zack replied, angrily.

"So do I. Let's wait a little longer. If there's no action by tonight, I've a small surprise for them. It should flush out Balaam, wherever he's lurking, and bring this affair to a head. In the meantime, I'm going for a walk."

"Do you expect to find some ruins?"

"No, but it will waste time."

Festus watched children floating down a stretch of rapids—giggling and screaming with delight, as the water tossed them about over the smooth rock bed. So much for the disappearance of the film and tapes being an accident, he thought. He spent the rest of the day surreptitiously studying the water systems. Late that night he scuttled out of his room a number of times. Each time he was carrying a large package.

That next day passed as unremarkably as the previous one, until the late morning, when there was a considerable amount of activity in the village.

"Watch them! Just sit and watch them!" Festus said as he shepherded the Texans into the square. "Let them know we're watching. Pan, why don't you play your harmonica? Something cheerful!"

"Typical Festus. You sit there smirkin'. Obviously, you've done somethin' sneaky but you won't tell us. Just like a child," Zack muttered with a mixture of frustration and amusement.

"It doesn't always pay for everyone to know my plans."

"I know, I know. But it still irritates the shit out of me."

"Not out of you. Out of them," Festus smirked.

"I've got it," Zack laughed. "You put something in the water, I bet! Look at that guy over there holding his gut."

Festus nodded. "You old bastard," chuckled Pan who had overheard the conversation. "Did you do the whole village? I guess not, or we'd be suffering too.

"I fixed the assembly house. Look, here's what I've been waiting for." He pointed. A door had opened in the building across the stream and Heraclio Balaam was standing by it, looking down on them. He walked across the bridge, down the steps, and approached them—with dignity, but stiffly, apparently controlling himself with some difficulty. Festus rose and met him.

"I underestimated you, Dr. Festus. There's no point in endless discussions. Frankly, I'd hoped the waiting would make you more amenable to working out a practical solution. Now, you and I must make a deal! W hat have you put in our water supply—dysentery, cholera? We didn't have a problem until you came."

"It's something for which only I have the antidote," Festus replied, deliberately trying to sound smug. "You've drugged our children. I hope you have an antidote for that. If you do, we can trade."

For a second, Balaam looked ready to make a sarcastic retort, but instead answered mildly. "It will be necessary to have the reawakening ceremony."

"Let me talk to Zachary Cronson," Festus said.

Festus found the Cronson men and explained the deal. Pan and Ari eyed him dubiously. It was obvious Zack didn't like having his authority preempted. "I don't see why he doesn't deal with me."

"It's simply fear of what I may have done, Zack," Festus reassured him. "He doesn't know what else I can do. We should trust him."

"No choice, I guess." Pan nodded and Ari followed.

Festus held out his hand. Balaam hesitated, and then shook it. "First we must talk privately…but in a minute," Balaam gasped, as he sped away to the assembly house.

Festus followed. The square was silent. All eyes watched them disappear into the building. "I hope he'll be all right," Pandora whispered to Rosie.

"Dr. Festus will be fine," Demos muttered. "It's us I'm worried about."

"You're worried about yourself," Rosie replied, angrily. "You set us up."

Festus blinked, waiting for his eyes to adjust to the dark. The room had stone and adobe walls supported sturdy wooden beams that carried the roof. A few oil lamps provided a dim light. At the far end of the room from the entrance was a dais and in front of it a large carved stone block.

"This is our room of ceremonies. We assemble here for meetings of the village elders, for special festivals, or for some emergency." Festus looked enquiringly. "The visit of your children was an unusual emergency. Though not quite as bad as when the Spanish arrived." Balaam added sarcastically.

"It seems to me you must have kept the Spaniards away. There's a noticeable lack of a church." Festus paused. "This new emergency must have occurred before you lured our children here?"

Balaam muttered to himself angrily, in his own language, and then recovered his composure. "To be precise, we lured Demosthenes Cronson here. He brought the others for protection. Unfortunately, I was not able to prevent them from finding our village. Believe me, I tried. It was not an accident, when his colleague was hurt."

"I wondered about that. What a pity. I'd convinced myself that even Demos couldn't be so callous. Why did you want him?"

"Surely, you know the answer?"

"I'm not sure. I know he's been using drugs. My best guess is that he found out something about your skill with them, or possibly he was lookin' for a market for your drugs to pay for his habit."

"Yes, but it's still not clear whether he wanted to sell the drugs or keep them for himself." Balaam looked disapproving.

"I suppose the book, which has now disappeared, led him to you?"

"That's correct, Dr. Festus. I suspect that you have heard what was in the book." Festus nodded. "The young couple were sick. My predecessor helped them. He gave them some mild drugs as part of their cure. Unfortunately, the young man saw one of our ceremonies. We use illusions in these ceremonies, to remind us of our history. They are a replacement for your home movies. He came away convinced that he had seen spectacular ancient ruins. It's our custom to give gifts to young married couples. My predecessor made the mistake of giving them a modest amount of gold to help them on their journey. We are not naïve. We expected them to tell of their experiences, but there are many ancient cities for people to look at. Back then, travel wasn't so easy. What difference would one more tale of ruins make? Particularly, if they didn't know exactly where we lived. I'll admit that my predecessor had not expected them to write a book. In fact, we did not realize they had done so until Demosthenes Cronson found a copy, believed their story and investigated. By the time we understood that he was after our drugs, he knew far too much about us. Anyway the book doesn't exist any more."

"It's a sad reflection on life that you're hurt because of acts of kindness." Festus stopped, searching for the right words. "Look, I need to know something. The kids are going out of their minds. When you treated the kids, did you expect the violent reaction they've had?"

Balaam looked embarrassed. "Frankly, no. They reacted far more strongly than our own people would have. We simply wanted to make them forget. I still don't understand what happened."

"Can you deal with the problem?"

"I think so."

"How can I help you?" Festus asked, innocently.

Balaam glared at Festus and rose to his feet. "Can you help us? What was it George Bernard Shaw said about the United States? Yes, I remember, 'The only country to have gone from barbarism to decadence without becoming civilized!' You come here to dig up our civilizations, but you seem to learn very little from that experience. I am Balaam the Olmec and take the form of Kukulcan, the bird-snake deity on earth. Your child, Pandora, is aptly named. She meddles and interferes following the path of her father. She found...stole is a better word, one of our books on medicines. If she had not done that, maybe we would have treated only Cronson. As for you, Dr. Festus, are you simply an actor in your Argos Play cycle, or are you really Hephaestus the god? You see I have researched you Greeks. Balaam stopped, reacting to some imagined slight in the way Festus was looking at him.

"In his greed, your Demosthenes might have revealed our existence. Why? We don't interfere with you. We're an ancient people. He wouldn't let us be." Balaam paused for a moment, his anger stifling the waiting words. "He dared to threaten me as if I were some poor peasant. We have techniques, carried from the past, to deal with such situations. The way you children responded is a reflection of their fears. You have tricked me with your drugs. We can cure them, but why should we?"

There was a long silence while Festus tried to muster his thoughts. "I had no idea your society had survived, secretly, for thousands of years. I'd be privileged to know more. However, it seems to me you're beginning to fall into the very trap that you must have avoided these many years. You are hanging onto the trappings of the past without having the ability to improve upon them. You have these drugs, but I suspect that you know very little about how to improve them. Your scientists also developed a phenomenally successful agricultural system. When civilizations disintegrate, it is because they have lost their drive to advance, and the tools that made them great become the tools for their destruction. Did the Maya fall into that trap? They had all the food, all the organization to continue as a great people, but they became bogged down in ceremony and ritual. I have heard that they ran out of energy, because they had denuded the landscape arounnd their cities, and had no trees for fuel. We run a similar risk."

"You're correct in part, but the Mayan situation was more complicated. Their energy problem, problem could have been solved. Some priests were inciting rebellion. We changed the drugs. The priests became mad and the system collapsed. We overreacted. Nevertheless, the culture would have recovered, given time." Balaam stopped for a moment. "Then we had the problem with the Aztec becoming too powerful. My forebears could have hamdled it but, with unfortunate timing, the Spanish came. That, we could not have anticipated. Ever since then we've been in what you call…a holding pattern. We will regain control, sometime." Balaam sighed and stood with head bent for a long time.

"We do need to change. I realized it some time ago and persuaded the council to let some of the young people study science. We can adapt, you see." Balaam looked searchingly at Festus for a moment as if he were trying to read his mind. He seemed to be satisfied with what he saw. "It is interesting you know. You are the only outsider I have ever talked to like this. For some reason, maybe because I sense you have a similar connection to the past, I feel the need to share my hopes with you. Come! Let me show you the rest of our empire. You'll be amazed. I guarantee it. We'll go to the house across the stream. I'm sure you're curious to find out what it contains."

When they returned to the assembly house, Balaam took Festus by both hands, holding on to them firmly. "We will hold a ceremony and release your children, but Demosthenes Cronson must be contained. I believe that is the correct jargon. You must all attend to ensure that you understand your responsibilities. Now, I give a word of warning. In our terms, I have lain in front of you, like a sacrifice, my chest is bared so that you may pluck out my heart. Do you understand what will happen if you let me down?"

"I'll do my best, but in our society, I don't have control of other people as you do. I will have to rely on Aristotle Cronson to control Demosthenes. If he fails, I will deal with the boy. Is that clear." Festus nodded agreement.

The next day, when Festus entered the assembly building, the tables had been rearranged, with a semi-circle of them facing the stone altar. Between this semi-circle and the altar was a single long table, its benches facing the front. Flowers decorated the room and the tables were laden with food. Through a side door, which led outside he could see a large open fire burning and, close by, chickens pecking busily at corn on the floor of their coops. By the door, a goat, tied to a metal ring let into the wall, looked at him with its keyhole eyes.

The Texans were ushered to the long table. Behind them, the senior men of the village filed in and took their places at the semicircle of tables. There were some new faces among the group. Elders from neighboring villages, Festus guessed.

"This is what happened before, Dad," Pandora whispered. She clasped his hand.

Festus nodded encouragingly, trying not to show his fear. "Let's hope it's the opposite of what happened last time."

On the altar, there were thirteen bowls of *zaca*, a mixture of cornmeal and water sweetened with honey, and piles of tortillas, thirteen high.

"Those stacks of tortillas are called *tutiwah*," Jack remarked. "There's a stack for each Mayan lord of the day. The tortillas represent clouds."

While the food cooked, male attendants offered more drink. This time it was *balche*, made from fermented honey and tree bark. They drank in near silence. The village women were cooking outside. The atmosphere was tense and the Texans were becoming more nervous by the minute. It was a relief when at last Balaam appeared. He was dressed in a white peasant costume. A garland of flowers was around his neck. In his right hand, there was an ornate fan of quetzal feathers, set in a silver handle. He stood in front of the table and motioned to Festus. "You and the Cronson brothers must help me in the ceremony! You will have the opportunity to protect these children. Come to the altar of sacrifice!" He smiled at the look of shock on the faces in front of him. "Don't worry, we're only a little as barbaric as you imagine."

The altar was carved from a single block of volcanic stone. On its sides, were the faint figures of humans and animals, intertwined and combined. The surfaces were all worn and the carved shallow basin of the top was discolored. Balaam took a position behind the altar and motioned for Festus and Zack to stand to one side with Ari and Pan on the other. He spoke in English. An acolyte translated for the villagers.

"Bring me the Cup of Forgetfulness." Young men came from the back of the room and handed small stone cups to the Texans. They gave Balaam a larger, more ornate cup. He motioned for all to drink. As they drank, he waved the fan in front of his face and started a chant. The villagers joined in what seemed like a chorus. He removed a garland of flowers, revealing a bright stone pendant on a gold chain.

Zack leaned across to Festus. "Am I seeing an illusion? Is that the Pendant of Cronos?"

Festus looked intently. "No, but it reminds me I need to look..." His voice tailed off. Balaam had removed the pendant and was swinging it gently. A single light behind the altar shone through the pendant and flashed in the faces of the assembly. The young village men, continually refilled the cups, averted their gaze.

Balaam continued his chant.

> "Oh great God! From you all of life comes.
> The blood that flows in our bodies.
> The heart that beats to drive it
> And the clouds above us.
> Through life we grow
> And our life is sustained by your gift.
> We live at your pleasure
> And in the end we must return your gift to you.
> All of us, priests, kings, men, women, children,
> Peasants, slaves will follow this road.
> There is escape for no one.
> This we understand.
> For those assembled here we ask continued health
> And we make this sacrifice
> As payment for continuing life.
> We ask also for forgetfulness for those whose minds
> Cannot live with the memory of your presence.
> To this end we drink your blood and eat your flesh."

Balaam raised his cup again. The young men brought the *tutiwah* forward. They placed half on the altar, half on the tables. They scooped out the *tutiwah* and filled them with pieces of chicken. Balaam motioned for all to eat and drink. Festus was glad to eat. He felt dizzy. Ari and Zack looked unsteady too. Pan seemed unaffected.

Balaam repeated the words and, as the drink took effect, Festus saw the scene change. The Greeks stood to the side, facing slightly towards Balaam as if to support him. Zack became Zeus, clothed now in a white tunic. A circlet of gold olive leaves shimmered on his head. He, Festus, was dressed in the dark purple cloak of the master smith, Hephaestus. A single jewel set in a headband on his forehead denoted his trade. Aristotle became Ares. Only Pan seemed unchanged. He had moved from the altar and was playing his harmonica.

Balaam appeared to grow in stature. His face was now part human-part animal. The gold of his ceremonial robes and jewels reflected the light set in the walls. Hephaestus watched as the members of the expedition were ushered forward. Pandora was wearing a short white skirt, but was naked above the waist. The room grew silent. Hephaestus felt panic, but his body would not move, nor could he speak. It was strange, the Chorus from the Argos play-cycle appeared in ceremonial clothes, feather headdresses, and, he looked down...Mayan sandals. This was insane, he thought. What were they doing here? He soon found out. As he stood immobile, watching in an apparently detached fashion, the Chorus brought Pandora to the altar and laid her on it. She did not struggle and to Hephaestus she seemed to be smiling at him. At that point he realized that the scene was an illusion, but one that could become reality if he did not act. He was still unable to move, but he concentrated on rejecting the image as Balaam reached down and withdrew an obsidian dagger from his belt. Balaam raised the dagger high above his head and plunged it towards Pandora's chest. The chorus, muttering morosely, disappeared. Pandora's body was less clear now and flickered in exchange with another shape. The dagger descended with agonizing slowness towards the bound body of the goat. Hephaestus had not completely shed the illusion for it seemed as if Balaam pierced the goat's chest and plucked out its heart, which was still beating. Balaam held it high for the assembly to see. There was a groan of shock and then a shout of exultation.

> "Oh great God, we have given of our blood.
> Give us forgetfulness!"

The light flickered to a dim glow. A shadow passed over the room. Festus lost consciousness. When he awoke, Balaam and most of the villagers had gone.

"Did you see what I thought I saw?" Zack asked, holding onto the altar.

"It was an illusion, boy. A very clever illusion, but you can't put old Pan down with a mere drink. He tried to make me see my Rosie being sacrificed," Panou

Cronson rumbled with amusement. "What did you see, Henry? Pandora being sacrificed? Look at the altar, man! It was a goat. Look! You all saw what you feared to see."

Festus approached the altar fearfully. A young white goat lay upon it. Its neck was slit and its blood was soaking into the stone. On the far side, Pandora lay asleep, blood dripping from the altar onto her shirt. In fact, Festus saw that all of the team was asleep, except Demos.

"Satisfied Dad?" Demos said to Ari.

"Son, you're responsible for this mess," Ari said, sadly.

"To hell with you!" Demos ran out.

Festus and Zack picked up Pandora and carried her to a table. Festus removed her bloodstained shirt, dressed her in his own shirt and held her.

"How are we going to get them out of here?" said Zack.

A village elder stepped forward. "We will help you. You must all leave the village now! We have stretchers. We will bring Demosthenes Cronson. We will give the children something to wake them when you are in Suchiapa."

Three days later, they were in Argos. The members of the expedition were sleeping well and looking fit. Even Demos seemed to have recovered and was his normal oily self. None of the team remembered much about Tam'oan Shan. While they had not found any ancient ruins, they had obtained agreement to write their term papers on other aspects of their expedition.

On their return, Festus took Ari aside. Ari looked haggard. "I hope it works out with Demos. I'm going to say it again. Balaam laid it on the line. If Demos causes him any more problems, he will deal with him."

"I heard you," said Ari. "I put him in this drug clinic. They won't let him out until he's clean. Yianna was furious. I even had a hard time persuading her that we have to keep him in Argos, when he returns. The woman talked about sending him back to college."

"Good luck." Festus patted his shoulder.

"Incidentally, did I imagine it or was Balaam wearing the Pendant. I really must check that Sam still has it. In some ways I wish that Marienna hadn't given it to her."

"I think it was another illusion. We saw what we knew. I hope that Sam is looking after it."

"You said nothing on the trip home and since then you've been avoiding me. Admit it!" said Zack. Festus hung his head in mock guilt. "I've been waiting to find out what really happened. Exactly what did you and Balaam discuss? Who is he? Are there really any ancient ruins in that area? Damn it! Stop looking so smug!" Zack decided to needle him. "I don't see how that apparently ignorant group of peasants could trick us. Anyway, it was another triumph for you, Hephaestus. It was clever of you to trick those primitive people by poisoning their water. How many Labors have you succeeded in now—eight? You'll be overtaking Heracles soon."

Zack's tactic worked. "Primitive people you say. Sweet Jesus, Zack! You have no concept of them." Festus retorted, angrily. "These Olmecs have survived through thousands of years. They've outlived the Mayans, the Aztecs, the Spaniards, the Industrial Revolution, a civil revolution and the interference of outside countries. They've retained the good features of their civilization, while shedding the vainglorious trappings."

Zack looked skeptical. "It was touch and go whether they would let us leave," Festus continued. "Balaam and the council believed that I understood some of their secrets. They held meetings, and they kept us waiting while they debated our future. They must have decided we could be trusted, or maybe that we wouldn't dare cross them—hence the demonstration of their power. They may also have been worried that our disappearance would lead to an unwelcome investigation." Festus paused wrestling with the decision whether to tell Zack the truth. "All right, I'll tell you. It's too much of a discovery for a scientist like me to keep to myself. I've already told you too much. Understand though; let the warning be clear. If you speak further of this they'll remove all of us. You're our padrone so I guess you should know. Anyway, I need to share my concerns about Demos with you. I've explained to Ari that he must keep Demos in Argos. If Ari loses control of Demos, Balaam will deal with him!"

"Are you serious?" Zack stopped, seeing through the cold eyes of Festus an image of the awful consequences.

"It has never been clear why the Olmec civilization ceased. They were more powerful than their neighbors were and more skilled. There's no indication of any internal dissension in the limited amount of information available. There's no indication of the kind of decay that rotted the Egyptian or Roman empires. They simply ceased, it seems, and later the Mayans arose. I will tell you Balaam's explanation.

"Something like two thousand years ago, the Olmec leaders concluded that they were not making adequate progress in their enclave around La Venta. Their neighbors—primitive tribes—continually harassed them. They deliberately divided their people into small groups, and left the homeland to spread their knowledge. The Maya were one outgrowth of that remarkable exodus. Today, there are a few villages scattered over southern Mexico, in which they sustain their civilization. Tam'oan Shan is the chief among them. They have influenced much of the development of Mexico from behind the scenes. The Spanish and some other recent developments have thrown them off the track on occasion, but they still exist. Balaam says that much more than a thousand years ago they realized that the vast cities, the gold, the trappings of advancement were holding them back and were making them more vulnerable. Their leaders believed that continued development, unrestrained in all directions would lead nowhere. They discussed the problem for more than a century. Then they made their second major decision; to withdraw from the coastal cities into these mountains."

"What about the Spanish?" Zack asked.

"Their arrival was a shock," Festus replied. "The Olmecs had no local enemies, more powerful than they but, since they did not know about Europe, they could not have foreseen the coming of the Spanish. The Aztecs were not one of their successes and Monteczuma had given part of the country away before they had a chance to fight back. The main strength of those latter day Olmecs lay not in military might, but in the skills of their brilliant chemists and agricultural geniuses. They developed the strains of corn and other vegetables that we use today. They returned to an apparently simple agricultural existence, which was straightforward as they had an abundance of food. An advanced medical system allowed them to handle many diseases. Finally they controlled use of hallucinogens and antidotes in ways that are outside our knowledge."

"Did Balaam explain what they did to the kids?"

"Balaam said that the problem with many hallucinatory drugs is that they leave significant brain damage, like LSD. This causes occasional relapses. They have a drug that accumulates in the body. It can be released from the organ it hides in, but only under the right conditions. For example, if someone has been conditioned to fear something. This drug plus hypnosis is what they used."

"What's the cure?"

"They have another drug that causes it to be flushed from the body."

"You're kidding?"

"A dumb example of such a thing is the use of beer in nuclear labs to flush out that heavy kind of hydrogen—tritium."

"Incredible!"

"Another amazing thing is their trick for recovering past monumental glories. To handle the need that the people still feel, to be reassured of their strengths they make 'Home movies'! It's so simple. In that building across the stream, they have exquisite models of their ancient cities, and vividly illustrated books recounting their history. This is what that young man, who wrote the book, saw when he witnessed a ceremony. There was a curious modern touch too. Balaam was serious about being a movie producer. He has modern movie cameras, the works. Apparently, he makes historic films regularly, to keep the past alive. Some of the profits are used to refurbish the ancient sites across Central America."

"I thought he was joking." Zack shook his head, disbelievingly.

"They have survived within our society—apparently a part of it but in fact beyond it. I wondered how they keep outsiders away from their village? Balaam told me that they have agents everywhere around them, controlling the whole area, in a loose kind of way. Like a protective blanket. Primitive! Oh, no! Zack. The Olmecs represent advanced civilization. We, in our headlong, non-thinking rush forward, represent the primitive past."

"An impressive tale, Fes. You spin it convincingly, but do you really believe it?'

"I don't know. Is some of it just another illusion woven by Balaam? Probably, in part it is. I guess I want to believe it, because it's a fantasy that resonates with the strange things that have happened to us."

"If they're so advanced how you could trick them?"

"They're advanced but, as I told Balaam, they've not been careful enough in protecting their scientific heritage. They use it, but more and more without understanding. Balaam says that he realized this and has begun to correct it. At the moment though, they have no experienced scientists. It was easy to use an old trick. Do you remember what we did to Lampasas High?"

Zack looked puzzled, and then beamed with delight. You don't mean putting phenolphthalein in the water? I assumed you had some incredible modern drug."

"So did they. So did they," Festus chuckled. "It was diluting and washing away as we had the ceremony. I also put in a neutralizer before we left."

"I bet that village council has the cleanest bowels in the Americas. Talk about Montezuma's revenge. How about the revenge of Hephaestus?"

Festus looked at him, sharply. Zack smiled urbanely and nursed his coffee.

36. The Pendant of Cronos

Festus pulled the lamp closer, to study the facsimile of the Phaestos Disk. "It's funny the way you're fascinated by that ugly thing," Dawn giggled. "Do you know what it means?"

"Not really. I'm tending to the view that the symbols are related to the intricate patterns executed by the dancers on a dancing floor. Was it at Knossos or Phaestos or…"

"How about that place where you got that weapon back from Duke?"

"Oh, you mean Aradin," Festus replied, remembering the dance that had occurred there. "Yes, that was something else."

"Have you worked out what any of the symbols stand for? Could they be like sounds or even letters?"

"It's possible, but with so many symbols, it's hard to know where to start. One thing I realized just yesterday. Or rather I should say that Marienna pointed out that there are some similar symbols on the gold that holds the stone in the Pendant of Cronos."

"Is she right?"

"I have vague memories of being fascinated by it when I was little, sitting in Mom's lap. I can still hear what she said to me, '*Maybe you will be bright enough to unlock the secrets of this bauble. It's very ancient, and it has seen many things*'. Boy, I wanted to have it then, but it wasn't to be. Mom added. '*I would like you to have it, but by tradition, it must go to Marienna and from her to Agamemnon Cronson's first granddaughter*'. That turned out to be Samantha. Now, I really need to study it," Festus said, ruefully. "I wish I'd made the connection earlier."

"I remember now," said Dawn. "The Pendant was a wedding present from Marienna to Sam. Why don't you call Sam and ask to look at it.

"I think they're still on vacation. I'll try Ari first."

The phone was answered immediately. "Ari, have you checked on the Pendant? You remember we thought we saw Balaam with it."

"No, not yet Doc. Sam and Ionides down on Mustang Island for the week with friends. Don't know their phone number. Sam said she'd call when they get back.

"Let me know as soon as you find out!" The next day, Ari returned his call. "Bad news, Doc. Sam kept it in safety deposit box in the bank in Austin. Smart enough not to keep it in her apartment. After I called, she went and checked. Pendant gone. Trying to find out who else has been in vault."

Festus stared bleakly at his desk. All these years he could have studied the Pendant, now it might be too late. He had to find it. In the meantime, he might as well think about the Disk. He tried, but couldn't think of anything useful through his growing headache. His unhappiness was compounded by the fact that it was October 28, a day that should have been for celebration. It was on this day, thirty seven years earlier, in 1940, when the Greek dictator, John Metaxas, dismissed the Italian delegate—who had the temerity to suggest that Italian troops would cross onto Greek soil—with the single word OçI, NO! The Italians tried and were soundly beaten. It was indeed a day for celebration, yet he felt tired and lonely, and, for some obscure reason, hungry, and considered going to the Kaffenion for a sweet pastry, coffee, and company. The old men haunted the place, a home from home. They would be happy to see him, bend his ear about the Labors, and reminisce about the war. They complained he rarely came any more. His headache was getting worse by the minute. The kitchen became more attractive than the Kaffenion. He ate a bowl of Cornflakes, took two aspirin with some grapefruit drink brought by Marienna the day before, then lay on his bed and slept.

His sleep was fitful, his mind too crammed with thoughts to allow a deep sleep. *He saw the dancing floor again, the dancers weaving their spiral pattern, slowly, with the music. It was Persephone orPandora or Aphrodite, he wasn't sure. The image was hazy, and all the dancers were wearing masks. Who was the master of ceremonies? He tried to turn his head. It was too heavy and it took a frustrating length of time. Had he seen Balaam? Yes, Balaam was directing the dancers. Balaam held the Pendant high. The rays of the sun focused on the path the dancers should take. The bull stood motionless in the shade, its eyes adapting to the sunlight. It watched the dancers curiously, without fear or anger. An acrobat, wearing a mask, gamboled by and struck it on the nose. The bull pawed with its right hoof, then charged. Other acrobats tried to distract it, but it followed the offender straight to Balaam. The acrobat jumped onto the dais and pulled the Pendant from Balaam's hand. The mask slipped. It was Demos. He vaulted over the bull and ran out through the door into the bull's den. The bull now focused onto Balaam and lowered its head. Balaam turned to look at the bull. Festus, facing him, could see the appeal in his eyes. The big gong rang out, signaling an emergency. Festus charged. He could not stop himself now. The bells rang and Balaam disappeared.* He hit the floor. The phone was ringing. His hand floated up to pick up the receiver. "Hello."

"Zack here. Ari called me about the Pendant. I had to stir things up. Fortunately, or maybe unfortunately, I know the owner of that bank in Austin. So do you. Remember the golf match at Stimpson?"

"Oh, yes." Festus chuckled.

"You're not going to like what I'm going to tell you, Fes. That damned kid, Demos, got out of the clinic and went to Austin. He was seen going into the vault with Wendell. Somehow, they managed to break into Sam's deposit box. I'm sure they have the Pendant." Zack paused. "I don't know if our banking friend is involved. For his sake he'd better not be."

"We must find Demos and the Pendant before he gets to Balaam or Balaam gets to him."

"You're sure the two are connected?" Zack sounded surprised.

"No, but it's a strange coincidence. I had this weird dream in which Balaam, the Pendant, and the dance were all mixed up."

There was silence on the other end of the phone before Zack responded. "Look, Fes. I can sorta understand Tam'oan Shan. We were drugged. I don't understand what happened in Crete. Do you think we're just dreamin' or are we hypnotizin' ourselves into some fantasy?"

"Zack, I'm becoming convinced that we're playing, or maybe replaying some game. We know our roles. We all have parts to perform in the plays. Marienna believes it."

"Marienna! It all comes back to her. Her plays. Her dance. Her fantasies."

"I worry about that too, but I think there's more to it. She had nothing to do with Balaam."

"We'll talk about it sometime." Zack hung up.

Dawn had overheard the discussion. "I didn't tell you, but something like that happens to me in the plays. I feel like I'm repeating something I did a long time ago."

Festus put his arms around her. "It's beginning to seem like we all do."

As he greeted Festus at his front door, Zack pulled him aside. "About our conversation last night. I was tired. Let's not talk about it now. Maybe some other time?" He looked at Festus for reassurance.

"All right. Sometime, though, we're going to have to face it, Zack."

"I know, but not now."

Elena, Ari and, to Festus' surprise, Angelica Cronson, were in the den drinking. Their conversation stopped when Festus came in. Angelica, the younger sister of Zack and Ari was wearing her customary tracksuit. She rose and embraced him.

"Still not a free man, Fes. I'm sorry," she whispered in his ear. He had dated both Angelica and her adopted sister Dawn when they were all teenagers. This was Angelica's normal greeting to him. He wasn't convinced that she really minded that he had married Dawn. Her sexual preferences were somewhat of a mystery to him, although he knew what the rumors were, and her clothes and manner certainly encouraged the belief that she preferred women. Festus pulled back and studied her. Her face had always fascinated him, with its high cheekbones, strong straight nose, and sparkling hazel eyes. "I think only of you Angel," he replied.

"You were always too good for her," Angelica said quietly, then pressed his arms with her hands and returned to her seat.

"I suppose you're looking to me for some answers," Festus started. "For once I'm not sure what to do. I guess Demos has the Pendant and we've gotta get it back. I need to look at it. I think he's after something from Balaam—presumably drugs. I can't believe he'd dare go back into Mexico. Do you know anything, Ari?"

"Tried to find him today. Kid has sixth sense to get out when in trouble. Reckon he's still in Austin. Can't wait to get my hands on him." Ari sounded sad rather than angry. "Came up with couple of things. Wendell Jameson's there, maybe his girlfriend too. Used to be at Stimpson's. Remember golf match, Amanda Ellesmere. Won beauty pageant. Was leading cheerleader. Birds they call them." Festus nodded. Ari continued. "Other thought. Pan has connections. Find Demos' drug dealers. Phoned him. He's asking around. Angry with Demos. Happy to help."

"Did you check around in Austin any further?"

"Not yet. Didn't want to scare Demos away. Have a chance of finding him, if he's in Austin. Don't know where to look if he leaves, except Tam'oan Shan. Not eager to go back. Seems to me that one person at Olympic Services might help. I mean Chuck. Knows a lot of people. Demos has hardly ever seen him."

"Good idea. We'll ask Chuck to help track Demos, while Pan looks into the drug connection. I just pray we can find him before Balaam does. We've got to bring him back here, or there'll be real problems."

Angelica was puzzled by the comment. "Why, Henry? What could this Balaam do?"

Her question put Festus in a very difficult position. He had agreed with Zack, Ari and Pan to limit the spread of the true story of their trip to Mexico. He looked to Zack for a lead. Zack nodded, so Festus gave a more detailed, but, nevertheless, expurgated account of the happenings in Tam'oan Shan.

Angelica looked startled. "I find this all very hard to believe, Fes."

"You're forgot something, Doc," Ari looked sad. "We think Demos has been involved with drug dealers."

"How awful. I'll do anything I can to help. I know he's a bit wild. I always felt he was simply trying to compete with your image of what he ought to be. I've always had a soft spot for him. You know, having no children myself," Angelica continued, diffidently. "None of these people know me. I could probably snoop around without being noticed. Please, let me do something to help?"

"Angel, we want your help but really don't think you should do that. Dangerous and could cause more problems. Appreciate offer. Could go and look together? Help Chuck"

Zack shrugged in agreement. "OK I guess. Let's say we find him. How do we persuade him to come back here? If we persuade him, how do we get him to stay?"

"May have to commit him to sanitarium. I think we could fix it," said Ari sadly. "Desperate end to come to. Might shake him up enough if we put him away for a year."

"That's a terrible idea, Ari!" Angel gasped. "Let him stay with me. I'll look after him."

"The problem is, you can't give him what he needs," said Zack.

"What's that?"

"Either imprisonment or sex and drugs."

Angel bridled at the suggestion. "I should hope not! But I can give him love and care. We need to find him a nice girl. I know a lot of nice girls in my volleyball team." She left.

Zack threw up his hands in despair. "Oh, shit! Sorry I agreed to bring her into this. I guess we'll have to take her, but God help us! Ari, you've got to keep her under control. The last thing we need is for her to wander up to some drug dealer and make demands."

They met at Olympic Services in Austin, to discuss progress. "Let me start this off," Zack said. "I've found out something that explains a lot of what's happened. I visited the bank where Sam and Demos have deposit boxes. As I told you before, Fes, I know the guy who owns it. We've had battles in the past. The problem isn't only him though. It's his cousin or nephew or something, that little creep, Wendell Jameson, who tried to set me up in that golf game some time ago. He works at the bank and I suspect he's the drug connection to Demos. In fact, I'll bet he was the drug supplier at Stimpson. It would explain a lot."

"I still don't see how Wendell could get into Sam's safety deposit box," Fes said curiously.

"Sam told me there was some problem with her original box. I guess Wendell…and Demos engineered it. They had to transfer Sam's belongings to another box. It was done in her presence. It appeared legitimate except that it seems likely that Wendell had a spare key for the new box. It wouldn't be difficult." Zack paused. "Let me get back to Wendell. Frankly, Ari, I'm not sure whether he leads Demos or Demos leads him."

"How about you, Pan, did you find out anything?"

Panou Cronson shifted his vast bulk in the chair, smoothing down his Hawaiian shirt before speaking. "Course I did, Fes. You're right, Zack, Wendell Jameson's a major supplier to the kids. First at Stimpson and now at the University of Texas. He uses his bank job as a cover. I don't think his uncle knows about it, though, he does use Jameson for dirty jobs. I reckon that Demos is working with Jameson to try to get Balaam's drugs. I guess it was Jameson who got him solidly hooked. They're all playing a dangerous game. I've found out who they're working with south of the border and I, sure as hell wouldn't like to mess with those guys."

"Chuck, have you got anything to add?" Zack asked.

"It wasn't difficult to find Mr. Cronson's son. He's holed up in South Austin, in that old apartment complex off South Lamar. You know, the fake Mex place—Hacienda Heaven. He's in apartment 223 with that…whore, Amanda. Jameson has her doing tricks for visiting businessmen and people he wants to influence. She's a good looking little…Well! I wouldn't give her more than five or ten years before she's worn out, from the drugs and booze. Let me say one other thing following what Mr. Cronson said," he indicated Pan. "We're not the only people looking for them. There are numerous southern gentlemen, who are snooping around."

"I found out some things too," Angel volunteered. "After Chuck pointed out that tramp Amanda to me, I followed her. I've a long list of addresses she visits regularly. You'd not believe who she sees," she said, obviously shocked by the knowledge. "Why old George…"

Zack stopped her at this point. "I think we've heard enough, Angel. Spreadin' this further ain't useful. You were fond of George, weren't you?" Angel turned her head away; her face set in a hard expression. "So, what are we going to do?" Zack asked. "Do you have any comments, Fes?"

"We've a real problem because I think I now understand why Balaam has been so worried about us. You see, if only Demos knew about the drugs, he could handle that. Now though, I'm hearing that Demos has connections to a major drug ring. As Pan told us, a drug ring in Mexico. That's much more dangerous for Balaam and his plans. He's going to have to remove not only Demos but Wendell and the girl also. If these guys have heard what Demos knows, we're all in deep shit; because Balaam may conclude that we're all a danger to him."

"Goddamn it, Fes! Why so depressing?" Ari barked. "Worried enough in the first place about Demos. Now it looks like a complete disaster! I vote we move in and take these kids away before it gets worse! What do you say, Zack?"

"I agree, Ari. We do it today. I want to keep it in the family though. It's not fair to involve Chuck. We sure appreciate what you've done. Won't forget it."

"Are you sure, sir? I could help."

"I'm sure you could, Chuck. Thanks, but his is a family matter from now on. Pan, I think you should keep out of it too. Your connections are too close to some of these bad guys." Zack looked searchingly at Pan.

Pan nodded agreement. "I don't want Rosie hurt."

"So that leaves Ari, and you, Fes and me," Zack said. "I say this with some reluctance but Elena, you and Angel should come with us to handle the girl." Angelica looked at Elena triumphantly. Elena appeared worried, but said nothing about her fears. "One final point, when are they likely to be there together?"

Angel answered quickly. "If that girl isn't laying someone, then early in the morning, say one or two, usually sees the lights out."

"They're usually all tucked up in bed by then." Chuck grinned.

The apartments of Hacienda Heaven were modeled on imaginary Mexican buildings. There were fake adobe walls with fake beams and an overabundance of irrelevant, wrought iron, railings and grills. The ironwork was inappropriate for decoration but convenient for people trying to raid a second floor apartment. Zack climbed up onto the balcony of apartment 223, while Ari and the rest of the raiders went to the front door.

Festus knocked on the door and in a drunken voice made his demands. "Where's that little bitch, Manda? She said she'd fuck me." He fell against the door, knocking feebly with his right hand as he clung to the ornamental wrought iron doorknocker with his left hand. Ari, Elena and Angel, stood out of sight to the side of the door. Festus could hear someone inside trying to see who was knocking, but Festus had cleverly sunk below the level of the peephole. He continued to repeat his demands, banging occasionally on the knocker. Persistence won out. Wendell opened the door.

"You old bastard! You're going to pay for this," Wendell said. As he unlocked the door, Ari put his considerable strength and weight into a push, shoving Wendell back against the wall. Festus fell to the floor and Wendell, recovering, was about to kick him when Ari stepped up.

"Hold it, Wendell!" Ari pointed a shotgun at Wendell's chest.

Wendell moved away, with Ari prodding him as he went. Festus, back on his feet, motioned the women to come in and closed the door. While all of this was happening, Demos had woken up, and reacting quickly, had gone to the balcony to escape. As he opened the sliding glass door, Zack reached around and locked his arms behind his back. "Not this time, Demos. This time you'll do it our way."

In one of the bedrooms, Elena and Angel found Amanda Ellesmere sprawled on the bed. She was snoring loudly. The state of the bed suggested that she'd spent an energetic night with Wendell, Demos or both of them. Angel pulled her up roughly. Elena put her hand on Angel's shoulder. "Don't take our problems out on her, Angel. She needs help. She's the one who's been exploited. Come on, we'll get some clothes on her." Throughout this discussion, Amanda remained unconscious. The bottles on the bedside table indicated the reason.

Festus stood by the glass door, holding the shotgun. Demos, looking surly and Wendell, looking worried, were seated on the sofa. Amanda, now dressed, was slumped in a chair. It worried him that he still didn't have a coherent plan to escape from this mess, and didn't know where the Pendant was.

"You can't kidnap us like this," Wendell said cautiously.

"Oh no?" Zack said. "Try me! We're law-abiding folk but we've had enough of your crap. I doubt you understand who you're dealin' with."

"You mean all that junk Demos sprouts about Balaam's power?" Wendell jeered. "You believe it, I suppose? It's just another drug ring, and I deal with tougher groups than those peasants from Chiapas."

"Fine, you're really tough. Now, where's the Pendant?" Zack demanded.

"So that's what you want. You let us go and I'll tell you," Wendell replied.

As he finished speaking, an arm came through the curtains by the sliding doors, clamping the shotgun to Festus' side. Before he could react, four men rushed into the room. Three carried handguns and one of them carried a machete.

"Shit!" said Zack, turning to look at them. He spoke bitterly to Wendell. "Which set of peasants is this, you son of a bitch!"

Wendell spoke to the intruders in Spanish. They ignored him. The leader of the group, carrying the machete, motioned towards the door. Wendell, Amanda and Demos were rushed out. Demos turned and shouted, "where's Aunt Marienna, she..." He did not finish as one of the captors clamped a hand over his mouth.

"What the hell does that mean?" cried Zack. It was too late to find out. Their captors separated Zack, Elena, Angelica, Ari and Festus from the kids and hustled them out of the building and into one of two small furniture trucks. The men bound their hands and feet and placed them behind a stack of boxes. After some six hours, the truck pulled off the paved road onto a dirt track. Their captors removed the bindings and pushed them out of the truck. It was early morning and the sun illuminated a decrepit ranch set in a desolate landscape desolate with a few cactus and scrub cedar trees. There was a second truck and a twin-engine plane parked by the side of a barn.

"We went west, Zack whispered to Festus. "I doubt we've crossed the border.

"I wonder who they are, Zack. Is it Balaam's crew or some drug ring?"

"God help us either way," Zack replied. "I suppose they found the Pendant. They must have been outside when I asked for it. What did Demos mean about Marienna? How the hell could Marienna be involved?"

"I know she can't stand Demos," Angel answered. "I was visiting her some weeks ago and Demos was just leaving. Marienna didn't see me. I heard her shout after him. *'Don't you threaten me, Demosthenes! You'll regret it!'* I don't know what Demos had done."

"She's stirring shit again," said Ari, bitterly.

Their captors motioned them to stand and they were shepherded around the barn and into the plane. Demos, Wendell and Amanda, their hands still bound were sitting under a tree. Amanda looked frightened. As he was shoved into the plane, Ari turned and looked at Demos, angrily. Demos' face, under his mop of black hair, was expressionless.

"Kid doesn't seem to care any more," Ari said, despairingly. "Should have tried to deal with his problems earlier."

"It's difficult with your own children," Elena sympathized. "We make too many allowances for them when they're not strong enough or experienced enough to handle life. We don't know where Duke is. I wish…" Her voice trailed off as the plane lumbered into the air and headed south. There were two stops, at which a guard gave them food and water.

"Guess we're following the drug route in reverse?" Ari surmised. "Though if we go much further south I suppose that means it's Balaam who's got us."

"Not necessarily," Zack replied. "A lot of the drugs come from further south—Guatemala for example. It could still be anybody behind this."

By now, they were over a densely forested area with mountains to their right. "This has to be the southern Yucatan," said Festus. "We've been traveling now for eight hours. Allowing for stops we've done about a thousand miles; more or less due south, if I've been judging the position of the sun correctly."

The plane stopped one more time, before continuing. "I guess we're over-shooting Balaam's domain?"

"It seems so, Zack." Festus agreed.

Finally, the plane descended over the treetops and landed in a small clearing by a river, and they were unloaded. Towering above the landing area was a magnificent stone temple. The river had eroded some layers of the underpinning structure, and its position looked precarious. As they came closer, staring in awe at the massive structure, they could see that work had been started to repair the depredations of the water. They looked up, responding to the sound of feet shuffling on the stones above them. A tall figure, dressed in a white suit with an open necked shirt, descended from the temple. Guards, carrying rifles, flanked him.

37. Copan

"Welcome to Copan." Heraclio Balaam spread his arms in a mock greeting.

"I'm glad to know it's you, rather than some primitive drug runners," Festus replied.

"You'll not be so relieved when you understand my plans for you," Balaam retorted. "You let me down Dr. Festus! You too Colonel Cronson!" His voice became angrier. "That damned child of yours, with his associate Jameson, talked to the wrong people. Jameson thinks we're a bunch of simple peasants. Unfortunately, their associates in my country are more thoughtful. I cannot have people snooping around!"

"We understand," said Zack sadly. "We blew it! Why the women? They're no danger to you?"

"How can I tell that?" Said contemptuously. "How do I know what they'll talk about at the bridge club?" Balaam pointed tat Angelica. "A grown woman, a teacher, running around Austin spying on a prostitute. God knows what else she could do."

"I'll do what I have to do to protect my family," Angelica retorted proudly.

"That's exactly what I mean," said Balaam.

"Then why did you bring us here?" Festus asked. "Surely if your plan was to dispose of us, you didn't need to go to all this trouble?"

"I don't plan to dispose of you," Balaam replied. "I plan for you to deal with the problem yourselves. We have traditional ways of handling these situations. I am obliged to follow our ancient laws and, for that matter, I do not wish to deviate from them." He paused. "You'll play the game. Do you understand what I mean, Dr. Festus?"

"I'm not sure. Ari, do you know?"

"Think so. Will we play against your team?"

"Unfortunately not," Balaam answered, dryly. "Otherwise, I could get rid of you all easily. No, in our system, Colonel Cronson, the people who cause a problem play the people who let them cause it. It's a remarkably fair approach. You'll play your son Demos and his friends. They'll be flown in today. My problem is to find a way to help you to win. I'm sure you don't want to die!" With this response, Balaam walked away, signaling for the guards to collect up the Eurysthesians and untie them.

"What the hell does he mean?" Zack asked.

"He's talking about the ancient ballgame—tlachtli," Ari said. "I don't like the sound of that at all. I guess it's better than immediate execution. Do you know what the Maya used to…?"

"Ari! Please stop! I don't want to hear it."

"Sorry, Elena."

They climbed up from the riverbed, and made their way to where restored buildings bordered a grassy area. The buildings had been constructed of green trachite, and looked as if they might have grown there. The guards pointed them to where four small tents were set up around a fire, and then moved a short distance away and sat at the base of a temple.

"Where's Copan, Ari?" Elena asked.

"In Honduras, near border with Guatemala. Trying to escape waste of time," Ari answered.

"Tell us about this game!"

"Let me think a minute, Zack. Tlachtli was a game played by the Mayans. I'm sure there is a ball court here." Festus smiled noting how Ari had lost his clipped manner of speech as he discussed his hobby. "As to the rules of the game? I'm not so sure. I recollect that the rules varied from city to city. I presume we'll have to play Balaam's rules. What do you know, Doc?"

"All I can recall is that it's similar to a more modern game, hulama, which is played by some of the Indians in the Yucatan."

"Right Doc. In addition I had the impression that tlachtli was only played by professionals. From what Balaam said, it must have been used to settle problems or arguments. The Maya used to gamble very heavily on it and even sell themselves into slavery if they lost. From what I've read the crowds were very unkind to the losers."

"In what way, Ari?" Angelica asked.

"They'd beat them, Angel, and strip their clothes as recompense for their losses, and sometimes the losers would be sacrificed." Ari replied. His companions looked thoughtful.

Zack broke the ensuing silence. "So it was like hulama. What the hell are tlacht...or hulama?"

"Well, let me see." Ari thought for a moment. "They use a court, say about one hundred, or sometimes more, feet long. It's generally shaped like a large letter 'I'. The length is three or five times the width. The top and bottom of the 'I' are about one width in length and two widths in breadth. Extending along the longer sides of the 'I' are the stands. These are stone structures. Sometimes the walls are vertical and sometimes they slope up and away from the court. Set in the middle of each wall, opposite the midpoint of the 'I' is a ring. The ring is mounted vertically."

"What do you mean, vertically?"

"Well, Zack, opposite way to a basketball hoop." Ari held his hand out flat and then rotated it so the thumb pointed up. "I should add that the ring is maybe eight feet of the floor of the court."

"Great!" Zack said, shaking his head.

"The two games are similar. Let me give a kind of composite picture. The number of players on each side generally varied from two to five though, on the bigger courts, it could be more. The idea was to get a small, hard rubber ball through one of the rings. It's not known whether each team had its own ring or whether either would suffice. Each side must stay to its side of the center of the court, which is marked on each side by the rings."

"That doesn't sound too difficult." Angel volunteered, hopefully. "I still play volley ball. So does Elena, though she's been a little lazy recently. We might be quite good at it. Certainly better than Demos, and that kid Wendell, who doesn't look like he's into sports."

"I agree with Angel," Ari said, harshly. "Demos always was a lazy little bastard. He used to be good at sports, though," he added, wistfully. Then subsided into silence, suddenly realizing that, when he played against his son, only one of them might come out alive.

"I don't want to disappoint you, Angel. Your athletic skills may be important to us. But there's one thing we haven't mentioned," Festus said.

"Oh God. Here we go." Elena laughed. "Don't tell me we have to head it through, like in soccer?"

"Unfortunately, no," Festus answered, quickly. "I'd have liked that. I used to play a little soccer and with my leg as it is, heading was one of my better skills.

No, it's worse. The one thing I do recollect about the game is that you may only strike the ball with your elbows, hips or legs. And when I say legs, I mean somewhere above the knees."

"Oh shit," Zack exclaimed. "This is going to be hell. If I understand brother Balaam right, it's our lives at stake in this game."

"Why don't we just refuse to play?" Angel asked. "Regardless of what Demos and Wendell have done, why should we allow ourselves to be pushed around like this?"

"You're right, you little darlin'," Zack said, angrily. "Why am I allowing myself to be bluffed by this peon?" He stood and paced around the fire. "I don't have to do a damn thing I don't want to."

"Maybe we'll all do it because we're not so confident that it's a bluff," Elena countered, gently, seeing that Zack was working himself into one of his famous tantrums.

"I think we should go along with Balaam for the time being," Festus agreed. "Let's face it; we're a long way from home, with no return ticket."

"Damn!" Zack's temper subsided as fast as it had risen. He reclined on the ground, looking into the fire. It was getting dark now and the red of the flames contrasted strangely with the green of their surroundings. "I wonder how Balaam will make up the teams." Zack mused.

"All of you will play, and I do not bluff" Balaam replied, as he stepped into the firelight.

"That makes five against three?" Festus queried.

"No, it makes five against five. Your Demos subverted two of my young people" Balaam answered, bitterly. That stupid boy Pacal and his girlfriend Cha will play with them. It will make it challenging for you. The boy was a good ball player before he took to drugs. He and the girl were two of the bright ones we sent to your University in Austin."

"I guess that means we'll lose," Festus said. "Surely, putting the ball through the ring is a difficult art? Pacal will have an enormous advantage."

"I thought of that," Balaam replied. "He'll play in the backfield and will have less opportunity to attempt a ring. You seem to understand the game. It is a little like volleyball, although we don't rotate the players. What else..."

Ari interrupted him. "Why don't you give us a complete description of the game? The Doc and I probably got it wrong."

Balaam's description of the game paralleled Ari's, the main difference being that scoring was not only by putting the ball through the ring. "The game is started by an umpire throwing the ball to the forwards on one side of the court.

The nearest player hits the ball to the other team. You must remember that you may only use your elbows, hips and thighs, at four fingers-widths above the knee, to strike the ball. The nearest player on the opposing team must receive the ball, either on the volley or on the first bounce. A point is scored against a side when it fails to return the ball to the other court within three strikes. Mishandling the ball leads to a penalty point. The first side to gain thirteen points wins."

Elena looked up at Balaam. "How about scoring through the ring?"

"After the ball has crossed the center line two times, a player may try and put the ball through the ring. The first side to do this wins outright, at any time in the game."

"Do players normally try for the ring each time it's permitted?" Zack asked.

"No, not usually, for two reasons. First, they may be out of position and second, if they miss-hit the ball, it may hit the ring and bounce back into their own court, which costs them a point."

"Can you play to your own side before returning the ball?"

"Certainly, Dr. Festus, but not on the first play when you must send the ball directly to the opposite side, and after that not more than two times—from say, the backfield to halfbacks then to the forwards. Or from one forward to another." Balaam paused for a brief period, going over the rules in his mind. "Oh, yes. I should add that only one ring counts. The one on the left hand side of the court when you're facing your opponents."

"You sound like my high school coach explainin' basketball." Zack commented wryly. "How can you be so cold blooded? Our lives are at stake in this game."

"This is an old tradition for me. I've taught the game for many years. Though rarely with such a serious end in mind. In that sense I am your high school coach."

Festus was worrying about the practicalities of playing the game. "How long will we have to prepare?"

"I'll give you five days. Beyond that I'll have a problem keeping you here."

"That's right," Angel snapped. "Why do you imagine you can get away with this? Somebody in Argos will surely miss all of us pretty soon. It will be in all the papers. I've heard of Copan. There are tourists here. Someone will see us."

"Mister Panou Cronson and that employee of yours have been advised to tell your relatives and friends that you're on location in the Yucatan, making a film about Mayan temples." Balaam smiled. "Funded by the Eurysthesian Foundation and Trust, of course."

"As to your being here, I have some influence on the local authorities. They agreed to keep tourist away for the eight days I said I needed to shoot scenes for my movie. If you try any tricks, you and they will be amazed at the realism of the death scenes. I should make one final point. In five days, you'll not learn to play tlachtli to any useful level, without coaching. Your opponents, who are practicing elsewhere, will have the advantage of playing with my ex-protege, Pacal, and his..." Balaam smiled, adding mockingly, "his fiancée. Tomorrow you'll see the court and we'll start practice. For now, there's some food coming and I expect you need sleep. If during the night you need to relieve yourselves, don't surprise the guards. They might shoot you!" Elena looked at Angel and made a small grimace then dropped her head and kept quiet.

The army issue tents were functional and kept out the multitude of bugs that were drawn by the fire. Even at the altitude of two thousand feet above sea level, the air in Copan was quite humid, and the sleeping bags were more to be slept on than in. They were just adequate to soften the hardness of the ground so that the Eurysthesians could sleep. Festus thought about Dawn and Pandora. Would they believe the story? He suspected not, even if they heard it from Pan, but what could they do? No sooner had he dealt with the eighth Labor than he was kidnapped to this godforsaken place, from which he might never return. He rubbed his tear-filled eyes and felt sorry for himself. To overcome the feeling he concentrated on thinking about the ballgame.

"Where's breakfast? Said Ari, emerging, groggily, from his tent.

"Looks like you had a bad night," Angel said, sympathetically.

"I had this damn nightmare. Pushed Demos off a cliff. I'd wake up each time he started falling. Couldn't shake it."

"You'll feel better soon." Angel pointed to where a guard was making coffee. On the ground near him, were plates of refried beans, shredded chicken, tortillas, and sliced mangoes.

When Balaam joined them, he and a guard were carrying a stack of leather gear.

Balaam held up a short leather apron. "We should start practice soon. You'll need to wear an apron. The ball is made of hard rubber and the apron and these elbow and knee guards will protect the joints. As to what else you wear, I leave that up to you. You men should be naked from the waist up. Women don't play except in unusual circumstances such as these." He pointed at Elena and Angel and uttered some quick phrase in dialect to the guards, who laughed.

"What did you say?" Angel asked, curiously.

Balaam hesitated. "I said that with your athletic build maybe you shouldn't wear a shirt, but Mrs. Cronson needed a retainer of some kind. Otherwise she might hit the ball illegally, by accident, with the upper portion of her body."

"Maybe I could distract the other team if I showed my boobs. What do you say, Zack?"

Zack laughed, nervously. "It might be the only good part of our game."

"While we're on the subject of clothes, please Mr. Balaam could you find us some tee shirts and shorts or skirts?" Elena bent her head and sniffed. "After a day or so our smell will be enough to drive the opposition from the court if we stay in these clothes."

"What do you think of these leather aprons," said Elena, tucking in the shirt Balaam had provided.

"Unnattractive, heavy, and it'll slow me down" Angelica replied, trying to turn her hips.

"I feel like an idiot," said Festus, pointing at the guards were dressed to play with them. Thank God for sneakers. I don't think I'd last long barefoot."

The site, notwithstanding the beauty of its surroundings, was a grim place. The two small temples they passed were ornamented with death's-heads carved in stone. Part human, part animal caricatures leered at them from every wall. They descended a magnificent staircase. The riser of each of the sixty-three steps was inscribed with Mayan glyphs. A stone monster, depicting the bird serpent, marked their way down the stairs. Seated stone figures, set down the descent, stared at them with cold blank faces. The stairs led to a wide grassy clearing with decayed stone structures and a few trees.

At the bottom of the steps, Balaam turned to his right, stopped, and spread out his hands indicating that they had reached their destination. "Isn't it magnificent? My crew has restored it to be like it was a thousand years ago. We're standing at the end of the ball court. There are stands for spectators on each side of the court. The shallow sloping sides of the stands you see here are typical of older courts. The poorer spectators can sit on them provided they don't get too close to the rings. Aristocrats and priests sit on top of the stands. You can see there is a stone ring held in the mouth of a jaguar on each side wall. Some time ago, for a previous game, we reconstructed them and repaired the floor. It was necessary to put them back for the film. It is interesting that under this court there are older courts going back to the time of the ancient Greeks. Maybe that has special significance?" Balaam added, smiling.

Festus acknowledged the thought with a lift of his eyebrows. Certainly, many of the gods were present. It was the time too for the ninth labor where, in legend, Heracles recovers the golden girdle of Ares for the daughter of king Eurystheus. There was a parallel, he thought. They were trying to recover the Pendant of Cronos, for whom—Festus or Hephaestus? No, strictly speaking it was for Samantha. He could feel Balaam studying him, and switched his attention back to the court.

"I should add that this is a relatively small ball court by some standards. It's thirty meters long and seven or so meters wide. At Chichen Itza, the court is huge—one hundred and sixty meters or more in length and about seventy meters wide. That was for a game played somewhat differently, the players were allowed to cross the centerline. It's rougher too and strictly for experts. With your total lack of experience and advanced age, you'll find a small court like this easier."

"I'm getting older by the minute. We'd better start learning soon if we have all these disadvantages." Ari barked. "Where's a ball, so I can practice?"

"We need some discipline. Each of you will go with one of my colleagues." Balaam motioned towards the guards who were dressed out. "I'll work with Dr. Festus." Balaam accompanied this statement by walking away with a pronounced limp. "First we'll try to strike the ball with the hip. This is basic play. Later we'll try the upper thigh and elbows"

The guards each took a ball and tossed it into the air. As the ball dropped, they leaned sideways onto one foot bringing the hip around to strike the ball. The motion was fluid and it all looked very easy. The Eurysthesians attempted to return the ball but without exception, their timing was off. Either they missed the ball or it bounced only a small distance in a random direction.

"Now you understand the difficulties, let us do some exercises to learn the motions!" Balaam and the guards illustrated the techniques and made them practice the various motions for both the right and left hips and to allow for a ball coming from different directions. By the end of the morning, even with long periods of rest, the Eurysthesians were exhausted. However, they had learned some basic plays.

Festus was glad he had been playing, occasionally, as full back in an amateur soccer league in Austin. At first, he could not resist kicking the ball. "Penalty," Balaam had shouted each time, laughing. For once, his shorter left leg was an advantage. He could strike a ball with his left hip very effectively because he was used to balancing on his longer right leg.

"It's customary following a game or practice to cleanse the body with a steam bath," Balaam announced. "I think you'll welcome it. I'm sure you're exhausted.

We'll put special herbs in the fire, you'll find them soothing." He pointed to Elena whose arms and thighs were heavily bruised. "I'm afraid the color will stay but you needn't feel so sore. Come; let's go to the steam house!"

The steam house was a low structure with an anteroom for changing. There were wooden benches around three sides of the room. On the remaining side, there was a bed of hot coals covered it with a stone. Pitchers of water and a stack of dried plants were laid out ready to be used. In the anteroom, Zack and Ari stripped rapidly and unselfconsciously. If I looked as good as Ari, I'd strip quickly, Festus thought.

"Come on Angel, this is no time for modesty," Elena said, as she removed her shirt, dropped her apron and panties, revealing a mature, womanly physique. "Only you all and my hairdresser know my secret," she giggled.

"Boy, I'm hurting," said Zack, throwing some of the plants on the fire and pouring on the water to replenish the aromatic steam. Balaam was right, their muscles felt more relaxed and the camphor like essence of the herbs soothed the pain.

Balaam let them rest during the heat of the afternoon but they were back at practice early in the evening. That night they slept well.

The same regime followed for two days. By the end of this period, they had mastered the basic techniques of tlachtli, and they could keep the ball in the air between them for ten or more volleys. Ari and Angel were the most skillful. They had even learned to use their elbows effectively. Zack and Elena were less skilled but steady players. Festus was the weakest, because while he could handle a ball coming from the left better than the rest of them, he had difficulty with a ball coming from the right. Unlike them, he did not play volleyball or basketball and he had poor judgment about the position of his arms. Therefore, his elbow shots were inadequate and he couldn't use this shot to compensate for his weak right hip shot.

On the third day, they played a game against the guards. Balaam acted as umpire. After a small amount of discussion, they decided to set Festus in the backfield, Zack and Elena at left and right middle field and Angelica and Ari as left and right forwards respectively.

Balaam started the game by throwing the ball to the right forward of the guards. The guard swung and hit up field to the Eurysthesians. Elena, stretching, was unable to set up the ball for her forwards, but succeeded in returning it. Their receiver rapidly popped it up, and the other forward smashed it down the center of the court for a point. Zack, diving, was unable to take the ball on the first bounce. Balaam restarted the game by throwing the ball to Ari. He made a good shot down to the back guard. He in turn elbowed the ball but only reached his midfield players. They scooped the ball to the forwards who then were only able to clear it back to the Eurysthesians. Elena, running to help Zack, was again able to pop it up to the forwards but Angel hit it directly back to the forward line of the guards. Again they scored.

At this point Balaam stopped the game. "See the point of the game? Set up the ball for your forwards, like volleyball. Let's stop for a short period and practice doing that."

They practiced on the court, for a while, passing the ball to the forwards, before finishing the game. The guards won easily, 13 to 2. No rings were made though the guards made a few attempts. For the first time the Eurysthesians realized that, like in racquetball, the walls of the court could be used. They had been surprised when the guards had used this ploy. Strangely, it was the one play Festus found easy to handle when the ball came off the wall from his left. He could see that to ring a ball it had to be hit high and long. On one occasion he had the time to move up and return the ball as it deflected, however, he did not get enough speed on the ball and it fell short of the ring. His colleagues did not realize that he had attempted it and put it down to a poor shot.

"Thank God we scored," Zack muttered, tiredly, at the end of the game."

After the game Balaam drew Festus aside. "I saw you miss that shot," he said. "Why don't you stay behind and let me coach you on the proper technique? I see that you find it easier to strike the ball coming from the left and you've got good balance. In fact you're nearly at professional level, at least," Balaam grinned, "if the ball comes to you at exactly the correct angle. What sport have you played that gives you this skill?"

"I play a little soccer. I learned to adjust to my uneven legs, while trapping the ball and shielding it. Look, I can see how to do the shot, but I don't have the speed. Teach Ari! He's the best athlete among us."

"I'll teach him, and you learn how to pass the ball at the right height."

They worked hard for two more days. Balaam took Ari aside and trained him in the technique for making a ring. "It should be automatic, Colonel Cronson," he said. "Automatic. You will not have time to think."

When they came for their final practice, Balaam surprised them by saying, "you've practiced enough. Rest up for the game tomorrow. Eat well tonight for tomorrow you'll only be allowed to drink a little. This is the custom. You're free to walk around Copan but don't go beyond your side of the ball court. Your opponents are camped in the main court beyond it. Have a good night and remember that it was also the custom to refrain from sex, though this custom was followed less than most."

"I'm going for a walk," Festus said, scrambling to his feet. "I need to think about strategy." He walked down to the river. Zack and Elena, without a word, also left. Ari and Angelica sat and looked at each other.

"Ari, I'm sorry about Demos."

"Angel, I failed him. Now we've got to play against each other in this damn game. Balaam's been teaching me how to shoot a ring. Don't know if I can do it. If I succeed, does it mean death for Demos?"

Angel grasped him firmly by the arms and looked steadily at him. "You must protect our family!" she said, forcefully. "You know that."

"I know," said Ari, wearily, "and the Doc too. Sometimes I hate that little bastard. He's too damned smart. I owe him one for getting us out of that mess in Tam'oan Shan. But Demos?" Ari looked teary.

Angel rose. "I need to talk to Fes. I don't like to leave you alone, but I've got to tell him something." Ari watched as she followed the path down to the river. Then he too wandered off, following the side of the temple to the east court. The guards watched but did not follow any of them.

Festus sat by the river. It was still light and he could pick out individual trees. Mahogany was the only one he could recognize. The first bats were appearing, ready for that night's feast of insects. Just in front of him, the water was trapped by rock and swirled slowly around before joining the main stream. As he stared at the smooth surface of the water, it appeared to mirror an image of a ball game. The players became more distinct. *He could pick out Demos and his team members. Wendell and Amanda he could more or less picture, but the two Olmecs were hazy. In his own team, he could clearly see Zack, Ari, Elena and Angel in their positions. In his position, he saw only a dark shape. I can see everyone I know except myself, he thought. The players finished warming up. The spectators cheered, it was the Chorus from the Play Cycle again, now dressed as Olmec peasants. Then a robed figure in the stands lobbed a ball down and started the game. He watched in horror as Demos and his team overwhelmed them. The crowd came out of the stands. He felt a hand on his shoulder.* The illusion *vanished.*

Angel backed away. "I'm sorry Fes. I didn't mean to startle you."

Festus wiped his hand across his forehead. "I was dreaming, Angel. Mesmerized by that little whirlpool."

Angel sat by his side. She looked at him, uncertainly. "I...I don't know how to say this, Fes." The words rushed out. "When you started going with Cathy

Schmidt, I was hurt, Fes. Cathy and I are close, very close, you know." Festus remained silent.

"I've dated a number of men but it hasn't worked. I'm more comfortable with women. But I've always loved you. I was really sick when you married Dawn." Angelica laughed, "Marienna was too."

"You're kidding! She's my godmother!"

"Well, I suppose it was your father Marienna loved and it sort of transferred to you. Anyway, now we're going to die tomorrow and I don't care anymore what anyone thinks."

Festus was silent for a moment trying to master a reply. "Angel, I'm very fond of you too. You're not going to die. It wouldn't make sense, regardless of what Balaam says."

"Are you sure?"

"No." Festus grinned, wryly.

They returned to the camp. Angel went to her tent. Festus sat looking at the fire. In the flames, he could imagine the ball court. There was a play to win. The main problem was getting the other team to lead into it.

"Talked to Demos, Doc. He told me it was my fault. They'll win and we'll all die." Ari's handsome face was haggard with strain. "Don't know if I can play to win against him. Deserves to lose but he's my son."

"If we die, our people will lose their identity."

"Our people, Fes? Who the hell do you think we are? Sometimes you act as if the plays are real. Are you Hephaestus the god? I'm surely not Ares the god. I'm poor damned Aristotle Cronson I run a farm and I'm in the Army reserves. I'm Zack's deputy in our businesses. Sometimes, I'm the sheriff. I'm interested in Central America. Not this interested. I coach high school football. I don't understand the dancing floor and the damn dreams." Ari looked embarrassed. "Yeah, I've had dreams too. This is reality. Tomorrow I may die and if I don't it's only because my son's gonna die."

"Ari, as I was telling Angel, I'm not convinced Balaam's going to have anyone killed," Festus said reassuringly.

"He didn't sound like he was joking to me."

"Think about it, Ari. If we disappear, there will be hell to pay. Pan knows what we we're doing in Austin and he knows about Balaam."

"You may be right." Ari looked relieved, but only for a moment. "What about Demos? Balaam's going to do something whoever wins."

Festus hung his head. "Can't argue with that. Implies it doesn't matter if we win."

"Ari shook his head. "Easy for you to say." He started to leave.

"Did you ask him what he meant about Marienna?" Festus called after him.

"What, Doc? Oh, sorta."

"What did he say?"

"Somethin' about Marienna's yard and...I don't know." Ari responded, tiredly, and left. The guards looked on, impassively.

Festus lay on his back trying to picture Marienna's yard. What had Demos meant? He wondered. A shadow passed across the side of the tent obscuring the light for a moment. He thought he could hear Balaam speak. "Sleep! Sleep well!" Festus concentrated on thoughts of Dawn. His eyes closed.

The ball court sparkled in the morning sun. The sandy floor had been freshly raked. Three zones were marked on each side of the centerline, which lay in a line with the rings. They helped the players retain position. Festus looked at his team. While he felt ridiculous in his leather apron and padding, they looked the part, athletic and fit—except for the incongruous looking sneakers. At least he felt fit. The steam house had relaxed his muscles. He glanced around him. For the first time they were not alone in the ball court, with only the guards and Balaam for company. Now, the stands were filling with people. All were dressed in Mayan costumes—a noisy crowd, shouting and betting. The thought that Balaam was taking this too far crossed his mind, until he remembered that it was real. A real game to the death, and Balaam really was making a film. He could see the cameras, set on rails, one across the top and back of a stand, others at each end of the court, ready to swing out to film the play.

Ari nudged Zack. "That Balaam must be mad. Thought he was joking about filming us. Ask him if we can have instant replay so that we can correct our mistakes! I'm sure as hell going to need help," Ari added wryly.

"It's too late for that, Colonel Cronson but I can use the film for coaching if at some later date I'm forced to set up another game such as this." Balaam commented as he walked past them on his way to a camera. He was dressed as a Hollywood director of the 1920's, in jodhpurs, boots and a white shirt. A referee's whistle hung around his neck and he held a megaphone in his hand.

"Order please!" Balaam shouted. The crowd noise ceased on cue. "There will be only one take of this game, so remember your instructions. You must strike that ball on the volley or on the bounce. If the ball remains on the ground in your part of the court, the other team gains a point. Thirteen points wins the game. If, at any time, you ring the ball in the ring at the left of your court, you win outright. When a point is won, I will throw the ball to the losing team. There will be a rest period after the first team has scored seven points. Now, let's toss a coin to see who receives. Colonel Cronson, you call!" Balaam flicked a silver peso in the air. "Heads," said Ari.

"Tails it is. Pacal's team will receive. Here! You keep the coin!" Balaam said, flicking it to Ari.

"Loser!" Demos shouted.

Each player faced his or her opposite number across the centerline. As Balaam had promised, the most experienced player, Pacal, was in the backfield. Festus was opposite him. Elena, at right midfield, faced Amanda Ellesmere. Opposite Zack at left mid field, was Wendell Jameson. As right forward, Angelica faced the Olmec girl, Cha. Aristotle was opposite Demos. Both of them were staring steadfastly at the ground refusing to look at each other. The two teams bowed. "You're dead, suckers." Wendell mouthed as he turned.

Balaam lobbed the ball down into the court area near Demos. He took it on his left hip and flicked it hard towards Elena. Elena managed to touch it with her left elbow and it took a low trajectory back towards Festus. Festus hip thrust desperately with his right hip, lost his balance, and fell to the ground. Elena despondently picked the ball up and threw it to a guard.

"Good try, Fes. I meant to hit it to Zack," Elena spoke encouragingly.

"Cripple!" Wendell shouted across the court. "I fucked your wife."

Festus stopped and stared at him in amazement. He couldn't imagine how this could have happened, and realized it was a ploy to upset him. "Dream on kid. I really do," he replied. "It's great." It was Wendell's turn to look surprised.

"I'll get you bastard! Shitface!" Ari shouted angrily.

"Come on team!" said Zack, wearily. "Don't be suckered by his childish cracks!"

The game restarted. Balaam threw the ball to Zack. Zack spun quickly and hit a long ball down to Pacal. Pacal, surprised at the strength of the shot, scrambled and just managed to knock it to Wendell. He in turn elbowed it to Cha. She had no chance at a scoring shot and returned the ball up court to Angelica. Angelica flicked the ball with her elbow back across to Ari. Ari succeeded in driving the ball hard down into the dirt at the feet of Demos. The score was now tied at one a piece.

"Take your time gettin' back to your places," Zack whispered. "This game is moving too fast. We musn't get tired."

Balaam threw the ball down to Cha. She spun quickly and hit the ball into the wall around Angel towards Zack. Festus ran forward. This time he was ready for the ball coming from his left. I must try a shot. Now, while the score is low, I can risk it, Festus thought. "It's mine!" Festus shouted. Zack stopped in surprise. Festus transferred his weight to his right foot and hit the ball back hard. It reached the wall and bounced against the jaguar head that held the ring. It fell to the ground. Festus hung his head dejectedly.

"Don't be too clever, Fes." Zack spoke softly, catching him as he staggered sideways. "Next time pass the ball and help set up a score." Festus waved his arm in apology.

Angelica received the next ball from Balaam and knocked it straight at Amanda. She panicked but succeeded in lobbing the ball up in the air. Pacal, to the surprise of the Eurysthesians, rushed from the back of the court, dove, and flicked it to Demos using his right elbow. Demos moved awkwardly, nevertheless he succeeded in dropping the ball between his father and Angelica for a score.

"Come on team," Ari shouted. "Keep it cool." He collected the ball thrown in by Balaam and again hammered it down court, this time over Demos' head at Amanda. Again, she appeared panicky but succeeded in keeping the ball in play. Wendell, anticipating her dilemma, caught the ball on his left thigh and pushed it up to Cha. Cha shot it hard at the space between Angelica and Ari. Angelica, learning from Pacal, threw herself head long and flicked it to Ari with her elbow, he smashed it with his left elbow into the ground behind Cha. From the score of three to two in favor of Pacal's team, the game went remorselessly against the Eurysthesians, to stand at seven to four.

Balaam called a break. The Eurysthesians gathered in the shade of the stand and sipped at cups of water.

"We've got to hold the ball longer," Zack commented. "It's the only way to catch up."

"I'm worried we won't catch up," Festus interrupted. "The odds seem against it. I believe we have to ring the ball."

Zack retorted angrily. "Oh, for God's sake, Fes! I'm not going to waste scoring opportunities so that you can try more idiot shots."

"You know Balaam coached Ari and me," Festus responded. "He believes it's the only way we can win. I haven't got enough speed. I'm sorry I tried it. Ari's our strongest player. He could do it, but he'll have to change position to sweeper or left midfield."

"Zack," Elena pleaded, "why don't we try it your way but, if we continue to fall behind, we should change the positions and let Ari try a shot?"

"It sounds risky, but I guess we have no choice. Hell! If this fiasco goes on much longer, we'll be desperate enough to try anything. I reckon Balaam's serious in his threats." Ari and Angelica nodded agreement.

Following the rest period, the Eurysthesians played better so that after the fifteenth game the score stood at nine to six in favor of Demos' team.

For the sixteenth play, Balaam threw the ball down to Elena who made a bad shot across the court to Wendell. Wendell flicked the ball across to Demos. He in turn pretended to take a scoring shot then elbowed the ball across to Cha. Zack and Elena were now out of position and Cha simply dropped the ball too far in front of Zack for him to reach it. The Eurysthesians were tired and making more mistakes. For the seventeenth play, Angelica received the ball and again trying a long shot, overbalanced and missed the ball, which dropped at Ari's feet. Ari wearily stooped to pick up the ball. As he straightened up, he could see Demos right in front of him.

"You're dead, old man," Demos whispered.

Ari tried to hide his feelings, but his anger showed when he hurled the ball back to Balaam. While this interplay was going on, Festus went over to Zack and Elena.

"Let Ari try the ring shot!"

Zack looked resigned. "If we lose two more plays, we're dead. We might as well try it, though heaven knows whether we're good enough. I'll tell Ari and Angel."

As Balaam threw the ball down to start the eighteenth play, he shouted. "The score is eleven to six in favor of Demos Cronson and his team. The game ends at thirteen, or," he looked in Ari's direction, "if a ring is made."

Zack, who had swapped places with Ari, caught the ball and for the second time in the game, succeeded in striking it long, down field to Pacal. He passed forward to Wendell, who misjudged the angle of the ball. Wendell was lucky to knock it forward far enough so that Demos, scrambling, could elbow it across the centerline to Angelica. Angelica, instead of taking a prime scoring opportunity, flicked it back to Ari. He was not ready for a ring shot and to the amazement of Demos' team, did not hit it far up court but spun and hit it of the wall towards Cha. Cha, surprised by the move, swung fast and hit the ball to the back of the court. Festus, popped it forwards, in the move he and Ari had practiced. Zack dropped to the ground as Ari rushed forward.

"Dad!" Demos screamed, realizing what was going to happen. Ari did not hesitate. The athlete in him and the training for the shot had taken over. He was totally committed to the play. "Oh God, help me make this one," Ari cried. Planting his weight on his right foot, he spun hard, catching the ball as it dropped towards him. The crowd was silent as the ball caromed off the hard, smooth face of the wall in front of the ring. Demos and his team stood transfixed, as the ball seemed to float in slow motion through the ring. It dropped at the feet of Cha. Balaam broke the silence.

"A ring has been made by the team of Zachary Cronson. They are the winners."

"I did it. We won," Ari screamed. "Fuck you, Wendell! That'll teach you bastards. You won't mess with me again." Ari ran towards the center of the court as if to attack Wendell, until he saw his son, when he stopped abruptly. Demos, sullen faced, was watching him. "You always win at sports. That's your...He didn't finish, for Cha had picked up the ball and hurled it out of the court, rushing to embrace Pacal. When Cha moved, the crowd erupted, descending on the hapless losers, ripping at their clothes and beating them. "Stop them!" Ari screamed at Balaam.

Balaam shrugged his shoulders. "It is the custom."

"I'll stop them then," Ari shouted as he rushed to help Demos. The crowd beat him off. At this point Balaam signaled for the guards to move. They restrained Ari and dispersed the crowd quickly, threatening them with their rifles. The rifles appeared incongruous in the setting of ancient Mayan costumes. The nearly naked losing team was bustled off the court.

The guards escorted the victors to the stream house. The hot, heavily scented vapor swaddled their bodies as they sat on the wooden benches.

"Thank God that's over." Zack said with relief. "I was sure we'd lose. Ari, you've done it again! Thank God somebody in the family can play sports!" Ari remained silent. Zack paid no attention, giving Festus a bear hug. Fantastic set-up, Fes."

"Watch it Zack, I've a few bruises you know."

"Me too," Elena echoed. "My body is one big bruise. God, this steam feels good. I could sit here for ever."

"It feels good but the scent's a bit strong for me today," Angelica added. "I feel dizzy."

"I do too," Festus mumbled. "Before I pass out. Thanks Ari."

"Doc! You set the ball up great. Fooled them completely." Ari sank wearily onto the bench. His handsome face, normally tanned and youthful looking, was gray. Not from exhaustion but from fear, thought Festus. The War God, victorious again, yet fearful of losing his most treasured possession.

"What happens now we've won, Doc? What happens to Demos and his team? Will Balaam really kill them or is this another of his tricks? Why did I do it?"

"I'm not sure about anything, Ari. Don't blame yourself," Festus responded quickly, seeing Ari's distress. "As Balaam told you, the shot had to be automatic. I'm not convinced we would have lost, regardless of the outcome of the game."

"I think Fes is right," Zack added. Elena and Angel nodded agreement. "Don't blame yourself, Ari. Balaam is making a movie. This is fantasy land."

Ari looked hard at him, and then went over to add more water. "Oh hell! There's no water left. I guess we'd better get dressed."

Their clothes had disappeared from the antechamber. White gowns were in their place. A jug of water and cups were set out on a low table. "That I need," said Elena, descending on the water and drinking rapidly. The rest of the team joined her.

Balaam was waiting for them outside. He was no longer dressed as a film director, but was dressed as an Olmec priest. He wore a cloth shirt—open to the waist—a tasseled leather belt, and a short apron. He wore a light wood headdress with long green quetzal feathers. At the end of each feather, there was a stylized, red snake's head. He also had heavy jade earrings and a jaguar skin cloak slung loosely over his shoulders. The Pendant of Cronos and a thin jade disk on a chain hung down to his bare chest.

"Congratulations to the victors. We must drink a toast to your success." The guards handed each of them a stone mug. Festus looked at it warily.

"I remember the strange effects of a drink you gave us before, Balaam. What is this?"

"This is innocuous," Balaam replied. "Come let us drink." Festus joined in but only pretended to drink. "What do you claim for your prize in victory?" Balaam asked.

"Freedom," Zack replied.

"Spare the losers," Elena added quickly.

"I regret that is not possible. You must know it." Balaam answered, sternly. "The game must run its course."

"What will happen to Demos?"

"You will see, Colonel Cronson."

"I would like the Pendant returned," Festus volunteered.

"Why should I give it to you?"

"Because we won."

"Freedom is not enough?"

"That is not yours to give," Festus replied, adopting Balaam's formal way of speech.

Balaam smiled. "Given that you are isolated and are surrounded by my people, I find that a remarkable statement."

"You know what I mean."

"Yes, maybe I do. I do not own you. You played my game and you won it. He gave the Pendant to Festus, and then held up the jade disk so that the sun shone through it onto the Eurysthesians. "Look at it. You will see the past too."

Mesmerized, the Eurysthesians watched the shiny object as he swung it slowly back and forth in front of them. Balaam was chanting in a strange language. The sight and sound was comforting and they now felt strangely euphoric. The scene took on a misty aura and they could sense what he was saying. *"Follow me," Balaam led them into the West Court.*

There was a roaring sound in their ears, from the wind that was growing in strength and from the crowd sitting on every vantage point around the court. Balaam indicated that they should stay with him as he climbed the steep steps of the temple. On the top sat an ornately carved altar and by it a small metal plate heated red by the fire. A limestone jar was under the altar. It contained a polished jade ball, the conjuring stone—satsun—used by a medicine man. Balaam took the satsun, and held it aloft, sweeping his hand in an arc to emphasize the act. Below them, Copan lay in its splendor. The ball court was empty now. The crowd had followed them into the west court and had spread out into the surrounding smaller temples. Behind them, the main temple dropped steeply down to a smaller courtyard and beyond it the river.

The crowd parted and the losing team was escorted into the court to face the temple. Balaam signaled for the first of them to be brought to the top up. It was Amanda. She appeared to be drugged as she allowed herself be led to the altar.

"Kneel!" Balaam said.

"Kneel!" repeated the priests, flanking him.

"Kneel!" chanted the crowd, the Eurysthesians joining with them in the chant. Amanda knelt down facing the court, her back to the altar.

"You are honored to be sacrificed to the gods," Balaam chanted.

They dragged Amanda to the altar. She lay supine, her face expressionless. She was naked above the waist. Balaam reached down to his belt. From it, he withdrew an obsidian knife and held it high. "Oh, Kukulcan accept this slave to your great court."

He plunged the knife into her chest, and tore it open, splaying her breasts aside. He paused, the bloody knife held aloft, then reached in and wrenched out the still beating heart. The crowd roared in approval as he tossed it to one of the priests, who dropped it onto the red-hot plate. As the heart burned and the smoke rose, Balaam chanted a paean in praise of Kukulcan. The other priests picked up the body and unceremoni-

ously hurled it down the backside of the temple, where it dropped into a small court-yard.

One by one, the victims were sacrificed until only Demos was left. He was led to the altar. His movements were lethargic. Then, as the priests moved to lay him \ on the altar, he swung around, pushing them aside. Demos ran to the back of the temple and started to descend. He tripped on the carved, glaring head of a jaguar and crashed down the side of the temple to join the other bodies. His neck was skewed to the side. Balaam watched this scene with surprising serenity. The priests dropped their heads in terror at this insult to the gods. The crowd was silent.

"Oh Kukulcan! Accept this sacrifice as it was intended. Forgive this insult." Bal-aam bowed his head. As he spoke, the sky darkened, as if on command. Rain poured onto Copan, fiercely, beating their shoulders. Flashes of lightning reflected from the standing water and blinded them, temporarily. The guards pushed the Eurysthesians to their knees, holding their heads down until, abruptly, the downpour ceased.

When they were able to lift their heads, the crowd was gone. The altar was no longer on top of the temple but was set in front of it in the west court.

"Was it real?" Zack cried. "Did he hypnotize us again?"

"That and special effects. He drugged us with the fumes in the steam house and with something in the water. I didn't drink the toast. Balaam told the truth then, we were already drugged," Festus answered. "Unfortunately, it wasn't all a dream. Look!" Festus pointed down to where the lone body of Demos lay, his dead eyes looking at the sky. Ari hung his head. Zack put his arm around him. "I'm sorry, but he brought it on himself."

Ari shook his head sadly. "Zack! It didn't have to happen. If only I'd been a better father." Ari descended slowly to his son, where he stood in silence for a long time, his head still bowed. When the tears had flowed enough for that moment, he reached in his pocket and removed the game coin, placing it on Demos' forehead. The Eurysthesians watched sadly.

"What happened to Wendell, Amanda and the Olmecs?"

"We'll probably never find out, Angel," Festus replied.

"Were they sacrificed?"

"I doubt it. The master of illusion tricked us again. I guess Balaam will…it sounds terrible to say it like this…will recondition them. What happens to them then, God only knows. Obviously, we've only his word for it that Pacal and Cha weren't actors. We'll never know."

"What will happen to us?"

"I think we'll be going home, Angel. See! The plane's down there," Zack replied.

Ari and Yianna butied Demos in Argos. Zack spread the story that Demos had slipped while climbing a temple in Copan. The ball game was never mentioned. Privately, people wondered if drugs were the cause of his death. Nobody questioned what the Eurythesians had been doing in Copan. They assumed it was another of Festus's weird schemes. The Greek community rallied around his mother. She had spoiled Demos, but who could fault a mother's love, they rationalized.

The bank reported to the police that Wendell was missing. Amanda's disappearance then came to light. After the police had made the connection to drugs, they questioned suspected dealers, but learned nothing. Eventually, with no progress made and despite the protestations of the families, the cases were filed. Festus told Dawn the true story.

Ari sank into a deep depression. He told his family that it did not matter whether Balaam would have let them win regardless of the outcome of the game. He did not believe Demos' death was an accident. He was the reason Demos had died. He retired to his ranch and, from then on, rarely came to Argos.

38. The Phaestos Disk

"Honey, I've got some good news." Dawn embraced Festus as he came in.

"What is it?" said Festus distractedly, thinking about the Disk.

"Pandora and Chuck are going to get married."

"Good."

"They'll be living together, until then."

"They'll what?"

"You heard me, and don't lose your cool!"

"When's the wedding?"

"They're planning on December."

Festus nodded. "That's fine. The next junket won't be until April. If I can get the Trust to support it."

"Where are you going?"

"Not quite sure. Getting close. Still working on it."

"You sound like Ari."

"God forbid!"

Festus fidgeted while Joe Maximos went through the usual business matters of the Breakfast Club. He smiled, picturing the look of discomfort on Harold Dexter's face when he had sat down, squashing the fart-cushion, secreted under the seat cover. Still sitting on it. Scared to move. Joe continued in, to Festus, excessive detail about finances. Festus was mounting pieces of sausage in a mound of scrambled egg and h potatoes and was tunneling under it, when Joe stopped talking. Festus looked up.

"Doc, I hope you can explain how to finance our Foundation as well as you know how to spend our money. Your turn, I hear you have some breakthrough."

"Sorry Joe, I'm a little distracted. No one understands the Club like you do. It's just that I think I'm on to something really important, as important as Che." He continued apologizing as he moved to the front. "I've solved the writing on the Phaestos Disk," he announced triumphantly. "Well, not all of it...but... enough to have uncovered some important facts."

"Some people may not know what Disk," Zack bellowed.

"It's an ancient clay tablet, found at the Palace of Phaestos. It's now in the museum at Iraklion. I have a replica of it with me and you can pass it around while I show some slides. Please be careful." Festus held the tablet, lovingly, for a moment. "Ionides, please turn on the projector."

The picture on the screen showed a round clay tablet. The surface was covered with impressed signs that spread out from the center between two spiral lines. The pictographs appeared to be of heads, people, fish, plants, buildings, weapons, tools, and other stylized images. The signs were in groups, with each group separated by short radial lines. The groups looked as if they might represent words or possibly sentences.

"There have been many suggestions, mainly fanciful, as to its meaning. Is it a list of possessions? Is it a game? The main problem in establishing its purpose lies in the symbols. Are they hieroglyphs or do they represent sounds?" Festus stopped to give his audience time to study the Disk. "Ion, please show you the other side"

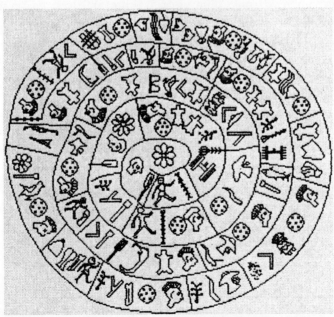

After a pause, he continued. "I have an advantage over the others who have attempted to translate the Disk. I have the Pendant of Cronos. It is the only other artifact that I am aware of that has an inscription that uses some of the Disk's symbols. On its own, that wouldn't help, but you see the Pendant's inscription is also in Hittite hieroglyphs. Seeing some uncomprehending faces, Festus tried another tack. "Maybe you've heard of the Rosetta Stone which has Egyptian hieroglyphs, demotic writing and Greek?" There were a few nods. "Interestingly, both the Egyptians and the Hittites are important to my translation. The Hittites ruled the area where Turkey and part of Syria are today. They were very powerful from at least as early as 1800 BC to 1200 BC. Particularly, because the Anatolian smiths had developed the techniques to work with iron, heralding the end of the Bronze Age. The pendant told me two things; first, the symbols are phonetic; and second, once I realized that one script was Hittite, it was a simple matter to obtain the excellent translations of Ignace Gelb and from those assign meanings to some of the symbols on the Disk.

"It really all sounds pretty simple, Henry. Put like that," Harold Dexter said, his face pinched in a token smile.

"Yes and no, Harold. One possibility is that the Disk is the work of a Hittite scribe, who employed some unfortunate Hittite practices. For example, they sometimes wrote down a different, but similar, word to the one spoken. Occasionally, they also lapsed into a form of shorthand in which a single symbol stood for a word. To compound the problem, they used both Akkadian and Sumerian abbreviations."

"So, what does it mean, Fes," Zack asked, irritably.

"It's not easy to answer. The Disk has about fifty different symbols and some are rotated in their positions, which may alter their meanings. It is relatively straightforward to look for a consistent translation for those that repeat a lot. Look at these ones on the next slide. I have managed to relate them to Greek letters, as indicated, and I have given them names to help me remember them.

flower ✿ (ου), skin ♋ (μ), soldier ✪ (s), shield ⊕ (o), boomerang ➤ (ρ) or (ερ).

The greatest difficulty lies in interpreting those signs that appear rarely. With an insufficient context to tie them down, they might be anything. Fortunately, the Pendant gave me the key. The most important discovery was that the Hittite symbols on the Pendant stood for Crete and Cronos. This established meanings for some of the Phaestos symbols—specifically, as shown here." Festus gave his audience a moment to look at the slide.

"Let me have the next slide, Ion. This shows the Phaestos symbols, the Greek letters, and the tentative English translation."

"The pronunciation, while strange by modern or even classical Greek standards, gave me the clue that the language was basically Greek. The analogy to the recent translation of the Aegean Linear B script by Michael Ventris is remarkable. Though, to give him credit, he did not have the benefit of a Rosetta Stone like the Pendant of Cronos." Festus paused to put up another slide. "With these symbols as a start, I tried various interpretations of the Disk. In particular, I looked for proper names from the period, around 1500 BC when, supposedly, it was made. It helped me, enormously, to know that there was a connection to the Hittites. Finally, I translated side of the Disk with a flower at the center. I have meanings for most of the symbols, but I cannot translate all the words yet. The running man is an abbreviation. It stands for χ(ω) ρ(α) or land. The ending varies depending on where the land is. A critical discovery was that ↳ ⬱ ◈ ⬥ stands for οδος the Greek for journey. It means journey from if the bird faces left, and it means journey to if the bird faces right. The scythe stands for θ or sometimes for τ. The skin at the end of a word stands for μα or μαι.

"It tells a fascinating story," Festus finished, proudly.

"Great," said Joe, "but what the hell does it mean?"

"Oh! I thought it was self-explanatory. The first point is that Alluwamnas was king of the Hittites from around 1500 BC for a decade or so. The name Hittite stands for the people of the tribe of Hatti, hence 'Hatti-land'. It seems that he, or more likely his personal boat, made a voyage from the port of Meranimos. The seafaring skills of the Phoenicians are well known, I hadn't realized that it started with the Hittites. The boat went to a land called Erythmos. It seems a leader, phonetically, K p i ch r, requested it."

"Wait up Fes! You've lost me. How do you know that word is a name? It could be anything. And one other thing, if you're right, was this person a Cretan?"

"Thanks, Alex. Both those points worried me for a long time. As to the first question, the answer lies in the position of the word in the sentence. It follows the words 'ibis guardian;' hence, 'ibis guardian Kpichr' implies a proper name. The word ibis hinted that the person might be Egyptian. That in turn led me to look at Egyptians from that period. Tuthmosis III was Pharaoh at the time and Rehkmire was his Vizier. In the necropolis of Rehkmire, there are pictures of Cretan traders, which confirm the connection. More important, there is a cartouche in the description of Rehkmire's deeds giving the name of one of his aides— Kapicher. It all fits very neatly"

"I have two other questions," Alex Platon was not satisfied with the answer. "Why did this Kapicher ask for help from the Hittites? And where is Erythmos?"

"It seems that the Egyptians lacked tin and made a secret deal. Now remember, this was the Bronze Age for most of the world. I'm pretty sure the Hittites had not divulged the progress they had made with developing iron. To make bronze you need both copper and tin. The Egyptians had access to the copper of Nubia and the Sudan. If however, their previous source of tin had dried up, for whatever reason, that would cause big problems. I assume that's what happened and they asked for help from their trading allies, the Cretans."

"Since it also appears that the Hittites helped with the boat, couldn't the Egyptians have gone directly to them, rather than to Crete? No, wait a minute I remember something, I guess they had a problem dealing with the Hittites? They were at war maybe?"

"Right, Harold" Festus smiled. "Good to hear that someone knows their history. They were at war when the Disk was made, or at least rivals for the land between them; where Israel, Jordan, Lebanon and Syria are today. This state of affairs continued until, at a later date, the army of Rameses II fought the army of the Hittite king Muwatalli at Kadesh in northern Syria; about 1300 BC, around the time of the demise of the Crete. The battle was a draw though, as depicted in the bas-relief at Luxor, the Egyptians claim a victory. Either way, it led eventually to what has been described as the worlds' first non-aggression pact. So, what does this have to do with the story?"

"You are going to tell us today? Aren't you?" Zack laughed loudly, emphasizing his irritation.

"Let me see, where was I?" Festus was momentarily startled by the aggressive tone. "So you see, I think the Hittites had access to some vast reserve of tin and the Egyptians used the Cretans as middlemen to obtain it. Oh yes, another important point on this side of the Disk is the reference to Erythmos. I believe that Erythmos was that 'Erytheia beyond the ocean stream' referred to by Apollodorus, and visited by Pythias the Greek in 400 BC."

"Great, Fes and where was that?"

"The West of England, by all accounts Cornwall. It all fits because, you see, Cornwall was a major source of tin in the Bronze Age. They're still mining tin today, some few thousand years later. So if..."

"Now that's where I'm sure you must be wrong," Harold Dexter interrupted, triumphantly. "It's a subject I have read about. It's true that the Phoenicians traded with Cornwall but, as you indicated, that was many centuries later. A major source of tin at the time you're discussing was Minorca in the Balearic Islands, off the coast of Spain. The Egyptians, Cretans, Hittites or whoever had no reason to go careering off to Cornwall, when Minorca was obviously far more convenient." Harold looked pleased on seeing the flicker of worry cross the speaker's face.

"A very good point Harold. It puzzled me when I made the translation. I...er...don't have a good answer." Damn Harold for knowing one of the few weak points in his theory! Better get off the topic. "Er...I can only surmise that for some reason the tin from Minorca wasn't accessible to the Egyptians or to the Cretans during that period. Maybe some hostile people had taken over the island?"

"Come on Henry, the fact is you really don't know what it means."

"Harold, let me finish giving you my interpretation before you dismiss it! You could have also asked why the Cretans, who were a great sea power, needed the Hittites to provide a boat. Certainly, they were capable of trading with Minorca. I conjecture, however, that they were not equipped to sail to Cornwall. Did they lack a navigator? Were they scared to leave the Mediterranean? I suspect the southern part of the Hittite Empire had made that connection, and their Phoenician descendants were the inheritors of the trade rather than its initiators. I'm sure you can think of good reasons why they couldn't have gone. Eh! Harold."

"It's a lot of suspicions and conjectures. I suppose you're going to propose that we all tear of to Cornwall on the basis of it?"

Joe Maximos was incensed. "Harold, please try and be a bit more positive?"

"Damn stupid, asinine, practical jokes. A...a...expletive-cushion, for Christ's sake!" Harold's face showed his anger as he stood up and removed the offending object. For a second it seemed that he would throw it at Festus, but he merely dropped it on the floor and sat down.

"I expect Fes will get to your point in a minute. You know, Harold, I sometimes think you forget the purpose of our Foundation. Doc has done an outstanding job of finding Labors that bring us credit and on average are financially rewarding. Let him explain it in his way. I'm sure it'll all be clear in a moment."

Festus smiled his thanks at Joe for the support, and continued, trying to avoid looking at Harold. "I believe the Egyptians came to the Cretans for help in finding tin. Presumably, they offered them a substantial payment. For some reason, they ruled out Minorca, and the Cretans turned to the Hittites for help. I speculate again that the Hittites may well have had other sources of tin closer to home but those were needed to meet their own demand. The Cretan request gave them a subsidized way to make use of this new source they'd discovered." Festus paused, expecting comments but none came. "It seems incredible I know, yet life is full of the incredible. Let me give you a modern day example. The Soviets and we are still in this Cold War. It has many of similarities to the state of the Egyptians and the Hittites back then. One area, in which each country takes great care to protect its interests, is that of nuclear fission, because of the bomb. Yet I read recently that enriched uranium fuel, in use in some power station on the East Coast, originated in the Soviet Union. The Soviets sold it to an Italian company. In turn, the Italians, acting as intermediaries sold it to the US. As has been said many times before, business is business. My discovery could be very important to us. I believe..."

Harold interrupted him again. "Important to you Henry. Important to your personal ambitions. I remember other trips which didn't help the rest of us."

Before Festus could reply, Alex spoke. "All right, we'll allow that you're correct Fes, but I must agree with Harold. I can see it will be of great interest to archeologists. I know a little bit of ancient history, but I'd never realized that the Hittites were great sailors. Nevertheless, though you've worked out a good excuse to go to Cornwall, by translating the Disk, I don't see how the Foundation can turn a profit from it."

Festus raised his arms in supplication. "If this works out we may be able to recoup everything. I interpret the Disk this way. If we follow the route of the journey it describes, we'll find the clues to the great treasure that the Egyptians paid to the Cretans and Hittites, and I suspect the Hittites then paid the Cretans for brokering the deal. More important though, I believe we may find an answer to all of those strange things that have happened to us. For example..."

Zack interrupted him. "Let me say that I think there's something to this treasure business," Zack, I...and Marienna...have been following up on rumors of a treasure for a number of years, and getting nowhere until now." Zack continued. "Fes, you'd better explain the other comment. I'm not sure everyone accepts what you're gettin' at.

Festus looked at the ground to hide his smile. He remembered a brief discussion with Duke before he had disappeared. This confirmed the suspicion that Zack was following a hidden agenda in his dealings with Crete. So this was it, the secret treasure of the Disk. It sounded like Marienna might be behind it. His face showed no further emotion as he spoke to the Eurysthesians. "Zack knows, Marienna knows, Peri knows, and I think, Harold, you know, but like many of us you pretend it doesn't exist. I mean our connection to the past."

There was silence. Each person in the room had lives in which flashbacks to ancient Crete had occurred. However, as Festus had correctly stated, few of them admitted to it. Apparently, for some it was an infrequent occurrence, for others, like Festus and Peri Dexter, it was a persistent situation.

"Festus means the feeling that we're leading double lives. That sometimes our Cretan or Greek past is repeating itself. I believed it was due to our involvement in the plays—a strange continuation of each role. Since I visited Crete, recently, I've had my doubts about that simple explanation for our situation."

"Maybe it isn't a fantasy," Alex interjected, flippantly. "I've always felt it was the other way around. I haven't been turning into my character Apollo. My character has been turning into me. I'm converting Apollo into a lawyer."

"God forbid! You're joking, yet I bet you of all people believe it. Our families have all had roles for many generations, going back to the earlier sketches. Zack's family has been involved for God knows how long. During recent years, our adventures have paralleled the plays in a remarkable way. Let me say it before Harold does, I set up the first Labor. I did nopt plan to match the Labors of Heracles or to follow the play cycle for the other activities. Yet in some odd manner, they do exactly that. Remember that in the final play of Marienna's tetralogy, Heracles and I go down to Tartarus," Festus grinned at Harold, "to take a treasure from Hades."

"Henry, I think you and Marienna suffer more from this weird illusion than any of us," Harold retorted. "Sometimes, despite all of your protestations to the contrary, I'm convinced that you've manipulated us through the Society to correct your image in the plays. The coincidences are incredible. You or Marienna tried to get the plays changed to emphasize your role, over that of Heracles, over that of Ares, and even over that of Zeus. When that attempt to change recorded history failed, you tricked us into setting up Olympic Services, and we all know how you manipulated the Foundation's trip to Blarney. I don't believe this nonsense about a strange connection to the past. There are some odd coincidences, but everything else you or Marienna have set up in some, typically, devious way."

"It's an easy solution, Harold, to lay all the blame on Fes. Is he responsible for your cemetery being across the Colorado River—your personal Styx?" Alex asked, slyly. "Does he force you to cross it daily in your rowboat, accompanied by that strange dog of yours?"

"Don't be stupid, Alex! You know damn well that fishing is my hobby. Peri doesn't enjoy fishing and my dog keeps me company. I resent your personal attack."

Zack motioned them to let the argument die, and acted quickly to restore order to the discussion. "As you say, Harold, it's a far fetched idea. Let's drop it for the moment and continue with the business in hand. Carry on, Fes. Tell us whereabouts in Cornwall you expect to find the clues to this treasure?"

"The last phrase on the Disk says, 'the host of Crete weapons contain.' I interpret this to mean the treasure is on Crete and guarded. I propose to follow the route of the Hittites and their Cretan allies back from Cornwall to Crete. I hope to find clues on Bronze Age stone monuments, which are near the tin mines in Cornwall. What I need is help in translating the obscure parts of the Disk, notably on the first side that phrase, 'journey to (?) Alluwamnas.' I think it refers to the intermediate stopping place between Cornwall and Crete. At that intermediate place there may be other clues to what to look for on Crete."

"What if you can't find this place?" Zack sounded skeptical.

"I'm embarrassed to mention it, but I'm assuming that is the beginning of the tenth Labor—the recovery of the cattle of Geryon. This limits the possibilities to the Pyrenees, Cadiz in Portugal, the South of France, and Sicily. That is to places between Greece and Cornwall which, in legend, Heracles visited in undertaking these Labors."

"Why didn't you just say Southern Europe, Henry?" Harold commented, crabbily.

"For God's sake cool it Harold! Fes is simply being frank with us. His hunches have paid off before. Let him continue! Can you narrow down those options?"

"I think so, Alex. It's likely to be a place with a good port. Notwithstanding the various legends, it should be on a sensible route from Cornwall to Crete. I favor Cadiz or Sicily.

"What if you can't find any more clues, even if you find this port?"

"Well, Zack, I've translated part of the second side of the Disk. Though I'm not in as good shape as on the first side. It does support the idea that the treasure is on Crete and there are hints that a dancing floor is involved. Unfortunately, I don't know where the floor is, or what to do if we find it. It might be one we visited before?"

"I have a question. How much money will we need this time? I guess as treasurer of our Trust it's time for me to start worrying about it," Joe volunteered, quietly.

"I haven't worked it all out yet except we may need to do some mining in Cornwall and it would be a good idea to have an ocean going boat to follow the trail of the Cretans and the Hittites. I guess a million or so might cover it," Festus finished, hesitantly.

"Is that all?"

"Yes, Harold, that should be enough. If we need more, Joe will come to see you." Festus replied, flatly. "Of course, we'll require a crew. I'm hoping the Club can provide that."

"We may even do better than that," Alex said. "You know, and I suppose you're angling for it, that I have a modest sailboat down in Corpus Christi. I could sail over and meet y'all in Cornwall. I've sailed to Europe before. Joe and Mary Beth could come. They've crewed for me in the Caribbean. At a squeeze, I could take another couple or two. That would save a fair bit of money."

"Thanks for taking the hook, Alex. Could you come for as much as six months, though? I think it will take that long.'

"Sure, I need another sabbatical. Business has been good recently. To be honest I've been waiting for an excuse to sail around Europe again. Now that I'm the senior partner I can lay work off on my associates, and get on with some serious laying of my own," Alex grinned broadly.

Senior partner thought Festus. How could anyone look that young? Maybe it came with the self-indulgent, bachelor life that Alex led—unencumbered by children. Plenty of time to indulge his superstitious nature, the only threat to his wrinkle free face.

"Don't forget Sam and me," Ionides interrupted, excitedly. "We can sail a bit too."

Festus smiled encouragingly. "Ion, I'm sure y'all get a chance to go on the boat later. First I'd like you to help me with the mining, and I need to start that before they join us."

"Mining, Fes! You'd better explain about the ancient stones you mentioned and this minin'. Why do you need to mine? Aren't these stones visible?"

"I'm not sure we have to mine, Zack. It may be that the inscriptions, assuming that's what I'm looking for, are on the exposed sides of the stones. Somehow I doubt it, because in none of the discussions of them which I've read, is there a mention of any inscription. I'm guessing that if they carry a message it's on the base of one or more stones. Their weight offers protection against a casual inspection. In my judgment, it would take a long time to get permission to lift the stones. The stones are a national treasure. So, I wrote to the local mining companies, asking for information. I said we had developed some new techniques for reestablishing abandoned mines, and were interested in testing them. One of the companies sent me detailed maps of the mines in the area. They show that there is one shaft with a gallery that goes towards the stones. I plan to extend the gallery, come up under the stones and study them from there."

"You're crazy," muttered Harold. "You talk about stones. What stones? You've told us nothing about them."

"Goddamn it, Harold! I would've told you if you'd allowed me to complete my talk in the way I planned it, without interruption."

"You don't need to shout at me, Henry. I've every right to ask. It's my money you want to spend. Tell me then, how in the name of God do you look at stones in Cornwall, from Texas, and decide that they have hidden Hittite inscriptions? And ano…"

"I thought a lot about where to look," Festus retorted, angrily. "There are a number of stone monuments in the area. Marienna helped me analyze and narrow down the possibilities. In fact, she suggested the inscriptions might be hidden. There are two groups of stones that I believe may connect with the Disk. They're both near the village of Morvah, which is a little north of Lands End on the Atlantic coast. One group is called Men-an-Tol; it consists of three stones in a row. The center one is a stone ring, which sits vertically across the line between the remaining two stones, which are sort of somewhere between rectangular and conical in shape. They're the main clue to the previous presence of the Hittites. You see, in Hittite writing two triangles with lines across them represent land or country. The symbols for god and sun both have the form of a ring."

"I see. So one simple interpretation of their significance would be that the Hittites left them to show they had been there or maybe to claim the land on behalf of their gods?"

"You took the words out of my mouth, Zack. If this is a correct interpretation, then we should see similar signs along the way."

"What about the other stones you mentioned."

"The second group's even more interesting. This is a set of eleven stones known, incongruously, as 'the Nine Maidens'. It's a significant name if, as I'm guessing, it refers to the nine maidens on the dancing floor."

"Surely there aren't usually nine?" Harold asked, in surprise. "I rarely remember seeing that many." No one answered him. "How do I know? I guess..." his voice trailed away slowly. He recovered quickly and spoke more brazenly. "You're right, Henry. I remember Marienna talking about that Royal Cretan dance she gets us to do. There were up to nine novitiate priestesses involved, though often less of them took the floor. However, if I assume your explanation's correct, I can't explain the eleven stones."

"You all know the answer, I suspect?" Festus replied. "The additional stones represent the high priestess and the bull master."

"You're right Henry that would make sense. Now then, do you know which stones to study, to find these inscriptions? Assuming there are any?"

"I'm afraid we'll have to look at all of them, Harold."

Harold Dexter had now recovered his composure and, irritated by his earlier admission of weakness, went on the attack again. "Let's get back to the question of money for a second. Therefore, in reality, you need maybe two million. Then all of us are going to trip around, like in Ireland, I suppose?"

"Oh, wrap it up, Harold!" Zack shouted. "Stop criticizing so much. You and Peri had a hell of a good time in Ireland and in Crete. I know that there were difficult moments on both trips. We had family problems to settle. Yet, despite that, everything worked out for the good in the end. You're being far too negative. Peri would love to return to Crete. Why don't you ask her?"

Harold's gray face took on a grayer hue. He pursed his lips in unspoken anger at Zack's criticism. Festus could tell that he was frightened for Peri's sake; her imagination made her so vulnerable. Yet she would want to go and there was no way he could prevent her from hearing about the plans. Harold hid his fears by again grumbling about the cost. "It's still a lot of money."

"Haven't you grasped it yet, Harold?" Joe Maximos retorted, sharply, irritated by the persistent carping. "It's money that would have gone in taxes. That's the point of the Foundation." He turned to Festus. "Don't worry, I'll raise the money. We still have royalties coming in from the Loch Ness film and there have been some spin-offs from the oil-eater. We should do this one properly. Hell! If you need more cash then people can fork it out of their own pockets for a change. Surely to God, a trip to the West of England, and around the Mediterranean, is worth something?"

Pandora and Chuck were married just before Christmas. Ionides was best man and the Cronson girls were bridesmaids. Dawn and Festus got on well with Chuck's parents. In a selfish way, Festus felt relieved. He liked Chuck and Pandora would be less of a drain on his time.

39. The Nine Maidens

The stark, windswept, landscape around the mines reminded Festus of Argos County, with its pockets of compact beauty in the areas that were protected from the wind. It was pity Dawn was not there to share in the Labor. They had recovered the lost joy of turning over in bed and encountering each other. She was adamant in insisting on their agreement that she would not subordinate her work to his.

His mind turned to thinking about the Nine Maidens. Were slaves sacrificed to appease the gods or to guarantee secrecy? Then there was the strange coincidence that this tenth labor of "Heracles" had a parallel in Celtic mythology. The Irish hero Cuchulain was reputed to have raided hell—Dun Scaith—and returned with cattle and a magic cauldron.

Marienna broke his train of thought, echoing his delight in the scenery. "This is a glorious place, Henry, and weird too, with its contrasts. It struck me when I first came here. I never expected to see palm trees and fuchsias so far north. Further inland there's a bamboo thicket at the start of a small creek. We must find time to go and see it. You could lose Cornwall in our part of Texas, yet somehow the variety of its scenery makes it feel much larger."

"It's the roads, Marienna," said Alex. "They're so narrow, it takes as long to travel ten miles here as it does to go from Argos to Austin."

"I'll be sorry when we have to leave. Henry, how long do you think it'll take to study the stones?"

"I'm not too sure, Marienna, but probably a couple of weeks more." Festus shrugged. "The gallery has progressed very well and we're preparing to support the first stone so we can study its base."

"I don't want to leave either," Mary Beth Maximos added, tilting her head with its distracting orange hair. "But I'm sure looking forward to something a little warmer. The Mediterranean sounds great to me."

"Back to the stones. Like, why are they here? Why do you think they relate to the treasure? Is it your legendary reticence, or don't you know?"

Festus grinned. "To be honest Alex, coming here is a long shot. I used the word treasure to get peoples attention, but often, ancient legends are based on real events. The…it sticks in my throat to say the words…Labors of Heracles, may not be an exception. For example, this treasure might be the "Golden Apples of the Hesperides". The Disk is like a crossword puzzle. There are hints about "a treasure" and hints about looking at the ends of the journey. My guess is that the Hittites and the Cretans left part of the information here in Cornwall and maybe some connecting information at an intermediate stop."

"Fes, if you've got some of the words wrong then your entire interpretation may be rubbish." Alex laughed.

"As I said, it's along shot. Enjoy your vacation! I'll need your help in a few days time, assuming there's something on the stones. Ion, Sam, and I can handle the work for the moment. By the way, what do you have planned?"

"We're all to go on playing the tourist, are we?" Alex asked. "Okay. Well, there's a place called Caerhays Castle, up the coast a ways. Marienna has researched it. It's Easter and the grounds are open. They're supposed to have the most incredible collection of rhododendrons, azaleas and magnolias. Magnolias here! I find it hard to believe, but the drive will be fun. These roads are like those in Ireland—a hole in the hedge. I shall drive with my friends and with great trepidation. Easter time makes me feel homesick for red eggs and *mayeritsa*. Cornish pasties are no substitute."

An image of the dining table at home with Dawn and Pandora, flashed into Festus' mind. It was laden with food, *mayeritsa*—a stew of liver and kidneys, flavored with thyme and topped with an egg and lemon sauce—a salad, cakes and wine, and the red eggs, symbolizing the blood of Christ. He was not religious, but he missed it and his family.

Their base was the tiny port of St Mawes. It occupies a promontory between the Percuil Creek and the river Fal, on the English Channel coast of Cornwall. Festus had chosen St Mawes as his base, because it offered a good berth for Alex's boat, and was more charming than the bleak area near the tin mines. Alex Platon's yacht lay at anchor behind them in a bend of the Percuil Creek, sheltered by the Saint Anthony headland.

Ionides and Samantha walked to the mine. Near the coast, the wind had bent the trees close to horizontal. Near the mine, other trees huddled for protection in hollows—like sheep. From the track, a patchwork quilt of stone-walled fields spread down to the gorse-covered headlands. The "Nine Maidens" stood in one of these fields. They could see the broken remains of an old mine a short distance away. The gaunt wheel of its hauling machinery hovered above a deep shaft. There were horizontal galleries radiating from the shaft, under the sea. They had been told that, on a rough day, the miners could hear boulders dragging on the seabed above them. The mine entrance they were using was very dilapidated. Its crumbled buildings were hidden from sight until the passerby came very close. They reached it just as Festus emerged from the mine entrance. He waved and shouted to them. "We're under the first stone. Come and look!"

The shaft dropped vertically for six hundred feet. Their crew of Cornish miners had blocked it at a depth of twenty feet. Years before, a gallery had been started in the rough direction of the "Nine Maidens." One of the miners speculated that there might have been plans for another shaft. This gallery would have allowed access with protection from the weather. Ion and Sam saw that the crew had completed a chamber under the stones. An array of pit props and steel beams supported the roof.

Festus pointed out the recent progress. "In the first phase, we left some six feet of earth between the roof and the stones. Well, we've excavated under the first stone and we've got a steel ring supporting it. I had a look from above and there's only a faint hint of subsidence. Oh, incidentally Ion, we put the vibrator on the stone, and used that microphone you built, to locate the base. It worked beautifully. See! We hit plumb in the center."

Ionides looked up toward the stone. Small areas of it were visible in a matrix of fine roots and pebbles embedded in clay. Ionides had enlarged the hole to a greater diameter than that of the base to accommodate a steel ring. The ring was mounted on two pit props and rising from it were prongs that, sticking through the clay, engaged the sides of the stone, leaving the base free. The view did not look particularly encouraging at this stage, he thought.

"By the way, Sam, you'll be relieved to hear we removed the bones."

"Like the bones of slaves sacrificed when the stones were put up?" Samantha asked.

"They're rather small, a child's maybe?" Festus watched her face wrinkled in distaste.

"Very funny Fes," Ionides applauded with a slow handclap.

"Sorry, bad joke."

"Ion shook his head. "Come on Sam, I guess we might as well get on with the cleaning, while Fes works on his humor."

Ionides and Samantha worked patiently, clearing away the debris from the base of the stone; taking turns scrubbing with a toothbrush. It was a slow and awkward procedure in the dank, cramped space beneath the stone. Early on, they had seen a pattern emerging but had said nothing. The pattern consisted only of an erratic looking, single line and at first they were not sure it was man-made. They watched in amusement as Festus paced, like an expectant father, below them. He became more and more anxious as time passed and asked, repeatedly, whether they had found anything. Finally, when they had completely cleaned the stone and it was clear that the line had been scribed deliberately, they put him out of his misery. "We've got somethin' now, Fes, but it ain't very excitin'," Ion announced as they scrambled down.

Festus studied the base. The four miners, who had been watching the interplay, while they cleared a passage below the second and third stones, looked at Ionides and grinned. Ionides smiled back. He knew what they were thinking. The previous day, he had taken them to their local pub for lunch.

What do you think about what we're doing?" Ionides asked.

There was a moment's silence then the foreman, Joe Nichols, spoke. "Slightly crazy, might sum it up, sir. Why doesn't Dr. Festus just lift the stones and look underneath them?"

"It's been done before," another miner added, looking slyly over the top of his beer mug.

"What does he mean?" Ionides said, in surprise.

"Never you mind Morley, sir, he confuses things. It was along time ago," Joe responded quickly. "Either way it makes no difference to us. The good mining is below, why go to all this bother for the stones."

"We're on a tight schedule. Fes didn't want an argument with the authorities. Ionides answered. "He's sure they have important inscriptions on them. He's usually right,"

"Like with the Loch Ness Monster?"

"You can't win them all." Ionides laughed. "You'll keep this to yourselves?"

"Don't you worry none. You know there is a streak of anarchy in us Cornish. We were isolated, independent for a long, long time. We'll stand by your story that Dr. Festus was testing ways of reviving the mines. It's a credible story. The price of tin's been increasing. Mines are being revived. South Crofty and Wheal Pendarves mines near Cambourne are operating and so is the Geevor-Levant mine near St. Just."

Ionides remembered another part of the conversation. It had been obvious that Morley Pascoe, a dark, intense, man, was less sure. When Ionides had gone to the men's room, in a small building behind the pub, Morley had followed, waiting outside. He had grabbed Ionides by the arm.

"Cornwall's not what it seems," Morley said. "You tourists see beaches, sports-fishing and cream teas. We're a society of old beliefs and customs. The Floral Dance is not an event cooked up for you lot. It's necessary to appease Mother Earth, ensure a good planting, and a good harvest in the following year. These stones are still important for us."

"It's serious for us too, Morley," Ionides reassured him.

"I told Missus Cronson. She said not to worry it was only part of a game. Talked about Greek gods. I don't know now't about them. I know my God don't approve of messing with the stones." Morley pointed up the hill to a tiny, tin-roofed, fundamentalist chapel near the mine. "My Chapel," he said. "Sunday's I pray 'forgive us our trespasses.' We're trespassing."

Ionides watched as Morley made the sign of the cross privately, and looked uneasily down the darkened tunnel. "There's things that live in the older passages," Morley whispered. "I've seen them in my nightmares."

Festus looked closely. There was a line, yet what did it mean? His experienced eyes picked up something that Ionides and Samantha had missed; a few small holes had been picked out around the rim. He called down to Ionides. "Bring up the camera so I can take some photos! Then I'd like you and Sam to tape tracing paper over the base and pencil over it to bring out all the markings. Incidentally, make sure to get the edge. There are some marks there you didn't spot."

From then on, Festus worked them all like a slave driver. He was anxious to complete the studies before someone in authority questioned what they were doing. He had brought in the remaining Eurysthesians to clean the stones, record the markings and to assist the miners in restoring the ground to its original condition. Consequently, ten days later the work was close to completion. The markings on each stone consisted of an erratic looking single line and a few small holes around each rim. Their significance remained a puzzle. His theory was that each line represented the path to be taken by a dancer on the dancing floor, though the seemingly random orientation made no sense. The ninth stone brought more confusion. On its base, the marking was not a continuous line but a dashed one.

Two stones remained. The miners gradually raised the steel supports as they picked away at the earth beneath the final stones. A miner inserted a thin metal probe to test the distance that remained to the base of each stone. His colleagues had filled the holes under the first nine and had raised the roof supports, so that the gallery resembled a wooden, underground version of Stonehenge. Festus listened for the gratifying sound of the each metal support, clinking as it met the base of its stone. He fidgeted impatiently, while the miners raised ladders so that he and Ionides could start the inspection.

"I'm hoping that these last stones will have some more useful clues, Henry," Marienna said. "There are nine dancers, and two who direct the dance. Leaving aside the question of that strange stone with the dotted line, it seems to me there's a good chance the remaining two stones will help tie together the other patterns."

"I hope so too," Festus replied, as he finished cleaning the base of his stone. The exercise required him to keep his head down, in order to avoid the shower of dirt created by the toothbrush. He let the dust settle, brushed the more obtrusive dirt from his hair and looked up.

He came close to falling off the ladder in his excitement. On the base of this stone, there were a few symbols from the Disk and accompanying them were Hittite hieroglyphs, whose meaning he knew. The hitherto untranslated fourteenth word—with its club and fish symbols on the side of the Disc with the flower at its center—stood for the Greek "υιοισ" or "to the sons". Therefore, the intermediate stop on the journey was "to the sons of Alluwamnas." Presumably, that symbolized a place settled by the Hittites. Cadiz and Sicily remained the most probable sites.

He shouted the news to his friends and the gallery resounded with their applause. Ionides shouted back that, by contrast, there were no markings on the bottom of his stone, only some holes around the rim. Ionides climbed down so that Festus could look. Festus saw that the holes were similar to those on the other stones but there was a small difference. Three of the holes were in a group above a barely discernible outline of a triangle. Festus called for the camera and tracing paper. Ionides passed Morley Pascoe on his way to get them.

Morley looked at him apprehensively. "It's not right he said." Suddenly, the lights dimmed.

"What happening?" Alex shouted, crossing himself.

"The Bull," screamed Morley. "The Bull's coming. Blow the trumpets!"

Thee darkness and those words created fear in the Eurysthesians. A fear that had its roots deep in their past. The passages of the labyrinth fell silent. They huddled instinctively to the sides of the cavern. There was a roar of air and the chamber filled with a dank, cold smell and then silence returned.

Morley Pascoe lay on the floor, curled into the fetal position. Marienna was also on the floor. Joe Nichols helped her to sit up. "Don't worry m'dear. It's a cave-in deep in the mine. They happen sometimes in the older part." He helped Marienna to stand "Don't you mind old Morley, ma'am. He had a bad experience with a bull when he was a little. He was in a field, picking mushrooms with his mother. They didn't realize there was a bull there. It charged. His mother managed to get Morley over the stile, but she was gored, badly. He's never forgotten."

"I hope that's the explanation," Marienna said, uncertainly. "It's a strange coincidence. What did he mean by 'blow the trumpets?'"

"Oh, that's now't to worry about, m'dear. Old Morley has a lot of imagination. Used to be, on Walpurgis Day in Penzance, the young boys would walk the town blowing tin trumpets; to scare the devil away."

"Look at the bright side," volunteered Ionides. "If it was a warning, then it shows we're on the right track."

"Are you all right, Marienna?" Festus asked.

"Don't fuss over me, Henry! In the commotion I slipped," she snapped at him. She stood unsteadily, carefully brushing dust from her clothes to hide her discomfort while she regrouped. "Come on," she said, let's get back to work!" Her words did not fool Festus. He suddenly realized how frail she had become. He had never thought of Marienna as getting older. Yet she was now over seventy. Her iron gray hair was turning white, and her commanding posture was deserting her.

Following the completion of the work on the stones, they moved to a hotel on Veryan Bay that had more space for their work. Festus was determined to stay until he had resolved enough of the puzzle to locate the intermediate, stopping place on the journey. He felt, unscientifically, that the Cornish atmosphere might help in this quest.

Alex joined him to look at the eleven tracings spread on the floor.

"Let's put the blank tracing in the middle, Alex," Festus said. "Maybe it's for the bullmaster because he determines his own path."

"That's possible, Fes. Or it is determined but to be found somewhere elsewhere."

"That still leaves us with the problem of what to do with the lines and dots. I just wish the dots had a more systematic pattern."

While they were talking, Marienna came silently into the room. She too had been studying the tracings. "Your comment on the bullmaster giving instructions might apply equally to the high priestess. I wonder whether those dots on the outside of the stone, which has no lines on it, set the relative orientations of the engravings on the other stones?"

Festus jumped to his feet and embracing her. "Thank God for you, Marienna! You've saved me again. I was thinking on similar lines, but I assumed there would be only nine dots on the rim of the high priestesses stone. If it's a code, then each grouping of dots should appear. Come on now! Let's look for a match."

They worked for a number of hours, but fitting the pieces of the puzzle proved to be more difficult than they had anticipated. Every attempt led to a dead end. "We'll have to be more systematic," said Festus. "It's all too easy to fit a few of the patterns, but if any one of them is wrong then it's a waste of time. Let me work up a system for classifying them! That should reduce the number of arrangements to a manageable level."

"Why don't we all take a break for a few days, Fes?" Alex cajoled him. "We've been working hard now for a long time and you, particularly, look exhausted. Come and visit some interesting arty folk I met in St. Anthony. A sculptor there really enjoys chatting to your godmother. They act like they're old friends."

"I'd like to Alex. I just couldn't enjoy myself. Not knowing the answer would bug me remorselessly. If Dawn were here, it would be different. You guys take a break! Enjoy yourselves! That's still the main purpose of our Trust. I'm sure the manager will know all the good things to do around here." Festus looked at them appealingly. His friends exchanged glances. Alex looked like he was going to try to change Festus's mind. Marienna shook her head.

The Eurysthesians went back to being tourists. From time to time, one or other of them would drop in on Festus and tell him of their discoveries.

"We just loved Veryan," Mary Beth Maximos gushed. Festus noticed that her hair was now a strange, streaky, blonde color. "Those little roundhouses on each road into the village"

"I like the idea of the crosses on top to ward off the devil, if he comes by road" Joe added. "We should put some up in Argos." He paused. "Of course, old Satan might fly in."

"Joe, don't be so silly! We took lots of photos and we talked to the locals. They speak real funny, Fes. It'll make a wonderful talk for my ladies club." Festus listened politely and returned to his work.

Not everyone liked Veryan. As Alex explained to Festus, crossing himself, "they have the roundhouses for a reason." Festus listened with resignation as Alex continued, extolling the virtues of a local fishing village—Portloe. "It's beautiful, Fes. Slate-roofed cottages huddled into the sides of a steep-sided valley. There's a tiny harbor in a break in the cliffs. Best though, there's an artists' colony. Marienna and I bought paintings to ship back to Texas." Alex tried one more time to talk Festus into accompanying them but he was still not ready to leave his work.

In truth, Festus was desperately tired and his head was dizzy from his efforts. Despite his systematic approach, he realized that he was now repeating some of his earlier incorrect arrangements. The plot of all the tracings showed, apparently random paths that meandered across the central area, which represented the combined faces of the stones. The paths started on one side of this area and finished on the other. Festus still believed that each line represented the ordained path of a dancer, and maybe also of each acrobat, on the dancing floor. How did they relate to the Phaestos Disk, other than it had hinted where to look. He tried overlaying the lines on photographs of each side of the Disk. There was no obvious connection between them.

By now, Festus was sufficiently frustrated that he agreed to spend an afternoon sailing with Ion and Sam, in the fishing dinghy they had rented in the nearby village of Portscatho.

The break in routine should have stimulated a new vigor in his work, yet on returning to the hotel, he was overwhelmed again with a feeling of the hopelessness of the task. Festus even considered withdrawing from the Foundation's work. He consoled himself with the thought that having ten projects completed was enough of an achievement. Like a child faced with a mountain of homework turning to an adult to provide the pressure to complete it, he turned to Zack Cronson. He sent a wire to him suggesting the suspension of the project. The return wire was an uncompromising order for Festus to continue.

> PROJECT NOT OVER STOP
> DO NOT CHANGE ARRANGEMENTS STOP
> CUT OUT SELF PITY STOP
> YOU WILL FIND WAY STOP
> ZACK STOP

When Festus received the wire, his first reaction was one of anger but, as he calmed down, it turned to a feeling of relief. Then, after numerous phone calls and pleading letters, Dawn agreed to join him in Crete. It gave him greater incentive to find the intermediate stopping place for the Hittites, quickly. He wired back

WILL DO STOP
SIR STOP

Festus reviewed his ideas with Marienna. "I heard an interesting thing, this morning. One of your friends told me that the Nine Maidens were also known once as "Naw Bugh Men" in Cornish—Nine Cow Stone—an appropriate name."

"Fascinating," Marienna looked amused. "So you have a parallel to the tenth Labor, where Heracles stole the cattle of Geryon, as his ritual feat for obtaining a bride."

"Yup. I have stolen the secret of the Nine Maidens, or Naw Bugh Men, to bring as a gift to Dawn in Crete."

"I have another coincidence, Henry. There is a Greek-style theater on the other side of Falmouth. I've booked seats."

"I'm not sure I…"

"Henry, you need a break!"

The Minnack Theater occupied a natural bowl in the cliffs near Porthcurnow. The theater offered a pretty view across the sea to a neighboring headland. In stark contrast, the play by Euripides was a miserable experience, and Festus returned to the hotel in a subdued mood, the final words of the Chorus ringing in his ears—"We go with grief and bitter tears, robbed of our great protector." Was it a warning of what would happen to him if he failed in his Labors?

He redoubled his efforts to solve the problem of the markings. The key point was the allusion to the land of the sons of Alluwamnas. There was the additional clue, which he had kept to himself, of the marking with three dots above the triangle, which might represent a hill if it was not part of the Hittite sign for country. In his mind, he flicked through his store of odd remembered facts. Something about the markings had seemed familiar. It was like doing a crossword puzzle, he thought, and he been waiting to understand some clues.

Nothing registered until he tried to connect it to Cadiz and Sicily—the two most likely intermediate, stopping places. Then he remembered the conference that he had attended in Erice; a village perched atop a mountain at the western end of Sicily. An area that had once been the land of the Elymians; a people who had come originally from the area of the Hittite empire, though the date for the settlement was generally believed to be later than the period he was investigating.

Elymians—Alluwamnians, people of Alluwamnas—in his mind the two words fused into one word. It was a plausible explanation, he thought. He would go to Erice as soon as the work cleaning up the mine was completed. However, he remembered that on the site of Cadiz there had been a Phoenician sanctuary, called Melkart. It would be sensible to stop in Cadiz, on the way, to confer with local archaeologists about a possible Hittite presence at an even earlier time. Nevertheless, he felt almost certain now that Sicily held the answers he was looking for. Maybe the triangular marking represented Monte Erice, but then what did the three dots represent?

Festus wired a message to a friend at the Majorana Center at Erice, Sicily. He sent a second message to Pandora and Chuck asking them to fly to Erice as soon as possible and start checking for signs of the Cretans and Hittites. Elena Cronson had already arrived to join Alex, Ion and Sam, and they would leave immediately to sail Alex's boat to Cadiz and on to Sicily.

"So, it looks like we're all ready to move on." He said to Marienna.

"Henry, I'm sorry," Marienna apologized. I need to return to Argos to deal with some matters. "I expect to rejoin you in Crete, with the Dexters."

"Pity, I can always use your help. We still have the problem that we don't know the place for the dance."

A final task remained. To supervise the completion of the work, restoring the mine to near its original condition. Festus enjoyed the weeklong effort as a kind of therapy. He took one last look at the stones, until he was sure they had no more to tell him, and then he signaled for the miners to start filling the space beneath them with rocks. Up to this point, the miners had been strangely reticent in asking about the project, believing it to be nonsense. Now as it was coming to an end and they had seen the inscriptions, it was as if an invisible barrier had broken. As they worked, they bombarded Festus with questions.

"How did you come to pick this site? Why were you so certain there would be inscriptions, Dr. Festus?" They appeared amused by his rambling answer that referred to various books discussing the connection of the tin mining to the Phoenicians. He did not tell them about the Hittites, or about the Phaestos Disk. He was glad he had sited the Society members away from the mine, to prevent too much social contact and idle talk. It had worked, he thought with satisfaction. The questions were good ones though. The truth was that the chance sighting of a photograph of the stone monument Men-an-Tol, and then the photograph of the Nine Maidens had led him to Cornwall. Although he tried to suppress the thought, there was the feeling that he had been there before—as Hephaestus.

40. Erice

On his way to Sicily, Festus had worried about leaving Cadiz after only cursory and fruitless inquiries. Now, the view of Monte Erice, looming two thousand feet above the plain, restored his confidence that he was on the right track. Festus felt an affinity with Erice, the home of the Cyclops; metal smiths whose symbol of office, a brightly colored spot painted in the middle of the forehead resembled a single eye. In legend, his namesake, Hephaestus, was the son of Arges the Cyclops.

His taxi had left the Trapani airport, apparently on two wheels. Now, as they passed the saltpans, that abutted the sea, it seemed as if the driver was preparing to engage in a head-on collision with a tractor. The saltpans and the port of Trapani at this far, western end of Sicily had been in use for thousands of years. The Phoenicians and the Greeks had visited the area. Earlier still, the Anatolian people, the Elyms, had established the towns of Erice and Segesta.

The taxi driver created and then negotiated each potentially dangerous situation with a casual skill. Soon they were climbing away from the outskirts of Trapani, and the olive trees and vineyards of the plain. They passed a man with a donkey. The donkey swayed under the weight of overloaded panniers.

The Ettore Majorana School in Erice was not in session, and Festus' friend had arranged for the Eurysthesians to stay at its San Rocco center for the early part of the quest. Alex and his crew had arrived in Trapani a day earlier.

The focal point of the courtyard of the San Rocco was a statue of the Saint carrying the baby Jesus. The saint and his precious cargo were sheltered from the sun by a dark green metal roof and by pink and white oleander bushes. Their slim branches sprouted through the flimsy six-sided, iron lattice that supported the roof. The hexagonal, ornamental garden contained a variety of trees and bushes and brief meandering paths. It was the kingdom of a family of timid cats.

Festus took his map of Sicily and the neighboring islands and laid it on a table. His friends clustered around him, impatiently waiting for clarification. Mary Beth Maximos concealed her irritation with difficulty as Festus toyed with the map. Elena Cronson smiled conspiratorially and mouthed the words, "I know what you're thinking." She looked fondly at the dark head studying the map.

Festus reviewed what had happened in Cornwall for the benefit of the newcomers. "Using the bi-syllabary on one of the Nine Maidens I was able to improve my translation of part of the Disk.

"Bi-syllabary? What?" Mary Beth shook her head.

"Don't worry about it, dear!" Elena interjected. "Let's hear the bottom line."

"Sorry for the jargon. The Disk has a hint about the intermediate-stopping place for the ancient people, who went from Hattiland to Cornwall for tin. The sons of King Alluwamnas of the Hittites settled it. This led me to make the connection to the ancient Anatolian tribe, the Elymians who settled here in western Sicily. My plan is to research the ancient sites, particularly those that had involved the Elymians, but also those of the Greeks, who settled the island later."

"Looks like a lot of potential sites," Alex said, pointing at the map. "It could take a long time?"

"I know." Festus shrugged. "We'll split up and start with the Elymian and Greek temples at Segesta, Seliunte and Agrigento. They're interesting in their own right, though, from our point of view, the issue is whether they carry signs of the Hittites. Signs like some of us saw in Cornwall, and those on the Disk." Festus sketched the triangular sign for land and the circular sign for god, on the edge of the map.

"If they did, wouldn't it have been noticed before?"

"Possibly, Alex." Festus looked uneasy. "Let me be honest and tell you that my best guess, is that they don't contain what we're looking for. We need to eliminate them as candidate sites, so please bear with me. The place we're looking for might be here in Erice, or it is on one of the Aegadian islands that are out to the west of us. There are grottoes on the islands and I'm hoping that one of them contains Hittite inscriptions."

"I'd like to investigate the temples," Elena volunteered. "I could go with Joe and Mary-Beth. If we see the slightest hint of the Hittites we'll get you to check it out."

"Sounds great to me," said Festus with relief, happy to offload a chore he viewed as a dead end. "In the meantime Elena and I will look around Erice for clues though, as I indicated, I don't think it's…"

Pandora interrupted him. "Chuck and I haven't wasted time waiting for you. We've already been out to the islands and we've seen some of the grottoes, like you suggested. There are some primitive cave paintings but nothing like a Hittite inscription. There was one strange thing though…" her voice trailed off.

"Come on Pandy!" Ionides prompted her after a long pause. "You can't stop on a remark like that. What was strange?"

"Well, on Levanzo. That's the nearest of the islands. We met this crazy guy when we were eating lunch. For God's sake! He came up and introduced himself. He was curious why we were there. Go on Chuck, you can do him, you tell it!" she bubbled excitedly, her blonde ponytail bouncing.

Chuck laughed. "He fancied you. The greasy slob couldn't take his eyes off you. I don't think there was any more to it than that. I mean. Look at her, folks! She was wearing those same shorts and that miniscule bikini she's wearing now. The creep was waiting for her to fall out of her bra." Chuck stopped in embarrassment remembering too late that Festus was there. Pandora smacked his hand hard. The other Eurythesians turned away to hide their amusement.

Festus waved his hand to dismiss the problem. "Chuck, it's never easy for any dad to say this but, I welcomed the day when you took over the responsibility for worrying about my daughter's effect on men."

Pandora hoisted up her skimpy bra and gave Chuck a passionate kiss. "You'd better keep a close eye on me honey, but don't waste time worrying about the Alfredos. You should worry that I'll meet someone smart and good looking, like my dad. Now, tell them about Alfie!"

"Alfredo Mokarta is about fifty, I guess. He's short, but he's broad; stocky isn't an adequate description. Curly black, oily looking hair, and a droopy moustache—gives him a lugubrious look when he's not smilin'. Chuck adopted a stylized pose and affected a strong Italian-American accent. "Hiya there. Y'all sound-a like Americans. I lived in the States once-a—Chicago, Kansas City, Newark New Jersey, Las-a-Vegas, Phoenix. I have-a a family in these-a places you understand. You tell-a me where-a you from, I've-a been there. We told him we were from Texas. He commented that his family didn't have much to do with Texas but we were welcome anyway. Pandora asked him what he did in the States."

"Alfie said he was a student," Pandora giggled. "Some-a student, eh! I asked him why he'd left. He muttered something about family business calling him back to Sicily and that he didn't get on with the U.S. government. No offense to us, he said. He was funny."

"I didn't think he was funny. The guy is obviously Mafia. Those places he lived. They're all Mafia centers."

"Could you find him again?" Joe asked. "He could be a useful contact. I've read that the Mafia is well wired in here."

"I guess so. I can't believe that anything moves on Levanzo without Alfredo Mokarta knowing about it."

"I'm a little confused Pandy. You said he was curious about you. Why? At least he seemed friendly?"

"Yes Dad, he was friendly when he thought we were simply tourists. But the minute we started asking about caves and things the average tourist wouldn't see, he changed the subject rapidly and recommended we stick to the standard tourist spots, preferably on the mainland."

"This is an area for smuggling, and it's on the drug route from the Middle East to the States," Joe added softly. "Maybe the kids got too close to some sort of an operation—a heroin lab or somethin'. That could be a problem, Fes, if it's where we need to go."

"I agree Joe, so next time we'll go in greater strength. We can also try out the power of the almighty dollar. It sounds like Alfredo may be able to help us."

"I need time to think of a strategy. We'd better delay confronting Alfredo. Let's leave it for a few days and get some of the other chores cleared up first. I guess you kids can find something to do?"

"We'll go out to San Vito Lo Capo. It's fantastic, Sam. It's like a set for a Spaghetti Western and there's this neat place on the beach—Ristorante Charlie Brown!" Pandora giggled.

Alfredo did not wait. He appeared while they were lunching at Ristorante Charlie Brown, and quizzed them in an idle fashion. Then, claiming an urgent appointment on the island of Levanzo, he rushed off. The rest of the party visited the temples but found nothing of use.

Elena loved Erice with its close walled, cobbled streets that weaved around the town. In the yellow, stone walls, there were ornamental gates that allowed glimpses of secluded gardens.

"I think we'll know when we're in the right place, Fes. I can sense the pull of the past, here at this end of Sicily," Elena said, as she and Festus toured the town. They passed through a courtyard on the southern tip of the mountain, where the remains of a Norman keep covered the earlier temple of Venus. From the battlements, there was a magnificent view of the western end of Sicily.

Elena said, "I don't think what we're looking for is in Erice. I'm drawn to the islands." She pointed to the sea beyond the town of Trapani that sprawled below them. A heat haze covered the sea so that the nearby islands of Levanzo and Favignana appeared as misty shadows, and the distant island of Marettimo might well not have existed.

The sight of the two islands jogged Festus' memory. He squinted, looking in vain for the third island. On thinking about the three islands, he made the connection to the inscription on the tenth stone in Cornwall. The triangle and the three dots could represent Mount Erice and the Aegadian islands. He was certain now that the islands were the place to look.

"We've got to explore the islands. I hope that Alfredo Mokarta knows something. I have no idea why the Mafia should be interested."

"On this site, it might be wise to ask Venus for help," said Elena.

"Help from Venus? No! From Aphrodite, yes? I wish Dawn were here."

"She's coming to Crete. Hang in there!"

"I'm trying to. Right now, I think we need to contact Mokarta. Though I'm worried about the apparent Mafia connection."

"Guess who's here, Dad?" Pandora looked pleased with herself."

"Alfredo?" Festus said, uncertainly.

"Much better," Pandora laughed. "Mom."

"How long have you known?' It was hard to feel angry, Fetsus thought.

"She called from the airport an hour ago."

Festus rose to his feet, stiffly. "I should help with the bags or something." He turned to find Dawn framed by the doorway. She was wearing a transparent blouse, a gaily patterned, gypsy skirt, and low-heeled sandals. A skimpy lacy brassiere barely contained her breasts. She looked as radiant and sexy as he had ever seen her.

"I couldn't wait for Crete. I...It's lonely in Argos with you and Pandora gone." She grabbed Festus. Festus struggled to draw breath as she worked her tongue around his mouth. She leaned back, her hips pushed against him. "You seem to be feeling well."

"Don't let go just yet," Festus whispered.

"You old goat," she whispered, holding him.

"We should go to our room, honey. I need to freshen up, and you seem to need to do something too." Dawn said.

Festus presided over a meeting of the Eurysthesians, at the Ristorante Ulisse. Tuna, pasta, salad, fruit and a formidable number of bottles of local white wine, Alcamo, covered the table. Pandora was telling how the cult of the goddess of fertility started in Erice. "I mean the cult of Aphrodite," she said, looking at her mother.

"I hope that's a good omen." Dawn winked at Festus.

"Anyone else with historical information?" asked Alex caustically. Nobody answered, so he quickly changed the subject. "I decide to follow up on our friend Alfredo Mokarta. Alfie may be vague about his stay in our great country but I'm pretty sure he must have been deported. I've cabled a friend of mine in the FBI in

Austin, asking him to check on him. He owes me a favor and I think he'll find out who Alfie is, and what he was doing in the US.

"Are you sure Alfie will help?"

"Not really, Elena. I reckon he's curious about us. He'd probably like to find out why we're here."

"He's very suspicious. I forgot to tell you Dad, he turned up again today at Charlie Brown's. I told him we were an amateur archaeological Society and he kept coming back to the question, 'what do you want?' I said we'd heard about a cave with fabulous drawings. I mentioned your name. It was weird, you know, he'd heard of you."

"Pandy I keep on telling you, your father's famous. I guess you didn't pay much attention to the Loch Ness business when you were traipsing around the islands…oof." Chuck stopped as Pandora pinched his thigh hard.

"Don't bring that up again Chuck! That's was years ago when I was only a kid. I know my Dad's famous, but to me he's still old Dad. Every time something like this happens I have to pinch myself."

"Rather you than me babe…oof."

"Will you never learn? Don't mock us Festus women. Alfie said he'd-a look-a into it-a."

"While we're waiting, let's check out the islands. There are three islands in the Aegadian group. Elena and you Joe and er…your…er…could go to Marettimo. It's the furthest island but it's a nice boat ride. Alex, Ion, and Sam could look into Isola Favignana. I'll go with Dawn, Pandora and Chuck to check on Levanzo. Pandora thinks Alfie lives there?"

The boat approached Favignana harbor. A single tree, a few red-tiled roofs and, in the background, the green and gold dome of a church colored the barren-looking island.

"What do people do?" Festus wondered, as the waited for the boat to Levanzo. "Suppose they must depend a lot on tuna fishing? Maybe they grow grapes somewhere. I guess there's tourism?"

The port on the island of Levanzo was large enough to shelter a few fishing boats. There were forty or so box-like houses clustered around it, and were terraced vineyards and olive trees on a hill to its left. To the right of the village, a dirt track edged the sea.

The bar-ristorante Tyrhennia, which they had seen from the boat, was at the front of the Pensione Tyrhennia, a tired looking, nineteen thirties building. A semi-circular patio with tables shaded by vine-covered trellises constituted most of the restaurant. The bar had white and blue tiles that covered the floor and continued half way up the walls, where grimy, flaking, blue paint took over. For decoration, there was a framed photograph of two overweight dogs and a few plates in the Erice style. On high shelves, there were dusty wine bottles, pieces of coral, a stack of sundae glasses, and shells. Two plastic deer heads were mounted on the wall above the dimly lit bar and refrigerator.

A plump woman was cleaning glasses behind the bar. She acknowledged with a smile that she had noticed their arrival and continued her polishing. When, finally, the woman shuffled out to the patio to take their order, Festus asked about Alberto Mokarta. Using sign language to supplement her torrent of Italian, she succeeded in transmitting the message that he was not there. She brought the wine and retired to her bar. There were the faint sounds of a telephone in use.

"Allo," Alfie said. "Is-a me you looking for?" He nodded at Alex and Festus, his eyes brushed past Chuck quickly, and he ogled Dawn and Pandora appreciatively. "Bella, bella is-a two-a Venus."

Festus remembered Chuck's description. Broad he had said. It did not do justice to Alfie's disproportionately large shoulders. "I think you've met my daughter and Chuck before. I'm...er...Dr. Festus," he continued, with his customary embarrassment at using the title, "and this is my wife."

Alfie clasped his hand reverently. "I have-a heard of you Dottore Festus, sir. Is-a great honor to meet you and welcome you to our island of Levanzo. I read all about the Loch-a Ness-a monster. They say we have a monster here-a too." He pointed vaguely out to sea. Is that why you are here?"

Festus released his hand slowly. "I think I've had enough of monsters Mister Mokarta. I'm more interested in cave paintings and carvings of an earlier era, before the Greeks came. Not prehistoric, you understand?"

Alfie's face remained blank. It was not clear to Festus whether or not Alfredo understood, or whether he didn't want to understand, so he tried a different tack. "We would be happy to pay a retainer for a guide and advice, say twenty dollars a day. Can you recommend someone?"

"Sir, I Alfredo Mokarta could be such a guide and advisor. And please, no more Mister Mokarta, you are from the States, in the States I am called Alfie."

"All right Alfie. What do you suggest?"

Alfie sat back and rubbed his forehead to signify that this was a weighty question. After a long pause in which it seemed that he must have been considering many options, he responded in carefully measured tones. Strangely, his accent was less pronounced as if he couldn't think, ogle Dawn and Pandora, and sustain it. "You should see our well known Grotta dei Genovese here on Levanzo. There is not much more to see here. Then, you should-a go to see the Grotto Marine on Marettimo. It is magnificent-a, but you should-a concentrate your efforts on Favignana. They have found fantastic paintings, just now." He said this earnestly to Dawn, who was lounging and looked negligently sexy, as always.

"Our other friends are looking at that cave on Marettimo and at caves on Favignana, today, Alfie."

Alfie looked pensive. "I know-a of other caves sir. It-a could be fixed."

"We'll wait for you to fix it Alfie. In the meantime could you show us Levanzo?"

"I will Dottore Festus. We will go to our famous Grotto dei Genovese and see its fine paintings."

They spent an entertaining but nearly unprofitable day with Alfie. He took them around the island by boat. From the boat, they could see the mantle of clouds that skirted the peak of distant Monte Erice. Clouds also formed and then vanished on the hilltops of Favignana. In contrast, the sky above Levanzo was cloudless. A sharp breeze chopped the blue sea, flecking it with white. On the western end of the island, there was a cove with low rocks and clear blue water, in which they swam. The promised cave was in the cliff. It contained Neolithic charcoal paintings of a pig, dolphins, bulls, and stick people. Given their 6000 BC origin, they were surprisingly fresh looking. The cave also contained an unusual red painting, in ochre, blood and animal fat, which had been dubbed "the goddess." An inscribed figure of a bull was so Cretan looking in its elegance that, for a moment, Festus felt that he had reached his goal.

"Is-a Paleolithic. Festus shook his head in disappointment.

They returned to the boat and continued their circumnavigation of the island. Festus was frustrated by the lack of progress and stared moodily at the steep cliff that marked the northern shore. The carried on around the eastern end of the island. The boat had nearly finished its tour before Pandora aroused him.

"Hey, Dad, look at that neat cemetery!"

Festus glanced up wearily. They were passing a small valley. Directly in front of him was a cemetery, set into the valley just below where it rose steeply to the dirt track. Inside a high stone wall, there were tombs, surrounded by trees.

"They look just like those Victorian bathing huts I saw in Cornwall," Festus laughed. "Celestial bathing huts. You go into them to change on your way to heaven."

Festus asked Alfie to take the boat into shore. Alfie looked uncertain, but Pandora pleaded with him and they came to shore. Large iron gates appeared to be the only access to the cemetery. They were locked. They could see well mown patches of grass under the trees. Oleander and bougainvillea were in bloom. A stream that bubbled from the rock at the upper end of the cemetery was the obvious cause of the lush vegetation.

Alfie reacted strangely when Chuck began to photograph the scene, grasping him by the arm to restrain him. With his composure restored he stopped, pretending it was all in play. "Hey, Chuck! my-a grand-a-father is-a buried here. You should not-a disturb him." His accent was very strong as if to emphasize it was all a joke.

"Was your grandfather an important man?" Festus asked, having observed that Alfie was easily distracted. Chuck took more photographs.

"My grandfather was the most important man in all of Western Sicily," responded Alfie proudly. "This was his world. He was the boss."

Pandora made a face at Chuck, behind Alfie's back, mimicking the words "the boss."

"How long has the cemetery been here?" Festus asked.

Alfie raised his hands in supplication. "For many centuries." He pointed to a smaller tomb at the upper end of the cemetery. "That one is-a fourteenth-a century. I have-a heard it said-a that there was-a older one on the same site before it."

Festus walked up the hill, slowly, to find a better view over the wall of the tombs. Alfie had implied older than the fourteenth century. Could it have been a burial ground for Romans, Greeks, Phoenicians and the Hittites before them. The bathing huts squatted below him, revealing nothing.

Samantha was wildly excited about the grottoes, which she had seen on Favignana, and started talking the instant the Eurysthesians reached the San Rocco. "There were these incredible cave paintings. Stick people chasing stick animals and fishing," she enthused. "They only found some of them recently and they're fantastically well preserved. They're beautiful in a skinny sort of way. Just like Ion." She hugged her husband before he could reply.

"Did you see anything…anything in our line?"

"Nothing. Sorry, Fes," Ionides replied.

"Did any of you have a feeling about any of the places you visited? A sense of having been there earlier?"

"I had feelings." Festus looked up with interest. "There was this funny little guide. He kept pinching me. I can't imagine why."

"I had to threaten the little bastard," Ion growled.

"Okay then. Let's continue with Elena's party. How did it go on Marettimo?"

"The island had a nice atmosphere. We had a great time. But no cookie."

"What do you mean?" Festus asked, in a distracted fashion.

"No prize. No great discovery. We also saw some nice drawings on the walls of a cave. Some of the figures appeared to be dancing. There were pictures of cattle too, which is interesting, given the distance from the mainland. Everything is pre-Cretan or pre-Hittite by a long time, though. It was fascinating, but there were no vibrations. How about you, Fes?"

"We had an interesting time too, in the company of our new friend and associate, Alfredo Mokarta. The cave paintings were fantastic, but they're Neolithic and Paleolithic. However, we may have struck pay dirt?"

"Dad means the cemetery." Pandora interrupted him, excitedly. "We saw a fantastic old cemetery. It had these crazy looking tombs. Dad called them celestial bathing huts. They're real cool. Aren't they, Chuck?"

"Yeah, really neat. I took some pictures." Chuck waved his camera.

"I was going to add," Festus continued, patiently, "that the cemetery did set up some vibrations. I…"

Chuck interrupted him. "I should add, there were fruit trees. Oranges I think."

"That's right," Dawn said. "I noticed them too, at the head of the valley, near those older tombs. You can only see the fruit if you get right up to the gates."

"I wish you'd told me before. That could be significant. You understand?" Festus managed to sound irritated while looking pleased.

"Oh yes, I think so, but it's a bit farfetched isn't it? You're talking three thousand years."

"What do you mean, Dad?"

Elena answered for him. "Your father is suggesting that the oranges are like the Golden Apples of the Hesperides. The Apples that Heracles stole in his eleventh Labor. I guess golden apples could have been a description of oranges?"

"Why not, eh?" Festus answered. "Given that we didn't get any other clue. I suggest we concentrate on Levanzo."

"Where can we stay?"

"There's a small hotel, Elena, the Pensione Tyrhennia. Some of us can stay there. The rest of us can probably fit on Alex's boat, one way or another."

41. Levanzo

Festus climbed the steps leading from the harbor to the Pensione Tyrhennia. Instead of entering it, he slipped around the side and climbed through a small pine thicket and scrub to the hilltop. From there, he could see the track to the cemetery. He did not try to go further, but mapped a route to it in his mind.

Alex had ordered dinner and, as he arrived at the patio, the proprietress laid a steaming bowl of pasta on the table. The pasta was touched with the flavor of a delicate seafood sauce, and the Eurysthesians disposed of it quickly. The woman served an anonymous, light dry wine, from often-used bottles. Following a concatenation of poor Italian and sign language, they determined that the wine was the owner's share of the produce of a vineyard on Favignana. After dinner, they took a few bottles with them and repaired to Alex's boat for private discussions.

"The more I think about it the more I become convinced that what we're looking for is in or near the cemetery. I checked earlier and it's possible to reach it by trekking over the hill behind the Pensione. It looks a bit rough, but it shouldn't be more than a half-hours walk, even in the dark. We could get to it by taking the track along the shore, but it's further."

"Do you want us to check it out Fes?" Ionides asked eagerly. "Sam, Pandy, Chuck and I could do it."

"Don't we need to get Alfie? Surely, Fes, the whole point of finding him was so that he could fix it for us?"

"Absolutely right, Elena, but we may only get one chance with Alfie. He really seemed very nervous when we were there earlier. The place may be used for smuggling. I think it was the thought of easy money that made him agree. I'd like to be prepared when we go with him."

"What exactly are we looking for?" asked Joe. Festus was silent.

"Oh, come on, Fes. Don't be so damned secretive!"

"I'm not sure, Joe. I was trying to think of a good answer. I guess I'm looking for two things. Alfie suggested that some of the tombs sit on top of older ones. The stream comes out of the ground, runs through the cemetery and disappears at the lower end. The limestone rock is obviously porous and there's a high probability of a cave. The structure of these islands is quite interesting you know. A long time ago…"

"Thanks for the preview, Fes. Save that speech for a conference," Joe laughed.

It took more than Festus' estimate of a half-hour for them to reach the cemetery. It was further, and the terrain tougher, than he had allowed.

"Dad, I wonder how Mom will like this stroll?" Pandora asked slyly. "It's not exactly her bag," she giggled.

"It's a pity that Dawn, Elena, and the Maximos didn't come. Heavens knows, maybe Mrs. Maximos, whatever her name is, will be the one to see the place as it was."

"Dad! You're terrible, pretending you don't know that nice woman's name. Why, er…well anyway she's very nice."

Festus pointed at the cemetery. "The only gate is on our side of the valley and it's set in that high stone wall, You can sorta tell from here, that the site is pear shaped, broadening as it approaches the sea. The stream starts just below us. It runs down towards the gate, and then it swings across to the other side, before snaking back again and disappearing at the lower wall. You can see the two largest tombs, which are set in the bends of the stream. Those tombs look relatively modern. I would guess they're 19th century. The tombs that interest me most are at the head of the valley, on the far side from us, up against the cliff."

"Are we going to break in?"

"No, Chuck, I think it's better not to. You go with Ion and the girls and circumnavigate the place. See what else you can find. Watch out for traps!" Festus called out, as an afterthought.

"I'll leave it to them," Alex said. He looked immaculate in a jaunty yachting cap, pale blue silk shirt, white trousers, and unblemished sneakers. "So, what's the plan, Fes?"

"Let's try and work our way above the top wall so that we can get a closer look at those older tombs."

"I can see them now. You mean the two smaller ones and a larger one, partly hidden by those trees. Hey! They are orange trees! Just like Chuck said." Alex grinned. "The allusion to the Golden Apples of the Hesperides makes more sense now. Like Heracles stealing the apples from Atlas, you Festus are going to steal them from Alfredo Mokarta." Alex continued sarcastically. "Have to say parallel seems weak."

"Alex, I don't have a clue what Alfie has that's worth stealing."

A little later, a noisy scuffling announced the arrival of Ionides and Pandora. Chuck and Samantha followed them, breathing heavily. "Some people are in shape," said Pandora doing a little dance around Chuck. He was too out of breath to respond.

"Did you find anything?"

"Yes, Fes" Chuck replied. "We found a way in. Pandora insisted that we take a look."

"It was spooky," added Pandora between gasps. "That's why we ran here."

Chuck continued. "That stream goes under the wall in a small cave. It reappears briefly before disappearing again. You can't see that until you're close."

"I'm surprised it isn't blocked off," said Festus.

"It was once," Ionides replied. "There are the remains of a metal grill, eroded by the stream."

"One of the bathing huts had a window. I looked inside, Dad. It was grisly. There are mummified bodies around the wall." Pandora shivered theatrically.

"That's one of the burial customs in Sicily, for example, the Capuchin Convent at Palermo. It was prestigious to be disposed of like that. Relatives would come to hold discussions near the remains of the deceased, in the hope of obtaining their influence in decision making."

"Gruesome," Samantha laughed. "Can you imagine the kinotitos holding a meeting in the cemetery in Argos?"

"Don't make mock, Sam. Harold Dexter does it all the time and look how rich he is," Alex retorted. "You know it's probably bad luck to break into a cemetery."

"Let's try it through the front door next time. Alfie is coming to see us tomorrow. We'll have to humor him by sending people to those other caves he mentioned. I'll pay him well. Then I'll hit him with the idea of coming back here."

The Eurysthesians spent a frustrating few days visiting the caves dredged up by Alfie. Elena, Joe and Mary Beth bore the brunt of the assignments. "I swear, if I have to crouch down or crawl through some damp orifice in the ground just one more time, I will scream," Mary Beth rubbed her thigh. "I'm bruised all over."

"Me too," said Elena. "It's time that Fes put a stop to this nonsense."

Festus thanked Alfie for all of his help. He told him how seeing the caves that were not known to the public, had been a valuable experience for the Society members and had fulfilled that part of their mission. "One more thing. Before moving on we would like to see something here on Levanzo that is typically Sicilian."

Alfie's eyes took on a wary look. "Yeah, boss and what-a is that-a?"

"Just over the hill behind us is that old cemetery you were kind enough to take us to last week. It was locked, you remember, so we couldn't see very much. Could you arrange for us to get in? We'd really like to study the place from close up. We'd be happy to cover any expenses. I'm sure you could arrange anything."

Alfie looked worried. "I am not-a sure. I would have to check-a with certain people. You understand the families might-a object. If I tell them it is you, Dottore Festus, who is interested it might-a help. Even so it could cost-a quite a lot to…um…handle their pride…You understand."

"You tell me what you need and, within reason, I can handle it."

"I will-a need to tell-a these people why you want to see our cemetery. There are many such places on the mainland. Can you explain-a to me the reason," Alfie asked, innocently.

"That's easy to answer, Alfie. As I told you before, the Eurysthesian Foundation provides support. We set it up in our home town of Argos, Texas, as a route to broaden the opportunities for travel and education of our people."

"It probably helps with-a the taxes too, yes," Alfie asked, grinning.

Festus looked at him sharply. I must be careful not to be taken in by his looks and strange accent, he thought. He is smarter than he appears. Festus continued. "In part also, because we are of Mediterranean heritage, we try to visit places which connect to our past. I guess, though it may sound silly, that we find a sense of belonging in those places. This place is one of them."

"Loch Ness in-a Scotland is such a place?" Alfie prodded, gently.

"No that was different. Though it was organized through the Foundation, we also do, which is my interest, some scientific research."

"Of course-a, you are scientist. This visit is-a different."

Festus could see that Alfie was not convinced by his explanation. He decided to volunteer more information to strengthen his story. "Our present journey started in Cornwall, in the West of England. From there we came here to Sicily and soon we will move on to our final destination Crete." Alfie appeared startled by the word Crete, but he remained silent. "You should understand Alfie that what I am going to tell you is not to be spread around." Alfie nodded, intently. "In the same way that I had a theory about the Loch Ness monster, so I have a theory about the ancient travelers. Do you know that well before the time of Christ, the Phoenicians traveled to Cornwall to trade for tin? It is generally believed that, on that long journey they stopped near Cadiz in Spain. I am almost certain that they stopped here too. The Elymians who ruled this area came originally from Anatolia, which was to the north of Phoenicia. I am looking for signs of such journeys."

"I understand-a better now your interest in-a the caves. It is-a puzzle to me-a why you like the cemetery so much-a."

"Because, as you pointed out to me, some of the tombs may be sitting on older tombs. In addition, there is a source of fresh water there. In ancient times, sailors would travel from one source of fresh water to another. They may have had a camp nearby. Maybe they even buried some of their ranks nearby, those killed fighting or dying from some disease. We really would appreciate the opportunity to see the tombs. It would make a great ending to what has been, with your help, a fascinating experience."

Alfie's face showed his unease. Festus guessed that he had worked out which tomb would be of interest and he knew his family would not like it shown. "Alfie, I would view it as a great honor to be shown the tombs by you."

Alfie seemed to be impressed that he, Festus, was asking the favor. "I don't-a know. Do you simply-a want-a to walk around?"

"Mainly, I would like the chance to see some of the tombs from close-up, though to be honest I really want to look in one of the older tombs. For example, that one you mentioned."

"I think you talk about-a the Mokarta tomb. Where my-a family is buried." Alfie rubbed his face with his hands and considered the request.

"I will talk to my grandmother. Possibly, she could persuade-a my uncle. The tomb-a has not been used since my grandfather was-a, how do you say it? Laid to rest-a there, yes."

"I am embarrassed to raise the question of recompense for your efforts, as you are a friend," Festus offered tentatively, "but our Trust believes in paying its way. Is there something we could donate? For Levanzo, perhaps?" He let his voice trail away, inviting Alfie to make a suggestion.

Alfie waved his hands deprecatingly. "It is only a pleasure for me to help-a such an eminent man-a as yourself. You should not-a mention to anyone our little agreement that I will let-a you peek into my family tomb-a. You-a understand."

"Naturally. It is very kind of you."

"If they agree, then a donation-a to the harbor improvement fund would be welcome. I would accept it on behalf of the fund," he stated, seemingly unembarrassed by the idea. "American dollars, cash or travelers checks, would be convenient, shall we say-a few hundred dollars?" Alfie looked at Festus closely and seeing no obviously negative reaction, continued, "Maybe five-a hundred? In cash!"

Festus showed his surprise. How could he pay such an amount on short notice? He would have to wire Zack for funds. But it would be worth it. He was sure now that the tomb held the answer. Alfie's demand showed that he and his family had something to hide. He prayed that the tomb hid more than some smuggling activity, or whatever it was that made Alfie scared. "Consider it done Alfie. I hope that this little deal can be kept strictly between you and me, right?" He hoped that, between himself and his family, he could raise the cash.

Alfie looked relieved. "Very certainly, sir. You can-a trust me."

It was a blisteringly hot day. The rocks and plants shimmered in the heat. There was a breeze and below them, the turquoise sea, ruffled by the breeze, murmured to itself. Dawn, wearing a plain white dress cut low at the back and front to show off the fullness of her brown body, clung to Alex's arm for support. Chuck and Ionides brought up the rear. They were loaded with torches, cameras, sketchpads and other paraphernalia. At the front, Alfie was wearing the black suit and hat appropriate to the visit. He stopped periodically, to mop his brow with a large, red spotted, white handkerchief, and to check on his brood. Festus followed with Pandora. His leg hurt and his limp was very pronounced. Pandora, seeing it, tucked her arm under his to steady him.

"You're worried, aren't you, Dad?" Pandora asked quietly.

"Why is Alfie nervous? Whatever it is, it seems that Alfie's greed exceeds his fear. Mainly I'm worried that there's nothing there for us. I'm not quite sure what to do next, other than go to Crete and hunt blindly for something or other. I need help to complete the translation of the Disk."

"Don't worry, Dad! You'll work it out. You always do,"

They reached the wall and the old, iron gate. It was cooler in the valley and they took the opportunity to rest in the shade of the hill, while Alfie produced a key ring, which carried a number of keys, selected one and opened the gate. The large key grated a little as he turned it, but the lock seemed to be in good condition for it opened easily, as did the gate. Alfie stepped aside and with a grandiloquent gesture ushered in the Eurysthesians. "Welcome to the resting-a place of my ancestors, ladies and gentlemen. Please-a stay with me in one-a group. I promised my family you would be-a good, don't-a let me down, eh!" To emphasize the need he added. "Some-a are not happy-a for you to be here. The older people, you understand-a. We have traditions."

As they toured the cemetery Alfie allowed them to peer into tombs, but he became very uneasy when Pandora tried to open a door. "Only the relatives are permitted in a tomb-a," he cautioned. "Look, don't-a touch!" He showed them the larger tombs. He was proud that they contained the dead of two very important families, connected by marriage with the Mokartas, who had left Levanzo in the 18th century and had settled on the mainland, he explained. At last, they reached the upper part of the cemetery and the three older tombs, set against the hillside, which interested Festus. The central tomb, though it was smaller than the two large tombs in the center of the cemetery, was nevertheless of impressive size. It stood some fifteen feet high. At the back, it abutted the cliff, which formed the head of the valley. In the center of the front wall was a solid looking wood door. He could see now the embellishments on the Mokarta tomb and on the two smaller tombs that accompanied it. It was a disappointing sight. From a distance, it had appeared that Hittite-like symbols had been carved in the stone lintel. On a closer inspection, the embellishments seemed to be merely geometric designs that fitted conveniently between the door and the roof. Festus stood back looking for other signs. He became aware again of the orange trees whose fruit hung invitingly nearby. Pandora had also noticed them. She sidled up to Alfie and put her arms around him. "I'm so thirsty Mister Mokarta. Can I pick an orange?"

Alfie was amused. "Are you not scared-a that the juice of the oranges is no more-a than the blood of my ancestors? What-a price would you pay-a for such an orange?"

Pandora quickly kissed him on the forehead. "That's my payment."

"No more-a?" said Alfie, in mock disappointment. Pandora shook her head.

"It's a deal-a." He walked to the nearest tree and selected three large oranges, and proffered them to her. "For-a my lady."

Festus watched the scene idly, his mind working on the problem of why there was no sign of the Hittites. The light reflected from the shiny skins of the oranges made them appear to dance as Alfie picked them. He remembered a previous casual discussion and certain images clicked together in his mind. Could it be that these *citrus aurantrum* were the Golden Apples of the Hesperides, the eleventh Labor of Heracles? Heaven knows how they came to this remote site so early in history, he thought, for by contrast oranges were only a recent import to Crete. Could this little grove have survived here for thousands of years? Festus supposed that at some time the site had become sacred and the picking of oranges a sacred rite for the priestess alone to conduct. The priestess picked the oranges and offered them to Hera. One should not offend the goddess. In panic he called to Pandora. "Give them to Hera!"

The Eurysthesians turned to look at him. "What did you say, Fes?" Alex asked curiously. Then he too realized the implication of the scene. He walked over to Pandora, took one of the oranges, and ceremoniously handed it to Elena.

"They should all be mine, I suppose," Elena said uncertainly. "However, seeing that Pandora and Chuck are well into eating the other two, I guess I'll have to be satisfied with only one."

Alfie watched the scene in seeming bewilderment. However, he sensed and reacted to the sudden change in character. "What do they say-a?" he asked Joe Maximos.

"They are talking about a play we perform back home. Our play involves golden apples not oranges. They were just acting out their roles."

"Oh! A play." Alfie giggled nervously. "You Americans are strange-a. I thought so when I lived-a in the States." He edged back towards the path. "Is there anything more to do here? There are very fascinating tombs below us near the wall."

"Yes," replied Festus, firmer now in his belief that he had reached his goal. "Yes, we can do more. I would like to see inside the Mokarta tomb, as we discussed. I believe that it may be more ancient than you realize. It could be an important archaeological find."

It appeared that Alfie had hoped that Festus would not hold him to the agreement that the Eurysthesians could enter the tomb. He edged further away, while his mind worked on the possibilities raised by Festus' statement. Festus worked hard on this chink in Alfie's resolve. "If, in fact, this is an older tomb than even you understand, it may surpass the grotto as a tourist attraction. It could mean a lot more business for the island. I need to study it to be sure." He signaled surreptitiously to Ionides, who sidled across to loom ominously over the startled Alfie.

"It would be a big disappointment for my friends to miss this opportunity to see your family's tomb, Mister Mokarta," said Ion, harshly.

Alfie wavered for only a moment. "Okay, anything for-a the ladies, but you must-a promise not to touch-a anything and stay-a close to me."

The latter request appeared to be the easier to meet for the tomb was only some twenty feet in width. Alfie selected a second key from the ring. The door, for all of its size, opened with remarkable ease. He motioned for them to enter.

Light was filtering in through small holes, set high in the walls. The breeze that had cooled them earlier, somehow penetrated even to this isolated spot, for the room seemed to breathe with every surge of the wind.

As their eyes adjusted, they could see that there were bodies all around the wall, like an extreme form of wallpaper.

"They must have hidden fastenings to hold them up," said Ionides, feeling behind a black-suited body.

"Don't touch," said Alfie and Alex in unison. Alex crossed himself. "It's bound to be bad luck."

The Eurysthesians pressed past Alfie then, following some unspoken yet instantaneous agreement, crowded the center of the chamber away from the dead. Dawn, as was her custom, made a big fuss about the situation to gain attention, and clung possessively to Festus. Alfie, unable to slow the initial rush quickly worked his way around them muttering worriedly until he stood between the group and the back of the tomb. He spread his hands expressively as if he, for the first time, was offering them the sight.

"Is-a magnifico, no?" Alfie turned and pointed to the back of the tomb. "My grandfather, he was a great-a man."

His grandfather's mummified remains were clothed in a baggy black suit that had the wide lapels and generous lapels of the 1940's. A wide gray fedora, stuffed with a thin layer of newspaper, was on his head. It was a ridiculous sight, though it seemed to please Alfie. "Some-a day I hope-a to take my-a place here-a," he announced proudly.

Alex observed Festus, whose face had the flat look that advertises disappointment. "It doesn't look like this is the place does it, Fes?" he whispered.

"No, Alex it doesn't. I have couple more ideas, but they're very weak. I was sure this was it. Unfortunately, the tomb isn't that old, late Medieval at the earliest," Festus concluded, leaning close to Alex to finish his comments as the noise of the wind increased.

Most of the Eurysthesians found their surroundings to be intimidating. They remained still and silent in the middle of the chamber, seemingly stuck together like candy in a child's pocket. Pandora on the other hand roamed about, feeling the clothing and peering up at the mummified faces, while maintaining a constant stream of excited chatter. "Wow! This guy's wearing a cravat. I wonder how old he is. Look at this one he's lost half his face."

"Leave them alone Pandy, they're tired," Chuck exclaimed in despair at her antics.

Alfie showed less concerned. Festus assumed that he was used to the Sicilian custom of talking to the dead. Alfie eyed Pandora appreciatively and complimented her in colloquial Italian on the neatness of her backside, adding in English. "It is-a good you-a talk to them. My grandfather likes that. Maybe you bring-a him back-a to life. He loved-a the ladies."

Pandora played up to his suggestion and proceeded to grandfather Mokarta. She jerked away suddenly and shrieked, "He moved! You weren't joking, Alfie. I saw him move."

"Don't be silly Pandy. That's not very funny."

"I wasn't joking, Mom. He moved." She edged back into the group, pointing at the mummy.

The Eurysthesians, who had turned as one when the commotion began, looked and, as one, they too reacted. It was true. The baggy suit was swaying at the waist and around the thighs. So too were the clothes on the bodies nearby. The movement was accompanied by an eerie scratching sound, as if the mummies were limbering up for dance. Outside, the noise of the wind increased further and the atmosphere in the tomb cooled appreciably. Even Alfie seemed disturbed. "Maybe we should-a leave now?" he requested, plaintively.

By contrast, Festus was elated. "No, there's nothing to be worried about," he said. "That noise is only the trees rubbing against the roof. It's a draft moving the clothes, so it seems the tomb may go back further."

"You're right, Fes. That would explain it," added Ion, moving across to Alfie and putting his arm around the broad shoulders. "Alfie, my friend, we need to move your grandfather."

Alfie shook his head mutely.

Ion rotated Dawn, who was clutching his other arm, to face Alfie. Dawn took the hint quickly, put her arms around Alfie and pulled him to her.

"I'm sure your grandfather would like company. Pandy and I can talk to him. He'd-a like-a that-a," Dawn said, making a face at Pandora, over Alfie's head.

Alfie, with his face pressed tightly against Dawn's magnificent breasts, looked as if he were in heaven. Dawn held him for a moment longer, then turned to his side retaining a grip on his left arm. Before his euphoria could evaporate, Pandora quickly grasped his right arm. Dawn and Pandora pushed Alfie closer to his grandfather.

The grandfather's body, hanging slackly in its suit was a cumbersome object to move. Nevertheless, eventually it was unhooked from its supporting ropes, and Festus and Joe handed it to Alfie. Hooks on the back of the suit had been hooked over ropes that were now visible. Behind the ropes, hiding the wall, there was a heavy brown curtain. Chuck took a flashlight from Ionides, and went down on his hands and knees to peer under the curtain. He was silent for a moment then, muttering excitedly, he crawled under it and disappeared. Festus declined to follow by that route and fussed with the curtain until he found an overlap in it. Alex and Joe helped him move more mummies aside to make the access easier. Then, one by one, the Eurysthesians entered the rear of the tomb, leaving Alfie alone in the center of the room, mournfully supporting his grandfather.

The opening behind the curtain led to a circular cave. It appeared in part to be natural, and in part to have been carved from the rock. A stone column supported the roof. They saw three wooden coffins resting on a shelf. The source of the draft, that had indicated the presence of the cave, was apparent now. Fissures, high in the walls, hissed gently in concord with the rise and fall of the wind as it swirled around the head of the valley.

"Don't touch the coffins!" Alfie shouted, as the curtains closed. They could hear his muffled voice say. "You have-a already insulted-a my grandfather-a, please respect our dead-a." Pandora looked through a hole in the curtain. Alfie was standing, nearly still, shuffling his feet for balance like some unfortunate in a dance marathon.

Festus paced around the coffins, arranging the flashlights to obtain a better look at them. "They don't look ancient," he said finally. "What do you make of these carvings, Alex? You know more about Italian stuff than I do."

"At a guess they're late nineteenth century."

"Damn it! I'm afraid you're right Alex. What the hell do we do now?"

"It's a pity they're not what you want, Fes, but I'm getting scared. Please can we get out of here?" Dawn said nervously.

"Just hang on a little longer, honey! Chuck, get some photos! I want to make sure we have records. Anybody who wants to help, do some tracing or whatever. I don't see any point in tracing the carvings, but what the hell. Maybe they'll show something." Festus slumped against the pillar.

"Fes, aren't you being far too hasty?" Elena said, seeing his disappointment. "I know when you found the cave you hoped for an instant sign of the Hittites. Life, in my experience, isn't usually that kind. Shouldn't we look inside the coffins? Alfie may be unhappy, but so what? We didn't come all this way to be put off by such a minor problem. Remember how the signs in Cornwall were hidden."

Festus jerked upright. "You're right. Everything's been too easy up until now. I hoped that whatever it is we're looking for would be sitting in plain view. I guess I'm uneasy about opening the coffins. Put it down to superstition. All right, finish the pictures first! Oh! Forget about the tracings! Chuck, have you got anything to pry them open with?"

"The general store has everything," Chuck answered confidently, pulling two tire levers from his backpack. "Let Ion and me see what we can do."

They removed the lid and saw a terracotta sarcophagus. There was a brief silence while the torch light played over the contents. "It's Minoan," Festus shouted. "Just like those in the museum at Iraklion. This is it. Look at the painting on the lid. Bless you sweet Hera. Look at the rim! See the Hittite signs!" Festus leaned weakly against the pillar as his friends clustered around to see for themselves. Sure enough, the lid carried a painting of spiral lines. In the center of the spiral were a caricature of a female figure and a few of the symbols from the Disk, juxtaposed with Hittite script. There were similar paintings on two of the remaining sarcophagi—although the central motif differed. In one case, the spiral contained a male figure. In the other, there was the head of a bull but no spiral. In addition, there were further symbols from the Disk and Hittite hieroglyphs.

The Eurythesians paid no attention to the contents of the sarcophagi. Pandora continued to fuss around them and eventually succeeded in raising a lid. Underneath was a layer of sackcloth. "Look what I've found," she said, brandishing an automatic weapon.

Alex picked one up and studied it. "I'm no great expert, but I think these are British Sten guns. I think we'd better get our photos and get out of here."

"We'll only be another minute," responded Ionides.

"What do we do with Alfie?"

"I don't think he knows we've seen the weapons, Elena," Festus said. "Maybe we simply leave and say…"

"I do know," said Alfie—his face and that of his grandfather, making an eerie sight as they poked around the edge of the curtain. "You should not-a have opened the coffins. I-a warned you." He noticed that Alex was about to speak and guessed the topic. "Money won't solve-a your problem now. I shouldn't have let you in the tomb-a," Alfie added sadly, pointing with his right hand. It was then that they noticed the gun.

"How in God's name did you miss that gun, Dawn?" Fes shouted. "You damn nearly raped the man."

"Darling, I didn't realize it was a gun. I honestly thought the poor man was excited. I have that effect on men, you know." Dawn finished lamely.

"Oh, shit."

"Alfie, let me hold your grandfather! All we want is photos of the pictures on the lids. The other is not our business. We won't talk."

Alfie trained the gun on Festus. "Stop! I cannot-a risk it. You come-a here slowly. The rest of you get behind the coffins! Don't anybody try-a anything or some of you will be joining my grandfather."

Though it was dark in the cave and both Ion and Joe fancied their chances at tackling Alfie, they held back for fear ta stray bullet would hit one of their company. With care to keep the gun pointed at Festus, Alfie pushed the body of his grandfather against Festus. He called to Joe. "There is a rope-a on the floor. You-a pick it up and tie my grandfather to the great-a Dottore Festus! Tie him tightly you understand!"

"Sorry, Fes," said Joe, shaking his head, as he bound the two bodies together.

Alfie checked the bindings and then he pushed Joe back towards his companions. He turned to Festus. "Now you will-a hold him up," he whispered. "I don't think you will-a drop him either. Eh!" Festus and the grandfather shrugged, wearily. He shuffled away from the curtain into the outer part of the tomb. The curtain closed. "He can-a do nothing. I will deal with him in a moment," he muttered, with satisfaction. "Show me these pictures that-a mean so much to you!"

Alfie studied the spirals disinterestedly. "I have seen these before. They are just the drawings of children." He brandished one of the weapons in his left hand. "This-a means something to our friends and relations on the mainland." He stopped, as if worrying he had said too much, and in a distracted manner dropped the rifle back into the coffin. "Put the lid on and close up the coffins! Stay on the far side! Right." He motioned to Dawn. "You come-a with me!"

Alfie retreated towards the outer tomb, keeping the gun pointed at her, and disappeared through the curtain. He assessed the scene quickly. The outer tomb was empty. Where was Festus? His grandfather's body was back against the wall, crowded in among the other bodies. "How did-a Dottore untie himself? No is possible" he muttered. Alfie sought counsel from his grandfather, quickly offering apologies for the insult that had been given him. "Is he outside, grandfather?" Is it-a what I would have done." His grandfather's head moved, acknowledging the apology. Alfie was pleased at the sign, until he understood what had happened. He started to back away, but he was too slow. His grandfather and the figure at his side moved faster. Automatically his arm went up to protect his grandfather and he dropped the gun. Dawn quickly grabbed it and stuck it in Alfie's ribs. "Untie him now!" she said.

Festus again handed Alfie his grandfather and took the gun from Dawn. She called to the Eurysthesians to come out.

"Oh, Dad," laughed Pandora. "You look like a relic from a 1930's gangster movie."

"You mean the hat?" Festus pushed the hat back from his forehead. "I put it on when I changed places with Alfie's grandfather. It was the only thing I could think of to fool him. I think it suits me. Joe, thanks for leaving the rope loose."

Joe laughed. "Old escapologist's trick, Fes. I had one hand under it when Alfie checked. When he was satisfied I removed it."

Joe took the gun from Festus and looked at it. "It's not loaded."

"Naturally," said Alfie. "What-a do you-a take me for-a?"

"We'd better get out of here," said Alex. "The boat can take all of us, if it's only for a few days. We can tie Alfie loosely. Even he isn't going to stand around forever holding his grandfather. If we lock him in we'll have to send someone to get him."

"Look, Alfie! We are not going to tell anyone about your secret. We've put everything back the way it was. We are only interested in those pictures. If you keep quiet, no one else will ever know. Now you think about it! I'm sure you'll make a sensible decision."

"You tricked-a me, Dottore Festus," shouted Alfie. "Maybe I will not tell my friends, but I will get-a you. You-a defiled the memory of my-a grandfather. I know where-a you are going. I have friends. We will meet again."

"What does he mean?" asked Elena, as Festus paused to pick an orange.

"I'm not sure. When he talked about the mainland, I thought at first he meant Sicily. Now, I wonder whether, some of the time, he meant Crete. Is it possible that the ancient connection between these islands and Crete never vanished?"

"Maybe the guns are for those crazy people that Duke was trying to help in Sfakia?"

Festus looked at Elena. "Not just for Duke? Eh!" Elena grimaced.

Alex's boat cleared the harbor at Trapani and headed east. Alex and Festus, sitting in the stern, watched the Aegadian islands disappear over the horizon.

"I'm relieved we've finished that phase," Alex remarked. "Though I suppose, if I take Alfie's threat seriously, it's not over yet. It's curious that his gun had no bullets in it. Strange?"

"Yes, it's odd," replied Festus, thoughtfully. Something worried him but he could not bring it into focus. "I don't think Alfie will do anything, unless he happens to cross our path by chance. When he's had a chance to reflect a bit I reckon he'll be too embarrassed to tell his family what happened. However, I'll be glad when we all meet again in Iraklion. I think our precaution should be sufficient to cope with any problems Alfie and his friends might cause, if I'm wrong about him. Incidentally, changing the subject, did you ever hear from your FBI friend who was going to check on Alfie?"

"Oh yes," replied Alex, laughing. "Alfie's on the FBI files; deported as an undesirable alien. You're going to like the description of his *modus operandum*." Alex paused for effect. "Alfredo Mokarta spent time in jail, when he was deported he was a hold-up man—just like Atlas!"

"That's great," Festus laughed.

"One other thing, Fes," said Alex, looking amused. "My contacts told me they'd heard that Alfredo was terminated by his Mafia colleagues a few years back!"

"Maybe they were misinformed?"

Alex shrugged. "It's too late to find out now."

42. Cerberus

Alex sailed his boat, close to the 36th parallel, from Trapani to Reggio di Calabria on the Italian mainland. The boat continued with a small crew to the tiny island of Sapienza. The stop at Sapienza was in part to break up the journey, and in part for Festus to see the 19th century lighthouse. The drive mechanism for the lamp was elegantly simple. It had a large weight that dropped over a twenty-four hour period, turned the petroleum powered light. A massive system of four lenses beamed the warning light for up to twenty miles. Nowadays, the optical signature of the lighthouse was different from the intent of its designers—three flashes for three minutes then blank for one minute. During the Second World War, the Germans had shot out one set of lenses.

Festus spent most of the voyage poring over the photographs and tracings from Cornwall and Sicily. The symbols from the Hittite monument in Cornwall had given him the clue to the find in Sicily. He was reasonably certain of his translation of one side of the Disk, the side with the flower at the center. Now he had further symbols from the Disk, along with their translation in Hittite hieroglyphs. He turned his attention to the second side of the Disk, pulling out a photograph to study it.

Zack was waiting on the dock in Iraklion. His booming laugh had already betrayed his presence long before Festus could see him. Festus knew that the laugh masked exasperation about something. He was right! Zack wasted no time on formalities. He launched into a long monologue about how great it was that the Greece was now in the hands of men who could put it back on the right course. By the time they had reached the hotel, Zack was ready to discuss the Foundation's business. Festus had the odd feeling that the two topics might be connected.

"Well, Henry, I hear you've unraveled the secret of the Disk? I've been waiting for you to get in touch with me and tell me about it."

Though forewarned by the dockside laughter and the use of Henry rather than Fes, Festus found the irritation in Zack's voice disconcerting. It seemed that Zack was placing considerably more importance on the quest than simply meeting the goals of the Foundation. "I'm sorry Zack. It got a bit hectic at the end. You see…"

"Tell me later! What about the treasure, have you worked out where it is?"

"Yes and no, Zack. I…"

"Come on, Henry! Yes and no, what the hell kind of an answer is that?"

"I think I understand most of the words and our successes in Cornwall and Sicily show we're on the right track. However, the Disk only hints at what the treasure is, and where it is. It seems that the dance will show the way to the treasure and so we need to try that route."

"Are there any other artifacts, say here in Iraklion at the Museum, which would shed light on the meaning of the Disk?"

"Not as far as I know. The Disk, the Pendant, the Nine Maidens and the sarcophagi in Sicily appear to be the main pieces of the puzzle. It's possible that there's some other clue from one of the palaces, Knossos, Phaestos, Mallia, or wherever, which hasn't been found or hasn't been recognized yet."

"So assuming we find nothing else, what's the main problem to overcome?"

"The main clues that I've not understood so far, are the spiral lines from Cornwall and Sicily. We think they may be patterns for the dancers and acrobats on the dancing floor. You know, like those pictures of footprints we used to follow as kids that showed the steps for a dance."

"I'll let you worry about that. Now, are you really sure there's nothin' else here?" Maybe I should talk to the director of the museum, or fly in some expert from Athens?"

Typical Zack, Festus thought, putting him down just to show he was boss. Elena saved him from having to reply.

"You've already talked to the director, haven't you, Fes?"

"Yes, I have." Festus smiled at Elena. "He's been very helpful. He's not aware of any other artifact with Hittite and Disk symbols on it. To be honest he's skeptical of my translation."

"You see my problem, Henry. If you'd bothered to keep me informed I wouldn't have to raise these questions. So, seeing you're in charge, what do you want us peons to do next?"

"Go back to the hotel. I've rented a meeting room. When all the rest of us peons are assembled, I'll go over my findings and we can make a decision on how to proceed." Festus replied, hastily, regretting his sharp answer as he spoke. Zack's belligerent attitude was worrying. It seemed unlikely that it involved Duke, since he had heard that Zack had resolved Duke's problem with the military.

Festus looked around the dining room of their hotel. Pandora and Chuck were at the back with Ionides and Samantha, all of them talking animatedly, while Ionides prepared the slide projector. In front of them, Peri Dexter was twittering to Marienna Cronson. Marienna seemed to have benefited from her rest in

Argos, but she was showing her age. The somber black robe covering her stooped figure gave her the appearance of a dowdy, elderly Cretan peasant woman. Beside her, and wearing his best black suit, was Harold making periodic comments to Angelica Cronson. The Maximos' completed the row. In the front row, Dawn sat with Alex Platon occasionally flashing sultry looks at Festus. Zack and Elena were in the middle of the front row, Zack fidgeting impatiently. The last of the group, Panou Cronson and Rosie arrived. Panou had forsaken his customary Hawaiian shirt for a black shirt and an embroidered Cretan waistcoat, which terminated a shade above his ornate leather belt. Jeans and Texan boots completed the outfit. Rosie joined Pandora. Pan dragged a chair to the front, bellowing greetings as he went.

"The first slide please, Ion. It shows what I call the first side of the Disk."

"You see those symbols that looked like a pear and three squiggly lines at the center. In my translation they are shorthand for κρητη or Crete—possibly in Crete or by Crete. The scythe could represent either θ or τ ; there might be no differentiation in writing the two sounds at that stage of development of the script. I also suspect that as with the Linear B script, translated by Ventris and his collaborators, there is a single symbol for [b] and [p] as well as only one for [l] and [r]."

"Tell your Japanese story, Dad."

"Pandy, I don't think…"

"Go on!"

"Okay. I was in Tokyo, and took a tour. The guide told us about the 'glandeur of the parace of the Clown Plince.' That's what I'm talking about."

After the laughter died down, Festus returned to his primary concern, the meaning of the second side of the Disk. "Next slide please. The find in Sicily gave me the meaning for the vertical broom symbol. It stands for β or π. This led to the name Cerberus, the three-headed dog that guarded the underworld—Tartarus—for Hades. The allusion to Cerberus was probably poetic license, meaning simply that the treasure was place in a cave. At that time, around 1400 BC, it was believed, commonly, that many caves led to Tartarus.

"What does it mean?"

"In a minute, Pan. Using δ for the symbol that looks like a turban worked well. It appears that the line attached to the bottom of the turban modifies the sound to δευ and δια; this finding led me to the name of Deucalion. The writing appeared to say that Deucalion had divided Crete. For some reason Deucalion had hidden the treasure in a cave guarded by gates. The implication is that the treasure is gold. The final words seemed to be a glorified 'no trespassing sign.'"

κρ ητη-θ ε λε ω - κ ε ου πτς -κ ερ βε ρ ω-δευ κα λη ω -λ ερ ε κα
in Crete-by sacred - (concealed) - Cerberus   -by Deucalion   -(boldly)
        rite   (with)

κρ ητη κα -(ου)ερ κω-τ ε λε μα -δια κα λ ω ην -κρ ητ η - α δε η
in a Cretan - swears -I (myself) -(I) divided - Crete - (by)
manner   accomplished   fearless

δευ κα λ ω-χρ μ ω ς -εις πε ριν ου πτς -χρ υς ω - ιερ υ α
Deucalion -(business) - I contrived   -with gold - a priestess

ο φε λ λ ης - χρ η-θυ μα - πι λ ο ς - ου π λα κα - θ ε λ ω
has the duty -necessary a - gates   -(has armed) - a cave
                sacrifice

αρ χρ α κα κας -οις πιο-χρ α   - μο ερ ε α - ο φε λ εις -μα θ υν
(causing evils) -(divine judgement) - destined - to profit in vain
        (country)

σι ε λ ς - ου ρκ ητη μα - κα π ω ο ς
prepare for -   dancing   - (???)

Harold was unimpressed and Festus could hear him muttering to Angel, throughout the analysis. Festus decided to call his hand. "Do you have a problem with my analysis, Harold? Have you got some other interpretation you want to share with us?"

"I could easily come up with another explanation of the facts you presented; even using a similar set of letters. I think you juggled everything to suit your particular fantasy."

"What do you mean?"

"Come on Henry! You believe you're repeating the Labors of Heracles. Obviously, you had to come up with the name Cerberus. This being, I suppose, your Twelfth Labor. I've done some reading about the Disk while you've been on your travels. What do you have to say about the translation of that Bulgarian Georgiev? He says the language of the Disk is Luwian—one of the Hittite languages. I suspect that's where you got your ideas from."

Harold's tone was insulting and Festus had a hard time keeping his temper. It was going to be difficult if both Harold and Zack were on the attack.

"I know of Georgiev's work, Harold. You're quite right it was one of my leads. To put the rest of you in the picture, Georgiev suggested that one side of the Disk described the fate of a leader called Yara who was banished to a castle after losing a battle, probably somewhere near Troy. Georgiev paper says that the Disk was made by a man named Santadimura. Yara assures this Santadimura that he will cause no more trouble."

"Well! What's wrong with that translation?"

"It's ingenious, Harold. Unfortunately for Georgiev, he didn't have the bilinguals, and his interpretation is incorrect."

"Arrogant rubbish!" Harold muttered.

"If you'd looked into it further, Harold, you might also have found out that some of the symbols appear on tablets found at Mohenjo Daro in the Indian subcontinent. I can't explain that, but it doesn't alter the validity of my translation. Have you any constructive comments?"

Marienna did not wait for Harold to answer. "Harold, I don't understand why you question Henry's judgment. It's almost as if you don't want him to continue. You seem to ignore all his successes. He was right about Cornwall. He was right about Sicily and I believe he's on the right track here in Crete. Let's hear what he wants to do and try and help him."

"Thanks, Marienna. I do need all of you to help. It seems there is a treasure but, honestly, I don't know what it is. It appears it's to be found in a cave, maybe in the labyrinth that was guarded by the Minotaur or the dog Cerberus. The problem is…where's the cave? The name Deucalion, the son of king Minos, suggests it could be at Knossos. There is a clue that the route to the treasure involves the dancing floor. I find that an appealing idea, given our previous experience. I believe the spiral lines, I showed you, to be the ordained paths for the dancers and acrobats. I just wish there were some way to relate them to the Disk."

"Would it help if we enacted them for you, Fes? Sort of went through the motions so that you could see them."

"Yes, Angel, that's exactly what I need. Marienna and I have some idea of how the dance starts. It is like the one we do in the Festival. However, even if we have the correct arrangement of all the lines, we don't know the pace of the dance or the relative timings of the dancers."

"I...I didn't find it difficult before, Fes," Peri ignored the angry look on Harold's face. "It all seemed to come back to me, if you know what I mean. I guess it's a lot like Marienna's dance we do at the Festivals. You know it too Harold, for all your talk. You got involved. Go on, admit it!" Harold, his head still bent, nodded grudgingly.

"Fes, why don't you show us whatever you have worked out on the spirals? Maybe we can see who should play each role." Zack's tone was conciliatory.

"What I plan to do is this, Zack. When we were in Cornwall, Marienna realized the significance of the pattern of holes around the edge of the Nine Maidens. She suggested that that they might be positions for the High Priestess, the King and the Bull Master. In Cornwall we found nine spiral paths and on the largest stone the words "of himself" and a complete pattern of holes. Using this last stone and overlaying the patterns from all the stones so that each group of similar holes is aligned, we found the relative orientation of all the spiral lines." Festus paused. "Now, from the lids of the sarcophagi in Sicily we obtained two more paths and in the center of them, supporting Marienna's thesis, were the stylized figures of a man and a woman. Strangely, I guess, with the figure of a bull there was no path. The additional symbols on the lids do not appear to have any special significance, but the bilingual helped in translating the Disk. As a final point, there is one odd feature about the lines. All of them are continuous except one from Cornwall, which is a dashed line."

"Come on, Fes, show us the pattern!" Zack said, impatient again.

"Here's the overlay of all the lines. It's a bit messy but if you study it carefully, you'll see the key features. There are two groups of spiral lines plus four individual paths. The latter four include the dashed path from Cornwall and the two paths from Sicily. The paths are spread over, what we are assuming to be the dancing floor. They are in pairs, with one path from each of the groups belonging to the High Priestess and the King."

"Why pairs?" Angelica asked.

"I believe one line represents a dancer, tripping across the floor on her prescribed path. The other line is for the acrobat, assigned to protect the dancer by distracting the bull. There are additional acrobats who try to keep the bull under control. It's curious..." Festus could tell that Zack had done enough listening and needed to assert his authority.

"Your description makes some sense, Fes. I guess the problem now is to explain the remainin' three paths. I probably shouldn't say anythin', given earlier comments, but I will. I know the significance of the path associated with the figure of a man; the King, as Marienna has correctly surmised. Don't you say a damn thang, Harold! Before the dance, the King walks to the center of the floor and back again to give the pace of the dance. Now let's turn to the path associated with the female figure. Do you want to comment Elena?"

"Yes. I think I know what the High Priestess does. She goes before the King, sorry dear. She can also change the difficulty because she sets the distance between the dancers. If the dancers are widely spaced it is easier for the acrobats to keep the bull away from them. If they are bunched together it's much more dangerous."

"Remember they start in the middle of the floor, so if they're lucky and the dance is quick, they'll have a chance to spread out before the bull charges for the first time," Angelica added. "Marienna mentioned it."

"Does anyone understand the dashed path and the lack of a path with the bull symbol?" For a moment, there was silence.

"I think I do in part, Zack." The voice came from the center of the room. It was a big surprise to the Eurysthesians.

"I think I understand the lack of a path for the bull," said Harold, standing. "In each dance, the Bull Master shows the path he wants the bull to take. He paces it out across the floor. Of course, the bull will charge in many directions. It is the job of the lead acrobats, those free from protecting a particular dancer, to keep the bull moving as close to the chosen path as possible, by forcing corrections each time it deviates. They are rewarded depending on how well they do. If the Bull Master wants to be unkind he brings the bull near the center of the floor at the start."

"How do you happen to know this, Harold?"

"Goddamn it, Zack! I don't really know. Maybe the plays, rehearsing with Marienna. Like Peri says, that damn Royal Cretan dance of Marienna's." Harold stopped, looking embarrassed. When Marienna didn't react, he continued. "Maybe because, like the rest of you, I sometimes get pulled back into the past. When I'm fishing, I daydream and I see the old times. I've learned a hell of a lot. I just don't glory in it like some of our number. I worry about Peri," he added softly. "I couldn't keep her away and she'll have to do the dance, and neither the King, nor the High Priestess, nor the Bullmaster can show her any favors. Let me tell you Zack, I'm not happy about what we're doing here. I don't think Henry understands what he's getting in to, which is odd in itself. Have you told him?" He stopped briefly under the influence of Zack's steady gaze.

"Have you told me what?" Festus said angrily.

Zack ignored him. "Harold, do you know who the Bullmaster is?"

"I know what he does, Zack, but I'm not sure who he is. I can't explain the broken line either. I feel I ought to know, yet each time I nearly have it, it escapes me. We'll have to wait for the dance, to find out."

"So we have to do the dance," said Zack, to no one in particular. "Then I must pick the players." He looked around the room. "Maybe it will be easier if people volunteer. As your leader I could order it, I guess." He laughed. "As a Texan I'll follow our standard anarchic policy and leave it up to you."

"Harold's right. I'm a dancer," said Peri firmly. There was silence.

"I'm a dancer too," Rosie added, in a whisper.

"No way!" Bellowed Panou, rising to his feet. "No way is my Rosie going on the dancing floor."

"Pan, you made a deal. You know why you're here? This must be done. It is destined."

"I didn't reckon Rosie would have to dance, Zack, or we would have stayed in Texas. It's damn fool plan that drives you, not destiny. Does Fes know?"

"That's enough! It's too late to change the plans now," Zack retorted.

Pan stood for a moment, rebellion showing in the set of his shoulders. "I'll be fine, Dad." Rosie spoke comfortingly. Pan shrugged, looked quizzically at Festus, and sat.

"Explain it to me Zack! What did he mean, 'does Fes know?'"

"Nothing for you to worry about Fes," Zack sounded conciliatory. "He's upset because we haven't consulted him enough, and I guess…you…about some help we've been giving to my…relatives…on a related matter. Now isn't the time to be fussing over detail. This isn't like those two times with our friends, south of the border. I'm convinced that no fantasy bull is going to hurt anybody. The way I see it, this business of reverting to the past is all in our minds. It's as if we are trying to correct some unfinished business. That's why we go into a kind of trance. Some form of self-hypnosis. Either way, this time I am convinced we're onto something big. Something of great historic importance, and we need to support Fes."

Festus was irritated by the way Zack seemed to be using him as a cover for his own plans. The odd comments from Pan and Harold implied that Zack had some grand plan in which his own search was a small part. Zack had conned Duke into stealing the Bullroarer. The logical explanation was that he intended to aid the Sfakians. To fight the Turks? That appeared ridiculous, but what other explanation could there be? Did he want to find the treasure for the same purpose? Clearly, Europa had screwed up the plan. When Zack had found out she was part of a German-Greek terrorist group, he had decided to abort that part of his plan. Then there was Sicily. "Do the weapons we found in Sicily have something to do with this? Do you know Alfredo Mokarta?'

"I can honestly say, no."

"I'm the third dancer," said Dawn.

"I'm an acrobat. I'll be with Dawn. You're an acrobat too, Angel." Angelica nodded agreement. Alex turned to look at Joe and Mary-Beth Maximos. "You two make up the set, I think."

"Seeing as I'm a 'foreigner' I'm flattered at being asked," Mary Beth said. She had dyed her hair black upon arriving in Crete, to appear more Greek looking, apparently. "I hope we're fit. Mind you, I've been going to the YWCA fitness class. It's Joe we should be worried about. He hasn't done a thing since he gave up tennis."

"I've been playing golf."

"From a cart, honey, it's not the same." Mary Beth patted his middle. "Maybe we should go jogging later."

"There are limits to what I'll do to prepare. How about a cold beer?" Joe paused, adding, "Maybe, I do remember something from the past. Make it two beers." Mary Beth mimed smacking his head.

"We should all be very careful, Joe. Each time we revert, things become more real. I wonder if at some point I might stay there."

"Don't be so morbid, Peri! You have far too much imagination."

"You would be wise to listen to her, Zack." Harold rose to his feet in anger. "You're taking something on with these games you and Festus are playing that could destroy us all. The way things are, I can't stop you. As you know damn well! This is my last warning."

"Come on Harold! You're so gloomy, anyone would think we were all gonna die. Mind you, in your profession you probably think that's an honorable solution. Give us a break!" Harold stared at him coldly for a moment, then, like Festus before him, he sat and rested his head in his hands. "Now where were we? Ah, yes. Alex, who do we have to play the free acrobats?"

"It's going to have to be Pandora, Samantha, and Ion. Chuck's never been in the plays or dance. I don't think he would know what to do"

"I agree." Chuck looked relieved.

"That leaves the question of who plays the King, the High Priestess and the Bullmaster. I think we all know your role Zack and yours Elena. This leaves the question of the Bullmaster." Festus looked around. "I would have said it was Ari, but he's not here. Is it you Harold or Pan? Or...me?"

"Not me," replied Pan. "You should all know what I do. I play the pipes and keep the rhythm started by the King. That leaves you two."

"Wait up! We haven't named the fourth dancer."

"I think it's me, Zachary."

"Marienna," Zack, struggled to find the right words. "I don't think...At your...It wouldn't be wise. You should advise the dancers. We'll work something..."

"Zachary, don't you tell me what I can or cannot do!"

Zack was saved from the argument by a voice from the back of the room.

"I've been outside, listening to your discussions. I was having difficulty deciding whether to come in. Frankly, if I hadn't a previous experience of what you've been talking about, I'd reckon you were all crazy. Like Mary-Beth, though I'm a foreigner, I've done it before. So I'm your fourth dancer."

"Why, it's Cathy Schmidt," Dawn said, sweetly. She was about to continue, when Angelica interrupted her. "Cathy's with me, Dawn. She can help."

"We'll go to Knossos tomorrow. I've arranged to get into the palace early, before the tourists arrive. They think we're making a film. I told them we would be rehearsing without cameras. Amazingly, they'll even let us put sand on the courtyard. I was lucky to find a local building contractor who was looking for a filler job for some of his men. He'll do the sanding the tonight and clean it up when we've finished." Zack looked around to see if there were questions. "Seeing as we have all the players settled, except the Bullmaster who can't or won't reveal himself, let's stop now."

Festus watched them leave and returned to studying his translation. One aspect still bothered him. The translation seemed very similar to parts of Marienna's fourth play, "the Goats." Was the whole thing an invention of Marienna's?

42. The Sacred Dance

The skeletons of half-built houses, constructed during good times by Cretan families as dowries for unwed daughters, waited patiently beside the road to Knossos for a marriage to occur. The Eurysthesians arrived at the skeleton palace that Sir Arthur Evans had constructed. Festus wondered what event it was awaiting—the dance?

"Your contractor's done a good job, Zack," Festus said, looking appreciatively at the artistically raked floor of the central courtyard of the Palace.

"What do we do now, Fes?" Alex asked with amusement. "I've come to the dance and my card is still empty."

"Mark out the spiral lines, first. Ion, please do what we discussed. I don't see Chuck anywhere." Festus watched them finish the job. It was hot. He took nervous sips from his flask. Alex looked at him impatiently. "Sorry Alex. I'm worried I'm missing something. What the hell! Come on everybody! Let's get the dancers and acrobats onto the floor. You know your positions. The other acrobats should spread out across the floor. Pan, get ready to provide the rhythm, as soon as Zack has set the timing! Zack, you should go to that balcony over the antechamber! Elena, you need to space the dancers! When you've completed that, join Zack on the balcony!"

Festus paced nervously round the edge of the sand-covered area. He wished he knew who the Bullmaster was and what his instructions would be. The only people he could see who were not involved in other activities were Harold and Marienna. It seemed unlikely that the Bullmaster would be a woman, and Marienna now walked with difficulty. She seemed to be in pain. That left Harold. He had to be the prime candidate. Festus reached the southern end of the courtyard and turned to check the scene. It did not look right. He shouted. "Are you sure you acrobats know who you're guarding? Please keep your positions."

"Don't worry Fes," Alex reassured him. "Ion and Pandora will be free agents, I will protect Dawn, the Maximos will attend to Peri and Rosie, and Angel will watch over Cathy."

Festus could hear the insistent sound of the pipes above the background chatter. He worked his way across the floor, offering words of encouragement as he went. At the center of the floor, he hesitated. Looking around, he saw Marienna beckoning him. He went towards her. His right foot was dragging on the ground, a sign that he was nervous, and the sand was heavily marked by his passage. The palace was completely quiet now, except for the lilt of the pipe. The dancers and acrobats were poised, seemingly frozen in their places, waiting for the signal to start. Festus felt dizzy. The scene started to flicker. He saw Chuck approaching. He looked different was his last thought before he reverted to the past.

"A crowd has gathered. Please explain again why we are here."

"Iolaus, this is the grand dance to elucidate the Mysteries, on behalf of King Minos," Hephaestus replied, pointing at the King. "Surely you remember that the King made an alliance some years ago with powerful nations across the seas. It is surely no secret now that, in payment for our work, they paid a vast tribute. Deucalion, his son, had hidden it and disappeared. As have all the others who helped him. It is not known whether they perished or, perchance, lost their memories in the waters of Lethe. It is said the dance is the key to its recovery." Hephaestus pointed again. "See, the dancers have started."

"Look, Hephaestus! In the shadow by the corner of the antechamber, the bull is ready."

"Who released the bull? If I knew that, I would know more about the treasure. There is such a crowd now; I cannot distinguish those around the King. What is the crowd chanting?" Hephaestus put a hand to his ear and heard.

"Oh, Lord Hephaestus, if the gods in their wisdom wanted you to find the treasure, they would open your eyes." The crowd chanted in unison. "Watch the bull! He has a problem too. His eyes are still accustomed to the dark. He sees only shadows, which make him fearful. See how he paws the ground in frustration!"

"Don't forget the dancers as they start on their merry path, scattering flowers as they go," Athena cautioned. "A merry path indeed, when all the time death careers around that path like a whirligig. See how they trip daintily along their ordained routes. This must indeed be a grand dance, for there are four of them; each accompanied, more or less light-footed, by a protector. That protector will bend the pace just a small amount, to slow or speed their progress and, with luck, they should evade death. Listen Hephaestus, the crowd knows what can happen!"

"Now the acrobats come, flowers still bright in their hair. They approach the bull. How will they look later, we wonder? Will each hold aloft the jeweled rewards of the spectators? Or will some lie with their tawdry plants, like broken marionettes, dusty and blood bespattered on the ground? For surely all of them will not complete this venture."

"Complete it they must. Yet see, she deviates from the planned path. The bull is charging. Watch out acrobat! The 'Bringer of Death' is to your left. Oh, gods protect him!" Hephaestus cried.

"He took a bad throw. Someone help the lad, while his fellow acrobats herd the animal away!" The crowd shouted.

"Well Hephaestus, the dance is over now," said Apollo, gasping for breath. The dancers failed to complete their paths. Could it be that some things are better left not understood?"

"I...I wish I knew. What is this? The palace is decaying around me. Who touched my shoulder?

"What are you doing here? Who put the sand down?" The guard sounded angry.

Festus looked startled but recovered, quickly. "We have permission to be here, to make a movie. That's why we put sand on the floor, to level it. Don't worry we'll get it cleaned up. This paper explains everything. I tried to find you when we arrived. I'm surprised you weren't expecting us."

"Someone should have told me. I've been sick the last two weeks. This is my first day back on the job. It isn't my shift, but I owe my mate, so we swapped."

"Well I'm sure it must have all been very confusing. This was our first rehearsal." Festus saw Zack approaching.

"Hi, Zack, I was explaining to our friend here that we're checking sites for a movie. What do you think so far?"

Zack nodded to the guard. "It looked good at the start, Fes. Then the dancers seemed to get disorganized and there was no pattern anymore."

"I'll still have to confirm your story," said the guard as he left. "Please wait here."

"Do you think we should try again?" Zack asked.

"The problem is that I don't know why we failed. I would quite like to try again, but I'm not sure how many dances our family can stand."

"They can stand it," Zack said, dismissively. "I'll get that contractor workin' on the courtyard at Phaestos. I've already fixed it with the authorities. Are you happy with using sand again to level the area?"

"Yes, it works quite well, Zack. You can still see most of the tracks left by the dancers. Don't forget that at Phaestos, he'll have to move some large stones, temporarily.

"The contractor knows. Now, let's get everybody together and go over what happened while it's still fresh in our minds."

Festus looked towards the northern end of the Central Courtyard at Phaestos. In the distance, he could see the peaks of Mount Ida tinted with orange by the rays of the rising sun. The Eurysthesians were making their way from the Grand Stairway through the remains of the Propylon, the old entrance hall, to join him. He continued to look around as he paced towards the northern end of the courtyard. He had misjudged the size of the courtyard. It was smaller than the one at Knossos. He was worried that it would be too small for the large number of dancers and acrobats, when there was a bull careering among them. This wasn't the same as Marienna's dance, he thought. Should he spend more time thinking about the place of the dance and less time in testing for the place, blindly? Before he could come to a resolution of the quandary, Ionides arrived.

"Do you want me to start laying out the patterns on the dance floor, Fes?"

"Oh, yes. I guess so. I was distracted. We should get on with it," said Festus, moving to the center of the floor. "Will you be okay for the dance? Your ankle, I mean?"

"It's fine Fes."

"Good. Now remember; don't put down the dashed line! We're still not quite sure what it's for. Did you find the guard? I don't want to repeat Knossos"

"Yes, he'll watch from near the entrance and keep any early visitors out."

"Okay. The center of the floor seems to be about here. When you've done the patterns, ask Elena to position the dancers and acrobats!"

The palace was silent except for the sound of the pipe, measuring out the rhythm of the dance. No one moved. The scene appeared to be stalled in time. Festus looked around. It seemed that only he and Pan were not trapped in the time lock. He stepped onto the dancing floor and walked, his feet scuffling in the sand, from the North Corridor, towards the southwest corner of the courtyard. He skirted the dancers and acrobats, who looked at him impassively. As he walked, he glanced from side to side. Marienna, *no Athena, was signaling for him to join her. By the time he reached her, the buildings seemed to be higher—one, two and even three stories high. She clasped his hands, briefly. You know what to do; she seemed to be saying. By the time his slow progress was complete, the shadows were receding across the floor, leaving the scene illuminated by sunlight. He reached the corner and turned. The sound of the pipes was more insistent now. The murmur of spectators picked up with the music.*

King Rhadamanthys, the brother of King Minos, signaled and the dancers set out along their ordained paths—pacing lightly across the floor, following the flowers strewn by Iolaus and the High Priestess. The guardian acrobats and the free acrobats glanced around warily, watching for the 'Bringer of Death'. They were almost caught by surprise. The bull came at a run from the northeast side of the courtyard, where it had been standing in the shadows. It charged straight at the dancers, who were circling outward on the eastern side of the floor. The spectators screamed in panic for the acrobats to take control. They reacted quickly. One of them ran directly at the bull and vaulted gracefully over the lowered head, twisting the right horn as he landed on the broad back. The bull veered to its right, barely missing a dancer. The crowd applauded and threw flowers. The bull skidded to a halt in front of Hephaestus, who jumped behind some pillars, flapping his cloak to shoo it away. The crowd roared with laughter.

The bull turned slowly and glowered at the scene. The dancers were further out now and they were spread more widely. The bull charged again. This time it was easier for the acrobats to distract it and they had more room in which to play their dangerous games. A girl, her blond hair streaming behind and her taut young breasts bouncing rhythmically, ran at the bull. She vaulted over its head and lay, momentarily, on its back, her legs splayed apart. A boy followed her vaulting high above the bull, so that for an instant he hovered above the girl, before both flipped quickly over its tail. This overtly sexual act was a favorite of the spectators. More flowers were thrown and among the flowers was jewelry.

Hephaestus watched the scene uneasily, relieved that his daughter Pandora had completed that dangerous stunt. He feared for her safety and for the safety of his wife Aphrodite as she spiraled steadily outward in the dance. A picture of their broken bodies flashed through his mind. He suppressed it quickly. He watched the bull complete its second run. It was curious how it had followed a similar path to its first run. Although, the second time, it had veered to the left instead of the right in order to follow the line. The bull turned to face him. It's looking at me, Hephaestus thought. Hephaestus raised his head and his hand, involuntarily, as if he were going to smooth his hair, then let his hand drop. The bull charged again. This time the acrobats were not so successful in guiding it around the dancers. It eluded them by darting first in one direction and then in another, tossing its head as it charged. It's going to attack her, Hephaestus realized in horror, as it bore down on his wife. She was close to him now, trapped upon the chosen path. "No, no, stop!" Hephaestus screamed, silently, the sound was locked in his head. He tried to move and succeeded, but only in slow motion. The scene froze around him. He floated towards the bull. It too was moving slowly. He struggled past Aphrodite and faced the 'Bringer of Death'. Its head was lowered, in readiness to slash at her. Hephaestus grabbed the horns and pulled down hard to his left dragging the massive head away from the prostrate woman. Thank the gods his arms were still strong, he thought, since his legs were too unbalanced for the vault. The bull sank to its knees. Strangely, it barely struggled. The scene became blurred.

The sun seemed to disappear for an instant. When it reappeared, Festus found himself on the ground, his arms around Deucalion Cronson. He had ceased struggling and seemed amused by the situation. "Hello, uncle Fes, how nice to see you again," he said, chattily. "Please would you let go of my neck, my gold chain is cutting into me."

Festus had no response. Suddenly he felt exhausted and he fell back toward Dawn, who caught him and lowered his head gently onto her lap.

"Is it over now, Fes? Can we stop?" she begged.

"I wish we could. I feel wrung out. These reversions to the past are a terrible emotional drain," Festus replied, sadly. "Fortunately, I've solved part of the puzzle. In a way, I wish I hadn't. I'm afraid this labor must be completed or there will be no peace for any of us."

Dawn studied his face. "Are you sure?"

"There's only one thing I'm more sure of, I don't want to lose you. Please stay with me through this."

"I love you. We can do it together," Dawn replied, smiling.

Festus scrambled awkwardly to his feet. Dawn put her arms around his waist to support him. Duke, having persuaded his captors to release him, stood up tentatively. He was watching his parents and Marienna approaching across the courtyard. Marienna walked with difficulty, and continued to hold onto Zack's arm after they arrived.

"Duke, where have you been? Your father and I have been very worried. You could at least have written."

"I did write, Mom, but I had to be careful with the army looking for me. I got friends to send the letters to Dad at the bank. I'm sure he..." Duke stopped in mid-sentence and looked at Zack. Zack looked away. "I couldn't go back to Argos, so I've been working for the cause. We Sfakians must work together to protect Crete against invaders. You've seen the problems in Cyprus. It could happen to us."

"Zack, why didn't you tell me?" Elena stormed away.

"Mom, you don't understand. You explain it, Dad," Duke called after her.

"Later son, later. There's something more important. I've got good news for you. Since we recovered the Bullroarer, I've been holding discussions with the...let me just say...authorities. They were embarrassed by the whole affair, not least because the weapon contravenes certain understandings. We agreed, mutually, to forget what happened and they gave you an honorable discharge. I've...um...been waitin' for the opportunity to tell you."

"You could have told me sooner! You have no idea what it's like being on the run." Duke started to follow his mother then sat with his rad in his hands.

Zack reached as if to pat the bowed head, then shook his head and turned to Festus. "You said just now that you'd solved part of the puzzle."

"The patterns. Look at the dancing floor! You can see the marks where Duke—the bull—followed my footprints in the sand. He went in a more or less straight line then veered briefly to his right."

"What does it mean?"

"I think it's a route on a map. It shows the path to take if you know the starting place and one other place on the route."

"How clever of you Henry," exclaimed Marienna. "It all adds up, doesn't it?"

Duke stood. "I know where the starting point is but, before I tell you, I want a guarantee that the interests of my friends will be protected."

"How could you know?" exclaimed Zack.

"I've heard our Sfakian friends discussing it."

"Agreed," Zack said, quickly." Don't forget, Duke, how this all started."

Festus wondered what Zack meant by the remark. The feeling that he was being used came back. It had been implied at various times. Unfortunately, ow was not ta good time to ask.

"From all accounts of the treasure there should be enough for everyone. Understand, though, that the Foundation has a sizeable investment in this venture, which it needs to recover."

Duke nodded his agreement. "There's a Sfakian legend of a great treasure hidden in a cave. They've been looking for it forever, unsuccessfully. It's not surprising they haven't been successful. The mountains are riddled with caves, particularly, at the head of the Gorge of Samaria. Who knows? This particular one may have been blocked at some time in the past. We've searched there and near Omalos and we've also scoured the Dhrakoloi or 'Dragon's Cave' as it's known. We found nothing."

"Get to the point, son! Where is it," Zack growled.

"The starting place is the Dancing Floor at Aradin," said Duke.

Festus visualized his map of the area and mentally traced out a route to the cave. He thought he knew where it would be. "That makes sense. Supposedly, Aradin is a Phoenician name, but I suspect it predates the Phoenicians. I'll bet it was started by the Hittites," said Festus. "Will your friends help us?"

"They will," answered Zack, not waiting for Duke's reply. "We'll make sure they get their fair share."

"Understand, Dad, if they don't, y'all won't leave this island alive," Duke added. "They've waited too long to be cheated of their treasure now."

"Put in such a charming way, Duke, we will find it hard to disagree with you." Alex laughed. "Now, the last time we went to Aradin, I remember climbing two thousand feet up some monstrous cliff from by the sea near Loutro. Can we find some more tractable route this time? I recollect seeing a track of some kind quite close to Aradin, near the top of the cliff. I guess it comes from Anapolis. Fes has a detailed map. Let's check it out."

"Good point, Alex," replied Zack. "I think we should try and get hold of a bus. We'll need it to carry our tents and provisions."

"Henry. You seem to have everything under control. You don't need me anymore. I am not up to making that trek again. I am going back to Argos. I have some things to settle. It will be tiring, so I will stay in Athens for a few days, with Nicholas and Maria." Marienna rose with difficulty. "Give your godmother a kiss! I have talked to Angelica. She will take my role if need be. Deucalion, would you help me back to the hotel please?" Festus watched sadly as Marienna. He wondered if he would see her again.

The bus ride from Khora Sfakion to the village of Anapolis was hair-raising. The dirt track snaked up from the sea along the side of the cliff. It was barely wide enough to accommodate the small bus. On the corners, the back of the bus projected well over the precipitous drop. The local driver drove with a ferocious intensity, as if he was competing in a rally. "I see now what Duke meant about the chances of getting out of here alive," Alex joked, nervously.

From Anapolis, the bus followed a narrow rock covered track for a further two miles and stopped by the ravine that rose form the sea to Aradin. From there they went on foot. The Eurysthesians pitched their tents beside the ancient ruins of Aradin. Alex Platon could not resist the opportunity to mock Festus. "Will you and Dawn be joining the rest of us, Fes? Or would you prefer a more secluded area." Festus gestured at him good-naturedly, with his index and little finger extended in the time honored sign.

"That's what I meant, Fes," Alex grinned.

Dawn put her arms around Festus and snuggled close to him, pressing her belly into him provocatively. "He's got a point, Fes. I haven't seen you so much recently, and you can be so noisy."

"Deucalion has brought us here to Aradin," Festus said. "It seems that the Sfakians are convinced that this is the starting point for the journey to the trea-sures of Deucalion. Assuming this is true; we may add the form of the path shown to us by the dance at Phaestos. The only question remaining is, where do we go, and how far? Down to the sea to Loutro? Back to Khora Sfakion? Up in the mountains behind us or across to Agia Roumelli?" Festus paused for effect.

"Henry knows the answer, why doesn't he spare us the suspense? It's probably in the Gorge of Samaria," Harold muttered, loudly, to Peri.

"Fair enough, Harold. I'll get to it," Festus retorted sharply, irritated at being upstaged. "The answer is on the Disk, where Deucalion says, 'gate (I have) armed.' It must refer to the Iron Gates, the Sidheroportes. In the Gorge, as Harold suggests. Then the cave lies somewhere in the Gorge by Iron Gates. I'm sure it's there, where the stream disappears. On its way to your place Harold—Tartarus."

"Are there caves, Duke? You've spent some time searching in the Gorge."

"Yes, Dad, there are a few caves and many small openings. If Uncle Fes is right, one of those openings may lead to a bigger cave. Possibly the entrance has been partially blocked. We didn't find anything before."

"I think I can pinpoint the section of the Gorge quite accurately using the track that was mapped on the stone. I'm hoping that once we get there it will be obvious to us," Festus said.

"Do we need to perform the dance again, here at Aradin?"

"No, Peri, I don't think so. We may have to enact the Sacred Rites to gain entrance to the cave. Like in Marienna's play."

"I'll help."

"Thanks. Let's walk a short way on the path to the Gorge. We can take turns with the parts. Do you remember them all?"

Peri smiled. It's the favorite part of my favorite play. I'll start.

> Now it is Boedromion, the time of fall.
> A time to tread this sacred hall.
> Measure by measure we advance,
> In a way that is planned,
> By Demeter's fair hand,
> In this mystic and holy dance.
> Your turn, Fes."

"Come, Persephone! Hear this chorus!
> Return now to Tartarus!
> Your light that shone above the rest,
> To launch the last year's harvest,
> Should now come here to shine.
> Come here to see how husband Hades pines!
> He misses you for half the year.
> Come now! You must reappear!"

"The banishing of evil comes next," said Peri.

> "Shed your light on this dark tomb,
> That now becomes the home
> Of those who venture here,
> To these depths and smoky air.
> Let them all soon be reborn,
> Oh, great Goddess of the Corn."

"I'll do the procession," said Festus.

> "Come now, all who follow
> To the depths of this dark hollow.
> Come, see the monument we make
> For Persephone's and Hade's sake.
> It's a simple matter, for sure.

You have arrived at his door."
"Now we depart for Thriasian Plain.
 Now, on and on we rush.
 Hey there! Don't push!
 There's time enough
 To traipse along this path.
 For we have sung our song
 And danced our dance.
 So now perchance
 We may get along.
 So long, so long."

"That so long, so long is really corny," Festus chuckled.
"Marienna put it in for the foreigners."
"Yeah. Well do you think it worked, Persephone?"
"I pray it did, Hephaestus." Peri hugged him. "I pray it did.

43. The Iron Gates

It was a very tough hike along winding trails, dropping 2000 feet from Aradin to the outskirts of Agia Roumelli and the lower end of the Gorge of Samaria. They were all tired and sore by the time they made a camp in the Gorge.

Sleep, for Festus, when it occurred, was fitful and dominated by a recurring nightmare in which he found the cave and the walls closed in and trapped him.

Now the rocky cliffs of the Sidheroportes—Iron Gates—oppressively towering hundreds of feet above him, gave him the feeling that he was truly about to live his nightmares. The stream now stretched from wall to wall, forcing them to walk in the water. Festus wondered about the name, Sidheroportes. Maybe once there had been gates of iron, to protect the treasure from marauders, coming from the sea. That would have been later than the time of the Disk, which he placed at around 1490 BC, for the Cretans were still in the Bronze Age. Only a few groups, including the Hittite smiths of Anatolia, had mastered the art of making iron. It was a curious description. He reached a place where the Gorge widened, and there were cypress, holm oak and oleander, forming a narrow band some thirty feet above the water. The gray waves of the limestone cliffs were horizontal. Ahead, the stream poured over the side of a massive boulder that had sheared from the mother rock and slipped to jam against the base of the cliff. For a moment, he wondered if the dark hole, formed by the boulder and the rock wall, was his entrance to Tartarus. A closer examination, however, showed only a blank stone face in the shadows. He quickened his pace to pass the donkeys.

The band of trees soon endedand the Gorge narrowed. The waves of limestone thrust upward. Festus again called a halt, sensing that they had reached their destination. The morning sun was now high enough to reflect from the tops of the larger boulders. To his left, there was a chimney of tortured rock that, in a strange optical illusion, seemed to spiral upwards. A shaft of sunlight illuminated the crags that towered above the chimney, giving the scene the appearance of the backdrop to a Wagnerian opera.

Shortly after, they reached the narrowest dry part of the Gorge, where the stream passed underground. Festus thought about the kri-kri, wild Cretan goats, still survived in this isolated area. Their spectacular leaps across the rocky crags were legendary. There were few left and they were rarely seen. Were they the spies of the gods, laughing at him?

"We'll stop here," said Festus. "We won't have a lot of time. The first tourists will be here within the hour."

"What are we going to do?"

"We'll pray to the gods for help, Dawn. I don't know what else to do. I'm hoping everything will fall into place, like it has in the dances." He drank from his flask and handed it to her. "Thank God, Angel has taken over from Marienna in this department. The juice even tastes the same"

"You're really hooked on it," Dawn laughed. "It's too bitter for me."

Close by, stood an outcrop of rock and dirt that supported a lone fir. The younger members of the party climbed to this point. Alex and Angelica were struggling to climb the chimney in order to reach a small ledge. The Sfakians clustered with the donkeys and quizzed Duke about what would happen. Duke gestured that Festus, who had clambered onto a large boulder, was going to tell them.

Festus crouched awkwardly on a rock. He was unsure of his balance, unsure of what to say, and in embarrassment looked upwards, away from his friends. If ever he had needed Marienna, it was now. She would have scripted what to do. He was not sure he was ready to take more responsibility, yet someone had to take control. His mouth felt dry and he took another long drink. In hesitant Greek, he made his plea to the gods. "Oh, gods, we have traveled far, following the instructions left on the Disk by your servant Deucalion. We have completed the sacred procession as you have guided us here from Aradin. Now we wait for further guidance in this hallowed spot where once the oracle of Apollo resided and where Artemis was born."

As Festus spoke, he scanned the Gorge. High up to his left the rays of the sun continued their daily descent of the spiral chimney. Duke, who was perched next to him, pointed out a lone kri-kri that had clambered down to the top of the chimney. As if this were the hoped for cue, the sun's rays reached down, illuminating the climbers like a spotlight in a theater. Festus had the illusion that Alex and Angelica were wearing white robes. *The spiral of rock seemed to open behind them. It was the entrance to a cave. There was the Minoan sign of the double axe, the labrys, carved into the rock. As Festus became Hephaestus, he had one last thought that it felt like Marienna's play, "The Goats." He started his climb.*

"Why do Hephaestus and Heracles seek the way to Tartarus?" Apollo shouted.

"We seek the treasure of Deucalion, at the command of King Rhadamanthys.

"Heracles, or should I also call you Deucalion, do you join in this search?

"Today, I play the role of Heracles. It is my nature to engage in great ventures such as this, to help the people," Deucalion answered.

"They are here on my behalf, to retrieve that, which was stolen by my ungrateful nephew, Deucalion," King Rhadamanthys shouted from the floor of the Gorge.

"The goats find it amusing. Listen to them," Artemis laughed.

It is a strange turn of events that Rhadamanthys should ask Heracles and Hephaestus to find the treasure. Life has gone full circle. It should be entertaining. Let the farce continue.

"Come, Apollo and you, Artemis! Lead us along the path to the underworld!"

"Rhadamanthys, you must wait," cautioned Artemis. "Two must start the journey, while others follow. Since this is an adventure, Heracles with club and lion's skin should lead the way. Limping behind will be the cunning Hephaestus, who resents his claimed accomplishments."

"Tell me, Artemis! What is the quickest way to Tartarus?"

"It is amazing that either of you would ask the way. You, Heracles, didn't you show the way to Dionysius? Aristophanes claims it is so. It seems from the puzzled look on your face that you have forgotten. So then, take Hephaestus and climb to the highest point of the cliff!

"To what purpose?"

"To discover if you can fly."

"But Artemis, if we fail, we will be dashed to pieces on the rocky floor of the gorge."

"And go immediately to your desired destination. It is an elegant plan."

"What way will you try?" Apollo asked.

"The way that succeeded before. Remind me of it!"

"Heracles, it is a dangerous voyage. First, you ascend to join Artemis and me. You can see now the sign of the labrys, marking the entrance to the cave that leads below.

"I noticed the sign," said Hephaestus. "Is this indeed the entrance to Tartarus, or is this the entrance to the labyrinth of the Minotaur?"

"It is both of them sir, though Minos had no hand in this. Far down in its depths there are many merry monsters including the Minotaur that you, of all people, should not fear."

"How is that so, Apollo?

"Because you took a hand in creating it."

"I did? I hope it was only my hands that were involved." Hephaestus scratched his head, as if doing so would help him to remember.

"Your hands made the contraption that seduced the bull into doing...you know what."

"Unfortunately, now I remember. We smiths do some things that we would sooner forget. I think I made Minos pay for it, but I can't remember how."

"Hephaestus, enough of this reminiscing about the good old days," Heracles bellowed. "Concentrate on climbing! Tell me Apollo! Is Cerberus, the three-headed dog, still down there? You see I know some history."

"You have forgotten your part in it. Let me remind you. Heracles! When you were in Tartarus, you killed that poor beast and carted its body away."

"With my help, most likely," Hephaestus snorted.

"I remember now. It was a fine animal. King Eurystheus made me do it."

"Cease this whining, both of you!" Artemis cried. "It is not other people who do these sad acts. It is you, Hephaestus, the conscienceless intellectual and you Heracles, the muscle-bound warmonger."

"Save your blame for those who exploit us, Artemis! Now tell me, what will I return with this time?"

"Precious little," chanted the goats, as Heracles followed by a gasping Hephaestus reached the entrance to the cave.

"Charon will take you down to Tartarus. See he is waiting," said Apollo. "A warm welcome awaits you. Good luck."

44. Tartarus

"What should I do now, Hephaestus?" Heracles looked at the door to Hades' house.

"Whatever you did before."

"It's coming back to me. One knocks brought that pretty girl. Two knocks and that unpleasant fellow Hades came. Or was it the other way around? I'll try two knocks.

"Who is there?"

"Oh, hell! It's the wrong one. It is I, Heracles."

"Heracles, you villain! Last time you were here, you took my dog, Cerberus. Now what do you want. Listen and you will hear my feet departing to fetch the Minotaur."

"What shall we do?"

"It seems to me that you were responsible for this Minotaur creature. Here, take my lion skin and club! You can be me if you insist on being so courageous. I'll be you and limp, and posture with fanciful notions."

"Good God! It's that dolt Heracles," said Dionysius, appearing round the side of the house with King Rhadamanthys. "Heracles, you were responsible for showing me how to get here last time. It cost me two obols on the ferry, when I could have walked around the water with my servant Xanthias. Then I played my flute for you to distract Hades, while you clobbered that poor mutt Cerberus. Come now! Repay me, or by Zeus, I'll sit on you until you do."

"How can such a sorry looking fellow have destroyed my dog?" Hades looked at the ill-clothed duo with amusement. "You are too small for your cloak and your club. It's a wonder you don't fall on your face. Your servant has more the figure of a man than youdo. What is he named?

"Why, Heracles, naturally."

"Then, who are you?" said Hades, with a sideways glance at Dionysius.

"I am Hephaestus, master of technology and reluctant aide to Heracles. It is I who conjured up the wherewithal that allowed him to complete the Labors.

"The Labors of Heracles. You are responsible for the death of my dog! Let us seize him!"

"Hold on! I didn't kill your dog. It's not the job of scientists to kill. We merely provide the weapons. Don't blame us if other people misuse them."

I will strike a bargain. Tell me why you are here, or I use some of your weapons on you and the person you claim is Heracles."

"I and Hephaestus search for the treasure that Deucalion took from King Rhadamanthys to help the people."

"I have a simple test." Hades grinned. "Tell me the nature of the treasure and it is yours. You, Heracles, what is your opinion? You should leave us Hephaestus while Heracles tells his story. I will call you back in a minute.

Heracles struck a pose like a nervous schoolboy. "Well, I um, let me see. As I understand it, King Minos agreed to help the Egyptians…who needed help. The Hittites were the only people who could help them, um…but they were at war. So er…Minos or maybe it was Rhadamanthys, with my help, arranged for the Hittites to get what the Egyptians wanted."

"Make up your mind, Heracles! Was it Minos or Rhadamanthys?" Rhadamanthys shouted.

"I...I meant Rhadamanthys, now I come to think of it. They are brothers you know.

"If any one would know better it could only be our mother."

"Yes, exactly. Therefore, they all got what they wanted. I remember now. Tin it was, for the Egyptians to use in making bronze. 'Contrived with gold,' it says on the Disk. The Egyptians paid a large sum in gold to King Alluwamnas of the Hittites. A portion of the gold was due to Rhadamanthys." Heracles looked at Rhadamanthys, who nodded his head.

"What happened to the treasure?" asked Rhadamanthys.

"Well, as we all know, Deucalion took it and brought it down here, and Hades has protected it since then."

"Thank you, Heracles. Hades turns and shouts. "You can come back, Hephaestus. Hephaestus rushed in. "Heracles has told us a fine tale. What do you have to say?

"I am beginning to remember. The Disk tells most of the story. I expect Heracles has said that the Egyptians needed tin, and came to Minos. He discussed it with his brothers Rhadananthys and Sarpedon. Then he sent his nephew Deucalion as an emissary to King Alluwamnas, offering him payment in gold and other valuables from the Egyptians. The Hittites, with Deucalion accompanying them, went to Erythria and obtained the tin. The Egyptians paid the fee." Hephaestus looked thoughtful, "You know I have a feeling I was involved in the deal."

"Maybe you were. Tell me then, what is the treasure? What was due to Rhadamanthys? What was he paid, and what part did you play?"

"Those are all good questions, Hades. I have a question for you. Why did Deucalion hide the treasure?" Hephaestus paused. "The Disk says, '(he) with gates has armed a cave'. The Iron Gates limit access from the sea. It seems unlikely that they were iron. Such gates would have been more valuable than any gold. I could have made bronze gates. I am also puzzled by the last words on the Disk. They seem to be familiar."

"What's all this business about gates?" Rhadamanthys showed his impatience.

"I suspect the symbols don't mean 'Gates of Iron', but rather 'Gates to the Iron'. It's coming back to me. The Egyptians made a great payment in gold and other valuables to the Hittites. Alluwamnas was happy to trade tin for gold, because his iron weapons were far superior. He did not fear the Cretans. Theirs was a small empire compared to the Egypt. The payment to Rhadamanthys was not gold from the Egyptians. It was from the Hittites as a reward for brokering the deal. It was in iron!"

"What do I care for iron? I want my gold." Rhadamanthys spluttered. Seeing that Apollo and Artemis had joined them, he added. "You tell them Apollo!"

"I will give answers to your questions in a minute. For now, let us congratulate Hephaestus. Hephaestus, the treasure is yours. Are you proud of yourself?"

"Yes, and rightly so. All of these years I have put up with insults and my achievements have gone unrecognized. You have all made fun of my deformity. You have done it to hide your fear of my knowledge and imagination. Nevertheless, you turn to me for help; the strong like Heracles; the cunning like Rhadamanthys and Minos; and even you Gods. I make your toys, your weapons, clean up your messes. Soon, I will have recovered three most precious things, my memory, recognition and my iron. You have no concept of what marvels I will work with the iron. I remember now, the Hittite smiths, my brothers, shared their skills with me. Now I will create plowshares and wheels, and many things of a magnificence that you have never imagined."

"You didn't mention weapons. Why do you think Deucalion hid the treasure? He hid it from you, Hephaestus. To prevent you from making weapons for Rhadamanthy; to use against his brother Minos, Deucalion's father. Isn't that right Apollo?"

"Nearly right, Hades. Nearly right. You see Phaes, here, helped to hide the iron.

"He did what?" shouted Rhadamanthys.

"Hephaestus helped to hide it from you Rhadamanthys, because he was fearful of what you, his master, might ask him to do with it. His skills are truly wonderful, but he has no control over his imagination, over his inventive genius. He might think of a way to make a stronger plough, or wheel rims for your chariot, or he might invent a terrible weapon." Artemis continued. "Like his daughter, Pandora, he is inquisitiv. He cannot resist opening the box of knowledge. His quandary is that once his mind releases an idea he must try it and then it will be known for all time. It is you, who control the purse strings, who should be the filter that directs his genius for the good of humankindd. Unfortunately, your ambition betrays both of you.

"Why don't I remember all Of this? I have a very good memory, Artemis." Hephaestus looked distraught.

Artemis smiled sympathetically. "You came to me and I gave you and Deucalion a potion that made you forget. Sadly, you couldn't stand the thought of losing that knowledge and you had already, secretly, created the Disk. Hephaestus' Disk', you called it. You invented the system of pictographs. You even signed your name on it, with a warning. The last word is not a single word, but the two words that you used as an abbreviation for 'against Hephaestus.' It was your warning to anyone who might decipher the Disk, to stay away from the treasure. My potion made you forget all you knew about the pictographs. You were obliged to work out their meaning using the clues you'd had a friend leave in various places."

"But it couldn't have been just Deucalion and I who did all this. Who was the Bullmaster—the controller of 'the Bringer of Death?'"

"It must have been Hades, skulking over there."

"Hephaestus you still don't understand, do you?" Hades said sadly. "You never did. Mine is an honorable profession. I receive the dead. I honor them. I don't kill. You were responsible for creating the Minotaur; that poor creature that is neither man nor bull. He is the 'Bringer of Death' surfacing in your nightmares. Now he is dead, he lives here with me. Theseus, the alter ego of Heracles killed the Minotaur with your help. I look after him.

"Then who is the Bullmaster?" Hephaestus sounded desperate.

"Don't you understand yet? It is you Phaes. Your dragging right foot makes the dashed line, showing the chosen path for the bull on the dancing floor. You created the 'Bringer of Death' for your master, Zeus or Minos or Rhadamanthys or Eurystheus, or whatever he called himself at the time. They control you and, in turn, you control it. Wake up to yourself! Hephaestus brought the sword to man. Hephaestus invented the shield to protect against the sword. You bring both the problem and the solution. With your gifts, you and the other thinkers have raised humans above the level of animals, whose lives are circumscribed by nature. Humanity is no longer controlled by nature, but equally it is not completely in control. Consider this awful possibility! You brilliant people may have to go on inventing forever to keep us from disaster."

"You should not lay blame only at us technologists! Those with a gift of oratory or a skill with the written word are as guilty as I am when they turn those skills against their fellow man. Just leave us intellectuals alone to paint, sculpt, write books and plays, compose music and devise artifacts to benefit all! Concern yourself too with those who do nothing but squander nature's riches; or who practice benign neglect, and return nothing to humanity. It is clear to me now that I should not take my treasure. Deucalion was correct in the first place. I will bring the Disk here and leave it and the treasure, and Artemis may make me forget again."

"Hold on, my friend!" said Rhadamanthys. "What is this talk of 'your treasure?' Hades may have chosen to offer it to you, but it is mine to hold on behalf of my people. They wait patiently to benefit from it. Isn't that so, Hades?

"Theoretically, yes…"

"So, now it is mine…er, my peoples and given that I may take delivery of it, may I tempt you to work with it, Phaes. If you choose not to it will be fine with us. We understand that you must stick with your principles. You shouldn't feel any pressure to help. I'm sure I can find others to do the work. I hear the Scythians have some fine craftsmen."

"No gold in the world would tempt me."

"I didn't for a moment think it would, but you did mention making iron plowshares and wheel rims and even I can see how they would be a wonderful help to our

valiant farmers. I have one question to ask. Do you have the right to deny such humble folk the benefits of your God-given gifts?"

"Your question is difficult to answer," Hephaestus mused, somberly. "There is an element of truth in the argument that I have no right to withhold my inventions." Hephaestus felt light-headed and continued in a brighter tone. "I really have thought of a fine way to make wheel rims and pots and pans, which would last a long time. Rhadamanthys has made me see that the choice is not mine, it is up to him and the people to see that my talents are not misused." Hephaestus saw his friends looking at him in horror. Everything became blurred. He felt he stone walls closing around him.

45. Samaria Canyon

Artemis:	Please, let me start the ceremony.
	All who bathe in Lethe's Water will forget what happened here.
	Please, Hephaestus.
	(There is a long silence while Hephaestus decides what to do.)
	(Athena descends among them, deus ex machina.)
Athena:	So! What will you do, little Hephaestus?
Hephaestus:	I cannot let it go. I must use this iron. Rhadamanthys has made it clear that I have no choice. I'll guarantee not to make anything that could harm the people. Anyway, you know the Hittites already have it, so we must keep up to their level. Otherwise, they may overrun not only the Egyptians but us also. Now, show me my treasure and leave me with it while I decide how to use it for the good of all.
Athena:	You have won your treasure, Hephaestus, and you have proved to all it was you not Heracles who masterminded the Labors. From now on let them be known as the 'Labors of Hephaestus'.
Hades:	Let me add my congratulations, Hephaestus. Come, get down on your hands and knees and take your treasure! There it is, pick it up and take it with you! It is all mixed up with goat manure. In these many years, since

you and Deucalion laid it here, the sacks have rotted and all the iron has disintegrated to become the rusty floor of this cave.

Chorus of acrobats, dancers, peasants and goats:

Poor Hephaestus, he's won but he's lost.

Can his ego stand the terrible cost

Of seeing his treasure turned to rust

As all of us will turn to dust?

The stage was in darkness. The canyon walls had echoed the applause of the audience. The players had all left quickly as was the custom in the Argos Play:

For the players merely impersonate the gods.
They should not receive glory in their place.

Festus remained at the edge of the darkened stage in a state of confusion. Had he been in the play, or was it one of his fantasies? Before her death, Marienna had changed the ending. Why? What was all the business about the Disk and the iron? The Cretan trip had finished that way. He recalled being in the Gorge of Samaria with his fellow Eurysthesians. He had regressed to the past and was reenacting the play, "The Goats," except it wasn't the same play. It had evolved into a nightmare, in which Balaam, Seamus, Georgina MacLeod, Spiros, Wendell Jameson...even the guide at Blarney Castle had appeared in various guises. They'd put him on trial, accused him of being a scientific prostitute. The last thing he could remember was the guide saying, "Stop it or I'll drop the bloody stone on you!" and then Athena had put an end to the nightmare. He had regained consciousness in the hospital in Iraklion, to see Dawn at his bedside. She said that he had fallen while trying to climb up to join Alex and Angelica. He had remained in a coma, while they struggled to get him to a doctor in Khora Sfakion. The doctor had arranged for the transfer to Iraklion. She told him that, apparently, Zack had continued the search for a few days but had found nothing. Dawn waited until he recovered to tell him her greatest concern.

"You seem to be back to normal, honey," she said, hesitantly.

"There's something else. Isn't there?"

"The people at the hospital said you acted like you'd been drugged. It made me think about what happened to you in Tam'oan Shan and Copan."

"How could that be? I'm sure Balaam wasn't involved."

"Marienna?"

"You're kidding! She wasn't there."

"I know. That leaves Angel. She prepared the drinks."

"No way she could know how to do it."

Dawn shook her head. "Then what was it?"

"I must have eaten something bad," Festus replied. He looked thoughtful.

In Argos, his companions were sympathetic, but not keen to rehash the strange things that had happened in Crete. Somehow, with Marienna's death, the illusions were evaporating. Marienna's dance at the Festival had been replaced by traditional Greek dances. Now he was back doing the Play Cycle, Festus felt drained and wondered if the other actors had the same kinds of reaction. It was easier for them, he thought. They strutted and pranced or floated delicately about the stage, while he hobbled awkwardly in his buskins. Crippled Hephaestus, the butt of ridicule, the thinker whose achievements were belittled by those with lesser abilities. The truth was many feared him. In real life it was little different from the plays. At least Marienna, bless her memory, had softened the original cruel treatment of Hephaestus, when she'd transcribed the plays into English. At the beginning, she had tried to show everybody his real self—the real Hephaestus. He did not like to think about the bitter old woman she had become at the end.

I will remember the Marienna that I knew as a child, he had said to Dawn at the funeral. It had been a grand affair. Bishop Platon came from Galveston to officiate. The congregation filled the little church in Argos. Leaving the church, Zack Cronson had said, "for some reason I feel relief. It is as if..." He was not able to complete the thought.

"I know what you mean. Marienna's manipulations, Zack," Elena had replied. "I wonder if we'll ever find out the extent of them."

Alex had set up the reading of Marienna's will on the morning the Festival.

"I'm not going to go over all the standard stuff," Alex said. "I'll go straight to the meat of it. Most of her estate is her share of the Cronson Enterprises. In addition she has a surprising amount in cash in her bank in Austin, over a million."

"What Bank!"

"You didn't know? Let's just say she needed it to pursue private interests." Alex shuffled the papers. He was trying not to smile. "She leaves her stake in Cronson Enterprises to her godson, Henry Everett Festus. She leaves all the cash to her longtime friend Jorge Vasquez. I am trying to contact Senor Vasquez."

There was a stunned silence.

"I often wondered why she took so many trips to Mexico," said Panou, laughing.
"So, who the fuck is Senor Vasquez?"

"I don't know. He lives in Mexico. The Will lists a contact address—a lawyer's office in Mexico City. I have spoken to office on the phone and they are trying to get hold of him."

"Get on with it Alex. Any other bombshells," Zack shouted, getting to his feet and pacing the room.

"She has left her house to Angelica. There is a comment that Angelica will know what to do with it."

"What the hell does that mean, Angel?"

"I think she wants me to keep the garden looking nice. She was very proud of it, Zack," Angel replied, without looking at him.

"She's hiding something," Dawn whispered to Festus.

"There is one other thing that she says that may help you understand." Alex reached under his desk and produced a great pile of school notebooks. They were in a dozen or so bundles, tied with string. "These are her diaries. This stack is for Zachary and Elena. This one is for Fes and Dawn. I'll get them delivered. I have already sent the rest to Senor Vasquez's lawyers, per her instructions. You will find that some of the books have been separated into individual pages. She also copied some pages to give to both of you. This is because you only get the bits that apply to you. In the Will, Marienna says it is up to y'all whether you want to share the information."

"God help us all, Alex. What does she say in the diaries?"

"I don't know, Zack. She made me swear I wouldn't look at them. I haven't."

"Why the hell did you send stuff to Vasquez before I could look at it?"

"I respected my client's wishes Zack," Alex replied, smugly.

As they were leaving, Zack grabbed Festus by the arm. "Marienna left you her share of the business. With what you already have, that adds up to a large stake. Too large"

"Tell you what, Zack. I'll give you Marienna's share and you give me Olympic Services. Deal?"

"I'll think about it."

Festus smiled at the memory. He still got a childish pleasure from seeing Zack put down. Dawn interrupted his reminiscing.

"Henry Everett Festus, what are you doing out here? I've been looking everywhere for you. For heaven's sake, you haven't changed yet!" Dawn chuckled. Then with more concern, she continued. "Are you sure you've got over your fall? The doctor said to take it easy."

"I'm sorry Dawn. I'm fine, you know how these plays always leave me emotionally exhausted. I was just daydreaming. I'm afraid I sometimes still can't tell what's real and what's only in my mind."

Dawn smiled at him fondly. "I know it's difficult for you doing the plays, but you do it so well. Everyone tells me it's as if you really are Hephaestus. I guess it's because you're very similar. Well you are my hero, darling."

"Without Hephaestus there wouldn't be any plays. He should be the hero. Since Marienna's death I've had to accept that they'll remain the way they are even though she tried to bring out his importance." Festus buried his head on her shoulder and continued quickly. "I love you, Dawn. I'm sorry about all this business with the plays. You know, getting too involved in Marienna's fantasy—that and my work. I neglected you and Pandora"

"It was a tough time darling, but I love you too. Otherwise I wouldn't have stayed. Pandora's worked out fine too. Thanks to Chuck."

Festus looked thoughtful. "You know, because he's a foreigner it could break the chain?"

"You mean, even if they have a son, he won't be Hephaestus?"

"Yeah." Festus looked sad for a moment. "But, there's still Ionides?"

"Enough," Dawn said, laughing.

Festus noticed the notebook she was holding. "Is that one of the diaries?"

"Oh, yes. Alex took his time sending them. They only came this morning, after you left. I've only had time to glance at this first one."

"Enough of the suspense! What does…?"

"She discusses the plays, how she adapted them year by year to take account of changes in Argos…to change our community, and to help you grow up and learn to use your talents properly."

"You and she have both helped me. Today, Zack asked me to work on a new project. He seems to have given up on taking over Crete. It seems he accepts Marienna's theory that if there was a treasure it was only iron. We did discover that didn't we? Or was it Marienna changing the play? I don't rem…"

"Fes, it doesn't matter. It's over. Tell me what Zack's after now!"

"There's an unbelievable amount of money being offered to prepare a new variant of the oil eater. Some nut has come up with another brilliant scheme for dropping it all over vast areas of Viet Nam, to help win the war. A simple calculation shows it would do more damage to us than to the enemy."

"Did you tell Zack?"

"Yes. Yet again! He said not to worry. It was somebody else's problem."

"What did you tell him?"

Festus smiled grimly, remembering his father's words, *"be your own man."* "I said No! In the words of John Metaxas, when he dismissed the Italian delegate in 1940, Oçl!"

MARIENNA

Marienna Cronson

Born 1895. Died 1969.

"I played Athena.
Athena played me."

46. Marienna

"It's amazing," said Dawn Festus. "I thought I knew Marienna, but this is wild. Fes, did you know she was treated for mental problems? After reading this first part of her diaries, I'm not surprised. Listen to this, from October 1920!" Dawn read from the first diary.

"It is encouraging that our biannual Greek Festival has become so popular. Even the local Texans—we refer to them as "foreigners"—seem to enjoy it. The dancing, the food and the puppet show have been a huge success. I wish I could say the same about what we choose to call "the Play." This collage of sketches about the ancient gods, resurrected from ancient Cretan tales, and including a primitive single act play, is a mess. I started thinking about rewriting them the year I reentered college and my godson Henry was born—a joyous year. It was a difficult time after my parents divorced and my father, Agamemnon, married Penelope Zolatas. Then, my father adopted Dawn. There is endless speculation in the community about whether she is his illegitimate child. Who could the mother be? Surely, she can not be local. I suspect he has a little friend in Crete. I heard that it was quite a business getting all the papers completed for the baby. I was so depressed that my mother persuaded me to see a psychiatrist. I emerged from that nonsense a stronger woman despite the incompetence of the man. Worse was to come, for my mother Olympia married again, to Argos Festus!

I can reveal here in the privacy of these pages that I love that man. He is the cleverest, kindest person I have ever met. Yes, he is sixteen years older than I am but it does not matter to me. I worry that in my depression I drove Argos away. Writing is a welcome therapy. If I cannot have Argos, at least I can dedicate something to his son. I think Olympia understands my feelings. She asked me to be his "synteknissa". I prefer the Cretan name to the Anglo-Saxon word, godmother. They called him Henry. I suggested they add the second name Everett. Olympia, like Queen Victoria, was not amused when she understood the pun H. E. Festus—Hephaestus. Argos, bless him, laughed and said that he hoped it would turn out to be appropriate.

Back to the plays. The sketches that our families act out every two years are very confusing. They appear to be bits and pieces of otherwise forgotten works of the ancient playwrights. I plan to rewrite them into a set of four plays, roughly in the style of Aeschylus, Euripides, Sophocles and Aristophanes, respectively.

It is amusing that the players seem to have become like the roles they play. My father acts like Zeus. Argos really is a wizard. He even limps like Hephaestus. I have heard that he was injured trying to help my father in some harebrained scheme. My mother had the role of Athena. It is mine now and I have played it once. Will I become Athena as Argos became Hephaestus? Hephaestus is treated as a buffoon in the sketches. How Argos can stand playing him I do not know; though he accomplishes it with good grace. In the new plays, Argos will be better treated and, in due time, Henry will inherit a much better role. In addition, I may be able to do something with the Labors of Heracles—Labors of Hephaestus sounds better! Obviously, there is a limit to how far I can adjust history! I will have to work out how to refine the relationship of the hierarchy of Greek gods to our real families in Argos. Families already have established roles in the sketches, and they resist every suggestion for change. I will tell you later, dear diary, how I succeed or fail in my plans."

"I guess I knew some of it. She used to tell me things when I was little," Festus said. I suppose I didn't understand what she meant."

"Did she tell you she loved your Dad?"

"No, not really, but she acted differently around him—coy, flirty even. I remember being embarrassed by it."

"I would love to see what she wrote about the rest of my family."

Festus snorted. "Just hope we get all the bits about us."

"Yeah, I wouldn't want anyone else to read what she thought about me." Dawn looked pensive. "Maybe, not even you honey."

"I'll show you mine, if you'll show me yours."

"How about right now?"

"The entry for May 1921 is interesting," said Festus, after they returned from the bedroom. "Marienna talks about the gods and fitting the roles to our relatives. Listen!"

"Dear diary:

I am not making good progress on the plays. Schoolwork and college have taken most of my time. The Greek myths are very confusing. The gods and goddesses evolved, as each successive City-State felt the need to personalize this panoply of beings. I have concluded, however, that there are only a few main characters.

A king: Cronos or Iapetus or Zeus.

His wife or the high priestess: Rhea-Hera-Athena.

The pretender to the throne or war chief: Ares-Heracles-Theseus.

A technologist or wizard: Arges-Hephaestus.

God of wine and revelry: Dionysius-Pan.

A god of the underworld: Erebus-Hades.

Goddess of agriculture and fertility: Demeter-Core-Persephone.

A god of the sea: Oceanus-Poseidon.

The Egyptians also had such gods and the Romans renamed all the Greek ones. Apparently a similar set can be found in Hittite and Norse legends. Even the Irish had such a group. In ancient Ireland they called the pretender the tanist. I like the name and will use it. Now, I will have to develop my own interpretation and find some way of folding in a number of other characters to accommodate my relatives and friends. I am not going to use a sea god. The memory of the disaster wrought by the Galveston hurricane is still strong. For the record, here are some of these relatives and the other pertinent members of the Greek community of Argos County."

"December 1922 carries on the theme."

"I have completed the rewrite (final version?) of the Greek myths, from the perspective of Hephaestus. It has taken far too long. Now, at last, after many refills of the inkwell, the story basis for the Plays lies in front of me and I can complete the first play. Let me be honest. I have found it necessary to take great liberties with the pantheon of gods to match them to the families of Argos County. If I took the myths seriously, I would have to have nearly everyone fathered by Cronus, Zeus or Iapetus! Of course, this image fits my father, Agamemnon, who generally takes those roles—much to the annoyance of Odysseus Maximos. I have written my version of how Hephaestus must have felt.

I wish Agamemnon and Odysseus would not fight so much. I believe that a lot of it stems from our Sfakian heritage. If only those other Cretans—Maximos—had resisted Turkish rule as we did. Thank God, America supported us. I have read that, in 1898, the year of our freedom from Turkey, the military commandant of Sfakia Province wrote to the American consul in Athens, offering to send five hundred men to fight in the Spanish-American War. The consul, a certain D. E. McGinley, expressed his thanks, regretting that he had no power to act in the matter—such is the way of bureaucrats!

It did not stop at where they came from in Crete. They disagreed on nearly everything. Old Max gave his allegiance to King Constantine and the royalists, while Agamemnon supported the liberal party of Eleutherios Venizelos—their fellow Cretan. The Greek-American newspapers that they had managed to obtain in the early days, for the 'real' news, were similarly polarized; Max took the royalist Atlantis, while Agamemnon read the liberal paper, the National Herald.

What a mess!"

Dawn unfolded a piece of paper from the diary she was studying. "Look here Fes, she's made family trees for the key people in Argos in 1920."

Agamemnon Cronson (Kronosakis)
+ 1. Olympia Platon (m. 1894)

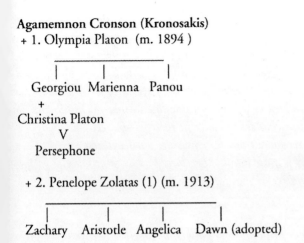

| | | |
Georgiou Marienna Panou
+
Christina Platon
V
Persephone

+ 2. Penelope Zolatas (1) (m. 1913)

| | | |
Zachary   Aristotle   Angelica   Dawn (adopted)

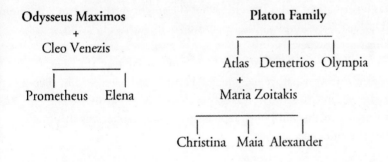

Odysseus Maximos
+
Cleo Venezis

| |
Prometheus   Elena

Platon Family

| | |
Atlas Demetrios Olympia
+
Maria Zoitakis

| | |
Christina Maia Alexander

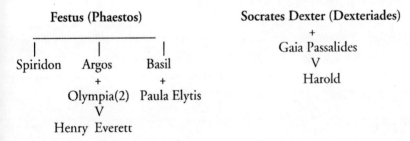

Festus (Phaestos)

| | |
Spiridon   Argos   Basil
+   +
Olympia(2)   Paula Elytis
V
Henry Everett

Socrates Dexter (Dexteriades)
+
Gaia Passalides
V
Harold

47. The Plays

"It's fascinating to see how she created the plays. I only remember them as fully developed. I never realized how difficult it must have been to write them," Dawn read from the diary. "It's December 1925.

At last, I have my BA in Liberal Arts. I also have a good draft of the first play, 'Zeus Bound.' It was an awkward task, even though some of the Argos sketches fitted quite well, and I had a play by Aeschylus to use as a model. The original sketches and my first draft of the play were in Greek. I had to translate it into English. For the benefit of the 'foreigners.' The translation does not have the rhythm of the original—just like other translations of the ancient Greek plays. I should add that my family has not helped. Every one of them wants changes to better fit their self-image! The thought of going through this business three more times is depressing, but I will not give up.

The cast of main characters is quite small. Therefore, I added a number of peripheral characters to satisfy my relatives.

Ares   Zeus
Hephaestus   Chorus of Priestesses
There are brief appearances by Aphrodite, Apollo, and Iapetus. The scene is a grove by my temple. Note to myself. I also appear. It is not an ego trip!"

"She was a very gifted lady. Imagine what she might have done in a different situation. Up East for example, rather than nowhere, north of Austin."

"Fes. This isn't nowhere."

"You know what I mean. This must be her first version of the play. Let's see how different it is from what we use today." Festus and Dawn read in silence.

"I hate the ending. It always leaves me depressed." Festus exclaimed. "It's engraved in my brain. Listen! Poor Hephaestus! Poor Hephaestus. It usually gets a laugh from the audience."

"I've noticed."

"Listen to this from April 1926," Dawn chuckled.

"Dear diary:

It is a disappointment that my family has not agreed to stage the play at the next Argos Festival. They say they need more time to think about it! In reality, they are using the time to jockey for the best roles. Heaven help me! I know who should play each part. For the record here they are. Time will show if I get my way.

ZEUS BOUND
Zeus   Agamemnon Cronson.
Ares   Georgiou Cronson
Hephaestus   Argos Festus
Athena   Marienna Cronson
Aphrodite   Penelope Cronson
Apollo   Atlas Platon
Iapetus   Odysseus Maximos

Chorus of Priestesses (whichever women I can talk into doing it).
On a cheerful note, Maia Platon married Prometheus Maximos. The dancing and
drinking carried on well into the night."

"Marienna had to wait until 1928 before they would let her stage it. This is
from August."

"*Zeus Bound*" *was a huge success at the Festival. It was a crowning achievement of
the long weekend of Greek dancing, singing and story telling. Even my father was
pleased. He did not say much to me, but I overheard him boasting to his cronies about
his clever daughter. Now that the play is doing well, the kinotitos has asked me to
improve the dances. They are a little disorganized. This is good. It could help with
some other plans I have been thinking about. I got all the players I wanted, except one.
Dad did not like the idea of my brother Georgiou playing Ares. Too close to home, I
guess. His excuse was that there were too many Cronsons in the play. He worked out a
deal with Odysseus, and Prometheus Maximos played the part. Prometheus was very
good. I wonder if Odysseus would have agreed if he had been playing Zeus!*

*It is interesting how people associate with the roles. In fact, it is weird the lives of
our families reflect what was in the sketches and is now in the play(s). I mean, beyond
what I have created. It is clear that my young half brothers Zachary and Aristotle will
fit perfectly as Zeus and Ares, respectively. Zachary is clever. Cunning might be a better description. Ari is already a fine athlete. Then there is Dawn. Though I cannot
accept that intruder into my family, I have to admit that she's only nine and already
beautiful. I am sure that she will take over the role of Aphrodite from Penelope. The
three children already seem to fit into my play. Three months ago, I caught Aristotle
with Dawn in the old barn at the end of my property. Dawn's pants were down
around her ankles. Aristotle said Dawn wanted to play 'doctor'! Dawn would not
speak to me. I sent Ari packing. Dawn was crying and tried to make me believe Ari
had forced her to do it. The little tramp! I smacked her bare bottom. Ari is into sports.
I do not believe he is interested in that other kind of thing. I told Dawn it was her
fault and not to tell tales.*"

Festus could see that Dawn's eyes were misting. "Dawn! I'm sorry. How could
she have done that to you?"

"I knew it. She hated me. I didn't say anything because Ari had hold of my
hand and was squeezing hard, warning me to be quiet. Ari not interested in that
kind of thing! Marienna must have had a sheltered upbringing. Ari was twelve.
He'd been fooling around with me for years. The saddest thing is that I believed
it was my fault. I didn't dare ask Mom for help. After what Marienna said, I was
scared to. I guess it wouldn't have done any good anyway. Mom spoiled the boys.
She would have blamed me too, I guess."

"Are you sure you want to go on reading these diaries? I could read them first if you like?"

"No! I'm a big girl now. It can't get any worse than that. Anyway, I wonder what she is going to say about you."

Festus laughed. "I wonder what she meant about the dances."

"Seeing what happened later, so do I. I need a break, Fes. I'm going for a walk."

"Want me to come?"

"No. We can get back to this later."

"March 1929, Dawn, and she's fussing about you and me."

I am worried about Henry. I have seen him playing with Dawn. I will speak to that little slut again. I will not have her perverting my godson. I dread the day when they are older. I will ensure that Henry takes over as Hephaestus from his father. Unfortunately, it does look like Dawn will inherit the role of Aphrodite from Penelope. If the future is predicted in the plays, the plot should deal with the relationship of Aphrodite and Ares. This business has helped me see how to handle the plot of the second play, which I have therefore titled 'Aphrodite and Ares.' Some of my relatives have carped about the first version of the play. They say it is too steamy for Texas. I do not agree at all. These are Greek myths. They are steamy! Nevertheless, I have toned it down a little. I am hopeful the play will go on as it is now. Here is the latest version."

"I've always liked this play. Except for the part when you're trapped on the bed with Ares."

"Tell me about it. With Ari it was like being in the back of a car on Prom night."

"Oh!" Festus frowned.

"With you honey. Remember?" Dawn giggled. "I think you had more hands back then."

"Look here, the characters don't seem to have changed!" Festus read the cast.

"APHRODITE AND ARES

Artemis	*Aphrodite* \
Ares	*Apollo*
Hephaestus	*Hermes*
Nurse	*Pandora*
Dionysius	
Chorus of Ocean Nymphs	
Aphrodite's retainers."	

Dawn skimmed through the pages of the Play. "Let's read it later. Now, who were who the actors? She's put a foot note."

"Note for myself. My relatives are still haggling over the roles. The older ones are concerned about the play being too bawdy. I am glad that Panou is helping me beat them into submission. He says it is not bawdy enough! I wrote a special part for him as a thank you.

This time I think I will get my way. My aim is to get the following people into the play. Last time, Prometheus Maximos was very good as Ares. It will be interesting to see how he and Penelope get on. Maybe he can succeed where his father failed. It is inconvenient that I had to put both his mother, Cleo, and his mother-in-law, Maria, in the play.

Artemis	*Gaia Dexter*
Aphrodite	*Penelope Cronson*
Ares	*Prometheus Maximos*
Apollo	*Atlas Platon*
Hephaestus	*Argos Festus*
Hermes	*Demetrios Platon*
Nurse	*Cleo Maximos*
Pandora	*Persephone Cronson*
Dionysius	*Panou Cronson*
Chorus of Ocean Nymphs	
Leader	*Maia Maximos*
Aphrodite's retainers	
Leader	*Maria Platon"*

"It is truly incredible, how much shit stirring that woman was doing. Do you remember the fuss about Prometheus and my mother?" Dawn asked.

"Vaguely. I wasn't into that kind of thing. You mean after the problem with the oil?"

"Yes. I guess it would have been then. I wonder what Marienna will have to say about that?" Dawn answered.

"Let's get onto the next chapter of this soap opera," Festus said, chuckling.

"Here we are, April 1929, when the oil was found. Let's see what she has to say about that."

"Dear diary:

No one expected to find oil, except Argos. He was the one who studied the geology of this whole area and realized the similarity to the oil-bearing areas to the south of us. It was a geographic anomaly, highlighted later in every textbook. Apparently, it was due to the erratic drift, in the late Paleozoic era, of land from another part of Texas—gen-

erally theorized to have been the Luling Fault to the south. It is exciting, except that so far the oil has been found only on Odysseus's land. Agamemnon is furious and has Argos working full time drilling all over his ranch. It is particularly frustrating because Odysseus's field is close to the boundary with our property. Odysseus boasts about his field so much that people are fed up with hearing about it. The Everyman Bore is now its nickname. I do not like to think what will happen if my father finds no oil. Odysseus will become much richer and his power will increase.

I hear from Georgiou that, in the kinotitos, the question has been discussed of whether to tax the Maximos Oil Company. Odysseus is stalling. I think he will win, as long as he is the only one with oil. I am furious that only men are involved in such discussions. I am much smarter than most of them! Agamemnon says it is not right for a woman to be involved. When I raised the point with Odysseus, he did not even reply. His cold stare gave the answer. I must make do with our women's society. Wonderful! Most of them seem to be totally dominated by their men folk.

I realized something interesting. It is not just our surnames that have changed over the years. There are many non-Greek first names in Argos County—Zachary, Dawn, Joseph, Rosie, and Samantha. I am responsible for Henry Everett. I have concluded that it was a consequence of the immigrants wanting to improve their command of the English language, mainly for business reasons. So, before the Greek-American newspapers were available to them, they read the local Galveston paper. On occasion, they were also able to obtain the "Rolling Stone" and the "Houston Post", and could enjoy, for a brief period in the 1890's, the humorous daily column of W.S. Porter, better known as O'Henry. From this start, they branched out into the Western stories of, not only, O'Henry, but also Bret Harte, Zane Grey and others. From the novels, they picked a smattering of English names for their children. They were influenced also by contacts with the American Hellenic Association, AHEPA, which promoted Americanization of the Greek immigrants."

"The rest of this part doesn't look interesting," Festus said. "Let's see what she has to say about the famous oil drilling incident."

"Not interesting to you, but that first bit explains her frustration."

"You're right we'll come back to it, Dawn. I'm hoping she will tell us the whole story about the oil. I think you've got the diary for September."

Dawn picked scanned her pile. "Here it is."

"The situation is very bad. It seems that Argos developed a way of drilling sideways so that he could tap into Odysseus's oil. I do not blame him. I am sure it was my father who demanded it. Odysseus' crew discovered what was happening and back pressured their well causing our rig to explode! Afterwards, there was a terrible fight. It has all been hushed up, but I have heard that some of the roustabouts were killed—maybe

some of our distant relatives! Agamemnon and Odysseus have agreed on a common story. The party line! Otherwise they are not speaking. The deaths have been attributed to the normal dangers of drilling. I wonder how they will deal with the injured. Surely, someone will talk. A more critical question for me is what it will do to the Play Cycle. I have tried to find out from Agamemnon, but he is too distracted by his failure to find oil. It is irrational he is blaming Argos for the fiasco. Argos is distraught and won't talk to me. Olympia says he is burying himself in his work. He looks haggard."

"It was a bad time. I saw it all from a distance. The fight looked bloodier than was told in the stories going around. Dad didn't like to discuss it. He felt responsible. Afterwards, he drove himself terribly. You know, I often wonder if he was less concerned about the way he was treated by Agamemnon Cronson, than that he had failed to find the oil. He was proud of how well his bias drilling had worked. That invention was worth a lot."

"Worth to whom, Fes?"

"To you Cronsons, Dawn. Thanks for reminding me."

"You're not still bitter about that, are you?"

"My father was. He only got ten percent of what Cronson Enterprises made. I have a better deal but Zack's still screwing me on my inventions. That will change, if he accepts my deal and I get Olympic Services."

"I hope it works out, honey." Said Dawn, hugging him. "Notice what really worried her, not the deaths or the problems for your father but her damn Play! I wonder if they staged it in 1930?"

"It's here, in the May and August diaries."

"Argos has found oil on our land. It was deeper than the first field on the Maximos' property. Dad was elated and I had no difficulty persuading him to provide additional support for this year's Greek Festival.

This question of funding has made me think about how we might secure a more permanent source of support. Though everyone loves the Festival, it is a challenge each time raising the money. With both clans having oil, it might be possible to get the Foundation to set up some kind of endowment. I need to talk to Atlas Platon about it. Rehearsals for 'Aphrodite and Ares' are going all right, given the circumstances. I wish I could have had all the players I wanted, but Old Max is still furious about the attempt to steal his oil and has withdrawn his clan.

Georgiou has agreed to play Ares, even though he is not well. Dad is in a good mood, he did not object. I will play the nurse in place of Cleo Maximos. Panou's new wife, Maria, will replace Maia Maximos as the leader of Aphrodite's retainers. I hear that Old Max bullied poor Maia into turning down the part. Fortunately, the rest of her blood relatives stuck with me, or I would have had trouble staging the Play."

Festus continued.

"The Festival is over. The reception for my new play was overwhelming! The drama critics of both the Austin and San Antonio papers raved about it! Now back to reality. I must complete the third play. Dear diary, you may not hear from me again until that work is complete.

I am tired and I need a break. I will go to Mexico for the rest of the month, to the Sierra Madre Occidental. A consortium of Hispanic clubs from a number of Universities has arranged the trip. I will be back in time to resume teaching in September.

Footnote: The vacation with the Huichol people was incredible. I met a shaman, mara'akame, in their language, who explained all about their use of the peyote cactus in their religious rituals. It has very interesting hallucinogenic properties. I have seen this cactus in Argos County! It may come in useful sometime. I will write more about the trip later. For the moment, I am too busy preparing classes.

One other thing I should mention. There was this most interesting handsome, young Mexican, Jorge Vasquez. He comes from Chiapas and is studying at Harvard. I was curious as to why a Mexican would come on an 'Anglo" trip. He explained it was a good opportunity for him to study the Huichol's. We agreed to keep in touch by letter. He was most interested to hear about my plays. Fortunately, his English is very good, so I will not have to improve my Spanish."

"That's odd," said Festus.

"What do you mean?"

"Heraclio Balaam was a Harvard graduate, class of 30-something, he said. It's hard to be sure of his age, though he seems to be of the right vintage."

"Do you think they could be the same person? And what about the peyote?"

"God knows! Maybe she'll tell us?" He started reading.

"August 1932.

Dear diary:

Another Festival has passed by. I was only able to stage the first two plays because the third play, "Hephaestus and the Cretans," is not completed to my satisfaction. I must have it ready for the 1934 cycle. My initial reorganization of the dancing went well. In addition to the traditional Cretan dances, I have introduced a new one that involves many of the actors. It symbolizes a ritual dance connected to the pictures of the bull and acrobats seen in Cretan frescoes.

On a good note, Odysseus and his Clan are back participating in the Festival, though he and Agamemnon are barely speaking. I Talked to Odysseus about supporting the Festival. He was noncommittal, but I could sense the wheels turning in his cunning little mind. I think it should be called the Eurysthesian Foundation, after the king who ordered some of the Labors of Heracles. Later, I will make the connection to the role of Hephaestus in those Labors. In the meantime, I will work on the other members of the kinotitos, to get their support. I have begun courses on a second degree—in chemistry! I fear it will take me a long time to complete it."

"Oh shit!" Festus shouted. "She set us up again. I remember discussing it after we'd done the ritual dance for the first time at Phaestos—how easy it all seemed because most of us had acted in Marienna's so-called "royal Cretan dance" during the Festivals. We put it down to coincidence because it didn't explain how Europa seemed to know what to do. Duke must have told her about Marienna's dance. I should have realized."

Dawn put her arms around him. "Honey, you better prepare yourself for more. I don't think she's finished explaining what really happened yet."

"The chemistry courses are tough going, but I must persevere. It will be easier now that 'Hephaestus and the Cretans' is completed. I like it except for the business of Artemis playing Hephaestus' love interest. Gaia Dexter insisted on having her part in the play. I had no choice because her husband Socrates was arguing that the play was like 'Aphrodite and Ares,' and too racy for Argos. I think Gaia put him up to the ploy but as they say, give up a battle to win the war. Other people must see that Gaia is too old and out of shape to play Artemis. My half-sister Angelica will be perfect for the role, in a few years. I suspect not so keen on boys."

"You know it's curious that Marienna hardly appears in the plays. She's not in the cast of 'Hephaestus and the Cretans,' there's only Silenus, Minos, Hephaestus, Artemis, and you, Aphrodite"

Dawn laughed. "That gave her more time to manipulate us. Boy, she was sneaky, changing Hephaestus' love interest from Artemis to a mortal girl."

"Dawn, I remember asking her why she did it. She gave me some excuse about Angel wanting to continue as Artemis, but not be Hephaestus' love interest. It's obvious she was just trying to get Cathy and me together."

"Fes, it makes me wonder what really happened to make Pandora run away. Cathy was ready to go with you. It was a helluva a coincidence!"

"Maybe, she'll tell us?"

"Here's June 1935."

"I have a marriage and a birth to report. On the depressing side, my niece, Persephone, married Harold Dexter. I cannot conceive what prompted her to do that. She is bright and cheerful. He is the most depressing individual. The event seemed to be straight out of the Greek myths. I am relieved that my plays to date have not involved Hades. Otherwise, I might have felt responsible. They are living over this undertaker's business. His mother Gaia is still there. Poor Peri!"

On the good side, Paula and Basil Festus had a boy. They have called him Ionides. Basil is quite old to be having children—fifty-five. Fortunately, Paula is a lot younger. It will be good for Henry, having a cousin. He is excited about it.

My chemistry courses are progressing well. I am beginning to grasp the subject. Argos has been a big help, though I think my knowledge will soon outstrip his. I have not told him about my new interest—PEYOTE.

On my trip to Mexico, I heard about how the Huichol Indians use this hallucinogenic cactus in their rituals. They collect peyote buttons, cutting them off just above ground level. If the roots are left, the plant will regenerate. They sometimes chew the plant, and sometimes grind it and put it in a drink. Jorge and I have a common interest in peyote. In one of his letters, he alerted me to a good scientific article that discusses its main ingredient—mescaline. I found the article at UT. It is not very explicit on how to extract the drug, but there is enough information to help me get started. Why am I doing this? I am not sure, but I feel it could come in useful. Jorge, who has no scientific background, has expressed an interest in my results. I wonder how he found out about the article. I will ask him when we meet in Tuxtla Gutierrez in August."

"You know, I wondered why she had this huge cactus garden," Dawn said. "She must have made it so large to hide the peyote. I remember she didn't like us kids playing there. Who would have guessed?"

"Apparently nobody," Festus chuckled. "Can you see anything resembling this picture of peyote in the National Geographic?'

"Look! They're all around the border of this bed."

"You're right, and someone has trimmed some of the buds. I have an increasingly uneasy feeling about where this is all heading."

"You mean, you think she was drugging us, Fes?"

"It surely would explain a lot. I need to find out more about peyote and mescaline. Who has the keys to the house?"

"She left the house to Angel. If Angel hasn't taken possession, you could try Alex."

Festus continued reading. "There's more here in September about her Mexican friend."

The two weeks I spent with Jorge were wonderful. We visited the canyons carved out by the Grijalva and La Venta rivers. Spectacular! The Grand Canyon has real competition. Then we left Tuxtla and he took me to San Cristobal de las Casas. We were able to visit the local villages because they look upon him as a friend. Jorge is a remarkable linguist. He seems to understand all the different dialects or languages. We both would like our people to recapture the glory of the past. I am attempting to do it through the Festival and the Plays. Jorge believes strongly that the villagers should continue to practice their old rituals. Both of us are frustrated by the slow progress. Jorge is convinced that hallucinogenic drugs help. I think he is right!

As an aside, we attended a Sunday service at the "Catholic" church in one of the villages. I put Catholic in parentheses because there was no priest present and the rituals were pure Mayan. The Indians assemble in family groups on the floor of the church, in front of the effigy of the saint of their choice. The women have brought eggs and sometimes a chicken, and, it is hard to believe, Coca-Cola! They use the aerated drink to help them to belch. The Mayans believe that evil spirits are expelled by the belching and enter the eggs or the chicken. They then break the eggs and kill the chicken. The evil spirits are destroyed. The local Coca Cola representative is the richest man in the area."

"It sure looks like Jorge might turn out to be my friend Balaam. Heraclio Balaam never sounded like a real name to me."

"Sure does," said Dawn. "Dual-identity! It's beginning to sound like the 'Mask of Zorro!'"

"It looks like we've got to the time where Zack has her diaries. These excerpts skip from August 1936 to July 1937 to February 1938 and to May 1939. Listen!"

"The Plays went very well. Having three of them now makes a much better Festival. I received many compliments. I have always provided soft drinks for the players. This time, for "Hephaestus and the Cretans," I put some peyote in the drinks. I could not use much because of its bitter taste. I disguised it with grapefruit juice. There were comments about the strange taste. I will have to spend more time refining the mixture. I hope that it will be easier when I have learned to extract the mescaline. More importantly, Jorge was in the audience. He loved the Plays. We agreed it was better not to let my family know about our relationship. Therefore, we spent time together in San Antonio. Jorge says that the Indians fast before using peyote in their rituals. I need to figure out how to get them to eat very little before a play.

Dear diary:

Finally, I have my chemistry degree! My family gave a party to honor me. Henry saved up the money he gets from his paper route and bought me some equipment I needed for my little laboratory. He was as excited as I was. Of course, he does not know what I plan to use it for...

...I am having no success in writing the fourth play. For some reason, I cannot focus on the plot. I feel it should be in the style of Aristophanes—something like "The Frogs." What is the point I am trying to make? Maybe it would help if I could come up with a translation of the Phaestos Disk. I am having trouble assigning a meaning—sounds or letters—to the many symbols. I need to do more research on languages in the UT library. Which reminds me that Henry will start at the University in the Fall. I am sure he will do well.

There is one interesting piece of gossip, Panou passed on to me. It seems that Zachary is secretly dating Elena Maximos. Odysseus Maximos would have a fit if he found out. I wonder if Cleo Maximos knows.

Dear diary:

The situation in Europe does not look good. Cleo did know about Elena and Zachary! The situation in Argos looked even worse when Odysseus found out! Unfortunately, Agamemnon worked out an arrangement. In the end, as far as I can tell, he and Odysseus agreed it would be good for business. Men! Zachary and Elena were married. It was a beautiful wedding and a bad day for me. Our little church was filled with flowers. Bishop Platon officiated. They are honeymooning in Crete. Zachary will be working on some business for Agamemnon. They'll be gone for a year."

"Fes, she doesn't say it, but I bet she was the one who made sure Odysseus would find out about Zack and Elena."

"Sure looks like it. I think she was worried about that Zack's power would increase." Festus continued reading. "Wait up! What's this about the Disk?"

"...I am making progress on the Disk, using the assumption that the symbols are related to ancient Greek. The trick is to have the symbols represent sounds such as ka and kr, rather than just have each symbol be a single letter like a k. In this way, I can accommodate all 45 to 51 of them. Note to myself. The number of different symbols is not clear because some of them did not print well and I may be misreading them. I am looking for words that might be useful—like Crete, Minos, Phaestos, Knossos, Hephaestus, Zeus and gold. So far, I have concluded that the symbol that looks like an animal hide may be a (μ). But I sense that two hides together does not represent ($\mu\mu$). I am working on the assumption that the 'words' should be read from the center, spiraling outwards. This would be consistent with the Egyptian system in which the writing goes in the direction in which the human figures are facing. In this case, there is a common ending of what I am calling a shield followed by a soldier's head. The easiest assumption to make is that this is a nominative ending ($o\sigma$).

Similarly, I am guessing that the symbol that looks like a dog's head is a genitive ending (ησ). It is too early to worry about the gender of the nouns. Tentatively, I am interpreting the third to last word on the side with a flower at the center as of (or from) Crete. The three symbols in the word are a bell with a tail (κρ), three squiggly lines (ητ), dogs' head (ησ), in total, Κρητησ i.e., Crete. I will have to see where this leads."

"Shit! It looks like she translated the Disk a long time before I did. Read on, Dawn! I need to find out how far she got."

"I've got August 1940 June 1942."

"Zachary and Elena returned from Crete. A great surprise was that they had a baby boy, Deucalion. It was not an easy trip with a newborn. They had to go through Morocco and the Azores.

We had the Festival this year, but it was a subdued affair. Everyone is worried about the War. I have started on the fourth play but it is slow going. I see Henry sometimes. He is doing well at the University. Unfortunately, it seems that he is still dating Dawn!"

"It is the best of times and the worst of times." My beloved Henry graduated from the university with an engineering degree. It is very exciting. He will go on now to do graduate work in engineering at the University of California at Berkeley. I am so proud of him. Why, oh why, did he have to ruin it all by marrying Dawn? I tried to get him interested in other girls. It was a waste of time. He will regret that he did not listen to his godmother. Then, there is the War. Aristotle loves it. He came back recently, on leave. I think it was to show off his uniform. It suited him."

"I don't regret it one bit," Festus said, hugging Dawn. "She was sure persistent. Marienna would ask me for help in her house. When I got there, she would have some girl for me to meet. I remember what's her name Patillis one time, and another time it was Gloria Elytis.

"Poor Fes. It must have been hell. Look! She's got more on the Disk."

"...I am making some progress on the translation for the Disk. Mainly, because a plot for the play is coming into focus. In my notes about "the ancient world according to Hephaestus," I have him developing this way of writing. The Disk will tell the story of a great treasure that he hid. The question now is from where did the treasure come? One possibility is a deal with another power. The Egyptians and the Hittites are possible candidates. I will look for a name of a country or a person outside Crete. The symbol of a "walking man" is interesting. It appears coupled a number of times with what I call a "thin fir". I will try interpreting them as place, land or country. Then the

walking man might represent (χω or χωρ) and the "thin fir" is (ρα or α). The latter option seems to fit better, where the symbols appear in other words."

"I thought the translation was mine." Festus sounded sad. "Obviously, she had already done it—at least this far."

"It does look like what you did?"

"So far, yes. She must have cleverly fed me her solution. We talked a lot when I was working on it."

"She did have the Pendant, but what about the stones in Cornwall and the stuff you found in Sicily?"

"I guess we'll find out. There's more in April 1943."

"Aristotle will be going to England with the Army. Before he left, he got married to Yianna Patillis. She has to be the dullest of women, pretty in a vapid way. It seems incredible, but I suppose he must have done it for the sex.

I am making progress with the Disk. I think the word that starts with what looks like a Mayan hieroglyph is a name. It is the third word on the side with a flower at the center. It goes "glyph", "wheat stalk", "weed", "skin", "skin", "shield", and "soldier's head". The two skins might represent (μν) rather than (μμ).

One possibility is an interpretation of the name of a Hittite ruler, king Alluwamnas (Αλουμνοσ)—glyph (α), wheat stalk (λ), weed (ου), skins (μν), shield (ο), and soldier's head (σ). I am trying to see how this will affect other words."

"She's got stuff here, in November 1940, on how she sowed the seeds of my problems with Zack."

"Dear diary:

I fear that I have caused problems for Argos. It seems the Plays really do live in our real lives. My father is dying and it looks like Zachary will become head of the family. I am the oldest of Agamemnon's children but Agamemnon refuses to consider me because I am a woman! Panou does not want the role. If I cannot have it, then I would prefer to have Aristotle lead the family. It will be much easier to manipulate him. The War will be over soon and Aristotle will be back soon. I persuaded Argos to speak to my father on behalf of Aristotle. Argos was not keen on the idea, but he worries, as I do, about how Zachary will treat Henry. Unfortunately, my father told Zachary. He was furious and blamed Argos, threatening to throw him out of the Company. I managed to prevent that, but I fear it will come back to haunt Henry when he takes over from his father."

"Listen to this from February 1945!" Dawn laughed.

"New children everywhere! Henry and Dawn had a daughter. They have called her Pandora. An unfortunate name! I hope it is not an omen. I had hoped they would call her Marienna. After all of these years, Panou and Maria had a child, a daughter

Rosalie. I am very happy for them. Aristotle and Yianna also had a daughter, Saman-
tha. It seems to be a habit occurring nine months after his previous leave. A year ago,
it was the same pattern with Demosthenes.

I have part of the fourth play completed. It will be like Aristophanes' play "The
Frogs". In my play, "The Goats", Hephaestus will journey to Hades."

"It's March 1945 and Agamemnon is dead. The end of an era."

"Dear diary:

My father is dead. Agamemnon and I have fought mightily over the years. Our
relationship was thorny but I shall miss him. Battling with Zachary will not be the
same. Where my father had the true confidence of the self-made man, Zachary has the
smugness of one who was groomed for power. Control of Cronson Enterprises will be
in his hands. With my share of the businesses, I will be a rich woman but it is poor
compensation for not having control. I must work harder to have my way. Argos and
Olympia have both aged a lot during the past year. Of their generation, only Old Max
will remain when they have gone. He seems to be indestructible.

Henry will finish his doctorate soon. He and Dawn plan to return home. Argos
says he will retire and then Henry will be working for Cronson Enterprises. At least, I
assume he will. I hear that he has had many offers of employment. I must make sure
that he sees the advantage of having the kind of authority he will start with in our
company. It should be possible to make it more attractive. I have been thinking about
how our companies might benefit from having some kind of broad-based, technical
support laboratory in Austin. That way it would be easier to use university faculty in
handling a wider ranging set of issues than Argos has been able to do on his own. I was
very impressed with one of my chemistry professors—Willard Mowlin. He told me of
an interesting possibility for using bugs to clean up oil spills. Argos thinks the labora-
tory is a good idea, but said he was too old to travel so far daily. Henry could do it. It
would allow him to work away from Zachary. It's a pity I can't use it for my own lit-
tle bits of research. Henry must not find out!

I may have made a breakthrough on the disk. The word, "walking man" (χρ),
"fish" (υσ), "dog's head" (ησ) could be interpreted as something to do with gold
(χρυσοσ).

If anyone reads this, they will see that I am having trouble with the endings.

I interpret the "bell with a tail" as (κρ). When "the bell" is without a tail, I am
guessing it stands for (κ). The fourth word on the side that starts "bell", 'squiggly lines'
begins with a (κ). To get the connection to the underworld, I am going to fit it with
Cerberus, Hades' dog. Then the 'angled lines' stand for (ερ), the "firebrand" is (βε),
the "ram's head" is (ρ), and the "harp" is some kind of an ending."

"What research is she talking about?"

"I guess she means extracting the mescaline," Dawn suggested.

"What about the oil bugs?"

"Could she have used Willard?"

"It's a possibility." Festus looked thoughtful.

"I wonder why she waited until the last Play to put herself in the limelight," Dawn asked, reading the from the December 1945 diary."

"Dear diary:

I have succeeded in preparing a first draft of "The Goats," even though I have not managed to finish my interpretation of the Disk. With luck, the play will be in a final version in time for this summer's Festival. The plot uses a translation of the word after Cerberus as Deucalion, the son of King Minos. This word, with a different ending, is also the thirteenth word on that side of the Disk. The plot centers on a treasure that Deucalion and Hephaestus have hidden from the king. My thesis is that the Disk tells where they hid it.

Cast of the Frogs.

Hephaestus	*Argos Festus.*
Heracles	*Prometheus Maximos*
Athena	*Marienna Cronson*
Minos	*Zachary Cronson*
Charon	*Joseph Maximos*
Hades	*Harold Dexter*
Persephone	*Peri Dexter*
Dionysius	*Panou Cronson*
Apollo	*Alexander Platon*

Other relatives act as the Chorus of Acrobats and Dancers. The children love playing the Goats."

"That's interesting. I'd forgotten. Ari was still playing at war. See here! Marienna wanted Zack to play Heracles. He agreed, then he read the part. He was livid. Said it made him look like an idiot. He insisted on playing Minos. That's why poor Prometheus had to step in. You notice, back then, Marienna had Minos. Nowadays, it's Rhadamanthys. Curious! Here's the actual cast in her August 1946 diary."

"It was a great Festival! Everybody was relieved about the War being over. Having the complete set of plays really made a difference. The theme of 'The Goats' was received well. I had the cast I wanted, though Zachary complained about the way I portrayed King Minos.

Hephaestus	*Argos Festus*
Heracles	*Aristotle Cronson*

Athena	Marienna Cronson
Minos	Zachary Cronson
Charon	Prometheus Maximos
Hades	Harold Dexter
Persephone	Peri Dexter
Dionysius	Panou Cronson
Apollo	Alex Platon

The only sad part was seeing Argos struggle through the complete cycle. I am afraid that he will not be able to do it again. It is time for Henry to step up to being Hephaestus, and in more ways than being in the Plays!

Our mother Olympia is showing her age too. I remember the proud woman who stood up to my father, and I cannot see her in the timid, uncertain person who remains. It will not be like that for me. I will be strong to the end.

I still look at the Disk in hope of completing the translation, but now the Play is done the motivation is missing. Maybe something will come up later to get me back to it.*"*

"Dad hated the ending too." Festus read from the manuscript.

"Hephaestus: I cannot let the opportunity go.

Minos has made it clear that I have no choice.

I'll guarantee not to make anything that could harm our people.

Now, show me my treasure and leave me with it

While I decide how to use it for the good of all.

Athena: Dear Hephaestus, I have protected you through all of your troubled years.

Now you have won your treasure and proved to all

It was not Heracles, but you, who masterminded the Labors.

From now on let them be known as the "Labors of Hephaestus."

Yet, at the same time you have lost.

In reality, you have no control over your inventive genius.

So the world will career on its merry path, staying one

Step ahead of disaster, while you and your fellow

Technologists will attempt to invent the way out of each crisis

As you invented the way into them."

"Marienna wouldn't change it"

"Why."

"She said it was his reality and would continue to be so until he dealt with it. He only played the part twice. I took over the role of Hephaestus in 1948, when Dad no longer had the strength to do it."

"In earlier diaries, she said she was going to use the plays to help improve the image of Hephaestus." Dawn chuckled. "She did a lousy job of it."

"You're right. Maybe she started with good intentions but it was too difficult to do, given what was in the original material." Festus paused. "You know, she does hammer one very important point."

"What's that?"

"We scientists and technologists get screwed by our masters—Hephaestus and Zeus, Eurystheus etcetera, Dad and Agamemnon, me and Zack. We have to find a way to escape."

"So, her plan worked."

"Festus smiled broadly. "It took a long time but it sure did."

"She's right you know. My mother became old quickly. It was hard on Dad. When she died, he went downhill fast."

"I remember. You went to Crete with him. Was it forty eight or forty nine?"

"Nineteen forty nine. He died there. I'm glad I went with him," Festus' eyes misted. "I don't think I ever told you how much I appreciated you letting me go."

Dawn hugged him. "Honey, I loved him too. He was like a real father to me."

Festus paused to scan the next part of the diaries. "Marienna discusses it all here. She mentions my mother leaving her the Pendant. Let's move on and see if she explains what she means about making me more like Hephaestus."

"I thought that would grab your attention," Dawn giggled. "I'll take these diaries and you take those."

48. The Labors of H. E. Festus!

After a while, Dawn tapped Festus on the shoulder. "I've found something interesting here about the Eurysthesian Society. Have a look."

"What date?"

"September, 1957. She's talking again about wanting to broaden the Foundation to do research."

"*...The time has come to put flesh on the idea that Hephaestus was critically important to accomplishing most of the so-called Labors of Heracles. My Henry is now solidly established as the principal scientist for the Cronson enterprises—fully meeting the standards of his father. But, like his father, he is not receiving proper credit. I am tired of hearing Zachary and Aristotle refer to his work as if he were some kind of clerk. 'Our pet technologist'. Even their use of the name Doc seems to be mocking him.*

I created the Eurysthesian Foundation. In a sense, I am Eurystheus. So in that role I will define a set of Labors. Henry will succeed in them and my story about Hephaestus will become reality. Henry will need better facilities for his research in support of the Labors. His light engineering works does not quite fit the bill. I must find a way to persuade Zachary to set it up through the Foundation..."

"My Henry! 'Our pet technologist'," Dawn laughed. "They're so patronizing."

"Yeah, except she's trying to be nice. I was like the son she never had. But what I'm reading is getting me worried." Festus shook his head. "I didn't grasp the extent to which she influenced me. I remember many talks about the Foundation and the Labors. When I was younger, she would tell me at length about how clever Hephaestus was and how he didn't get proper recognition. She was continually bitching about the men in her family. I guess I saw many things through her eyes. When she suggested a separate laboratory, to be in Austin, I jumped at the idea. Now, I understand that she had ulterior motives."

"You mean like driving a wedge between you and me."

"Sorry, that too. I meant it was a way for her to get scientific things done."

"Like what?"

"She used to work with Willard. Remember! He was her professor at UT. I guess he helped her with extracting mescaline. Which reminds me, she hasn't talked about that in these more recent diaries. Let's get back to that topic when we find something. Another thing, she was the one who pressured us to work on the oil bug. The basic idea came from Willard. I got too much credit for the success."

"What about putting out the oil well fire?"

"Thank God! That was my idea." Festus paused. "I think?"

"I think that's all in this diary," said Dawn, scanning the remaining pages. "Oh no it isn't. Look here! She comments on changing 'Hephaestus and the Cretans' to replace Artemis with a mortal girl. That would have taken place in 1958."

"You're right. That's when Cathy Schmidt started. I remember Marienna introducing her. She was such a pretty girl. Perfect for the part."

"Fes!"

"Just kidding."

"There's more on Cathy in July 1958." Dawn giggled as she read.

"The Festival is over. Cathy did very well. Henry seems to like her. He is really getting involved in his role. I could see it clearly on the last day at the end of "Zeus Bound." Which reminds me. I have found the best way to use 'the juice', as I call it. At the end of the play, I dispense it to the ones I want to affect, when they have not eaten for a while and are thirsty. From occasional comments, I can tell that the each actor is becoming more and more like his role. On that last day, I even overheard Zachary comment on feeling like Zeus."

"So that's how she got us to feel our parts were reality. My God!"

"Wait for the next bit," said Dawn, after scanning ahead.

"I am close to persuading Zachary to set up "Olympic Services" as a vehicle for the Society to pursue projects. Alex Platon has been a huge help. He is a smart young man. While I do not approve of his social behavior—his apparent predilection, on occasion, for young men—he is very likeable (and good-looking). In turn, Alex has persuaded Joseph Maximos and through him Prometheus. Zachary is working on Odysseus. As usual, that old man is suspicious about the idea. Some things do not change! Harold Dexter may be an obstacle. So far, we have kept him out of the loop. Zachary believes he will be negative regardless of when he finds out. So, we might as well spring it on him in public or at least at the Breakfast Club. That way he will find it harder to object. Naturally, Aristotle is opposed, but he will have to go along with Zachary.

I have written my own version of the pantheon of the gods and the role of Hephaestus in the Labor: Hephaestus—the true story: according to Marienna Cronson.

I talked to Henry at length about possible projects—Labors. For Henry, hunting the Loch Ness monster comes to the top every time. I would love to see Harold's face when he finds out. Beyond that, I see the oil-eating bug offering a potential for a Labor.

It was fortuitous meeting Georgina MacLeod those many years ago. I am glad I kept in touch. I will be visiting her next month. She seems to be excited about helping. Probably needs the financial support. I hope she is a good actress..."

"I am beginning to wonder if anything was real. Georgina MacLeod should have been on the stage. Old people are dangerous, you know. You don't expect them to be playing games."

"The way she talks about the juice. I wonder how much she used." Dawn shook her head.

"She came to me after nearly every performance. It was a funny tasting drink. Refreshing in a strange way."

"She never offered me a drink."

"You're lucky. I guess she didn't want you to become Aphrodite. Well, she failed. That's who you are to me—the most beautiful woman in the world."

"Fes, do you think it will have a long-term effect? Like you'll really believe you're Hephaestus."

"God knows!" Festus grinned. "There must be benefits to being all powerful. Aphrodite, I am Hephaestus and I need you to work your magic now."

"I am at your command, oh powerful one."

"Great!"

"After a long interlude in the bedroom, they continued reading.

"*...Now, back to the Phaestos Disk. I have started priming Zachary with the thought that there is a treasure on Crete and the Disk holds the clue to where it is. I have not told anyone else, not even Henry. It fits in with Zachary's ambitions to do something for our homeland. He has become obsessed, partly with my prompting, with the idea that the Turks might invade. He views the problems in Cyprus as a reason to be worried. Unfortunately, he has taken the idea far beyond my plan to support public works. Zachary does not know that I know but I received a letter from Crete, from my very good friend, Theodora. She says that he now wants to use the supposed 'treasure' to arm the citizens of Sfakia. I am beginning to wonder if 'the juice' is affecting his judgment. I need to get him back on track, and then find a way of turning it into Labors for Henry.*"

"It only took her until May 1959 to get agreement to the start of the Labors."

"*Dear diary:*

Success! They will set up Olympic Services, despite complaints from Harold and Aristotle. Even Odysseus gave a cautious blessing. He must see some angle in it. Henry and Ionides will be leaving for Scotland shortly. Georgina is performing magnificently. She has found a submarine for sale and a place in Inverness that can do the modifications Henry wants. I have to find a way for Henry to learn about this without him knowing where the information came from. I shall have to be inspired..."

"Shit! There she goes again."

"Fes! You've got to admit it's funny. What was the name of that Scottish guy?"

"You mean Hamish McDougall?"

"Yes, Hamish. I wonder if he was working for Marienna too."

"I'm not sure I want to know."

"*...One bad thing about the Loch Ness Labor is that Henry and so many of the key people will be in Scotland next year that it has been decided to defer the Festival until*

1961. A small price to pay if the Labor goes well. Which comment makes me think about what if it does not go well? I must admit I have not given much thought to the question of failure. Frankly, Henry believes in it, and has ideas about how it can survive, but I doubt that the beast exists. I will have to come up with a solution for that eventuality!"

"Shit! Shit! Shit! I saw it. I know I did."

"Fes! Marienna can't change that. What could she have done?"

"God knows, but it doesn't sound good." Festus held up his hand. "Hold on! The phone's ringing."

Dawn continued trying to read, while hearing what sounded like an argument from the other room. When Festus returned, he looked angry.

"Who was it?"

"Zack. He's been reading his part of the diaries. It seems what she wrote about him is as entertaining as what she wrote about us. He wants to see our diaries."

"What did you say?"

"I said, not until we have read all of them and then maybe not at all. He was furious. I think he's worried about how much of his stuff is in our set of diaries. I'm not happy about that either. You know, Zack learning how she manipulated me. I asked if we could see his set."

"And?"

"The bastard weaseled! Screw him."

"Do you think we should destroy them when we finish?"

"It might be a good idea, Dawn. In the meantime, let's carry on reading. I'd like to finish them today."

"Tonight, I'll hide them, just in case Zack tries something."

"Her spies kept her informed about your progress, Fes. Listen to this from Septmeber 1959!"

"I received a letter from Georgina. It seems that Henry is going to do what I wanted. He is ensconced, for his work, at McDougall's Yard and the submarine that Georgina found has been purchased. I had to offer to underwrite some of the cost to get the funding in place so quickly. Henry does not know. Finally, the base for the hunt will be Urquhart House! It is all working out. Now, there will be a real Labor."

"There's more on the first phase of the hunt in January 1960."

"Dear diary:

Henry and Ionides came back for Christmas. It is wonderful to see how excited he is. McDougall's Yard and the submarine are working out very well. He needs to do more work on the net. I would like to suggest improvements to the Rube Goldberg device he has come up with for catching the monster, but I must be quiet. Henry seems happy with Urquhart House. He is curious about how well I know Georgina, and quizzed me at length. He seems suspicious. I told him what he already knew about meeting Georgina and her husband at the Festival. I went on at length and he became bored with the subject. It is a ploy I must remember to use again."

"There's a brief comment in the June diary about looking forward to being in Scotland," said Dawn. "Have you found anything?"

"Unfortunately, yes. She writes here, in May, about how our marriage is in trouble. There is a brief comment about her getting Ari to help you with something. It isn't explicit. She mentions Cathy Schmidt, and is unhappy the plays won't bring us together until the next year. Interestingly, she actually seems sympathetic to your need to go back to university. She talks about taking Pandora to Scotland."

"Does she say anything else?"

Festus leafed through the remaining pages. "No. This is mainly about the need to replenish 'the juice'. I guess to have some to use in Scotland?"

"Did she use it?"

"It's a few years ago. I don't remember anything. I think we'd done well enough on scotch. Look she continues in August 1960."

"Things are not going well. We did not find the monster. It is hardly surprising given the short time of the hunt. Of course, Zachary does not understand the slow pace of research. He wanted to pull the plug on the Labor and sell the submarine. I had to threaten him. I alluded to his plans for Crete. He probably thinks I know more than I do. It worked. I will need to get more information to hold over him. He must not find out that my source is Cousin Theodora. Her husband would be furious if he knew.

Henry will return in September. I really need to get him to deal with the situation of Pandora and Dawn. Angelica is helping temporarily with Pandora. As for Dawn, a permanent solution is called for! It is some way off, but I will try to get the rehearsals for the Plays started earlier. I can argue that with the extra one-year's gap more time will be needed for rehearsals. With Dawn away a lot, Catherine and Henry will have time together. In the meantime, Catherine and I will be back at school, and I can find pretexts to have them both in my house. I am an old woman. They can help in the yard."

"The scheming old bitch!" shouted Dawn. "She played on our weaknesses."

"Fortunately, it didn't work out the way she wanted. I can't take much credit for that," Festus said, ruefully. "You had every right to go back to university. You gave up a lot for me. I should not have let Marienna encourage my...my...my mindless drive to show how smart I was."

"You didn't need to. Look at all you've done."

"All that Marienna's done?"

"Very funny, Fes. You know what I mean. Come on! Let's see what else she did. Here's April 1961"

"Dear diary:

It is frustrating. I have arranged numerous times for Henry and Catherine to be at my house. Supposedly, to help me do some chore. Henry pays no attention to her. He is only interested in talking about his damn polygraph. He uses Pandora and Catherine as guinea pigs. I will not allow him to subject me to that contraption. It would help if Angelica did not come with Catherine. They are only interested in talking about sports.

Henry told me about explaining his plans for Blarney to the Breakfast Club. I wish I could have been there. Apparently, Harold gave a stellar performance. I will be in Blarney."

"And she did, but not before stirring things up." Dawn laughed, bitterly.

"July 1961.

Dear diary:

The Festival is over and next week I will go to Blarney. I believe that Henry and Catherine have noticed each other at last. The rehearsals helped. In 'Hephaestus and the Cretans' they seemed positively amorous. Angelica commented on it. Catherine responded well to 'the juice'. She told me that she felt like one of us for the first time— no longer a foreigner."

"I remember that," Festus said thoughtfully. "Marienna changed the play, replacing Artemis with a mortal girl."

"You don't have to remind me again, Fes."

"She also had us embracing."

"I noticed."

"There was this sudden change when we were doing the play. She started looking at me differently."

"How about you?"

"Yes. I'm embarrassed to admit it, me too." Festus smiled, sheepishly.

"You old devil."

"Yup! Right in the middle of the play. It's a good thing I play a cripple. The audience thought my being doubled up was brilliant acting."

"Did it go any further?"

"No. Not then."

"But later?"

"When we were separated. You know it didn't work out."

"Yes." Dawn hugged him.

"I guess we'd better see what she has to say about Blarney."

"I've got it," said Dawn, "September 1961. You're not going to like it."

I am not given to vulgarity, but the shit has really hit the fan. In Blarney, I found out that Henry had hired our agent, Seamus O'Flaherty, to trap Dawn and Aristotle in flagrante delicto. It cost me a lot of money! Nothing would have happened if I had not taken action. First, I arranged for Peri to take Samantha shopping. Then I used the pretext of looking at a pretty cottage to get Dawn and Ari to come for a walk with me. At the last minute, I said I could not come. As I had planned, they carried on. Seamus followed them. Afterwards, he gave me the photographs that showed Aristotle assaulting Dawn. I do not think Aristotle needed much encouragement, but I am sure the juice helped. I selected the most damaging ones for him to give to Henry. I must admit that did not realize that he would humiliate Dawn and Aristotle in public. Nevertheless, it finished their marriage. Good! But Henry may have permanently alienated Zachary, the Foundation Board, and the other members on the kinotitos. Bad! I will have to put a lot of effort into mending fences. I will need to pay closer attention to what he is doing. I cannot have him deciding how to do the Labors! It could interfere with my plans."

"She must have been insane, even then," Festus looked sad. "I loved her. How could she do that to us."

"She was jealous and hated me."

"I could kill Seamus. The bastard!"

"I guess everyone has his price?'

"Dawn. I would have given him more if I had known."

"You don't know how much Marienna paid."

"True, but it wouldn't have mattered."

"I guess not. This is interesting."

"...Henry cannot face being in Argos. He has gone back to the Loch. I wonder when I will see him again. Angelica is looking after Pandora. I must persuade Zachary to let the hunt for the monster continue. Success would change everything."

"It' May 1962 and she's still pushing Cathy."

"Elena and I will take Pandora to stay with my cousin Nicholas in Athens. Dawn has gone to California. Henry has now been separated from them for a large part of a year. Success! Catherine will join me in Loch Ness. Maybe this time she and Henry will do something. Unfortunately, Catherine will be going on to a job at a base in Germany. There is not much time. I live in hope."

"She was remorseless."

"It seems so, and I was incredibly naïve. Now, seeing it written down, I remember how often Marienna would ask me for help on something at her house and Cathy would be there. It wasn't until the play in 1961 that I took any notice."

Dawn raised her eyebrows."

"I know. I was an idiot. I'm up to August 1962. Let's see what she has to say about Pandora."

"Dear diary

I have really stuck my neck out. Pandora has run away and Henry has gone to find her. I persuaded Catherine to help him. The family was not happy. Elena is suspicious about what I am trying to do. We had strong words. Fortunately, nobody else was available and Catherine knows Pandora well from school. I misjudged what that young gardener of Nico's would do when I encouraged him to be friendly with Pandora. So this will be Henry's next Labor. It is not one that I would have chosen..."

"The old bitch," Festus cried. "She was the one responsible for Pandora running away."

Dawn put her arms around him. "Honey, she wasn't alone. It was my fault too. Marienna only built on what I'd done."

"I guess so," Festus said, calming down. "I didn't help. Even so I..."

"Let's move on. September 1962"

"Henry has found Pandora and will be coming back soon. Thank God! An oil well on the Everyman Field has blown up and Odysseus blames us Cronsons. I am worried he will do something rash. He will not accept our help. I wonder whether we can do something from a distance by using bias drilling to intercept and divert the oil and put the fire out. I must talk to Henry as soon as he returns. Maybe, I can find out also what happened between him and Cathy. Her letter was not forthcoming."

"Great minds think alike," Festus said, sadly. "I thought of it before I talked to her and I came up with the idea of the flame suppressant."

"Fes! You shouldn't take it so seriously. She is the one with the monster ego problem."

"You're right. My ego problems are less than hers are. The diaries are a hell of an ego trip. I wish she didn't take such pleasure in putting me in my place."

"I wonder if it affected her sanity? It must have been very frustrating for her having to work through other people."

"We'll find out. It's January 1963. Read on!"

"Dear diary:

Hooray! Henry put out the fire. He used my suggestion for bias drilling and then, brilliantly, added a flame suppressant. He is becoming Hephaestus. Dawn and he seem to be truly separated. Good! The romance with Catherine was going well. Then it foundered. Bad! Neither of them will talk about it. Catherine is in Germany.

Henry is in Scotland. Fortunately, I am only working part-time now so I can join him. The 'benefit' of being over sixty-five. Maybe, Georgina and I can find out what happened."

"Pressing right along, her's March 1963."

"We are all back in Argos. Zachary has ordered it. It is what I feared. Erhard Mitterer is going to unveil his work on the oil-eating bugs. Willard and I agree, the man is a fool and dangerous. He does not understand what he will be unleashing. We must find some way of getting hold of a sample so that we can do our own tests. That way we may be ready with an antidote, in case they mutate and run wild."

Dawn patted Festus on the back. "See! She gives you credit for the flame whatsit"

"Yup, and I should give her and Willard credit for the bugs. They were way ahead of me on that one."

"It all worked out in the end. Can you count it as a successful Labor, Hephaestus?"

"Very funny. I did work out how to get a sample." Festus hesitated. "I think I was the one who worked out that the anti-fouling paint on the buoys was causing mutations. I don't think it was Willard or Marienna?"

"So you can score a half-Labor?"

"But that means I still have another half a Labor to do."

"So far!"

"You're right. Maybe it'll get worse."

"April 1963.

Dear diary:

We are now set up to work on the oil-eating bugs. I have never seen Willard so excited about anything as his part in obtaining a sample of Mitterer's bug. Men! Children to the end. Panou has used his dubious contacts to find out what enzyme they are using. We managed to get samples from the test at sea. Now the hard work begins."

"July 1963.

Dear diary:

I took one last shot at bringing Henry and Catherine together through their roles in 'Hephaestus and the Cretans'. It did not work, even with a liberal use of 'the juice'!. Reluctantly, I must admit failure in that effort. Since I do not have another foreigner for the role I may have to revert to the version with Artemis. I think Angelica would like that. She has a soft spot for Henry. I owe her a favor for helping me with the garden. Which reminds me. As a favor to Aristotle, I have let Demosthenes help her. It's part of Aristotle's plan to help that boy shape up. Good luck to him. He is a strange boy. I do not trust him. So he only works in my front yard. I will not have him in my cactus garden."

"Before we move on, Fes. Do you think that comment on helping Marienna with the garden means that Angel knew about the peyote?"

"Could be. It might explain stuff that happened later."

"Like when?"

"In Crete."

"How about Demos?"

"Yes indeed, how about him? I fear we will hear more." They read in silence.

"This November diary has stuff on Kennedy's assassination." Festus continued reading. "She has a comment that it will be convenient having Lyndon in charge." He paused again. "Now she's going on at length about dealing with the oil disaster. I don't see any surprises."

"Do you think she had anything to do with what happened in Dallas?'

"Don't even think about it!"

"Anything more about Cathy or Angelica?" Dawn giggled.

"Not yet. What have you found?"

"On Cathy and…?"

"No. On the oil."

"Nothing yet. Here's March sixty four."

"The oil catastrophe will be resolved. We have come up with a solution. Henry and Willard will demonstrate it tomorrow. Appropriately, their demonstration will be in the same place as Mitterer's. I plan to be there, in the back, just like the last time.

Zachary is causing problems. He wants Henry and Willard to turn our solution into a weapon. He is being very persistent. I tried to talk him out of the idea. He told me to "Butt out!" I will not be talked to in that way. He forgets who I am. I will teach him a lesson."

"What does she meant? Teach him a lesson."

"I have no idea. But then I had no idea she was at Mitterer's demonstration either."

"I can't wait to find out."

"Here it is, Fes, in the June 1965 diary. Boy she is patient in getting her revenge. You remember how surprised we were that she had all that money in the bank in Austin. The one with that banker Zack hates."

"You mean Howard Clements. He and Zack had a bet on the charity golf match. It was right at that time?"

"Yes. Well, obviously money talks. It was Marienna's idea to con Zack."

"Dawn, I bet she told old Howard she'd remove her money if he didn't cooperate."

"She had to do more than that."

"You're right. She must have set up that deal with Wendell and the cheerleaders."

"With help from Demos?"

"It's possible, or maybe the banker. He knew Wendell."

"Either way, Demos would have known," said Dawn, thoughtfully. She continued reading. "There's more. Let me read it." Festus handed her the diary. And she started reading. 'The golf match was a fiasco. Henry saw what was happening, and enlisted our relatives to help Zachary win. It seems that he knew some local shopkeeper, who sold practical jokes. I heard he used itching powder to rout the Band and the cheerleaders. Then he clinched the match for Zachary by showing him some trick shot. Howard said it was amazing. He even seemed amused. It is not amusing, but I will set it aside."

"Gracious of her," Festus laughed. "What's next?"

"There was one good aspect to all this. In gratitude for Henry's help, Zachary has agreed to let the Foundation return to Loch Ness. On the down side, Henry says that he will leave before the Festival. I am furious. It means that Ionides will play Hephaestus. I am not optimistic about his capabilities. To cap it all, it seems that Henry and Dawn have made up. I shall have to resign myself to that also. There is no hope of involving him with Angelica. But even these irritations pale besides the problem that I will have such little time to find a solution to complete the Loch Ness Labor."

"Have you noticed how the tone in her diaries changed with time?" Festus said.

"A little, I guess."

"It's subtle, but she is referring more and more to how things affected her than to how they affected me."

"My poor baby. Do you feel neglected?"

"It's not funny. Look at what she says here, 'She will have to find a solution that completes the Loch Ness Labor'. Not, Henry or Hephaestus will! I am very worried about where all of this will lead. Press on!"

July 1965.

Dear diary:

A very serious matter has arisen. Demosthenes found out about my involvement in the golf match. In an unsubtle way, he tried to threaten me. I suspect he also knows about the peyote. Some buttons were cropped. Not by me! I acted as if I did not under-

stand him. The child is dangerous. The analogy of my family to the gods is becoming too real. As a son of Ares, he could turn out to be Diomedes king of Thrace, a truly unpleasant individual. I will let it rest for the moment but, if he does anything more, I will act."

"That sounds ominous, given what happened later in Copan."

"You're not saying she planned that too?"

Festus shook his head. "When we started reading I would have said not. Now I'm not so sure. We'll have to see what she says later, but first the ned of the Loch ness hunt."

"November 1965.

Dear diary:

I feel that this is the end of an important period in my life. Finally, the Loch Ness Labor is completed. Did we find a monster? I do not know. I have looked at the pictures many times. It is not clear what one is looking at. There is a huge controversy about the "tail." Is it the monster, or a large eel, or a piece of weed? The poor quality of the pictures allows all of those interpretations. There was quite a large eel caught by the net. Henry called it Elmo! Men are so childish! He seemed happy. Maybe, that is all that matters? As the saying goes, "it is all in the eye of the beholder." Georgina is as excited as I am about how we were able to help. The "juice" worked its wonders again."

"I can still remember feeling lightheaded in the submarine. I told you about seeing Aphrodite." Festus thought for a minute. "You know, she took a hell of a chance, doping me up when I made those scuba dives."

"That's scary, honey. Do you think the drugs made you...? I don't know how to say this. Create in your own mind the images you saw. Like that first time, when you and Hamish were underwater?"

"It must have had an effect. Enhancing what ever happened." Festus smiled. "At least, I have this grand reputation now. But what did I really do? How many of my brilliant efforts were drug created or Marienna created fantasies?"

"I think you're being hard on yourself. So far, her diaries have covered six Labors. Let's see what she has to say about the final six!"

49. Athena

"March 1966.

Dear Diary:

I will be going to Crete next week. I wish it were a happier occasion. My nephew Deucalion has run away from his army post in Germany. Supposedly, to go to Crete.

Aristotle tells me the correct word is AWOL, Absent Without Leave. It is a typical military distortion of the English language! Zachary is very tight lipped about it, but I hear from my contacts that Duke has stolen a new weapon—the Bullroarer. I am worried that Zachary may have put him up to it! This may explain why he will not use our Cretan relatives to find Deucalion. Instead, we members of the Argos clan are going to scour the island until we find him.

Henry has been told to make this hunt a Foundation activity. So, we will visit all of the ancient sites. Ostensibly to do research. I managed to persuade Zachary to allow us to reenact the Dance as one of the activities. A side benefit is that I will be able to look at the Phaestos Disk. It is most important that I now finish my translation. I know that Henry is back working on it since he and Pandora returned from Crete. It is important that his version bears my stamp.

I have made a lot of juice to take. Fortunately, it is quite concentrated. I will get bottles over there and make up my usual refreshing drink to enhance the archaeological experience for my relatives.

There will be a big surprise waiting for Henry in Crete. Catherine will be there. It was not easy, but I persuaded her to extend her vacation and join me. Zachary will be furious. I will have to feed him plenty of juice!"

"It's becoming more and more obvious that she spent years setting us up for the dance," siad Festus, putting down the diary. It makes me wonder what she did with the Disk."

"I bet she'll tell us. Let's see what April 1966 has too say."

"Everything is going very well. The Director of the Museum in Heraklion was most helpful. I told him I was from New Orleans and most interested in learning about Dancing Floors. I worried he might say something to Henry, but I have heard nothing. Good...

...I am camped by the sea near Loutro. It is a beautiful site. The juice is working miracles. All of my relatives are falling under its spell. We reenacted the Dance at Phaestos. It was spectacular. Remarkably, Catherine was able to play her part. I hardly dare to say it, but the return to the past seemed to be real, not simply my invention working through the mescaline and the dance at the Festival. I am beginning to feel that, truly, I am Athena. I must be careful. Rhadamanthys is an arrogant king. He was very angry that I had introduced a mortal girl into the proceedings. I reminded him of his need for my help in finding the treasure. We have an uneasy truce.

I am wandering. Let me return to the present. Alexander told me that Zachary, Aristotle and Henry came across Deucalion in the Gorge. He used the weapon against them. They were lucky to survive. I have to reassess Zachary's role. Is it possible that Deucalion did this on his own? Or, was using the weapon a part of the plan?"

"So, Marienna doped us there too. I should have guessed when she insisted we all eat lightly in deference to the traditions. I remember Harold, bless him, saying, 'Marienna, I have no recollection of fasting being mandatory before the Dance'. You could tell she was furious that her authority was being questioned."

"What did she say?"

"She basically told him to shut up. Very unlike her to be so obvious. What was even more amazing, he did!"

"I get it. Fasting makes the drug more effective. The Indians do it."

"Right."

They continued reading, sitting at the table their heads together.

"See here! She did the same thing before the dance at Aradin."

"Fes, she's doing it again. There's a subtle change in the way she's writing about herself?"

"You mean the bit about her being Athena."

"That and the more hostile tone towards her family. It's obvious Harold wasn't the only one to get on the wrong side of her. Look at this stuff about Aristotle screwing up the Dance by firing the Bullroarer."

Festus read from the diary. "The Dance should have been allowed to run its course. A death is required."

"I wonder which century she was in when she wrote that—twentieth AD or fourteenth BC?"

"God knows! Let's move on. I'll make some coffee." Festus went into the kitchen.

"There's a lot more here, Fes, on the Disk. It's in the November 1966 diary."

"Let's have a look!"

Festus read for a long time before he spoke. "She did my translation, more or less," he said, shaking his head. "Maybe I should say that I recreated hers."

"How did she get you to follow the same approach?"

"She says here, 'I am making slow progress in persuading Henry to arrive at my interpretation of the Disk. It is difficult, because he must not know that I have my own version. He is so stubborn.'"

"She got one thing right."

Festus was not paying attention. "She goes on to say 'I must find a way to have Henry adopt my interpretation of some key symbols'. She specifically mentions the pear shaped symbol being (kappa), the skin being (mu), and the two lines at an angle being (epsilon) and (rho). I remember arguing with her." He continued reading, in silence. "Here it is. The bottom line is she wants me to make the connection to that scene about the treasure that's in in the 'Goats.'"

"Does she say how she'll do it?"

"Yes, she writes about having the Pendant remounted, with the pattern around the edge now showing a few symbols from the Disk with their Greek equivalents. She says here that Jorge Vasquez will help her find a jeweler in Mexico."

"What puzzles me Fes, is why you didn't notice the change. You've told me about remembering your mother wearing it."

"I was a little kid. All I remembered was a worn Greek inscription. Only a few letters showed clearly. There was a funny pattern too. Marienna was very clever in helping me to accept her version. Having it stolen. I was so eager to have it I didn't think."

"What about Cornwall and Sicily?"

"There is nothing about Sicily, but she mentions Erythmos here. You can see the importance of the symbols for er and m!"

"Is there any more?"

"No. She finishes with a line about there being a big problem. I wonder what it was."

"Listen to this from February 1967," said Festus, after they had read for a while.

"My worst fears about Demosthenes have been realized. His drug habits are far more serious than I knew. Now, he has used a book he found at the University as a pretext for an expedition to go to Chiapas. I am certain he is after drugs. From whom, I do not know. It seems that Pandora and Rosalie will also go. I dare not tell Henry and Panou, let alone Aristotle, or Demosthenes will reveal my little secret. I must protect Athena's image. I have asked Jorge for help."

"She knew and she didn't tell us. How could she have been so selfish," Dawn cried.

"She explains it, Dawn. Protecting Athena. She might as well have written, 'I dare not tell Hephaestus and Dionysius, let alone Ares, or Diomedes will reveal my little secret."

"You think she was that far gone?"

Festus thought for a moment. "I think she was so committed to her plan for the Plays, the Dance, the Labors, and us Eurythesians that it was all she was living for. I really believe that she was living her dreams through my father, and then through me. The diaries show that, as time went by, it was progressively more about her and her role as Athena. She couldn't let anything get in her way. Remember what happened to Demos! There's more."

"*March 1967.*

Dear diary:

I have just returned from Mexico. Jorge contacted key people in Chiapas. Curiously, they knew about Demosthenes. I wish I could have found out more. Either way, between us we have worked out a good way to handle the situation.

On the way home, I visited Taxco. The jeweler has done a wonderful job with the Pendant. The mounting looks just like the original except for the small modifications around the edge. It was very clever the way he gave it an aged appearance. Now I must find a way for Henry to discover it. I have already given hints about the inscription being curious. He has not reacted yet, but I know he hears everything. The processing is sometimes slow!"

"You don't have a comment?"

Dawn laughed. "No. It would be too easy."

Festus shook his head. "You take April and I'll take May. Let's see what she has she has to say about Tam'oan Shan."

"It's here at the end of the April diary," said Dawn, who had been scanning the book. "Marienna writes, 'As I expected, Demosthenes was after drugs. It seems Jorge was right. The Indians in Chiapas have more sophisticated potions than my 'juice.' As the expedition found out in Tam'oan Shan, with the help of somebody called 'Heraclio Balaam.'" I love that name, even though it sounds contrived. In two words, it unites the mythology of the Greeks and the Mayans. I wish I could meet him. I am becoming more convinced that Heraclio and Jorge are the same person.

The family is in an uproar. Doc Maximos is concerned about the nightmares Pandora and Rosalie are suffering. Elena tells me that Zachary, Panou, Henry and Aristotle will take the expedition members back and try to get treatment. I would love to go, but I need to keep a low profile. They must not learn of my role. One good result of this mess is that my relatives are beginning to grasp that Demosthenes is a little swine. I even heard Yianna criticize him. They had better deal with him soon or I will have to act!'

"Interesting, she also thought that Heraclio Balaam was a made up name, and that his Jorge Vasquez might be the same person?"

"She also talks about Jorge knowing about the drugs."

"Yes, it all adds up." Festus paused. "Why don't you see what's in the June diary? I'm still working on May."

Some time later, the doorbell rang. It was Zack.

"I don't like being stiff armed," he shouted. "What the hell does she say about me?"

"That you're a loud-mouthed bully. Who should have better manners than to come into our house and talk like that," Dawn retorted, sharply.

Zack raised his hand in anger then, as rapidly, calmed down.

"Not very much in our diaries," said Festus. Except, she does mention your interest in Sfakia and the business with Duke. Nothing new there, I'd already worked out you got Duke to steal the Bullroarer."

"Oh! You knew! Did you tell anyone, Fes?"

"Only Dawn."

"Zack, these are diaries about us, but, mostly, they are about Marienna. They are private and we're not going to let you read them."

"Does, she mention 'the juice?'"

"Yes."

"She could have caused serious damage. I still get weird dreams, and not only at night. This fantasy about us being the Greek gods. She went too far."

"We could talk to Doc Maximos about it."

Zack shook his head. "No. We'll keep this between the four of us. I don't want it getting out."

"The four of us? How about Angel, Georgina MacLeod, and the ubiquitous Jorge Vasquez?"

"There's nothing we can do about them. We just don't need to add anybody." Zack was silent. He seemed to be struggling with what to say next. Festus and Dawn watched in amusement.

"Give me Marienna's share of my companies, and you can have your damned Olympic Services!"

Festus grinned. "It's a deal." Zack grunted. He did not look pleased.

"Now! What are you going to do with the diaries?"

"Before I answer that. What does she say about me…I mean us?" Festus asked.

"Other than trying to screw up your marriage?" Festus nodded. "She talks about your being Hephaestus to my Zeus. She has this stuff about Heracles not doing the Labors and you will get a chance to repeat them. I was thinking she was completely nuts, but she describes how you would end up doing them—Loch Ness, Blarney, the fire, the oil-bug and so on—generally ahead of the events. What with the dreams and the Dance and…Heraclio Balaam I wonder if she's right."

"On the matter of Balaam. We think he and this Jorge Vasquez may be the same person."

"It's a possibility. I've got people tracking him down. We'll find out. I want those diaries, Alex stupidly sent him. Now about your diaries."

Festus looked at Dawn. "I think we'll keep the original versions of the plays and burn the rest." Dawn nodded.

"Good. I've already burned mine. Fine. Just wanted to see how things were going." Zack looked relieved. "One other thing, towards the end, her diaries seem incoherent. Have you found that?"

"Not yet. More strident, maybe, talking about her role."

"Fes, I didn't tell you this before. In those last days in Crete she was ill and left us, but she didn't come straight back to Argos. She went to Athens first and had Nicholas take her to Delphi." Zack grinned and went to the door. "I'll let myself out."

"What?" Festus shouted at Zack's retreating back. Zack turned and grinned but said nothing.

"Are you really going to burn them, Fes?"

"Yes. Why did she go to Delphi? I guess we'll find out. Let me tell you what she says in May."

"She doesn't say much about Tam'oan Shan. Mostly, she complains about the difficulty of arranging things from a distance. She's obviously frustrated about not having control. I have the impression she didn't know exactly what would happen. There's an interesting note here. She sent Balaam a facsimile of the Pendant to use in the ceremony. She must have had that jeweler in Taxco make it. Boy, she planned everything. I wonder how she managed to get it to him. Jorge, I guess. What does she say in June?"

"She's still complaining. She writes, 'I need more information about what happened in the ceremony. How did they reverse the effects of the drugs? Pandora and Rosie have recovered. They do not remember much of what happened. I could use those skills.' She's curious about what you did. She guesses it was phenolphthalein, and she's angry you won't tell her. Berates you for acting like a schoolboy."

"She made me feel like one."

"Then she goes on about you showing renewed interest in the Pendant. She says, 'my little fake bauble worked.'"

"The final pages discuss the Festival and the difficulty of getting us all to rehearse. That's it."

"Olympic Services! What a reward for all those years." Dawn pulled Festus onto the floor and kissed him passionately.

"I have an idea for another reward."

"You've got it."

Festus rolled over and patted Dawn's bare bottom. "I hate to suggest it, but we need to get back to the diaries. September 1967 is the next one."

"Time for a quickie first."

"Sure."

"Dear Diary:

Demosthenes has gone too far. He has worked out that I was involved in the business in Tam'oan Shan. He even spotted the copy of the Pendant. I let him think I would do what he wanted. Athena can dissemble if she needs to. He does not know what he has unleashed. I have a plan. Henry asked to see the Pendant. He was furious because I had already passed it on the Samantha. She has put it in a safety deposit box in my Austin Bank. I have given Demosthenes the impression that Balaam would like it. I am sure that evil child will find a way, probably with his equally venal friends, to steal the Pendant. The slut Amanda is bedding my "old friend" Howard. I hope the information and funds that I have sent through Jorge will have them taken out of the country, where they can be dealt with properly. Henry and my other brothers will have to take their chances. It is costing me a fortune and it is frustrating, but I must stay away from the action. Angelica will have to stand in for me.

I am assuming Henry will get out of this business alive, and use the Pendant to discover for himself the clue to go to Erythmos, or as it is known today—Cornwall. I hope he does not take too long. I am feeling old and tired. On that self-pitying note, I must return to arranging my tour of relevant sites in Europe."

"Jesus, Fes! 'Henry and my brothers will have to take their chances.' Look here! She knew what was going to happen to y'all in Copan. It looks like she paid for it!"

Festus winced. "At least she hoped I'd come out alive."

"Yeah! So you could play the next part of her game. I wonder which relevant sites she was talking about."

"Maybe she says something in September. You're quicker than I am. Have a look!" Festus tossed the diary to Dawn.

"She's put September and October together. She visited her buddy Georgina, and then went to Cornwall. She comments on the interesting prehistoric sites and going to an artist's colony. Then she went to Sicily."

"Did she go to Erice?"

"No, she spent her time mainly on the eastern end of the island around Mount Etna. Apparently, she didn't find what she needed. There are some disparaging remarks about Palermo, and Agricento. She does say she needs to go back and check out the western end of the island."

"What about Crete?"

"She stayed with our relatives and she mentions looking for the best Dancing Floor. That's it."

"It says a lot."

"There's a bit more on poor Demos in December."

"Dear diary:

Demosthenes is gone. I heard through my sources that it was not the way that had been planned. Demosthenes slipped to his death. Pity! I have heard that Balaam was disappointed the ceremony could not be completed correctly. My hallucinating relatives remain confused about the whole business. Ares is convinced his athletic prowess caused the death of Diomedes. From what I have heard, Balaam's script was written to accommodate a win or a loss. Either way is consistent with a Mayan practice. In some cities, the vanquished were sacrificed. In others, the victors were sent to 'heaven' to receive their rewards. I, Athena, ordained that Diomedes would die whatever the result. I am elated by the demise of Demosthenes. I am sad that Ari believes he was the tool of his death. Ari has retired to his ranch and we rarely see him anymore. I have considered telling him the truth, but it would expose my involvement. He leaves me with a huge problem. Who will play Ares? Angel has volunteered. It could be the best option! Maybe, I should agree with her on the condition that she helps me with the cactus garden. I am finding it hard to do the work. I will have to trust her!"

"She's losing it. Isn't she?"

"Yeah. It's sad to read."

Dawn continued reading. "Fes, there is a comment here about how fortunate she is to have encountered a group of people who revere the past as she does. There are comments on the parallels between the ancient Mexican pantheon of gods and those of Greece."

"That could explain a lot. The use of the present tense is intriguing, Dawn, 'fortunate she is,' and so on. It could imply she only met them recently. Presumably, because of Demos finding that book in the UT library. So we're back to the problem of Jorge Vasquez. How does he fit in? Is he Balaam? I hope Zack's people track him down. I have a lot of questions I'd like to ask him."

"There's something here about the Pendant. Now the good bit." Dawn chuckled. "She wishes you would be quicker in understanding how to use it."

"Let me see that!" Festus read for a moment. "I was exhausted after Copan," he muttered defensively. "She kept on bugging me about the Disk. I remember being irritated. I guess she knew she didn't have much time left."

"She says it here in June 1968," said Dawn.

"I hate feeling so old. It is becoming harder to complete the tasks I have set myself. At least, Erythmos is complete. The Cornish crew and my new friend Geoffrey did a fine job. Morley Pascoe complained the whole time. It was easier than we thought to lift the stones and have Geoffrey inscribe my patterns on their bases. Fortuitously, he also knew how to make them look old. Geoffrey told me how much he enjoyed my little game. It reminded him of his work during the Second World War. He was in a special unit, forging material to fool the Germans. There was one awkward moment when an officious local busybody wanted to know what we were doing. Threatened to go to the police. I explained that we were part of new show for television, featuring a treasure hunt. The fool believed me. He thinks he will get to play a role. I will have to keep him on the hook until Hephaestus has completed this Labor. I wish he would hurry up and finish the translation. He continues to flounder.

I can only rest for a while, before I go back to Sicily. Now that the clues are marked on the Nine Maidens, I have no choice but to make Sicily the last stepping-stone. After doing a lot of reading, I think I know where to site the final pieces of information."

"She had the stones lifted. So simple! Like an idiot, I burrowed under them. I remember Ionides telling me that one of the Cornish miners asked him I didn't lift them up. It didn't mean anything to me at the time. Obviously, they knew it was easy to do. I met this Geoffrey guy when I went with Alex went to some artist's colony. Alex bought one of his sculptures. He showed great interest in our activities; all the time laughing at my antics, I guess. As for Marienna, you've got to hand it to her. She was a very smart old lady. Even with her clues and prompting, it took me until early this year to recover her translation. I must have been stupid."

"Fes, you couldn't have known. This whole business is unbelievable. Now I can't wait to find out what she did in Sicily."

"But first a comment on Chuck."

"...Pandora was married. Chuck Steeger seems like a nice enough young man, but he is a 'foreigner.' I am not sure their children will be able to take a role in my plays. We are losing our identity..."

"We're getting near the end—January 1969.

"Dear diary:

Now all I can do is wait. At last, Henry has understood how to translate the Disk. He is talking about going to Cornwall. I will help him persuade the Council. I think he has also grasped that he will then need to go to Sicily. Fortunately, he has been there before—to Erice. This will be a perfect base for exploring the area. I have completed my arrangement. The clues are placed in a cemetery on the island of Levanzo. Again, I used the ploy that this was part of a new television program. My contributions to "local charities" helped persuade the locals to support my venture. Then, I had the good fortune to become acquainted with a fine Italian actor who, as they say in the business, was resting. Ettore was happy to have guaranteed employment until the affair is over. Hopefully soon! He has developed this marvelously funny character, 'Alfredo Mokarta,' based on a real mobster—now departed. As befits a stand-in for Atlas, Alfredo was a hold-up man. He will ensure that Hephaestus finds my clues. To complete the analogy with this Labor, I had some orange trees planted near the tomb. I hope nobody looks at them too closely."

"I should have guessed. Alfredo Mokarta was such a ludicrous character."

"Maybe that's why we believed he was real," said Dawn laughing. "Do you remember that ridiculous scene in the tomb with his…grandfather?"

"Unbelievable, I am amazed that this Ettore was out of work. He was incredible. We ought to go back there. See if we can find him and offer congratulations."

"I'll come with you."

"Good. I am going to need a break. My world is being torn apart. I thought I knew who I was. Being Hephaestus doing the Labors gave me a purpose. Now I am back to being Henry Everett Festus, servant to the Cronsons."

"Fes. Stop being morbid! That's not what you said a couple of days ago. You did do the Labors. So, Marienna created some of them? So what? It was traditional for the 'gods' to create Labors."

"So, I was still a puppet, working for the Cronsons. What difference does it make—Zachary or Marienna?"

"Or me?" Dawn patted his hand tenderly.

"You know what I mean. Come on! Let's finish! There are only two diaries left. You take June. I'll read July. Boy, her handwriting is getting hard to decipher."

"This is very rambling and hard to follow," Dawn said. "She wrote it in Argos, after returning from being in Cornwall with you. There's a comment about someone called Morley Pascoe having a fit in the tunnel you'd dug—something about a bull. She viewed it as an important omen. She was very relieved he didn't spill the beans. Her words. She talks about getting drunk with that guy Geoffrey. I can't imagine Marienna drunk."

"Nor can I. What did they talk about?"

"You. But I can't make out her writing very well. Something…hilarious…best fun, I guess, since War."

"Great, very uplifting. Anything else?"

"Doc Maximos told her she had advanced cancer. He gave her a few months to live."

"This is the end—July 1969."

"Dear Diary:

This is my final entry. The various pills and potions that Doc Maximos gave me to handle the pain have allowed me, more or less, to complete my mission. I was not able to go to Sicily, but Ettore, Atlas, has written me copious notes on the Labor. I laughed so much it hurt. He described a scene in the tomb that should be in the movies. He tells me that the discovery of the guns lent it a greater reality. He assumes that I know where they came from. I have not told him that I have no idea. I supposed that it was connected to a local faction. When I rejoined my clan in Crete, they confirmed what had happened. Hephaestus has a different interpretation for the weapons. He thinks they were bound for Crete, to defend against the Hittites. It is easier for me to place them in those terms. It fits with my story.

My last days in Crete were wonderful. We performed the Dance twice, at Knossos and then Phaestos. Finally, Hephaestus got the point about the dashed line showing the way to Tartarus Bless Deucalion for his help in that! I have no idea what he will find when he gets there. Will my story match the reality? Angelica has the 'juice' and will dispense it liberally. I may never know what happened—at least not in this life. The pain is becoming unbearable. I have my pills. It should be over quickly.

This is the end, the last words of my last diary.

Hephaestus! Let me set the record straight. I wrote the Plays, hoping to improve the role of Hephaestus. My fantasy, expressed in 'his words' was that he wanted credit for the so-called Labors of Heracles. I did this originally for your father, Argos, whom I loved. Henry inherited the role. Through my efforts, he was able to complete twelve Labors, more or less successfully. When I look back, I realize that they were my Labors. I invented most of them. I brought them to a conclusion. The last time I left Crete, I did not come straight home. But went to the Oracle at Delphi. Through 'the juice,' I could recreate this ancient place and was able to talk to the Pythoness herself. She told me that I would have the opportunity to prove that it was I, Athena, who accomplished the Labors."

50. Jorge Vasquez

"Those seem to be the key points, Zack. I couldn't read the other parts of this diary. It's incoherent."

"It's plenty enough," said Zack, darkly. "Will you tell me what's in the other diaries?'

"No, Zack. It's personal. "I didn't know whether you knew about the cancer."

"Doc told me privately. I didn't tell anyone else. He didn't tell me she had committed suicide. Though I guess, I knew. What do you make of this Athena business?"

"The diaries show her becoming steadily more and more enmeshed in the concept that we are reincarnations of the gods," Dawn replied. She starts referring to Fes as Hephaestus. You are Zeus or Rhadamanthys, Aristotle is Ares and she even has Demosthenes pegged as Diomedes, king of Thrace."

"Wait up a second. What does she say about Demos?"

Festus replied cautiously, realizing that Zack didn't know what Marienna had done. "Oh she was upset by his drug dealing, and…"

"She was upset by his drug dealing!" Zack expostulated. "What about hers?"

"I guess she viewed that as different."

To their relief, Zack moved on to another topic. "What about Senor Jorge Vasquez?" He asked caustically.

"Very little. She doesn't seem to have had much contact recently." Festus kept away from the business with the Pendant, recognizing that it could lead back to a discussion of Demos.

"Do you think he and Heraclio are the same person?"

"It's not clear. I don't know who else it could be."

"We've got to find him. And I am going to have words with Angel about this juice stuff. We'll have no more of that," Zack said firmly, terminating the discussion.

Dawn waited until he had left. "I think we should destroy the diaries now. The family mustn't find out what she did."

"I agree, right now. But we'll keep the Plays.

Festus and Dawn watched as the last page of the diaries turned black, crumbled and disintegrated. Festus stamped out the fire. "It's the end of an era." He shrugged his shoulders. "Now that I've read the diaries, I need to say goodbye to Marienna again. Will you come with me? I loved her, you know." Festus could not hold back his tears.

"Of course, Fes. And whatever she may have done, she loved you too. That's why she set up the Labors."

"Yeah."

"Do you think you completed them?"

"Define complete!" Festus laughed. "If you mean unaided. No. With help, yes."

"What about Loch Ness? If only you could have found Che."

Festus did not reply immediately. Dawn was surprised that he seemed to be considering his response. She had given up on getting an answer and was leaving the room when he spoke.

"I did."

"Dawn looked at him in amazement. "What do you mean? I was there. When?"

"In front of y'all."

"I don't understand."

"Do you remember Elmo the eel?"

"How could I forget? You and Ion were a riot. Covered in weeds, with ole Elmo thrashing about. It was hilarious."

"It wasn't an eel. She was long and thin, like an eel. We caught her with a mass of weeds. It's amazing nobody questioned why the weeds were sticking to her. People just assumed Elmo was an eel. Her skin was smooth, but not slippery. She had bumps. Which I guess were vestigial flippers. It was the baby Chekkush. I would love to know how she will evolve as she grows. Will there be flippers? Ow! You didn't have to punch me."

"I'm angry. All these years and you never told me."

"I haven't told anyone until now. The small skin sample I collected was enough to prove it was a different species."

"Does Ion know?"

"A good question. He's never said anything. It was all pretty hectic. The difference is that I went into the tank suspecting that Elmo was Che and Ionides didn't."

"Why, didn't you tell the world? You would have been really famous."

"You mean, as opposed to being viewed as an interesting nut case?"

"Yes."

"The scene with the reporters was a circus. They didn't care about Che. Some idiot was trying to grab the toy dinosaur as a souvenir. I suddenly realized that if they knew what Elmo was, other idiots would have tried to capture her. I couldn't let that happen. I know what I found. That's enough."

Dawn hugged him. "I am so proud of you. I don't think you could have done that at the start of the Labors."

"We will give thanks to Marienna for helping me grow up."

They walked, hand in hand, through Argos and crossed the bridge to the cemetery. There was a car at the gate. A man knelt by the new grave. From a distance, they could not make out who it was. The man heard their footsteps and stood up slowly with the aid of a cane. He peered at them with interest as they approached and spoke first.

"It is a pleasure to meet you at last Dr. Festus and you Senora Festus," he said, flourishing his hat. "Over the years, I have heard so much about you. I am Jorge Vasquez, a friend of Marienna's. I was paying my respects. Sadly, it was not possible for me to attend her funeral."

He waited for Festus to speak. Festus was strangely silent. He seemed to be mesmerized by the mustachioed face in front of him.

"It's a real pleasure to meet you, Senor Vasquez," Dawn replied. "We've heard a lot about you too."

"I interpret that as meaning you have read the diaries."

"We sure have. It was a surprise."

"I am certain it was. Marienna was a remarkable woman." Jorge Vasquez paused, pointing at the gravestone. "Her epitaph says a lot, you know. He read slowly,

'I played Athena.
Athena played me.'

"She lived through her fantasies. You Doctor Festus were the vehicle to realize them."

"And how," said Festus, ruefully. "But, I am..."

Vasquez interrupted him. "Don't take it badly. Your godmother was unfortunate to have been born into a society that was unable, or unwilling to make proper use of her talents."

"She went too far. And I have a..."

"I agree. I fear she began to lose her reason. I think it started during your final adventures in Scotland. Then you all went to Crete. I am sad to say our communications were not very good after that. You went to Mexico and..."

"That's it," Festus shouted. "You're not Heraclio Balaam!"

"He isn't?" Dawn exclaimed.

"I'm not...? Oh! I think I know what you are asking." Jorge looked expectantly at Festus.

"Heraclio Balaam was the key figure in the Labors that took us to Mexico and Copan. You weren't a part of that?"

"Not really. There was some problem with her nephew. I do not recollect his name."

"Demosthenes, or Demos."

"Yes, that was it. I passed on some messages for Marienna...and money. I have not been well in recent years. I was in a nursing home at the time and could not do more. As I said, my contacts with Marienna have been very limited in the past three or four years. Then, her letters became quite strange as she became," he pointed at the gravestone, "Athena!"

"What about the Pendant of Cronos? Did you have anything to do with that?"

"I remember. Marienna wanted to have the Pendant remounted. I suggested a jeweler in Taxco. It was the last thing I did for her. Tell me about this Heraclio Balaam or rather Hercules Jaguar, a strange name. What do you mean by Olmec? The Olmec civilization was a very long time ago. As for me, I am proud of being part Xoque"

"Would you do us the honor of coming to our house? I would like to learn more. My brother in law, Zachary Cronson, very much wants to speak with you."

Jorge Vasquez shook his head. "I am sorry Doctor Festus. There is nothing more I am prepared to tell any of you. I now realize that I may know this Balaam. There was a very interesting compatriot of mine at Harvard, a true visionary. He saw a better, even glorious, future for Mexico, that was tied to its past. In his own way, he had dreams similar to your godmother's. Possibly, in his mind, he was an Olmec. Who is to say he was wrong?"

"You won't say more."

"I cannot." He offered his hand to Dawn "Please help me to the car. It will be my fondest memory of Argos. Leaving on the arm of Aphrodite."

Festus and Dawn watched the car until it disappeared over the hill. "Zack will be furious he missed Senor Vasquez."

"I don't give a shit," said Festus. "I agree with the Senor. There are some things we should not understand completely. As far as I am concerned, Marienna was, or is, Athena. Balaam is the reincarnation of Kukulcan. Most important, you are Aphrodite and I am Hephaestus. We will carry on. I still have Labors to complete"

51. Hephaestus—the true story: according to Marienna Cronson

I Hephaestus, son of Arges the Cyclopes and the Titaness Rhea, have prepared this record to set down the truth about my life and works. My role has been diminished, as a result of ignorant scribbling and corrupt translations, and I am going to set the record straight. I am a technologist and an inventor. My work is well regarded from one end of the world to the other; from Erythria to the land of the Sumerians, who know me as Enkil; in the land of the Hatti; and from Scythia to Egypt, where I am known as Ptah.

If I have one weakness it is that I am a poor scribe. Yet here my inventiveness has helped again. I have made some small punches, each of which carries an embossed picture. These punches are used to imprint the reverse of the pictures onto tablets of wet clay. Each picture signifies a particular sound, and groups of pictures constitute words. To ensure that my system will be used widely, I have assigned symbols to represent some of those sounds that are not a part of my own language. In this way my writings will reach a larger audience. I am confident that this technique will become commonplace and you the reader will have no difficulty in understanding my message. Obviously I am right, because here you are reading my story.

[Note to self: I am thinking here of that strange terracotta Disk found at the Cretan Palace of Phaestos. I will relate it to Hephaestus. I hope I have not challenged myself too much.]

I am not as proud of the weapons that I have created, as of my other inventions such as this writing, my tools, and my toys. Unfortunately, for creative people such as I, there seems to be little choice but to invent whatever each master demands. There is another problem. All of my masters have needed my support, but each of them has been fearful and jealous of me and has preferred that my works would go unrecognized. This is a source of great frustration for me since my technical skills are used in resolving the regular conflict between the king of the moment and his tanist, as Zeus and Ares know well. The candidate kings come to me as they prepare to undertake their ritual tasks. Ask any of them—King Eurytheseus or King Minos of Crete—and, if they are honest, they will agree with my view. One person, more than any of them, is indebted to me. Which brings me to the so-called "Labors of Heracles."

[Note: I am going to use the Labors as a device to show the contributions of Argos. He works for my father (Agamemnon/Zeus!) who treats him just like Zeus treated Hephaestus.]

Heracles is, and I shall not mince my words, a shambling dolt, and an inveter-
ate liar and braggart. He rambles around the countryside, belting people with his
absurdly large club, and assaults any female who cannot run faster than he can.
He would never have survived his dealings with various monsters, those so-called
"Labors," if I had not fixed things to his advantage, using all the technical tools at
my disposal. Heracles needs help putting on his sandals!

Why then did I help this fool Heracles in the few Labors that involved him?
First, I thought that my contributions would be recognized and, second, to be
honest I had to keep on good terms with his adoptive parents, Zeus and Hera. I
have worked for many kings, yet my first allegiance is to Zeus, the king of us
gods. When Zeus told me to protect his 'baby boy' I jumped into action. Nevertheless, I have found life so unbearable since sorting out the idiot child's problems that I have asked the gods for another chance to demonstrate my skills; to
make the world aware of the truth—that I, Hephaestus, am responsible for the
successful completion of the Labors! As you may imagine, Zeus and Hera were
uneasy about the idea, but my protectress, Athena and my friends, Apollo and
Artemis, persuaded them to support me.

[I expect to inherit the role of Athena from my mother. Atlas Platon, a truly
good looking man, plays Apollo, and Gaia Dexter usually plays Artemis—not a
good fit.]

This is a good place for me to pause in my story and clear up some of the mysteries regarding the interrelationships of the gods that have influenced my life.
Regardless of the claims for accuracy of storytellers such as Homer and Apollodorus, many of the commonly accepted 'facts' are in reality propaganda put out
by Zeus and other gods and goddesses to save themselves embarrassment.

Principal characters

I will set down the truth in an orderly and unsensational manner. For instance,
Zeus is said to have coupled with Metis, Leto, Maia and Hera, to name only a
few, and to have fathered, Athena, Persephone, Artemis, Ares, Dionysius and
Apollo, to mention even fewer of his supposed children. Ridiculous! Ares and
Artemis are, respectively, his brother and sister, Dionysius is his half-brother and
Athena his half-sister. Apollo is a cousin, the son of Atlas and Leto, and contrary
to common wisdom Artemis is not Apollo's sister. They merely played together
as children. The whole set of stories was spread to make Zeus appear to match the
image of that rogue, his father Cronus. Cronus is said to have laid every female he
sighted.

Mother Earth gave birth:

To the Cyclopes, who were created in Thrace and moved to Lemnos, Crete and Sicily;

To Erebus, the god of the night, who inhabited the underworld;

To the Titans, who resided at various places over the whole Mediterranean region; and

To the Giants, of whom Atlas is the one best known to me.

A discussion of all of them would be too confusing. In the various stories, many of them have been counted twice because like me—Hephaestus-Enkil-Ptah—they were known by different names in different places. So I will tell you only about those whose lives and actions bear upon mine.

Cronus was the youngest of the Titans. By Rhea he had three children, Poseidon, Hestia, and Dionysius. There is a widespread misunderstanding that Hestia and Athena are different women. So, for example, it is said that Dionysius took the place of Hestia among the twelve gods and goddesses on mount Olympus. Not so, Hestia is mentally disturbed and Athena is her second personality. What happened was that Hestia-Athena insisted on having two of the twelve seats on Olympus. Because Dionysius was often traveling, arranging drunken orgies, it usually didn't matter. When Dionysius stopped traveling extensively, he demanded his seat back. Since, by this time Hestia-Athena was becoming steadily more Athena than Hestia; Dionysius took the seat claimed by Hestia. As an aside, their dual personalities caused many problems, not only to those taught by Athena, but also to her men friends who would become engaged to Athena only to be rejected by Hestia. I have heard that this happened to my father. It is the primary reason why Hestia-Athena never married. Nevertheless, Athena and I get along very well. She has been my mentor. We even shared temples in Athens.

[Note to self: I have written an explanation of why Athena did not marry Arges the Cyclopes. I am not happy with it.]

Cronus was persistently unfaithful and Rhea divorced him. He married again, the Titaness Phoebe, and by her he had two sons, Zeus and Ares. They also had a daughter, Artemis, a person for whom I have a high regard. She has taken a vow of celibacy. Subsequent to the birth of Artemis, another child joined the family, but who the mother was is not known! We have our suspicions of course, but I don't want to be a gossip. I will just say that Cronus came home one day and said, calm as a sunning snake, "This baby girl is called Aphrodite. I have adopted her." Phoebe was furious and threatened to divorce him, but he sweet-talked her out of the idea.

In the meantime, Rhea, by now feeling completely free of Cronus, had married my father Arges. I was born a few years later. In fact, I am younger than Aphrodite!

Some years later, Cronus was killed. Zeus is reputed to have done it, but he was far too young at the time, being only four years old. I suspect the husband of the unnamed lady who bore Aphrodite, of the deed.

Several of the children of Cronus married and produced offspring. Poseidon was married briefly to Demeter. Before she left him they had a daughter, Persephone. As I said before, Zeus and Hera had no children of their own and Hestia-Athena never married. Dionysius married Ariadne and they had numerous children.

Ares married Pyrene, a pathetic little thing who for some baffling reason could intimidate him. They had two children, Diomedes, later king of Thrace, and a daughter Alcippe. Diomedes was an unpleasant child and an even more unpleasant adult. He persistently pursued my daughter Pandora and encouraged her willfulness. By contrast, his sister is a delightful girl, who eventually married my cousin and principal assistant Iolaus.

Aphrodite is my wife. I sometimes wonder why she married me. I suspect that she could see that even Zeus was apprehensive about my skills. It gave me an aura of power. I married her to prove something to the other gods. They all desired her, and it felt good to know that she was mine any time I wanted her. Well, to be truthful, nearly any time. In fact, it was more than that. Most of them cannot see beyond her beauty. Aphrodite is clever, and she listens to my ideas and makes useful suggestions. She is a lot smarter with people than I am. Unfortunately, our marriage is not well founded any more, and this has proved very damaging for our only child, Pandora. As a reaction to her mother's affairs and, I regret, to my being immersed so much in my work, she has become rather wild. Her main problems are her inquisitiveness, which she inherited from me, and that unpleasant youth Diomedes who encourages the willfulness that Pandora inherited from her mother.

I have one other relative worth mentioning. My young cousin, Iolaus, the son of my uncle, Brontes, is a good lad. He helped me handle the Lernean Hydra.

Some additional family history is needed to maintain the logic of this tale. Hera, Zeus's wife, and her brother Prometheus were the children of Iapetus the Titan and the nymph Clymene. Iapetus and Cronus did not see eye to eye on anything, for a range of reasons. It all started when Cronus took Phoebe, whom Iapetus fancied, for his second wife. The problems were compounded when Zeus eloped with Hera.

Their children continued this rivalry and, as a result, Prometheus suffered very badly at the hands of Zeus. I am not proud of my part in the matter. Earlier, Prometheus married Maia and she bore him a son Hermes, a good friend of mine.

Maia and Demeter are the daughters of a kindly couple, the giant Atlas and his wife Leto. When Hades eloped with Persephone, Demeter must have believed the poor girl to be dead. It all seems to have worked out now, and Persephone visits her once a year. They have an unmarried brother Apollo, a fine musician. He spent far too much time in his youth playing with his flute...if you know what I mean!

This leads me back to Hades, the son of Erebus and Gaia. He is really not a bad sort, although I think he has a limited sense of humor. But, living down in Tartarus, he leads a pretty dull life and I guess that is why he looks so glum. All those bodies he has to cope with could dampen the spirits of even the most cheerful god.

If you have been following my narrative, you will remember that I, Hephaestus, am the son of Arges the Cyclopes and Rhea, who left Cronus following the 'appearance' of Aphrodite. There is a general misconception held about Cyclopes. I expect that you imagine my father having only one eye? Right! Let me correct this impression. The confusion arose because he and his brothers, Steropes and Brontes, were bronze-smiths. As in much technological work, there are certain rituals to be followed. My father would paint a ring on his forehead in honor of the sun, the source of the fire in his forge. I am proud to be carrying on the tradition of my family, though I do not follow all of the customs. I am self-conscious and having paint all over my face can make me look silly. However, I sometimes wear an eye patch as a safety precaution.

There are unpleasant rumors that Aphrodite has other children, by Ares and various mortals. I believe that she has had a number of affairs. Haven't we all? She had a strange long-term affair with Ares, that I dealt with very cleverly, but no children came of it. Thank Zeus! Enough said about Aphrodite, the thought of her still hurts. Until now, my life has been mainly my family and my work although, recently, I have found a new love, a mortal. No, I will not tell you her name!

The Labors

At this point, I, Hephaestus, will take the opportunity to refresh your memories on the content of the Labors. I will not describe them in great detail but I will remind you, occasionally, of my part in them. One point I should make, at the beginning, is that the whole exercise came about because Heracles was attempting to usurp the throne of my master. At that time, by order of Zeus, it was king Eurystheus. To accomplish his goal, Heracles had to complete various Labors ordered by the existing king; an odd custom, I think! At the same time I was under orders, from Zeus and Hera, to protect Heracles. It was altogether a messy situation.

In the First Labor, the slaying of the Nemean Lion, the labor was not really the slaughter of that beast by Heracles. Let me set that lie to rest immediately! No, it was the creation of a massive bronze urn by bronze-smiths, working under my direction. We built it for king Eurystheus so that he could hide when Heracles returned to claim his throne. Eurystheus feared Heracles, who had a great knack for killing. When it appeared that Heracles would complete a labor, he would remain in the urn until he could think of another labor that he hoped Heracles would fail. In that way, Eurystheus was able to remain as the king.

I did not play a direct role in the destruction of the Lernean Hydra, the Second Labor. Rather, I instructed my cousin Iolaus to take various actions that ensured the "boy-wonder's"safety, while he thrashed around destroying the monster.

The Third Labor, capture of the Ceryneian Hind, was quite simple. It was necessary only to drive the poor animal and ambush it. I made sure that it crossed the path of Heracles. I wonder sometimes if his eyesight is quite normal, for he missed it with his net, and was obliged to pin it with an arrow. There, I will admit, he has skill on occasion, despite his poor eyesight.

Among my many inventions are some cunning chains that lock automatically around any object on which they are laid. I made the mistake of showing them to Heracles. For the Fourth Labor, he took them without my permission and used them to capture the Erymanthian Boar. As has been the case in most of his "adventures" he has failed to acknowledge my help.

The cleaning of the Stables of Augeias was beyond the limited capabilities of "the lout'" and he came to me in desperation for aid. It was a challenging problem. Again I found a solution for this Fifth Labor in the diversion of two rivers that rapidly swept away all the muck. I sent Iolaus to ensure that he did not make a mess of it.

Heracles was in dire straights in his attempt to rid the Stymphalian Marsh of an extremely unpleasant flock of birds. The idea for this Sixth Labor was a stroke of genius on the part of Eurystheus. By the time we came to deal with the problem I was ready to let Heracles perish, because I was so irritated by his cocky attitude. In retrospect, I suppose I am lucky that Athena gave him some brass castanets, which I had made for her. He used these to terrify the birds and when they took to the air, en masse, they were so closely packed that even he could not miss them with his arrows.

When I was principal advisor and bronze-smith to King Minos of Crete, a massive bull appeared, which ravaged the countryside. I offered to capture this Cretan Bull but, to my annoyance, Minos insisted on calling for Heracles for help; stating publicly that the job was beyond my capabilities. Heracles succeeded in this task with great ease and returned the beast to Sparta. He received many honors for this Seventh Labor and swaggered around boasting of it for an interminable time. What I did not discover, until many years later, was that Zeus and Minos set up the whole exercise. It was Heracles who had brought the animal to Crete in the first place; on the orders of Zeus, who likes to embarrass me occasionally to show that he is still in charge. Minos was happy to agree because he was in disfavor with his people. By obtaining the services of Heracles on such short notice, he demonstrated how essential he was to their well being.

The Mares of Diomedes were kept by that unpleasant youth, the king of Thrace who, as I mentioned earlier, is the son of Ares. Diomedes raised the mares on human flesh, usually that of unsuspecting guests. King Eurystheus, who had lost quite a few friends and relatives to these mares, ordered Heracles to capture the beasts for his Eighth Labor. Heracles had no clue what to do for while, in his brutish way, he could easily have slain each of them he had no concept of how to capture a demented mare. He lost the ends of a couple of fingers while trying to put a bridle on one of them. Fortunately, I was there to help him. A fact he chose not to mention later. I studied the matter carefully and concluded that, since horses do not normally eat people, they were being drugged. It was then a simple matter for me to substitute a different drug, a tranquilizer, so that Heracles could capture them. Heracles then took revenge on Diomedes, following the orders of Eurystheus, by setting him in a field with the Mares after the tranquilizer effects had dissipated.

I had no part in the Ninth Labor, the taking of the girdle of Hippolyte, queen of the Amazons. It was altogether a sad affair; for she was destined to be the bride of Heracles. However, Hera was fearful of any woman who might steal the affections of her son and spread rumors that the Amazons planned to attack Heracles and his men. Heracles heard the rumor just before he met with Hippolyte to receive her girdle, a token of her submission to him. She gave him the girdle and he killed her, but not before he had taken advantage of all of her favors! Nice guy! In fact, I did have some connection to the Labor. I made the girdle in the first place, at the request of Ares.

The final three Labors are, in reality, all a part of the same task. While Heracles was engaged in the Tenth Labor to fetch the Cattle of Geryon, Eurystheus informed him that he would not count two of the earlier Labors as meeting his challenge. I believe that Eurystheus had uncovered some of my role in the affair. I was accompanying Heracles again and had constructed a boat to take us to Erythria. On the return journey, after Heracles had slaughtered various unfortunates who stood in our way, he managed to get lost. It was while we were in Sicily, on our random wanderings, that a messenger from Eurystheus told him that he would have to do two more tasks. In the first of these, the Eleventh Labor, he should obtain some of the Apples of the Hesperides. Eurystheus wanted them in Crete, as a present for king Minos, in whose palace he was a guest. I helped get the apples by tricking poor Atlas into picking them. We then proceeded to Crete, where Eurystheus had left another message that Heracles should purify himself by attending the Greater Mysteries, and then descend into Tartarus to capture the dog Cerberus for the Twelfth Labor. There were also instructions to me, regarding the setting up of an amazing treaty that I am unable to divulge. It was indeed the month of Boedromium, by the time my particular task was completed, and the time of the Greater Mysteries, which Heracles and I attended. We then descended into Tartarus. Neither of us remembers what happened there since, as I understand it, we bathed in Lethe, the river of forgetfulness, at the command of Artemis. However, I am sure that I made a record of my work. I always keep notes, but I cannot remember where I put them.

[Note to self: Again, I do not know how I will be able to do it, but I need to make this part of the story told by the Phaestos Disk.]

The Oracle at Delphi

I, Hephaestus, have discussed those characters relevant to my story, barring a few mortals, and can return to the main point about my obtaining a second chance to get recognition for my contributions to society. I have asked the gods for it and Zeus and the whole motley crew have agreed. I just wish I knew when it will occur and how I will be challenged. That is a real problem, for when we reappear under new circumstances we do not generally remember who we are. So I may not be able to savor my success, unless I am lucky enough to come across the tablets and other clues I am preparing, and can understand them.

I have some idea about my future for I have consulted the Oracle at Delphi and she helped me look into the sacred flame. Poor girl, as is the custom the elders dragged her from her village. To prepare her for being the Pythoness they doped her with drugs, dropped her into a nearby ravine, and then kept her there

458   Marienna's Fantasy

for a few days. It is amazing she did not succumb to exposure in addition to losing her mind. Fortunately, she owes me a favor because I built the bronze temple that protects her from the elements. It protects both the Pythoness and the sacred flame that she tends. I also built the elegant, round, three-legged table that holds the fire. I painted it red white and black to brighten the place.

I chose a day when it was raining to visit her, in the hope that she would be appreciative of the fact that it was owing to me that she was dry. Regrettably, she was still high on her favorite potion of mushrooms and laurel leaves. She sat wild-eyed, glaring balefully at me until recognition dawned.

"What does Hephaestus want?" she asked in that drunken, slurred speech that mortals mistake for the sound of the gods.

I explained my dilemma and she nodded sagely. I thought she was thinking of a suitable reply, but discovered that she had drifted into a trance. We gods are not in awe of the Oracle as are those mortals. I took a stick and prodded her, at which point she woke up and started babbling. My recollection of the verses she intoned may not be accurate but, with some attempt at rhyme, here they are:

> "Look to a star alone
> Your dreams to realize.
> Follow the chosen path
> To reach again the skies.
>
> Six labors you will try
> And memory return in part.
> A mortal girl you will meet
> And she will turn your heart.
>
> Six more labors to be done
> As god-like you become.
> Beware conceit my lord
> Or you'll be overcome."

While she was speaking, I looked into the sacred flame. I have a hazy recollection of what I learned in addition to her words. I think I saw images of my return and triumph, in strange clothes and in a strange land. Though it may have been wishful thinking or the narcotic affects of the fumes.

Then, the Pythoness staggered to her feet and rambled on in a nearly incomprehensible way. The only words I could understand were "A star alone" which she repeated continually while raising both hands to shoulder level and pointing the index and little finger at me—an unpleasant gesture. I do not understand the significance of her words or actions, except that, obviously, I will fall in love with a mortal girl and must be careful not to become conceited at my successes. I am not concerned about the latter part of the message. It is unlikely. I believe I have a very balanced view of my genius.

As to my future, Zeus says that we gods will live forever in the great works of the Greek writers, though I have my doubts, given their self-seeking and incompetent attempts to date in describing my role. Notwithstanding that comment, there are some plays that spotlight my skills, for example, "Zeus Bound" by Aeschylus, which might have been better titled the "Cunning of Hephaestus." This continuing problem with Zeus and Ares was on my mind when I visited the Oracle. We technologists have difficulties with those who wish to use our creative talents and technical skills for their own ends. If any of you, who read these tablets, realize that I am completing my Labors again, please set the record straight and describe my successes so that all may marvel at my skill and ingenuity.

Pantheon of the Gods: according to Marienna Cronson

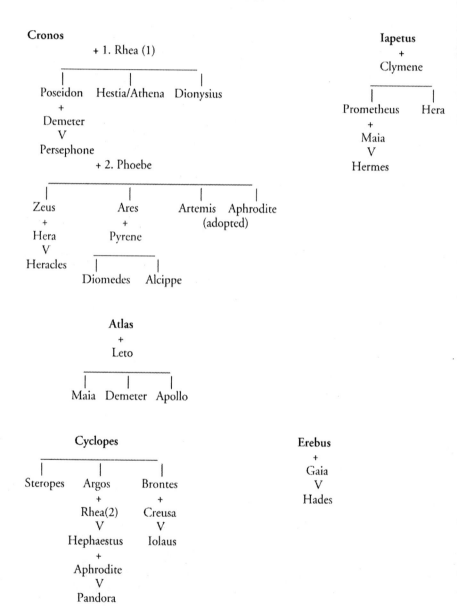

0-595-33345-1

Printed in the United States
26353LVS00002B/34-102